P9-DOH-136

Also by Colleen McCullough

The October Horse

Morgan's Run

Roden Cutler, V.C. (biography)

The Song of Troy

Caesar: Let the Dice Fly

Caesar's Women

Fortune's Favorites

The Grass Crown

The First Man in Rome

The Ladies of Missalonghi

A Creed for the Third Millennium

An Indecent Obsession

The Thorn Birds

Tim

THE TOUCH

COLLEEN
McCULLOUGH

Simon & Schuster

NEW YORK LONDON TORONTO SYDNEY SINGAPORE

SIMON & SCHUSTER
Rockefeller Center
1230 Avenue of the Americas
New York, NY 10020

Book design by Ellen R. Sasahara

Manufactured in the United States of America

ISBN 0-684-85330-2

FOR DR. KEVIN COOREY

who manages to keep me alive;

with love and gratitude

to a terrific bloke.

CONTENTS

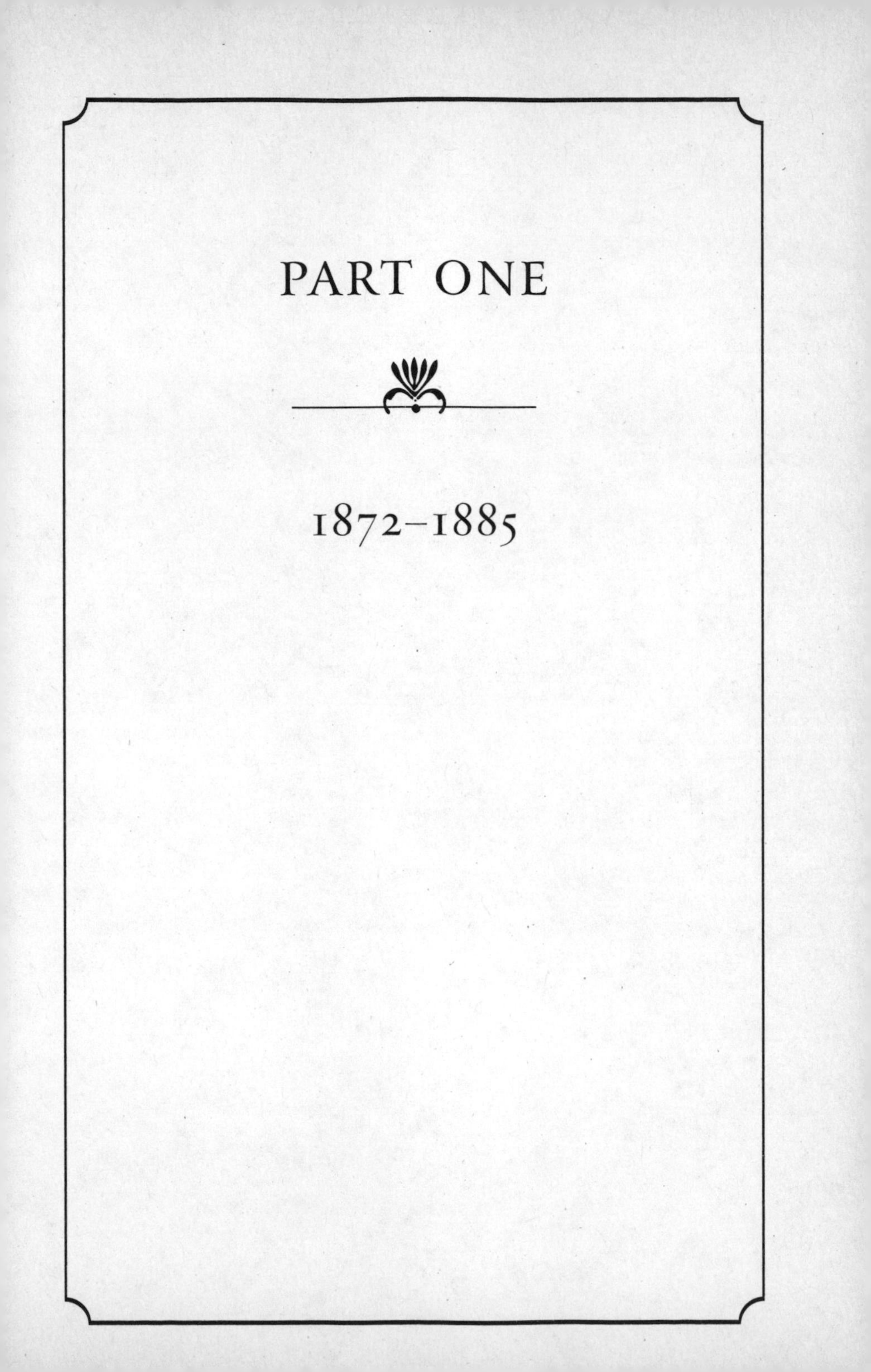

PART ONE

1872–1885

One

A CHANGE OF FORTUNE

"YOUR COUSIN Alexander has written for a wife," said James Drummond, looking up from a sheet of paper.

The summons to see her father in the front parlor had fallen on Elizabeth like a blow; such formality meant a lecture for transgression, followed by a punishment appropriate for the offense. Well, she knew what she had done—over-salted this morning's porridge—and knew too what her punishment was bound to be—to eat *un*salted porridge for the rest of the year. Father was careful with his money, he'd not spend it on a grain more salt than he had to.

So, hands behind her back, Elizabeth stood in front of the shabby wing chair, her mouth dropped open at this amazing news.

"He asks for Jean, which is daft—does he think time stands still?" James brandished the letter indignantly, then transferred his gaze from it to this youngest child, light from the window pouring over her while he sat concealed by shadows. "You're made like any other female, so it will have to be you."

"Me?"

"Are you deaf, girl? Aye, you. Who else is there?"

"But Father! If he asks for Jean, he'll not want me."

"Any respectable, decently brought-up young woman will do, judging by the state of affairs in the place he writes from."

"Where does he write from?" she asked, knowing that she wouldn't be allowed to read the letter.

"New South Wales." James grunted, a satisfied sound. "It seems your cousin Alexander has done well for himself—made a wee fortune on the goldfields." His brow wrinkled. "Or," he temporized, "at least has made enough to afford a wife."

Her first shock was dissipating, to be replaced by dismay. "Wouldn't it be simpler for him to find a wife there, Father?"

"In New South Wales? It's naught but harlots, ex-convicts and English snobs when it comes to women, he says. Nay, he saw Jeannie when he was last home, and took a strong fancy to her. Asked for her hand then. I refused—well, why would I have taken a shiftless boilermaker's apprentice living in the Glasgow stews for Jeannie, and her barely sixteen? Your age, girl. That's why I'm sure you'll do for him—he likes them young. What he's after is a Scots wife whose virtue is above reproach, whose blood he shares and can trust. That's what he says, at any rate." James Drummond rose to his feet, brushed past his daughter and marched into the kitchen. "Make me some tea."

Out came the whisky bottle while Elizabeth threw tea leaves into the warmed pot and poured boiling water on top of them. Father was a presbyter—an elder of the kirk—so was not a drinker, let alone a drunkard. If he poured a dollop of whisky into his teacup, it was only upon the receipt of splendid news, like the birth of a grandson. Yet why was this such splendid news? What would he do, with no daughter to look after him?

What was really in that letter? Perhaps, thought Elizabeth, accelerating the steeping of the tea by stirring it with a spoon, the whisky would provide some answers. Father when slightly befuddled was actually talkative. He might betray its secrets.

"Does my cousin Alexander have anything else to say?" she ventured as soon as the first cup was down and the second poured.

"Not very much. He's no fonder of words than any other of the Drummond ilk." Came a snort. "Drummond, indeed! It's not his name anymore, if you can believe that. He changed it to Kinross when he was in America. So you won't be Mrs. Alexander Drummond, you'll be Mrs. Alexander Kinross."

It did not occur to Elizabeth that she might dispute this arbitrary decision about her destiny, either at that moment or much later, when enough time had passed to see the thing clearly. The very thought of disobeying Father in such an important matter was more terrifying than anything she could imagine except a scolding from the Reverend Dr. Murray. Not that Elizabeth Drummond lacked courage or spirit; more that, as the motherless youngest, she had spent all her little life being tyrannized by two terrible old men, her father and his minister of religion.

"Kinross is the name of our town and county, not the name of a clan," she said.

"I daresay he had his reasons for changing," said James with unusual tolerance, sipping at his second tipple.

"Some sort of crime, Father?"

"I doubt that, or he'd not be so open now. Alexander was always headstrong, always too big for his boots. Your uncle Duncan tried, but couldn't manage him." James heaved a huge, happy sigh. "Alastair and Mary can move in with me. They'll come into a tidy sum when I'm six feet under."

"A tidy sum?"

"Aye. Your husband-to-be has sent a bank draft to cover the cost of sending you out to New South Wales. A thousand pounds."

She gaped. *"A thousand pounds?"*

"You heard me. But don't get your head turned around, girl. You can have twenty pounds to fill your glory box and five for your wedding finery. He says you're to be sent first-class and with a maid—well, I'll not countenance such extravagance! Och, *awful!* First thing tomorrow I'll write to the Edinburgh and Glasgow newspapers to post an advertisement." Down came his spiky sandy lashes, a sign of deep thought. "What I want is a respectable married couple belonging to the kirk who are planning to emigrate to New South Wales. If they're willing to take you along, I'll pay them fifty pounds." His lids lifted to reveal his bright blue eyes. "They'll grab at it. And I'll put nine hundred and twenty-five pounds in *my* purse. A tidy sum."

"But will Alastair and Mary be willing to move in, Father?"

"If they're not, I'll leave my tidy sum to Robbie and Bella or Angus and Ophelia," said James Drummond smugly.

Having served him two thick bacon sandwiches for his Sunday supper, Elizabeth threw her plaid around her shoulders and escaped on the pretext that she'd better see if the cow had come home.

THE HOUSE wherein James Drummond had brought up his large family lay on the outskirts of Kinross, a village dignified with the status of market-town because it was the capital of Kinross County. At twelve by ten miles, Kinross was the second-smallest county in Scotland, but made up for its lack of size by some slight degree of prosperity.

The woollen mill, the two flour mills and the brewery were belching black smoke, for no mill owner let his boilers go out just because it was a

Sunday; cheaper than stoking from scratch on Mondays. There was sufficient coal in the southern part of the county to permit of these modest local industries, and thanks to them James Drummond had not suffered the fate of so many Scotsmen, forced to leave their native land in order to find work and live, or else subsist in the squalor of a reeking city slum. Like his elder brother, Duncan, who was Alexander's father, James had worked his fifty-five years at the woollen mill, turning out lengths of checkered cloth for the Sassenachs after the Queen had brought tartan into fashion.

The strong Scottish winds blew the stack-smoke away like charcoal under an artist's thumb and opened the pale blue vault to near-infinity. In the distance were the Ochils and the Lomonds, purple with autumn heather, high wild mountains where crofter's cottages swung decayed doors on nothing, where soon the absentee landlords would come to shoot deer, fish the lochs. Of scant concern to Kinross County, in itself a fertile plain replete with cattle, horses, sheep. The cattle were destined to become the finest London roast beef, the horses were brood mares for saddle and carriage horses, the sheep produced wool for the tartan mill and mutton for local tables. There were crops too, for the mossy soil had been extensively drained fifty years ago.

In front of Kinross town was Loch Leven, a broad, ruffled mere of that steely blue peculiar to the Scottish lochs, fed by translucent amber peat streams. Elizabeth stood on the shore only yards from the house (she knew better than to disappear from sight of it) and looked across the loch to the verdant flatlands that lay between it and the Firth of Forth. Sometimes, if the wind blew from the east, she could smell the cold, fishy depths of the North Sea, but today the wind blew off the mountains, redolent with the tang of moldering leaves. On Lochleven Isle a castle reared, the one in which Mary Queen of Scots had been imprisoned for almost a year. What must it have been like, to be both sovereign and captive? A woman trying to rule a land of fierce, outspoken men? But she had tried to bring back the Roman faith, and Elizabeth Drummond was too carefully reared a Presbyterian to think well of her for *that*.

I AM GOING to a place called New South Wales to marry a man I have never met, she thought. A man who asked for my sister, not for me. I am caught in a web of my father's making. What if, when I arrive, this Alexander Kinross doesn't like me? Surely, if he is an honorable man, he will send me home again! And he must be honorable, else he would not have sent for a Drummond bride. But I have read that these rude colonies so far from home do indeed suffer a scarcity of suitable wives, so I suppose he will marry me. Dear God in Heaven, make him like me! Make me like him!

SHE HAD GONE to Dr. Murray's school for two years, long enough to learn to read and write, and she was well, if narrowly, read; writing was more difficult, since James refused to spend money on paper for silly girls to despoil. But provided she kept the house spotlessly clean, cooked her father's meals to his liking, didn't spend any money, or hobnob with other, equally silly girls, Elizabeth was free to read whatever books she could find. She had two sources: the texts in the library of Dr. Murray's manse and the drearily respectable novels that circulated among the feminine members of his massive congregation. No surprise, then, that she was more informed about theology than geology, and circumstance than romance.

That marriage would be her lot had never occurred to her, though she was just beginning to be old enough to wonder about its pleasures and perils, to look at her older siblings' unions with fascinated interest. Alastair and Mary, so different, always arguing, yet, she sensed, enjoying some deeper communion; Robert and Bella, perfectly matched in parsimony; Angus and his twittery Ophelia, who seemed determined to destroy each other; Catherine and her Robert, who lived in Kirkaldy because he was a fisherman; Mary and her James, Anne and her Angus, Margaret and William. . . . And Jean, the oldest daughter, the family beauty, who at eighteen had married a Montgomery—an enviable catch for a girl of good enough blood but absolutely no dowry. Her husband had removed her to a mansion in Princes Street, Edinburgh, and that was the last time the Drummonds in Kinross ever saw Jean.

"Ashamed of us," said James with contempt.

"Very canny," said Alastair, who had loved her and was loyal.

"Very selfish," said Mary, sneering.

Very lonely, thought Elizabeth, who remembered Jean only vaguely. But if Jean's loneliness became too much to bear, her family was a mere fifty miles away. Whereas I will never be able to come home, and home is all I know.

It had been decided after Margaret married that Elizabeth, the last of

James's brood who lived, was to remain a spinster at least until her father died, which family superstition believed would not be for many years to come; he was as tough as old boots and as hard as the rock of Ben Lomond. Now all of it had changed, thanks to Alexander Kinross and a thousand pounds. Alastair, James's pride and joy after the death of his namesake, would override Mary and move her and his seven children into his father's house. It would go to him anyway in the fullness of time, for he had cemented his place in James's affections by succeeding his father as loom master at the mill. But Mary—poor Mary, how she would suffer! Father deemed her a shocking spendthrift, between buying her children *shoes* to wear on Sundays and putting *jam* on the table for breakfast as well as for supper. Once she moved in with James, her children would wear boots and jam would appear only for Sunday supper.

The wind began to bluster; Elizabeth shivered, more from fear than the sudden chill. What had Father said of Alexander Kinross? "A shiftless boilermaker's apprentice living in the Glasgow stews." What did he mean by shiftless? That Alexander Kinross stuck to nothing? If he was shiftless, would he even be there to meet her at journey's end?

"Elizabeth, come inside!" James was shouting.

Obedient, Elizabeth ran.

AS THE DAYS flew by they conspired to give Elizabeth little time for reflection; try as she did to stay awake in her bed and think about her fate, the moment she lay down, sleep claimed her. Every day saw quarrels between James and Mary; Alastair, away to the mill at dawn and not returning until after dark, was fortunate. All of Mary's own furniture had to be moved to her new residence, and took precedence over James's chipped, battered pieces. If Elizabeth wasn't running up and down the stairs with armloads of linens or clothing (including shoes) or on one end of the piano, the bureau, the chiffer-robe, she was outside with one of Mary's rugs spread over the clothesline, beating it within an inch of its life. Mary was a cousin on the Murray side, and had come to her marriage with a certain amount of property, a small allowance from her farmer father, and more independence of mind than Elizabeth had credited any woman could possess. None of which had impinged on her in the way it did after Mary came to live with Father. Who didn't always win the battles, she was amazed to discover. The jam stayed on the breakfast table every morning and was there again every night. The children's shoes went on their feet before service at Dr. Murray's kirk on Sundays. And Mary flirted her shapely ankles in a pair of exquisite blue kid slippers with heels high enough to turn her walk into a mince. James spent much of his time in towering rages and soon had his grandchildren in healthy fear of his stick, but Alastair, he was learning, had become putty in Mary's hands.

Elizabeth's only chance to avoid this domestic turmoil were visits to Miss MacTavish's establishment in Kinross's main square. It was a small house whose front parlor, opening straight on to the pavement, bore a big glass window in which stood a sexless dummy clad in a very full-skirted pink taffeta dress—it would never do to offend the kirk by showing a dummy with *breasts.*

Everyone who didn't make her own clothing went to see Miss MacTavish, an attenuated spinster lady in her late forties, who, upon inheriting a hundred pounds, had given up employment as a seamstress and opened her own business as a modiste. It and she had prospered, for Kinross contained women able to afford her services, and she was clever enough to produce magazines of ladies' fashions that she insisted were sent to her from London.

Five of Elizabeth's twenty pounds had gone on tartan wools from the mill, where Alastair's position allowed her a small but welcome discount. These and four house dresses in coarse brown linen she would craft herself, together with her unbleached calico drawers, nightgowns, chemises and petticoats. When the expenditure was totted up, she found that she had sixteen pounds left to spend with Miss MacTavish.

"Two morning gowns, two afternoon gowns, two evening gowns and your wedding dress," said Miss MacTavish, enchanted with this commission. She wouldn't make much of a profit on the exercise, but it wasn't every day that a young and very pretty girl—oh, such a figure!—was thrust into Miss MacTavish's hands without a mother or an aunt to spoil her fun.

"As well," the modiste chattered as she wielded her tape measure, "that I am here, Elizabeth. Were you to go to Kirkaldy or Dumfermline, you'd pay twice as much for half as much. And I have some lovely materials in stock, just right for your coloring. Dark beauties never go out of fashion, they don't fade into their surroundings. Though I hear that your sister Jean—now there was a fair beauty!—is still the toast of Edinburgh."

Staring at herself in Miss MacTavish's mirror, Elizabeth heard only the last part of this. James wouldn't brook a mirror in his house and had won that particular encounter with Mary, who, when James produced Dr.

Murray as reinforcements, was obliged to keep her mirror in her own bedroom. Beauty, Elizabeth sensed, was a word that tripped easily off Miss MacTavish's tongue, and served as a balm to soothe a customer's misgivings. Certainly she saw no sign of beauty in her reflection, though "dark" was accurate enough. Very dark hair, thick dark brows and lashes, dark eyes, an ordinary sort of face.

"Och, your skin!" Miss MacTavish was crooning. "So white, and quite flawless! But do not let anybody plaster you with rouge, it would ruin your style. A neck like a swan!"

The measuring done, Elizabeth was led into the room wherein Miss MacTavish's bolts of fabrics were arranged on shelves—the finest muslins, cambrics, silks, taffetas, laces, velvets, satins. Spools of ribbon in every color. Feathers, silk flowers.

Elizabeth sped straight to a bolt of brilliant red, face alight. "This one, Miss MacTavish!" she cried. "This one!"

The seamstress-turned-modiste went as red as the cloth. "Och, dear me, no," she said, voice constricted.

"But it's so beautiful!"

"Scarlet," said Miss MacTavish, shoving the offending bolt to the back of its shelf, "is not the done thing at all, my dear Elizabeth. I keep it for a certain element in my clientele whose—er—*virtue* is not what it should be. Naturally they come to me at a prearranged hour to spare embarrassment. You know your scripture, child—the 'scarlet woman'?"

"Ohhhh!"

So the closest to scarlet that Elizabeth came was a rust-red taffeta. Irreproachable.

"I don't think," she said to Miss MacTavish over a cup of tea after the choices had been made, "that Father will approve of any of these dresses. I won't look my station."

"Your station," said Miss MacTavish strongly, "is about to change with a vengeance, Elizabeth. You can't go as the bride of a man rich enough to send you a thousand pounds wearing naught but tartan from the mill and plain brown linen. There will be parties, balls, I imagine, carriage rides, calls to pay on the wives of other rich men. Your father ought not to have kept so much of what, I am sure, is *your* money, not his."

That said (for it had burned to be said—what a miserable old skinflint James Drummond was!), Miss MacTavish poured more tea and pressed a cake on Elizabeth. Such a beautiful girl, and so *wasted* in Kinross!

"I really don't want to go to New South Wales and marry Mr. Kinross," Elizabeth said unhappily.

"Nonsense! Think of it as an adventure, my dear. There's not a young woman in Kinross who doesn't envy you, believe me. Think about it. Here, you will not enjoy a husband at all, you will spend your best years looking after your father." Her pale blue eyes moistened. "I know, believe me. I had to look after my mother until she died, and by then my hopes of marriage were gone." Suddenly she sighed, beamed. "Alexander Drummond! Well do I remember him! Barely fifteen when he ran away, but there wasn't a female in Kinross hadn't noticed him."

Stiffening, Elizabeth realized that at last she had found someone who could tell her a little about her husband-to-be. Unlike James, Duncan Drummond had had but two children, a girl, Winifred, and Alexander. Winifred had married a minister and gone to live near Inverness before Elizabeth had been born, so that was her best chance gone. Quizzing those of her own family old enough to remember Alexander had produced curiously little; as if, for some reason, the subject of Alexander was forbidden. Father, she realized. Father didn't want to give back his windfall, and was taking no chances. He also believed that ignorance was bliss when it came to marriage.

"Was he handsome?" she asked eagerly.

"Handsome?" Miss MacTavish screwed up her face, shut her eyes. "No, I wouldn't have called him *handsome.* It was the way he walked—a swagger. He was always black-and-blue from Duncan's stick, so sometimes it must have been hard to walk as if he owned the world, but he did. And his smile! One just went—weak."

"He ran away?"

"On his fifteen birthday," said Miss MacTavish, and proceeded to give her version of the story. "Dr. MacGregor—he was the outgoing minister—was quite heartbroken. Alexander, he used to say, was so terribly clever. He had Latin and Greek, and Dr. MacGregor hoped to send him to university. But Duncan wouldn't have that. There was a job for him in the mill here in Kinross, and with Winifred away, Duncan wanted Alexander here. A hard man, was Duncan Drummond! He'd offered for me, you know, but there was Mother to care for, so I wasn't sorry to refuse his offer. And now you're to marry Alexander! It's like a dream, Elizabeth, it's just like a dream!"

That last remark was true. In what corners of her mind the constant hard work permitted her, Elizabeth thought about her future much as clouds passed across the high, wide Scottish sky; sometimes in airy, light-hearted wisps, sometimes sad and grey, sometimes stormily black. An unknown severance with unknown consequences, and the limited ken in which she had spent her barely sixteen years could offer her neither comfort nor information. A tiny thrill of excitement would be followed by a bout of tears, a spurt of joy by a dizzying descent into despond. Even after intense perusal of Dr. Murray's gazetteer and *Britannica,* poor Elizabeth had no yardstick whereby to measure this complete and drastic upheaval.

THE DRESSES got made, including her wedding dress, every item folded between sheets of tissue paper and packed in her two trunks. Alastair presented her with the trunks, Mary with a veil of white French lace to wear at her wedding, Miss MacTavish with a pair of white satin slippers; all the members of the family save James managed to find something to give her, be it Cologne water, a scrimshaw brooch, a pin cushion or a box of bonbons.

James's respectable Presbyterian married couple answered one of his advertisements from Peebles, and after several letters had traveled back and forth between Kinross and Peebles, said that, for fifty pounds, they would be pleased to take custody of the bride.

Alastair and Mary were deputed to take Elizabeth on the coach to Kirkaldy, where they boarded a steam packet for the journey across the Firth of Forth to Leith. From there several horse-drawn trams took them into Edinburgh and to Princes Street Station, where Mr. and Mrs. Richard Watson would be waiting.

Had she not been felled by the choppy ferry crossing, Elizabeth would have been agog; in all her life she had never been as far afield as Kirkaldy, so the huge city of Edinburgh ought to have transfixed her, if her delight at seeing Kirkaldy was anything to go by. Catherine and Robert lived there and had put them up, shown Elizabeth the sights. But she could summon up no enthusiasm for Edinburgh's bustle, its wintry beauty, wooded hills and ravines. When the last of the trams deposited them at the North British Railway station, she let Alastair guide her, install her in the tiny, boxlike second-class compartment she was to share with the Watsons all the way to London, and left him to search the jam-packed platform for her tardy chaperones.

"This is quite tolerable," said Mary, gazing about. "The seats are well padded, and you've your rug for warmth."

"It's the third-class passengers I don't envy," Alastair said, pushing two cardboard chits into Elizabeth's left glove. "Don't lose them, they're for your trunks, safely in the luggage compartment." Then he slipped five gold coins down inside her other glove. "From Father," he said with a grin. "I managed to convince him that you can't go all the way to New South Wales with an empty purse, but I'm to tell you not to waste a farthing."

The Watsons finally arrived, breathless. They were a tall and angular couple in shabby clothes that suggested Elizabeth's fifty pounds had promoted them from the horrors of third-class to the relative comfort of second-class. They seemed pleasant, though Alastair's nose wrinkled at the liquor on Mr. Watson's breath.

Whistles blew, people hung out of the carriage windows to exchange screams, tears, frantic clutches and final waves with those on the platform; amid huffs and explosions, clouds of steam, jerks and clangs, the London night train began to move.

So near, and yet so far, thought Elizabeth, eyelids drooping; my sister Jean, who started all of this, lives in Princes Street. Yet Alastair and Mary have to hire a room in the railway hotel, and will go back to Kinross without so much as setting eyes on her. "I am not receiving," her curt note had said.

The eyelids fell, she crashed into sleep sitting curled in one corner with her cheek against the icy window.

"Poor little thing," said Mrs. Watson. "Help me make her more comfortable, Richard. It is a sad state of affairs when Scotland has to send its children twelve thousand miles to find a husband."

SCREW-DRIVEN steamships cut their way across the North Atlantic from Britain to New York in six or seven days, but there was no coal to fuel a steamship en route to the opposite end of the world. That was still served by sail.

Aurora was a four-masted barque with double topsails, square-rigged on her foremast and mainmast, fore-and-aft-rigged on her mizzens, and she completed the twelve thousand miles to Sydney in two and a half months, stopping only once, in Capetown. Down the Atlantic, then across the Southern Ocean into the Pacific. Her cargo consisted of several hundred water-flushing ceramic toilets and cisterns, two barouche carriages, suites of expensive walnut furniture, cotton and woollen fabrics, bolts of fragile French lace, crates of books and magazines, jars of English marmalade, tins of treacle, four Matthew Boulton & Watt steam engines, a consignment of brass doorknobs, and, in her strongroom, many very large cases marked with the skull-and-crossbones. On her way home, she'd carry thousands of bags of wheat and her strongroom would exchange cases marked with the skull-and-crossbones for gold bullion.

Much against the will of her master, a fanatical woman-hater, *Aurora* took a dozen passengers of both sexes in some degree of comfort, though she owned no staterooms and her cooks were of the plainest kind—plenty of fresh-baked bread, salty butter kept in insulated firkins, boiled beef and whiskery potatoes, and floury puddings laced with jam or treacle.

Though Elizabeth found her sea legs halfway across the Bay of Biscay, Mrs. Watson did not, which meant that Elizabeth's time was taken up in ministering to her. Not a distasteful duty, as Mrs. Watson was a kind soul who seemed to labor under many burdens. The three of them had one cabin blessed with a porthole and a small maid's cubicle opening off it; *Aurora* hadn't entered the English Channel before Mr. Watson announced that he would sleep in the passengers' saloon to give the women privacy. At first Elizabeth wondered why this news distressed poor Mrs. Watson so, then realized that much of the Watsons' poverty stemmed from Mr. Watson's penchant for strong drink.

Oh, but it was cold! Not until they passed the Cape Verde Islands did the winter weather finally lift, and by then Mrs. Watson was coughing badly. At Capetown her frightened husband sobered sufficiently to call a doctor, who pulled his mouth down and shook his head.

"If you want your wife to live, sir, I suggest you bring her ashore here and sail no farther," he said.

But what to do with Elizabeth?

Fortified by half a pint of gin, Mr. Watson didn't stop to ask himself this question, and Mrs. Watson, lapsed into stupor, couldn't ask it. The two of them were off the ship with all their belongings not half an hour after the doctor had departed, leaving Elizabeth to fend for herself.

If Captain Marcus had had his way, Elizabeth would have been bundled after them, but he reckoned without taking one of his three other women passengers into account. She called a meeting between herself, the two married couples, the three sober single gentlemen, and Captain Marcus.

"The girl goes ashore," *Aurora*'s master said, tone adamant.

"Oh, come, Captain!" said Mrs. Augusta Halliday. "To put a sixteen-year-old ashore in a strange place without a soul to protect her—for the Watsons are no fit guardians—is quite unconscionable! Do it, sir, and I will report you to your owners, to the Master's Guild and whomsoever else I can think of! Miss Drummond stays aboard."

As this announcement, delivered with a martial glare in Mrs. Halliday's eyes, met with murmurs of agreement from the others, Captain Marcus understood that he was beaten.

"If the girl is to stay," he said between his teeth, "I'll have no contact between her and my crew. Nor any contact between her and any male passenger, married or single, drunk or sober. She will be locked in her cabin and take her meals there."

"As if she were a prisoner?" asked Mrs. Halliday. "That is disgraceful! She must have fresh air and exercise."

"If she wants fresh air, she can open the porthole, and if she wants exercise, she can jump up and down on one spot, madam. I am master of this vessel, and my word is law. I'll have no harlotry aboard *Aurora*."

So Elizabeth spent the last five weeks of that interminably long voyage locked inside her cabin, sustained by the books and magazines Mrs. Halliday sent her after a hasty trip ashore to Capetown's only English bookshop. Captain Marcus's sole concession was to agree that Mrs. Halliday could escort Elizabeth twice around the deck after darkness fell each day, and even then he followed behind, barking at any sailor who came near.

"Like a watchdog," said Elizabeth with a chuckle.

Once the Watsons quit the ship she had recovered her spirits, despite imprisonment; that she understood, knowing that both her father and Dr. Murray would have approved of the captain's edict. And it was bliss to have her own domain, a larger one than her little room at home, which she was forbidden to enter until it was time to go to bed. If she stood on tiptoe she could see the ocean through her porthole, a heaving vastness that stretched forever, and during the nightly walks on deck she could hear its hiss, the boom it made when *Aurora*'s bows hammered down.

Mrs. Halliday, she learned, was the widow of a free settler who had made a modest fortune in Sydney by opening a specialist shop that catered to the best people. Be it ribbons or buttons, stay-laces or whalebone insertions, stockings or gloves, Sydney society purchased them at Halliday's Haberdashery.

"After Walter died, I couldn't wait to go home," she said to Elizabeth, and sighed. "But home wasn't what I expected. So very peculiar, that what I had dreamed about all those years turned out to be a figment of my imagination. I have become, though I knew it not, an Australian. Wolverhampton was full of slag heaps and chimneys, and would you believe that I found it hard to understand what people said? I missed my children, my grandchildren, and the *space.* We tend to think that, just as God made Man in His image, Britannia made Australia in her image. But she has not. Australia is a foreign land."

"Isn't it New South Wales?" Elizabeth asked.

"Strictly speaking, yes. But the continent has been called Australia for a long time now, and whether they're Victorians or New South Welshmen or Queenslanders or from the other colonies, people call themselves Australians. Certainly my children do."

Alexander Kinross came up in their conversation frequently. Sadly, Mrs. Halliday knew nothing of him.

"It's four years since I left Sydney, he probably arrived in my absence. Besides, if he's a single man and doesn't go into society, only his colleagues would recognize his name. But I am sure," Mrs. Halliday went on kindly, "that he is above reproach. Otherwise, why send for a cousin to marry? Scoundrels, my dear, tend not to marry at all. Especially if they live on the goldfields." Her lips drew in, she sniffed. "The goldfields are dens of iniquity plentifully supplied with shady women." She coughed delicately. "I hope, Elizabeth, that you are acquainted with the duties of marriage?"

"Oh, yes," Elizabeth answered tranquilly. "My sister-in-law Mary told me what to expect."

WHEN *AURORA* entered Port Jackson she was taken in tow by a steamboat; plagued by the presence of a pilot he detested, Captain Marcus was too engrossed to notice that Mrs. Halliday had liberated Elizabeth from her confinement, taken her up on deck to point out with proprietary pride the landmarks of what the good lady called "the grandest harbor in the world."

Yes, Elizabeth supposed that it was grand, gaze absorbing massive orange cliffs crowned by thick blue-grey forests. Sandy bays, gentler slopes, increasing evidence of habitation. The trees, tall and spindling, became replaced by rows and rows of houses, though on some foreshores they remained around what were majestic mansions, whose owners Mrs.

Halliday named with succinct comments that ranged from defamation to condemnation. But the air swam with moisture, the sun was unbearably hot, and over all the beauty of this grand harbor lay a terrible stench. Its water, Elizabeth noted, was a dirty, detritus-laden brown.

"March is not a good month to arrive," Mrs. Halliday said, leaning on the rail. "Always humid. We spend February and March praying for a Southerly Buster, which is a south wind that cools everything down. Is the smell bothering you, Elizabeth?"

"Very much," said Elizabeth, face pale.

"Sewage," said Mrs. Halliday. "A hundred and seventy-odd thousand people, and it all flows into the harbor, which is little better than a cesspool. I believe that they intend to do something about it—but when is anybody's guess, my son Benjamin says. He is on the city council. Water is a difficulty too. The days when it cost a shilling a bucket are gone, but it is still expensive. Few save the colossally rich have a supply laid on." She snorted. "Mr. John Robertson and Mr. Henry Parkes don't suffer!"

Captain Marcus descended, roaring.

"To your cabin, Miss Drummond! At once!"

And there Elizabeth remained while *Aurora* was towed to her berth; then all she could see through the porthole were masts, all she could hear were bellowing voices, the chug of an engine.

When, it seemed hours later, the knock fell on her door, she leaped off her bunk, heart thudding. But it was only Perkins, the passengers' steward.

"Your trunks have gone ashore, Miss, and so must you."

"Mrs. Halliday?" she asked, following him into a chaotic world of winches lowering crates in rope baskets, ruddy-faced men in flannel shirts, sailors whistling and jeering.

"Oh, she disembarked a long time ago. Asked me to give you this." Perkins fished in his waistcoat pocket and handed her a small card. "If you need her, you can find her there."

Down the gangplank, across the filthy boards of the wharf between high stacks of crates and cases—where were her trunks?

Having found them in a relatively peaceful corner against the wall of a tumbledown shed, Elizabeth sat on one, put her purse in her lap and folded her hands on top of it. Where to go, what to do? Thinking that if Alexander Kinross saw the Drummond tartan he would recognize her at once, she was wearing one of her home-made dresses, but this was not the weather for serge wool; in fact, she thought, dazed with heat, little of what reposed in her trunks was suitable for this climate. Sweat dewed her face, ran down the back of her neck from her hair, confined inside a matching bonnet, and soaked through her calico underwear into the Drummond tartan.

And after all that, it was she who recognized him in an instant, thanks to Miss MacTavish. She sat looking down a narrow lane between the off-loaded cargo and saw a man who walked as if he owned the world. Tall and rather slender, he was dressed in clothes strange to her eyes, used to men in working flannels and caps, or in the splendor of kilts, or in somber suits over shirts stiff with starch and stiff hats upon their heads. Whereas he wore soft trousers made of some fawn-colored skin, an unstarched shirt with a scarf at its neck, an open coat of the same skin that dangled long fringes from its arm seams and hem, and a soft fawn hat with a low crown and wide brim. Under the hat was a thin, deeply tanned face; his hair was black sprinkled with grey and curled on to his shoulders, and his black beard and mustache, greyer than his hair, were carefully trimmed into the exact same style as the Devil wore.

She rose to her feet, at which moment he noticed her.

"Elizabeth?" he asked, hand out.

She didn't take it. "You *know* that I am not Jean?"

"Why should I think you Jean when you're obviously not?"

"But you—you wrote for—for Jean," she floundered, not daring to look at his face.

"And your father wrote offering me you instead. It's quite immaterial," said Alexander Kinross, turning to signal to a man in his wake. "Load her trunks into the cart, Summers. I'll take her to the hotel in a hackney." Then, to her: "I'd have found you sooner if my dynamite hadn't chanced to be aboard your ship. I had to clear it and get it safely stowed before some enterprising villain got to it first. Come."

One hand beneath her elbow, he guided her through the aisle and out into what seemed an enormously wide street that was as much a depot as a thoroughfare, littered with goods and crowded with men attacking the wood-block paving with picks.

"They're putting the railway through to the docks," Alexander Kinross said as he thrust her upward into one of several loitering hackneys. Then, as soon as he was seated beside her: "You're hot. It's no wonder, in those clothes."

Finding her courage, she turned her head to study his face properly. Miss MacTavish was right, he wasn't handsome, though his features were regular enough. Perhaps that they were not Drummond or Murray features? Hard to believe that he was her own first cousin. But what chilled Elizabeth was his definite resemblance to the Devil. Not only in beard and mustache; his brows were jet-black and sharply pointed, and his eyes, sunk deep between black lashes, were so dark that she could not distinguish pupil from iris.

He returned her scrutiny, but with more detachment. "I'd expected you to be like Jean—fair," he said.

"I take after the Black Scot Murrays."

Came a smile; it was indeed, as Miss MacTavish had said, a wonderful smile, but no part of Elizabeth's anatomy went weak at the sight of it. "So do I, Elizabeth." He reached out a hand and put it under her chin to turn her face to the brilliant light. "But your eyes are remarkable—dark, yet not brown or black. Navy-blue. That's good! It says there's a chance our sons will look more like Scots than we do."

His touch made her uncomfortable, so did his reference to their sons; as soon as she felt he would not take offense, she pulled away from his fingers, stared at the purse in her lap.

The cab horse was plodding uphill away from the wharves and into a genuinely big city that seemed, to Elizabeth's unschooled eyes, quite as busy as Edinburgh. Carriages, sulkies, gigs, hackneys, carts, drays, wagons and horse-drawn omnibuses thronged the narrow streets, lined first with ordinary buildings, but then with shops rendered alien by awnings that jutted to the edge of the pavement; their presence hid the contents of the shop windows from any traveler on the road, a frustration.

"The awnings," he said, it seemed able to read her mind—yet another characteristic of the Devil—"keep shoppers dry when it rains and cool when the sun shines."

To which Elizabeth made no reply.

Twenty minutes after leaving the dockside the hackney swung into a wider street flanked on its far side by a sprawling park wherein the grass looked absolutely dead. Twin tracks ran down the middle of this street; here the horse-drawn public transport took the form of trams. Their driver drew into the curb outside a large yellow sandstone building with Doric pillars around its entrance, and a marvelously uniformed man helped her out of the hackney. His bow to Alexander was deferential, but became even more so after Alexander slipped a gold coin into his hand.

The hotel was incredibly luxurious. An imposing staircase, plush crimson everywhere, huge vases of crimson flowers, the glitter of gilt from picture frames, tables and pedestals. A colossal crystal chandelier blazed with candles. Liveried men bore her trunks away while Alexander led her not to the staircase but to what looked like a gigantic, lacy brass bird cage, where another liveried man waited with his gloved hand on its open door. As soon as she, Alexander and the attendant were inside it, the cage jerked and quivered, then started to rise! Half fascinated, half terrified, Elizabeth looked down on the receding lobby, saw the cross section of a floor, a crimson hallway; creaking and groaning, the bird cage continued to rise. Four, five, six floors. Shuddering, it stopped to let them out.

"Have you not seen a lift, Elizabeth?" Alexander asked, his voice amused.

"Lift?"

"Or, in California, an elevator. They're governed by the principle of hydraulics—water pressure. Lifts are very new. This is the only one in Sydney, but soon all commercial buildings will grow higher and higher because their occupants won't have to climb hundreds of stairs. I use this hotel because of its lift. Its best accommodation is on the top floor, where there's fresh air, a view, and a lot less noise." He produced a key and used it to open a door. "This is your suite, Elizabeth." Out came a gold watch; he consulted it and pointed to a clock ticking on the marble mantel. "The maid will be here shortly to unpack for you. You can have until eight o'clock to bathe, rest, and change for dinner. Evening dress, please."

That said, he vanished down the hall.

Her knees were weak now, but not due to Alexander Kinross's smile. What a sumptuous room! A pale green color scheme, a vast four-poster bed, and an area containing a table and chairs as well as something that looked like a cross between a narrow bed and a sofa. A pair of French doors led out on to a small balcony—oh, he was right! The view was wonderful! Never in her life had she been up more than one flight of stairs—if only she could have seen Loch Leven and Kinross County from such a lofty eminence! The whole of eastern Sydney was spread before her—gunboats moored in a bay, many rows of houses, forests on the distant hills as well as along the foreshores of what did indeed look, from so high up, the grandest harbor in the world. But fresh air? Not to Elizabeth's sensitive nose, still able to smell that fetid stink.

The maid knocked and entered bearing a tray of tea, little sandwiches and cakes.

"But have your bath first, Miss Drummond. The floor butler will make the tea when you're ready," said this dignified person.

Elizabeth discovered that a huge bathroom lay through a door beyond the bed, together with what the maid called a dressing room, replete with mirrors, cabinets, bureaux.

Alexander must have explained to the maid that all this was strange to his intended bride, for the woman, expressionless, took over—showed her how to flush the water closet, drew her a bath in a massive tub and washed her salt-caked hair as if she saw naked women every day and thought nothing of it.

ALEXANDER KINROSS, thought Elizabeth later, sipping tea. Impressions can be treacherous, shaped by accident and gossip, ignorance and superstition. It was Alexander Kinross's misfortune that he happened to be the image of a head-and-shoulders sketch of the Devil that Dr. Murray had deliberately hung on the wall of the children's Bible-study room. Its aim was to terrify the children of his congregation, and it succeeded: the thin mouth with its slight sneer, the horrible dark pits of eyes, a malignancy suggested by shrewd lines and shadows. All Alexander Kinross lacked were the horns.

Common sense told Elizabeth that this was sheer coincidence, but she was far more a child than a woman. Through no fault of his own, Alexander entered Elizabeth's life with an ineradicable handicap, and she took against him. The very thought of marrying him terrified her. How soon? Oh, pray not yet!

HOW CAN I look into those diabolical eyes and tell their owner that he is not the husband I would choose? she asked herself. Mary told me what to expect in the marriage bed, though I already knew it is no joy for a woman. Dr. Murray made it clear to me before I left that a woman who enjoys the Act is as loose as a harlot. God gives pleasure in it only to husbands. Women are the source of evil and temptation, therefore women are to blame when men fall into fleshly error. It was Eve who seduced

Adam, Eve who entered into league with the serpent, who was the Devil in disguise. So the only pleasure women are allowed is in their children. Mary told me that if a wife is sensible she separates what goes on in the marriage bed from the person of her husband, who is her friend in all else. But I cannot envision Alexander as my friend! He frightens me more than Dr. Murray does.

HOOPS, MISS MACTAVISH had remarked, were out of fashion now, but skirts were still voluminous, held out by layer upon layer of petticoats. Elizabeth's petticoats were singularly unlovely, made of unbleached cotton without embellishment. Only the evening dress itself had been crafted by Miss MacTavish, but even it, Elizabeth sensed as the maid helped her into it, was unimpressive.

Luckily the gas-lit hall was dim; Alexander's gaze passed over her and he nodded in apparent approval. He was clad tonight in white tie and tails, a masculine fashion she had seen only in magazine illustrations. If anything, the black and white served to enhance his Mephistophelian quality, but she put her hand on his arm and allowed him to lead her into the waiting lift.

When they arrived in the lobby she understood a great deal more about the limitations of rural Scotland and Miss MacTavish; the sight of the ladies strolling about on gentlemen's arms reduced her pride in the dark blue taffeta dress to nothing. Their arms and shoulders were bare, one separated from the other by a puff of silk or a froth of lace; their waists were tiny, their skirts gathered at the back into huge humps that cascaded frills into trains sweeping the floor behind them; their matching gloves came up past their elbows, their hair was piled high and wide, half-naked bosoms blazed with jewels.

When the pair entered the dining room, it stilled. Every head turned to survey them; men nodded gravely to Alexander, women preened. Then the whispers began. A toplofty waiter guided them to a table at which two other people already sat, an elderly man in what she was to learn to call "evening dress" and a woman of about forty whose gown and jewels were superb. The man rose to his feet to bow, the woman continued to sit, a fixed smile on her otherwise unreadable face.

"Elizabeth, this is Charles Dewy and his wife, Constance," said Alexander as Elizabeth sat in the chair the waiter drew out.

"My dear, you're charming," said Mr. Dewy.

"Charming," Mrs. Dewy echoed.

"Charles and Constance are to be our witnesses when we marry tomorrow afternoon," Alexander said as he took the menu. "Do you have any preferences in food, Elizabeth?"

"No, sir," she said.

"No, Alexander," he corrected gently.

"No, Alexander."

"Since I know all too well the sort of fare you ate at home, we'll keep it simple. Hawkins," he said to the hovering waiter, "a flounder meunière, a sorbet, and roast beef. Well-done for Miss Drummond, rare for me."

"Sole," said Mrs. Dewy, "doesn't exist in these waters. We make do with flounder. Though you should try the oysters. Quite the best in the world, I venture."

"WHAT ON EARTH is Alexander about, to marry that child?" asked Constance Dewy of her husband as soon as the lift had deposited them on the fifth floor.

Charles Dewy grinned, raised his brows. "You know Alexander, my dear. It solves his problems. Puts Ruby in her place and at the same time gives him someone young enough to mold to his liking. He's been single far too long. If he doesn't begin to raise his family soon, he'll not have time to train sons to run an empire."

"Poor little thing! Her accent is so thick that I could hardly understand a word she said. And that awful dress! Yes, I do indeed know Alexander, and his taste runs to opulent women, not dowdy misses. Look at Ruby."

"I have, Constance, I have! But only with a spectator's lust, I swear," said Charles, who stood on excellent and humorous terms with his wife. "However, little Elizabeth would be a real stunner if she were made over, and do you doubt that Alexander will make her over? I do not."

"She's afraid of him," Constance said positively.

"Well, that's only to be expected, isn't it? There's no sixteen-year-old in this iniquitous city half as sheltered as Elizabeth obviously has been. Which is why he sent for her, I'm sure. He may philander with Ruby and a dozen others, but he's not a man who'd want anything but complete innocence in a wife. It's the Scots Presbyterian in him, protest though he does that he's an atheist. That's a church hasn't budged an inch since John Knox."

* * *

THEY WERE married in the Presbyterian rite at five the following afternoon. Even Mrs. Dewy had no silent criticism to level at Elizabeth's wedding gown, very plain, high to the throat, long-sleeved, ornamented only by tiny covered buttons down its front from collar to waist. Its satin rustled, the calico underpinnings didn't show, and the white slippers emphasized ankles that Charles Dewy judged promised long and shapely legs.

The bride was composed, the groom imperturbable; they made their vows in firm voices. When they were pronounced man and wife, Alexander lifted Elizabeth's lace veil off her face and kissed her. Though the salutation looked innocuous enough to the Dewys, Alexander felt her shiver, her tiny withdrawal. But the moment passed, and after warm congratulations outside the church from the Dewys, the bridal couple and their two witnesses went their separate ways, for the Dewys were going home to somewhere called Dunleigh while Mr. and Mrs. Kinross walked back to the hotel for dinner.

This time the other diners applauded when they entered, as Elizabeth was still clad in her wedding dress. Red-faced, she kept her eyes on the carpet. Their table bore white flowers, chrysanthemums mixed with feathery white daisies; sitting down, she admired them for something to say, something to alleviate her embarrassment.

"Autumn flowers," Alexander told her. "The seasons are reversed here. Come, have a glass of champagne. You will have to learn to like wine. No matter what you might have been taught at the kirk, even Jesus Christ and his women drank wine."

The plain gold wedding band seemed to burn, but not as much as the other ring on that same finger, a diamond solitaire the size of a farthing. When Alexander had given it to her during lunch, she hadn't known where to look; the last place she wanted to look was into the little box he held out.

"Don't you care for diamonds?" he had asked.

"Oh, yes, yes!" she managed, flustered. "But is it proper? It's so—so *noticeable.*"

His brow creased into a frown. "A diamond is traditional, and *my* wife's diamond must be fitting for her station," he said, reaching across the table to take her left hand, slide the ring on to its third finger. "I know all this must be very strange for you, Elizabeth, but as my wife you must wear the best, have the best. Always. I can see that Uncle James didn't endow you with more than a small fraction of the money I sent, but I suppose I expected that." He smiled wryly. "Careful with his bawbees, is Uncle James. But those days are over," he went on, turning her hand within both of his. "From today, you'll be Mrs. Kinross."

Perhaps the expression in her eyes gave him pause, for he stopped suddenly, got to his feet with unusual clumsiness. "A cheroot," he said, going to the balcony. "I like to smoke a cheroot after I've eaten."

And that had been the end of the subject; the next time Elizabeth saw him was inside the church.

Now she was his wife, and had somehow to eat a meal she did not want.

"I am not hungry," she whispered.

"Yes, I can imagine that. Hawkins, bring Mrs. Kinross some beef consommé and a light savory soufflé."

The rest of their time in the dining room became locked in a mental cupboard she could never afterward pry open; later she would understand that her confusion, the agitation and alarm within her, were due to the swiftness of events, the crush of so many foreign emotions. It wasn't the prospect of her wedding night that lay at the base of her state of mind, it was the prospect of a lifelong exile with a man she couldn't love.

THE ACT (as Mary phrased it) was to take place in her bed; no sooner was she in her nightgown and the maid had withdrawn than a door on the far side of the room opened, and her husband came in wearing an embroidered silk robe.

"Into bed with you," he said, smiling, then went around all the gas jets, turning them out.

Better, much better! She wouldn't be able to see him, and, not seeing him, might manage the Act without disgracing herself.

He sat sideways on the edge of the bed, turned with one knee under him to gaze down at her; apparently he could see in the dark. But her desperate attack of nerves was abating; he seemed so relaxed, so loose-boned and calm.

"Do you know what must happen?" he asked.

"Yes, Alexander."

"It will hurt at first, but later I hope you'll learn to enjoy it. Is wicked old man Murray still the minister?"

"Yes!" she gasped, horrified at this description of Dr. Murray—as if it were Dr. Murray who was the Devil!

"There's more blame for human misery to be laid at his door than at the doors of a thousand decent, honest heathen Chinee."

Came the rustle of silk, his full weight on the bed, movement in the coverings as he slid beneath them and gathered her into his arms. "We're not here together just to make children, Elizabeth. What we're going to do is sanctified by marriage. It's an act of love—of *love.* Not merely of the flesh, but of the mind and even the soul. There's nothing about it you shouldn't welcome."

When she discovered that he was naked, she kept her hands as much to herself as she could, and when he tried to take the nightgown off her, she resisted. Shrugging, he peeled it up from the hem and ran those rough hands over her legs, her flanks, until the change came that prompted him to mount her and thrust hard. The pain brought tears to her eyes, but she had known worse pangs from Father's stick, falls, bad cuts. And it was over quickly; he behaved exactly as Mary had said he would—shuddered and swallowed audibly, withdrew. But not from her bed. There he remained until the Act happened twice more. He hadn't kissed her, but as he left he brushed her lips with his.

"Goodnight, Elizabeth. It's a fine start."

One comforting thing, she thought drowsily; he hadn't *felt* like the Devil. Sweet of breath and body scent. And if the Act was no more fearsome than this, she knew that she would survive—might even, eventually, enjoy whatever life he intended her to lead in New South Wales.

FOR THE NEXT few days he stayed with her, chose her maid, supervised modistes and milliners, hosiers and shoemakers, bought her lingerie so lovely that her breath caught, and perfume and skin lotions, fans and purses, a parasol for every outfit.

Though she sensed that he thought himself considerate and kind, he made all the decisions—which of the two maids she had liked would get the job, what she would wear from colors to style, the perfume he liked, the jewels he showered on her. "Autocrat" was not a word she knew, so she used the word she did know, "despot." Well, Father and Dr. Murray were despots, for that matter. Though Alexander's imperiousness was subtler, sheathed in the velvet of compliments.

At breakfast on the morning after that surprisingly bearable wedding night, she tried to find out more about him.

"Alexander, all I know about you is that you left Kinross when you were fifteen, that you were an apprentice boilermaker in Glasgow, that Dr. MacGregor thought you very clever, and that you have made a wee fortune on the New South Wales goldfields. There must be far more to know. Please tell me," she said.

His laugh was attractive, sounded genuine. "I might have known that they'd all shut their mouths," he said, eyes dancing. "For instance, I'll bet they never told you that I knocked down old man Murray, did they?"

"No!"

"Oh, yes. Broke his jaw. I've rarely felt such pleasure. He'd just taken over the manse from Robert MacGregor, who was an educated, cultured and civilized man. You might say I left Kinross because clearly I couldn't stay in a town of Philistines led by the likes of John Murray."

"Especially if you broke Dr. Murray's jaw," she said, feeling a secret, guilty satisfaction. Most definitely she couldn't agree with Alexander's opinion of Dr. Murray, but she was beginning to remember how many times he had made her miserable, or shamed her.

"And that's really the sum of it," he said, lifting his shoulders. "I spent some time in Glasgow, took ship for America, went from California to Sydney, and made somewhat more than a wee fortune on the goldfields."

"Will we live in Sydney?"

"Not in a fit, Elizabeth. I have my own town, Kinross, and you'll live in the new house I've built for you high on Mount Kinross and out of sight of the Apocalypse—my mine."

"Apocalypse? What does it mean?"

"It's a Greek word for a frightful and violent event like the end of the world. What better name is there for something as freeing and earth-shaking as a gold mine?"

"Is your town far from Sydney?"

"Not as distances go in Australia, but far enough. The railroad—railway, I mean—will take us within a hundred miles of Kinross. From there we will travel by carriage."

"Is Kinross big enough to have a kirk?"

His chin went up, making the beard look more pointed. "It has a Church of England, Elizabeth. I'll have no Presbyterian parsons in *my* town. Far sooner the Papists or the Anabaptists."

A suddenly dry mouth made her gulp. "Why do you wear those strange clothes?" she asked to divert him from this sore subject.

"They've become an idiosyncrasy. When I wear them, everyone deems me an American—thousands of Americans have come here since gold was discovered. But the real reason I wear them is that they're soft, supple and comfortable. They don't chafe and they wash like rags because they're chamois skin. They're also cool. Though they look American, I had them made in Persia."

"You've been there too?"

"I've been everywhere that my famous namesake went, as well as places he didn't dream existed."

"Your famous namesake? Who is that?"

"Alexander . . . the Great," he added when her face remained blank. "King of Macedonia and just about the whole known world at the time. Over two thousand years ago." Something occurred to him, he leaned forward. "You *are* literate and numerate, I hope, Elizabeth? You can sign your name, but is that the size of it?"

"I can read very well," she said stiffly, offended, "though I have lacked history books. I did learn to write, but I haven't been able to practice—Father kept no paper."

"I'll buy you a copy-book, a book of example letters that you can use until your thoughts go down on paper easily—and reams of the best paper. Pens, inks—paints and sketchbooks if you want them. Most ladies seem to dabble in watercolors."

"I have not been brought up as a lady," she said with as much dignity as she could muster.

His eyes were dancing again. "Do you embroider?"

"I *sew,* but I do not embroider."

And how, she wondered later in the morning, did he manage to deflect the conversation from himself so neatly?

"I THINK I may be able to end in liking my husband," she confided to Mrs. Augusta Halliday toward the end of her second week in Sydney, "but I very much doubt that I will ever love him."

"It's early days yet," said Mrs. Halliday comfortably, her shrewd eyes resting on Elizabeth's face. There were big changes in it: gone was the child. The masses of dark hair were piled up fashionably, her afternoon dress of rust-red silk had the obligatory bustle, her gloves were finest kid, her hat a dream. Whoever had wrought the image had been wise enough to leave the face alone; here was one young woman who needed no cosmetic aids, and Sydney's sun didn't seem to have the power to give her quite extraordinary white skin a glaze of pink or beige. She wore magnificent pearls around her neck and pearl drops in her ears, and when she drew the glove off her left hand Mrs. Halliday's eyes widened.

"Ye gods!" she exclaimed.

"Oh, this wretched diamond," said Elizabeth with a sigh. "I really detest it. Do you know that I have to have my gloves specially made to go over it? And Alexander insisted that the same finger on the right-hand glove be similarly made, so I very much fear that he intends to give me some other huge stone."

"You must be a saint," said Mrs. Halliday dryly. "I don't know of any other woman who wouldn't be swooning over a gem half as splendid as your diamond."

"I love my pearls, Mrs. Halliday."

"So I should think! Queen Victoria's aren't any better."

But after Elizabeth had departed in the high-sprung chaise drawn by four matched horses, Augusta Halliday succumbed to a little weep. Poor girl! A fish out of water. Loaded down with every luxury, thrust into a world of wealth and prominence, when by nature she was neither avaricious nor ambitious. Had she remained in her Scottish ken she would no doubt have continued to look after her father, then turned into a maiden aunt. And yet been comfortable with her lot, if not idyllically happy. Well, at least she thought she could like Alexander Kinross, and that was something. Privately Mrs. Halliday agreed with Elizabeth; she couldn't see Elizabeth coming to love her husband either. The distance between them was too vast, their characters too much at odds. Hard to believe that they were first cousins.

Of course by the time that Elizabeth came to visit in her chaise-and-four, Mrs. Halliday had found out a great deal about Alexander Kinross. Quite the richest man in the colony, for unlike most who found paydirt on the goldfields, he had hung on to every grain he dredged from the alluvium, and then sniffed out the reef. He had the Government in one pocket and the Judiciary in the other, so while some men might suffer shockingly from claim-jumpers, Alexander Kinross was able to deal with them and other nuisances summarily. But though he went into society if he was in Sydney, he wasn't a society man. Those worth knowing he tended to beard in their offices, rather than wine and dine them; sometimes he accepted an invitation to Government House or to Clovelly at Watson's Bay, but never to a ball or soirée held just for enjoyment. Therefore the general consensus was that he cared about power, not about people's good opinion.

CHARLES DEWY, Elizabeth discovered, was a minor partner in the Apocalypse Mine.

"He's the local squatter—used to run two hundred square miles until the gold arrived," said Alexander.

"Squatter?"

"So called because he 'squatted' on Crown Land until—as possession does indeed tend to be nine-tenths of the Law—he virtually owned it. But an Act of Parliament changed things. I softened his attitude by offering him a share in the Apocalypse, and thereafter I can do no wrong."

They were leaving Sydney at last, no grief to Mrs. Kinross, who now owned two dozen large trunks, but no personal maid. Having, it appeared, made a few enquiries about the town of Kinross and its location, Miss Thomas had quit that morning. Her desertion did not distress Elizabeth, who genuinely preferred to look after herself.

"Never mind" was Alexander's response to the news. "I'll ask Ruby to find you a good Chinese girl. And don't start saying you would rather not have an abigail! After two weeks of having your hair dressed, you ought to know that you need a pair of hands to do it that are not attached to your own arms."

"Ruby? Is she your housekeeper?" Elizabeth asked, aware that she was going to a house staffed with servants.

That made Alexander laugh until the tears ran down his face. "Ah—no," he said when he was able. "Ruby is, for want of any better words, an institution. To refer to her in a less grand way would be to demean her. Ruby is a master of the acid remark and the caustic comment. She's Cleopatra—but she's also Aspasia, Medusa, Josephine and Catherine di Médicis."

Oh! But Elizabeth had no opportunity to pursue this avenue of conversation because they had reached Redfern railway station, a bleak area of sheds and braided iron tracks.

"The platforms here are rather derelict because they're always talking of erecting a palatial terminus at the top of George Street—but that's all it is, talk," said Alexander as he helped her down from the chaise.

The aftermath of seasickness had rendered her incapable of curiosity when she boarded the London train in Edinburgh, but today she gazed at the Bowenfels train in awe and amazement. A steam-wreathed engine mounted on a combination of small wheels and huge ones, the latter joined together by rods, stood panting like a gigantic and angry dog, wispy smoke curling from its tall chimney. This infernal machine was linked to an iron tender full of coal, behind which were eight carriages—six second-class and two first-class—with a caboose (Alexander's word) on the back to hold the bulky luggage, freight, and the conductor.

"I know the back of the train moves about more than the front, but I'm compelled to lean out the window and watch the locomotive working," said Alexander, ushering her into what looked like a plushly comfortable parlor. "For that reason, they couple one first-class car behind all the other cars. This is really the Governor's private compartment, but he's happy to let me use it whenever he doesn't need it—*I* pay for it."

At seven o'clock on the dot the Bowenfels train pulled out of the yard, with Elizabeth glued to a window. Yes, Sydney was big; it was fifteen minutes before the houses became scattered, fifteen minutes of rattling along, clickety-click, at a breathtaking pace. An occasional platform flashed past after that to mark some small town—Strathfield, Rose Hill, Parramatta.

"How fast are we going?" she asked, liking the sensation of speed, the swaying motion.

"Fifty miles an hour, though she's capable of sixty if they really stoke the boiler. This is the weekly through-passenger train—it doesn't stop before Bowenfels—and it's a lightweight affair compared to a goods train. But our speed slows down to eighteen or twenty miles an hour once we begin to climb, in some places less than that, so our journey takes nine hours."

"What does a goods train carry?"

"Down to Sydney, wheat and produce, kerosene from the shale works at Hartley. Up to Bowenfels, building materials, stock for country shops, mining equipment, furniture, newspapers, books, magazines. Prize breeding cattle, horses and sheep. Even men going west to prospect or find work on the land—the fare is uncollectable. But never," he said emphatically, "dynamite."

"Dynamite?"

His eyes went from her animated face to several dozen big wooden cases stacked from floor to ceiling in one corner, each one marked with the skull-and-crossbones.

"Dynamite," he said, "is the new way to blast rock apart. It never leaves my custody because it's so scarce that it's nigh as precious as gold. I had this lot shipped from Sweden through London—it was with you on *Aurora.* Blasting," he went on, voice growing more excited, "used to be a risky and unpredictable sort of business. It was done with black powder—gunpowder to you. Very hard to know how black powder would fracture the rock, what direction the explosive force would take. I know, I've been a powder monkey in a dozen different places. But recently a Swede had a brilliant idea that tamed nitroglycerin, which of itself is so unstable that it's likely to explode if it's jarred. The Swede mixed nitroglycerin with a base of a clay called kieselguhr, then packed them in a paper cartridge shaped like a blunt candle. It can't go off until it's detonated by a cap of fulminate of mercury tightly crimped on the end of the stick. The powder monkey attaches a length of burnable fuse to the detonator and produces a safer, far better controlled blast. Though if you have a dynamo, you can trigger the blast by passing an electric current down a long wire. I shall be doing that soon."

Her expression provoked a laugh; she was amusing him a lot this morning. "Did you understand a word of that, Elizabeth?"

"Several," she said, and smiled at him.

His breath caught audibly. "That's the first smile you've ever given me," he said.

She found herself blushing, looked out the window.

"I'm going to stand on the plate with the engineers," he said abruptly, opened the forward door and disappeared.

The train had crossed a wide river on a bridge before he came back; ahead of it now lay a barrier of tall hills.

"That was the Nepean River," he said, "so it's time to open a window. Our train has to climb a gradient so steep that it has to zigzag back and forth. Within the length of much less than a straight mile, we will ascend a thousand feet, rising one foot for every thirty feet traveled."

Even at their much reduced speed, opening a window was ruinous to one's clothes; big particles of soot flew in and landed everywhere. But it was fascinating, especially when the track curved and she could see the locomotive laboring, black smoke pouring out of its chimney in huge billows, the rods attached to its big wheels driving them around. Occasionally the wheels would slip on the rails, losing traction in a flurry of staccato puffs, and at the end of the first zigzag the train went up the next slope backward, the caboose leading and the locomotive bringing up the rear.

"The number of reversals has the locomotive leading again at the top," he explained. "The zigzag is a very clever idea that finally enabled the Government to build a railroad over the Blue Mountains, which aren't mountains at all. We're ascending what is called a dissected plateau. On the far side we descend on another zigzag. If these were real mountains we could travel in the valleys and go through the watershed in a tunnel—a far easier exercise that would have opened up the fertile growing country in the west decades ago. New South Wales yields nothing easily, nor do the other colonies of Australia. So when the Blue Mountains were finally conquered, the men who worked out how to do it had to abandon all their European-based theories."

So, she was thinking, I have found one of the keys to my husband's mind—and to his spirit, if not to his soul. He is enthralled by mechanical things, by engines and inventions, and no matter how uninformed his audience, he will talk and teach.

The scenery was spectacularly outlandish. The heights fell away many hundreds of feet in dramatic precipices to mighty valleys stuffed with dense grey-green forests that became blue with distance. Of pine, beech, oak and all the familiar trees of home there were none, but these alien trees had their own beauty. It is grander than home, she thought, if only because it is so limitless. Of habitation she saw no sign apart from a few tiny villages along the train line, usually associated with an inn or a mansion.

"Only the natives can live down there," said Alexander when a big clearing gave them a particularly wonderful view of a vast canyon ringed with perpendicular orange cliffs. "Soon we'll pass a siding called The Crushers—it's a series of rock quarries—and on the valley floor beyond there is a rich coal seam. They're talking of mining it, but I think the cost of bringing it a thousand feet straight up will be prohibitive. Though it will be cheaper to ship to Sydney than the Lithgow coal—hauling that up the Clarence zigzag is very difficult."

Suddenly his hand swept in a grand gesture, encompassing the world. "Elizabeth, *look*! What you see is the geology of the earth in all its glory. The cliffs are early Triassic sandstone laid atop Permian coal measures, under which lie the granites, shales and limestones of Devonian and Silurian times. The very tops of some of the mountains to the north are a thin layer of basalt poured out of some massive volcano—the Tertiary icing on the Triassic cake, now all but eroded away. Marvelous!"

Oh, to be that enthusiastic about anything! How could *I* lead a life that would enable me to know the tiniest fraction of what he knows? I was born to be an ignoramus, she told herself.

AT FOUR IN the afternoon the train arrived at Bowenfels; this was as far west as the train went, though the chief town was Bathurst, forty-five miles farther on. After an urgently needed visit to the lavatory on the platform, Elizabeth was bundled into a carriage by an impatient Alexander.

"I want to be in Bathurst tonight," he explained.

At eight they reached the hotel in Bathurst, Elizabeth reeling with fatigue; but at dawn the next morning Alexander was bundling her back into the carriage, insisting that the convoy start moving. Oh, another day of perpetual travel! Her carriage led the way, Alexander rode a mare, and six wagons drawn by draft horses carried her trunks, cargo from the Rydal rail depot, and those precious cases of dynamite. The convoy, said Alexander, was to deter the attentions of bushrangers.

"Bushrangers?" she had to ask.

"Highwaymen. There aren't many left because they've been hunted down remorselessly. This used to be Ben Hall country—he was a very famous bushranger. Dead now, like most of them."

The cliffs had been replaced by more traditionally shaped mountains not unlike those in Scotland, for many were cleared of trees; here, however, no heather grew to lend the autumn some color, and what grass grew was lank, tufted, brownish-silver. The deeply rutted, potholed track wound aimlessly to avoid big boulders, creek beds, sudden plunges into gullies. Perpetually jerked and tossed, Elizabeth prayed that Kinross, wherever it was, would soon appear.

But it did not until nearly sundown, when the track emerged from a forest into open space and became a macadamized road lined with shacks and tents. If all that had gone before was utterly strange, it paled compared to Kinross, which her imagination had visualized as Kinross, Scotland. Oh, it was not! The shacks and tents turned into more substantial wooden or wattle-and-daub houses roofed with a rippled iron or sheets of what looked like tree bark strapped and sewn down. Habitation straggled down either side of the street, but a few side lanes revealed wooden towers, struts, sheds, a bizarre landscape whose purpose she could not guess at. It was ugly, ugly, ugly!

The houses became commercial buildings and shops, all sporting awnings held up by wooden posts; no one awning looked like its neighbors, nor was joined to them, nor had been erected with any attention to symmetry, order or beauty. The signs were roughly hand-painted and announced that here was a laundry, a boarding house, a restaurant, a bar, a tobacconist, cobbler, barber, general store, doctor's rooms, an ironmongery.

There were two red-brick buildings, one a church complete to spire, the other a two-storied block with its upper verandah lavishly adorned by the same cast-iron lace Elizabeth had noticed all over Sydney; its awning was of curved rippled iron, had iron posts holding it up, and yet more lavish application of cast-iron lace. An elegantly lettered sign said KINROSS HOTEL.

Not a single tree stood anywhere, so even the foundering sun beat down like a hammer and turned the hair of a woman standing outside the hotel to pure fire. Her attention riveted by the martial posture, the sturdy air of invincibility the woman exuded, Elizabeth craned her neck to watch her for as long as she could. A striking figure. Like Britannia on the coins or Boadicea in illustrations. She gave what seemed a mocking salute to Alexander, riding beside the carriage, then swung to stare in the opposite direction from the convoy. Only then did Elizabeth notice that she held a cheroot, her nostrils trickling smoke like a dragon's.

There were plenty of people around, the men shabbily clad in dungarees and flannel shirts, with soft, wide-brimmed hats on their heads, the women in much laundered cotton dresses thirty years behind the times, shady straw hats on their heads. And many were unmistakably Chinese: long pigtails down their backs, quaint little black-and-white shoes, hats like conical cartwheels, women and men in identical black or dark blue trousers and jackets.

The convoy passed into a wilderness of machinery, smoking chimneys, corrugated iron sheds and high wooden derricks, then came to a halt at the bottom of a sloping cliff that ascended at least a thousand feet. Here railway tracks actually ran upward until they disappeared from sight among welcome trees.

"Journey's end, Elizabeth," said Alexander, lifting her out of the carriage. "Summers will let the car down in a moment."

And down the tracks it steadily came, a wooden conveyance not unlike an open omnibus on train wheels, for it had four rows of plain plank seats-for-six as well as a long, highly fenced tray for freight. But these seats were built at an impossible angle, so that sitting in one tilted the passenger far backward. Having closed the end of their seat with a bar, Alexander slid down beside Elizabeth and put both her hands firmly on a railing.

"Hang on and don't be afraid," he said. "You won't fall out, I promise."

The air resonated with sounds: the chug of engines, a quite maddening constant, thumping roar, metallic screeches, the slap-slap of rotating belts, crunches and grinds and howls. From high above came a separate noise, one lone steam engine. The wooden car began to move over the level ground to where the rails curved up, gave a lurch, and started to ascend the incredibly steep slope. Magically Elizabeth went from almost lying down to sitting upright; her heart in her mouth, she gazed down as the town of Kinross spread before her, widening in scope until the fading light turned its unlovely outskirts to impenetrable shadow.

"I didn't want my wife down there," he said, "which is why I built my house on top of the mountain. Apart from a snake path, this car is the only way up or down. Turn your head and look up—see? It's being pulled by a heavy wire cable that's wound or unwound by an engine."

"Why," she managed, "is the car so big?"

"The miners use it too. Apocalypse's poppet heads—those derricks holding winches—are on that wide shelf we just passed. Easier for the men than going in through the tunnel at the bottom because of giant ore skips and the close proximity of locomotives outside. Cages let them down into the main gallery and bring them up again at the end of the shift."

A coolness descended as they passed into the trees, as much, she divined, from altitude as from the sheltering boughs.

"Kinross House is over three thousand feet above sea level," he said with that eerie habit he had of reading her mind. "In summer, comfortably cool. In winter, much warmer."

THE CAR RAN on to flat ground at last, tilting them, and came to a halt. Elizabeth scrambled out before Alexander could help her, marveling at how quickly night fell in New South Wales. No long Scottish gloaming, no witching hour of soft radiance.

Hedge screened the car siding; as she came around it she stopped dead. Her husband had built a veritable mansion in this remoteness, of what looked like limestone blocks. Of three full stories, it had big Georgian-paned windows, a pillared porch at the top of a sweeping flight of steps, and an air of having stood there for five hundred years. At the foot of the steps was a lawned terrace; a great effort had been made to create an English garden, from trimmed box hedges to rose beds and even a Grecian temple folly.

The door was open, light streamed from every window.

"Welcome home, Elizabeth." Alexander Kinross took her hand and led her up the steps and inside.

Everything of the best, brought here at what her Scottish canniness said was astronomical cost. The carpets, furniture, chandeliers, ornaments, paintings, drapes. *Everything,* including, for all she knew, the house itself. Only the faint reek of kerosene gave the lie to its being situated in a gas-lit city.

It turned out that the ubiquitous Summers was Alexander's chief factotum, while his wife was housekeeper; an arrangement that seemed to give Alexander a peculiar pleasure.

"Begging your pardon, Marm, would you like to refresh yourself after your trip?" asked Mrs. Summers, and led Elizabeth to a properly functioning water closet.

Never had she been more grateful for anything than for that invitation; like all carefully brought-up women of her era, she sometimes had to go for hours upon hours without any opportunity to empty her bladder, thus dared not drink so much as one sip of water before leaving on an expedition, no matter of what kind. Thirst led to dehydration, concentrated urine to bladder and kidney stones; dropsy was a great killer of women.

After several cups of tea, some sandwiches and a piece of delicious seed cake, Elizabeth went to bed so tired that she remembered nothing beyond the foot of the staircase.

"IF YOU DON'T like your quarters, Elizabeth, please tell me what you'd prefer," said Alexander over breakfast, taken in the loveliest room Elizabeth had ever seen; its walls and roof were of glass panes joined together by a delicate tracery of white-painted iron, and it contained a jungle of palms and ferns.

"I like them very much, but not as much as this."

"This is a conservatory—so named because in cold climates it conserves frost-vulnerable plants from death during winter."

He was dressed in his skins, as Elizabeth had privately christened them, his hat dumped on a spare chair.

"Are you going out?"

"I'm home, so from now on you'll not see much of me until the evening. Mrs. Summers will take you over the house, and you must tell me what you don't like about it. It's your house far more than it's mine—you're the one will do most of the living in it. I don't suppose you play the piano?"

"No. We couldn't afford a piano."

"Then I'll have you taught. Music is one of my passions, so you'll have to learn to play well. Do you sing?"

"I can carry a tune."

"Well, until I can find you a teacher of piano, you'll just have to pass your time in reading books and practicing your penmanship." He leaned to kiss her lightly, clapped his hat on his head and vanished, hollering for his shadow, Summers.

Mrs. Summers appeared to conduct "Marm" over the house, which held few surprises until they reached the library; every room was sumptuous in the style of the Sydney hotel, even echoing the form of its main staircase, a splendid affair. The large drawing room held a harp as well as a full-sized grand piano.

"Brought the tuner all the way from Sydney once the piano was put in the right place—a fair nuisance it is too, what with not being allowed to move it a hair to clean under its legs," said Mrs. Summers, disgruntled.

The library was definitely Alexander's lair, for it didn't have the contrived look the other rooms displayed. Where its vastness wasn't dark oak bookshelves and dark green leather easy chairs there was Murray tartan—wallpaper, drapes, carpet. But why Murray? Why not his own tartan, Drummond? Drummond was a rich red checkered with multiple green and dark blue lines—a very striking pattern. Whereas Murray had a base of dull green more distantly divided into checks by thin red and dark blue lines. It hadn't escaped her that her husband's taste ran to splendor, so why this muted Murray?

"Fifteen thousand books," said Mrs. Summers, voice awed. "Mr. Kinross has books on everything." She sniffed. "Except he ain't got a Bible. Says it's rubbish. A godless man—godless! But Mr. Summers has been with him since some ship or other they was both aboard, wouldn't hear of leaving. And I expect I'll get used to being a housekeeper. House ain't been finished more'n two months. Until then I just kept house for Mr. Summers."

"Have you and Mr. Summers any children?" Elizabeth asked.

"No," said Mrs. Summers shortly. She straightened, smoothed her spotless starched white apron. "I hope, Marm, that youse'll find me satisfactory."

"I'm sure I will," Elizabeth said warmly, and produced her widest smile. "If you kept house for Mr. Summers, where did Mr. Kinross live before this house was built?"

Mrs. Summers blinked, looked shifty. "At the Kinross Hotel, Marm. A very comfortable establishment."

"Does he own the Kinross Hotel, then?"

"No" was Mrs. Summers's answer; no matter how hard Elizabeth probed, she refused to be more forthcoming on the subject.

The other servants, the mistress of Kinross House discovered as the tour progressed to kitchen, pantry, wine cellar and laundry, were all Chinese men. Who nodded, smiled, bowed as she passed.

"Men?" she squeaked, horrified. "You mean that *men* will clean my rooms, wash and iron my clothes? Then I shall deal with my underthings myself, Mrs. Summers."

"No need to make mountains out of molehills, Marm," said Mrs. Summers, unperturbed. "Them heathen Chinee been washing for a living long as I know of. Mr. Kinross says they wash so well on account of they're used to washing silk. It don't matter that they're men—they ain't *white* men. Just heathen Chinee."

ELIZABETH'S PERSONAL MAID arrived just after lunch, a female heathen Chinee who to Elizabeth's eyes was ravishingly beautiful. Frail and willowy, a mouth like a folded flower. Though Elizabeth had never seen Chinese before today, something about the girl said that there was European in her ancestry as well as Chinese. Her eyes were almond shaped, but were widely opened and possessed visible lids. She wore black silk trousers and jacket, and did her thick, straight black hair in the traditional pigtail.

"I am very pleased to be here, Marm. My name is Jade," she said, standing with her hands clasped together and smiling shyly.

"You've no accent," said Elizabeth, who in the past months had heard many different accents without realizing that her own Scots accent was so thick that some of her auditors didn't understand what she said. Jade spoke like a colonial—a trace of East London Cockney intermixed with North of England, Irish, and something more distinctively local than any of those.

"My father came from China twenty-three years ago and took up with my mother, who was Irish. I was born on the Ballarat goldfields, Marm. We've been following the gold ever since, but once Papa fell in with Miss Ruby, our wandering days were over. My mother ran away with a Victorian trooper when Peony was born. Papa says that blood calls to blood. I think she was tired of having girl children. There are seven of us."

Elizabeth tried to find something comforting to say. "I won't be a hard mistress, Jade, I promise."

"Oh, be as hard as you like, Miss Lizzy," said Jade cheerily. "I was Miss Ruby's maid, and no one's as hard as her."

So the Ruby person was a hard woman. "Who's her maid now?"

"My sister, Pearl. And if Miss Ruby gets fed up with her, there's Jasmine, Peony, Silken Flower and Peach Blossom."

Some enquiries made of Mrs. Summers revealed that Jade was to occupy a shed in the backyard.

"That isn't good enough," said Elizabeth firmly, surprised at her own temerity. "Jade is a beautiful young woman and must be protected. She can move into the governess's quarters until such time as I need a governess's services. Do the Chinese men live in sheds in the backyard?"

"They live in town," said Mrs. Summers stiffly.

"Do they ride up from town in the car?"

"I should think not, Marm! They walk the snake path."

"Does Mr. Kinross know how you run things, Mrs. Summers?"

"It ain't none of his business—*I'm* the housekeeper! They are heathen Chinee, they take jobs away from white men!"

Elizabeth sneered. "I have never known a white man, however poor and indigent he may be, willing to soil his hands on other people's dirty clothes to earn a living. Your accent is colonial, so I presume you were born and brought up in New South Wales, but I warn you, Mrs. Summers, that I will have no prejudicial treatment of people of other races in this house."

"SHE REPORTED me to Mr. Kinross," said Mrs. Summers angrily to her husband, "and he got the pip something horrible with me! So Jade gets to live in the governess's rooms and the Chinee men get to ride the car! Disgraceful!"

"Sometimes, Maggie, you're a stupid woman," Summers said.

Mrs. Summers sniffed. "You're all a pack of unbelievers, and Mr. Kinross is the worst! Consorting with that woman, and marrying a girl young enough to be his daughter!"

"Shut your mouth, woman!" Summers snapped.

AT FIRST IT was difficult for Elizabeth to fill in time; in the wake of that exchange with Mrs. Summers, she found herself disliking the woman so much that she avoided her.

The library, for all its fifteen thousand volumes, was not much of a solace; it was overloaded with texts on subjects that did not interest her, from geology and engineering to gold, silver, iron, steel. There were shelves of various committee reports bound in leather, more shelves of New South Wales laws bound in leather, and yet more shelves filled with something that rejoiced in the title of *Halsbury's Laws of England.* No novels of any kind. All the works on Alexander the Great, Julius Caesar and the other famous men he mentioned from time to time were in Greek, Latin, Italian or French—how educated Alexander must be! But she found a simple retelling of some myths, Gibbon's *Decline and Fall of the Roman Empire,* and the complete works of Shakespeare. The myths were a delight, the others hard going.

Alexander had instructed her not to attend service at St. Andrew's (the red-brick Church of England with the spire) until she had been in residence some little while, and seemed to think that Kinross town contained no inhabitants with whom she would care to associate. A suspicion began to grow in her that he intended to isolate her from ordinary folk, that she was doomed to dwell on the mountain in solitude. As if she were a secret.

But as he didn't forbid her to walk, Elizabeth walked, at first confining herself to the beautiful grounds, then venturing farther afield. She found the snake path and negotiated it down to the shelf where the poppet heads of the mine reared, but could find no vantage point from which she could watch the activity unobserved. After that she began to penetrate the mysteries of the forest, there to find an enchanting world of lacy ferns, mossy dells, huge trees with trunks of vermilion, pink, cream, blue-white, every shade of brown. Exquisite birds flew in flocks, parrots in all the colors of the rainbow, an elusive bird that chimed like fairy bells, other birds that sang more melodically than a nightingale. Breath suspended, she saw little kangaroos leaping from rock to rock—a picture book come to life.

Finally she went far enough to hear the sound of roaring water, and came upon a clear, strong stream that tumbled in lacy leaps down a monstrous slope, down to the wood and iron jungle of Kinross below. The change was dramatic, horrific; what atop the falls was paradise was transformed at the mountain's foot into an ugly shambles of slag heaps, detritus, holes, mounds, trenches. And the river down there was filthy.

"You've found the cascades," said Alexander's voice.

She gasped, whirled around. "You startled me!"

"Not as much as a snake would have. Be careful, Elizabeth. There are snakes everywhere, some capable of killing you."

"Yes, I know there are. Jade warned me and showed me how to frighten them away—you stamp very hard on the ground."

"Provided you see them in time." He came to stand beside her. "Down there is the evidence of what men will do to lay their hands on gold," he said. "Those are the original workings. They haven't yielded placer in two years. And yes, I'm personally responsible for a great deal of the mess. I was here for six months before the word leaked out that I'd found paydirt on this wee tributary of the Abercrombie River." He put a hand under her elbow and steered her away. "Come, I want you to meet your teacher of piano. And I'm sorry," he continued as they retraced their steps, "that I didn't think to bring in the kind of books I should have known you'd prefer. A mistake I'm busy rectifying."

"Must I learn the piano?" she asked.

"If you wish to please me, yes. *Do* you wish to please me?"

Do I? she wondered. I hardly see him except in my bed, he doesn't even bother to come home for dinner.

"Of course," she said.

MISS THEODORA JENKINS had one thing in common with Jade; they had both followed the gold from place to place in company with their fathers. Tom Jenkins had died of liver failure due to strong drink when he reached Sofala, a gold town on the Turon River, leaving his plain, timid daughter with no roof over her head nor means of support. At first she had taken employment in a boarding house, waiting on tables, washing dishes and making beds; it gave her that roof over her head and her keep, if not more than sixpence a day in wages. As her leanings were religious, church became her great comfort, the more so after the minister discovered how well she could play the organ. After the Sofala gold failed she moved to Bathurst, where Constance Dewy saw her advertisement in the *Bathurst Free Press* and brought her to Dunleigh, the Dewy homestead, to teach piano to her daughters.

When the last of the Dewy girls went to boarding school in Sydney, Miss Jenkins returned to the drudgery of teaching piano and taking in mending at Bathurst. Then Alexander Kinross had offered her a little house in Kinross plus a decent salary if she would give his wife daily lessons on the piano. Hugely grateful, Miss Jenkins accepted instantly.

She was not yet thirty years old, but she looked forty, the more so because her coloring was nondescript and her skin, after constant exposure to the sun, was seamed with a network of fine lines. Her musical gift she owed to her mother, who had taught her to read music and tried to find a piano for Theodora to play on whichever goldfield they happened to be living.

"Mama died just one day after we arrived in Sofala," said Miss Jenkins, "and Papa followed a year later."

This kind of nomadic existence fascinated Elizabeth, who had never been more than five miles from home until Alexander had sent for her. How hard it was for women! And how pathetically glad Miss Jenkins was for the chance Alexander had offered her!

That night in bed she turned of her own volition into her husband's arms and put her head on his shoulder.

"Thank you," she said very softly, and pressed a kiss on his neck.

"For what?" he asked.

"For being so kind to poor Miss Jenkins. I will learn to play the piano well, I promise. It is the least I can do."

"There's one other thing you can do for me."

"What?"

"Take off your nightgown. Skin should feel skin."

Caught, Elizabeth obliged. The Act had grown too familiar to provoke embarrassment or discomfort, but skin on skin didn't make it more pleasurable for her. For him, however, this night clearly marked a victory.

OH, BUT LEARNING to play the piano was difficult! Though she wasn't entirely without aptitude, Elizabeth didn't come from a musical environment. For her, it meant starting from absolute scratch, even in rudimentary matters like the forms music took, its vocabulary, structure. Days and days of stumbling up and down the scales—would she ever be ready to play a tune?

"Yes, but first your fingers have to become more nimble and your left hand has to get used to making different movements from your right. Your ears have to distinguish the exact sound of every note," said Theodora. "Now once again, dear Elizabeth. You are improving, truly."

They had passed from formality to calling each other by their first names within a week, and had established a routine that did much to alleviate Elizabeth's loneliness. Theodora came up on the car at ten o'clock each weekday morning; they did the theory of music until lunch, which they ate in the conservatory, then transferred to the piano for those interminable scales. At three Theodora took the car down to Kinross again. Sometimes they walked in the garden, and once took the snake path until Theodora could point out her little house to Elizabeth; she was entranced with it, so proud of it.

But she didn't invite Elizabeth to visit it, and Elizabeth knew better than to ask. Alexander had been firm on that point; his wife was not to visit Kinross for any reason whatsoever.

WHEN ELIZABETH missed her second lot of courses, she knew that she had conceived. But what she didn't know was how to tell Alexander. The trouble was that she still didn't really *know* him, nor was he the kind of person she thought she might want to know. Rationalize her fears though she did, he still loomed in her mind as a rather remote figure of authority, immensely busy—she didn't even know what to talk to him about! So how could she give him this news, which filled her with secret joy that had nothing to do with the Act or with Alexander? No matter which way she turned it over in her mind, she couldn't find the words.

Two months after she arrived in Kinross House, she played *Für Elise* for him; for once he had come home to dinner. Her performance delighted him, as she had wisely waited until her fingers could negotiate the keyboard without a mistake.

"Wonderful!" he cried, plucked her off the stool and sat down in an easy chair with her on his lap. First he chewed his lips, then cleared his throat. "I have a question to ask."

"Yes?" she said, expecting a query about the piano lessons.

"It's two and a half months since we married, but you've had no monthly courses. Are you with child, my dear?"

Her hands clutched at him, she gasped. "Oh! Oh! Yes, I am with child, Alexander, but I haven't known how to tell you."

He kissed her gently. "Elizabeth, I love you."

Had the interlude continued with Elizabeth cuddled on his lap and tenderness flowing in him—had he only confined what he said to the delight of a coming baby and the sweet fact that this girl, still half a child herself, was ripe for closer intimacies—who knows what might have happened to Elizabeth and Alexander?

But suddenly he jerked her to her feet and stood before her with grim face and angry eyes that she took as evidence that she had in some way displeased him. Elizabeth began to shiver, to shrink away from his hands, which were squeezing hers convulsively.

"Since you are to bear my child, it's time that I told you about myself," he said in a hard voice. "I am not a Drummond—no, be still, be *quiet!* Let me talk! I am not your first cousin, Elizabeth, just a distant cousin on the Murray side. My mother was a Murray, but I have no idea who my father was. Duncan Drummond knew my mother had been seeing some other man for the simplest of reasons—she had refused to sleep in his bed for over a year, yet grew heavy with a child he knew he hadn't generated. When he taxed her, she wouldn't say who the man was—only that she had fallen in love and couldn't bring herself to be intimate with Duncan, whom she had never loved. She died giving birth to me, and carried her secret to her grave. Duncan was too proud to say that I was not his son."

She listened torn between relief that he wasn't angry at her and horror at the story he told, but most of her was wondering why he had destroyed her lovely moment of feeling enfolded and enfolding. Someone older, more mature, might have asked why this news couldn't have waited for another day, but all Elizabeth knew was that the devil in him was stronger than the lover. *Her* baby was less important than his secret illegitimacy.

But she had to say something. "Oh, Alexander! The poor woman! Where was the man, if he let her die like that?"

"I don't know, though I've asked that question of myself many times," he said, voice harder still. "All I can think is that he cared more for his own skin than for my mother or me."

"Perhaps he was dead," she said, trying to help.

"I don't think so. Anyway," he went on, "I spent my childhood suffering at the hands of a man I thought my father, wondering why I could never please him. From somewhere I had a mulish streak that wouldn't let me cower or beg, no matter how hard or how often Duncan beat me, or what foul thing he put me to do. I simply hated him. *Hated him!*"

And that hate still rules you, Alexander Kinross, she thought. "How did you find out?" she asked, feeling her heart slow a little from its frantic tattoo.

"When Murray arrived to take over the kirk, Duncan found a soul mate. They huddled together from Murray's first day, and the story of my parentage must have been told almost at once. Well, I was used to half living at the manse, studying with Dr. MacGregor—Duncan wouldn't go against his minister—and was naïve enough to assume that Murray would continue. But Murray banished me, said he'd make sure I never went up to university. I saw red, and hit him. Broken jaw and all, he managed to spit out that I was a bastard, that my mother was a common whore, and that he would see me in hell for what I and my mother had done to Duncan."

"A terrible story," she said. "So you ran away, I was told."

"That very night."

"Was your sister kind to you?"

"Winifred? In her way, but she was five years older than I, and married by the time the truth came out. I doubt she knows to this day." He released her hands. "But *you* know, Elizabeth."

"Indeed I do," she said slowly. "Indeed I do. I sensed that there was something wrong from the moment I met you—you didn't act like any Drummond I knew." A smile came, dragged up from some reservoir of strength and independence that she hadn't known she possessed. "In fact, you reminded me of the Devil, with that beard and those eyebrows. I was absolutely terrified of you."

That provoked a laugh, a look of astonishment. "Then the beard comes off at once, though there's not much I can do about the eyebrows. At least there can be no doubt of the identity of this child's father."

"None at all, Alexander. I came to you untouched."

For answer he lifted her right hand and kissed it before he turned and left the room. When she went up to bed he wasn't there, nor did he come that night. Elizabeth lay wide-eyed in the darkness, weeping. The more she found out about her husband, the less she believed she could ever come to love him. His past ruled him, not his future.

Two

IN THE FOOTSTEPS OF ALEXANDER THE GREAT

WHEN ALEXANDER ran away from home on the night of his fifteenth birthday, he took nothing with him except a loaf of bread and a hunk of cheese. The only decent clothes he had were those he wore to the kirk, everything else too torn and ragged to bother packing. Though he wasn't massively built, the life his father had forced on him had endowed him with more than usual strength, so he ran at a lope all through the dark hours without needing to stop to catch his breath. Other Kinross boys had absconded occasionally, but they were always found a mile or two from home; Alexander fancied that in their hearts they weren't committed. Whereas he was absolutely committed, and when he paused at dawn to suck water from a brook, he was already seventeen miles from Kinross. What did that place hold for him if he couldn't leave it to go up to the university in Edinburgh? To spend his life working in the tartan mill was worse than a sentence of death.

It took him a week to reach the outskirts of Glasgow—he couldn't bear to head for Edinburgh—where he hoped to find some sort of employment. He'd chopped firewood or hoed gardens for food as he traveled, but these were activities he could perform in his sleep. What Alexander wanted was a chance to work at something he could learn, something that required intelligence as well as brute strength. And he found it as soon as he reached Glasgow, the third-largest metropolis in the British Isles.

The thing sat inside a yard forcing air into a foundry, its stack smoking, its round girth wreathed in white vapor. A steam engine! There were two steam engines in the Kinross flour mills, but Alexander had never laid eyes on them—nor ever would have, had he stayed in Kinross. Mill territory was divided up among the local families, and Duncan and James Drummond were denizens of the tartan mill, which meant their children were too.

Whereas I, thought Alexander, am going to follow in the footsteps of my namesake, the Great, by striking into completely unknown territory.

EVEN AT FIFTEEN, he had a way with him. Until now it had been directed at no one save the departed Robert MacGregor, but when he sallied into the foundry yard he found a new target—and not the grimy figure shoveling coal into the boiler's flaming, hideously hot maw. A better dressed man was standing by, a rag in one hand, a spanner in the other, but doing nothing.

"Excuse me, sir?" asked Alexander, smiling at the idle one.

"Yes?"

"What do you make here?"

Why, thought the man later, did I not just put my boot up his arse and send him flying on to the road? As it was, he lifted his brows and smiled back. "Boilers and steam engines, laddie. There's no' enough boilers and steam engines, no' enough."

"Thank you," said Alexander, slid past him and walked into the cacophony of the foundry.

In one corner of this inferno was a flight of wooden steps that led upward to a glass-windowed eyrie from which everything going on could easily be seen. The manager's lair. Alexander leaped up the steps four at a time and banged on the door.

"What?" asked the middle-aged man who opened it.

He was clearly the manager, for he wore pressed trousers and a laundered white shirt, its sleeves rolled up, its collar not attached—well, it would wilt in the heat, and who here cared?

"I want to learn how to make boilers,sir. Then, as soon as I can make boilers, I want to learn how to make a steam engine. I can live in a hole and do without a bath, so I don't need much of a wage," said Alexander, producing the smile again.

"A shilling a day—that's a penny an hour—and free salt tablets. What's your name, laddie?"

"Alexander"—he almost said Drummond, but changed his mind in a split second—"Kinross."

"Kinross? Like the town?"

"Aye, like the town."

"We can do with an apprentice, and I'd rather take on one who came asking for a job than have one brought to me by his dad. My name is Mr. Connell, and don't hesitate to ask questions. If you don't know how, don't do it until you've asked. When can you start, laddie?"

"Now," said Alexander, but didn't move. "I have a question, Mr. Connell."

"Aye?"

"What are the free salt tablets for?"

"To swallow. A man working in here sweats gallons. Taking salt means he doesn't get muscle cramps."

NOT ONLY did the new apprentice learn quickly; he also had the happy knack of making the other men like him despite his evident excellence, excellence being a quality that usually tended to irritate other, less clever or willing workers. Perhaps they saw no danger in him, thanks to his making no secret of his desire to move on once he had learned everything to be learned from Lanark Steam. His abode was a corner of the yard adjacent to the steam engine producing compressed air; it was sheltered from the elements by a sheet of iron and warm enough provided he kept the boiler stoked during the night—a favor Mr. Connell deemed worth the accommodation.

In that year of 1858, when Alexander first arrived, Glasgow was an appalling city; it had the highest death rate in Great Britain—and the highest crime rate—because the bulk of its residents were jammed into waterless, sewerless, lightless slums that formed a tortuous maze no policeman or official would dare enter. The city fathers talked of mass demolition, but, as in most places, talk was never allied to action; it was just a way to appease the ever-growing number of well-to-do people who were developing a social conscience. The iron and coal industries were of paramount importance because of Glasgow's proximity to both these raw materials, which meant that a suffocating pall of noxious smoke blanketed the entire city, made worse by the fumes of a thriving chemical industry that specialized in substances calculated to corrode the stoutest lungs.

Not a place wherein Alexander wanted to linger, yet he knew he must remain there long enough to earn his ticket and a good reference, a written testament that he was thoroughly conversant with boilers and steam engines.

Once he had graduated from the foundry floor and was put on constructing the engines themselves, his busy brain saw many ways to improve the product. Of course he was well aware that, as an apprentice, his ideas were the property of Mr. Connell, who took out the patents on his series of inventions. Strictly speaking, that meant that Mr. Connell was not obliged to give Alexander even a tiny share of the profits, but he was a fair man for his times; every so often he would slip this wonderfully gifted lad ten gold sovereigns by way of thanks. He also hoped that when Alexander was out of his apprenticeship, he could be persuaded to stay; those inventions had pushed Lanark Steam well ahead of its competitors. Further to this, Alexander's wages went from a shilling per twelve-hour day to five shillings in his second year and a pound in his third. Mr. Connell *needed* him.

But Alexander had no intention of staying. Almost everything he earned went into his secret cache behind what looked like all the other bricks in the yard wall. He didn't trust banks, especially the Glaswegian ones. Eighteen fifty-seven had seen the collapse of the Western Bank, with terrible consequences to industry, commerce and the savings of ordinary people.

He still lived in his corner, bought secondhand clothes, and once a month caught a Caledonian train into the countryside to wash his clothes and himself in a quiet glen stream. Food represented his greatest expense; he was growing so fast that his belly growled perpetually from hunger. Sex hadn't entered his life because he was too permanently tired to seek it.

Came the day when he received his piece of paper from Mr. Connell, who pleaded in vain that he stay. The paper said that he had served a three-year apprenticeship with satisfactory results; that he could weld, braze, operate a steam hammer and a rolling mill, bend pipes and sheet iron, and, if put to it, construct a steam engine from its component parts; that he understood the principles, theories and mechanics of steam and had a talent for hydraulics.

That his knowledge went far beyond that of anybody else at Lanark Steam, even Mr. Connell, was due to his studying in the Glasgow University library on Sundays; a more fruitful exercise, he was sure, than attending the kirk. To use this library was absolutely forbidden to all save university members, but, nothing daunted, Alexander had filched an accreditation from an undergraduate whose steady drinking prevented his using it.

WITH THE SECRET compartment beneath the false bottom of his tool chest loaded with gold coins, Alexander walked across Cumberland in the direction of Liverpool as if he carried a feather. For those few sweet days he reveled in the superlative beauty and peace of this loveliest of all English counties, then entered Great Britain's second-largest city, quite as filthy as Glasgow, if a trifle healthier.

Not that he intended to remain in Liverpool. Alexander was looking for a ship bound for California and the goldfields, and found the *Quinnipiac* tied up. She was that new sort of ship, a wooden three-masted sailer with a steam engine driving a screw rather than a paddle wheel. Her Connecticut-born captain/owner was pleased to obtain the services of a young man who really did know marine steam engines, as he proved to *Quinnipiac*'s engineer when put through a rigorous examination on site. No Yankee trusted a piece of paper.

Quinnipiac's cargo was mixed—mining equipment like battery stampers and huge cast-iron retorts whose purpose Alexander could not guess at, steam engines, rock crushers—but she also carried brass fittings, Sheffield cutlery, Scotch whisky, curry powder.

"It's the Civil War," the engineer explained. "All the iron and steel in the Union is going into guns and other war matériel, so the Californians have to buy what they need from England."

"Will we be going to New York?" asked Alexander, dying to see that fabulous city of hopes and dreams.

"No, to Philadelphia, but just to take on more coal. We make sail only when we have to—steam's quicker and straighter, no tacking to find a wind, no battling contrary currents."

ONCE *QUINNIPIAC* emerged from the Irish Sea to enter the Atlantic Ocean, Alexander understood why the captain had been so delighted to have a capable second engineer; Old Harry, as he was universally known, succumbed to racking seasickness, staggering about his duties clutching a bucket into which he spewed.

"It'll pass," Old Harry gasped, "but it's a fucken nuisance."

"Go to your bunk, you cantankerous old donkey," Alexander ordered. "I'll manage."

But, having found out that coaxing a mechanical beast under pressure to give of its best in a heaving sea was a full-time job for two men, Alexander was relieved when Old Harry reappeared two days later, apparently over his malady. The big end bearings on the con rods driving the crankshaft had a tendency to run hot due to poor lubricating oil—not Old Harry's fault, but a problem in all the available oils. The boiler had a habit of building up too much pressure, and one of the two stokers, having gotten into the Scotch whisky, almost drank himself to death. Which led to Alexander's first observation about Americans: they were not as class-conscious as the English or the Scots. Though a master engineer, Old Harry cheerfully took his turn shoveling coal into the firebox, and so, after the second stoker mysteriously fell overboard after winning an acrimonious card game, did *Quinnipiac*'s three mates. No English or Scots engineer or ship's officer would ever have demeaned himself by doing manual labor, whereas these practical men preferred to shovel coal than order the crew to do it; the crew were sailors in the true sense of that word, and resented the imminent death of their profession due to some panting, dangerous thing stuck down in the ship's bowels.

They docked on the Delaware twelve days out from Liverpool, but Alexander never got ashore to see Philadelphia. Deputed to supervise the loading of coal, he spent his time watching colliers upend hessian sacks into the coal hold while Old Harry and the senior officers went off to dine on some sort of crab they craved.

Chugging south in better weather and calmer water, the trim ship burned less coal than Old Harry had expected because she had a good wind in the right direction, on the leading edge of her sails, thus augmenting her steam power; she was off Florianópolis in southern Brazil before the boiler had to be shut down.

Much to his surprise, Alexander learned that South America was rich in coal and every kind of mineral wealth. Why do we from Britain, he wondered, think that all the world's industrial assets are limited to Europe and North America?

A paddle steamer took *Quinnipiac* in tow at the mouth of a long, placid inlet on the Uruguayan border called Lagoa dos Patos, and at Porto Alegre she took on a full load of coal.

"It used to be wet, gassy stuff because the better seams are upcountry," said Old Harry, "but some English company has the mining concession now and gets the coal down by rail."

Rounding Cape Horn, however, was done under sail—that was a grand experience! Mountainous seas, howling gales; everything that Alexander had read about Cape Horn was true.

The boiler wasn't stoked again until after *Quinnipiac* left Valparaíso in Chili, which the locals spelled Chile.

"Chilian coal is the last we'll get," Old Harry said sadly. "Even when we reach California, there's no decent coal—just lignite loaded with water and low-grade bituminous coal loaded with sulfur—no good for marine steam engines, you'd die of the gases. We'd have to go on to Vancouver Island to pick up the best of a lousy choice, so it's back down the western Pacific under sail all the way to Valparaíso."

"I wondered why the steam engines we're carrying are built to burn wood," said Alexander.

"There sure is wood, Alexander! Thousands of square miles of it." Old Harry's shrewd grey eyes twinkled. "You're planning to make a fortune on the goldfields, huh?"

"I am."

"The alluvium's all gone long since. It's an industry now."

"I know. That's why I think a steam engineer has a chance to do well."

SAN FRANCISCO had quadrupled in population since the gold rushes of 1848 and 1849, and displayed all the features of such a huge influx over such a short period of time. Shacks and huts abounded on its periphery, most long deserted. In the city's hub it was easier to see the power of gold, for it owned some pretensions to architectural beauty. Many of those who had forged west had ended in settling there to do more prosaic things than prospect for gold, but with the outbreak of war between the North and the South on the other side of the Rockies, a certain number had gone back east to fight.

Yes, he was as careful with his bawbees as his uncle James, but Alexander knew that the best place to find a couple of willing seekers after gold was in a bar, so to a bar he went. Not at all like a Glasgow pub! No food was served, vulgar-looking women waited on the tables, and whatever the customers drank came in small glasses. He ordered a beer.

"You're real cute," said the waitress, thrusting out her breasts. "Want to take me home when this joint closes?"

He considered her through half-shut eyes, then shook his head emphatically. "No, thank you, madam," he said.

She bristled with outrage. "What's the matter, Mister Weird Accent, ain't I good enough?"

"No, madam, you are not good enough. I've no wish to acquire syphilis. You've a chancre on your lip."

When she brought the beer she slammed the mug down on the table, slopping it, stuck her nose in the air and flounced off. An action which had two men in a dark corner staring.

Alexander picked up his beer and strolled over; gold fever was written all over them. "May I?" he asked.

"Sure, have a seat," said the slight, fair one. "I'm Bill Smith, and this hairy guy is Chuck Parsons."

"Alexander Kinross from Scotland."

Parsons chuckled. "Well, friend, I knew you were from real foreign parts. You don't have the American look. What brings you to California?"

"I'm a steam engineer with an urge to find gold."

"Say, that's dandy!" cried Bill, beaming. "We're geologists with an urge to find gold."

"A useful profession for it," said Alexander.

"So, friend, is steam engineering. In fact, with two geologists and one steam engineer on board, a gold train might not be a figment of the mind," said Chuck, and waved his horny paw at the other drinkers in the bar, a morose lot. "See them? Down on their luck and trying to get home to Kentucky or Vermont or whichever state they came from. Wouldn't know schist from shit, greenhorns pure and simple. Any fool can swill a pan or build a flume, but working vein gold is for men who know what they're doing. Could you build a steam engine, Alex? Keep it going?"

"Given the parts, I could."

"How much money have you got?"

"It depends," said Alexander warily.

Bill and Chuck exchanged a wise nod. "You're smart, Alex," said Chuck, grinning through his wild bush of beard.

"In Scotland, the word is canny."

"Right, then let's talk turkey," said Bill, hunching over the table furtively and lowering his voice. "Chuck and I have two thousand dollars each. Match that figure, and you're in."

Four dollars to an English pound: "I can just match it."

"Then it's a deal?"

"It's a deal."

"Shake."

Alexander shook their hands. "How do we go about it?"

"A lot of what we need we'll get for nothing on abandoned workings along the American River," Bill said, sipping his beer.

None of us, thought Alexander, is fond of the drink. That augurs well for this partnership. They're a sanguine pair, but not fools. Educated, young, hardy.

"Exactly what do we need?" he asked.

"The parts for that steam engine, for one thing. A rock crusher. Wood already cut to make flumes and the like. A battery mill. Those we can pick up on workings where miners hoped to find reef gold. Also extra mules—the abandoned ones are still up there," Chuck said. "Our money will go on what we have to buy here in Frisco—kegs of black powder, which is made locally and kinda cheap, considering the war back east. The salt-peter comes from Chili, there's plenty of sulfur in California, and good charcoaling trees grow everywhere. Cartridge paper to hold the charges. Fuse. The biggest expense will be flasks of mercury, but luckily it's found on this coast too."

"Mercury? You mean quicksilver?"

"That's it. If we're going after gold embedded in quartz, we have to get it out of the quartz, and you can't do that with a tom or a rocker. You break up the quartz to two-inch pieces in a crusher, then pound those to powder in a stamper mill. It's fed with a constant stream of water in which mercury is suspended in fine droplets. You see, gold amalgamates with mercury, and that's how it's leached out of the quartz." Chuck frowned. "We won't be able to drag the cast-iron retorts that separate the gold from its mercury amalgamation—they weigh literal tons and can't be broken down into component parts. Besides, I doubt any will be lying around for us to grab. So when we find a vein, we'll have to keep our gold amalgamated until we run out of mercury."

"Mercury's very heavy, I know that," said Alexander.

"Yeah. One flask of it weighs seventy-six pounds. But that amalgamates a helluva lot of gold, Alex—up to fifty pounds of it. We'll be rich before we need to separate," Bill said.

"What else is bought here? I have my own tools, by the way."

"Food. Much cheaper here than in Coloma or any other gold town. Sacks of dried beans and coffee beans. Bacon. Edible green stuff grows wild, and there are plenty of deer. Chuck's a crack shot." Bill lifted an eyebrow. "One of us has to be. The bears are bigger than a grown man, and the wolves hunt in packs."

"Should I have a gun?"

"A revolver, sure. Leave the rifle to Chuck. No man goes unarmed in California, Alex. Pack it where folks can see it."

"And six thousand dollars will buy all of that?"

"Sure. Including three horses for us to ride, and mules to carry what we buy in Frisco."

IF ALEXANDER was skeptical about any of these logistics, it was the blind faith Chuck Parsons and Bill Smith had in the propensity of disappointed prospectors to abandon immensely precious machinery. But as they rode toward the foothills of the Sierra Nevada, he began to see why they were so optimistic; already the terrain was cut up into gorges they called canyons, an indication that indeed a consortium of disillusioned men might be tempted to leave most of what they owned behind.

Sure enough, wherever the American River foothills suggested the presence of a quartz vein, they found the remains of steam engines, rock crushers and battery stamper mills, not so much rusted as abused, as if the men who had operated them didn't know enough about them to keep them working. The country of the river's course looked as Alexander imagined country would look after a terrible war waged with cannon had gouged it up, scattered its rocks and gravels, deflected its streams, blasted out holes, pits, caves. Fallen flumes, sections of pipe, spintered toms, rockers, cradles. A profligate land: if it couldn't be made to work, walk away and leave the thing to rot, melt, disintegrate.

Of the men who had wrought this destruction they saw no signs; some had gone back to San Francisco, some had gone up into the high gravels, there to get at the buried placer with huge jets of water projected against a gravel wall, while yet others had gone even farther afield in search of the mother lode, the elusive veins of quartz that harbored free gold. These last were the most determined men, the real sufferers from gold fever.

As they rode, the two geologists taught the avidly listening Alexander the basics of their science.

"There hasn't been much work published on California's rocks," said Bill, the more studious of the pair, "but to start from the beginning, there's a minister of religion called Fisher in Europe somewhere who says that the globe has a flexible crust of rock and an inner, rigid nucleus.

Between the two is a molten, viscous fluid that erupts from volcanoes as lava. It's a pretty daring theory, but it kinda sounds right to us."

"How old is the earth?" asked Alexander, it never having occurred to him before to wonder about the globe he lived on.

"No one honestly knows, Alex. Some say two hundred million years, others reckon about sixty million years. But it's sure been spinning around for a lot longer than the Bible says."

"That makes sense," said Alexander. "There were no geologists around when the Bible was written." Something else popped into his mind. "And the crust? Is it entirely rock? Where do the minerals come from?"

"Minerals in a mass *are* rocks."

Chuck took over. "The crust is layered in what the paleontologists call strata, according to what fossils are found in the rock. That's how we know Darwin is right about evolution. The older the rock, the more primitive the life forms preserved in it are. Some rock—they call it fundamental gneiss—is so old that it contains no fossils at all, but nobody's ever found any of this fundamental gneiss, though there's a red sandstone in Britain that's so old it's lifeless."

"But," objected Alexander, "almost every cliff in every canyon we see isn't in nice flat layers at all. In fact, it's hard to see *layers.*"

"The crust's moving all the time from earthquakes," said Bill, "so after they've been formed the rock layers get shifted, crumpled, contorted, dislocated—you name it, it's done to them. They're also worn by wind and water, or else they're under a sea at one moment, above it at another. When it comes to rocks, the earth is a real busy old ball."

California, Alexander learned, was quite young, especially along its coastline. And—though he personally hadn't felt any since his arrival—it was convulsed by frequent earthquakes.

"The coastal mountains are extremely young—sandstones and shales, but northward they're broken up by intrusions of granite that turned them on their edge during the Pliocene era—very recent. There are limestone outcrops in the Sierra foothills, but the range itself seems almost pure granite. It's in granitic country that you find the quartz veins containing pure gold, and they're what we're looking for," said Bill.

IT IS SAID that some men have a nose for the presence of gold, and swear that they can actually smell it, even under the ground; Alexander turned out to be such a one.

They rode south from the American River in that early spring of 1862, shepherding a huge mule train carrying their purchases from San Francisco as well as everything they had scavenged from abandoned workings, including a broken-down battery stamper mill, a rock crusher, and, on a rough frame that dragged its back legs over the ground, a medium boiler for the steam engine Alexander would build. Bill and Chuck were in favor of plunging into the high Sierras, but the prudent Alexander said no, not when it would be winter before they were really mining. He was, besides, edgily conscious that he could smell the same odor as emanated from a gold filling in one molar. *It* oozed out of a valley that looked no different from a hundred others—granite boulders dewed the slopes, which were clear of forest in places.

"We try here first," he said, adamant. "If we find nothing, we go higher, but I think there's gold here, and close to the surface. See that outcrop, Chuck? Go look at it. This is where we stake our first claim."

Beneath the leaf mold and soft earth at the base of the outcrop was an unmistakable thick vein of quartz that sparkled when Chuck scrubbed it clean and chipped it.

"Jesus!" he breathed, sinking back on his heels. "Alex, you're a witch doctor!" He sprang to his feet, did a dance. "Right, we're gonna be here for a whiles, so we build a good hut and a corral for the horses—the mules won't stray too far, this is wolf country. Alex, get started on the engine."

"Later on," said Alexander, curiously unexcited, "you'll have to teach me to blast."

SUMMER WENT by in a frenzy of construction; many trees had to be felled to season for burning in the engine firebox, that shack had to go up, and the machinery readied to deal with the increasing piles of fragmented rock Chuck and Bill first dug out with picks, then, following the vein inward, by small blasts of black powder. There were the inevitable accidents; Chuck barely escaped serious injury when a charge exploded early, Bill badly cut his leg plying an axe, and Alexander was scalded by a gush of steam. Bill sewed up the rent in his leg with an ordinary darning needle, and Chuck, hobbling around on a home-made crutch, produced some foul-smelling bear grease to anoint the burn. But the work went on remorselessly, for who could tell when some men would ride into their valley and discover what they were up to?

By the time the rainy, sleety winter came down, they were in full production, breaking up the rock, pounding it to powder under the iron shoe of the stamper, their engine huffing and roaring away. This was a land prodigiously endowed with water, more than enough to wash through the stamper cylinder and force the free gold to amalgamate with the droplets of mercury inside the chamber. What gold didn't amalgamate there ran through as slurry on to a sloping apron, at the bottom of which a copper plate covered with more mercury captured it.

High spring saw the end of the mercury, piled now in flaky, yellowish masses under a covering of brush.

Alexander had just had his twentieth birthday, and had developed the wiry, sinewy body of one reared on hard labor; at just over six feet, he knew he had stopped growing.

But, he thought, I am tired of this life. For almost all of the past six years I have had no roof over my head that kept out the cold, or didn't leak when it rained—even *Quinnipiac* dribbled water on my hammock because her deck wasn't properly caulked. If a deck ever can be properly caulked. I eat until my belly is full, but in Glasgow the food was ninety-five percent flour, and here it's eternal beans and venison. The last time I had roast beef and roast potatoes was at a Kinross wedding. Bill and Chuck are good men, intelligent and well read on geology, but they know far more about George Washington than they do about Alexander the Great. Yes, I am tired of this life.

So when Chuck spoke on that clear May morning, Alexander listened as if to the sound of a distant, melodious horn.

"That," said Chuck, gazing at their haul, "is one helluva lot of gold. Even if we get closer to thirty than forty percent of bullion from the amalgam, we'll be rich men. It's time to let the cat out of the bag. One of us will have to ride into Coloma to get separation retorts. Two will have to stay here to deal with claim-jumpers."

"I'll go because I want to go," said Alexander. "I mean I want to leave permanently. You can buy me out with one-third of our amalgam, which I'll take with me. You can deed my share of the mine to whoever is willing to bring up the retorts, and a man who can keep the engine running. Give me a pound of good ore for assay and you'll be overwhelmed with potential partners."

"But the vein's not worked out yet by a long shot!" cried Bill, horrified. "Alex, the deeper we go, the better the yield! We'll never get other partners as hardworking and easygoing as you! Why do you want out, for God's sake?"

"Och, I guess I'm just footloose. I've learned all I can, so it's time I moved on." He laughed. "There's more gold under more mountains someplace else. I'll send you guys the separated mercury back if it hasn't sickened."

ALEXANDER HAD his third of the amalgam separated in Coloma, and kept fifty-five of the sixty pounds of gold it yielded as bullion. It traveled with him hidden in the false bottom of his tool chest loaded on a mule as he rode out of town. Of course the word was out that he had gold, but within a mile of the last shack he had eluded those who pursued him, to vanish without a trace.

By the time he attached himself to a large and well-armed party of men journeying east to get in on the dying throes of the Civil War, Alexander was faultless in the role he had assumed, that of disgruntled and luckless prospector. Even so, he slept each night cuddling his precious tool box to him, and grew used to the discomfort of the gold coins sewn into his clothing. Nor did he ever look as if overburdened.

Once the high Rockies were traversed he was fascinated to see Red Indians in their natural state, magnificently haughty men riding their ponies bareback, clad in buckskin that was sometimes intricately beaded, their lances flaunting feathers, bows and arrows at the ready. But they were too wise to attack this big, warlike party of the hated white men, just sat their ponies to look at the intruders for a while, then disappeared. Buffalo in hundreds roamed the grasslands together with deer and other, smaller creatures; one little burrowing fellow would sit up on his haunches like a gnome, which enchanted Alexander.

As European settlement grew more widespread, they passed through tiny villages of a few tired wooden buildings grouped on either side of a muddy track; here the Red Indians were clad in the white man's garb, shambling along in a drunken haze. Strong drink, reflected Alexander, has been the ruin of the world; even Alexander the Great had died of a ruptured stomach after a gargantuan drinking binge. And wherever the white man goes, he brings cheap strong drink in his train.

They were following one of the wagon trails, though, thanks to the war, they encountered few settlers going west in the long convoys that gave them some protection against Indian raids. It crossed Kansas to

Kansas City, a biggish town at the junction of two great rivers. Here Alexander said goodbye to his companions and followed the Missouri River to St. Louis and the Mississippi. These must be the greatest rivers in the world, he thought, awed, and marveled again at the bounty Nature had given America. Rich soil, any amount of water, a good growing season even if the winters were far colder than those in Scotland. Which made little sense, as Scotland was much farther north.

He deliberately avoided the war zones, having no wish to become embroiled in a struggle he felt he had no part in, nor any entitlement to. Then, crossing northern Indiana, he stopped at a lone house coming on dusk with his usual request: a meal and a bed in the barn in return for whatever hard labor might be needed around the place. With so many of the menfolk away, this worked very well; women trusted him, and he never betrayed their trust.

The woman who answered his knock held a shotgun, and he quite saw why: she was young and beautiful, and there were no sounds of children anywhere. Alone?

"Put the gun down, I'll not harm you," he said in that Scots burr so strange and attractive to American ears. "Give me food and shelter in the barn for the night, and I'll chop wood for you, milk the cow, take all those weeds out of your vegetable patch—whatever you need, madam."

"What I need," she said grimly, propping the gun against the wall, "is my man back, but that's not going to happen."

Her name was Honoria Brown, and her husband of a few weeks had been killed in a battle called Shiloh; she had been alone ever since, scraping a living off what soil she could till herself and resisting the pleas of her family to return to them.

"I like my independence," she said to Alexander over a good dinner of chicken, fried potatoes, green beans from her garden and the best gravy he had tasted since leaving Kinross. Her eyes were the color of an aquamarine, thickly fringed with lashes so fair they looked made of glass, and they held humor, hardness, indomitability. A new expression entered them, of speculation; she put down her fork and stared at him intently. "However, I'm wise enough to know that once this war is over and the men start drifting, I can't exist here alone. I don't suppose you're looking for a wife who owns a hundred-acre farm?"

"No," said Alexander gently. "Indiana isn't journey's end for me, nor will I ever be a farmer."

She shrugged, the corners of her lush mouth turned down. "It was worth a try. You'll make some woman a good husband."

The meal done, he sharpened her axe and chopped wood for an hour by lamplight, swinging the instrument easily, tirelessly. Toward the end, she appeared at the back door and watched him.

"You've worked up a sweat," she said when he put the axe down, sharpened it again. "It's cold, so I've put a little hot water in my tin kitchen bath tub. If you bring in more water from the well, you can have a bath in the warmth while I wash your clothes. They won't dry before morning, and that means you can't sleep in the barn. You can sleep in my bed."

The kitchen, wherein they had eaten, was spotless again when he entered, the dishes done, the big cast-iron cooking range giving off enough heat to make the air comfortable; her tin tub stood before it, the bottom filled with hot water from her huge iron kettle, which he refilled from the well before adding more water to the tub. Her hand out, she stood while he gave her his clothes—jean trousers, jean shirt, flannel long johns—then smiled appreciatively.

"You're very well made, Alexander," she said, turning to a small washtub on the deal table.

It felt so good to squash himself down into warm water that he lingered, sitting hunched with his chin on his knees; his eyelids drooped, closed.

The feel of her strong, rough hand on his back woke him.

"It's the one bit you can't do for yourself," she said, fingers kneading his flesh.

She spread a big braided rag rug on the floor under his wet feet, draped a huckaback towel around him, rubbed briskly.

Where before he had been exhausted, now he was alive, alert, all his senses leaping. He turned inside the towel to face her, and kissed her awkwardly. That brought a huge response from her, deepening the kiss to a dark web of the most intensely physical emotion he had ever known. Her shabby dress came off, her shift and drawers, her home-knitted stockings, and for the first time in his life Alexander Kinross felt a naked woman against him. Her full breasts enthralled him, he couldn't get enough of them, buried his face between them, brushed her nipples with his palms. It all progressed so naturally; he didn't need prior experience to sense what she wanted, what he wanted, and the climax when it came was shared, a light-filled ecstasy that bore no relation to the shame of stimulating himself to climax.

At some time during the night they transferred to her bed, but Alexander kept on making love to this wonderful, passionate, beautiful woman who was as starved as he.

"Stay here with me," she pleaded at dawn when he started to put on his clothes.

"I can't," he said through his teeth. "This isn't my fate, it isn't my destiny. Were I to stay here, it would be Napoleon electing to stay on Elba."

She didn't weep or protest, but rose to make him breakfast while he went out to saddle his horse, load his mule. For the first and only time during his American odyssey, the gold had lain forgotten all night under the straw in the barn.

"Destiny," she said thoughtfully, loading his plate with eggs, bacon, grits. "It's a funny word. I've heard it before, but I didn't know men could think about it the way you do. If you can, tell me what your destiny is."

"My destiny is to become great, Honoria. I have to show a narrow, vindictive old Presbyterian minister what he tried to destroy, and prove to him that a man can rise above his birth." Frowning, he gazed at her rosy face, all aglow from the splendor of the night. "My dear, get yourself four or five big, nasty dogs. You're a fierce woman, they'll respect you and do as you tell them. Train them to go for the throat. They'll be better protection than a shotgun—use it to feed them rabbits, birds, whatever you can find. Then you can live here alone until that husband comes along. He will. He will."

When he left she stood on the height of her porch to watch him for as long as she could see him; he wondered if she had any idea how massive was the change she had wrought in him. What had been an inchoate ache at his core was now conscious knowledge. She had opened Pandora's box, Honoria Brown. Yet thanks to the kind of woman she was, he would never go the way so many men did, willing to beggar their pride for the chance to have a woman whenever they could.

His greatest grief at the parting was his awareness that he couldn't do what he burned to do—leave her with a little bag of gold coins to tide her over if times grew harder. Had he offered, she would have rejected them and thought the worse of him, and had he left them for her to find later, her memories of him would be tainted. All he had been able to give her were firewood, a weedless garden, a well pulley that worked much better now, a sharp axe, and the essence of himself.

I will never see her again. I will never know if I quickened her, I will never find out what her destiny is.

TO ALEXANDER'S horror, New York proved to be a city much like Glasgow or Liverpool in that its teeming hordes were pent up in stinking slums. Where it differed, however, was in the cheerful mood of its poor, convinced that they wouldn't be at the bottom of the human rubbish heap forever. Some of that was due to the polyglot nature of these people, who hailed from all over Europe and clustered according to nationality. Though their living conditions were appalling, they lacked that awful hopelessness the British poor had aplenty. A poor Englishman or Scot never even dreamed of getting out, of rising up, whereas everyone in New York seemed sure that times would improve.

Or at least this was what he concluded in his very brief progress through the city; he had no intention of being parted from his horse and mule until he walked up the gangway of a ship bound for London. The better class of people who frequented the wide avenues of the commercial area smiled at his appearance, judging him some yokel from plains country, with his buckskins, his weather-beaten steed and that patient, plodding mule.

And so finally he docked in London, another fabulous urban sprawl he had never seen.

"Threadneedle Street," he told his hackney driver, keeping the tool chest bearing his gold inside the cab with him.

Still wearing his buckskins and his soft, wide-brimmed hat, he hefted the chest into the revered portals of the Bank of England, dumped it on the floor and stood looking around.

Its acolytes would not have dreamed of being rude or even verbally contemptuous to any man who entered their temple precinct, thus Alexander found himself confronted by a clerkly dumpling who smiled at him.

"An American, sir?"

"No, a Scot in need of a bank."

"Oh, I see." Sniffing wealth, the clerkly dumpling didn't make the mistake of palming this peculiar-looking man off on some minion; he bade Alexander be seated until a deputy manager was free to attend to him.

A short time later an Important Personage appeared. "How may I help you, sir?"

"My name's Alexander Kinross, and I want your bank to hold my bullion for me." The toe of Alexander's scuffed boot nudged the chest. "I've fifty-five pounds of it."

Two minions picked up the chest by its handles and lugged it into Mr. Walter Maudling's office.

"Do you mean to say, Mr. Kinross, that you have physically carried fifty-five pounds of gold from California all the way to London?" asked Mr. Maudling, round-eyed.

"I've carried a hundred pounds. My tools are atop the gold."

"Why not a San Francisco bank, or at least a New York one?"

"Because the Bank of England is the only one I trust. I figure," said Alexander, unconsciously using the forms of speech of the land he had just quit, "that if the Bank of England goes under, the world will stop spinning. I'm no' a man who esteems banks, as I have already told you."

"The Bank of England is highly flattered, sir."

Hammers, wrenches, files and more esoteric items were strewn all over the floor; Alexander lifted the chest's false bottom to reveal its dully gleaming contents, eleven little gold bricks.

"I separated it from the amalgam in Coloma," said Alexander chattily, stacking the bars on the desk and replacing the false bottom and tools. "Will you keep it for me?"

Mr. Maudling blinked. "Keep it? Like *that*? Don't you wish to cash it in and earn something on it?"

"No, because while it's like *that* it says what it is. I've no intention of exchanging it for numbers written on ledger paper, Mr. Maudling, no matter how many noughts follow them. But, as I don't want to keep on dragging this with me, will you keep it?"

"Of course, of course, Mr. Kinross!"

And that, thought Walter Maudling as he watched the tall, rather catlike figure stride out of the Bank of England, is the oddest client I have ever encountered. Alexander Kinross! A name the Bank of England is going to hear quite often in the years to come, I'd bet the contents of his tool chest on it.

THE FOUR HUNDRED pounds in gold sovereigns that he obtained for his American dollars were not wasted on luxurious hotels or high living, nor did Alexander buy a conforming suit. Instead he bought washable clothes of dungaree and cotton, new flannel underwear, and put up in a

Kensington boarding house that offered very good home cooking and clean rooms. He visited the museums, art galleries public and private, the Tower of London and Madame Tussaud's waxworks; in a private gallery he paid fifty of his precious pounds for a painting by someone named Dante Gabriel Rossetti because the woman in it looked like Honoria Brown. When he presented it to Mr. Maudling for storage in the Bank of England, that gentleman never batted an eyelid; if Alexander Kinross paid fifty pounds for a painting, it was sure to end in being a masterpiece. The work was, besides, quite lovely, lyrically romantic.

Then, after criss-crossing England on trains, heading ever northward, Alexander arrived at the village of Auchterderran in Kinross County, a short distance from Kinross town.

What had really happened and would happen to Alexander Kinross were never imparted to Elizabeth; what she learned was semi-myth. His intention in returning was to obtain the promise of a wife. That he didn't want to marry just yet was due to his ambition to follow—literally—in the footsteps of Alexander the Great; to retrace the tortuous route the King of Macedonia had taken in his conquests. Not a journey that a young woman would relish, he was sure. So he would marry on his return and take his bride with him to New South Wales. He had her picked out already: she was Uncle James's eldest daughter, Jean, whom he remembered as if he had last seen her yesterday. An exquisite, precocious ten-year-old who had gazed at him adoringly and told him that she loved him, that she would always love him. Well, that would make her sixteen now—the perfect age. By the time he had done with this new expedition, Jean would be eighteen and old enough to marry.

He rode a hired horse into Kinross on a Sunday afternoon and went to see Uncle James. Who greeted him with distaste.

"You look as shiftless as ever, Alexander," said James as he led his visitor into the front parlor, then hollered for tea. "I had to pay for your father's funeral, since you'd disappeared off the face of the map."

"Thank you for your tact in breaking this news to me, sir," said Alexander, poker-faced. "How much did it cost?"

"Five pounds I could ill afford."

Alexander fished in the pocket of his fringed buckskin coat. "Here are six pounds—the extra pound represents interest. Is it long since he died?"

"A year."

"I suppose it's too much to hope that old man Murray has followed Duncan to hell?"

"You're a maggot and a blasphemer, Alexander. You always have been. I thank God that you're no kin to me."

"Murray told you that, did he? Or was it Duncan?"

"My brother died with his shame still his own business. Dr. Murray told me at his funeral, said *someone* had to know."

At which moment Jean walked into the parlor bearing a tray of tea and cake. Oh, she was beautiful! Grown up exactly as he had imagined, with Honoria Brown's glassy lashes and aquamarine eyes. But he couldn't delude himself that Jean even recognized him, let alone remembered that she had said she would always love him. The stare she directed at him was cursory, uninterested, then she pranced out of the room. Well, that was understandable. He had changed a great deal. Best get down to the bargaining.

"I've come to ask for Jean's hand in marriage," he said.

"I hope you're joking!"

"Not at all. I'm here in all honor to ask for Jean, though I'm aware she's not old enough yet. I can wait."

"You can wait until the worms eat you!" James snapped, eyes flashing. "Give a Drummond to a bastard? I'd sooner give her to an Anabaptist!"

Somehow he suppressed his anger. "No one knows that story except you, me, and old man Murray, so what does it matter? I'm on my way to being a very rich man."

"Tosh! Where did you go when you ran off?"

"To Glasgow, where I was apprenticed as a boilermaker."

"And you think to make a fortune at that?"

"No, I have other strings to my bow," Alexander began, intending to tell James about the gold. That would shut him up!

But James had had enough. He rose to his feet and stalked to the front door, threw it open dramatically and pointed to the road. "Out you go this minute, Alexander whoever-you-are! You'll no' get Jean or any other young Kinross woman! If you try, Dr. Murray and I will pillory you!"

"Then I make you a promise, James Drummond," said Alexander, biting off his words. "At some time in the future, you'll be glad to give me one of your daughters in marriage." He walked down the path, mounted his hired horse and rode away.

Now where did he learn to ride so well, and where did he get his clothes? wondered James, too late.

Elizabeth, five years old, was in the kitchen with Jean and Anne, learning how to make scones. Because Jean neglected to mention the visitor in the parlor, Elizabeth never knew that only one room had separated her from that shiftless boilermaker's apprentice, her cousin Alexander.

IT HAD BEEN a foolish impulse, Alexander admitted to himself as he nudged the horse to a canter. A little serious thought would have told him what James Drummond would say to his offer, but all he could think about had been immature little Jean's resemblance to Honoria Brown.

I would have married Honoria Brown, except that I could tell she was wedded to her patch of Indiana earth.

THERE DIDN'T seem any hurry now to make his next fortune; Alexander put his western saddle on a good hack, stowed his belongings in two saddlebags and set off across Europe, seeing the march of history as he rode: gothic cathedrals, half-timbered towns, immense castles, and, when he reached Greece, once-glorious temples felled by the movements of Mother Earth. Still under the sway of the disintegrating Ottomans, Macedonia held more evidence of Islam than of Alexander.

In fact, he realized as he wandered through Turkey, poked about in Issus, followed the line of his namesake's march south to Egypt, little physically remained of Alexander the Great. Whatever of the world's ancient history had visibly endured was constructed of massive stone, be it pyramid, ziggurat, sanctuary, or a red sandstone gorge whose very walls had been carved into majestic temples. Babylon was a city of mud brick, its hanging gardens evaporated into the mists of time, giving nothing of Alexander's death away, or of the life he had lived there.

Slowly the pilgrimage became something else, an insatiable curiosity about Asia rather than an attempt to turn back the clock of the centuries. So he went wherever he fancied, whether Alexander the Great had been there or not. Because he had been told that it couldn't be done, he rode over the mighty peaks of eastern Turkey to see that, yes, the snow on the mountain flanks was indeed a rich pinkish-red from sand blown all the way from the Sahara desert. What awed him now was the power of Nature's world, and how humanity had coped with it.

Though the war had been over now for ten years, he deemed it imprudent to visit the Crimea, so he turned eastward over the Caucasus instead, and came down to the Caspian Sea in a Russian outpost named Baku. This was the northern branch of the ancient silk route from China, a bleak and almost rainless place whose tiny capital, also Baku, was a jumble of disintegrating houses stepped on top of each other up a hill. And there he found two wonders. The first was caviar. The second was how the local people ran their Caspian paddle wheelers, their locomotives, their fixed steam engines. For neither trees nor coal were to be found anywhere near Baku.

The entire area was littered with soak-wells of what some called naphtha, others bitumen, and chemists petroleum. Many of these wells burned brilliantly, great gouts of flame leaping skyward—not the petroleum itself, he was able to ascertain, but the gases it gave off. On his return from Egypt he had ridden down the Arabian coast of the Red Sea intending to visit Mecca, when a seasoned English traveler advised him against it; infidels were not welcome there. But here in Baku was a different religious sect's equivalent of Mecca, or Rome, or Jerusalem: adherents of Mazda, the fire god, came from all over Persia to worship the burning gases, lending an already exotic little place additional nuances of sound, color, ritual.

Unfortunately Alexander couldn't speak Russian, French, Farsi or any of the languages understood in Baku, nor could he find one other English-speaker who did. All he could do was make what assumptions he could about the fact that somehow these unsophisticated people, deprived of wood or coal, had learned to use the petroleum as fuel to heat their boilers. Going on the evidence of the burning wells, Alexander thought that what burned to turn water into superheated steam were the gases emitted by the petroleum, not the substance itself. That meant that once the gases in the boiler chamber above the tray of petroleum started to burn, the petroleum must keep on giving off gas. What was more, he noted, fascinated, this oil—for so it looked—produced far less smoke than either coal or wood.

FROM BAKU he went south into Persia, through more mountains quite as rugged as the Rockies. Where they became a range known as the Elburz—lower, less craggy—he saw, amazed, evidence of this petroleum again. The ruins around Persepolis were highly satisfying, but a personal need drove him north again to Tehran; his buckskins had reached the end of their useful life, and in Tehran, a big city, he would find someone able to make him new clothes out of chamois. This exquisitely fine, soft leather was so comfortable to wear that he paid the delighted tailor to make more and send them to Mr. Walter Maudling at the Bank of England to keep until he collected them. This was typical Alexander; he trusted the tailor and saw nothing inappropriate in having his banker act as his depot. So accustomed was he by now to communicating in a mixture of sign language and drawn pictures that, he thought whimsically, were he to be marooned in a colony of bears, he would be able to make the bears understand him. Probably because he was alone, looked ordinary if utterly foreign, he was never threatened by the people he encountered on his travels; as had been his way since he was fifteen, he tried to earn what he ate by performing some kind of helpful manual work. People respected that, and respected him.

Other items than chamois suits were shipped to Mr. Maudling from time to time: two icons that he bought in Baku, a perfect marble statue from Persepolis, a huge silk rug from Van, and, in an Alexandrian bazaar, a painting that the vendor said originally came from an officer in Napoleon's army, loot from Italy. It cost Alexander five pounds, but his instinct said it was worth far more, for it was old, had a little the look of his icons.

He was thoroughly enjoying himself, the more so because he had never enjoyed his childhood, or those years in Glasgow. After all, he was still in his middle twenties; he had time on his side, and his common sense said that every new thing he experienced contributed to his education—that, between all of this travel, his Latin and his Greek, one day men would defer to him for other reasons than mere wealth.

HOWEVER, ALL things must end. For five years he wandered around the Islamic world, central Asia, India and China, then took ship for London out of Bombay. A quick and easy voyage now that the Suez Canal was open.

As he sent word to Mr. Walter Maudling that he was coming to the Bank of England at two in the afternoon, that gentleman had time to prepare a homily upon the etiquette of dumping all his acquisitions at Threadneedle Street. It also gave him time to have one of those acquisitions removed from the attic in his own house and couriered to his office, where it sat, a big and bulky package sewn up in canvas, by the side of his desk.

The skin-clad Alexander strode in and slapped a draft for fifty thousand pounds in front of his banker, then sat in the visitor's chair, eyes laughing.

"No bullion?" asked Mr. Maudling.

"Not where I've been."

Mr. Maudling took in the weather-beaten face, the neat black goatee, the hair curling over Alexander's shoulders. "You look astonishingly well, sir, considering the places you have been."

"Never had a day's sickness. I see that my chamois suits have arrived. Did my other things reach you?"

"Your 'things,' Mr. Kinross, have caused this bank no small inconvenience. It is not a *poste restante*! However, I took the liberty of calling in a valuator to see whether I should put your 'things' in some external storage facility, or send them to our vaults. The statue is second century B.C. Greek, the icons Byzantine, the rug has six hundred double knots of silk per square inch, the painting is a Giotto, the vases are mint-condition Ming, and the table screens—also in mint condition—are some dynasty of fifteen hundred years ago. Therefore they went into our vaults. The parcel you see here I stored in my own attic, having ascertained that it is new, if peculiar, clothing," said Mr. Maudling, trying to look severe. He picked up the draft and flicked it. "What does this represent, sir?"

"Diamonds. I sold them to a Dutchman this morning. He's made a nice profit on the deal, but I'm happy with the price. I had the pleasure of finding them," Alexander said, smiling.

"Diamonds. Don't you have to mine for them?"

"You can, but that's very recent. I found mine where most have been found since Adam was a boy—in the gravelly beds of sparkling little rivers that flow down from the Hindu Kush, the Pamirs, the Himalayas. Tibet had very good pickings. Rough diamonds look just like pebbles or gravel, especially when they are crusted with a layer of some iron-rich mineral. If they sat there glittering, all of them would already have been found, but some of the places I went were pretty remote."

"Mr. Kinross," said Walter Maudling slowly, "you are a phenomenon. You have the Midas touch."

"I used to think that myself, but I've changed my mind. A man finds the treasures of the world because he looks at what he sees," said Alexander Kinross. "That's the secret. *Look* at what you see. Most men don't. Opportunity doesn't knock once—it beats a perpetual tattoo."

"And does opportunity now drum out the financial realms of London?"

"Good lord, no!" said Alexander, shocked. "I'm off to New South Wales. This time for gold. I'll need a letter of credit to some Sydney bank—try to find me a decent one! Though my gold will come here."

"Banks," said Mr. Maudling with dignity, "are mostly above reproach, sir."

"Rubbish!" said Alexander scornfully. "Sydney banks will be no different from those in Glasgow or San Francisco—susceptible to theft from the top." He rose to his feet and effortlessly hoisted the parcel into his arms. "Will you keep my treasures until I decide what to do with them?"

"For a modest fee."

"That, I expected. Now I'm off to the *Times.*"

"If you tell me whereabouts you're staying, Mr. Kinross, I will have your clothing sent."

"No, I've a hackney waiting outside."

Curiosity piqued, Mr. Maudling couldn't resist asking. "The *Times*? Are you planning to write an article on your travels?"

"I should think not! No, I want to place an advertisement. If I have to spend two months on a ship to New South Wales, I refuse to be idle. So I'm going to find a man who can teach me French and Italian."

THOUGH JAMES Summers spoke English with a broad and vulgar (according to the People Who Mattered) Midlands accent, his French and Italian were a pleasure to hear, said his references. His father, he explained, had run an English ale house in Paris for more than the first ten years of Jim's life; he then transferred to a similar establishment in Venice. That Alexander chose him out of the many who applied was due to the man's curious dichotomy. His French mother had been from a good family and insisted that her son read all the French classics; then, when she died and his father married an equally cultivated Italian woman, her childless state caused her to focus all her attentions on her stepson. Yet James Summers had absolutely no scholarly leanings!

"Why did you apply for this job?" Alexander asked.

"It's a way to get to New South Wales," said Summers simply.

"Why do you want to go there?"

"Well, with my accent I'm not going to get a post at Eton, Harrow or Winchester, am I? My English is pure Smethwick because that's where my dad came from." He shrugged. "Besides, Mr. Kinross, sir, I'm not cut out for life in a classroom, and I'd never get employment in a private house teaching the daughters, now would I? Truth is, I like hard work—work with my hands, I mean. At the same time, I'd like some responsibility. And New South Wales might be the answer. I hear tell that how a man speaks doesn't tell against him, for one thing."

Alexander leaned back in his chair and studied Jim Summers intently. Something in the man appealed to him strongly—a kind of natural independence mixed with a degree of humility that said he needed to rely on someone he regarded as his superior in ability and intelligence. His father, Alexander suspected, must have been a hard man, but a fair one, and just possibly that true rarity—a purveyor of liquor who didn't indulge in it himself. So his son equated his education with the softness of women, yet yearned to be like his father. A servant who was not subservient.

"The job is yours, Mr. Summers," said Alexander, "though it may be that I won't discharge you after we reach Sydney. If, that is, you find that you like working for me. Once I have mastered French and Italian, I'm going to need a Man Friday, and I don't mean that in a derogatory sense."

The plain but attractive face lit up; Summers beamed. "Oh, thank you, Mr. Kinross, sir! Thank you!"

THEY ARRIVED in Sydney on April 13 of 1872, which happened to be Alexander's twenty-ninth birthday. In the end the voyage had consumed over a year because Alexander's progress in French and Italian was slower than he had expected, and also, more importantly, because he had never seen Japan, or Alaska, or the Kamchatka Peninsula, or northwestern Canada, or the Philippines.

In Jim Summers he had found a perfect foil for his own restless energy; the man relished everything they did, every place they went, yet was content to do whatever Mr. Kinross wanted to do. He addressed Alexander as "Mr. Kinross" and preferred that Alexander call him "Summers" than the implied ease and camaraderie of "Jim."

"At least," Alexander said to Summers at the end of their first day in Sydney, "San Francisco stands on a peninsula jutting into an enormous bay, so its sewage drifts out of nose range. Whereas Sydney hugs its harbor, so its sewage stays inside a much smaller body of water. I can't stand the stench here—it's as bad as Bombay, Calcutta or Wampoa. And to prevent your escaping the fug by moving inland from the harbor, the fools have erected a vile sewer vent chimney at the far end of the main park! Ugh!"

Privately Summers thought that Mr. Kinross was a mite too hard on Sydney, which he deemed very beautiful. But then, he had noticed, Mr. Kinross's smelling apparatus was extremely keen. So sensitive was it, said Mr. Kinross one day in the Yukon, that he could sniff gold, and there was a lot of gold in the Yukon.

"But as I've no wish to spend more bitter winters in cold latitudes, Summers, we'll not stay here," he had announced.

LITTLE WONDER then that as soon as he had presented his letter of credit to the bank Mr. Maudling had recommended, Alexander took the train and then the coach west to Bathurst, a town literally surrounded at all points of the compass by goldfields. Despite which, Bathurst itself was not a mining community—that, in Alexander's estimation, made Bathurst orderly, neat, benign.

Instead of seeking accommodation at a hotel or boarding house, he rented a cottage set in several acres of land on the outskirts and installed Summers in it.

"Find a woman to keep the place clean and do the cooking," Alexander instructed, handing Summers a list. "Pay her a little more than the going rate and she'll be anxious to keep the job. While I scout the goldfields I want you to shop around for the things on this list. Here's a letter of authority that will let you draw on my bank. If you can't keep accounts, you're going to have to learn. Find a bookkeeper and pay him to teach you." He swung into the American western saddle he had brought with him, his necessities in saddlebags; the nice bay mare he rode he had found locally, but there was no doubt that for long days of riding through rough country, an American western saddle was more comfortable than an English one. "I don't know when I'll be back, so expect me at any time."

And off he trotted in his skins and wide-brimmed hat.

His week in Bathurst had been filled with activity, chiefly the seeking of information from town and shire officials, three members of the local landed gentry, shopkeepers and inhabitants of various hotel bars. The alluvial gold had mostly run out, he learned, but reef gold was being worked in Hill End and Gulgong, generating a second gold rush.

In the early days of the first placer strikes, the New South Wales Government—and the Government in Victoria, where even bigger finds were made—had been so greedy to milk revenue from this bonanza that it had levied the astronomical sum of thirty shillings for a prospector's license that lasted only one month. In Victoria the outrage among prospectors combined with the ruthless methods of the Government's collecting agents had culminated in a near revolution. With the result that the license fee had been reduced to twenty shillings and lasted for a year. Still, Alexander didn't need a license yet—why tip his hand?

The road to Hill End, no better than a track, was thronged with traffic; huge flat-bedded drays pulled by ten to twenty bullocks; what looked for all the world like an American stagecoach with the words Cobb & Co on its side; horse-drawn wagons, carts and sulkies; men on horseback or on foot, and many women and children. The attire of the men went all the way from smart city suits and bowler hats to ragged dungarees, flannel shirts and wide-brimmed hats, whereas the women were more uniform in drab gingham or calico dresses, shady straw hats or poke-fronted bonnets, feet in men's boots. The children were of all ages from babies through to youths and nubile girls, mostly clad in little better than scrupulously mended rags. Boys of eight and nine smoked pipes or chewed tobacco like veterans.

This, Alexander thought, is what the roads to the fields in California must have looked like at the height of that gold rush. And how American it is! From stagecoach to wagons to the look of the people, frontier American. Yet in Sydney everyone I met was pretending to be English—not very successfully. How sad. This is just too far away to attract the non-British, so the city people have decided to cling to class-consciousness.

THE TOWN of Hill End was like all its brethren elsewhere: gouged, rutted streets that must be a mire in wet weather, the same shanties, huts, tents. It did, however, possess an imposing red-brick church and one or two other brick buildings, including one that announced it was the ROYAL HOTEL. Chinese abounded, some clad like coolies and sporting pigtails, others in British business suits and clipped hair beneath their bowlers. Several of the boarding houses were run by Chinese, also a number of shops and restaurants.

The air reverberated with familiar sounds: the maddening boom-boom-boom of battery stampers, the grating roar of crushers. The noise emanated from Hawkins Hill, where the reef gold lay—an ugly shambles of diggings, poppet heads, derricks and an occasional steam engine. Most of the claim owners, however, used horse power. It didn't take him long to ascertain that this was no land of bounteous water; there could be no pressure-hosing the gold out of gravel banks here, for the river, a thin and shallow stream, was the only water available for all purposes. As for the wood—as hard as iron, he was told.

"Thankless fucken hard work. This is a fair cow of a place," his informant summed up.

Very depressed, Alexander eyed the Royal Hotel and decided that it was not for him. Just off Clarke Street he saw a much smaller hotel of well-applied wattle-and-daub colored a pale pink, with a corrugated iron roof, an awning covering a boardwalk outside its door, a hitching rail and a horse trough. The sign said, in bright red letters, COSTEVAN'S. This will do fine, he said to himself, hitched the mare so that it could drink, and walked through the open front door.

At this hour most of the Hill End men were working their claims, so the cool, surprisingly elegant interior was almost deserted. A red cedar bar ran down one side wall and the big room held, besides the tables and chairs common to every saloon anywhere, a piano.

None of the half-dozen drinkers looked up, probably because they were too inebriated to do so. A woman stood behind the bar.

"Ahah!" she exclaimed triumphantly. "A Yank!"

"No, a Scot," said Alexander, staring at her.

She was well worth staring at. A tall woman, she had a lush body nipped in at the waist by a corset, the top half of creamy breasts bursting out of the décolletage of her red silk dress, its brief sleeves slipped down to bare her magnificent shoulders. Her neck was long, her jawline remarkably clean cut, and the face above them was beautiful enough to be called stunning. Full lips, a short and straight nose, high cheekbones, a wide brow, and green eyes. He hadn't thought that genuinely green eyes existed, but her eyes were genuinely green. The same color as a beryl or a peridot. The mass of hair that framed this ravishing face was a reddish-blonde, like pink gold.

"A Scot," she said, "but a Scot who's been in California."

"Some years ago, yes. My name is Alexander Kinross."

"I'm Ruby Costevan, and this"—she swept a shapely hand about—"is my place."

"Do you have accommodation?"

"A few rooms out the back for those who can afford to pay a pound a night," she said in a deep, slightly raspy voice whose accent was English-inflected New South Wales.

"I can afford to pay that, Mrs. Costevan."

"*Miss* Costevan, but just call me Ruby. Everyone else does unless they happen to go to church on Sundays. The Bible-bashers call me scarlet, not ruby." She grinned, displaying even white teeth and a dimple in either cheek.

"Are meals included in the tariff, Ruby?"

"Brekkie and dins, but not lunch." She turned to the array of bottles. "What do you drink? I've got home-brewed beer on tap as well as hard stuff—Alex, or Alexander?"

"Alexander. Actually I'd rather have a cup of tea."

Her eyes widened. "Jesus! You're not a Bible-basher, are you? You can't be!"

"I'm a child of the devil, but a fairly continent one. My consistent vice is a cheroot."

"Ditto," said Ruby. "Matilda! Dora!" she bawled.

When the two girls came through a door at the back of the saloon, Alexander suddenly understood one of the main functions of Costevan's. They were young, pretty, and looked clean, but they were unmistakably whores.

"Yeah?" asked Matilda, who was dark.

"Take over the bar, there's a good girl. Dora, go and ask Sam to make some afternoon tea for Mr. Kinross and me."

The fair one nodded and vanished, Matilda manned the bar.

"Take the weight off your feet, Alexander," said Ruby, arranging herself at what was probably the boss's table, better grained and polished than the rest of the saloon furniture. She pulled a slim gold case from a pocket in the side of her skirt, opened it and offered it to Alexander. "Cheroot?"

"Tea first, thank you. I've swallowed a pound of dust."

She lit one for herself, inhaled deeply and let the smoke trickle out through her nose. The thin, pale grey tendrils swam about her head, gave him the same kind of painful, gut-wrenching thrill he had sometimes experienced in Muslim lands when he met the kohl-rimmed eyes of some utterly alluring woman. They can smother them in all the veils they like, but there are women who can conquer any attempt at harness. Ruby is one such.

"Did you strike it lucky in California, Alexander?"

"Yes, as a matter of fact. My two partners and I found a vein of gold-bearing quartz in the Sierra foothills."

"Enough to be a rich man?"

"Moderately rich."

"Didn't piss it all away, eh?"

"I am nobody's fool," he said softly, black eyes flashing.

Startled, she began to say something, but at that moment the back door opened and a boy about eight years of age came out wheeling a cart on which stood a big teapot in a home-made cosy, a fine bone china tea set for two, an assortment of dainty little sandwiches and a cream sponge cake.

Ruby's eyes had lit up at sight of the boy, who was the most unusually beautiful child Alexander had ever seen. Exotic, slim, graceful, immensely dignified and self-possessed.

"This is my son, Lee," Ruby said, drawing the boy to her for a quick kiss. "Ta, my jade kitten. Say hello to Mr. Kinross."

"Hello, Mr. Kinross," said Lee, smiling Ruby's smile.

"Now scoot. Go on, quick-smart!"

"So you have been married," said Alexander.

Her pale brows lifted haughtily. "No, I have not. There's no power on earth could make me marry *anyone,* Alexander Kinross—no power on earth! Put my neck under some man's yoke? Hah! I'd sooner die!"

The violence of her answer didn't really surprise him; he instinctively knew the important things about Ruby already. The independence. The pride in ownership. The contempt for virtuous citizens. But the boy was a puzzle: that dark beige skin, the way his green eyes were set in their orbits, the absolute black of his straight, glossy hair.

"Is Lee's father Chinese?" he asked.

"Yes. Sung Chow. But he agreed that our son should be Lee Costevan, and that he be brought up British—provided that I make him a gentleman." She poured the tea. "Sung Chow used to be my partner in this enterprise, but after Lee was born I bought him out. Oh, he's still in Hill End, but he owns and runs a laundry, the brewery, and several boarding houses. We're good friends."

"Yet he consigned his son entirely to you?"

"Of course. Lee's a half-caste, so he can't be a Chinese. Sung sent to China for a wife as soon as he had the money, so he has two Chinese sons now. His brother, Sam Wong—Sung is the surname, but Wong decided to be Sam—is my overpaid cook, being the younger of the two Sungs. One of them has to go home to China to placate the ancestors, and that's Sam. So he only takes half his wage, I bank the rest for him—the more he takes home, the greedier the relatives will be." She snorted with laughter. "As for Sung—the only way he's ever going home to China is as ashes in a gorgeous dragon-wreathed jar."

"What do you hope for your son, then, if he's to be reared a gentleman?" he asked, knowing the fate of bastards.

The lustrous eyes swam with sudden tears; she blinked them away. "I have it worked out, Alexander. In two more months he won't be with me." The tears gathered again, were mastered again. "I won't see him for ten years. He's going to a very exclusive private school in England. It's a school that specializes in foreign pupils—the sons of pashas, rajahs, sultans, all sorts of Oriental potentates who want English-educated sons. So Lee won't stand out, except that he's *hugely* clever. You see, his school friends will be potentates themselves one day, all allied to the British Crown. They'll be able to help Lee."

"You're asking a lot of a little boy, Ruby. How old is he, eight or nine?"

"Eight, soon nine." She poured him a fourth cup of tea and leaned forward earnestly. "He *understands* his situation—the half-caste business, my society shortcomings—all of it. I've never concealed anything from him, but I've never let him become ashamed either. Lee and I face what we are with fortitude and a practical outlook. It's going to kill me to live without him, but I will, for his sake. If I tried to send him to school in Sydney, or even in Melbourne, someone would find out. But no one will find out if he's in a school for foreign royalty in England. Sung has a cousin, Wo Fat, who is to go with Lee as his servant and protector. They sail early in June."

"It will be harder for him, even if he does understand."

"Do you think I don't know that? But because he understands, he will do it. For me."

"Think of this, Ruby. When he's grown-up, will he thank you for taking him away from his mummy at such a tender age to throw him into the lion's den of an English public school? Surrounded by great wealth, aware that if his fellow pupils knew his real circumstances, they'd cut him dead—oh, Ruby, it has its dark side," said Alexander, though why he was fighting so hard for a child he'd scarcely seen, he didn't know. Only that something in the boy's eyes, so different from Ruby's in their soul's reflection, had drawn him strongly.

"Persistent blighter, aren't you?" She got up. "Have you a horse? If you do, there's a stable in the backyard. Just take the beast down the lane and hand it over to Chan Hoi. Feed is expensive in Hill End, so a horse will cost you five bob extra a night. Matilda, take Mr. Kinross to the Blue Room. He deserves blue—he's a cheerless bugger." And off she went to the bar. "Dinner's whenever you want it," she said as he followed Matilda through the back door.

The Blue Room was indeed a rather depressing blue, but it was big and comfortably appointed. He got rid of the lingering Matilda by brushing past her and going to attend to his horse; the girl clearly had hopes of largesse for services rendered.

There was a bathroom two doors down from the Blue Room, as good, he suspected, as any bathroom in Hill End. The lavatory was an earthen pit in the backyard—no water closets in Hill End! Water was, beyond any doubt, Hill End's most serious problem.

After a bath and a shave he lay down on the blue bed and slept deeply.

The noise awakened him: Costevan's had come alive, which meant that most of the town's miners had finished working. He lit the kerosene lamp, dressed in a fresh suit of skins, and went to find dinner. Wherever the whores did business, it was not in this wing housing the five paying guests Ruby could accommodate. When stabling his horse he had noted that the kitchen was a separate building to ensure that a kitchen fire wouldn't burn the whole place down, and he had noted too that another wing branched off the main building opposite from his. She had an organized mind, did Ruby, as well as a ruthless one. That poor little boy!

The saloon was packed. Men stood three-deep along the bar, and every table except the boss's was occupied. Matilda and Dora were flouncing about; so were three other girls. Presuming that he sat at the boss's table to eat, he ensconced himself there to an accompaniment of many curious glances; most of the influx of customers were still fairly sober.

"I'm Maureen," said a red-haired girl in green lace; she had more freckles than anyone Alexander had ever seen, and looked as if she was trying to get a smooth brown complexion by joining them up. "There's roast leg of pork with crackling, roast spuds and boiled cabbage for dins, and a spotted dog with custard for pudden. If youse don't fancy them, Sam can make something else."

"No, they'll do fine, thank you, Maureen," he said. "I know Matilda and Dora, but who are the other two?"

"Therese is the one with the brown hair and cross-eyes, Agnes is the one with the tattoos on her arms." Maureen giggled. "She used to work the sailors' pubs at the Rocks in Sydney."

So Ruby's girls weren't as clean as they looked. But, as he had no intention of purchasing their services—how much did they cost in Hill End?—he concentrated on devouring a really excellent meal. Sam Wong might be overpaid, but he certainly could cook. Maybe before he left he could coax Sam into making him some genuine Chinese food.

Ruby herself was behind the bar, so busy that all he got was a wave; he wondered if every saloon in Hill End was as well patronized as Costevan's, and decided not. The five girls were doing a roaring trade, disappearing with a victim to reappear within scant minutes, only to find another victim waiting. Of course there had to be a constabulary in the town; presumably Ruby bribed to stay in business.

Stomach pleasantly full, he sat back in his chair to enjoy a cheroot and a cup of tea and watch the antics. Payment for a girl's services, he noted, was made to Ruby beforehand.

Then, the drinkers mellow, Ruby moved to the piano. It stood just inside the entrance door and was angled so that whoever played it could be seen by the whole room. She arranged her skirts to free her feet, put her hands on the keys and began to play. Alexander stiffened, possessed by an absurd impulse to scream at the drinkers to pipe down and listen—she was so *good*! The music consisted of ordinary popular tunes, but she embellished them with complicated passages that said she was capable of doing justice to Beethoven or Brahms.

Until he went to America, Alexander had never paid much attention to music, simply because he never heard any. But in San Francisco he had gone to a concert of Chopin only because he was passing the hall, and discovered in himself a passion for music. Since then, he went to every concert in every place he could find one—St. Louis, New York, London, Paris, Venice and Milan, Constantinople—even in Cairo, where he heard the first performance of *Aida,* Verdi's commemoration of the opening of the Suez Canal. He didn't care what kind of music it was—opera, symphony, instrumental solo or the songs everybody sang in places like Costevan's. Music, *all* music.

And here, in Hill End, was a master pianist playing "Lorena" and singing the same wistful, melancholy verses he had heard sung by all kinds of people during his American odyssey, usually without accompaniment, or to the thin, plaintive strains of a concertina or harmonica.

> *"We loved each other then, Lorena,*
> *More than we ever dared to tell;*
> *And what we might have been, Lorena,*
> *Had but our loving prosper'd well.*
> *But then, 'tis past—the years are gone,*
> *I'll not call up their shadowy forms;*
> *I'll say to them, 'Lost years, sleep on!*
> *Sleep on! Nor heed life's pelting storm.'*
> *I'll say to them, 'Lost years, sleep on!*
> *Sleep on! Nor heed life's pelting storm.'"*

When she finished singing that last verse in her honeyed, strong contralto, the weeping miners applauded hysterically, begged for more, wouldn't let her go.

I could love her for the music alone, thought Alexander, and beat a cowering retreat to the Blue Room before he said something to her that later he would regret.

Someone had lit a fire; May was cold after dark in Hill End, for it was drawing close to winter. Thank God for that! I don't have to sleep in my underwear, the room is warm. He stoked the grate with more coal—coal, how interesting! Where did it come from? This wasn't carboniferous country and there was no railway closer than the siding at Rydal, a terrible drag away.

Perhaps because he had slept during the late afternoon, he wasn't very tired; he dug in one saddlebag for his Plutarch, adjusted the kerosene lamp so that he could see to read, and climbed, naked, into a bed that had very recently felt the touch of a warming pan.

Only when the door opened did he look up, startled; he had locked it, he knew. But of course the owner of the premises had a key to every room. Ruby came in wearing a lacy, frilly robe that parted as she walked to the bed to reveal a pair of long, shapely legs and feet pushed into feathered, high-heeled mules. Her fabulous mane of hair tumbled about her, almost as long as Lady Godiva's.

She peered over his shoulder to see what he was reading, and squeaked. "It's gobbledygook!" she said.

"No, it's Greek. Plutarch's life of Pericles."

She shoved his body aside with her hip and sat on the edge of the bed, undoing the ribbon that held her peignoir together. "You're an enigma, Alexander Kinross. See? I do know some big words, even if I never got much of an education. But you must be a real swell. Greek, eh? Latin too, I suppose?"

"Yes. And French. And Italian," he said, unable to keep the pride out of his voice.

"And you've been to a lot more places than California, I'll bet. The minute I set eyes on you, I knew you were a swell." The ribbons were undone; she slipped the robe from her shoulders to bare her breasts, which were full, high, perfectly shaped. Nor did her waist need much nipping in from that corset; it was small and her belly flat.

"Yes, I've been to many places," he said with more calm than he felt. "Have you come to seduce me, or just to tempt me?"

"You've been around the Bible-bashers somewhere, Alexander."

"I grew up in a nest of them."

"It shows, though you don't like being told that. I want you to make love to me—and don't you dare say a word about the price! When you're the madam of a brothel, you pay other girls to do the humping, you don't do it yourself. I'm so fussy that it's over nine years since I had a bit, so feel honored, sport."

"Lee's father, you mean. What do I have in common with him?"

"If you'd sneered when you said that, I'd clout you, but you didn't. I like the way Chinese look, and some of them are very handsome—tall too. You don't look Chinese, but you are real dark—a bit like Old Nick." She chuckled and threw the robe on the floor. "I'll bet you've deliberately cultivated the devilish appearance, Alexander Kinross." The green eyes glowed. "Well, how about it? In the mood for love?"

Even if his mind wasn't, his body certainly was, and even an Alexander Kinross couldn't always rule what the Presbyterian in him called his baser instincts. Though Ruby could have induced a saint to make love to her, and he was no saint. There had, of course, been other women since Honoria Brown: women of diverse nationality, appearance, circumstance. All of them with that special, intangible *something* that some women possessed, but most did not. And Ruby was irresistible.

She was gorgeous, passionate, sensuous and skilled; either the mysterious Sung Chow was a master of the art, or, despite her long abstinence, Ruby had had plenty of experience. Alexander wallowed in her, his fastidiousness thrust from all conscious thought. And if he knew that he had started something that would be impossible to terminate, he didn't think of that either.

"Why have you not given yourself since Sung Chow?" he asked, winding her hair around one arm.

"I've spent them here in Hill End, and I practice the old saying—never shit in your own nest."

"Then why me, in Hill End?"

"You won't stay in Hill End, you're a rolling stone. A day or two more, and you'll be gone."

"So you wouldn't want to continue this with me?"

"Bloody hell, of course I would!" She sat up indignantly. "But you won't be here. Just come back to see me sometimes, eh? It has to be you comes to me, because I can't pick up my traps like a Gypsy and trail along behind you—I have a son to educate. I *need* my business."

"How much is this school going to cost?"

"Two thousand pounds a year. He'll have to stay there in the holidays, you see. Some of the other boys stay as well, so he'll have company. And Wo Fat."

"That's a twenty thousand pound investment in an unknown quantity," said Alexander's canny side.

"I am not a stingy Scot like you, Mr. Kinross! If you open your wallet I'll bet the moths fly out, but I'm not like that. I come from a long line of thieves and spendthrifts. And I'm a woman. What men I give my heart to, I'll beggar myself to see prosper. You're a man, one of the lords of Creation. Other men see the iron in you, and surrender to your power. You must know you have it, because you use it. But my only power is in how I look—what other power can a woman have? Yet I've got a good business brain, and I've used it to exploit my only asset." Her breath caught on a sigh. "After, that is, I learned how not to be exploited."

"How old are you, Ruby?"

"Thirty. If I was peddling myself, I'd be looking at five more years of good money, then I'd dwindle to a raddled, clapped-out old tart lucky to get sixpence. Well, I saw that early, and decided to be the one running other girls. There's no age limit on that, I can only get bigger and better."

"Until Hill End becomes an upright community of Bible-bashers because the gold is a memory," he said. "Then you'll have to move on to some other wide-open mining town."

"I've taken that into account," said Ruby Costevan. "If you find gold somewhere, how about remembering me?"

"How could I forget you?"

FOR THE NEXT few days Alexander explored the length of the Turon River, amazed at how like the Californian gold country it was. Though this was a much smaller stream flowing from heights that weren't feet deep in winter snow, or even drenched with a heavy rainfall. New South Wales was a dry place away from the narrow coast, which hampered the mining of gold lodged in gravel. In California they had wasted millions upon millions of gallons of water—more wasted, probably, than had ever existed here. A passing botanist with a thick German accent took a room at Costevan's, and explained to him that Australian trees and plants in general were designed to survive a semi-waterless environment.

From Ruby, who had been on the goldfields since the alluvial rush of 1851, he learned that all the rivers flowing west from the Great Divide (an imposing title for a comparatively low range of mountains) in this segment of New South Wales had held alluvial gold—the Turon, the Fish, the Abercrombie, the Lachlan, the Bell, the Macquarie. None, when it came to water volume, in the league of the huge deep American rivers. There were times, she said, when drought turned them into a string of waterholes and not a blade of grass was left for a sheep or cow to eat.

But he couldn't smell a new reef anywhere on the Turon; its wealth had already been plundered.

When he asked Ruby if he might take Lee along on his last day in Hill End, a Saturday, she agreed immediately. He had thought to sit the boy in front of him on his own mare, but Lee turned out to have his own pony and was a good rider.

It proved to be a wonderful day; the more he saw of Lee, the more he liked him. Perhaps loved him. And, stingy Scot though he was, he found himself longing to help ensure that Lee got his precious English education.

The child talked frankly of his coming separation, with a maturity and fatalism that Alexander found sorrowful.

"I'll write to Mum every week, and she's given me a diary ten years long—it's a *huge* book! Then I'll always know exactly how long it will be before I see her again."

"Perhaps she'll be able to visit you in England."

The exquisite face darkened. "No, Alexander, she can't do that. To them, I'll be a Chinese prince with a Russian mother of high estate. Mum says that if I'm to keep up the fiction, I must live it as if it were absolutely real. *Believe* in it."

"She could pretend to be a friend of your parents."

He actually laughed. "Oh, come, Alexander! Does Mum look as if she's the friend of princes and princesses?"

"She might, if she tried."

"No," said Lee firmly, squaring his slight shoulders. "If I saw her, it would all come apart. The only possible way we can get through this is not to see each other at all. We've talked about it over and over."

"Then the pair of you are best friends with no illusions."

"Of course," he said, surprised at Alexander's denseness.

"I may have to visit England from time to time in years to come. Would you object if I came to see you?—properly dressed like a Scottish gentleman, naturally. The odd thing is that it's no social impediment in England to have a Scots accent. They regard us as foreigners who've shed far too much English blood, which gives us all kinds of advantages in dealing with them."

Eyes sparkling, Lee smiled joyously. "Oh, Alexander, that would be first-rate! Please!"

SO WHEN Alexander Kinross rode away from Hill End as the church bells were summoning Ruby's foes to Sunday service, his mind was filled with images of Ruby Costevan and her formidable son. The boy was even more intelligent than his mother believed, though his inclinations lay in engineering, not in the cultural subjects she yearned for. Once he discovered that Alexander knew all about engines, their ride up the Turon became questions and answers. This, he thought as Hill End disappeared, is the kind of son I hope to have when I find me a Drummond wife, as I must.

Back in Bathurst he found Jim Summers immersed in studying bookkeeping; the requirements on his list had been attended to, either sat in the backyard or were on order. The housekeeper was a young widow named Maggie Murphy; her education was sparse, but she cleaned house with energy and skill, and she cooked plain but delicious meals. The way she looked at Summers and the way he looked at her told Alexander which way the wind was blowing, but when Summers didn't mention his intentions, Alexander didn't ask. When the time came, he'd be told.

His next expedition was to the Abercrombie River, with a stop on the Fish River en route. There were a very few and very small gold hamlets; otherwise the country, he found out, was extremely wild, virtually unsettled.

The only village was Oberon, atop the Great Divide on the border between the granite intrusions to the west and the dissected sandstone plateau to the east. At one point before reaching Oberon he looked over the most magnificent valley he had ever seen, but its thousand-foot cliffs were Triassic sandstone, and their bases held coal and oil shale, not gold. The residents of Oberon catered to a small number of intrepid tourists who wanted to visit the Fish River caves, something that had to be done on horseback over a rough-hewn bridle path. However, he was assured, the caves were worth the journey, a vast limestone fairyland of stalactites and stalagmites. No cave lover, Alexander rode on.

Realizing that this expedition was going to be a long one, he led a pack horse (mules were impossible to come by) and ate sparingly; of game there was none, since he didn't fancy dining off the little rock kangaroos which abounded. No deer or rabbits, and no edible plants. The Colt revolver sat on his hip unused. He had a map he had acquired in Bathurst, but it was singularly devoid of names or information. When, many miles to the south of Oberon, he came upon a small but strongly flowing river that headed west, he could find no sign of it on the map. The lofty highlands around it weren't cleared, nor did he find excremental evidence of sheep or cattle sent up here to graze.

Oh, but his nose was filled with the smell of gold! So he turned and followed the stream westward until he arrived at the top of a cascade. The water didn't spill over a sheer cliff in a drifting veil of mist, it leaped and frothed from shelf to shelf of a very steep slope for perhaps a thousand feet. Below it was a broad valley; the river gurgled across the flat and meandered off between gentler, more rounded hills strewn with granite outcrops and boulders.

Someone had partially cleared the valley and the gentler hills, but for grazing, Alexander presumed, as there was no sign of gold workings anywhere. A consultation with his map and a sight of the sun through his sextant revealed that, whatever else it was, this whole area was unalienated Crown Land.

It took him the best part of two days to negotiate a way down from the heights to the valley floor, where he camped on hard ground beside the river in sight of that wonderful cascade. There is alluvial gold here for sure, he thought, but my nose says there's a vein of gold-bearing quartz inside that mountain. My nose—well, it's as good a way as any of explaining gut instinct.

For two more days he panned the river gravel and obtained a hundred troy ounces of gold dust and tiny nuggets. Time then to go to Sydney.

He erased every sign of his presence, even cleared the horse manure away and scattered gravel on the few places where hoofprints showed. Then he rode northwest toward Bathurst, and into another forest. Whoever the squatter was who "owned" this tract of land, he obviously "owned" vaster tracts elsewhere.

Casual questions in Bathurst yielded the name of the squatter who leased (for a pittance) most of the country between Blayney and a point somewhere north of a village called Crookwell. However, this Charles Dewy hadn't tried to squat on the mountains east of the region's gentler hills—cattle or sheep hauled up there, said the squatter imparting his knowledge to Alexander, would disappear forever into the impenetrable bush.

Armed with accurate latitudes and a set of survey figures he had no intention of divulging, Alexander set out for Sydney and the Department of Lands.

For once he put up at an exclusive hotel on Elizabeth Street opposite Hyde Park, and paid a willing Levantine tailor to make him the appropriate clothes in a very short time. Stingy he might be (Ruby's word still stung), but these outlays were in the nature of an investment. So when he presented himself at the Department of Lands he had no difficulty in securing an interview with one of the senior officials.

"We're trying to break the power of the squatters," said Mr. Osbert Winfield, "for several reasons. One is that they have accrued too much political power when compared to the far bigger population of Sydney. Another is that they pay a minute lease fee for unalienated Crown Land. The Government, of which I am a paid servant, wants to encourage city workingmen and ex-miners to take up small parcels of land. Oh, large enough to be viable, of course, but not hundreds of square miles."

"These are the selections?" Alexander asked.

"Precisely, Mr. Kinross. In 1861 a new law was introduced, the Crown Lands Alienation Act, which has since been amended to reduce the time span of a squatter's lease of Crown Land to a five-year maximum. He can renew, but the lease can be terminated if some person buys unsurveyed land on his lease."

"And how," asked Alexander guilelessly, "does a man go about buying such a piece of unsurveyed Crown Land, thereby alienating it from the Crown? I have a mind to buy a selection."

Out came the maps and Alexander's latitude figures. The Department of Lands maps were far better than any he had found in Bathurst, but he was interested to see that his river bore no name other than "tributary of the Abercrombie River."

"How much land can I buy in this way?"

"No more than three hundred and twenty acres, sir, at one pound per acre. You are required to pay a cash deposit of one-quarter, and you can pay the other three-quarters off within a period of three years."

"That's three hundred and twenty pounds in toto. I would pay for it in a lump sum now, Mr. Winfield."

"Where is it?" Mr. Winfield asked.

"Right there," said Alexander, a finger on his river at the base of the mountain.

"Hmmm," said Mr. Winfield, perusing the map through his half-glasses. The eyes he raised to his visitor's face were twinkling. "That's an excellent site to prospect for gold, isn't it? Hasn't been touched in that respect, either. Very shrewd, Mr. Kinross—*very* shrewd! However, you may only buy if you sign a declaration witnessed by a Justice of the Peace to the effect that you intend to fence your land, improve it, and live on it."

"Naturally I intend to fence it, improve it, and live on it, Mr. Winfield." Alexander's own eyes twinkled. "And how would I buy *this* land?" he enquired, pointing to the mountain. "As far as I can ascertain, it's not leased by Mr. Charles Dewy, who does lease the valley and river area. It's steep, thickly forested and quite useless, but I've taken a strong fancy to it."

"It would have to go for auction, Mr. Kinross, after due notification in the appropriate journals. I take it that you would want it to be contiguous with your selection boundary?"

"Naturally. How much of it can I buy?"

Osbert Winfield shrugged. "Pretty well as much as you can afford. If someone else bids, it might go for several pounds an acre, or, if nobody else bids, for ten shillings an acre. I doubt that there will be other bidders. I'm no expert, but I do not think you'll find gold on it."

"True. Alluvial gold settles in sandy, pebbly beds where gravity favors a halt to its progress down the river."

That evening he invited Mr. Osbert Winfield to dinner at the hotel he was to make his permanent headquarters in Sydney, a gesture that the senior public official found welcome. The documents deeding him his three hundred and twenty acres would be ready to sign on the morrow, and the auction would occur in two weeks' time. After some thought, Alexander had decided to bid for ten thousand clearly delineated acres.

"I should warn you, Alexander," said Mr. Winfield, blooming under the superb port, "that things become somewhat different if a township should spring up on your land. Town land has to be subdivided—well, that stands to reason, eh? Naturally you retain ownership of the unsequestered subdivisions, but certain allotments will be reserved by the State for its own purposes—post office land, police station land, school land, hospital land, church land. The town council will also want some land."

"I don't object to any of that," said Alexander, then bared his teeth in a snarl. "Except for the church land. The Church of England I can tolerate, or even the Catholics, but I'm *damned* if I'll see the Presbyterians move in!"

"Personal grudge, eh? I'm Church of England, so . . . It's fairly easy to deal with, actually. We can use all the church land up on the Church of England and the Catholics, if that's your wish. You cannot, of course, exclude the Presbyterians, who have *some* political clout. But they'll have to acquire private land, and if you won't sell to them, they're in the wilderness."

"Osbert," said Alexander, smiling, "you're a positive mine of helpful information." He frowned, wondering how frank he dared to be, and decided to be reasonably delicate. "I am not short of money, my dear chap, so if—er—you should ever suffer any financial embarrassments, I'd be delighted to assist you."

Whereupon Osbert Winfield proved himself a true official of a colonial governmental body. "As a matter of fact," he said, clearing his throat, "I am a little overdrawn at my bank."

"Would a thousand pounds alleviate the crisis?"

"Oh, definitely. Most generous! *Most* generous!"

Alexander ushered him off the premises feeling a glow of achievement. He had just bought himself the first of what he hoped would be many useful senior civil servants and members of the two New South Wales houses of parliament.

THUS DID Alexander Kinross become the legal owner of 320 acres of prime land including frontage on what was now entered on the Department of Lands maps as the Kinross River, and of 10,000 acres of the mountaintop, including the slope and the cascades, the latter bought for ten shillings an acre at auction. He had a license to prospect for gold in his river, and had enriched New South Wales to the tune of £5,321 including his gold license fee of £1. He had also learned that if he struck subterranean gold on his own property, it was, since it lay under ground inalienably his, his to mine exclusively.

IN AUGUST of 1872 he rode back to Hill End, where he found a disconsolate Ruby, bereft of her son and in no mood to be optimistic about anything. Though she was very glad to see him.

"I give Hill End another two years at the most," she said later in the night, sitting up in the Blue Room's bed smoking a cheroot. "I could go to Gulgong, I suppose—it's going to last longer. But after it peters out, where?"

"I wouldn't worry about that if I were you," he said, and changed the subject. "Ruby, I want to meet Sung Chow."

"Sung Chow? Why?"

"I have a business proposition for him that may well flow on to a business proposition for you."

Knowing Ruby's tastes by now, Alexander found Sung Chow much as he had expected: six feet tall, fair-skinned, handsome, about forty years of age. His office was in his brewery, and he himself chose to wear the Chinese garb, though not a coolie's drab attire. His long robe was of peacock blue silk embroidered in flowers, the slim trousers beneath it were dark blue silk, and his slippers embroidered.

"I am Mandarin," he said, ensconcing Alexander in a lovely lacquered chair. "I hail from the city you call Peking, where an unhappy incident deprived me of my entitlements. That is why Lee speaks Mandarin and will pass for a Chinese prince, even if there are other Chinese at his school. His colonial English accent we will blame on a governess. He will, besides, soon lose it."

"You speak almost accentless English yourself. What brought you to New South Wales?" Alexander asked.

"An abiding horror of the spreading rot the British East India Company has fostered in China—opium," said Sung Chow. "I would not kowtow to the British diplomats, so I resolved upon the honorable alternative of emigrating in search of gold."

"Did you find any?"

"Enough to go into business. My brewery, my laundry, my boarding houses and my restaurants generate a stable income, if not a princely fortune." He sighed. "There is no hope of more gold in Hill End—or Gulgong, for that matter. Sofala has died. To be a prospector *and* a Chinese is difficult and dangerous, sir."

"Alexander, please. Do go on, Mr. Sung."

"Sung is acceptable. The Chinese, Alexander, are extremely hardworking as well as frugal. But because xenophobia exists everywhere, those who look and sound like utter foreigners become the target for local men and women who either do not work hard or do not save what they earn. We Chinese are *hated*—it is not too strong a verb, believe me. We are beaten, robbed, even tortured, and sometimes murdered. British justice is not available for us, as the police are often our worst tormentors. Therefore the price of prospecting for gold is too high to pay for men like me, who have other talents and good business instincts." Sung spread his long-nailed hands. "Ruby said you had a proposition for me."

"I do, but I must warn you that it consists of prospecting for alluvial gold, at least in the beginning. However, not on any established field. I've located a new find in remote country southeast of Bathurst—a tributary of the Abercrombie that I've had the hubris to name the Kinross River." Alexander raised his pointed brows, grinned. "I could keep it a secret from all other men, but I'd rather share my secret with a small group of other men—Chinese men. I've been to China, you see. I know a little about the Chinese, and I get on well with them." He looked quizzical. "Why does Ruby get on well with the Chinese?"

"She has a cousin who accidentally spent ten years in China—a man named Isaac Robinson who is now living on Norfolk Island. He was running guns and opium on an American clipper that sank in the South

China Sea. When some Franciscan friars rescued him, he entered their monastery in the Shantung peninsula. But the life of a monk palled, he got into trouble and fled. Between China and his new home, he visited Hill End to see Ruby, whom he liked very much. They had an affinity for each other, which may well be how she obtained her penchant for the Chinese." Sung got to his feet, folded his hands inside the capacious sleeves of his robe, and paced up and down. "This is a very interesting and generous proposition, Alexander, and it tempts me greatly. What are your terms?"

"We split whatever we find two ways. Half for you, half for me. Out of your half you'll have to work out compensation for the other Chinese you'll bring with you. Out of my share I'll compensate Ruby for leading me to you." Eyes never leaving Sung, Alexander leaned back in his chair. "If there's as much placer as I think, a town is bound to spring up. That would enable you personally to be in on the ground floor of local commerce, and Ruby to own a better hotel than Costevan's. As one man, Sung, my grasp on the inevitable settlement will be nonexistent. But if there are a solid group of us in on the ground floor—and provided that the rest of you are willing to accept my leadership—then the settlement will always remain in my control."

"You have it all worked out," said Sung softly.

"There's no point in going off half-cocked, my friend. So think about it, will you? Twenty men, no women, and at first it won't be all panning for gold. By law I'm obliged to fence my land and build some sort of house on it. That comes first, then we're legal and aboveboard. We'll have to be, because there's a local squatter who's going to be very upset."

"JESUS!" WAS Ruby's reaction. "Are you mad, Alexander?"

"Sane as"—he grinned—"well, as sane as *something.* Sung came to see you, did he?"

"Yes. That's second nature for both of us."

They were leaning over the stall door apparently saying hello to Alexander's mare, a place where no one would overhear a word they said.

"And the stingy Scot," hissed Ruby, eyes blazing, "intends to give an ageing whore charity! Well, I can do without your fucken bawbees, Mr. Kinross! You don't fool me! Scratch your surface, and the Bible-basher is scrabbling to get out. I may have started out on my back and now make a living from employing other women to lie on their backs, but at least it's honest work! Yes, *honest*! Once a woman's married she doesn't want to do her marital duty—I don't blame her for that because her old man is probably too drunk to get up more than half a stiffy, or else he rations her housekeeping money but not his own tobacco and booze money—pah! So he goes somewhere else to get rid of his dirty water. If you don't even know a man, let alone love him, why *shouldn't* you be paid to get rid of his dirty water? Eh? Eh? Tell me that, you sanctimonious prick!"

Alexander had collapsed on the stable door, crying with laughter. "Oh, Ruby, I like you best when you're on your soapbox!" He wiped his eyes, took her hands and refused to let her snatch them away. "Listen, you idiotic bigot! *Listen!* Some people cause a chain of events to begin, and you're one such. Without you, I would never have been inspired to form an alliance with Sung Chow, and that in its turn would have led to troubles aplenty for me in this new enterprise. I'm not paying you for the divine pleasure you give me, but for doing me an invaluable business service. It's true that I'm a stingy Scot, but the Scots are generally honorable, as am I. I have needed to be stingy to get where I am, but once I can afford not to be stingy, I won't be. This is a deal that you deserve to be a partner in, Ruby—even if, for the time being, you're only a sleeping partner."

That last phrase, so blatantly provocative, made her laugh; the tempest was over. "All right, all right, I see your point, you bastard. Let's shake."

He shook her outstretched hand, then pulled her into his arms and kissed her. How easy it would be to love her!

AN ALLIANCE between a Scot and a Chinese meant extreme care in planning and an obsession with secrecy. Sung announced to the Chinese community of Hill End that he was going to visit China for six or eight months, and was taking a bodyguard with him; his wife and children would remain behind in the custody of Sam Wong, Chan Hoi and several other relatives.

Sung's twenty men were young, strong, and, so Alexander suspected, bound to the patrician Mandarin by ties that could never be plumbed by anyone not Chinese. They were probably his to the death. Though they all spoke better English than most goldfields Chinese, they were dressed as coolies.

The mission to China set off in state on the Rydal road, always busier than the Bathurst road, since Rydal was the rail depot for Hill End. Nearing Rydal, the party let darkness fall before leaving the road to disappear into the forest.

Alexander had left a day earlier, and waited for them in a clearing well away from habitation. With him was Summers and a string of pack horses loaded with rolls of wire, a post-hole borer, heavy wooden posts, tents, square five-gallon tins of kerosene, lamps, axes, picks, mattocks, hammers and an assortment of saws, the latter to prepare more fence posts from local trees. Sung's carved chests contained nothing but food: rice, dried fish, dried duck, onion and celery seeds, cabbage seeds, various bottled sauces and a gross of eggs preserved in isinglass.

"We travel on tonight," said Alexander to Sung, who was now in peasant garb. "We'll be able to continue in daylight tomorrow, then we'll rest the following night. A hard slog, but I want to get as far from civilization as possible before we halt."

"I agree."

Alexander introduced Summers. "He'll be our contact with Bathurst, Sung. I've a house on its outskirts where the rest of what we need is waiting. Summers will fetch it a little at a time, always leaving Bathurst in the wee sma's. I've sent my housekeeper to Sydney armed with a very long shopping list and instructions that she's to stay with her relatives there until I want her back."

Sung frowned. "Is she a weak link?"

Summers grinned. "No, Mr. Sung. She's promised to me in marriage, and she knows which side her bread is buttered on."

"Good."

BY THE END of January 1873 the fence was finished and Alexander's slab house almost finished. He and half the Chinese were already using the sluicing devices called toms, a great improvement over pans and rockers. The gravel was rich with gold, richer indeed than Alexander had originally thought; it seemed to be present far past his western boundary, which meant that the first horde of prospectors would stay long enough to put up a town. Sung and his twenty men all had prospecting licenses, but a claim once staked was only twelve feet square. They pegged their claims contiguously at the foot of the cascade, but until others discovered what was going on, the twenty-two men scattered down the river skimming off as much gold as they could outside their claim areas. Which left plenty; under the surface alluvial layer were deeper ones, and not restricted to the present riverbed—riverbeds moved around a great deal over the millennia.

Now they varied their diet with fresh eggs and chicken from a fifty-hen coop, duck and goose meat, pork from a pig sty, and a host of different vegetables from a thriving garden. Alexander loved Chinese food, though Summers, he noted with amusement, was not so keen. The Chinese tents were spread in an encampment some distance from Alexander's slab house, which he shared with Sung. Summers elected to be perpetually on the move.

At the end of six months they had retrieved 10,000 troy ounces of gold dust, tiny nuggets, a few larger ones, and an awesome beauty that weighed over a hundred pounds. Thus far their finds were worth £125,000, but more gold came in every day.

"I think," said Alexander to Sung, "that it's time I paid a visit to Mr. Charles Dewy, who used to lease this land."

"It surprises me that he hasn't yet descended upon us," said Sung, raising his thin, elegant brows. "Surely he would have been notified that you bought a selection on his leasehold?"

Alexander laid his index finger against the side of his nose, a universal gesture that Sung entirely understood. "Yes, you'd think so, wouldn't you?" he asked, and went off to saddle his mare.

DUNLEIGH'S HOMESTEAD overlooked the Abercrombie River to the west of Trunkey Creek, a gold-mining settlement that had made the magical transition from placer to reef gold in 1868. It had greatly irked Charles Dewy that Trunkey Creek became an official goldfield, but when the gold-bearing quartz vein was discovered, Dewy invested heavily in several of the Trunkey Creek mines; so far they had returned him a profit of £15,000.

Unaware that Mr. Dewy was a gold investor, Alexander rode up to what was an imposing collection of well-kept buildings inside an immaculate white post-and-rail fence. In front of the stables and sheds stood a magnificent two-storied mansion of chased limestone blocks. It flaunted towers and turrets, French doors, a covered verandah, and a slate roof. Mr. Dewy, thought Alexander as he alighted from his mare, is a wealthy man.

The English butler conceded that Mr. Dewy was at home, all the while eyeing the visitor askance—such peculiar apparel, an ungroomed horse!

However, as Mr. Kinross exuded a calm dignity and authority, the butler agreed to announce him.

Charles Dewy looked anything but a man of the land. He was short, stout, white-haired, wore prodigious side whiskers but no beard, and a Savile Row suit; the collar of his crisp white shirt was starched within an inch of its life, his cravat silk.

"You've caught me in town clothes—just returned from a junket to Bathurst for a meeting. The sun," Dewy continued as he ushered Alexander to his study, "is well and truly over the yardarm. Therefore a drink is called for, don't you think?"

"I'm not an habitual imbiber, Mr. Dewy."

"Religious scruples? Temperance and all that?"

Charles Dewy fancied that, had he been out of doors, Kinross would have spat upon the ground; as it was, he lifted his lip. "I have no religion and few scruples, sir."

This rather antisocial reply didn't dismay Charles in the least; of a sanguine temperament, he tolerated his fellow men's foibles without judging them. "Then you may drink tea, Mr. Kinross, while I drink the nectar of your native peat streams," he said cheerfully.

Settled in a chair with his Scotch whisky, the squatter regarded his visitor with interest. Striking-looking chap, with those pointy black eyebrows and natty Van Dyke beard. Eyes that gave nothing away but saw everything. Probably highly intelligent and educated. He'd heard of this Kinross in Bathurst; people talked about him because no one knew what he was up to, yet everyone knew that he had to be up to something. The American frontier clothes meant that the popular guess was gold, but, though the man had been to Hill End several times, rumor said that the only gold he had paddled in was Ruby Costevan's hair.

"I'm surprised that you haven't paid me a visit, Mr. Dewy," said Alexander, sipping his Assam tea appreciatively.

"A visit? Where? And why should I?"

"I bought three hundred and twenty acres of your leasehold almost a year ago."

"The devil you did!" Charles exclaimed, sitting up straight. "This is the first I knew about it!"

"Surely you had a letter from the Department of Lands?"

"Surely I should have, but surely I have not, sir!"

"Och, these government departments!" said Alexander, tongue clicking. "I swear that they're even slower in New South Wales than they are in Calcutta."

"I'll have words to say about this to John Robertson. It's he who started this nonsense with his Crown Lands Alienation Act—*and* he's a squatter himself! That's the trouble with going into parliament, even a hamstrung one like ours—the members become blind to everything except ways of raising revenue, and the ten pounds a year a squatter pays for his leasehold isn't much help."

"Yes, I met John Robertson in Sydney," said Alexander, putting down his teacup. "However, this isn't a mere courtesy visit, Mr. Dewy. I'm here to inform you that I've discovered gold placer on the Kinross River, where my selection is."

"The Kinross River? *What* Kinross River?"

"It was an unnamed tributary of the Abercrombie, so I gave it my name. I will die, but I hope my river will flow forever. It's full of gold, phenomenally so."

"Oh, Christ!" Dewy moaned. "Why do so many gold strikes have to happen on *my* leasehold? My father took up this land in 1821, Kinross, and squatted on two hundred square miles. Then came the gold and John Robertson. Dunleigh is shrinking, sir."

"Dear, dear," said Alexander mildly.

"Whereabouts did you buy?"

A Department of Lands map came out of one saddlebag; Dewy set down his drink, hooked a pair of half-glasses behind his ears, and came to peer over Alexander's shoulder. The man smelled sweet, he noticed—the leather suit was leather fragrant, and its wearer liked to wash his body too. The long, well-shaped and clean hand pointed to the very edge of Dunleigh's eastern boundary.

"I cleared a bit of that when I was still half a boy," Dewy said, returning to his chair. "Before anyone even dreamed of gold. And I don't think I've ever bothered to go back. The wild mountains start there, so I can't graze sheep and cattle—they scramble up into the native forest and disappear. Now you tell me that the creek is full of alluvial gold. That means an officially declared goldfield, a shanty town and all the hideousness of a collection of human beings thrown together by mutual greed."

"I also bought ten thousand acres of the mountaintop at auction," Alexander went on, pouring himself more tea. "I'll build a house up there to get away from, as you put it, all the hideousness." He leaned forward, looked earnest. "Mr. Dewy, I don't want to make an enemy out of you. I'm geologically knowledgeable as well as an engineer, so there was method in my apparent madness, paying five thousand pounds for a useless mountain I've named Mount Kinross. Any town that grows up on the goldfield will also be named Kinross."

"It's an unusual name," said Dewy.

"It's mine, and mine alone. In the general scheme of things Kinross town ought to die when the gravel is mined out. However, it isn't the placer gold concerns me, though I've already made a lot of money from it. Inside my mountain is what the Californians call the mother lode—a reef of quartz containing free gold—that is, gold unassociated with pyrites. As you know, any man can extract placer gold from gravel, but to mine a deep vein in solid rock is beyond the financial resources of the men who flock to a goldfield. It needs machinery and too much money to be privately funded. So when I'm ready to mine the mother lode on my own land, I'll be looking for investors to form a company. I assure you that every investor in that company will end richer than Croesus. Rather than have you agitating against me among your political friends in Sydney, Mr. Dewy, I would prefer to have you as my ally."

"In other words," said Charles Dewy, refreshing his drink, "you want investment money from me."

"When the time comes, of course. I don't want my company owned and controlled by people I don't know personally and can't trust, sir. It will be a private company, therefore not publicly funded. And who better to be a shareholder than the man whose family has been in the district since 1821?"

Dewy rose to his feet. "Mr. Kinross—Alexander, if you'll call me Charles—I believe you. You're a canny Scot, not a visionary." He heaved a sigh. "It's too late to oppose the rush, anyway, so let the locusts gather to strip the alluvium as quickly as possible. Then Kinross town will settle to proper mining, just like Trunkey Creek. My investments in the Trunkey Creek mines have paid for this house. Will you stay the night, share our dinner?"

"If you will excuse my lack of evening dress."

"Of course. I won't change either."

ALEXANDER CARRIED his saddlebags upstairs to a beautiful room whose windows revealed the surrounding hills and the sadly dirty waters of the Abercrombie River, polluted by a dozen gold discoveries farther up toward its sources.

Prepared to think poorly of Alexander Kinross, Constance Dewy ended in liking him very much. A good fifteen years her husband's junior, she had been a great beauty in her youth, now twenty years in the past. Hers, Alexander divined, was the hand that had shaped this house with such good taste, for she was superbly gowned in ecru satin flaunting the rudimentary bustle just coming into fashion. She wore rubies at her throat, in her ears and over the wrists of the ecru satin gloves that sheathed her arms to the elbow. She and Charles, he noted, stood on very good terms with each other.

"Our three daughters—we have no sons—are away at school in Sydney," Constance said, her breath catching. "Oh, I do miss them! But a governess can educate them only so far. Once they turn twelve, they have to learn to mix with other girls, make the social connections that will help them when they're old enough to think of marriage. Are you married, Alexander?"

"No," he said shortly.

"Too busy to meet the right girl, or does the life of a gay bachelor appeal more?"

"Neither. My wife is already picked out, but marriage is for the future, when I can build her a house like this. It's limestone, Charles, but where on earth did you find the masons to finish and lay the blocks so professionally?" Alexander asked, changing the subject neatly.

"In Bathurst," said Charles. "When the Government put the railway over the Blue Mountains, the zigzag down the western escarpment from Clarence had to be partially built on three high viaducts. They could quarry the sandstone fairly nearby, but the engineer, Whitton, could find no masons. He ended up importing them from Italy, which is why the viaducts and this house are built to metric measurement, not imperial."

"I noticed the viaducts when I came up from Sydney—as perfect as if they'd been built by the Romans."

"Quite so. After the job was done some of the masons chose to settle in Bathurst, where there's enough work to keep them occupied. I opened a limestone quarry near the Abercrombie Caves, excavated my blocks, and hired the Italian masons to build this."

"I shall do the same," said Alexander.

Later the two men repaired to the study, Dewy to enjoy his port,

Alexander to puff on a cigar. It was then that Alexander broached a touchy subject.

"It has not escaped me," he began, "that there is a great deal of ill feeling in New South Wales against the Chinese. I gather also in Victoria and Queensland. How do you feel about the Chinese yourself, Charles?"

The elderly squatter shrugged. "I don't hate the heathen Chinee, that much I can say. After all, I have very little to do with them. They congregate on the goldfields, though there are a few small Chinese-owned businesses in Bathurst—a restaurant, shops. From what I've seen, they're quiet, decent, mind their own affairs and harm no one. Unfortunately their capacity for hard work irritates many white Australians, who would rather not work terribly hard for what they receive. Also, they don't care to intermingle and they aren't Christians. With the result that their temples are usually called joss houses—a term that hints at nefarious activities. And, of course, the final indignity is that they send money home to China. This is seen as sucking Australia's wealth out of Australia." He giggled, a delightful sound. "In my view, what's sent home to China is a drop in the bucket compared to what gets sent home to England."

Knowing that his own money resided in the Bank of England, Alexander shifted restlessly. Charles Dewy was clearly one of that emerging breed, the Australian patriot at odds with England. "My partner is Chinese," he said, "and I will stick to him through thick and thin. When I was in China, I found that the Chinese share some qualities in common with the Scots—that capacity for hard work, and frugality. Where they beat the Scots hollow lies in their happy temperament—the Chinese laugh a lot. Och, but the Scots are dour, dour, dour!"

"You're a cynic about your own people, Alexander."

"I have good reason to be."

"I HAVE A feeling, Connie," said Charles to his wife as he vigorously brushed her long hair, "that Alexander Kinross is one of those extraordinary people who cannot put a foot wrong."

Constance's response was a shiver. "Oh, dear! Isn't there a saying that goes 'Take what you want, and pay for it'?"

"Never heard of that one. Do you mean that the more money he makes, the bigger the spiritual price he'll be called on to pay?"

"Yes. Thank you, my darling, that's enough," she said, and turned from her dressing table to face him. "It isn't that I dislike him—far from it. But I sense that he has many dark thoughts churning around in his mind. About personal matters. It's in personal matters that he'll go tumbling down, because he thinks that he can apply the same sort of logic to them as he does to his business enterprises."

"You're remembering that he said he'd picked a wife."

"Exactly. An odd way to put it. As if he hasn't bothered to consult her wishes." She nibbled at a nail. "If he weren't a rich man, that would solve itself, but rich men are greatly sought after as husbands."

"Did you marry me for my money?" Charles asked, smiling.

"The entire district thinks so, but you know very well that I didn't, you fraud." Her eyes softened. "You were so jolly, so unruffled yet efficient. And I loved the way your whiskers tickled my thighs."

Charles put down the brush. "Come to bed, Constance."

Three

FINDING A REEF AND A BRIDE

A YEAR AFTER Alexander Kinross discovered placer gold on the Kinross River, he finally returned to Hill End and the Blue Room at Costevan's.

Ruby greeted him coolly yet warmly: the kind of reception that said he was most welcome as an old friend, but that his chances of her climbing into the blue bed were—well, not good. Pride dictated her attitude; the truth was that she had hankered for him constantly, the more so because Sung and Lee were gone too. The natural attrition of disease, disillusionment and discontent meant that all five of the girls who had worked for Ruby a year ago had decamped, replaced by five new girls.

"I suppose I should say *fresh* faces, but they're really the same old things the cat dragged in," Ruby said a little wearily, pouring Alexander's tea. "I've been in the game too long—when the bar's busy I can't remember which one is Paula and which one is Petronella. Petronella! I ask you! Sounds like something you rub on to discourage mosquitoes."

"That's citronella," he said gently, fished in his jacket pocket and produced an envelope. "Here, this is your share of the proceeds thus far."

"Jesus!" she exclaimed, staring at the bank draft. "What sort of percentage does ten thousand pounds represent?"

"One-tenth of my share. Sung has used part of his share to buy a three-twenty-acre selection on top of a hill four miles from town, where he's building a pagoda city in miniature—all glazed ceramic tile and brick in wonderful colors, with curled eaves and tiered towers. He's donated me a hundred coolies to build a dam wall out of mixed mullock and rock at the outlet of a valley that will make a perfect dam. When they're done, they'll go up on top of my mountain to divert a part of the untainted river into the dam. And after that, they'll be part of an all-Chinese work force constructing my railroad. On white man's wages, I add. Yes, Sung's as happy as the Emperor of China."

"Dear Sung!" She sighed. "That tells me why Sam Wong is looking so restless. I can do without Paula, Petronella and the others, but I can't do without Sam or Chan Hoi. They're both muttering about going home to China."

"They're rich men. Sung registered claims on their behalf, as any brother or cousin would," said Alexander slyly, regarding her through half-closed eyes. "Kinross is one goldfield where the Chinese are in on the ground floor and are treated properly."

"You know perfectly well, Alexander, that Sam isn't any brother of Sung's, nor Chan any cousin. They're his—serfs—bondsmen—whatever the Chinese word is for freed slaves still under his authority."

"Yes, of course I know. However, I can understand why Sung perpetuated that fiction. He's a feudal lord from the north who clings to his dress and customs, and demands that his people do the same. The Chinese who've gone British have no love for him."

"Perhaps so, but don't get the idea that Sung has no sway over the Chinese who cut off their pigtails and put on starched shirts. The common enemy is the white man." She took a cheroot from her gold case. "You haven't done the Chinese any favors by going into partnership with them and treating them like white men."

"I could trust them not to talk, which gave me six months' headway," Alexander said, flicking the bank draft. "The size of that is largely due to Sung's hold over his people. The secret didn't get out until I registered our claims."

"And now you have a tent town of ten thousand."

"Absolutely. But I've already taken measures to discipline that. It will be many years before Kinross is a beautiful town, but I've planned how it will look, subdivided my land with the right amount sequestered for town and state governments—*and* brought in six good policemen. They're hand-picked, and know they can't prey on the Chinese. I've also hired a health inspector whose only job for the moment is to make sure that the cesspits are dug where they won't contaminate the groundwater. I want no typhoid epidemics carrying off Kinross's residents. There's a sort of a road to Bathurst—fit to take a Cobb & Co stage, at any rate—and another to Lithgow. Cabbages are selling for a pound each, carrots for a pound a pound, eggs for a shilling each, but that won't last forever. The good thing is that we're not in drought, and by the time we are, the dam will be full."

The green eyes surveyed him with mingled exasperation and amusement; Ruby guffawed. "Alexander, you're unique! Any other man would simply rape the place and get out, but not you. The mystery is why you called your town Kinross. Its rightful name is Alexandria."

"You've been doing some reading."

"I am now an expert on Alexander the Great."

"Right on the corner of Kinross Street and Auric Street I've reserved a particularly enviable piece of land. It has a one-hundred-foot frontage on to both streets, and space behind for stables, sheds, a yard. It's entered on the town plans as the Kinross Hotel, owner/licensee R. Costevan. I suggest that you build in brick." His gaze grew stern. "And one other thing—leave your whores behind in Hill End."

Her eyes blazed, she opened her mouth to roar, but Alexander got in first. "Shut up! Think, you prickly, pigheaded harridan, *think*! A woman doesn't usually personally administer a hotel she owns, but it's a respectable profession if the hotel is a bona fide business. A profession that won't handicap Lee when he's old enough to make his way in the world. What's the point in pouring so much money into your son's education if, when he's trying to establish himself in his chosen field, his mother is the proprietress of a goldfields brothel? Ruby, I'm offering you a new start in a new town, and I want you to be a citizen in good standing there." Came that wonderful, charming smile. "If you open a brothel in Kinross, one day you'll be forced to leave. The Bible-bashers will accrue the power to drive shady ladies out, probably tarred and feathered. And I can't imagine my life without you in it. After all, if I lose you, who will I have to listen to me when I rail against the way the Bible-bashers have appointed themselves the moral police of my town?"

She laughed, but sobered quickly. "To build the kind of hotel you're talking about would cost me a third of what you've given me. I can't do that. Here are half Lee's school fees—and right at the very moment when I was seriously wondering how I would ever scrape the money together. Hawkins Hill production is down, and Hill End is dying along with it. A good many Hill Enders are either already in Kinross, or on their way. So I'll be frank with you. First of all, thanks to them, my reputation will follow me. Secondly, I'm planning to go to Kinross myself very shortly, but to build in wattle-and-daub and put my girls to work at the only trade they know. I can see the sense in what you say, your majesty, but I can't follow your orders. Next year you might be able to give me another dividend, but that will be the end of it. The placer will be exhausted."

"Let's go outside and say hello to my dear old mare," he said, on his feet and holding out his hand.

HALF AN HOUR later a dazed Ruby went to her room to change into the dress she had hoarded against the day Alexander would return to see her—velvet the color of marmalade, stylish enough to be worn by a cabinet minister's wife. Perfect for the lady mistress of the Kinross Hotel.

A reef. He said there was a reef on his land.

She studied herself in the mirror with complete detachment. No, I don't look thirty-one. Twenty-five, more like. One of the advantages of an indoor life is a skin unravaged by the sun. Oh, those poor bitches hoeing their vegetable patches while their men are off at the diggings, unable to pay what Hee Poy or Ling Po charge for produce from their market gardens! A couple of toddlers hanging on to their skirts, another bun in the oven. Hands rougher than the hands of their men. I don't know why any of them put up with it—I bloody wouldn't. Love, I suppose. If it is love, then I will never love any man that much, from Sung to Alexander. Some of them used to be as lovely as I still am. *Used to be.*

Review your thirty-one years, Ruby!

I'm a shining example of the fact that sin does pay. If I'd let myself go like those women in their vegetable patches, neither of the men who have helped me would ever have noticed me. They say birth is an accident of fate—well, fate puts a hell of a lot more penniless women on the face of the earth than women whose backgrounds let them make comfortable marriages. Alexander says too that some women go to university, but their parents are rich enough to send them. Whereas the only place my mother ever sent me was to the pub for a jug of beer. I never knew my father, a ne'er-do-well named William Henry Morgan. Cattle thief and jailbird, the son of a convict. He already had a wife, so he couldn't marry my mother, who came out a convict. She died of gangrene after she broke her leg falling-down drunk. My half sisters are drunks and whores, my louts of half brothers are in jail and branded recidivists.

So why did *I* survive? Where did I get the strength to get out, better myself?

My brother Monty raped me when I was eleven—probably a good thing. Once the flower is plucked, the battle is over. No bloodstain on the sheet the morning after the wedding night, so no hope of a respectable husband. Men with marriage on their minds like to be sure they got there first. I'll bet that's true of Alexander Kinross!

What I dreaded was syphilis. All my life it's been around me, lurking. Monty didn't have it when he took me, but a year later he was poxed. I didn't wait. Once my flower was plucked, I ran off to Sydney and found myself a rich old man to keep me in style. He couldn't get it up unless I sucked it—nothing a female enjoys, but a good way not to have babies. When he died, he left me five thousand pounds—oh, the fuss his family made over that! They'd see me in hell before I got a penny of it. But when I read out his letters to them and said I'd read them out in court, they decided not to contest. Paid up without another murmur. The sucking bit clinched things.

So I came back to Hill End with the money to set up in the only businesses I know—pubs and prostitution—and fell in love with Sung. A beautiful man. A prince. But as canny as Alexander. Still, he gave me a gift beyond price—Lee. My baby, my hope, my future. And I'll never tell Lee that on his white side, he's descended from a lot of no-good convicts. Thanks to Alexander Kinross, Lee will escape the taint.

Does Alexander know I love him? Maybe, maybe not. Alexander might even love me back. But the good thing about us is that marriage isn't in the cards. He'd try to own me and I'd refuse to be owned. I pity his wife when he takes one, but I'll hate her far more for stealing him.

A reef. He swears it's there, he swears today's dividend is just the tip of the golden iceberg floating my way. Do I trust his word? Do I believe in him? Yes, a thousand times yes! So I'll do as he wants and build the Kinross Hotel in fancy brick, be a leading citizen of Kinross.

She got up from her dressing table and swirled the massive train of her skirt behind her, then went down to dinner.

"They're making excellent bricks in Lithgow," said Alexander over dinner, "and they can come by bullock dray over the Lithgow track. By the time the Kinross Hotel is finished, there will be a town water supply, gravity fed from the dam site. The sewers may well be finished too. I've found an ideal spot for a sewage farm, and God knows there are more than enough Chinese to make the farm produce. Vegetables will be very cheap on the purified—oh yes, the principle of a sewage farm is to treat and purify—human waste. What's more the site is on the lee side of town, so the winds will blow the smell away."

He will talk about bloody Kinross from now until the cows come home, thought Ruby. It's not the gold that drives him, it's what he can do with the money the gold brings in.

ALEXANDER FOUND the mother lode in February of 1874. Three months earlier he had begun tunneling into the rock about a mile to the north of the cascades, careful that his adit was on his own land. He worked the slender, man-high tube alone, doing all the blasting, shoring up and digging himself, his only aid besides black powder a set of two-foot rails and a single skip into which he shoveled the fragmented rock and dumped it outside the adit.

Fifty feet into the base of the mountain he came upon the vein of quartz at the blind end of his tunnel after a small blast that sounded duller, more crumpled. Two feet wide, it ran higher on the left, sloping to lower on the right. Sifting through the detritus by the wan light of a kerosene lantern, he found almost friable lumps of ore intermingled with slate as well as quartz. El Dorado! *How* did he know where to dig? Working swiftly, he threw the ordinary rock into his skip, piled the ore to one side. Then, holding a piece of the ore in one hand, he walked, a little unsteadily, out into the brilliant light of day and stared at what he held, mesmerized. Jesus! It would assay half gold!

Then he lifted his gaze to the mountain, smiling, shaking, weak at the knees. It goes upward and downward, and I know it goes a long way farther in. It may be only one of a dozen veins—Mount Kinross is literally a mountain of gold. The bastard child of an unknown father is going to be such a power in this land that he will buy and sell whole governments. The smile faded; he wept.

And when the tears dried he looked southwest across Kinross town, which wasn't going to die, oh no. It would be a Gulgong, its roads paved, its buildings imposing. An opera house? Why not? A thing of beauty shaped by a mountain of gold. His sons and his sons' sons would be proud to bear the name of Kinross.

THE FOLLOWING Sunday at dawn he brought Sung Chow, Charles Dewy and Ruby Costevan to see his find.

"Apocalyptic!" Charles cried, grey eyes round with wonder. "This has to be where God has dumped the wherewithal to rebuild the world after He's destroyed it. Oh, man alive, Alexander! It's like—like honey crumble! At Trunkey Creek the gold is so finely distributed in the quartz that you can hardly see it, but this looks almost more gold than quartz."

"Apocalypse," said Alexander thoughtfully. "A good name for it and us. The Apocalypse Mine, Apocalypse Enterprises. I thank you, Charles."

"Am I in?" Charles asked anxiously.

"Were you not, I wouldn't have shown you."

"How much do you want?"

"A capital fund of at least a hundred thousand pounds to begin with, at ten thousand pounds a share. I intend to buy seven shares and retain control of the company, but if any of you wants to buy two shares, that will simply increase our capital. Partnership is limited to the four of us, apportioned by the number of shares each of us holds," said Alexander.

"I'd be happy to see you in control even if you weren't the major shareholder," said Charles. "I'll buy two shares."

"And I will buy two shares," said Sung, nostrils flaring.

"Just one share for me," said Ruby.

"No, two shares for you. One you'll buy, the other is for Lee, to be held in trust by you until he comes of age."

"Alexander, no!" Ruby clutched at her chest, for once too shocked to be angry. "You can't be so generous!"

"I can be anything I like." He turned to lead them into the dazzling light, and there turned to face her. "Ruby, I have a feeling in my bones about Lee. That he has a role to play in the Apocalypse—yes, Charles, it's a brilliant name. This is not a gift, my dear friend. It's an investment."

"Why so much capital?" Charles asked, doing a few mental sums to see how he could come up with twenty thousand pounds.

"Because the Apocalypse is going to be mined with absolute professionalism from its beginning," said Alexander, starting to pace. "It will need miners, powder monkeys, carpenters, mill hands, at least a hundred employees on good money. I've no wish to be a target for those rabble-rousers who specialize in stirring up discontent among workers. I want a twenty-head series of battery stampers, a dozen crushers, and enough mercury to keep up with the amount of gold. Separation retorts. Steam engines to drive everything, and a mountain of coal. There's a lot of coal in Lithgow, but the uphill zigzag makes shipment to Sydney so expensive that the place can't compete with the northern or southern coalfields. We start immediately on the construction of a private standard-gauge railway from Lithgow to Kinross—why? Because we're going to buy a coal mine near Lithgow, and bring in our own coal. Burning wood is wasteful and unnecessary. We'll have gaslight for the town, coal for the steam engines, and coke for the separation retorts. We won't be using black powder much longer—I'm going to bring in the new Swedish wonder, a blasting substance called dynamite."

"I am answered," said Charles wryly. "What happens if the vein peters out before we make a profit?"

"That will not happen, Charles," Sung said positively. "I have already consulted my astrologers and the I Ching. They say that this locality will yield huge amounts of gold for a century."

THE KINROSS HOTEL was open for business, though Ruby still awaited some furniture and fittings for the lesser accommodation. Alexander had a suite of rooms on the top floor, and today had solved the riddle of whereabouts he had been for such long hours over the past three months. Finding the reef. Secretive bastard!

"I hope," she said to him over dinner à deux in the Ruby Room, "that the rest of my stuff comes soon. Once the word leaks out about the Apocalypse, we'll have the journalists back here in droves. Yet another gold rush."

"A few may come, but this is subterranean gold on private property that's owned by a company. A company that will have the mining rights to the whole of Mount Kinross." He smiled, lit up a cheroot. "Besides, I have a funny feeling that there's no gold anywhere off Mount Kinross. No doubt other companies will buy adjoining land and try, but they'll find nothing."

"How much money have you actually got?" she asked curiously.

"A lot more than the seventy thousand I've put into Apocalypse Enterprises. That's why I've hired some of Sung's surplus men to erect a cable railway to the top of my mountain. I want a mansion built a thousand feet up by next year. Kinross House." He rolled it off his tongue. "Because of the way this vein travels—there are many others—I intend to put the poppet heads on a limestone shelf about two hundred feet up. The limestone travels west, but I'll use the shelf as a quarry for blocks to build my mansion, which will enlarge the shelf nicely. The tube you inspected this morning will turn into number one tunnel. Fifty feet below it, on ground level, there will be a big adit with skips towed by cable to where locomotives can pick them up—to the crushers if it's ore, to the dam if it's rock. Since we found a tributary that flows directly into the dam valley, we can raise the dam wall. The cable car will haul the miners and their gear up to the shelf and the poppet heads, then go on up to my house site. I have it all worked out," said Alexander complacently.

"When don't you? But why build a mansion? What's wrong with my hotel here in Kinross? Aren't you comfortable?"

"I can't put my wife in a mining town hotel, Ruby."

Her jaw dropped, a numbness crept through her face. "Your *wife*?" The eyes went the same color as a cat's, narrow and feral and dangerous. "I see. All picked out, is she?"

"Picked out for years," he said, clearly enjoying himself. A puff of smoke gushed ceilingward; a ring followed it.

"At the moment," she said calmly, "the Church of England is still abuilding and your town improvements haven't gone beyond a water supply and sewerage. That you and I are lovers is common knowledge and offends no one. But once you have a wife, that will change. Jesus, Alexander, what a fucken *bastard* you are! I let you buy me, I let you put me in a position where I can't protest! Well," she said, rearing to her feet so quickly that her chair toppled and every other diner in the Ruby Room was staring, "I suggest you think again, you lump of shit, you—you snake!"

"Carry on like this," he said mildly, "and you won't become a partner in Apocalypse Enterprises."

Whack! Her hand struck his face so hard that the pendants on the chandelier tinkled. "That suits me fine! You can shove your fucken gold so far up your arse that you vomit it!"

She stormed out, the marmalade velvet dress a blur of melted gold air. Alexander regarded the rest of the diners with his brows up, put the cheroot in a crystal ashtray, and followed her out at a leisurely pace.

He found her on the verandah upstairs, pacing up and down, fists clenched by her sides, her teeth grinding audibly.

"I think I love you best when you're spitting mad, darling Ruby," he said, voice oozing charm.

"Don't you cozen me!" she growled.

"I'm not cozening you, I'm speaking the truth. If you weren't such a delectable termagant I wouldn't bother provoking you, but och, Ruby, you're a nonpariel when you're in a rage."

"Bully for me!"

"The best thing is that you can't keep the boiler pressure in the red zone for very long." He caught her hands and held them easily. "You run out of steam," he whispered as he kissed her burning cheek.

Her teeth snapped, missed. "Oh, *fuck* these ridiculous big skirts!" she cried, fingers curled into claws. "If I could, I'd kick your balls so hard you'd need neither wife nor mistress! Alexander Kinross, I hate you!"

"You don't," he said, laughing. "Come, let's kiss and make up. Whether you like it or not, you're committed to Apocalypse Enterprises, and you'll just have to get used to the idea of my wife. We can be friends, if not lovers."

She stared at him scornfully. "I'd sooner be friends with a Bible-basher!"

"To repeat my eternal refrain, Ruby, *think*! I can't marry you, that's manifest. As husband and wife we'd murder each other. But I've just found what I think will be the biggest gold mine in the world, and to whom am I going to leave my interest in it? I need a wife to sire sons. You have an heir. Sung has plenty of heirs. Whereas I have no heirs whatsoever. Be fair, dear one."

"Yes, I can see that," she said, beginning to tremble as she came down from the peaks of her rage. "Are you hinting that it's me you love, not her?"

"How can I possibly love a girl I've never seen?"

"Never seen?"

"I'm sending to Scotland for a bride. A cousin. Someone who knows nothing about New South Wales—or Australia, if you prefer that name—and nothing about me. I hope she'll be a nice little thing, but she's a pig in a poke. Certainly she's bound to be virtuous." He pulled a face. "And certainly she'll be soaked in Presbyterianism, but I can break her of that. As she will be the mother of my children, I hope to learn to love her. I hope she'll be a dutiful wife. That's highly likely—the women of my clan are brought up dutiful. Which is more than I can say for you, Ruby. Your virtue is nonexistent, and the duties of a wife would bore you to perpetual rebellion."

She fumbled in the pocket of her skirt and stamped a foot. "Oh, bugger, I've lost my cheroots! Give me one, Alexander."

He struck a match, held it while she puffed. "Down out of your high flies, Ruby?"

"With a wallop." Up and down the verandah she went, cheroot to and from her mouth. Then, some distance from him, she halted and turned to face him. "Alexander, this is madness. A pig in a poke? What a way to describe a wife! Marriages of convenience abound, but usually the parties to one know each other a little. Why don't you go to Sydney and find a suitable wife there? Charles and Constance have two or three girls who are 'out,' I think they phrase it. Sophia would be good for you, you'd learn to love her."

His face went flinty. "No, Ruby. My wife is not a subject I care to discuss with you any further. I've told you what I intend, and why I intend it."

"And are relegating me to the role of friend."

"I know that lot in Scotland," he said, plucking the burned-out stump from her fingers, "and whoever my cousinly bride will be, she'll never hold a candle to you. Besides, I'm not married yet, so friendship is for the future."

Her arms stole around him, her eyes went from cat to kitten. "You can't be sure she'll be charmless, Alexander. What if she turns out to be Delilah?"

The wall was near; he pushed her against it and wrenched the top of her dress down to bare her breasts. "There is only one Delilah, Ruby, and she's you."

THE LETTER that Alexander Kinross sent to James Drummond, the one that Elizabeth yearned in vain to see, went as follows:

My dear James,

I write requesting one of your daughters as my wife. Jean will do nicely if she is not yet married, otherwise another will suit me equally well.

Last time we met you said you'd sooner see a child of yours married to an Anabaptist, and I promised you that one day you would change your mind. This is that day.

The boilermaker's apprentice has done extremely well for himself, James. Not only did he find gold in California—a fact you wouldn't let me tell you—but he has found a whole gold mine in New South Wales. Alexander Kinross is a hugely wealthy man.

Kinross? I hear you say. What is this Kinross? Well, the Drummonds according to you have disowned me, so I chose a new name for myself. Your daughter will live the life of a great lady. New South Wales, from whence I write, has no suitable wives to offer—its women are whores, convicts or English snobs.

I am enclosing the sum of one thousand pounds to cover the cost of sending my bride out first-class, and accompanied by a trained abigail, as these females are also scarce here.

Write to me at once to tell me which of your girls I am to meet when she arrives in Sydney. You may expect five thousand pounds in the future if she pleases me.

He signed his name with immense satisfaction and sat back to reread it with a smile. So much for you, money-grubbing old sod that you are, James Drummond! And so much for you, John Murray!

Summers took the letter into Bowenfels to post, though there was a Royal Mail concession on the Cobb & Co coach to Bathurst. Its passage to Scottish Kinross was painfully slow; mailed in March, it reached James Drummond in September. James's answer informing Alexander that he was sending his sixteen-year-old youngest, Elizabeth, traveled much faster. It arrived in New South Wales a week before *Aurora* was due to sail from Tilbury.

KINROSS HOUSE stood atop Mount Kinross, finished in a frenzy. How Maggie Summers had wailed at the prospect of becoming its housekeeper! Not that her carryings-on had gotten her anywhere. Jim Summers said she was to do as she was told, and that was that. Poor woman, she seemed doomed to be barren; no children by her first husband, and none by Summers.

He had left it until late to tell Charles and Constance Dewy about his impending marriage, uncomfortably aware that it would sound most peculiar. Constance had tried her best to interest him in her eldest, Sophia, who she privately considered was an ideal match for Alexander—fetchingly pretty, clever, educated, a grand sense of humor and a nice touch of worldliness. But, though Sophia had yearned for Alexander, he did what Constance feared—looked through the poor girl as if she wasn't there.

Ruby Costevan was a social difficulty that the Dewys had gotten around the way a cat gets around a puddle: by wary side-stepping that pretends to be the route chosen ten thousand years before the puddle ever existed. Charles met her whenever the Apocalypse board met at the

Kinross Hotel, Constance only when the Apocalypse board threw a reception at the Kinross Hotel. What they, all of Hill End and all of Kinross town knew was that Ruby Costevan belonged to Alexander body and (if she had one) soul. What they couldn't even guess at was how Alexander was going to treat Ruby after he married, as marry he must.

When Alexander told the Dewys of Elizabeth's imminent arrival in Sydney, they were flabbergasted.

"Good lord, man, you're closemouthed," Constance said as she plied her fan vigorously. "A bride from Scotland."

"Yes, a cousin. Elizabeth Drummond."

"She must be lovely to catch *you.*"

"I wouldn't know," said Alexander imperturbably. "I knew her eldest sister, Jean—a beautiful, sprightly girl. But this one wasn't far out of the nursery when I was last in Scotland."

"Uh—really? How—how old is she now?" Constance faltered.

"Sixteen."

Charles choked on his whisky, which permitted a little time to elapse before a reply had to be made.

"Nearly half your age," said Constance, and beamed her widest smile. "That's delightful, Alexander! A very young girl will suit you. Charles, don't *guzzle*! It's whisky, not water."

AN ODD CHANCE, that his dynamite should be on the same ship; he had his bill of lading for it in the same postal delivery that brought James Drummond's letter. News that she was booked on the *Aurora* didn't please Alexander; *Aurora* took only a dozen passengers, which meant second-class accommodation, facilities and food. Plus a two-and-a-half-month voyage around the Cape of Good Hope instead of a brisk passage through the Suez Canal.

Once he had cast the die and couldn't retreat he had grown nervous, anxious, snapped at everyone including Summers. Was his pricked pride leading him into something he would bitterly regret? Why hadn't he realized how young she was bound to be? Why hadn't he counted up the years? The only young girls he knew were the Dewy daughters, and that was a matter of saying hello, then quite forgetting they existed. Every time he saw Ruby she was in a new mood: Cleopatra out to sexually please a jaded Caesar, Aspasia wanting a debate about politics, Josephine sure that he would abandon her, Catherine di Medici contemplating the contents of her poison ring, Medusa with a stare that reduced a man to stone. And Delilah, out to betray.

So he set out for Sydney halfway through March to find the coastal plain a swimming sea of humidity, and Sydney's sewerage problems still on everybody's lips. However, he did what he could to cushion Elizabeth's shocks, for he knew how James would have brought her up. Well, wasn't that why he was marrying her? Virginal and virtuous, unschooled, untried, a wee country lassie who got jam on the supper table on Sundays only and a roast dinner when the family celebrated some unusual event. A world he knew all too well, and had hated. What he hoped was that Elizabeth hated it too, had jumped at the chance to get out, start afresh.

When he saw her sitting primly on her trunk with her hands folded over her purse, clad in that unbearably hot, heavyweight Drummond tartan from head to foot, he knew that these hopes were unfounded. Her whole pose was that of an orphan cast adrift in a world she didn't know and didn't want. A mouse. Spirit broken by her father and—no doubt whatsoever—by her minister of religion. That knowledge prompted him to be businesslike and brisk toward her, while his heart squeezed up in dismay. Och, this wasn't going to work!

There was no wise and experienced older woman to tell him that he was going about it all the wrong way, so he had no idea that he was going about it all the wrong way. He proceeded according to plan: meet her and marry her as soon as possible.

The literal day that he spent with her before he married her he found encouraging in some ways, discouraging in others. Though her clothes were awful and her coloring too like his own to have instinctive appeal, a good look at her told him that she had the potential to be a very beautiful woman. And he liked her eyes, wide apart and big, their irises a genuine navy-blue. Once she was fashionably dressed and dowered with striking jewels, he'd have no cause to be ashamed of her appearance. The shyness and quietness, he told himself, would vanish in time, and her unintelligible Scottish accent would lessen. Her reception of the diamond ring was exasperating, but in the two weeks that followed their wedding she didn't object to being made over.

He had approached bedding her with the confidence of a man skilled in making love, whose experiences were wide enough to encompass womankind. But he failed to take into account the fact that all of his conquests were of women who had invited him into their beds—that is, women who desired him. And he had pleased every one of them, had them begging for more. Of course he knew that Elizabeth was too young and too ignorant to be in a receptive state of mind before the bedding took place, but he had no doubt that within a couple of minutes she would be aroused and ready for him. When that didn't happen, he was left without resources: no Don Juan, Alexander Kinross. Just a brilliant engineer with a powerful sexual drive so far channeled into mutual pleasure. But the silly girl wouldn't even let him remove her nightgown! Nothing he could do aroused her! At sixteen women were supposed to be absolutely at their ripest, but Elizabeth was a sour, very green cherry. She endured his attentions politely, in that she didn't reject him outright; clearly she was prepared to do her matrimonial duty, duty plain and simple though it was. So, after three assaults on the citadel of his new wife, Alexander left her bed a bitterly disappointed man. But more than that: he left her bed wondering if he had been mistaken all these years—was it possible that the women who had *seemed* to be aroused by his lovemaking were counterfeiting pleasure?

Reflection in his own sleepless bed reassured him on this last point. A man who knew gold from fool's gold wouldn't be so easily hoodwinked, and memories of Ruby in his bed laid those particular doubts to rest. No fake climaxes there, she was too juicy, too downright greedy. Och, but it was humiliating to realize that he wasn't such a great lover after all! Why couldn't he rouse Elizabeth? I'm not a vain man, he said to himself, having no idea that some would call his buckskins evidence of vanity, I'm not a vain man, but I have a good body and a fairly reasonable sort of face. I'm rich, successful, well liked. So why am I failing with my wife?

A question he couldn't answer.

Nor was it answered by the time that they left Sydney, though he had made love to her dozens of times, always without response. She just lay there and suffered it.

Had Elizabeth only realized it, she couldn't have found a better way to intrigue her husband than to be what she was: a woman he couldn't wrap around his finger, charm with that irresistible smile, drive into a fury that led to passion and wild pleasure. To him, it was a little like being married to an icicle that wasn't ice all the way to its core; if he could only find the key to what would melt her, he would be king of the world. He fell in love with her because he couldn't move her, he couldn't make her eyes light up when he entered the room, he couldn't elicit any response save uncomplaining duty.

On the night she turned to him and kissed him as thanks for his kindness to Theodora Jenkins, he had made a terrible mistake by calling in the debt at once.

"Take off your nightgown. Skin should feel skin."

Thinking that skin on skin was bound to light a spark in her, because it always did in him. But it hadn't. The stoical duty was still a duty. Elizabeth, he knew by now, not only didn't love him; she would probably never love him. He was her burden.

So he hadn't broken off his liaison with Ruby after all, and that in turn led to the complication of making sure that Ruby remained his secret. If he permitted Elizabeth to go about the town without him beside her, some vindictive old tabby would stick her claws in; it was even possible that Ruby would introduce herself. For of course Ruby had winkled the true situation out of him the moment he returned to Kinross and her, the woman he couldn't live without.

"You've fallen out of love with me and into love with your frozen wife," she said maliciously.

"It's worse than that," he said gloomily. "I'm in love with two women at once, for different reasons and with different objectives. Well," he asked, propping himself up on an elbow, "isn't that natural? You're about as different from each other as women can get."

"How would I know?" she asked, sounding absolutely bored. "I've never met Mrs. Kinross."

"And you never will!" he snapped.

"Sometimes, Alexander, you ooze shit."

HOWEVER, NONE of it mattered when he realized that Elizabeth was pregnant. She'd fallen at once, which boded well for a large family of boys and girls. One every twenty months or so. That would give her sufficient rest between their births. She may not be interested in the act of love, but she will make a wonderful mother, and she'll be queen in this house, he said to himself. His delight at the news of her pregnancy had driven him to tell her right then and there how far he had come, from what ignominious origins he had sprung. It had burned to be said as if a part of the sacrament of conception, which was logical to a man like Alexander, whose own conception was shrouded in mystery, whose mother had kept the identity of her lover a secret so close that not even Pinkerton's, when he put them on to it, had been able to break the silence of that little Scottish community. What he didn't know was that his confession destroyed the moment for Elizabeth, drove her even further away from him. He had intended to bridge the gap with it, not widen it.

Yes, he repeated to himself, Elizabeth will make a wonderful mother, and she'll be queen in this house. It took courage to put Maggie Summers in her place over Jade and the manservants. The hide of that woman to do such things behind my back! Why *do* women as common as Maggie Summers look down on the Chinese as their inferiors?

And my wife thinks that I look like the devil. If only I'd known! If only I'd known!

The beard and mustache came off on his next visit to Joe Skoggs the barber.

Elizabeth actually smiled when she saw his face, dark bronze and sickly white.

"Like a piebald pony," she said. "Thank you, Alexander."

Four

HOME TRUTHS AND AN UNEXPECTED ALLIANCE

THANKS TO Miss Theodora Jenkins and Jade, Elizabeth's life in Kinross House was not quite as lonely as it had been when she first arrived, but time still hung heavily on her hands, so used to being busy. Apart from a visit by the Dewys, during which Alexander gave a dinner party, she continued to see no outsiders. Sung Chow, who came to the dinner party, fascinated her, but his conversation was so erudite and his English so scrupulously correct that after the Dewys departed Elizabeth spent all her spare time reading, trying to improve her vocabulary and the way she expressed her thoughts—and in mitigating her accent. When she demonstrated no talent for watercolor painting or drawing, Alexander suggested that she take up embroidery.

"You're going to get heavier and more uncomfortable as the months go on, my dear, so some fancywork might vary your days," he said, striving to be kind and sympathetic, but very aware that he wasn't building his own life around his pregnant little wife.

It was from Jade that Elizabeth finally found out all about Ruby Costevan. The formal nature of their relationship was hard to break down due to Jade's terror of overstepping the familiarity mark, but finding Elizabeth in tears after a particularly trying attempt to do padded satin stitch on an embroidered butterfly's body, formality flew out the window in a trice. Jade mopped up the tears and spoke her mind, which dwelled on the coming baby.

"Oh, Miss Lizzy, I've always wanted to be a nurserymaid! Please may I look after your baby? Please? Pearl can come and maid you, she's been dying to ever since I told her how nice you are," Jade pleaded with fervor.

Elizabeth saw her chance. "Only," she said with a touch of iron in her voice, "if you tell me all about this Ruby Costevan woman. You can start by explaining why all her employees are Chinese."

"Because of Miss Ruby's ties to Prince Sung."

"*Prince* Sung?"

"Yes. He's from Peking, a Mandarin prince. We—all of his people—are Mandarin, not Cantonese." Jade sighed, fluttered her delicate hands. "So handsome, Miss Lizzy! Didn't you think so when he came to dinner? A great lord. Two years ago I was hoping that he would choose me as a concubine, but he liked my sister Pink Bird better."

"Concubine? It's a word in the Bible that no one has ever explained to me. What is a concubine?"

"A woman who is a man's property but is not well born enough to be one of his wives."

"Ohhhh . . . So what are Miss Ruby's ties to Prince Sung? Is she one of his concubines?"

Jade giggled. "Oh, Miss Lizzy! No! Miss Ruby owns the Kinross Hotel now, but she used to own a hotel in Hill End, where Prince Sung used to be too. They have a son. Lee."

"So she's one of Prince Sung's wives."

Jade's merriment increased. "No, no, Miss Lizzy! Miss Ruby has never been anyone's wife or concubine. She's from Sydney, but her family moved to the goldfields when she was a little girl. In Hill End her hotel was a house of ill fame. She isn't Chinese, but she smokes tiny black cigars and breathes fire like a dragon."

The woman outside the Kinross Hotel! That was exactly my own thought—she breathes fire like a dragon. So beautiful, so wild looking, so arrogant. A child by a Chinese prince!

"Where is this son, Jade? Here in Kinross?"

"Lee is at a school for swells in England. Miss Ruby reared him British and he goes by her name, Costevan."

"How old is Lee?"

Jade frowned in concentration. "I'm not sure, Miss Lizzy. About eleven, I think."

"And is Miss Ruby still tied to Prince Sung?"

"By friendship only."

Down went the embroidery needle; Elizabeth shoved the tambour frame away impatiently—what a bother fancywork was! "Then tell me, Jade, what Miss Ruby is to Mr. Alexander. Are *they* friends?"

"Um—I suppose so."

"Have they been lovers?"

"Um—I suppose so."

"Are they still lovers?"

"Oh, please, Miss Lizzy! Miss Ruby said that if I told tales out of school, she'd cut my throat with a razor—she would too!"

Elizabeth held up her folding embroidery scissors. "If you don't tell me, Jade, I'll use these to cut your throat. They'll hurt a great deal more than a razor, but I *will* do it!"

"Your accent, Miss Lizzy! I can't understand you!"

"Rubbish! I work on my accent every day, and you've had no trouble with it before. Stop beating around the bush, Jade, and tell me the truth. Otherwise you're dead."

"They've been lovers ever since Mr. Alexander went to Hill End about three years ago," Jade babbled. "When he came here, Miss Ruby followed him and built the new hotel. He wouldn't let her open a house of ill fame, but she doesn't need to earn money that way anymore—she's a partner in the Apocalypse Mine."

"She's a harlot. She sells her body," Elizabeth said in a flat tone. "She's lower than the things that crawl in slime."

"No, Miss Lizzy, she isn't a harlot!" Jade cried, distressed at such a judgment. "She has *never* sold her body! She kept a stable of girls and sold *their* bodies! She's only ever had two lovers that I know of—Prince Sung and Mr. Alexander. My father, Sam Wong, is her cook." A look of puzzlement crossed Jade's face. "Nowadays she calls Papa a chef, whatever that is. He likes it—his pay has doubled."

"Then she's much worse than a mere harlot. She profits from the harlotry of others," said Elizabeth, stony-faced. "And my husband consorts with her to this day?"

Jade solved her dilemma by bursting into tears and fleeing.

Elizabeth kicked the tambour frame so hard that it broke, then got up and walked to the window, staring out at the garden through a red haze.

So that's why he doesn't want me going into Kinross town! she thought. By accident I might encounter his mistress. Or she might accost me—the vile creature can have no pride, no respect for the niceties. And how he would hate the townsfolk to witness our meeting! Many of them are his employees. It's as I suspected. Alexander is like a rolltop desk—a multitude of compartments inside, each one for a different purpose. His mistress compartment is labeled Ruby Costevan. His wife compartment bears my name. Oh, how much I've learned since I left Scotland! But even there, even if one is barely sixteen, one knows that men keep mistresses. The Bible can be quite explicit on the subject—look at David and Bathsheba, and what Bathsheba did to a fine man's scruples!

ALEXANDER HAD said that he would be in to dinner early, as he had a gift for her. She donned a new dress from Sydney—burgundy silk shot with purplish black, cut to reveal more of her breasts than she liked. Jade had sent Pearl to help her, do her hair; the minx was taking no chances that Elizabeth might succeed in milking more information out of her. Pearl strung garnets around her neck, pushed pendants through the holes in her earlobes. The diamond in her engagement ring gathered all the light into itself, blazed it back in brilliant rainbow rays. By now Elizabeth knew that garnets were not very valuable, but she had loved them, chosen them herself when her husband had wanted to buy her rubies. Even then, some alarm had gone off, warned her against anything named ruby.

"My dear, you look magnificent," said Alexander, his chin and upper lip now the same shade as the rest of his face. She thought he was handsomer clean-shaven—why do men wear facial hair if they have no flaws to hide? she wondered.

"A sherry before dinner?" he asked, feeling very urbane.

"Thank you, I'd enjoy that," said Elizabeth composedly.

Suddenly he frowned. "Ought you, in your condition?" It came out sounding as if she were a drunkard.

"I imagine that a little of anything is all right."

"True." But he poured her only half a glass of amontillado.

She drained it at a gulp and slapped the glass down on the low table between them. "More, please."

"More?"

"Yes, more! Don't be a skinflint, Alexander."

He studied her as if she had bitten him, then shrugged and refilled her glass to the same level. "That's all you're getting, so stretch it out. What's upsetting you?"

Elizabeth drew a big breath and looked straight into his eyes. "I've discovered exactly who and what Ruby Costevan is. Your mistress and a brothel keeper. You still look like the Devil, Alexander, because you've got two faces."

"Who's the little birdie chirped this story?" he asked with suppressed anger.

"Does it matter? Some little birdie was bound to chirp it sooner or later. What a—an *abominable* situation! You keep a harlot mistress down in the valley, and a virtuous wife up on the heights; and never the twain shall meet! If she's Cleopatra, Medusa and I forget who else, what does that make me?"

"A pain in the arse!" he snapped.

She began to pleat the folds her skirt made across her lap, head down and concentrating on the task. "For all my ignorance, I begin to see the way your mind works, Alexander. You need heirs from an unimpeachable woman, and Ruby has already been impeached. I am not stupid, just young and inexperienced. Two qualities I am rapidly losing."

"I apologize for my language of a moment ago, Elizabeth."

"Don't. It was how you felt, therefore it was truthful. You shouldn't apologize for speaking the truth, it's too novel and refreshing," she said, voice dripping acid that she hadn't known she contained. "Tell me the truth about you and Miss?—Mrs.?—Costevan."

He might have started to win her then if he had thrown himself upon her mercy, begged her forgiveness, but he had far too much stubborn Scottish pride. Instead, he went on the attack, determined to put her in her place, which was exactly what *he* decided her place should be.

"Very well, if you insist," he said calmly. "Ruby Costevan is my mistress. But don't be too quick to judge her, my dear. Consider first what you might have become yourself if your own brother had raped you when you were eleven years old. Consider what you might have become yourself if you were, like Ruby—and like me!—a bastard. Even including Honoria Brown, I admire Ruby Costevan more than any other woman I've ever met. Certainly more than I admire you. You're saturated in the petty bigotries and hypocrisies of a small town dominated by a fanatical minister of religion who instills shame into innocent children. Who would burn Ruby Costevan at the stake if he had the chance."

Her color had faded, she looked ill. "I see. I do indeed see. But how are you better than Dr. Murray, Alexander? You bought me for your own purposes, and with no more compunction than you would have bought a side of beef."

"Don't blame me for that. Blame your avaricious father," he said, deliberately cruel.

"I do! I do!" Her pupils had dilated, her eyes seemed as black as his. "I wasn't offered a choice because it's clear that women don't have choices. Men make the choices for them. But if I had been given a choice, I wouldn't have married you."

"That speech rings ominous, but there's truth in it, I admit. You were simply told what your destiny was." He filled her sherry glass, wanting her head to spin. "What other choice did you have, Elizabeth? Spinsterhood, the fate of a maiden aunt. Would you really choose that over marriage to me, over motherhood?" His voice softened, dropped in tone. "The odd thing is that I love you. You're so thoroughly *nice,* despite the prudery." The smile flashed, disappeared. "I deemed you a mouse, but you're not, though you have more fortitude than courage. You're a quiet lion. That appeals to me. It warms my heart. I'm very glad that you're the mother of my children."

"Then why Ruby?" she asked, finishing the sherry.

Och, patience! He just didn't have it when it came to women, to women's troubles. Why was she putting *him* in the wrong? "You must understand," he said, the words clipped, uncompromising, "that a man's physical desires are much as that old horror Murray says. Why shouldn't I go to Ruby's bed, when there's no pleasure to be had in yours? Try though I do to arouse you, to satisfy you, I can't. You go away somewhere, I make love to a tailor's dummy. I want physical desire to go both ways, Elizabeth! You *tolerate* my invasions of your bed because you've been taught that a wife does have conjugal duties. But that kind of lovemaking is awful! Your coldness reduces the act to mechanics for generating children! It should be far more—a mutual and passionate pleasure, a joy for both of us! If you offered me that, I'd have no need to seek solace with Ruby."

This interpretation of the Act fell upon Elizabeth like a bolt from the blue. What he was saying ran counter to everything she had been taught, and to her own feelings when he made love to her. What he did was endurable only because it was how God had designed the generation of children. But to expect her to grunt and wallow and participate in what he did—! To think that when his fingers plundered the most secret parts of her, he truly believed that she could welcome them? No, no, no! To like the Act for its sensations, its carnal nature? No, no, no!

She licked her lips, strove to find words he would accept as final. "No matter what you say about choices, Alexander, you were not my choice. You would never have been my choice. Far sooner spinsterhood, the fate of a maiden aunt. I do not love you! Nor do I believe that you love me. If you did, you would not go to Ruby Costevan. And that is all I have to say."

He rose to his feet, pulled her up with him. "In which case, my dear, there's no more to be said, is there? I'm not about to justify myself one millimeter further. What it amounts to is this: you've married a man you're going to have to share with another woman. One for the pleasure of begetting children, one for the pleasure of the flesh. Shall we go into dinner?"

I lost, she was thinking. I lost—but how can that be? I have been shown that I am wrong, which makes a mockery out of all that I believe in. How did he defeat me? How did he manage to justify his continued connection with a harlot like Ruby Costevan?

At her place stood a small velvet box. Heart sinking, she opened it to see a ring sporting an inch-long rectangular stone. It was sea-green at one end, and subtly shaded through to a rich pink at the other. Diamonds surrounded it.

"A watermelon tourmaline I bought from a Brazilian trader," he said as he went to his place. "A gift for the mother-to-be. Green for the boys you'll have, pink for the girls."

"It's lovely," she said automatically, and slid it on to the third finger of her right hand. Her gloves would fit now.

She sat and ate cold chicken mousse with a caperish sauce, the acidic sorbet her husband was adamant must be served between courses, then unenthusiastically eyed the filet mignon. What she yearned for was a piece of fish, but the river fish were all dead and Sydney too far away to ship fish. One look at the yellow béarnaise sauce and she bolted for her bathroom, there to lose the mousse and the sorbet.

"Too much sherry or too many home truths?" she panted.

"Possibly neither," said Alexander, sponging her face. "It might simply be morning sickness in the evening." He lifted her hand and lightly kissed it. "Go to bed and sleep. I promise I won't disturb you."

"Yes," she said, "go down to Kinross and disturb Ruby."

I wonder, went her last conscious thought, what Ruby's son by Prince Sung is like? What an exotic combination. Eleven years old, and in a school for swells in England. I suppose his mother sent him to school so far away in order to conceal his far-from-swell origins. Clever of her.

But Alexander didn't go straight down to Kinross to disturb Ruby; first he went out on to the terrace where the light from the house spread golden bars across the lawn.

Tonight has been a bitter blow, he thought. Elizabeth does not love me. Until tonight I had believed, running my hands gently and lusciously across the body she now bares for me, that my day would come. That she would awake to my touch, arch her back, moan and murmur, use her own hands and lips to explore my body, caress the parts of it that she recoils from if I try to guide her there. But tonight has shown me beyond all shadow of a doubt that my wife will always recoil. What did you do to her, Dr. Unspeakable Murray? You poisoned her for life. She equates sex with corruption, so what sort of fellow would she fall in love with, if she ever did? God help him if he tried to touch her!

"I TOLD YOU, she's frozen" was Ruby's verdict when he ended his tale of the exchange between himself and Elizabeth. "There are some women whom nothing on earth can arouse. She is one. An iceberg. You're an adept at the art of love—if you can't provoke her into a response, no one can. Take what you need where you can find it, Alexander." A throaty laugh erupted. "She's up there in heaven, I'm down here in hell. I always knew that hell had to be more exciting than heaven—must be, holding such a motley lot. You're just going to have to make do with two women. Oh, what a terrible prospect!"

A COOLNESS entered Alexander's attitude toward Elizabeth from that confrontation on, though if anything he came home for dinner more often, and spent the evenings in her company. Her skill on the piano was increasing as she developed a love for music, but, said Alexander, who had begun to enjoy needling her,

"You play the same way as you make love. Without passion. Indeed, one might almost say, without expression of any kind. The technique is a credit to Miss Jenkins, who must have to work very hard. It's a pity you're not prepared to give a little of your inner self away, but you like to keep your secrets, don't you?"

That hurt, but if Alexander had become coolly cruel, Elizabeth had become extremely controlled.

"Does Ruby play?" she asked politely.

"Like a concert pianist, with the whole range of emotions."

"How nice for you. Does she sing too?"

"Like an operatic diva, except that she's a contralto—not a great many principal parts are written for contraltos."

"I'm afraid I don't know the word."

"Her voice is deep. I haven't heard you sing yet."

"Miss Jenkins doesn't think I ought to sing."

"I'm sure she knows best."

Since there was no one to whom she could confide these short exchanges, Elizabeth got into the habit of discussing them with herself—an unproductive business, yes, but at least some kind of relief.

"It's better to have Ruby out in the open, don't you agree?" asked Elizabeth One.

"She's certainly something to talk about—nothing ever happens that's worth talking about," said Elizabeth Two.

"I've stopped even liking Alexander," said Elizabeth One.

"With good reason," said Elizabeth Two. "He torments."

"But I am carrying his child. Does that mean I won't like his child? Does it?"

"I don't think so. After all, look at his contribution—heave, grunt and groan for about a minute, that's all. The rest is you, and you like yourself, don't you?" asked Elizabeth Two.

"No," said Elizabeth One sadly. "I want a girl to like."

"So do I. *He* doesn't want a girl," said Elizabeth Two.

THE SINGLE track of standard-gauge rail line between Lithgow and Kinross left Lithgow traveling west-west-south for 25 miles before turning south-south-east to run its last 70 miles home. The speed of its construction stood in triumphant contrast to the sluggish progress of the Government railway between Lithgow and Bathurst, its mere 50 miles started in 1868 and still uncompleted.

At 1 in 100, the average gradient was excellent; Alexander had engineered the line himself, choosing to set it in the flanks of the mountains a hundred feet above the valley floors to keep it as level as possible. The track traversed ten stout, high wooden bridges over flood-prone creeks, and went through two 300-yard tunnels as well as nine cuttings. Because he used Chinese labor, he had no work problems; they were, he thought, consumed with admiration, like engines made of living tissue, just kept on going as if there was no word for exhaustion in Mandarin.

It had been costed at £8,000 per mile and it came in at £841,000—an enormous sum of money that Apocalypse Enterprises condescended to borrow from Sydney banks rather than the Bank of England—in return for concessions on the tax it paid to export gold to the Bank of England, which went guarantor. No surprise; the Bank of England already held more Apocalypse gold than that as collateral, and Mr. Walter Maudling confidently informed his directors that the gold would keep coming for many years yet. Alexander and Ruby were its customers. Charles Dewy preferred to bank in Sydney, Sung Chow to bank in Hong Kong, the up-and-coming new entrepôt in eastern Asia.

Alexander bought two similar but superseded locomotives from the Great Northern Railway in England, now doing well from amortizing its older stock, still in excellent condition and a great deal cheaper for a colonial railway company to buy than factory-new models.

Rolling stock came from a different English source. One car was a refrigerated van, as Mr. Samuel Mort's freezing works in Lithgow and Sydney were now fully operational; Apocalypse Rail could rent the van out to the Government railway when it wasn't needed, which would be most of the time. All rolling stock were fitted with spring-buffers at each end and spring draw-bar connections. Alexander's greatest worry was the braking system, that of Fay and Newall: a continuous rod that passed under the train had to be triggered by several men at different parts of the train, which meant it could not be halted much short of a mile, and that men had to ride the train for no other reason than to apply the brakes if necessary. When he read of Mr. Westinghouse's compressed air brake, he put in an order for Westinghouse air brakes, to be shipped from Pittsburgh, Pennsylvania, as soon as possible.

The single passenger car was a new one, thirty feet long and eight feet wide, mounted on bogied wheels. It had a private compartment for the Apocalypse directors, and well-padded seating on either side of a central aisle for other passengers, who would pay a second-class fare. It also had something absolutely revolutionary: a lavatory cubicle, thanks to Ruby's nagging.

"You can witter on all you like about bogies, locomotives and brakes that work by air," she said at a very early meeting of the board, "but it's a disgrace that the men who design and own and run trains do not provide a lavatory for passengers. Oh, just lovely for you men! You nip out the carriage door on to the plate and pee to your heart's content! You can even drop your trou and take a shit if you're caught short. While we women sit in agony for nine hours between Sydney and Bowenfels unless the train stops, when there's a stampede for the station lav. Well, I can't do anything to boot the Government railway up the arse, but I can definitely boot the Apocalypse railway up the arse! I'm warning you, Alexander, put in a lavatory! Otherwise your life won't be worth living."

By the time the line was opened that late October of 1875, the bill stood at £1,119,000. That sum included the locomotives, the rolling stock, passenger car (with lavatory), refrigerated van, locomotive turntables, loading facilities at the Apocalypse coal mine and unloading facilities at Kinross, locomotive sheds, points systems and dozens of minor necessities. Despite this gargantuan expenditure, none of the Apocalypse directors deemed the railway a silly mistake; in the years to come it would pay for itself ten times over in the cost of shipping coal alone. For gold continued to come out of the mountain in ever-greater amounts, some of the ore so rich that whole chunks were lifted out hardly adulterated by quartz or slate, and the original vein had been joined by several more of equal quality.

The residents of Kinross town scarcely believed their luck. With the exhaustion of the placer fields its population had dwindled to 2,000 souls, all of whose work force was employed by Apocalypse in one way or another. Though Alexander chose not to sit on the town council, Ruby and Sung did, and one of Sung's nephews, Sung Po, was the town clerk. He had been educated at a private school in Sydney, spoke English with a clipped Anglo-Australian accent, and was remarkably efficient. The miners and workshop hands were mostly white, the council employees Chinese, who were happier digging and hoeing than underground or whanging away at machines. Sung Po's job, as spelled out by Alexander, was to dismantle the ugly relics of alluvial mining days, macadamize the streets with rock excavated from the mine and specially crushed, see to the erection of a town hall and offices, and badger the New South Wales Government for contributions toward a school and a hospital. A school for the 300 children of the town was already in place, but housed in a wattle-and-daub hall, while the hospital was still a wooden cottage next door to Doc Burton's residence. There was to be a park in a central square around which the town hall, the Kinross Hotel, the post office, the police station and an assortment of shops would stand.

Of course the arrival of coal by train meant gas lighting for Kinross's streets; Po hoped to find the funds to pipe gas into private dwellings within two years, though (of course) the Kinross Hotel piped it in immediately, much to Sam Wong's delight; cooking on gas stoves was wonderful.

The only rumbles about the high Chinese population came from transients like commercial travelers, who soon learned to button their lips; the white Kinrossians knew well that the real power in the town, Alexander Kinross, would not tolerate anti-Chinese attitudes. For which reason, probably, it was the Chinese segment that grew in numbers, especially among Mandarins, in far fewer numbers than Cantonese throughout Australia. Here in Kinross they could live peacefully, go about their business without the risk of being arrested by the police, or beaten up in some alley. Like the white children, Chinese children went to school from the age of five to the age of twelve. One day Alexander hoped to see a high school come into being, but be they white Kinrossians or Chinese Kinrossians, the adults of the town saw no virtue in keeping their children at school for years and years. The best that Alexander could do was to offer scholarships to schools in Sydney for the very few children with educational aspirations. Even this was sometimes opposed by parents who didn't want their sons or (horrors!) daughters talking down to them. Such feelings of inferiority appalled Alexander, who came from a country that prized education above all else; Australians, he had noted, were not on the whole enamored of educating their children to a higher level than they were themselves. And the Chinese felt the same. Time, he thought; that's all it will take. One day they'll all prize education the way we Scots do. It's a ticket out of poverty and ignominy. Look at my poor little wife, with her two years of reading and not much writing or arithmetic. She may say that she would have preferred not to marry me, but her education has resumed since she has married me. Better words, better expressions—look at how well she attacked me over Ruby! She couldn't have done that in Scottish Kinross!

BY LATE OCTOBER, when the Apocalypse railway opened, pregnant Elizabeth was too uncomfortable to attend, though she was able to be hostess at a dinner for the various dignitaries who came from Sydney, some of them red-faced because Kinross had a train before Bathurst did. In Lithgow, citizens of Bathurst picketed.

And finally Elizabeth met Ruby Costevan, who couldn't possibly be omitted from the guest list. The only invitees who actually stayed in Kinross House were the Dewys; everybody else was at the Kinross Hotel.

The guests arrived on top of the mountain breathless and exclaiming; the ride up on the cable car was so novel that the ladies especially were as enthralled as frightened by it. Elizabeth wore an artfully cut dress of steel-blue satin and a new suite of jewelry Alexander had given her for the occasion: sapphires and diamonds set in white gold, the sapphires paler and more translucent than those inky stones tended to be. And, of course, her diamond ring on one hand and her tourmaline on the other.

Pregnancy had enhanced her beauty, and her slowly stiffening pride meant that she held her lovely head high on its graceful neck, her black hair piled up in rolls surmounted by a sapphire and diamond ornament. Be regal, Elizabeth! Stand beside your unfaithful husband at the door and smile, smile, smile.

Though naturally she didn't credit Ruby with tact, Ruby did possess tact when she felt it called for, so she came up on the last car in the last place, escorted by Sung in full Mandarin glory. She had pleaded with Alexander to be excused, to no avail.

"In which case," she had said, "you really ought to have offered your wife the opportunity to meet me in private before this pretentious affair. It's hard enough for the poor little bitch to have to deal with this train-load of toffee-nosed swells without her having to deal with me as well."

"I prefer that your first meeting with Elizabeth be among a crowd of strangers," said Alexander in the voice that brooked no arguments. "She's a trifle fey."

"Fey?"

"Away with the fairies. Talks to herself a lot, so Summers tells me—Mrs. Summers is quite afraid of her. It wasn't as bad when she could sit at the piano for music lessons, but once Miss Jenkins ceased her visits, she went downhill."

"Then why," Ruby had asked, exasperated, "didn't you keep Theodora coming, even if she can't teach the girl piano? Your poor little wife must be desperately lonely."

"If you're implying that I'm not paying Miss Jenkins, Ruby, you're wrong!" Alexander snapped, nettled. "She'd saved a bit for a holiday in

London, so I gave her the rest as well as a comfortable stipend. I am *not* stingy!"

"No, you're not stingy! You're just a prick!"

Alexander had thrown his hands in the air and given up. No matter what a man did, he couldn't please a woman.

Ruby arrived dressed in ruby velvet and wearing a fortune in rubies; she looked magnificent, deliberately so. If Elizabeth had been forced to meet her amid a crowd of strangers, some of whom knew that Alexander still consorted with her, then she would at least show Elizabeth that she wasn't the common alley trollop Elizabeth's imagination no doubt pictured. The gesture was as much to salve Elizabeth's pride as her own; though, she thought wryly as she walked up the steps on Sung's arm, Alexander's wife probably wouldn't get the message.

Her own curiosity was piqued, of course. Gossip said that Mrs. Kinross was quite lovely in an understated way—understated because she was terribly quiet and reserved. But the truth was, as Ruby well knew, that no one in Kinross had seen her at all. Mrs. Summers was everyone's source of information, and in Ruby's opinion Maggie Summers was a spiteful bitch.

So when Ruby set eyes on Elizabeth she saw a great deal more than Alexander, for one, would have wanted. Her lack of height was a handicap, but she held herself very well, and she was indeed beautiful. The skin was white as milk and unsullied by rouge or powder, the lips naturally red, the brows and lashes too black to need enhancing. But in the very dark blue eyes there lurked a panicked sadness that Ruby instinctively knew was not on her account. Alexander took her hand to draw her forward, and those eyes flared distress, that mouth formed itself into an almost invisible moue of distaste. Oh, Jesus! thought Ruby, her heart melting. Physically she *loathes* him! Alexander, Alexander, what did you do when you chose a bride you'd never seen, didn't know? Sixteen is such a sensitive age, it makes or breaks.

Elizabeth saw the dragon woman on the arm of a man clothed in dragons, both of them tall and majestic. Sung in royal red and yellow, Ruby in ruby. But Sung she knew; her gaze moved to Ruby and assimilated those extraordinary eyes, so incredibly green, so incredibly *kind.* That, she had not expected. That, she had not wanted. Ruby pitied her as woman to woman. Nor could she be dismissed as a trollop, from garb to manners to a deep and slightly husky voice. Her speech, Elizabeth noticed, was surprisingly well rounded for someone from New South Wales—especially someone from her background. She didn't flaunt her voluptuous body, but moved it in a queenly fashion, as if she owned the world.

"So good of you to come, Miss Costevan," Elizabeth whispered.

"So good of you to receive me, Mrs. Kinross."

As this was the last pair of guests, Alexander moved away from the door on the horns of a hideous dilemma: should he give his arm to his mistress, his wife, or his best friend? Custom said that it ought not to be his wife, but custom also said that it could not be his mistress. Yet how could he leave his wife and his mistress to walk together behind him and Sung?

Ruby solved it by giving Sung a shove between the shoulder blades that propelled him toward Alexander. "Go on, gentlemen!" she said cheerfully. Then, sotto voce to Elizabeth: "What an interesting situation!"

Elizabeth found herself smiling back. "Yes, isn't it? But I thank you for making it easier."

"My poor child, you're a Christian thrown to the lions. Let us demonstrate that it's Alexander thrown to the lions," Ruby said, linking her arm through Elizabeth's. "We'll shine him down, the bast—reprobate."

So they entered the large drawing room arm in arm, smiling and looking well aware that every other woman in the room was cast into permanent shade, even Constance Dewy.

Dinner was announced almost immediately, much to the hired French chef's horror; he had counted on thirty minutes, so the spinach soufflés weren't anything like ready. He was obliged to fling cold prawns on small plates and slop a dollop of pedestrian mayonnaise on each—*merde, merde, merde,* what a culinary fiasco!

This was Alexander's ruse to separate his mistress from his wife, as they were, naturally, seated far apart. Elizabeth sat at one end with the Governor, Sir Hercules Robinson, on her right, and the Premier, Mr. John Robertson, on her left. Because Sir Hercules governed too autocratically, he wasn't getting on with the Premier, so it fell to Elizabeth to maintain the social decencies. A task made harder by Mr. Robertson's cleft palate and speech defect, not to mention the rate at which he consumed wine, and the tendency of his hand to stray on to her knee.

Alexander sat at the other end of the table with Lady Robinson on his right and Mrs. Robertson on his left. Though a notorious womanizer and drinker, John Robertson was a nominal Presbyterian; his extremely retiring Presbyterian wife was ordinarily never present at any public function, so to get her to Kinross was a mark of Alexander's standing in the State.

What, wondered Alexander as he stared at his cold prawns, am I going to say to this sophisticated addlepate and this kirk-bound martyr? I am not cut out for this.

Midway down the table, Ruby had Mr. Henry Parkes on her right and Mr. William Dalley on her left, and discreetly flirted with both men, to their high delight. So well done was it that the women in her vicinity felt more eclipsed than outraged. Parkes was Robertson's political foe and the state premiership had a habit of oscillating between them; if Robertson was up at the moment, Parkes would likely be up the moment after. It was as necessary to separate Parkes and Robertson as it was to keep Elizabeth and Ruby apart. Of course Sung was his usual charming self; no one made the mistake of deeming him a heathen Chinee, even though he was. Immense wealth could gild far less promising lilies than Sung.

The spinach soufflés when they finally appeared were worth waiting for; so too the sorbet, made from pineapples shipped by refrigerated van from Queensland, where such delicacies grew. Poached coral cod followed, then roast rack of baby lamb; the repast ended with a salad of tropical fruits arising from whipped cream like volcano peaks from a bed of cloud.

All this took three hours to eat, three hours during which Elizabeth grew more and more at ease with her duties as hostess. They might be disgruntled with each other, but Sir Hercules and Mr. Robertson responded to their beautiful companion like bees to a flower laden with nectar, and if Mr. Robertson was dismayed at so much Presbyterianism in this delectable woman, he wisely obliged her fancy—after all, he had one at home.

Whereas Alexander floundered, trying to make harmless chitchat with two women who weren't in the least interested in steam engines, dynamos, dynamite or gold mining. Compounded by the fact that he was anticipating a verbal drubbing from Premier John Robertson, and was looking forward to slapping Robertson down. This verbal drubbing would take place as soon as the ladies left the room, to the tune of: Why wasn't there land for a Presbyterian church in Kinross? How had the Catholics got enough land to build a school on *as well as a church* without paying a penny, while the Presbyterians were quoted an astronomical price for a postage stamp–sized piece of urban Kinross? Well, if Robertson thought that Alexander was going to back down, then Robertson could think again! Most of Kinross was either Church of England or Catholic, its Presbyterian element amounting to four families. So he shut out the women talking children across him, and dreamed of how he was going to tell John Robertson that he was going to donate land to the Congregationalists and the Anabaptists.

It went the way all formal dinners did; the moment the port decanters appeared, the ladies rose as one and retired to the large drawing room, there to wait a minimum of an hour for the men to join them. This was a custom designed to afford the ladies time to empty their bladders without the embarrassment of having men watch them come and go; as most of the ladies were dying to come and go, a procession began.

"Just as well there are two water closets downstairs," said Elizabeth to Ruby, "but if you'd like to come with me, we can go upstairs to my bathroom."

"Lead the way," said Ruby, grinning.

"I never thought for one moment that I'd like you," Elizabeth said as they prinked in front of a plethora of mirrors.

"There, that looks better," said Ruby, twitching the feathers springing from her ruby and diamond aigrette. "Well, I thought I'd detest you—tit for tat. But the moment I saw you, I just wanted us to be friends. You've no friends, and you need them if you're going to survive Alexander. He's a locomotive, rolls over all opposition."

"Do you love him?" Elizabeth asked curiously.

"To death and beyond, I suspect," said Ruby honestly. Her face changed, became defiant, but Elizabeth fancied that her eyes held pain. "But my loving him wouldn't make a marriage with him work, even if I wasn't a glorified tart, which I am. You've been raised properly to be a wife. I wasn't brought up, I was dragged up. To be Alexander's mistress is more than I expected out of my life, so I'm happy. *Very* happy."

We are at exactly opposite ends, thought Elizabeth with newfound wisdom; I am his wife and would be free of him if I could, whereas she is his mistress and would be tied closer to him if she could. It isn't fair.

"We'd better go down," she said with a sigh.

"Provided that we can find a sofa for two. I want to know all about you, Elizabeth. Are you well, for instance?"

"Quite well, though my feet and legs are swollen."

"Are they? Here, let me look." Down went Ruby on her knees at the top of the staircase to lift Elizabeth's hem and probe the puffy flesh that bulged above her shoes. "You're very dropsical, sweetheart. Hasn't he had a doctor to see you? Not that old Doc Burton in Kinross is any expert—a typical country quack. You need a specialist from Sydney."

They proceeded downward. "I'll ask Alexander."

"No, I'll *tell* Alexander," Ruby said with a dragonish snort.

Elizabeth giggled. "I'd love to see it," she said.

"It would offend your lovely little shell ears. I'm on my very best behavior tonight," Ruby announced as they walked into the drawing room. "Under ordinary circumstances I have what's called a salty tongue. Happens when you run a whorehouse."

"I was so disgusted when I found that out."

"But not so disgusted now, eh?"

"Definitely not so disgusted. Actually I'm dying of curiosity—how *does* one run a whorehouse?"

"With a bloody sight more efficiency than a government runs a country. A horsewhip helps."

They settled together on a sofa, oblivious to the stares of the lady visitors; Mrs. Euphronia Wilkins, wife of the Reverend Peter Wilkins of Kinross's Church of England, had seized the opportunity offered by their absence to acquaint Lady Robinson, Mrs. Robertson and others with Ruby's past and present history. These made Mrs. Robertson feel faint enough to ask for smelling salts, whereas Lady Robinson was highly intrigued and amused.

Burdened with a very dreary woman who was espoused to a cabinet minister, Constance Dewy eyed the pair with envy. Who could ever have predicted this? she asked herself, nodding and smiling at the litany of woes beside her. Elizabeth and Ruby have decided to be bosom chums, and oh, won't that make dear Alexander hopping mad? Serves him right, isolating that poor child up here without companionship!

When the men arrived from the dining room surrounded by a miasma of cigar smoke and vintage port, Elizabeth rose to her feet, some small corner of her mind wondering why Alexander looked so smug, and Premier Robertson so put out.

"I've heard, Ruby, that you play and sing beautifully," she said. "Would you honor us tonight?"

"Certainly," said Ruby, displaying none of the obligatory bashful modesty. "How about Beethoven and some Gluck arias, then Stephen Foster for dessert?"

Elizabeth led her to the grand piano and drew up a chair for herself beside it.

Eyes hooded, Alexander chose a seat next to Constance, who had ejected the dreary lady when the men came in. Charles sat on Constance's other side.

"They have taken to each other like ducks to water," said Constance rather loudly as Ruby launched into the "Appassionata." "Fortunate that Elizabeth's so obviously with child, Alexander—otherwise people might think you were running a *ménage à trois.*"

"Constance!" Charles squeaked, horrified.

"Sssssssh!" hissed Constance.

Alexander flashed Constance an appreciative smile, his eyes twinkling, and settled to hear the bravura performance, enhanced for him by the stunned looks on some of the women's faces. They would hear no better musician in London or Paris.

Sonata and arias ended, Ruby began to play and sing popular songs, while Elizabeth sat raptly watching and listening. How grossly unfair are the accidents of fate! she was thinking. This woman ought to be a duchess at least. How often I have thought about an eleven-year-old girl raped by her own brother, and been distressed by it despite my bigotry. But now I truly understand how cruel life can be. Oh, Ruby, I am so sorry!

Having noticed that Elizabeth was in considerable pain from those swollen feet inside pinching shoes, Ruby suddenly stopped.

"I need a cheroot," she said, and lit up.

Gasps from a dozen pairs of female lungs accompanied this, yet, noted a tickled Constance, Ruby somehow managed to make a woman's smoking a little black cigar look absolutely the done thing. Ruby, I have to know you better! No more avoiding you at Apocalypse receptions.

An imperious gesture of the cheroot brought Alexander to the piano, his expression informing the guests that every man's wife and mistress ought to be on the best of terms with each other.

"Time Elizabeth was in bed, Alexander," said Ruby. "Take her upstairs and tuck her in."

Elizabeth leaned to kiss Ruby's cheek, then left the room on her husband's arm while Ruby resumed her recital.

"Why didn't you tell me how nice she is?"

"Would you have believed me, Elizabeth?"

"No."

Jade and Pearl were waiting, but Elizabeth detained him with a hand on his coat. "Once my baby is born, Alexander, I shall go into Kinross whenever I feel like it," she said, chin up. "*And* I intend to see a lot of Ruby."

He looked bored. "Whatever you wish, my dear. Go to bed."

Five

MOTHERHOOD

THE OBSTETRICAL specialist from Sydney examined Elizabeth thoroughly, then summoned Alexander into the bedroom.

"You should both hear what I have to say," he began, manner grave but not ponderously so. "Mrs. Kinross, you are suffering from pre-eclampsia, a very dangerous malady."

"Very dangerous?" asked Alexander, looking shocked.

"Yes. I see no point in deprecating its seriousness either to my patient or her husband," said Sir Edward Wyler bluntly. "If I had been able to bring my more delicate apparatus with me, I could be slightly more certain—it would, for instance, be useful to ascertain your blood velocity with my rheometer, Mrs. Kinross. However, I can say that your condition can lead to fully fledged eclampsia, which is usually fatal." The patient, he noted, assimilated this without change of expression, whereas her husband's eyes were filled with horror. "As far as we know," he went on, "eclampsia is a disorder of the kidneys seen only in pregnancy, commonly the first pregnancy."

"What exactly do the kidneys do?" Alexander asked, face pale.

"They filter bodily fluids and excrete toxic elements via the urine. Therefore one must assume that there is a lack of harmony between Mrs. Kinross and the child in her womb. That, it may be, she isn't managing to eliminate the child's noxious wastes, which in consequence are poisoning her."

"What is fully fledged eclampsia?" Alexander asked, starting to pace the room. "How do we know if it develops?"

"Oh, you will know, sir. It is heralded by severe headaches, abdominal pain, nausea and vomiting. These are succeeded by strong convulsions that, if unremitting, cause the patient to lapse into a coma from which recovery is quite impossible."

"But all Elizabeth has are swollen feet and legs!"

"That is not what she tells me, Mr. Kinross. There have been episodes of headache, abdominal pain, nausea and vomiting over the past three weeks. In your wife's case, the edema—swelling—is dropsical in nature, not postural," said Sir Edward firmly.

Elizabeth lay, wide-eyed, listening to the dispassionate voice telling Alexander that there was every likelihood that she would die. A part of her didn't mind this news; death was one way out of her predicament. The part that protested at this verdict was the part that wanted badly to bear a living, healthy baby and have someone to love. What might have happened if she hadn't mentioned her puffy feet and legs to Ruby? When she had asked Mrs. Summers about them two weeks ago, the housekeeper had assured her that all was fine, she mustn't worry her head about a little swelling. But Mrs. Summers was barren. Did that mean Mrs. Summers was envious enough to wish her dead?

"What must I do, Sir Edward?" she asked.

"First of all, retire permanently to bed, Mrs. Kinross. As much as possible, lie on your left side—that assists your heart and kidneys—"

"Limit the amount she drinks," Alexander interrupted.

"No, no!" cried Sir Edward. "On the contrary, it is vital to keep the kidneys functioning, which means plenty of plain water in, and plenty of urine out. I'll bleed her to lessen the volume of blood her vascular system has to cope with. A pint today, and thenceforward half a pint a week. If we can get her to labor without the prior onset of convulsions, she has a good chance of getting through the birth process." Sir Edward turned to the bed. "You are, I would say, Mrs. Kinross, in about your thirtieth week. Ten more weeks to go. I cannot emphasize too strongly that they must be spent in bed. The only time you may get up is to evacuate your bowels—for urine, use a bedpan. Eat plenty of vegetables, fruit and brown bread, and drink copious amounts of water. I'll send a nurse from Sydney to teach a number of local women how to take care of you."

"Mrs. Summers will be ideal," said Alexander quickly.

"No!" Elizabeth cried, sitting bolt upright. "Alexander, I beg you, no! Not Mrs. Summers, please. She has too much to do already. I would prefer Jade, Pearl and Silken Flower."

"They're silly girls, not mature women," Alexander objected.

"So am I a silly girl. Humor me, please!"

FACE DRAWN, Alexander accompanied Sir Edward out. "If my wife should develop eclampsia, what will happen to the child? Is there any chance for the child?"

"If she goes to term and then suffers a status epilepticus proceeding to irreversible coma, then the child can be removed by Caesarean section before she expires. That will not guarantee its survival, but it represents the only chance."

"Can't that be done while *she* has a chance to live?"

"No woman has ever survived Caesarean section, Mr. Kinross."

"Julius Caesar's mother did," said Alexander.

"She cannot have. She lived to be seventy years old."

"Then why is it called a Caesarean section?"

"There were many Caesars after Julius," said Sir Edward, "so perhaps it was a different Caesar born that way. One whose mama died at his birth. For the mother must die—*must!*"

"You'll return for the confinement?"

"Alas, no, I cannot. This trip was hard enough to fit in. I have a very busy practice."

"The child is due around New Year. Come up after Christmas and stay until it is born—bring your wife, your own children, whomever you like! Think of it as a holiday in a delightfully cool environment—no stupefying heat and humidity up here, Sir Edward," Alexander cajoled.

"No, Mr. Kinross. Truly, I cannot."

But by the time Sir Edward Wyler boarded the train, he had agreed to return after Christmas. The price negotiated for his services was one of Alexander's two Byzantine icons—a curio, not a fee. Sir Edward was a collector of icons.

ALEXANDER COULDN'T face Elizabeth, couldn't look at that sweet wee face, so young, so vulnerable. Seventeen last September, and, it seemed, unlikely to live to turn eighteen.

It hasn't gone well, he admitted to himself. Something about me revolted her from the beginning—no, no, not that idiotic business of the devilish beard! What did I do wrong? I was kind to her, generous to her, set her up in a style she would never have known in Scotland. Jewels, clothes, extreme comfort, no drudgery of *any* kind. But I have never come at the core of her, drawn a single spark from those still sapphire pools of eyes, felt her heart leap at my touch, heard her breath catch. She's harder to grasp than a will-o'-the-wisp, her spirit is in a coma already. My Elizabeth who is not my Elizabeth. And now this terrible and unexpected illness that threatens my wife and my child. There is nothing I can do beyond put my trust in Sir Edward Wyler—how can I be sure he knows what he's doing?

"How *can* I be sure?" he cried to Ruby, tormented.

"You can't," she said bluntly, wiping her eyes. "Oh, what a pisser! I tell you what *I* will do, Alexander—ask old Father Flannery to say mass for her, light a pound's worth of candles every day, and hire the poor old bloke a decent housekeeper."

Alexander gaped at her, aghast. "Ruby Costevan! Don't tell me you're a Papist!"

She blew a rude noise. "No, I'm a nothing, just like you. But I swear, Alexander, that those Catholics have the inside running with God when it comes to miracles. Lourdes?"

Only his extreme misery prevented laughter. "Superstition, then? Or listening to too many Irish drunks at the bar?"

"More listening to my cousin Isaac Robinson—I asked Sir Hercules if they were related, by the way, and he said not, with a face puckered up like a cat's freckle. A few years with the Franciscans in China converted *him* to Papism, and I never met a more bigoted C of E lot than the Robinsons."

"You're trying to cheer me up."

"Yep," she said jauntily. "Now go away, Alexander, and mine another ton or two of gold. Keep busy, man!"

The moment he had gone, Ruby burst into tears. "However," she said to herself later, putting on hat and gloves, "I don't see what harm a few masses and candles can do." She paused at the door, face thoughtful. "And maybe," she continued to herself, "I ought to hector Alexander into giving the Presbyterians land in Kinross. Why offend anybody's idea of God?"

ON THE MORROW she descended upon Elizabeth's sickbed, armed with a huge bunch of gladiolus, snapdragons and larkspur from the absent Theodora Jenkins's garden.

Elizabeth's face lit up. "Oh, Ruby, how good to see you! Did Alexander tell you what's wrong with me?"

"Of course." The flowers were thrust at a stiffly disapproving Mrs. Summers. "Here, Maggie, find a vase for these—and take that look off your mug, you remind me of a caterpillar."

"A caterpillar?" Elizabeth asked as Mrs. Summers stalked off.

"I was really thinking of a slug, but enough's enough. You have to live with the woman."

"She terrifies me."

"Don't let her. Maggie Summers is sour, but she'd not do anything active against you, she's too much under her husband's thumb. And he's under Alexander's thumb."

"She's jealous of the baby."

"That I can understand." Ruby settled in a chair like a fabulously gorgeous bird upon a roost and smiled at Elizabeth, dimples denting her cheeks, eyes glowing. "Now come on, pussycat, no doldrums! I've sent telegrams to Sydney for books I know you'll love to read—the spicier, the better—and I've brought a pack of cards to teach you how to play poker and gin rummy."

"I don't think Presbyterians are allowed to play cards," said Elizabeth provocatively.

"Well, at the moment I'm trying to stay on the right side of God, but I'm buggered if I'll put up with that sort of rot!" said Ruby roundly. "Alexander says you have ten weeks of lying here doing nothing except drinking at one end and peeing at the other, so if cards can help to pass the time, we play cards."

"Let's talk first," said Elizabeth, heart full. "I want to know all about you. You have a son, Jade says."

"Lee." Ruby's voice softened, so did her face. "The light of my life, Elizabeth. My jade kitten. Oh, I miss him!"

"He's eleven now?"

"Yes. I haven't seen him for two and a half years."

"Have you a photograph of him?"

"No," said Ruby harshly. "Too much torment. I just close my eyes and picture him. Such a gorgeous little bloke! Sunny."

"Jade says that he's amazingly clever."

"Picks up languages like a parrot, but according to Alexander he's not cut out for Greats at Oxford, which was what I wanted. He's more likely to study sciences at Cambridge, it seems."

This subject, Elizabeth saw, was very painful for Ruby, so she changed her tack. "Who," she asked, "is Honoria Brown?"

The green eyes widened. "You too? I have no idea who she is, except that Alexander considers her a paragon of all the female virtues. I am a nothing compared to Honoria Brown."

"His opinion of you to me was somewhat different. He told me that he admired you even more than he did Honoria Brown. Are you *sure* you don't know her?"

"Positive."

"How can we find out?"

"Ask," said Ruby.

"He won't tell us, he'll be enigmatic."

"Bloody secretive bastard!" was Ruby's rejoinder.

THE WEEKS went by with surprising swiftness thanks to Ruby, books, poker—and Constance Dewy, who arrived to stay for the last five of them. Elizabeth's condition remained much the same; the constant bloodletting rendered her a little languorous, but the swelling went down a trifle, and the attacks of abdominal pain and vomiting ceased to occur. The nurse from Sydney was a brisk, no-nonsense Florence Nightingale–trained woman who drilled the three Chinese girls like a sergeant-major his worst troops, then departed to inform dear Sir Edward that Mrs. Kinross would be looked after at least as well as she would be in Sydney.

It was Alexander who suffered the most, shut out of his wife's daily life first by Ruby, then by Ruby and Constance, a formidable alliance. However, their company did keep Elizabeth's spirits up; gales of laughter erupted from her bedroom whenever he passed it by. As pass it by he did—scuttling, he told himself disgustedly, like a whipped cur avoiding its master. His only solace was work; the Westinghouse air brakes had finally arrived, so he had something interesting to do by installing them.

"I have discovered," he said to Charles Dewy, "that when a man marries, peace of mind and freedom go out the window."

"Well, old boy," said Charles comfortably, "that's the price we have to pay for having company in our old age and for ensuring that we have heirs to follow us."

"The companionship I grant you, but your only heirs are daughters."

"Actually I've come to realize that daughters are not a bad thing. They marry, you know, and—if my girls are anything to go by—they probably bring more able men into the family than a man's sons might have been. You can't stop your sons from exploring booze, loose women and gambling, whereas your daughters are excluded from all that and don't prize such vices in their husbands. Sophia's fiancé is a prince of a fellow with a shrewd business head, and Maria's husband runs Dunleigh better than I ever did. If Henrietta picks as good a man as her sisters have, I'll be a very happy chappie."

Alexander frowned. "That's all very well and sensible, my dear Charles, but girls can't perpetuate the family name."

"I don't see why they can't," said Charles, surprised. "If the name means so much, what's to stop at least one son-in-law from adopting it? Don't forget that the amount of a man's blood in his grandchildren is exactly the same for son or daughter—half. Are you hatching a bee in your Scottish bonnet about Elizabeth's having daughters rather than sons?"

"Thus far it's been an unfortunate marriage," Alexander said honestly, "so if fate goes on being ironic, that possibility may become a probability."

"You're a doomsday prophet."

"No, I'm what you said, a Scot."

Still, he thought later as he labored in the locomotive shed, Charles was right. If Elizabeth did have girls, then they must be reared to choose superior husbands who would be willing to change their names to Kinross. That meant educating his girls to university level, yet simultaneously making sure that tertiary education did not turn them into mannish dons.

Bang, bang, went his hammer; Alexander Kinross resolved that *nothing* was going to beat him, from an eclamptic wife who didn't love him, to a possible tribe of daughters and no sons. His life had a purpose of its own, just as he was driven to achieve it, and one of the major aspects of that purpose was to make sure that the name he had chosen for himself never died.

SIR EDWARD WYLER and his wife arrived just after Christmas and were put in the North Tower, a suite of rooms that had Lady Wyler swooning with joy. Not only had she been afforded the chance to leave Sydney at its summer worst, but a considerate God had landed her in the lap of a luxury that Sydney could not provide: Sydney servants were a cheeky, aggressive lot who came and went as they pleased, whereas Kinross House ran on wonderfully nice and attentive Chinese servants who were not a scrap servile. They comported themselves like well-paid people who liked their work.

For Elizabeth the festive season was simply a continuation of bed-bound incarceration; she was so heavy and lethargic that even Ruby's banter was losing its power to charm.

Though he flashed her a smile, Sir Edward paid scant attention to his patient when he entered with Jade, Pearl and Silken Flower, the girls carrying dishes, bottles, jugs, jars. He took off his frock coat, donned a clean white apron, rolled up his shirtsleeves to reveal brawny forearms, and washed his hands thoroughly. Only when his appurtenances were arranged to his satisfaction did he draw up a chair to sit beside Elizabeth.

"How are you, my dear?" he asked.

"Not quite as well as I was before Christmas," Elizabeth said, liking her accoucheur as much as she trusted him. "I have a very bad headache, pains in the stomach, I'm sometimes sick, and I have black spots before my eyes."

"I must see how your baby is doing first, then we can talk at greater length," he said, proceeding to the end of the bed and gesturing to Jade and Pearl to untuck the covers. "I'm a Lister man," he said chattily as the gentle examination went on, "so you must forgive the reek of carbolic. It will be here until well after delivery."

Finished, he sat down again. "The head is engaged, and I think your water may break at any time." His voice changed, became serious. "Now, Elizabeth, I have to explain what I might have to do in case, when the time comes, you're not able to follow me. You heard me tell your husband that, should you go into convulsions, there is a chance that you will not come out of them. It is generally left to the husband alone to take all the decisions at that point, but in my experience husbands are rarely up to the task unless I can assure them that the wife wishes me to do what should be done." He cleared his throat. "There have been a few recent publications that advocate the administration of magnesium sulfate if eclampsia begins, though I must warn you that this treatment is not proven."

"What is magnesium sulfate?" she asked.

"A relatively harmless salt."

"Administration? What does that mean? I drink it?"

"No, you'll be beyond swallowing any fluid. The salt is given by parenteral injection—that is, through a syringe attached to a hollow, sharp needle that is pushed into the abdominal cavity. There, the magnesium sulfate mixes with the body's own fluids and passes quickly into the bloodstream. One day I believe these hollow needles will be slender enough to insert directly into a vein," he added wistfully. "Naturally I will tell your husband about this, but first I must know how *you* feel about it. The life and the baby at stake are yours. I note too that you're in a mental decline approaching neurasthenia. Are you willing to let me administer magnesium sulfate injections if I need to?"

"Yes," said Elizabeth without hesitation.

"Excellent! Then we will wait and see what happens." He took her hand, squeezed it tenderly. "Be of good cheer, Elizabeth. Your babe seems strong. So must you be. Now, if you're up to it, I will introduce my wife to you. She acts as my midwife."

"Is that how you met her?" Elizabeth asked.

"Of course. Doctors while young have to work so hard at their profession that they rarely have a chance to meet young ladies who are not nurses or midwives. I am very fortunate," said Sir Edward sincerely. "My wife is a wonderful companion as well as a highly skilled midwife."

ALEXANDER LEFT it until the following day to see Elizabeth, Sir Edward having spoken to him at some length and advised him to wait until Elizabeth awoke from a laudanum-induced sleep.

The room had changed out of all recognition, he saw at once. Surplus furniture had been removed, what remained was draped in clean white sheets, a crisp white screen stood across one corner, Jade and Pearl wore white overall aprons, and a faint mist of carbolic hung in the air.

What a coward I am, he thought, approaching the bed. I have avoided her as much as possible for ten whole weeks. Her skin was yellowish, the whites of the eyes turned to him were red with ruptured vessels, and, even though she lay on her left side, he could see the distended belly beneath the light coverlet.

"Sir Edward has told you," she said, licking crusted lips.

"About his hypothetical treatment? Yes."

"I want him to go ahead with it, Alexander, if it becomes necessary. Oh, I am so tired!"

"You're full of laudanum, so that's to be expected."

"No, no, I don't mean tired in that way!" she said fretfully. "I am *tired*! Tired of lying in bed, of lying on my left side, of drinking gallons of water, of feeling sick and miserable all day, every day! It is a torture! Why did this have to happen to me? It doesn't run in Drummond or Murray."

"It doesn't run in families, Sir Edward told me, so you mustn't blame inheritance for your malady," Alexander said with an impassive face. "Your babe is healthy and strong, Sir Edward says, but what he wants to see is an improvement in your spirits."

Tears gathered, ran down her face. "I have offended God."

"Oh, claptrap, Elizabeth!" he snapped before he could stop himself. "Sir Edward blames a long sea voyage in some discomfort, a radical change of climate and eating different food for this illness. Why the hell blame God? That's illogical!"

"I don't blame God, I blame myself for not being true to God."

"Well," he said, teeth bared, "here are some gladsome tidings for you. I've donated a good piece of town land on which *I'm* building a Presbysterian kirk. So you can spend the rest of your life pandering to John Knox's idea of a god, all right?"

Her jaw dropped. "Alexander! Why?"

"Because that pest Ruby Costevan never lets up on me!"

"Dear Ruby," said Elizabeth with a tremulous smile.

"Has it ever occurred to you that, if it's God plagues you, maybe He's irked by the friendship you've developed with Ruby?"

That provoked a laugh. "Don't be silly," she said.

He swung sideways on the chair and stared out the window, which looked south across the gardens to the forest, his hands balled into fists. He knew he shouldn't talk harshly to her, but—"I don't begin to understand you," he said to the scenery, "nor understand what you want from a husband. However, I've come to accept the limitations of this marriage, just as apparently you've come to accept the presence of my mistress. I can even see why you've accepted her—she relieves you of the burden of physical love any more often than is necessary. And look at you, as sick as a poisoned pup because you did your marital duty! It must be a vindication to you, proof that disporting yourself in bed is sinful. Jesus, Elizabeth, you should have been born a Catholic! Then you could have gone into a convent and been safe. Why do you bring so much misery on yourself? If you learned to enjoy your life, there'd be no eclampsia, that's what I think."

She listened to this without pain, knowing that his bitter diatribe arose out of an anguish not in her power to assuage.

"Oh, Alexander, we are doomed!" she cried. "I can't love you, and you are beginning to hate me!"

"I've good reason. You reject every overture I make."

"Be that as it may," she said steadily, "I have told Sir Edward that I want to undergo his injections if he feels they are necessary. Do you agree?"

"Yes, of course I agree," he said, turning to look at her.

"Though," she went on, "in a way it would solve all of our troubles if I died. Even if the baby died too. Then you could find a more congenial wife."

"Alexander Kinross," he said, "does not surrender. You are my wife, and I will do everything I can to make sure that you live to remain my wife."

"Even if our child doesn't live, or I can't have more?"

"Yes."

ELIZABETH WENT into labor on New Year's Eve. Her condition had deteriorated to a remorseless headache, dizziness, vomiting, and pain in the area of her upper abdomen, but grew no worse as she went through the early stages of her confinement. Then when her eyes began to roll and her face to twitch, Sir Edward took the syringe from his wife, plunged it rapidly through Elizabeth's abdomen wall, retracted its contents a little to make sure he was not inside bowel, and injected five grams of magnesium sulfate. The convulsion proceeded from face to arms and hands, then to a stiffening of her whole body, followed by massive jerks. Her mouth was jacked open with a wooden gag, her limbs tied down to prevent injury. But she came out of it, face blue-black, breathing stertorously. A second injection was administered before a second convulsion came on, while the baby, now Lady Wyler's responsibility, continued to fight its way through a birth canal without assistance from its mother. Elizabeth, though not yet lapsed into coma, was hardly conscious of the labor pains.

Ruby and Constance waited downstairs in the drawing room, while Alexander shut himself in his library.

"It's so *quiet* up there," said Constance, shivering. "No screams, no howls."

"Perhaps Sir Edward's put her under chloroform," said Ruby.

"Not from what Lady Wyler says. If Elizabeth is convulsing, she'll have enough trouble continuing to breathe without making it harder for her to breathe by using chloroform." Constance reached out to take Ruby's hands. "No, I think the silence says that our darling girl is having fits."

"Jesus, why did it have to happen to her?"

"I don't know," Constance whispered.

Ruby looked at the grandfather clock. "It's past midnight. The child will be born on New Year's Day."

"Then let us hope that 1876 is a lucky year for Elizabeth."

Mrs. Summers came in bearing a tray of tea and sandwiches, her face so blank that neither Ruby nor Constance could read it.

"Thank you, Maggie," Ruby said, lighting one cheroot off the stub of another. "You've heard nothing?"

"No, madam, nothing."

"Don't approve of me, do you?"

"No, madam."

"That's too bad, but remember one thing, Maggie—my eye is on you all the time, so behave yourself."

Head in the air, Mrs. Summers marched out.

"Well, you have created some difficulties, Ruby," Constance said wryly. "Isn't it wonderful how wealth can alter a woman's social status?"

"That's true. Being a director of Apocalypse Enterprises certainly beats sucking someone's dickie under a table for a five-quid tip," said Ruby, blowing smoke.

"Ruby!"

"Yes, all right, I'll behave," Ruby said, scowling, "but only because that poor little sweetheart upstairs might be in extremis, for all we know. I can't help myself, I like to shock."

ONE PART of Alexander desperately wanted to be up there in Elizabeth's room, but a bigger part of him accepted the fact that men did not witness this woman's business unless they happened to be doctors. Sir Edward had promised to keep him informed, and did so through Jade, who skittled up and down the stairs every half an hour, eyes round with terror and suffering. So he knew that the convulsions had started, but that there was some space between them, and that Sir Edward hoped to deliver the baby soon.

Was it true, what Elizabeth had said? That he was beginning to hate her? If hate was indeed in what he felt, then it had crept in, existed because he couldn't bear to think that he, Alexander Kinross, was incapable of solving the problem his wife represented.

Fifteen, I left home at fifteen, and in all the years since I conquered everything I embarked upon. Soon I will be thirty-three, and I have done more than almost all other men can do by their seventieth year. My will is iron, my power is profound, I can dictate terms to most of those fools in Sydney because they have pinned their hopes on politics and live high without enough income to sustain that. I am the major shareholder in the most productive gold mine in the history of the world, I have interests in coal, iron, land, I own a town and a railroad. Yet I cannot make a seventeen-year-old girl see reason, or win her liking, let alone her heart. When I give her jewels, she looks sick. When I touch her, she freezes. When I try to have a conversation with her, she answers my questions passively and offers me nothing to think about except her aloof disinterest. The only friends she wants are women—she seized upon Ruby like a greedy child, and that's a fine kettle of fish.

And so went his thoughts, round and round, until Sir Edward appeared in the library doorway shortly after four in the morning. He wore no coat and his sleeves were still rolled up, but there was no bloody apron, and he was smiling.

"Congratulations, Alexander," he said, coming forward with hand extended. "You are the father of a healthy eight-pound girl."

A girl . . . Well, he had expected that. "Elizabeth?" he asked.

"The eclampsia has settled, though it will be another week before I can pronounce her out of danger. The convulsions can begin again at any time, though my personal feeling is that the magnesium sulfate did the trick," said Sir Edward.

"May I come up?"

"I'm here to escort you."

The room still reeked of carbolic, not a pleasant smell, but not suggestive of blood or decay. Elizabeth was lying on her back in the bed, washed and freshly clothed, her belly flat again. Alexander approached warily, nothing in his life having prepared him for this confrontation. Her eyes were open, her skin greyed with exhaustion, the corners of her mouth split and oozing.

"Elizabeth?" he asked, bending to kiss her cheek.

"Alexander," she said, summoning a smile. "We have a little daughter. I am sorry she isn't a son."

"Och, I am not!" he said with genuine pleasure. "Charles enlightened me about girls. How are you?"

"I feel much better, actually. Sir Edward says I might have more convulsions, but I don't think so."

Alexander picked up her hand and kissed it. "I love you, little mother."

The luminous eyes went flat. "What shall we call her?"

"What would you like to call her?"

"Eleanor."

"She'll get Nell when she goes to school."

"I don't mind Nell either. Do you?"

"No. They're both good names, neither ludicrous nor pretentious. May I see my daughter?"

Lady Wyler came forward with a tightly wrapped bundle and put it into Elizabeth's arms.

"I haven't seen her either," said Elizabeth, plucking at the swaddlings. "Oh, Alexander! She's *beautiful*!"

A mop of thick black hair, eyes screwed up against the glare of gaslight, sleek and dusky skin, a tiny O of a mouth. "Yes," said Alexander with a catch in his throat, "she's beautiful, our little Eleanor. Eleanor Kinross. It has a ring to it."

"She'll be a daddy's girl," said Lady Wyler cheerfully, reaching out to take Eleanor. "The first girl always is."

"I look forward to that," said Alexander, and left the room.

Education, education . . . First a governess, then a tutor to prepare his daughter for university. Education was everything.

She isn't going to be sent to school in Sydney, I don't trust that place. Nell—yes, I like that better than Eleanor—will stay under my eye, no matter how often Constance tries to tell me that girls need to mingle with other girls and learn to be pert flirts, society snobs. Yes, my daughter's future is mapped out already: a tertiary education in languages and history, and then marriage to Lee Costevan. If my luck hasn't utterly deserted me, Elizabeth's next child will be a boy, but I shall hedge my bets with Nell and Lee. Their children will fuse my blood with Ruby's—och, that's a formidable inheritance!

SIR EDWARD and Lady Wyler departed eight days after the birth of baby Eleanor; Elizabeth had suffered no more seizures, and was recovering rapidly. The obstetrician had advised that no conjugal intercourse take place for six months, but was of the opinion that a second pregnancy would proceed smoothly. Eclampsia was a disorder of first pregnancies.

His only qualm lay in Elizabeth's choice of a wet nurse, as she had no milk of her own. She had grabbed at a cousin of Jade and Pearl's, Butterfly Wing, who had lost her own baby at about the moment Eleanor was born. *Chinese* milk?

"You don't know what that might do to your child," said he, voice reasonable. "The races of Man are distinct and different, so it may well be that the mother's milk of one race is not suitable for the child of another race. Please I beg you, Mrs. Kinross, try to find a white wet nurse!"

"Rubbish," said Elizabeth, looking as stubborn as any Scot ever did, and that is stubborn. "Milk is milk. Why else can a cat nurse puppies or a dog nurse kittens? In America, I have read that Negro women nurse white babies. Butterfly Wing has enough milk to feed twins, so my Eleanor won't want."

"Have it your own way," said Sir Edward with a sigh.

"They are very peculiar," he said to his wife as they boarded the train for Lithgow. "Doesn't Alexander Kinross listen to the politicians of all persuasions? Robertson, Parkes, even those crass fellows who woo the working class are adamant that the Chinese are a danger, that the immigration of Chinese to Australia must stop. Many want to deport the Chinese already here. Yet Kinross has built his empire on Chinese, and his wife wants her child suckled by a Chinese, for pity's sake! If they persist in this attitude, there will be trouble."

"I fail to see why," said Lady Wyler placidly. "If Alexander exploited his Chinese, that would be a weakness in his armor. But he doesn't, which gives no one any reason to interfere with him."

"My dear, some politicians don't need reasons."

BABY ELEANOR thrived on Chinese milk and behaved perfectly. At six weeks of age she was sleeping through the night, and at three months she was able to sit up.

"A very forward little thing, aren't you, snookums?" cooed Ruby, kissing the chipmunk cheeks. "Auntie Ruby's darling—oh, Elizabeth, she brings back memories of what it was like to mother my jade kitten! He was so adorable."

"Her eyes are going to be blue," said Elizabeth, feeling no jealousy at the way Eleanor had taken to Ruby. "Not navy like mine, nor the sky of my father's. Deep yet vivid. Though I think her hair will stay black, don't you?"

"Yes," said Ruby, handing Eleanor to her mother. "Darker skin than yours, more like Alexander's. Except for her eyes, she looks more like him than you all round—that long face."

The eyes under discussion were fixed on Ruby with what did seem cognizance, though babes of three months were not supposed to do that. As if, Ruby fancied, the mite understood what was being said. Ruby dug into her purse and produced a letter.

"I received this from Lee," she said. "Would you like to hear it, Elizabeth?"

"Please," said Elizabeth, playing with the baby's fingers.

Ruby cleared her throat. "I won't bore you with the first paragraph, I'll just read out snippets. The second paragraph says 'I have now moved into the senior school, and have commenced Latin and Greek. My house master, Mr. Matthews, is a decent sort of chap who doesn't believe in the cane, though I suspect that canings at Proctor's are rather frowned upon because the pupils are all foreigners of exalted station. Don't you like that phrase? I am better at Maths than I am at English, but that means I am expected to work harder at English. Mr. Matthews says that no boy under his tutelage will emerge a literary idiot! He has set me to a special course of reading the English Classics, from Shakespeare and Milton to Goldsmith, Richardson, Defoe, and about a hundred others. My reading, he says, is not yet up to speed, but will be. I like history better, I confess, though not those interminable English struggles like the Wars of the Roses. They're mostly just crusades, battles and treachery—not enough science involved for me. I like the Greeks and the Romans, who fought under far better generals and for nobler causes. Scientific warfare.'"

"How old is he now?" Elizabeth asked, smiling at the pride in Ruby's voice.

"Twelve in June," said Ruby, eyes shimmering with tears. "The time drags for me, but not for him, which is the important thing. Shall I read more?"

"Yes, please."

"'I shall post this in the village so that I can write with frankness. No one at Proctor's would dream of censoring one's mail, but I am never *quite* sure that mail handed in to the school post isn't opened and read. There are all sorts of boys here, and not every one of them is either a good swot or an admirable character. When I first went to the junior school, I learned that the sons of maharajahs and princes sometimes covet the property of others to the point of stealing it, and are at least as clever at lying as the English. So it may be that the masters open and read our letters home, if only to monitor the currents and eddies among the pupils. I have prized Alexander's letters because they are so full of good advice and good sense.'"

"Alexander writes to him?" asked Elizabeth, surprised.

"More often by far than I do. He's Alexander Kinross, owner of the world's most productive gold mine—irreproachable as a correspondent. I don't know why, but he took to Lee when he met my jade kitten in Hill End."

"Go on," Elizabeth prompted.

"'My life at Proctor's is very easy since the gold. I can look any of the other chaps in the eye and not suffer, for I am quite as able as they to have my school suits made in Savile Row or pay for my share of a box at some play or opera in London to which the masters escort us. Mum, I would so much like to have a photograph of you now that you can wear lots of jewels and look like a real Russian princess! And a photograph of Papa, please.'"

"I hope you're doing that," said Elizabeth.

"Yes, I am. Sung is rather tickled at the thought of posing for the next itinerant photographer in his most majestic robes."

"More of Lee, Ruby. How well he writes!"

"'My Maths are so good that I am already being tutored with the chaps preparing to go up to Cambridge. Mr. Matthews says that I have a Newtonian grasp of mathematics, but I suspect that he is simply trying to ease me into an academic career. I have no yearnings in that direction. Engineering is more exciting by far. I want to build things out of steel.

"'My best friends remain Ali and Husain, who are sons of Shah Nasru'd-Din of Persia. Life there is pretty hectic; it seems someone is always trying to assassinate the Shah, but he doesn't look very likely to die in this way, he's too well protected. Not to mention that the would-be assassins are executed in public—a deterrent, Ali and Husain tell me.'"

Ruby laid the letter down. "And that's all that would be of interest to you, Elizabeth. The rest is motherish stuff, and if I read it out, I'll cry." She preened, lifted an arm to her head. "Do you think I could pass myself off as a princess of Russia? With a new dress from Sauvage, of course. And my diamonds and rubies."

"I'll lend you that ridiculous diamond tiara Alexander just bought me," said Elizabeth. "I ask you, Ruby, a *tiara*! Where on earth am I to wear the thing?"

"When some royal prince comes out to visit the colonies," said Ruby nonchalantly. "Alexander's bound to be invited to lick the royal bum."

"Where *do* you get your metaphors?"

"In the gutter, dear Elizabeth, where I grew up."

CONNUBIAL DUTY resumed for Elizabeth six months after Eleanor was born, with no pretense on Elizabeth's side that she welcomed it. What flummoxed her was how, knowing very well that she found his attentions distasteful, Alexander managed to do his duty. He always did, loveless and pleasureless though the exercise was. An instinct that, if he found out she had discussed this with his mistress, Alexander would be furiously angry, drove Elizabeth to ask *him* how this could be.

"You say I am cold, that there is no pleasure in the Act for you because there is none for me. Yet you come to my bed and you produce your—your seed. How can you do that, Alexander?"

He laughed, shrugged. "It's how men are made, my dear. If presented with a naked female body, a man will react."

"What if the naked female body is repulsively ugly?"

"I have no idea of the answer to that, Elizabeth. So far none of the naked female bodies I've encountered have been ugly or repulsive. One speaks as one finds," said Alexander.

"I can never best you in an argument!"

"Then why try?"

"Because you're so *complacent*!"

"Actually I'm not. That's only how you see me thanks to the state of affairs between us. You threw down a gauntlet, Elizabeth, and I picked it up. It wasn't I wanted a war. All I wanted was a loving wife. I've not ill treated you in any way, nor will I. But children I will have."

"How much did my father receive for selling me?"

"Five thousand pounds, plus whatever he kept of the thousand I sent to bring you out."

"Nine hundred and twenty pounds."

He leaned to kiss her forehead. "Poor Elizabeth! Between your father, old man Murray and me, you haven't been very lucky in your men." He sat up in the bed and crossed his legs like a pasha. "Who would you have chosen as a husband, if you'd had a choice?"

"No one," she muttered. "Absolutely no one. I'd sooner be Theodora than Ruby."

"Yes, that makes sense. The perennial virgin." He held out a hand. "Come, Elizabeth, let's admit that what we do in bed pleases neither of us, and try to get along with each other when we're not in bed. I haven't forbidden you to consort with Ruby, or indeed with anyone. Though it hasn't escaped me that, since the Presbyterians got their kirk and minister, you haven't once attended a service there. Why?"

"Your godlessness, as Mrs. Summers calls it, has rubbed off on me," she said, still ignoring the hand. "In all honesty, I just don't want to go to kirk anymore. What's the use? Will you have Eleanor raised a Presbyterian? Or anything else?"

"No, of course not. If she's of a spiritual bent, she'll find her own way to God. If she takes after me, she never will. But subject her to the prejudices, hypocrisies and clannishness of any specific religion, I will not. I notice that since our daughter's birth you've taken to reading the Sydney newspapers, so you must have read enough to see how riddled with religious dissension this colony is—as the whole of Australia is. Well, I may be godless, but at least I stand above all that. And so will Eleanor. I'll have her tutored in philosophy, not theology. On that kind of platform, she'll be intellectually equipped to choose for herself."

"I agree," said Elizabeth.

"You do?"

"Yes, I do. I have grown enough to realize that breadth of knowledge is more productive of freedom than narrowness. I would have my daughter free of the shibboleths that dog me. I want her to amount to something. To be able to talk geology and mechanics with you, literature with poets and essayists, history with true historians, and geography with those who have traveled."

He burst out laughing, hugged her. "Elizabeth, Elizabeth! That I should live to hear you say such things!"

But the hug broke the moment; Elizabeth withdrew, turned on her side and pretended to sleep.

ELEANOR'S PROGRESS suggested that all these parental hopes had some basis in fact, for she continued to develop ahead of her age. At nine months she began to talk coherently, which enchanted her father, who from that time on began to pay the nursery little visits during the day, when she was awake and alert. She adored him, so much was plain in the way she held out her arms the moment he entered, clutched him as soon as he picked her up, chattered away rather unintelligibly. Her eyes were her most striking feature, widely set, widely opened and the deepish blue of a cornflower; they would fix on him as intently as intensely, her infant prettiness in full bloom at Dadda's advent. Soon, he would think, she will have to have a kitten, a puppy; I'll have no child of mine grow up petless, as I did. She must learn that death is a part of life through the demise of beloved animals—far rather that, than through the demise of a parent.

MUCH TO Jade's dismay, Butterfly Wing had graduated from wet nurse to nurserymaid; Eleanor was passionately attached to her, and would not be parted from her. Indeed, in many ways she seemed to love Butterfly Wing and her father more than she did her mother, who was pregnant again and not thriving. So it was Butterfly Wing who took the child out into the garden, stripped her naked for ten minutes' worth of sun, guided her first tottering footsteps, gave her her food, her baths, her herbal medications for teething and colic. Alexander approved, delighted that Eleanor would grow up bilingual; Butterfly Wing spoke to her in Chinese, he spoke to her in English.

"Mum is sick," she said to Alexander at twelve months of age, brow wrinkled in a frown.

"Who told you that, Nell?"

"No one, Dadda. I can see it."

"Can you indeed? How?"

"Her skin is quite yellow," said the child with all the aplomb of a ten-year-old. "And she vomits a lot."

"Well—you're right, she is sick. But nothing that won't pass. She's expecting a baby brother or sister for you."

"Oh, I know *that,*" said Nell scornfully. "Butterfly Wing told me when we were picking carnations."

So much precociousness had Alexander at a loss, particularly because he had come to realize that his daughter seemed more interested in maladies than in toys; she knew when Maggie Summers had a headache or Jade pain in her arm from an old break. More disturbing was her observation that Pearl suffered a depressed mood at regular intervals, though of course Nell knew nothing of monthly courses. How long, wondered

Alexander, has this tiny creature been watching us with a thinking mechanism behind her lovely eyes? How much *does* she see?

It was certainly evident that Elizabeth ailed; when her morning sickness continued into her sixth month, Alexander sent for Sir Edward Wyler.

Who said, "As yet she isn't pre-eclamptic, but I think I ought to come up to see her in another month. She feels the child move, which is a good sign as far as the child is concerned, but her own constitution isn't strong. I don't like her color, yet so far her feet and legs are not edematous. It may just be that Mrs. Kinross doesn't carry easily."

"You haven't really allayed my fears, Sir Edward," Alexander said. "I thought she wouldn't have a second eclampsia?"

"It is very rare, but at this stage I do not know. Until—or if—she develops swelling, I would rather that she kept moving about, exercising her limbs."

"Get her through it, Sir Edward, and you have another icon."

WHEN THE swelling appeared in her twenty-fifth week, Elizabeth took to her bed voluntarily. Fifteen weeks of it this time.

Oh, will I never be rid of this bed? Will I never be able to do all the things I want to do, from playing the piano to learning how to ride a horse, drive a buggy? My daughter is being brought up by others, she hardly knows that I'm her mother. When she toddles in to see me, it's to ask me how I feel, demand to see my feet, quiz me as to how many times I've vomited, or if I have a headache. I don't know where she gets this preoccupation with diseases, yet I'm too miserable to fish in her mind. Such a sweet little thing—so like me, Ruby insists. But I think her mouth is Alexander's—straight, firm, utterly determined. And she has inherited his intelligence, his curiosity. I had wanted her to be known as Eleanor, but somehow she has decided to be known as Nell. I suppose the Chinese find it much easier to say, but I suspect it was Alexander started it.

As with the first pregnancy, it was Ruby who comforted her, Ruby who spent long hours by her bed playing poker, reading to her, talking. When she wasn't able to come, Theodora Jenkins took her place—less stimulating company, but since her trip to London and the Continent, Theodora was able to talk about more than the flowers in her front garden or the plague of cabbage moth in her vegetable patch.

Everyone worried constantly about Elizabeth save Mrs. Summers, enigmatic as ever, proof against the most charming of Nell's wiles. Elizabeth had hoped that in Nell Mrs. Summers would see the child she hadn't been able to bear, but her behavior gave the lie to any such hope; Maggie Summers was retreating, not advancing. As well then for the four Chinese women, upon whom Elizabeth depended for everything; they never let her down.

"Miss Lizzy, you have to try to eat," said Jade, holding out a dainty triangle of prawn toast.

"I can't, not today," said Elizabeth.

"But you must, Miss Lizzy! You're getting so thin, and that is no good for your baby. Chang will cook you anything you fancy—all you have to do is ask."

"Baked custard," said Elizabeth, who didn't want that either, but knew she had to voice a wish for something edible. At least it would slide down easily, and perhaps it would stay down. Eggs, milk, sugar. Nourishment for a bedridden invalid.

"With nutmeg on top?"

"I don't care. Just go away and leave me alone, Jade."

"I VERY MUCH fear," said Alexander to Ruby, "that Nell is going to be motherless." His face twisted, tears gathered; he put his head on Ruby's breast and wept.

"There there, there there," she crooned, rocking him until he quietened. "You'll get through this, and so will Elizabeth. What *I* very much fear is that she's doomed never to carry a child without coming to death's door."

He pulled away, mortified at displaying such vulnerability, mopped his face with a hand. "Och, Ruby, what can I *do*?"

"What are the latest pearls of wisdom from Sir Edward?"

"That if she comes through this confinement, she ought not to try to conceive again."

"I've just said the same thing, haven't I? I doubt the news will break her heart."

"There's no need to be bitchy!"

"Swallow it, Alexander. Give up this particular fight, it's one you can't win."

"I know," he said stiffly, put on his hat and departed.

Leaving Ruby to pace up and down her boudoir, no longer sure of anything beyond her ineradicable love for him. Whatever he wanted or needed from her, whenever he wanted or needed it, she would be there to give it. Yet her affection for Elizabeth kept increasing, and that was a mystery. By rights she should be contemptuous of the girl's inadequacies, her weaknesses, her sad and passive disposition. Perhaps the answer lay in her extreme youth—not far past eighteen years of age, expecting again, and facing death again. Never having really *lived.*

I suppose what I'm feeling is what her mother would feel. What a joke! Her mother who is sleeping with her husband. Oh, how much I would like to see Elizabeth happy! See her find a man she could love. The world has to hold a man in it somewhere whom she can love. That's all she wants, all she needs. Not wealth, not high living. Just a man she can love. One thing I know: she will never love Alexander. And how wretched for him that is! The injury to his iron Scottish pride, the taste of defeat in a mouth unused to it. How do these things happen? We go round and round and round, Alexander, Elizabeth, and I.

When she went to see Elizabeth on the morrow she was toying with the idea of speaking to her about the deteriorating situation between her and Alexander, which Ruby was positive lay like a foundation stone at the bottom of Elizabeth's illness. Oh, not that the illness was imagined! But Ruby had dealt with women of all kinds for more years than she cared to count. Then as she entered Elizabeth's room she changed her mind. To speak about it, she would have to divorce herself from it, and that she couldn't do. Perhaps she would accomplish more if she persuaded Elizabeth to eat her lunch.

"How's Nell?" she asked, settling by the bed.

"I have no idea. I hardly see her," said Elizabeth tearfully.

"Oh, come, sweetie-pie, look on the bright side! Only six or seven weeks left! As soon as this is over you'll bounce back."

Elizabeth managed a smile. "I am a misery, aren't I? I'm sorry, Ruby. You're right, I will bounce back. *If* I live through it." Her hand went out, so thin it resembled a claw. "That's what terrifies me—that I won't live through it. I don't want to die, yet I have an awful feeling that an end is coming."

"Ends are always coming," Ruby said, taking the hand and chafing it gently. "You weren't there when Alexander showed us—Charles, Sung and me—the reef of gold he'd found inside the mountain. Charles called the find apocalyptic—you know Charles, it's the sort of word he'd use. If he hadn't chosen it, he would have said cataclysmic or mind-boggling. But Alexander seized on the word, said apocalypse was Greek for a colossal event like the end of the world. Though when I wrote that to Lee, he said it really meant an ultimate revelation—and he had no Greek then, isn't that amazing? Anyway, Alexander thought that his discovery of this gold mine was a colossal event, and that's how the Apocalypse got its name. But it hasn't really been an end, has it? More a beginning. The Apocalypse has changed all the lives it touches. Without it, he wouldn't have sent for you, I'd still be keeping a brothel, Sung would still be an ordinary heathen Chinee with grand ideas, Charles would be a simple squatter, and Kinross would be a ghost town exhausted of placer."

"The Apocalypse is what the Catholics call the Book of Revelation," said Elizabeth, "so Lee's definition is the right one. It's an ultimate revelation, Alexander's gold mine. It has shown us what we really are."

Good, good! thought Ruby. She's more animated than I've seen her in weeks. Maybe this is a subtle way to dig up that foundation stone. "I didn't know it was biblical like that," she said with a grin. "I'm a religious ignoramus, so explain."

"Oh, I know my Bible! From Genesis to Revelation, how I know it! As far as I'm concerned, nothing was ever better named than Alexander's mountain of gold. Revelation upon revelation of beginnings *and* ends." Elizabeth's voice took on an eerie tone, her eyes glowed feverishly. "There are four horsemen riding through it, Death on a pale horse and three others. The three others are Alexander, you, and I. Because that's what we're doing—riding out the Apocalypse. It will make an end of me, of you, and of Alexander. None of us is young enough to survive it. All we can do is ride it out. And maybe, when we end, the Apocalypse will swallow us, hold us as its prisoners."

And how do I deal with this—this prophecy?

Ruby dealt with it by snorting and giving the hand a tiny slap. "What nonsense! You've gone what Alexander would call fey." A noise at the door came as a salvation; Ruby turned and beamed. "Lunch, Elizabeth! I declare I'm starved, and you look as if you're riding Famine, so eat."

"Oh, I see! You dissimulated, Ruby. You do know about the four horsemen of the Apocalypse."

Whatever had provoked Elizabeth to speak in a prophetic tongue, Ruby didn't know, but perhaps the foundation stone had shifted a little, for Elizabeth ate a good lunch, kept it down, and afterward was able to lie next to Nell on the bed and talk to her for half an hour. The child made no objection to her prone position, nor displayed any restlessness; she lay looking into her mother's face with what, in Ruby's opinion had Nell been much older, was an almost infinite compassion. Perhaps some Scots are fey, she thought. Elizabeth and her daughter have an otherworldliness about them, and how can a crusty engineer like Alexander cope with that?

SIR EDWARD WYLER arrived back to see Elizabeth on April Fool's Day, looking rather embarrassed. Lady Wyler was with him.

"I—ah—had a gap in my appointment book," he lied, "and I knew today there was a train to Kinross, so I decided to pop up and see how you're going, Mrs. Kinross."

"Elizabeth," she said, smiling at him fondly. "Call me that all the time, not merely when I'm at my worst. Lady Wyler, it's so good to see you. Please tell me that the gap in your appointment book is big enough to stay for a few days."

"Well, candidly, Lady Wyler has felt the summer heat in Sydney this year. In fact, it's quite worn her down. So if you don't mind, Elizabeth, she would like to stay a few days. Alas, I can't spare the time, so I'll just see how things are going and catch today's train back."

Having pronounced her reasonably well, if too thin, and taken a pint of blood from her, Sir Edward departed.

"Now that he's gone," said Lady Wyler in a conspiratorial whisper, "you can call me Margaret. Edward is a very dear man, but ever since his knighthood he's been wafting a foot off the ground, and will persist in addressing me as Lady Wyler. It's the way the title rolls off his tongue, I think. He was a poor boy, you know, but his parents scraped and screwed to put him through Medicine—his father worked three jobs and his mother took in washing and ironing."

"Did he go to Sydney University?" Elizabeth asked.

"Oh, dear me, no! It has no faculty of Medicine—in fact, when he was eighteen there was no Sydney University at all. So he had to go to St. Bartholomew's Hospital in London—it's the second-oldest hospital in the world, eleven hundred and something, I think. Or perhaps that's the oldest hospital, the Hotel Dieu in Paris. Whatever, Bart's is very old. Obstetrics and gynecology were very new specialties and puerperal fever raged if a woman was hospitalized for her labor. Most of Edward's patients had their babies at home, so he used to run from one alley to another with his black bag—it was appalling, but very valuable experience. When he returned home—he was born in Sydney in 1817—he found it difficult at first. We're both Jewish, you see, and people tend to despise the Jews."

"Like the heathen Chinee," said Elizabeth softly.

"Exactly. UnChristian."

"But he succeeded."

"Oh, yes. He was so good, Elizabeth! Head and shoulders above the—the *veterinarians* who called themselves accoucheurs. Once he saved the life and baby of a woman prominent in society, his troubles were over. People flocked to him, Jewish or no. He had his uses," said Margaret dryly.

"And you, Margaret? Were you born in Sydney? You don't have a local accent."

"No, I was a midwife attached to Bart's, and met him there. We married and I came back with him." Her face lit up. "He is a reader, Elizabeth! Every new advance is absorbed and becomes a part of his obstetrical arsenal. For instance, very recently he read of a woman's surviving a Caesarean section in Italy last year. So in September we're off to Italy to speak with the surgeon—another Edward, though of course Dr. Porro says Eduardo. If my Edward could save women and babies by Caesarean section, he'd be the happiest man in the world."

"What happened to his parents?"

"They lived long enough to enjoy the fruits of Edward's success. God has been very good."

"How old are your children?" Elizabeth asked.

"Ruth is almost thirty, married to another Jewish doctor, and Simon is in London at Bart's. He'll join his father's practice when he's finished."

"I'm very glad you're here, Margaret."

"So am I. If you can put up with me, I'd like to stay until your confinement and go back to Sydney with Edward."

A smile curled around Elizabeth's lips. "I think Alexander and I can both put up with you very well, Margaret."

TWO DAYS LATER Elizabeth's condition suddenly deteriorated; the eclampsia was back together with the onset of an early labor. Alexander sent an urgent telegram to Sir Edward in Sydney, but knew that the obstetrician couldn't possibly arrive in under twenty-four hours. Saving Elizabeth and the baby devolved upon Lady Wyler, who chose Ruby as her chief assistant. The same urge that had prompted Sir Edward to come to Kinross had also caused him to pack everything his wife might need in the event that he himself wasn't there. So Margaret Wyler took his place to give Elizabeth the injections of magnesium sulfate and cope with her seizures, while Ruby dealt with the birth process, barking questions to the official midwife and obeying barked replies.

There were more seizures this time, and closer together; Elizabeth was still fitting when the baby was born, a tiny, thin creature so blue and congested that Margaret Wyler was forced to leave Elizabeth to Jade and help Ruby try to resuscitate this second girl. For five minutes they toiled, slapping and massaging the frail little chest, before the baby gasped, jerked, began to wail faintly. Then it was back to Elizabeth, leaving Ruby to do what she could for the child. Two hours later the seizures came to an end, however temporarily; Elizabeth was still alive, and not quite passed into the terminal coma.

The two women paused to gulp a cup of tea Silken Flower brought, tears streaming down her face.

"Will she live?" Ruby asked, so exhausted that she sank into a chair and put her head between her knees.

"I think so." Margaret Wyler looked down at her hands. "I can't stop the tremor," she said, wonder in her voice. "Oh, what a terrible business! I never want to go through anything like this ever again." She turned to smile at Jade, beside Elizabeth. "Jade, you were marvelous. I couldn't have managed without you."

The little Chinese girl glowed, her fingers on Elizabeth's wrist to feel a pulse. "I would die for her," she said.

"Have you time to look at the baby?" Ruby asked, getting up.

"Yes, I think so. Jade, if her condition changes by so much as a whisker, yell." Lady Wyler moved to the crib, where the wizened scrap lay mewling, her skin gone from blue-black to a pinkish mauve. "A girl," she said, removing the linen Ruby had wrapped loosely about her. "About eight months, perhaps a little more. We have to keep her warm, but I don't want Elizabeth any warmer. Pearl!" she said loudly.

"Yes, my lady?"

"Have a fire lit in the nursery immediately, and put a warming pan in some kind of small bed. Then heat a brick and wrap it in plenty of cloth so it won't burn. And hurry!"

Pearl flew off.

"Jade," said Margaret Wyler, moving back to the bed, "as soon as Pearl says the baby's bed is ready, I want you to take her to the nursery and put her in it. Keep her warm, but make sure the bed isn't too hot. She's your responsibility now, I can't leave Elizabeth, and nor can Miss Costevan. Look after her as best you can, and if she turns blue again, call us. Nell will have to sleep in Butterfly Wing's room, so tell Pearl to move her cot out as soon as you bring the baby to the nursery."

It seemed to be done in the twinkling of an eye; Jade changed places with Lady Wyler and went to the crib, where Ruby gathered the baby up and handed her to Jade. Who looked down into the agonized tiny face with profound awe. "My baby!" she crooned, cuddling the bundle delicately. "This one is *my* baby."

Off she went, leaving Lady Wyler and Ruby to station themselves on either side of the narrow bed to which they had transferred Elizabeth the moment her travail had started.

"I think she's just sleeping," said Ruby, looking across the inanimate form at the midwife's drawn face.

"So do I. But be ready, Ruby."

"No more children for Elizabeth." Ruby made it a statement.

"That is so."

"Margaret, you're a woman of the world, aren't you?" Ruby asked, trying to make the question sound inoffensive. "I mean, you've seen a lot in your time, you must have done."

"Oh, yes, Ruby. Sometimes I think I've seen too much."

"I know *I* have."

Having put this gambit forward, Ruby fell into a silence, sat chewing her lip.

"I can assure you that nothing you say will shock me, Ruby," said Lady Wyler gently.

"No, this isn't about me," said Ruby, taking all propensity to shock as her province. "It's about Elizabeth."

"Then—tell me."

"Um—sex," Ruby blurted.

"Are you asking if sex is now prohibited to Elizabeth?"

"Yes—and no," said Ruby, "but it's a good place to begin. We know

Elizabeth can't possibly run the risk of having more children. Does that mean she must avoid the sex act as well?"

Margaret Wyler frowned, closed her eyes, sighed. "I wish I had the answer to that, Ruby, but I don't. If she could be sure that the sexual act didn't result in conception, then yes, she could lead a normal married life. But—"

"Oh, I know all the buts!" said Ruby. "I ran a brothel, and who better to know every trick in the book to avoid conception than a madam? Douches, the right days in the cycle, the man's withdrawing before he ejaculates. But the trouble is that sometimes none of the tricks works. Then it's a dose of ergot at six weeks and pray the stuff does its job."

"Then you know the answer to your question already, don't you? The only absolutely sure way is not to have intercourse."

"Shit," said Ruby, then straightened her shoulders. "Her husband's downstairs waiting. What do you want me to tell him?"

"Let him wait another hour," said Lady Wyler. "Then if Elizabeth's condition hasn't changed, you can tell him that she will be all right."

SO ANOTHER hour elapsed before Ruby entered the dull green Murray tartan room with a soft, warning knock.

He was sitting where he usually did, at the big window that looked across Kinross toward the distant hills. Night had not yet fallen; severe though Elizabeth's crisis had been, time had telescoped the past nine hours into an eternity. His book had fallen into his lap and his face was tinged with the dying gasp of the setting sun as he stared sightlessly at the angry sky. Her knock made him jump; he turned, got to his feet awkwardly.

"She's come through it," said Ruby gently, taking his hand. "Not out of danger yet, but Margaret and I believe she'll be all right. You're the father of another little girl, my dear."

He sagged, sat down abruptly. Ruby took the chair facing him and managed to smile. He looked older, greyer, as if, for all his strength and power, he had finally confronted a greater foe, and lost the battle.

"If you can summon up the wherewithal, Alexander, I am in desperate need of a cheroot and a *huge* snifter of cognac," she said. "I can't close the door because I might be needed again, but I can drink and smoke with one ear cocked."

"Of course, my love. You *are* my love, you know," he said, producing a cheroot and lighting it for her. "There can be no more children," he went on as he walked to the sideboard and poured two balloons of cognac, "that is manifest. Och, poor wee Elizabeth! Perhaps now she'll know some peace. Perhaps now she'll start to enjoy her life. No Alexander in her bed, eh?"

"That's the consensus of opinion," said Ruby, taking the glass. A big swallow and she exhaled deeply. "Jesus, that's so good! I never want to go through this again. Your wife suffered terribly, yet knew no pain. Isn't that extraordinary? It's all that kept me going. When one has a baby oneself, one doesn't see what it's like. Though Lee's birth was easy."

"He must be—what? Twelve? Thirteen?"

"Changing the subject, Alexander? He'll be thirteen on the sixth of June. A winter baby. Easier to carry through autumn, though God knows Hill End was hot enough."

"He'll be my major heir," said Alexander, sipping his drink.

"Alexander!" Ruby sat up straight, eyes wide. "But you have *two* heirs now!"

"Girls. Who, as Charles says, may well end in bringing far better men into the family than my own sons might have been, men who would even be willing to change their names to Kinross. But I think I've always known that Lee would end in being more to me than simply the son of my most beloved mistress."

"And which horse is *he* going to ride?" asked Ruby bitterly.

"I beg your pardon?"

"It doesn't matter." Ruby buried her nose in her snifter. "I love you, Alexander, I always will. Yet we shouldn't be saying these things with your wife at death's door. It's not—right."

"I disagree. So, I think, would Elizabeth. We've all admitted that my marriage was a mistake, but I brought it on myself. I am to blame, no one else. My pride was mortally injured. I wanted to show two terrible old men that Alexander Kinross was king of the world." He smiled, looked suddenly very much at peace. "And, for all the misery my marriage has caused, I can't help but think that I rescued Elizabeth from worse misery back in Scottish Kinross. She wouldn't see that, but it's a truth. Now that I'm out of her bed for good, she'll do better. I'll accord her all honor and respect, but my heart belongs to you."

"Who," she asked, seeing her chance, "is Honoria Brown?"

He looked blank, then laughed. "My first woman. She had a hundred acres of good Indiana farmland and she gave me shelter for the night. Her husband had been killed in the American Civil War. She offered me not only herself, but everything she had if I would stay, marry her, and farm her land. I took what I wanted—her body—but declined the rest." He sighed, closed his eyes. "I haven't changed, Ruby. I doubt I can change. What I told her was that it wasn't my destiny to be an Indiana farmer. And rode off in the morning with my fifty-five pounds of gold."

The green eyes glistened with tears. "Alexander, Alexander, the pain you bring upon yourself!" she cried. "Oh, and the pain you bring upon your women! What happened to her?"

"I have no idea." He put the empty balloon down. "May I see my wife and my new daughter?"

"Of course," said Ruby, climbing wearily to her feet. "I should warn you that neither will know you're there. The baby came out the color of Elizabeth in a fit—blue-black. It took Margaret Wyler and I five minutes to make her breathe. She's a month early into the bargain, so she's very small and frail."

"Will she die?"

"I don't think so, but she's no Nell."

"And no more marital duty for Elizabeth?"

"Lady Wyler says that. The risk is too high."

"Oh, yes, far too high. I must content myself with two daughters," said Alexander.

"Nell is very gifted, you know that."

"Of course. But her mind is slanted toward living things."

Ruby walked up the stairs slowly. "At fifteen months of age, Alexander, it's astonishing that she's slanted toward any sort of thing. Lee was a bit the same, though, come to think of it. I daresay what it really means is that Nell is permanently ahead of her years, just as Lee is. As to what her slant might be later on, you don't know. Children have fits of enthusiasm."

"I intend her to marry Lee," he said.

Ruby propped at Elizabeth's bedroom door, face like thunder, and took Alexander's hair in both hands so fiercely that he flinched. "Listen to me, Alexander Kinross!" she hissed. "I'll hear no more of this! No more of this, *ever*! You can't plan people's lives as if they were mines or railways! Leave my son and your daughter to find their own mates!"

For answer, he opened the door and went in.

Elizabeth had regained consciousness, turned her head on the pillow to see them, and smiled. "I've done it again," she said. "But I thought it was an end, and it isn't. Margaret says we have a new daughter, Alexander."

He leaned to kiss her brow tenderly, take her hand. "Yes, my dear, Ruby told me. That's wonderful. Do you feel strong enough to think of a name for her?"

Came a faint frown; Elizabeth's lips worked in and out. "A name," she said, as if puzzled. "A name . . . I can't think."

"Then we can leave it."

"No, she should have a name. Tell me some."

"How about Catherine? Or Janet? Elizabeth, after you? Anna? Or perhaps Mary? Flora?"

"Anna," she said with satisfaction. "Yes, I like Anna." Her hand lifted his to her cheek. "I'm afraid we'll have to find another wet nurse. I don't seem to have any milk again."

"Mrs. Summers has found someone, I believe," Alexander said, gently disengaging his hand; hers felt like a vulture's. "An Irishwoman named Biddy Kelly. Her child died of the croup the day before yesterday, and she mentioned to Mrs. Summers that she would nurse our child if her milk lasted. Well, our Anna has come very early, so she'll still have milk. Shall I hire her, Elizabeth? Or would you rather I asked Sung to find a Chinese wet nurse?"

"No. Biddy Kelly sounds ideal."

Only Ruby frowned; Maggie Summers had found a way to wriggle back into the center of things. This Biddy Kelly was undoubtedly a crony from the Catholic church who would tattle every morsel she overheard. A snooper in the house for at least six months. Many cups of tea in the kitchen, many whispered secrets. What Kinross didn't already know, it soon would.

Six

REVELATIONS

IF JADE HAD begged in vain to be let become a nurserymaid before Nell was born, the advent of baby Anna granted her most ardent wish. Biddy Kelly did her duty and nursed the child efficiently for seven months, at which point Anna was put on cow's milk without any adverse reaction. A disappointment for Mrs. Summers in losing her crony, perhaps, but a relief for Jade and Ruby. It pleased Ruby to see the housekeeper deprived of her principal source of upstairs information, but Ruby's emotions were mild compared to Jade's. Anna now belonged entirely to her.

Elizabeth recovered slowly but without setbacks; by the time her second daughter was six months old, she was able to behave as a healthy young woman ought. The piano lessons resumed, she took trips down into Kinross, and Alexander found her a trustworthy man to teach her equestrian skills as well as how to drive an elegant trap drawn by two high-stepping creamy ponies. She also had a white Arabian mare with floating mane and tail which she named Crystal, and developed a passion for grooming the beast until its coat was like satin. While she spent hours in the stables ministering to Crystal, she spent no time at all ministering to Anna. A large part of her neglect of the child's welfare stemmed out of Jade's possessiveness, for Jade made it very plain that she regarded Anna's mama as a rival. Still, Elizabeth was honest enough to admit that this state of affairs in the nursery suited her very well.

Alexander had caused a macadamized road to be excavated down into Kinross; though it wound back and forth and covered five miles before it reached the town, it freed Elizabeth from the cable car. To use that, she had to inform Summers or one of his sullen lackeys to have the car brought up from the poppet heads to the house, whereas she could ride off on Crystal or gee up her trap by asking at the stables, not in Summers's control. A huge bonus! In fact, life for Elizabeth had suddenly opened up, especially because her own body had liberated her from all save a distant relationship with her husband.

When Ruby, deputed to be the bearer of the tidings, broke the news to her that Sir Edward Wyler and his wife did not think it wise for her to continue her conjugal duties, Elizabeth had to suppress a cheer and keep her eyelids lowered. Ruby seemed to think she would miss the Act, but Elizabeth knew she wouldn't.

Horseback was her favorite mode of escape, since riding the mare meant she didn't have to adhere to the road, could push and poke into the forest wherever the undergrowth permitted. That in turn led to the discovery of nooks and dells whose beauty overwhelmed her; she took to spending hours sitting on some natural rock chair watching the passing parade of myriad creatures from lyre birds to wallabies to amazing insects. Or else she brought a book and read without fear of disturbance, ceasing occasionally to lift her head and dream of true freedom, the kind of existence these gorgeous birds, animals and insects surely regarded as their right.

Then she came upon The Pool. Quite a long way up the river, she found it during a stubborn mood by persuading Crystal to walk in the creek bed whenever the banks prohibited negotiation; a worse than usual attack of wanting desperately to fly away from all constraints. From the moment she encountered The Pool, she went nowhere else if riding.

It occupied a small subsidence that gave it considerable depth, and was filled by a little cascade that tumbled over big boulders amid native maidenhair ferns and thick long mosses of a kind Scotland did not possess. Its water was so clear that every stone on the pool bottom leaped into sight, and it held fish as well as minute shrimps transparent as the finest glass, their pinhead red hearts frantically beating. Though trees shaded it, around noon the sun streamed down in rays dancing with motes that touched The Pool's surface and struck it to pure molten gold. Every kind of life came there to drink; Elizabeth found a comfortable spot for Crystal far enough away from The Pool to pose no audible threat to its winged, walking and crawling visitors, then found a comfortable rock seat for herself, there to let her soul fly away.

The Pool was hers, entirely hers. The forest of the mountaintop was forbidden to all save Mr. and Mrs. Kinross, but even if a trespasser were to gain access to it, he would never find The Pool. Too far upstream, too difficult to reach.

WHAT ALEXANDER thought was impossible for others to tell. He had, it seemed to the occupants of the house, decided upon a courteous and civilized communion with his wife, one that went no further than the table and postprandial chats about the mine, the time of year, some new project of Alexander's, what the papers said, Sir Henry Parkes's rise to head the floundering government, or the elevation of Mr. John Robertson to the rank of a Knight Commander of the Order of St. Michael and St. George.

"Sir John Robertson," said Elizabeth thoughtfully. "I am a little surprised at the Queen's awarding him a knighthood. He isn't Church of England, nor is his reputation with women good. That usually sinks a man very low in her estimation."

"I doubt she's been informed of his womanizing," Alexander said dryly. "However, his knighthood doesn't surprise me."

"Why is that?"

"Because John Robertson has outlived his political usefulness. The moment a man does that, they petition the Queen to knight him. It's the signal that he must retire from the electoral arena, you might say."

"Indeed?"

"Oh, yes, my dear. You can't have failed to notice that the all too frequent governments-in-the-plural are utterly devoid of real objectives. Mark my words, Robertson will retire from the Legislative Assembly shortly. They'll probably appoint him to the upper house for life and keep him on the Executive Council. Parkes will be left to king it in the lower house." Alexander snorted. "Pah!"

"But Parkes is also a knight now," Elizabeth objected, "and I see no sign that *he* intends to retire."

"That's because Parkes's head is too swollen." Alexander grinned. "His eyes can't see for all that puffed-up flesh around them. Metaphorically speaking, of course. He's puffed up, is Sir Henry. Always was, always will be. He also lives too high—dangerous in a politician with no personal wealth to fall back on. Robertson is a rich man, Parkes is a relative pauper. On the face of it there's no money to be made as a member of parliament, but there are investment tips, perquisites for a premier—" He shrugged. "Ways and means, Elizabeth."

"I quite liked him, that night he came to dinner."

"Yes, he's charming. And I applaud his attitude toward the education of the State's children. What I don't trust is his willowy nature. Sir Henry bends with whatever wind blows."

AT THE END of January of 1878, when Anna was ten months old, Nell sought out her father in his library.

"Dadda," she said, climbing on to Alexander's knee, "what is wrong with Anna?"

Arrested, Alexander turned the two-year-old mite toward him and stared at her. His daughter's face was becoming more and more like his own, had the same pointed black brows and long, lean look to it; not becoming in a small child, but perhaps unusual and interestingly attractive in a grown woman. The eyes, startlingly blue, were steady of gaze and, at the moment, looked worried and anxious in a way not appropriate to a toddler.

"What do you think is wrong with Anna?" he asked, suddenly very aware that he hardly saw his second daughter.

"Something," Nell said positively. "At her age, I remember that I could talk, because I remember everything you said to me and I said to you, Dadda. *Everything!* Yet Anna can't even sit up. Jade cheats, she holds her up whenever I come in to say hello, but I see it. Anna's eyes don't work properly, they roll around. She dribbles a lot. I was sitting on a potty to do poohs, but Anna can't. Oh, Dadda, she's such a dear little thing, and she's my baby sister! But something is wrong with her, truly."

His mouth was dry; Alexander licked his lips and tried to seem—not unconcerned, more as if this wasn't such a shock. "What time is it?" he asked.

This was a game; he had taught Nell to read the hands of the grandfather clock that lived in one corner of the library. She was never mistaken, nor was she now.

"Six o'clock, Dadda. Butterfly Wing will be coming for me"—she giggled—"any old tick of the clock."

"Then why don't you find Butterfly Wing for once and surprise her?" Alexander asked, tipping Nell on to the floor. "If it's six, I must find your mother. Auntie Ruby is coming to dinner in an hour."

"Oh, I wish I could stay up!" cried Nell. "I love Auntie Ruby almost as much as I love Butterfly Wing."

"And is that more than Mumma? More than me?"

"No, no, of course not!" Nell produced a new concept. "It is all relative, Dadda, you know that."

"Off with you, wee pedant," said her father with a chuckle and a gentle push.

BEFORE HE sought out Elizabeth he went to the nursery, to which room Nell had never returned after Anna's birth, as Lady Wyler had felt that a noisy toddler would interfere with the demanding care a sickly premature baby needed. Butterfly Wing kept Nell with her, but of late Nell had been pressing to be given a room all to herself.

Now that he thought about it, Jade hardly left the nursery night or day; she had handed the maiding of Elizabeth over to Pearl and Silken Flower, devoted herself entirely to baby Anna. It was so subtle, so invisible—what father, he asked himself, is consumed with interest in a baby, even one he has sired? Especially when the baby is another girl? Nell was different—vital, intelligent, curious, busy, intrusive. Nell wouldn't let him ignore her existence, never had, even when she was newborn. The fingers curled around one of his, the fixed and cognitive regard, the bubbles, smirks, gurgles, coos. Whereas Anna had disappeared from sight, sound, presence. There always seemed to be a reason why he wasn't welcome in the nursery.

Tonight he didn't knock, didn't ask Jade's permission; he simply walked in. Jade was sitting with Anna on her knees, one hand supporting the child's neck, feeding her some kind of mush from a spoon. A startled face lifted; Jade jumped.

"Mr. Kinross!" she said, gasping. "Mr. Kinross, you can't see Anna now, I'm feeding her!"

For answer Alexander walked to a wooden kitchen chair, took it by its back and positioned it in front of his child and her nurserymaid. He sat on it, face stony.

"Give me the baby, Jade."

"I can't do that, Mr. Kinross! Her nappy's dirty, she'll make you all smelly!"

"I've been smelly before, I'll be smelly again. Give her to me, Jade. Now."

Transferring Anna was difficult; the child lolled like a rag doll and was unable to support her own head, but it was done at last. Bereft, Jade stood trembling, her delicately lovely features frozen into a mask of fear.

Alexander looked at his second daughter properly for the first time, and saw at once how right Nell was, despite the fact that at ten months Anna was a prettier baby than Nell, chubby and well cared for. Black hair, black brows and lashes, grey-blue eyes that didn't focus, couldn't seem to focus. That *some* thought processes lay within her skull was obvious in the way she recognized that the hands holding her were alien, the lap on which she sat not Jade's. Wriggling and flopping in this awkward grasp, she began to wail.

"Thank you, Jade, you can take her," Alexander said, alert to see how quickly Anna's sense of disorientation faded. Almost immediately; the moment Jade held her, she stopped crying and opened her mouth for more mush.

"Now," he said quietly, "I want the truth, Jade. How long have you known that Anna isn't what she ought to be mentally?"

The tears rolled down Jade's cheeks unchecked; she needed both hands to manage the baby. "Almost at once, Mr. Kinross," she sobbed. "Biddy Kelly knew too. So does Mrs. Summers. Oh, how they laughed about it in the kitchen! But I got out my dagger and told them I'd cut their throats if they ever breathed a word about Anna to anyone in Kinross."

"Did they believe you?"

"Oh, yes. They knew I meant it. I'm a heathen Chinee."

"What can Anna do?"

"She has improved, Mr. Kinross, honestly! But everything takes a long, long time. She can eat off a spoon now—see? It wasn't easy, but she *can* learn. I talked to Hung Chee in the medicine shop and he showed me how to help Anna exercise her neck so that one day she will be able to hold up her head." Down went Jade's cheek to rest against the black curls. "I love looking after Anna, sir, I swear it! Anna is *my* baby, she doesn't belong to Pearl or Butterfly Wing or anyone except me. Oh, please, oh, *please* don't send me away from her!" The weeping broke out afresh.

Alexander got up like an old man, put out a hand and rested it briefly on Jade's head. "Don't worry about that, my dear. I won't send you away from Anna. What kind of thanks would that be for so much devotion? You're right, Anna is your baby."

From there, down a short flight of steps to Elizabeth's suite of rooms, which he hadn't entered since she was able to leave her sickbed. It had changed, he noticed. His own attempt at furnishing it through the offices of his Sydney hotel had gone by the wayside in favor of what were obviously Elizabeth's preferences—less gilt, fewer mirrors, chintz instead of brocade, all of it blue, blue, blue. The color Ruby called cheerless.

What is the matter with me, that all this can have gone on since Anna's birth, and I, the master of this house, have had no knowledge of it? Yes, I am away a lot—who else can I trust to survey and build the road to Lithgow? But no one asked me, no one told me. Except, finally, my two-year-old daughter. I am an outsider in a house full of women. Maggie Summers . . . A fat spider in my web. I ought to have known that. Elizabeth never cared for her, now I see why. Well, she and Summers can move out of the third floor, find a house in Kinross. Let her keep it. I'll hire a new housekeeper. Go on hiring new housekeepers until I find one who suits all of us. Who doesn't loathe the Chinese, who doesn't have cronies like Biddy Kelly who go to church on Sundays to spread the gossip.

"Elizabeth?" he called, going no farther than the boudoir.

She appeared at once, still dressed in her wine-red riding habit, her eyes wide.

"That's a foolish color to choose for a habit when you ride a white horse," he observed, bowing to her. "It's smothered in white hairs."

A rueful smile flickered; she inclined her head. "You're absolutely right, Alexander. The next one will be bone-colored."

"And do you ride every day?" he asked, strolling across to the window. "I like the summer, it stays light much longer."

"I like the summer too," she said nervously, "and yes, I do ride almost every day. Unless I fancy driving down to Kinross."

A silence fell; he continued to stare out the window.

"What's the matter, Alexander? Why are you here?"

"How much do you see of Anna? Do you, for instance, see as much of her as you do of your horse?"

Her breath caught audibly, she started to shake. "No, I suppose not," she said dully. "Jade has taken Anna over to the point where I always feel a little unwelcome in the nursery."

"Coming from the child's mother, Elizabeth, that smacks of an excuse. You're perfectly aware, I'm sure, that Jade is your servant and obligated to obey orders. Did you try very hard?"

Two crimson spots flared in Elizabeth's bleached face; she flinched, turned in a tight circle as if nailed to the floor through one foot, squeezed her hands together. "No, I didn't try very hard," she whispered.

"How old are you now?"

"I'll be twenty in September."

"How time flies. Twice a mother at nineteen, twice almost dead from the business, and now free of it forever. No!" he barked. "Don't cry, Elizabeth! This isn't a moment for tears. Hear me out, then you can cry."

From where she stood Elizabeth could see only the back of him. What was it? Why was he suffering? Because he was badly suffering. She watched him gain control of himself, square his shoulders; when he spoke again it was more gently.

"Elizabeth, I don't blame you in the least for handing your children over to women as devoted and single-minded as Butterfly Wing and Jade, especially because you've never had a girlhood. I would think that these daily rides, the drives into Kinross, the sheer and sudden freedom have gone to your head like champagne. Why should they not? You've done as much of your duty as even old man Murray's god could ask, and now the duty's over. Were I in your shoes, I'd kick up my heels a little too." He sighed. "However, though your duty to me is a thing of the past, your duty to your children is ongoing. I'm not forbidding you to go riding, or driving, or walking, or whatever else takes your fancy, because I know your pleasures are innocent. But you must have a care for our daughters. In two or three years Nell will be old enough for me to take her off your hands, but I am afraid that Anna is no Nell."

The crimson spots had faded; Elizabeth dropped into a chair, cradling her cheeks in her hands. "You've seen it too."

"So you haven't been completely blind?"

"No, though Jade always tells me that Anna is having a bad day, or has a cold, or has hurt her back. I've wondered, but I've never put my suspicions to the test. And you are too kind. I deserve every reproach, every criticism you must be thinking. How did you come to realize that Anna is a little backward?"

"Nell came to see me this evening and asked me what's wrong with Anna. She can't hold her head up, her eyes roll, said our elder daughter. So I went and forced the truth out of Jade." He turned to confront her, face calm, eyes remote. "Anna isn't a little backward, Elizabeth. She's—mental."

Elizabeth began to weep, but silently. "It happened at her birth," she said clearly. "Margaret and Ruby worked on her for five minutes before she took a breath. It isn't hereditary, Alexander, I'm *sure* it isn't hereditary."

"Och, so I am sure of that!" he said impatiently. "I daresay there's a purpose behind it all, though what the purpose could be, I don't know. We have one very clever little girl, and one mental little girl. Maybe that evens up the odds, who can tell?"

He moved away from the window in the direction of the door, then stopped. "Elizabeth, look at me! *Look at me!* Before this goes on any longer, we have a decision to make. Namely, what to do with Anna. We can keep her here, or put her into a home. If we keep her, you and Jade are facing a lifetime of caring for a poor wee soul who can't care for herself. I'm sure that we can find a home where she won't be mistreated—in matters like this, money is all-powerful. What do you want to do?"

"Which would you choose, Alexander?"

"To keep her, of course," he said, surprise in his voice. "However, it's not I will bear the brunt of her. If anything ever happened to Jade, what would you do? What could you do?"

"Keep her," said Elizabeth. "I will keep her."

"Then we are at one about it. By the way, I'm going to sack Maggie Summers. That will inconvenience us for a while—I want her out of here tomorrow, not a day later. I feel sorrier for Summers, he likes to be at my beck and call and will resent an exile to Kinross. But it has to be. I'll advertise in the *Sydney Morning Herald* for a housekeeper."

"Why not use an agency for domestic servants?"

"Because I'd rather do the interviewing myself." He took out his gold fob watch, flicked its cover open and consulted it. "You'd better hurry, my dear. Ruby is due at seven."

"I'm not going down to dinner, if you'll excuse me. I have to find Jade and talk to her. And start to know Anna."

He picked up her hand and kissed it lightly. "As you wish. Thank you, Elizabeth. I couldn't have blamed you had you chosen to put Anna in a home, but I'm very glad that you didn't."

THE NEWS about Anna fell upon Ruby like a shower of boiling water. Alexander didn't mention it until they were in the library with cheroots and fine old cognac, having passed off Elizabeth's absence as a slight indisposition. Her sensitive nose had sniffed a domestic problem because she knew Alexander far better than his wife ever would; he got a certain look in his eyes, a certain expression on his face. Since the advent of Anna she hadn't seen these signs in him, as if he had given up the ghost on Elizabeth, had relegated her to some unimportant corner of his mind. Now they were back.

The reason for their presence was revealed when he told her about Anna—how he had come to make the discovery, how Elizabeth had reacted. But it took a large swallow of cognac to nerve Ruby into a reply.

"Oh, my love, my love, I am so sorry!"

"No sorrier than I or Elizabeth. Still, it's a done thing, it can't be altered or ignored. Elizabeth thinks, and I agree with her, that the damage was done at birth. She bears none of the usual stigmata most mental children do—in fact, she's very pretty and well proportioned. If she's lying down in her crib, you'd never know unless you looked at her eyes. As Nell said, they roll around aimlessly. Jade says she does learn, but that it takes a long, long time to teach her even something as simple as eating from a spoon."

"The secretive little bitch!" said Ruby, taking another gulp of cognac. "Jade, I mean," she added when Alexander looked at her with brows raised. "Not, mind you, that knowing about it earlier could have helped. Elizabeth's right, the child didn't breathe. Had I known, perhaps I wouldn't have tried so hard to make her breathe, but I wasn't to know. I just wanted Elizabeth's ordeal to be for something rather than nothing."

"But it was, Ruby, it was," he said, and reached out to take her hand, squeeze it. "The ancient Greeks said that hubris in men was a crime against the gods and would be punished. I've grown hubristic—too much success, too much wealth, too much—*power*. Anna is my punishment."

"I've heard not one whisper of it in the town, though Biddy Kelly nursed her for seven months."

White teeth flashed in a broad smile. "That's because Jade caught her and Maggie Summers having a laugh about it in the kitchen. Out came her dagger on the spot! She told them she'd cut their throats if they tattled, and they believed her."

"Good for Jade!"

"Maggie Summers moves out tomorrow. I've told Summers."

Ruby shifted in her chair as if it were uncomfortable, then took both Alexander's hands in hers. "So are you going to try to keep Anna's condition a secret?"

"Och, no, of course not! That would be to imprison the wee mite. There's no shame involved, Ruby. At least *I* don't think so. Nor, I imagine, does Elizabeth. I want Anna to be able to go about when she learns to walk, as walk she will, I'm sure of it. I want all of Kinross to know that wealth and privilege cannot insulate a family from tragedy."

"You haven't really told me how Elizabeth feels, Alexander. Did she know that Anna is mental?"

"I don't believe so. She'd convinced herself that the child was a little backward. A little backward!" He laughed, not a happy sound. "My wife has been too busy worshipping that wretched horse as if it were a goddess. Combing it, brushing it, stroking it—what *is* it between young women and horses?"

"Power, Alexander. Muscles moving under a beautiful skin. Being dwarfed by power. Clever of you to give her a mare—the sight of a stallion's prick might have been too much."

"You're a most unsatisfactory confidante, Ruby. Can't you ever phrase things nicely?"

"Hah!" said Ruby, her fingers playing with his. "What's the point of being nice?" She transferred to his lap and pillowed her face on his hair—so grey, so suddenly! "Are you any closer to knowing how Elizabeth's mind works?"

"No, not a bit."

"She's different since Anna's birth. Her contacts with me are absolutely general—she invites me to lunch if Theodora is here, otherwise to dinner when you are. She's unwilling to be intimate the way she used to be, when we had—oh, such conversations! About everything and anything. Nowdays she's gone into realms entirely her own," said Ruby sadly.

"I need you," Alexander said, face between her breasts. "I could come down to Kinross later tonight, if you'll have me."

"Always," said Ruby. "Always."

She went down alone in the cable car, looking across gas-lit Kinross, a sprinkling of greenish sparks. The engines chugged, the satanic glow of fires illuminated the sheds wherein Apocalypse ore was transformed into Apocalypse gold, and far off on Sung's hill the pagodas glistened as the moon soared to its zenith. I am a part of it, though I never wanted to be. What awful vengeance love wreaks! Were it not for Alexander Kinross, I would be no more than fate intended me to be—a shady lady living on the edge of expulsion, if not of extinction.

FROM THAT day when Anna's disability was made manifest to her, Elizabeth began to go to church. But not to the Presbyterian kirk; she appeared the following Sunday at St. Andrew's Church of England holding Nell by the hand, and with Anna in a perambulator Jade pushed as far as the church gate, there to wait for service to end, a wisp of a Chinese girl trying to make herself invisible.

Astonished and overjoyed, the Reverend Mr. Peter Wilkins greeted Kinross's first lady with becoming deference, made sure that she understood that the front pew on the right had always been reserved for the residents of Kinross House. The town was buzzing with the news that Mrs. Summers had been sacked, with unsubstantiated rumors that something was amiss in the Kinross family; all of which made the minister even more attentive.

"Thank you, Mr. Wilkins," said Elizabeth coolly, "but I would much prefer to take a pew at the back. My younger child, Anna, is mentally very slow, so I would rather be where I can wheel her outside if she isn't happy."

And so it was done. Kinross town learned that Anna Kinross was mental in a way that negated gossip, which spiked Maggie Summers's guns beautifully.

The exchange with Jade hadn't been acrimonious; after a bout of tears the two women amicably agreed to share custody of Anna so that Jade could have some respite while Elizabeth wasn't deprived of Crystal or The Pool. This venture to church was the start of a new regime at Kinross House, a public declaration of Anna's handicap as well as a notification that Mrs. Kinross was, now that she had recovered her health, not as godless as her husband. Glory be to God!

Perhaps that glory was a little tarnished if any of the churchgoers saw Elizabeth's first stop after service was ended; she called into the Kinross Hotel for lunch with Ruby, who welcomed her fervently, kissed her, hugged her.

"Does this indicate that you're back to normal?" Ruby asked, holding her at arm's length, eyes shining.

"Yes," said Elizabeth, smiling, "if by that you mean we are the best of friends as well as holding equal shares in Alexander. I've finally grown up."

"Oh, that's a shame." Ruby plucked Anna out of her pram. "No, no, snookums, bubba mustn't cry! You're going to have to get used to more people than Jade and your mama. Elizabeth, pay a mind to Nell when you speak—little pitchers have big ears, and this little pitcher is clever. What's for lunch? Mushrooms on toast and then grilled spatchcock.

Don't pull faces, Nell! A day may come when you'll think back on this menu with longing. Well do I remember when a hunk of stale bread and a bit of sweaty cheese tasted better than nectar and ambrosia."

ELIZABETH TOOK Alexander's reprimand about her neglect of Anna so much to heart that she refused to leave her children to accompany him on trips to Sydney. He was an ardent fan of music, theater and opera, and, since he didn't see why he should forgo these pleasures, he got into the habit of taking Ruby to Sydney instead. As 1878 turned into 1879, these visits became more frequent because, as he said,

"New South Wales is now close enough to Great Britain to permit opera and theater companies the chance to perform here. There are coal-bunkering facilities for steamships on the way out, which cuts the passage to five weeks via Suez."

He and Ruby saw a fine performance of *The Merchant of Venice,* every opera that came to town, and a sparkling musical play called *H.M.S. Pinafore* by a relatively unknown pair of composers, Gilbert and Sullivan. They also went to see the Sydney International Exhibition, housed in a grand palace built for the occasion. The venue was harder to get to than of yore; Alexander had had to change his hotel. The old one was rendered uninhabitable by the new steam trams that roared along Elizabeth Street emitting choking black smoke and swirling showers of sparks.

They were strolling through the exhibition palace, admiring the various pavilions, when Alexander spoke.

"I'm going to England very shortly."

Ruby stopped to look at him. "What provoked this?"

"Honestly?"

"Yes, always honestly."

"I'm tired of a house full of women. Soon we'll be entering a new decade and the new century will be a mere twenty years away. I want to see what's happening in England, Scotland and Germany—there are new furnaces for steeling iron, new ways to build bridges, methods of generating electricity that will turn it from a toy into a mighty force, and even rumors of new, quite revolutionary engines," said Alexander, eyes alight. "Were it not for Anna, I'd take Nell and Elizabeth with me, put them in a good house in the West End of London, and use it as my base. But that can't happen, and—*honestly*—I'm profoundly glad for it. I need a long respite from women, Ruby, even you."

"I understand completely." She commenced to walk. "If it should be possible, will you visit Lee?"

"Visiting Lee is the first item on my agenda. In fact, whenever he has school holidays, I intend to take him with me. It will be valuable experience for a budding engineer."

"Oh, Alexander, that's wonderful! Thank you!"

Now he stopped to look at her. "There's a question I've never asked you, Ruby, I suppose because Lee left so soon after I met him, and you and I in those days were not—well, the rather bigamous couple we've become. What I want to know is how Lee can pose as a Chinese prince when his name is Costevan?"

Her laughter was so spontaneous and attractive that the crowd in their vicinity turned to stare at them openly; naturally Alexander Kinross with a strikingly beautiful woman on his arm drew stares, but usually they were furtive, as gossip said this particular woman was not his wife.

"Alexander, Lee's nearly fifteen! It's taken you six long years to ask! On Sung's advice I simply told Proctor's that Lee was incognito to protect his father from enemies who would go to any lengths to get at him, including the kidnapping of his son. The whole school is in on the secret, and Lee derives great fun from listening to their guesses as to his true identity. If there were other Chinese there, it would be harder, but until recently Lee was the only one. There are two more this year past, but they're the sons of *merchant* princes from Wampoa who Lee says are sublimely indifferent to Peking."

"Well, well," said Alexander, grinning.

"You'll miss some important legislation," she said. "I hear that Parkes is going to strip financial aid from the Catholic schools—and from schools of other denominations. But they don't matter as much because they're funded by wealthy snobs. The children who go to Catholic schools come from a poorer background."

"He's a shocking Protestant bigot," said Alexander.

"There's a new land bill mooted, and one to limit Chinese immigration. Oh, and a few electoral bills—why do politicians fiddle with electorate boundaries?"

"To get more votes, Ruby. Don't ask rhetorical questions."

"Humph! The one that worries me is the liquor bill if it offers districts the right to go dry—bloody wowsers!"

"Rest easy, Ruby," he said, cuddling her arm. "Kinross won't vote to go dry, the place is too continent already, what with all the non-drinking Chinese. The wowsers won't get enough votes to send Kinross dry because the Chinese don't have a vote and the town's whites like their liquor too much."

"Anyway, I'm a residential hotel, not a pub. And I can slip the constabulary a bribe, shades of Hill End."

"You won't need to, I assure you." His voice changed. "Don't be surprised if I'm away for quite a long time."

"What do you call quite a long time, Alexander?"

"Two, three, even four years."

"Jesus! By the time you come home it will have grown back again—I'll be a virgin for the fourth time."

"I shall treat you as such, my darling."

"Does that mean you'll be there to settle Lee into Cambridge?"

"Yes. Perhaps Apocalypse Enterprises can endow a professorial chair, or build a research laboratory."

"Lee is very lucky. I pray he knows it," said his mother.

"Oh, I think he does," said Alexander, smiling.

THOUGH HER husband's departure toward the end of 1879 came as a shock, Elizabeth was not sorry to see him go. It was Nell who mourned inconsolably; her father had begun to take her with him to the workshops, the ore treatment plant, and even down into the mine since she had turned three last New Year's Day. What would she do, stuck in the house day in, day out?

Alexander's answer was to hire not a female governess but a male tutor who would teach her to read and write, commence her in Latin, Greek, French and Italian, and occupy her restless, ever-enquiring mind. The tutor was a bashful young man named William Stephens, whom Alexander set up in a large room on the third floor of Kinross House. Sung sent him three brilliant Chinese boys, the Reverend Peter Wilkins sent him his son, Donny, who was very bright, and Alexander managed to find three white girls whose parents said they could go to school on the mountain until they turned ten or thereabouts. Nell was the youngest; the three Chinese boys, Donny Wilkins and the girls were all five to her almost four.

After several days of tears and tantrums, Nell showed how like her father she was by stiffening her little shoulders and accepting her lot. One day she would be old enough to go away with Daddy; until then, the only way she could maintain her place in his heart was to excel in the schoolroom.

Half a dozen housekeepers had come and gone before Mrs. Gertrude Surtees arrived and fitted into the family like a hand into the right-sized glove. A fifty-year-old widow whose two children were grown up and married, she had been managing a seedy boarding house in Blayney when Constance Dewy found her. Mrs. Surtees was cheerful, unshockable, took no nonsense from Nell or Chang the cook, handled the rest of the Chinese servants deftly and kindly, and even contrived to get on the right side of Jim Summers. This last was rendered even more important after Alexander announced that he was going away, as Summers, for once, was not to go with him; Maggie Summers was suffering from a mysterious illness that her husband wouldn't talk about.

Though executive power in Alexander's absence did not devolve upon Summers. Sung doffed his embroidered silk robes and took over the running of the mine and all the other Apocalypse concerns: coal, iron and bricks in Lithgow; cement not far from Lithgow at Rylstone; several large wheat properties around Wellington; a tin mine in North Queensland; a steam engine factory in Sydney; and a new bauxite mine. Among other things.

As if to answer Alexander's restlessness with some unrest of her own, Elizabeth decided to tear Kinross House apart while he was away and fit it out with the colors, fabrics and furniture *she* liked. Alexander had told her that she might indulge her fancy to the top of her bent, on two conditions: the first, that she left his library severely alone, and the second, that nothing was blue enough to cause an emotional decline.

"He loves red, you know," said Ruby.

"Well, I don't," said Elizabeth, who had never gotten over finding out that scarlet was a color for whores. She looked dreamy. "Some rooms are going to be apricot and lavender-blue, others plum and butterscotch with a hint of yellow, and one or two chartreuse and deep cobalt with touches of white."

"Modern, but nice," Ruby admitted.

As Ruby and Constance both adored to shop, the three women gathered up Anna, Jade, Pearl, Silken Flower and Peach Blossom and periodically descended upon Sydney to pick over fabrics and exclaim at wallpapers, not to mention drive furniture salesmen mad when they weren't being fitted for dresses or trying on shoes and hats. An unregretful Nell was left behind in the care of Butterfly Wing, Mrs. Surtees and Mr. William Stephens.

EVERY DOCTOR reputed to be versed in mental children had seen Anna, but the verdict was always the same: hope of recovery should not be entertained, as those who failed to walk and talk by two years of age were definitely going to be mental for life.

She did, however, improve; at fifteen months she was able to hold her head up and focus her eyes on any person trying to capture her attention. Her beauty became more marked once she focused her eyes, large and well opened like her mother's, a light blue-grey between preposterously long black lashes.

By two years of age she could sit unsupported in her high chair and feed herself—a messy business that Jade regarded as a triumph and Elizabeth found turned her stomach. Anna's attachment to Jade was complete, though she began to recognize Elizabeth shortly after she went into the high chair. Talk she would not, walk she would not. Nell was in a special category to Anna, who greeted her with frenzied screeches of what seemed joy.

Jade persisted gently and firmly, guided by Hung Chee in the Chinese medicine shop; his Oriental wisdom seemed of more benefit to Anna than any of the drafts and nostrums the Sydney doctors prescribed, for Hung Chee preached exercise, patience, diet and repetitive teaching. He had also porcupined the little girl with thin, whippy needles he stuck into her skin to help her lift her head. Elizabeth had pondered the efficacy of this, but not forbidden it, so when Anna could lift her head and Hung Chee wanted to embark on a new course to help her walk, Elizabeth gave him permission. Oddly enough, Anna enjoyed being porcupined with needles, possibly because she loved Hung Chee.

Oh, the elation when Anna learned to sit on a potty! Admittedly, six months went by before she associated this activity with defecation, but she did—most of the time. Shortly after Alexander left at the end of 1879, when Anna was almost three years old, she began to try to say a few words. "Mum," "Jade" and "Nell" were the sum total of her vocabulary, but each was directed at the right person. The next word, added when she was three and a half, was "dolly," the dirty and beloved rag creature she slept with and insisted stay with her through everything from sessions with the needles to eating and sitting in her high chair. Dolly had to be washed at least once a week, but when Elizabeth tried to substitute a new dolly, Anna screamed the house down until she got the old one back.

"That's good," said Ruby. "Anna knows the difference."

"Mrs. Surtees suggests that I have Wing Ah at the Chinese tailor's copy Anna's dolly down to fading the fabric and putting all the marks we can't get out on it. That way, when dolly falls apart, as she must, we can quietly substitute a new old dolly."

"Good for Mrs. Surtees! She's a treasure, Elizabeth."

ELIZABETH STILL had time to ride Crystal to The Pool twice a week, which was all that really kept her going. As the horse disliked wading upstream, Elizabeth took a machete and cleared a bridle path through the forest, though with one part of her she feared that its presence would lead Alexander to discover her secret place once he returned home. Still, that was for the future; Alexander, away already for eighteen months, was in no hurry to come back to Kinross, so much was plain from his letters.

Those to his wife were brief and their language bordered on curt, whereas those he wrote to Ruby were longer, newsier. Full of Lee, who turned seventeen in 1881.

"You did well to send him away, Ruby," one letter said, "though I suspect that he has missed his Mama acutely. Whatever I can tell him about you is sucked up like water into a sponge, and the photographs I gave him occupy pride of place in his room. As a senior boy, he now has a bedroom and study of his own, with the two Persian princes one on either side of him. His English is rounded, very upper-crust, and his manner royal in a completely unarrogant way. I enclose a photograph of him taken in his new school suit; he was reluctant to have it taken, as he seems to have absorbed some of his fellow pupils' superstitions, and rather fears that the camera will steal his soul. Luckily he has too much engineer in him to *quite* believe this, hence the photograph.

"He is already six feet tall, and has a lot of growing yet to do, his house master says—I daresay the fellow has a great deal of experience with boys and youths, and knows what he's talking about, so you may expect a moderate giant when you see him. In his rowing attire you can see that he has a very good physique that doesn't go to pieces below the thigh like white men's legs. His calf muscles are pure Chinese, massive. With the result that he is a champion sprinter and rows superbly well. Cricket has become a passion—he bowls as efficiently as he bats. He hopes to row for Cambridge when he goes up, and to play cricket for his college at least. That college will probably be Caius, as it doesn't mind foreigners. From all of which you will deduce that he is very much looking forward to going up in October of next year. I am nosing around the Cambridge Powers That Be to see what I can do to ease his path there, as he isn't, for all his accent, an *English* gentleman. The two Persian boys have also elected Cambridge; they lean on Lee quite a lot, as do some of the other Proctor's pupils. Your son has a quality I'd call steadfast strength."

Ruby took the letter back from Elizabeth and gave her the photograph, beaming in pride. "Lee at last," she said.

The picture showed Lee seated on a chair, his legs crossed at the knee; Elizabeth studied it intently, trying not to be influenced by Ruby's patent pride or Alexander's rather surprising tendency to lyricism. Never, she had to admit, had she seen such a handsome youth, nor one so exotic. Not even Sung, whom Lee resembled, could boast such fine features. But Ruby was there too; Lee faced the camera with a faint smile that hinted at Ruby's dimples, and the Caucasian eyes were obviously light in color. More importantly, they held great intelligence.

"He's remarkable," she said, handing the photograph back. "Are his eyes green like yours?"

"Not the same green, yet just as green. Is that sensible?"

"Oh, yes. His hair is combed back as if he loaded it with macassar oil—he must need antimacassar flaps on the back of tall easy chairs."

"No, there's no oil. He has a pigtail."

"A pigtail?"

"Yes. Sung wished it."

"So eight years are gone, and only four remain before you'll see him again."

Only four years to go, thought Ruby as she took the cable car back to Kinross. An eternity to add to the eternity passed. I never heard his voice break, or saw the first bristles on his chin, or experienced that enthralling, heartbreaking moment when a woman's son suddenly excludes her from the sight of his manhood. Every letter he has written to me is tied in jade-green ribbon and put in its jade chest, every word of every one of them I know by heart, and yet when he returns to me it will be as a relative stranger. How could I tell Elizabeth that I hardly recognized him in the photograph? That I wept for hours, mourning his and my loss? My only consolation is that the eyes in his picture are steady, tranquil, without pain or insecurity. Well, once he got over the initial wrench of parting, his life at Proctor's must have been fascinating and fulfilling. I can ask no more than that, save to hope that when he chooses a mate, he does so for the right reasons. Alexander hankers for her to be his Nell, though I'm not sure Nell will turn out the kind of woman he will find alluring. Even at five, she's brisk and no-nonsense, very much an independent soul. Well, Elizabeth has had to devote her time to Anna, which has left Nell to find her own way. She's so like Alexander, and while Lee adores Alexander, I find it hard to imagine that he'll adore Nell. Still, these are all questions for the future. It will be four years before I really find out what sort of man my son is. When Lee returns, he will be twenty-one years old, and his own master. My baby will be a legal man, and I will sign over his share of Apocalypse Enterprises to him. He will sit on our board of directors as a stranger to me.

Perhaps because these musings were so painful, Ruby switched her attention to Kinross. How it had changed! The ugliness had gone, replaced by macadamized roads, curbing and guttering, tree-lined streets, a few fine brick buildings including the Kinross Hotel and St. Andrew's church. On one side of Kinross Square, now green and gardened, a new structure was rising: Alexander's precious theater and opera house. Why should Gulgong have the only opera house, why should Bathurst have three theaters and Kinross none? All the houses were wooden, the last wattle-and-daub effort torn down when the school was moved to a much larger, more imposing brick home. Even the hospital was respectable. And the river flowed between concrete embankments equipped with park benches, trees and ornamental gas lamps, though its water, alas, was as dirty as ever.

For between the town and the base of the mountain lay an industry, with rail tracks, machines, engines, the refinery plant, dozens of corrugated iron sheds and belching chimneys. The gold continued to come out in the same quantity, but its attendant structures had been joined by a gasworks, a dynamo house, and the refrigeration unit. Kinross now shipped in fresh milk and meat from Bathurst, as well as fish and fruit from Sydney.

What would this colony have done without people like Alexander and Sam Mort the freezer king? In England they would probably have moldered, but here in New South Wales they have put their hands on mighty undertakings and prospered. I wonder what my convict grandfather Richard Morgan and my convict mother would say could they only see what has become of the place they were sent to as a punishment? And look at me, Ruby Costevan: once an old man's darling; then a madam; now a company director. Men cannot help it. They put their hands on things and change them forever. Especially Alexander Kinross and Samuel Mort. So thought Ruby, going home to her posh hotel.

TIME REELED on, its public facets very discouraging due to the flaws in public men. The Irish-ancestry part of Kinross's population seethed with indignation when Premier Sir Henry Parkes, speaking in the parliament, informed its members that Irish immigration must be held down in order to make sure that the proper British feel of the colony be preserved, together with the dominance of Protestant religions. It was his wish, he said, to ensure the teaching and influence of the Protestant ethic, therefore no favors could be extended to the Irish and Catholicism that would alter the status quo, already too Irish and Catholic. A stupid statement that only exacerbated the widening rift between the Irish Catholics and their Protestant cousins from other parts of the British Isles; it also widened the rift between the working class and the classes above them, as Irishness and Catholicism were at their most numerous among the working class. There were also mutterings about the "Mongol and Tartar hordes," who weren't even Christians of any kind. But when the bigotry and intolerance stemmed from persons as exalted as state premiers, it simply indicated just how widespread these retarding sentiments were, and how indifferent public men were to uniting rather than dividing people.

In January of 1881, an intercolonial conference had met in Sydney to discuss restricting Chinese immigration and submitted a paper to the British Government complaining that the Australian colonies should not have to adhere to the British policy toward China, which was conciliatory. It also protested against the Government of Western Australia's decision to assist Chinese immigrants willing to work as farm laborers or domestic servants.

Sung joined with several other prominent Chinese businessmen to submit the Chinese side of the question, and drew the colonial conference's attention to the fact that it was foolish to antagonize a country of so many millions in such close proximity to a vast and largely unpopulated land:

". . . if you substitute arbitrary violence, hatred and jealousy for justice, legality and right, it may be that you will succeed in carrying your point; it may be that a great wrong will be accomplished by the exercise of sheer force, and the weight of superior numbers: but your reputation among the nations of the earth will be irretrievably injured and debased, and the flag of which you are so justly proud will no longer be the standard of freedom and the hope of the oppressed, but will be associated with deeds of falsehood and treachery."

In fact, this new decade that Alexander had had such hopes for had commenced in a mood of bitterness and resentment between many different groups in the Australian community. Women began to protest that they were unfairly treated when it came to education, so tellingly that Sydney University decided to open all its faculties to women students—with the exception of Medicine, of course; the very thought of a female medically qualified to inspect, handle and probe the penis and scrotum was horrific.

Because most Kinrossians read the newspapers (joined now by the *Daily Telegraph* and a weekly magazine of comment, the *Bulletin*) all these events and opinions were assimilated and discussed, but as far as Ruby and the town's publicans were concerned, those wretched wowsers were gaining too much power in the parliament; legislation was passed forcing hotels and bars to close at 11 P.M. from Monday to Saturday, and all day on Sunday. Like many of her confederates state-wide, Ruby informed the Liquor Commission that, as liquor licenses under the old law were valid until June of 1882, the old drinking hours would prevail until June of 1882. So there.

FOR ELIZABETH, time was mostly a matter of birthdays. Nell turned six on New Year's Day of 1882, and Anna turned five on April 6. It was like being in the middle of some extraordinary play dreamed up by the irreverent and earthy eighteenth-century comic theater, only it wasn't funny: Nell had acquired a polysyllabic vocabulary and could already make sense of trigonometry and algebra, whereas Anna had not yet learned to walk and still said "Mum," "Jade," "Nell" and "dolly." However, Anna was saving up a surprise; on her fifth birthday she crawled across the nursery floor, laughing and squealing, to Jade, coaxing her.

Elizabeth did her duty unflaggingly, but found it very hard to like that duty. Jade obviously didn't mind in the least, so Elizabeth felt that something must be wrong with her, the child's mother. Of course she knew that Anna was the spike that nailed her forever to life as Alexander Kinross's wife. It had occurred to her during those interminable weeks in bed before Anna's birth that if she saved the very generous allowance Alexander gave her, one day she would be able to leave him, disappear back to Scotland and live there in a cottage as a respectable maiden lady. Her children, she had thought, would survive very well without her; Nell already did. But then she looked at Anna properly and saw the shape of her fate. How could she leave this poor, helpless little creature who was doomed to be a lifelong burden? She could not. She just could not. Which meant that she loved Anna, no matter how she detested looking after Anna.

Oh, the uselessness of crouching on a toy chair at Anna's level repeating the same words over and over again, words like "wee-wees" and "poohs" and "yum-yum"! Sometimes she thought she would go mad from the sheer futility of it. Yet Ruby's fabulous earthiness encompassed mental children as easily as it did the monumental follies of men. Ruby never turned a hair when Anna dribbled down her expensive dress, or threw up on it, or smeared it with feces in an ecstasy of happiness. Whereas when Anna did those things to her, Elizabeth had to bolt from the room fighting nausea and a deeper revulsion. And, being Elizabeth, she told herself that she was lacking in common decency and humanity, that her churning stomach and appalled disgust were evidence that she might love Anna, but that love wasn't enough to quell the horrors of looking after a mental child.

Alexander once called me nice, but I'm not, she castigated herself. I am that worst of all women, an unnatural mother. Mothers are supposed to be able to cope, yet here am I unable to cope with either of my children. If Anna is a crawling lump of dough, Nell is a frighteningly superior being with whom I have absolutely no communion. Give Nell a doll, and she operates on it—takes a sharp knife and slits it down the middle, pulls out its stuffing with learned remarks about the state of its innards. Then she goes off and fashions accurately painted body parts for it from that ghastly atlas of anatomy Alexander won't part with because its etchings are by Albrecht Dürer, whoever he may be. And if she isn't doing that, she's out of her bed at midnight on the flat part of the roof with the telescope Alexander gave her, looking at the moon or raving about something's rings. I have given birth to a minature Alexander and a cabbage, and I cannot find it in me to like caring for either of them. I just love them because I carried them, they are a part of me.

With Anna, who knows what she thinks, if indeed she can—Jade swears she can. Yet in her way Nell is as much a monster as Anna—imperious, restless, arrogant, determined, insatiably curious, fearless. Though her eyes are blue, not black, when Nell looks at me from under her pointed brows, it's Alexander I see staring at me. Six years old, and she considers her mother only a few degrees higher in intelligence than Anna. She hates being cuddled, she hates being kissed, and dismisses feminine activities with scorn. The box of my discarded clothes I gave her last birthday to play at dressing up sits there unopened—oh, the scathing glance she shot me for what any other little girl her age would have deemed a treasure chest! As if to say, Mum, who do you take me for, an idiot like Anna?

I can love both my daughters, but I cannot like one of them because she has a gigantic mind and I cannot like the other because her habits revolt me.

Oh, dear God, tell me where I go wrong? What do I lack?

When she said some of this to Ruby, Ruby snorted in derision.

"Honestly, Elizabeth, you're too hard on yourself! There are people like me who have strong stomachs and don't mind dirt and messes, probably because we grew up surrounded by dirt and messes. You grew up in one of those immaculate Scottish houses, I suppose, everything swept and mopped and dusted. No one vomiting up too much booze, or shitting in a drunken stupor, or forgetting to wash the dishes until they grew mold, or leaving the garbage to rot inside the house—Jesus, Elizabeth, I grew up in a cesspit! And if your stomach's weak, it's weak. You can't control that, pussycat, no matter how hard you try. As for Nell, I agree with you—she's a sort of a monster. She's never going to be a person everybody takes to at a glance, she's more likely to put most people off. You suffer because you had very little education, and Alexander made you feel that. I had no education either, but I wasn't an immature girl of sixteen when I met him. Cheer up, and stop this self-castigation. To love your children is far more important than liking them."

WE NEED RAIN, Elizabeth thought one May morning in 1882 as she mounted Crystal to ride the three miles between the house and The Pool.

The Pool saves my sanity. Without it, I would be shut up, gibbering, in a place where they hosed me into submission. Still, then I wouldn't know anything, and that is a kind of peace. *Self-pity, Elizabeth!* The worst of all crimes because it leads to delusion, imagined injuries and loss of contact with the feelings of others. Whatever you are, whatever you go through, you have brought on yourself. You could have said no to Father—what could he have done, apart from beat you and send you to see Dr. Murray? You could have said no to Alexander—what could he have done except send you home again in disgrace? Ruby is right, I think too much about myself and my faults. I must think about The Pool instead. There I can forget.

She pushed the mare along the track, now so well worn that anyone might have followed it had anyone had a wish to, or been allowed to. Yet it had never once crossed her mind that The Pool might be invaded by any person other than herself.

Until, perhaps three hundred yards from it, Elizabeth heard the sound of a man's laugh, lighthearted, joyous. Her reaction contained no fear, but she didn't ride on. Instead, she slipped off Crystal and tied the animal to a tree branch, patted its shiny white hide and walked on softly. Her temper was up: how dared this fellow trespass on Kinross property? No fear, but prudence all the same. It dictated that first she should see who the interloper was. If, for instance, some party of bushrangers had discovered it, she would retrace her footsteps undetected and ride back to the house, there to use the new toy Alexander had installed before he left—a telephone linked to the Kinross police station and Summers's house. It went nowhere else, but its ability to summon help was instantaneous. The other possibility was a group of natives, but they rarely if ever came close to white settlements in this area, and were afraid of the mine; there were so many hundreds of square miles of uninhabited forest that these far from populous people preferred to safeguard their tribal identity by avoiding the white man's corruption.

No horses tethered nearby, no signs of desperadoes or of natives. Just one man, standing with his back to her on a rock that jutted out over The Pool like a flayed shoulder blade. Her breath caught, she slowed and stopped. He was naked, the light streaming over golden skin and a mane of straight black hair that fell down his spine to far past his waist. *A Chinese?* Then he turned in her direction, lifted his arms above his head and dived in a blur of movement to disappear with hardly a splash under the surface of the water. Her attention was focused on his face as he swung around, and she knew it as if it were her own in a mirror. Lee Costevan! Lee Costevan was home. Her knees gave way; she sank to the ground in a heap, then realized that the moment he came up for air, he would see her. Oh, what a confrontation! What an embarrassment for both of them! What could she *say*? Scrambling, she wriggled into the shelter of the undergrowth just in time.

His private delight was almost painful to witness as he projected himself out of the water in a leap as high and powerful as one of the fish that lived in it; then, flinging back his soaking hair from his face, he lifted himself effortlessly out of the water on to the rock, gazed about, entranced, and stretched himself flat to bake in the sun. Elizabeth stayed where she was, immobile as a lizard, until he decided to go back into The Pool. Then she crept away.

The ride back to the house got itself done—how, she never afterward knew. Her eyes, her mind, her very soul were possessed by the memory of that beautiful, wonderful body that had no flaw, its muscles liquid beneath the smooth skin, the face rapt, frozen in perfect pleasure. All her life she had yearned for freedom, but had never encountered it personified in a human being until now, and it was unforgettable. A revelation.

Lee Costevan was home.

Seven

A NEW KIND OF PAIN

RUBY APPEARED not long after Elizabeth had bathed and changed into an afternoon dress.

"Lee's home!" she cried, face transfigured. "Oh, Elizabeth, Lee's home! I didn't expect it, I had no idea!"

"How wonderful," said Elizabeth automatically, forming the words as if they were wool in her mouth. "Some tea, Mrs. Surtees."

She ushered a fizzing, exalted Ruby to the conservatory and persuaded her to sit in a chair for more than a second at a time, finding it easier now to smile. "Ruby, dear, calm down. I want to hear all about it at once, but you're in no fit state to talk."

"He just appeared off the Lithgow train last night, out of the blue—I wondered why it ran so late, but of course it waited for him to make the connection off the slow train from Sydney. I was in the lounge with the C of E bishop and his wife—he's visiting the parish," babbled Ruby.

"I know he is. He's coming here to dinner tonight, don't you remember? Now you can come with Lee."

"And in walked Lee! Oh, Elizabeth, my jade kitten is a man! So *handsome*! So tall! And you should hear him speak—vowels as round as the toffiest toff in England!" She brushed away tears, smiled ecstatically. "Bishop Kestwick positively fell all over himself the moment he heard Lee speak, and when he realized that this was my son—oh, I soared in his estimation!"

"I didn't know that was an ambition of yours," Elizabeth said, willing her heart to stop beating so fast.

"Well, it isn't, and the old boy is very confused about my place in the Kinross scheme of things, but he knows better than to treat me like a scarlet woman when I'm on the Apocalypse board and a potential donor to the church. Anyway, once he set eyes on Lee he decided that I was very wronged—my son had gone to none other than Proctor's. Oh, Elizabeth, I'm so happy!"

"A blind man could see that, darling Ruby." Elizabeth wet her lips. "Does this mean that Alexander is coming home? Is he in Sydney and arriving later?"

Some of Ruby's animation died as she saw the expression in Elizabeth's eyes, the way her face had donned its old mask. "No, sweetie-pie, Alexander stayed in England. He sent Lee home for the English summer because that's Alexander—his letter says that he couldn't contemplate my going another three and more years without setting eyes on my jade kitten. Lee is home until the end of July, when he sails again."

The tea arrived; Elizabeth poured. "So what are you doing here, Ruby? Why aren't you spending every moment with Lee?"

"Oh, Lee's joining us here," said Ruby, who looked a mere twenty-five years old, glowing with youth. "You don't think that I'd wait until dinner time to introduce you to my son, do you? He set off to explore Kinross, and promised that he'd turn up in time for tea." She mock-frowned. "The wretch! He's late."

"We'll make more tea when he comes."

That was half an hour later, by which time Elizabeth had composed herself. A little surprised, she had discovered a small twinge of regret when Ruby said Alexander wasn't coming home; Nell at least would have been delirious to see him. Though she could understand why Ruby wasn't very perturbed; it would be awkward to juggle a son and a lover who were the best of friends, keep the knowledge of what Alexander was to her from Lee.

Who walked into the conservatory with his hair braided into its pigtail, clad in a pair of old but clean dungarees and an open-necked cotton shirt with its sleeves rolled up. Not realizing that her face froze immediately into an expression of cool remoteness, Elizabeth rose to her feet and extended one hand to the young man with an aloof smile on her lips and no smile in her eyes. Ruby was right, he was handsome, strikingly so; a look of Sung as well as of his mother, Sung in the sharply delineated features and patrician air, Ruby in the grace of movement and the spontaneous charm. But his eyes were all his own, their light green irises surrounded by much darker green rings that gave his regard a piercing quality. Yes, pale eyes set in black lashes and bronze skin were unsettling, fascinatingly incongruous.

"How do you do, Lee?" Elizabeth asked, voice colorless.

His delight in the day waned, his head went slightly to one side as those eyes inspected her with a touch of bewilderment.

"I'm very well, Mrs. Kinross," he said, shaking her limp hand. "And you?"

"Very well, thank you. Please call me Elizabeth. Do sit down. Mrs. Surtees will bring fresh tea shortly."

He sat where he could see both women and let his mother do the talking. So this was Alexander's wife, of whom Alexander hardly ever spoke. No wonder, Lee reflected. She wasn't a warm or womanly woman, though an arctic composure suited her style. Quite the most beautiful woman he had ever seen, with that milk-white skin, black hair and very dark blue eyes. A lush mouth disciplined into a firmness alien to its natural contours, a long and graceful neck, and lovely hands on whose third fingers those massive rings looked out of place. Elizabeth Kinross wasn't a splashy person, but of course Alexander would have given her the rings, and he was definitely a splashy person. I wish he had come with me, Lee thought. I miss him, and I suspect that in his absence I am missing the essence of Kinross. His wife doesn't want me here.

"How is Alexander?" she asked when she could get a word in.

"Thriving," said Lee with a grin that displayed Ruby's dimples. "He's with the Siemens Brothers in Germany for the summer."

"Looking at engines and machines."

"Yes."

"Do you know if he's been to Kinross in Scotland?"

Lee looked surprised, his mouth open to say that surely Alexander wrote of such things, then he closed it; when he did answer the question, it was directly. "No, Elizabeth, he hasn't."

"I imagined that. Have you spent much time with him?"

"Every moment that Proctor's granted me."

"So you like him."

"He's more a father to me than Sung, though I don't say that with bitterness or mean to imply a criticism. I love and respect my blood father, but I am not Chinese," said Lee stiffly.

Ruby was looking from one to the other with dismay—this was not how she had imagined the meeting of her most beloved son and her most cherished friend! They weren't making a connection—worse, Elizabeth was radiating dislike. The ice was back with a vengeance. Elizabeth, don't do this to me! Don't reject my jade kitten! She jumped up, put on her hat.

"Oops, it's late. Up with you, Lee, while there's still a sandwich left on the plate. Bishop Kestwick is coming to dinner here tonight, so you and I will be returning with the episcopal couple at half past seven."

"I look forward to it," said Elizabeth woodenly.

"WHAT DID you think of Alexander's wife?" Ruby asked her son as they traveled down to Kinross in the cable car.

Lee didn't answer for a moment, then turned his head to look into his mother's eyes. "Alexander has never discussed her with me, Mum, but meeting her has made me understand why you're still his mistress."

Her breath caught. "So you know that."

"He made no secret of it because he knew that sooner or later I'd find out. That's what he said when he told me. We had a long talk about you, and I loved him for it. He spoke of you with such deep affection, said that you were the light of his life. But he didn't bring Elizabeth into it, or explain *why* he was still with you, except to say that he couldn't live without you."

"Nor I without him. I gather you don't disapprove?"

"Of course I don't, Mum." He smiled at the town, drawing closer. "It's his and your business, not mine, and it doesn't affect you and me, does it? Except that I'm so enormously pleased to think that my mother and my self-chosen father are in love."

"Ta, my jade kitten," she said huskily, squeezing his hand. "You're so like your self-chosen father in many ways—you both have a practical streak a mile wide, and that in turn gives you the detachment to accept the things that can't be changed."

"Like you and Alexander."

"Like me and Alexander."

They got out of the car and walked between the huge corrugated iron sheds that housed the Apocalypse activities, emerged on to the streets of Kinross.

"Did you explore the ore plant, the gasworks, the retorts and all the rest this afternoon?" she asked as they crossed the grass of Kinross Square.

"No, I went bush, Mum. Europe is full of factories, but it has no bush. That was what I wanted first—the sight of our own animals running wild, the smell of eucalyptus, birds that have all the colors of the rainbow in their plumage. European birds are rather dismal, though the nightingale has a beautiful song."

"And you didn't see Elizabeth?"

"No. Should I have?"

"Not really, except that today was a riding day, and she always goes bush."

"A riding day?"

"Some days of the week she relieves Jade in the nursery to look after Anna. I presume you know about Anna?"

"Oh, yes."

They entered the foyer of the hotel. "You're bound to meet Nell this evening—Elizabeth lets her stay up long enough to see the dinner guests." Ruby smiled wryly. "I think that's her way of demonstrating that one of her children is very clever, even if the other is mental."

"Poor Elizabeth," he said. "Formal evening dress, Mum?"

"Oh, yes."

"Will Sung be there? I feel a little guilty at going bush instead of paying my respects to him in that amazing pagoda city on top of the hill."

"You can do that tomorrow, Lee. His pagoda city is amazing, isn't it? But Sung won't be at Kinross House tonight—he's a heathen Chinee. The guests all have something to do with the C of E in Kinross." She giggled. "Except for the Costevans! We are not Chinese, but we are definitely heathens."

"Very wealthy heathens!" came his voice as he disappeared down the corridor to his room.

There are no flies on you, Lee, for all the years you've been away, thought Ruby, fancying that the air still contained some of his essence. He flattened me, she thought; I didn't know how big he was, how strange a mixture of Sung and me he'd be. Lee, my Lee!

AFTER A VISIT to the nursery Elizabeth went to her rooms and sat looking out a window. But she didn't see the vista of forest and mountain; her vision was inward, and occupied by Lee Costevan at The Pool, an image of beauty, masculinity, utter freedom. I have been visiting The Pool for years, yet never once did it occur to me to strip off my clothes and frolic amid the fish, a fish myself. Not all of The Pool is deep, I might have kept to the shallow end. I could have known what he knew today. Oh, Elizabeth, be honest with yourself! You didn't because you couldn't. You're not free to frolic, even on the days when you can ride Crystal. You're tied to a husband you can't love and two children you do love but can't like, and that weighs you down like an ingot of lead. So get on with your life, and go away, Lee Costevan!

Even so, she took particular care that evening to choose a dress—pale navy-blue taffeta, its bustle trimmed with chiffon frills that were repeated at her bosom and formed small sleeves just below her white shoulders. She shaved the hair in her armpits these days, a trick she had learned from Ruby, who deplored those women who, she said, "Lift an arm in their daring gown and display a thick bush that destroys their attractiveness completely. Pearl can use a razor, have her keep your armpits shaven, Elizabeth. It permits the sweat to get away, you'll smell sweeter."

"What about the downstairs department?" she had asked with a wicked smile.

"I don't shave it because it itches dreadfully growing back, but I do trim it with a pair of scissors," said Ruby, unabashed. "Who wants a sticky beard down there?" She giggled. "Unless it's a man's sticky beard."

"Ruby!"

At least, she thought, I am educated in such matters thanks to Ruby. There. The sapphire and diamond suite looked very well with this dress—hair ornament, earrings, necklace and two wide bracelets. She hadn't done her hair in the customary puffs and rolls, but swept it back into a braided bun atop her head. No need to be ashamed of her ears or her neck, so why dwarf her face with a bouffant hair style? A touch of jasmine perfume, and she was ready to face the Kinross Church of England.

Who, of course, felt utterly eclipsed by the two most important women in the district, if not in all of New South Wales.

"You must forgive the lack of a host, your lordship," said Elizabeth to the Bishop, "but I feel that this first visit to our little township should include dinner at Kinross House."

"Of course, of course," burbled the Bishop, staggered by so much beauty displayed with so much elegance and refinement.

"Lee, you are welcome," she said then to Ruby's son, looking as if he didn't know what dungarees and a limp cotton shirt were. His evening dress had been tailored in Savile Row, his tie a big affair in silk brocade, just as the latest fashion magazines depicted. Haughty was a new word she found for him; yet he radiated charm in Ruby's manner, and soon had the Bishop wrapped around his finger. The Costevans are shameless.

Elizabeth sat with Bishop Kestwick on her right and the Reverend Peter Wilkins on her left; the other guests were seated down either side of the table, extended to accommodate the eleven diners. Alexander's place at the other end was vacant. For a moment she had toyed with the idea of putting Lee there, then decided against it—he was, after all, not yet eighteen years of age. A fact that the Bishop chose to comment upon.

"Aren't you a little young to be drinking wine, sir?"

Lee blinked, flashed the clerical guest a particularly sweet smile. "Jesus," he said, "was a Jew in a country and at a time when wine was healthier to drink than most water. I imagine that He drank wine after His bar mitzvah conveyed official manhood on Him. That is, after He turned twelve or thereabouts. It would have been watered until His sixteenth birthday—or thereabouts. Wine is God's gift, my lord. Taken in moderation, naturally. I will not become inebriated, I promise you."

A reply that had the Bishop floundering, since it was given courteously yet firmly.

Grinning from ear to ear, Ruby blazed green fire at her son and mouthed, "That fucked him, Lee!"

Oh, dear God, thought Elizabeth, reading Ruby's lips, let me get through this disaster unscathed! Having two Costevans and the Church of England at the same table is a recipe for disaster.

However, Chang was in fine form and produced a superb meal: a French country terrine finished with tinned truffles; fillets of John Dory grilled to perfection; the obligatory sorbet; roast beef from a beast fattened with a diet of corn; and ice cream splattered with passion fruit.

"Wonderful, wonderful!" cried the Bishop, tasting the dessert. "How do you keep it frozen, Mrs. Kinross?"

"We have a refrigeration works, your lordship. After Mr. Samuel Mort established his freezing plant in Lithgow, my husband saw the virtue of it. I used to long for a piece of fish, but there is none up here. Now we can bring it from Sydney without fearing that it will poison us."

"But there are fish here," said Lee, eating with gusto but careful of his manners. Difficult for a seventeen-year-old.

"No, there aren't," said Ruby.

"I assure you, Mum, there are. I found them today when I went bush. In a glorious pool way up the river." He smiled at Elizabeth meltingly—

why wouldn't she thaw? "You must know of the pool, Mrs. Kinross. I followed a bridle path that I imagine only you could have made."

I see that in company I am not Elizabeth. How clever of him. "Yes, I do know of the pool and its fish, Lee. Yet no matter how I longed for fish—acutely, in the old days—I couldn't bear to catch them. They are so free. So untrammeled. So joyous. Were they leaping out of the water today?"

He flushed, looked contrite. "Er—no, I'm afraid not. I frightened them pretending I was a fish too."

I have found a chink in her armor, he thought. A chink found by a Chink. Quite a good pun, Lee, if unintentional. She envies the fish, she doesn't feel free, or untrammeled, or joyous. This house and her life are a prison she can't escape. Poor Elizabeth! I wonder how old she is? It's hard to tell a woman's age once she's dressed in all this clobber women have to wear. Mum is pushing forty, but Elizabeth is younger. About thirty-two or thirty-three, perhaps? "She walks in beauty, like the night of cloudless climes and starry skies." How did Byron know what the nights are like in Australia? She's unforgettable, but that's because of her remoteness. The likes of me don't exist for her. I wonder does Alexander?

When the men arrived in the drawing room after their port and cigars, Lee found Elizabeth seated in a chair for one, and drew up another close to it. Ruby cast him a look of gratitude, at liberty to sit at the piano and earn her dinner.

"You know," said Lee to Elizabeth in a low voice, "my mother is a truly great musician, and I'm sure that her skill has as much to do with her acceptance by the society of this town as her money does. I overheard some of the other guests as they left the car, all hoping ardently that she would play and sing."

"I am aware of her talent," said Elizabeth primly.

"I usurped your favorite spot today," he said, "and I am sorry for it. I won't go back, I promise. Your fish can leap in peace."

"It is of no moment," she said. "I cannot ride every day, just Wednesdays and Saturdays. On Sundays I go into Kinross to church, and on Thursdays I spend a few hours with your mother at the hotel. If you like, visit The Pool when I cannot—Mondays, Tuesdays, Thursdays, Fridays. I have a feeling that you are not a churchgoer, so Sundays are possible too."

"That's kind of you, but I can go elsewhere."

"Why? It might do the fish good to be stirred up."

It would do *you* good to be stirred up, he thought. So calm, so polite, so indifferent. That pool means a lot to you, Elizabeth Kinross, but you can't—or won't—let me see it.

"I would like to meet your children," he said.

"If you plan to eat lunch at the hotel tomorrow, you will. The children and I always have Sunday lunch with your mother."

"YOU'RE VERY silent," said Ruby to her son as they strolled the gardens of Kinross House waiting for the car to return. The huge clumsy dresses women wore took up more room than miners or men in evening dress, so they had let the car go down without them.

"I was thinking about Elizabeth."

"Were you? What, exactly?"

"How old she is, for one thing. Alexander doesn't talk of her, you know."

"Elizabeth will be twenty-four in September."

"You must be joking!" he said with a gasp. "But she's been married for over seven years!"

"Yes. She was sixteen when Alexander married her. He brought her from Scotland sight unseen. If he doesn't talk about her, it's because the union never prospered. Why else does he still see me? And no doubt has a few feminine consolations in Europe."

"You're wrong there, Mum. He's as celibate as a monk." Lee grinned. "Which didn't prevent his hiring the most magnificent bird of paradise to initiate me into the mysteries of sex."

"Oh, that was kind of him," she said sincerely. "I worried about that—the clap, the pox, unsuitable girls, gold-diggers. They must mill around a school like Proctor's just waiting to snare inexperienced boys who have money to burn."

"So Alexander thought. Be discriminating in the right sense, he said. Love will rule you, but sex never should."

"He's right. Have you a bird of paradise at the moment?"

"Oh, I still have the same one—I like dallying in a woman's arms, but I'm not promiscuous. Just one at a time. I keep her in a nice flat far enough away from Proctor's to be decent, and when I go up to Cambridge I'll put her in a bigger flat there. I'll be able to have my friends around," said Lee, sounding pleased.

"She's likely to cheat in your absence."

"No, she won't. She knows which side her bread is buttered on, Mum. Particularly as it comes sprinkled with diamonds."

"And what else were you thinking about Elizabeth?"

"Oh, nothing much," he said vaguely.

A lie he knew his mother would see through, yet somehow he didn't want to share any more of his thoughts with her. A mere twenty-three years old! Straight from the schoolroom to the marital bed. That answered many of his questions, for he knew quite a number of sixteen-year-old girls. Some were the sisters and cousins of his schoolmates, but nationality didn't matter—girls tended to be girls, and these girls were largely immune to the restraints that poverty and strict religious observance put on the humbler people of their realms. So they giggled a lot, were addicted to gossip, swooned when they saw young men they fancied, and dreamed of marriage romantically, despite the fact that it would be an arranged marriage. Unless the bridegroom was already known, they could always hope he would be the handsome young son of a nobleman rather than an ancient friend of their father's, and chance was on their side. More married handsome sons than ancient advisers. Besides these girls, Lee knew the girls who attended Miss Rockleigh's Academy for Young Ladies, situated in the neighborhood. Proctor's had an arrangement with Miss Rockleigh's, whereby the pupils of the two schools attended very proper dances together as well as a ball held every May Day. It was called grooming the pupils for their societal debut.

That kind of existence, he divined, had not been a part of Elizabeth's life. More than instinct told him this: Alexander had once delivered a diatribe against Scottish Kinross, its Presbyterian minister and the clan of Drummond, to which Elizabeth belonged. If Alexander spoke the truth, the girls were kept in something akin to purdah. From that to marriage with a man years older than she; Alexander had turned thirty-nine last April. She wore her beauty like a garment she had donned the way a man did a uniform, to tell the world who Alexander thought she was.

Why does she dislike me? Because I'm a half-caste? No, I can't credit that my mother would love her the way she does if Elizabeth were a bigot. Though it's an odd alliance! She must know of the relationship between my mother and Alexander.

"Does Elizabeth know about you and Alexander?" he asked.

"Oh, yes. He tried to keep us apart, but he failed. We took one look at each other and were firm friends," said Ruby.

Another question answered. Yet the mystery grew thicker and thicker, the convolutions more tortuous. What are they all going to say tomorrow at lunch when I explode my charge of dynamite? I can hardly wait.

The last thing Lee saw as he drifted into sleep was Elizabeth's mouth, and the last thing he thought was what it would be like to kiss it.

"ODD THAT Nell wasn't present before dinner last night," said Ruby, greeting Lee with a hug. "How was Sung?"

Lee returned the hug, yanked at his stiff collar. "Must I stay in this getup for lunch, as it's Sunday?"

"Yes, you must. Elizabeth goes to service at the C of E, so she'll be in a good dress, hat on her head. You didn't tell me how Sung was."

"In excellent form, of course. Plutocracy suits Papa more than being a Pekinese prince did, I suspect. *Very* pleased with me! I rather think he rues the day that he disowned me."

"Well, he wasn't to know what the future held when you were a gorgeous fat baby," said Ruby, smiling. "His loss, my gain."

"I remember your saying that Nell would be there last night, Mum. Was it odd that she wasn't?"

"Yes, decidedly so. Perhaps Nell's in a Darwinian mood and would have refuted the C of E tenets about the Creation."

"At six? Really, Mum!"

"Nell is a genuine prodigy, my son. Her interests are mostly scientific, but she also draws, paints, sculpts, and plays the piano and the harp extremely well. When her fingers can span an octave, I'll have competition. I like her, but many people don't." Came a smile. "To shock is her besetting sin—does that sound familiar? Come to think of it, of course that's why Elizabeth barred her last night. Nell would have gotten the Bishop's measure inside one minute, then given a dissertation on the penis in its flaccid and erect states. She dotes on anatomy, and did not take long to realize that certain aspects of it are social dynamite if the audience is right."

Lee burst out laughing. "She's a minx! I'll like her too."

"I know Elizabeth has had a hard life," Ruby said, "but I very much fear that Nell's life will be harder."

"And her a Kinross? Mum, Nell's Australian nobility!"

"She may be a Kinross, but she's a female, Lee. A female who is interested in subjects men regard as their exclusive prerogative. She's such a blue-stocking! Alexander is delighted at it, naturally, but he can't shelter her from ill treatment and opposition all her life."

So when the church party came in, Lee looked at Nell with great curiosity, and saw Alexander. Cut her hair off and put her in short trousers, and there would stand a six-year-old Alexander. That provoked a rush of love in Lee, but Nell wasn't about to love him back until he passed her examination.

First, however, he had to say hello to Elizabeth and Anna. A truly beautiful child, Elizabeth's image save for the eyes.

"Meet Lee, Anna," said Elizabeth, holding Anna in her arms. "Lee. Can you say Lee?"

"Dolly," said Anna, waving it.

"May I have her?" Lee asked.

"She'll cry, and I can't allow that." Curt, dismissive.

"No, she won't," he said calmly, plucking Anna from her mother's grasp. "See? Hello, Anna-wanna." He kissed her all over her face, which entranced her. Does no one kiss her like this? "I'm Lee, Anna-wanna. Can you say Lee? Lee, Lee, Lee."

Anna turned to put her arms about his neck, and discovered the pigtail. "Snake!" she said, tugging it.

Elizabeth gaped. "Jade, I didn't know she could say snake!"

"Neither did I, Miss Lizzy," Jade said blankly.

"Not snake, pigtail. Oink, oink," Lee grunted, not wincing at the healthy force exerted on his hair. "I'm Lee. Lee, Lee."

"Lee," said Anna, hugging him. "Lee, Lee."

Exclamations of delighted amazement all around. Chagrin too.

How dare the interloper, Lee thought, giving Anna to Jade, who went off kitchenwards with her to spend the time with Sam Wong.

Lee, Ruby, Elizabeth and Nell sat down at the table in Ruby's private dining parlor, Nell elevated on a cushion.

"What's my daddy doing, Lee?"

"Inspecting the very efficient German telegraph system with Ernst and Friedrich Siemens."

"Oh yes, Siemens and Halke," said Nell, and frowned. "*I* think the one named Wilhelm is the most interesting Siemens."

"I agree wholeheartedly, Nell. It's just that Wilhelm has become William and lives in England—better patent laws than Germany."

"It's barely a united nation," said Nell, "that's why."

"Give Count von Bismarck time, Nell."

"His Christian name is Otto."

"You're conceited," said Lee, voice normal.

"I am not conceited!"

"Yes, you are. Truly erudite people don't overwhelm their less knowledgeable brethren with unnecessary facts. You know his Christian name is Otto, and I also happen to know his Christian name is Otto. But I'm not compelled to air my erudition for the sake of impressing my audience."

She shut up like a sensitive plant at a touch, face scarlet, lids lowered, lips compressed to Alexander's straight line. A silence fell while the two women debated what to say, what to do; in the end they ignored this monumental slap at Nell's dignity, Ruby because she thought it would benefit Nell in times to come, Elizabeth because it thrilled her that someone had done what she couldn't—put that awful child in her place. While Lee blithely ate his Chinese omelet as if nothing had happened.

Facing him across the little round table, Elizabeth couldn't not look at him, dwelling upon the curious intimacy of watching him eat; the way his mouth moved, the play of muscles in his cheeks, the smoothness of a swallow. Economical yet thorough, immaculately done. He looked up and into her eyes so suddenly that she was sure he could read her thoughts in them; she didn't blush, but for a moment he glimpsed an atrociously shy creature surprised at a spring. Then the shutters came down, she ate her omelet with what he knew was feigned enjoyment. What does go on behind your façade, Elizabeth? What were you thinking when you studied me just then? Tell me about your secret self!

"The pity of your going to school in England, Lee," Ruby was saying, "is that you have no friends your own age in Kinross, so I'm afraid your eighteenth birthday party will consist of boring old women like Elizabeth and me. We could always invite the C of E minister, and of course the mayor will come—he's Sung."

"I really don't need a birthday party, Mum."

"No one *needs* a birthday party, but that doesn't alter the fact that you're going to have one." Ruby looked impish. "A pity you didn't bring your bird of paradise with you."

Elizabeth looked puzzled. "Bird of paradise?"

"Nell, don't fiddle with your food. Push off outside."

Nell went, casting Ruby a look of burning reproach.

"A bird of paradise," said Lee as soon as Nell disappeared, "is a lady of more allure than virtue. I have one in England."

"My! You Costevans start early!" said Elizabeth bitingly.

"At least we Costevans aren't dried up!" Lee snapped.

Elizabeth rose to her feet with a face like flint. "I must go home." And out she marched, calling for Jade.

Lee stared at his mother, one brow raised. "I finally got a reaction out of Madame Glacier," he said, still looking annoyed.

"It was my fault, I shouldn't have brought the subject up. Oh, Lee, I wasn't cut out to associate with proper people!" Ruby cried. "All I want is to liven up that poor, squeezed-up girl's hideously monotonous life! Usually she finds my vulgarity highly amusing, even when I shock her. But apparently not today."

"I'm the difference, Mum. For some reason Elizabeth doesn't like me." He hunched his shoulders. "Still, I wasn't going to let her get away with that slur on you. Evidently no one's taught her that if you give it, you'd better be prepared to take it too."

"Oh, Lee, I so hoped you and she would get along!" Ruby's hands clutched at his arm. "I think we ought to apologize."

His eyes went frighteningly icy. "I'd sooner die!" he said savagely, got to his feet and stalked out.

Ruby sat amid the ruins of the first course, elbows on the table, her face between her hands, and scowled at her plate. No birthday party, so much was sure.

Changed into dungarees and an old shirt, Lee went down to the locomotive shed, deserted on a Sunday, and found one of the iron horses partially dismantled. He could see what the trouble was, and worked off his spleen by fixing it. Only hours later did he realize that he hadn't exploded his dynamite. Now that Elizabeth had broken off even diplomatic relations with the awful Costevans, how was he going to achieve Alexander's ends?

THERE WAS not much to choose between Elizabeth's degree of offended anger, and Nell's. The family went back to Kinross House in a thunderous silence broken only by Anna, who kept saying that arrogant stripling's name over and over, "Lee! Lee!" until Nell, less inhibited than her mother, finally shouted at Anna to shut up. A phrase the child recognized because of its emotional load; she began to howl instead.

Well, I asked for it, Elizabeth fulminated, mixing with that lot down at the Kinross Hotel. Ruby is enough in and of herself, I don't need another smutty clown in her precious son. All that education, all that upper-crust manner, and the best he can do is insult me. I suppose he's aware that Alexander and I don't sleep together, but how *dare* he imply that I'm dried up? Finished, on the shelf, no wife anymore—him and his birds of paradise!

She was still stewing when Nell asked in a small voice, "Am I conceited, Mum?"

"Yes! Abominably so! You're a bigger braggart than your father, and God knows he's conceited enough for a hundred!"

More howls; Nell ran ahead, stormed up the stairs to her room and slammed its door in Butterfly Wing's face. Which left Elizabeth, freed from Jade and Anna, to go to her own rooms and weep. When the tears ceased to flow, there he was back in her mind, standing on the rock above The Pool. He has ruined it for me, she thought miserably. I can never go back there again.

That night two lights burned, one in Ruby's bedroom at the hotel, one in Elizabeth's bedroom at the house; both women paced up and down, up and down, sleep impossible. Tired out from his labors, Lee slept as if dead, no dreams of Elizabeth to plague him. His path was already chosen: from now until his return to England, he wouldn't go near Alexander's wife for any reason.

Further to this, in the morning he kissed his mother goodbye and set off on horseback for Dunleigh and the Dewys, who were dying to meet him. Ruby elected to follow in a carriage; she would celebrate his birthday at Dunleigh. Henrietta was just a trifle older than Lee and had met no one who tempted her. Who knows? asked Ruby of herself. They might take to each other. I don't think the Dewys would object.

But it was Alexander and Sophia all over again. Henrietta was enormously attracted to Lee, who didn't even notice her.

"Oh, what is it with children?" Ruby demanded of Constance.

"In a nutshell, that they are not us, Ruby. However, it is not Henrietta and Lee bothering you, so what is it?"

"Lee and Elizabeth have decided to dislike each other."

"Hmmm" was Constance's comment on that piece of news.

She set out to fish with the most subtle of baits in Lee's waters, and by dint of roundabout questions and the interpretation of roundabout answers soon learned that he liked Elizabeth far too much. Therefore, deduced Constance, it was equally possible that Elizabeth liked Lee far too much. As they were both honorable people, they had—entirely unconsciously, Constance was sure—manufactured a quarrel that would keep them apart. You're luckier than you know, Alexander, she thought.

SO LEE'S two and a half months at home were spent elsewhere than in Kinross. With an ecstatic Ruby in tow, he oscillated between Dunleigh and Sydney—parties, the theater, operas, balls, receptions, flocks of young women eager to have him stay in Sydney, or invite him to Daddy's property in the country. Using his mother as his chaperone, he threw himself into gaiety and nonsense without, it seemed to her, a care in the world. Any of half a dozen girls dreamed that it was she he was interested in, but he was too clever to be trapped. With young men he wasn't nearly as popular until one, just a little the worse for drink, invited him outside to take the hiding of his life. Lee went, and demonstrated that Proctor's might have been a toffee-nosed school for swells, but its pupils were adept at defending themselves with their fists. Not that Lee confined his tactics to his fists when his opponent played dirty; he had learned a few tricks from the Chinese as well. After that, he was considered a capital chap, pigtail and all. Rumor said that he was, besides, Alexander Kinross's major heir in the absence of Kinross sons.

IT SEEMED to end so suddenly. One moment the weeks were crowded with social commitments, the next it was time for him to sail. That meant a return to Kinross couldn't be avoided. And there was the matter of a charge of dynamite, still unexploded. In the end he decided to split its effect into two smaller blasts: tell his mother first, and then seek an interview with Elizabeth to tell her separately.

"Mum, I'm under orders from Alexander to deliver a message," he said, drawing a breath. "Next February you're to sail for England with Elizabeth, Nell and Anna."

"Lee!"

"I know it's a shock, but if you don't go, Alexander won't be pleased. He wants to show you Great Britain and Europe before he comes home."

"Oh, that's wonderful!" The delight faded from her face. "But what will Elizabeth say? Our friendship is quite ruined, Lee."

"Nonsense! I'm the fly in Elizabeth's ointment, not you, and I won't be there. I'll be up at Cambridge, far too busy to entertain Alexander's entire ménage. Just you, Mum, whenever you can find the time to visit me."

"Does Elizabeth know yet?"

"No, I'm off to tell her now." He looked wry. "And mend my fences if I can. Once she realizes that she won't see anything of me, I'm sure she'll be entranced at the idea."

He went to see her clad in old working clothes, stood in the portico with his battered hat in his hand and asked Mrs. Surtees if Mrs. Kinross could spare a moment to see him in the garden. The housekeeper stared at him oddly, but nodded and trotted away; he retreated to the rose beds, each plant pruned and bare.

"Roses do well at this altitude—it's cooler," he said when Elizabeth appeared looking wary.

"Yes. They'll bud soon. Spring comes early in Australia."

"A very short winter compared to Scottish Kinross."

"I'd rather say, no winter at all."

This is not good, he thought, despairing; we can't spend the time talking about the seasons. So he smiled at her, well aware of the effect his smile had on females of all ages. To find that all it did to Elizabeth was poker her up even more. Lord, how did one reach her?

"How are you?" he asked.

"Very well. Kinross has seen little of you and Ruby."

"Selfish of me to steal my mother from you, but she needed a respite from the same old round."

"I daresay we all do."

"Including you?"

"I daresay."

He took the plunge. "Then I come bearing good tidings. A message from Alexander, actually. Next February he wants you, Nell, Anna and my mother to sail for England. A respite."

This time the creature looked out of her eyes in a panic so great that he fancied she mentally blundered into one wall, then another, caroming off them without caring how badly she injured herself. But when he moved to support her, she backed away as if he intended to murder her.

"No, no, no, no!" she cried, quiet screams.

Confused, at a loss, he stood staring at her as at a stranger. "Is it me?" he asked. "Is it me, Elizabeth? If it is, there's no need for this. I won't be with you, I'll be up at Cambridge with my—with my bird of paradise. You'll never see me, I swear it!" He wept the words, brokenhearted.

She had covered her face with her hands and spoke through them. "It has nothing to do with you. Nothing!"

Dashing his tears away, he took one step toward her, stopped. "If it isn't me, then why? Why, Elizabeth?"

"There is no why."

"That's rubbish, of course there's a why! Tell me, please."

"You're a boy. You're nothing to me, nothing!" Down came the hands to reveal stony eyes. "There is no why that you could understand. Just tell Alexander that I can't. I won't, I won't!"

"Come, sit down before you fall down." Summoning up more courage than he ever knew he had, he took her shoulders between his hands and forced her to the grass—oh, she felt so thin, so frail! Curiously, she made no attempt to wrest herself away from his grasp, even leaned into it until he could smell her—jasmine and gardenia, but faint, not overpowering. His hands fell, he folded himself, cross-legged, near her but not too near.

"I know I'm only a boy. I know I'm nothing to you. But I'm old enough to have a man's feelings. You have to tell me why—if you do, I can mend your fences as well as my own. Is it the children? The hardship of bringing them to a new place when Anna is such a trouble?" When she didn't answer, he hurried on. "It will be easy, I promise. Alexander intends that five of the Wong sisters should go with you as well as Butterfly Wing. He's reserved a whole deck of staterooms for you on the ship—you'll travel in the lap of luxury. When you reach London, you'll live in a huge house he's rented on Park Lane right opposite the park gates. It has stables, riding hacks, carriages and horses, a resident staff from butler to skivvies. The lap of luxury!"

Still she said not a word, just stared at him as if at a stranger who wasn't a stranger—how could that be?

"My mother, then? Is it my mother? I give you my word that Alexander won't embarrass you with my mother. She'll be your best friend to everyone you meet, traveling with you for company because of the children. It won't be like Sydney, he's sworn to be the soul of discretion. So if it's my mother, don't worry."

Her face didn't change as he ran down, desperate to find a magic fact that would persuade her to go.

"I don't want to go!" she said between her teeth, for all the world as if she had read his mind.

"That's silly. You need a holiday, Elizabeth. Imagine the people you'll meet! The Queen is old and tired, but the Prince of Wales is very much the center of good society, and Alexander knows him quite well already."

Silence. Lee ploughed on. "You'll visit the Lake District, Cornwall and Dorset—Scotland and Kinross if you want. You'll see Paris and Rome, Siena, Venice, Florence—castles in Spain and Saracen fortresses in the Balkans. Cruise the Greek islands, go to Capri and Sorrento. Malta. Egypt."

Still she sat voiceless, staring at him in that odd way.

"If you won't do it for Alexander," he said, "then do it for my mother. Please, Elizabeth, please!"

"Oh," she said wearily, "I know I have to go. It came as a shock, that's all. If I didn't go, it would only make matters much worse. After all, I can't run away. I have two children. One of them would like living without me, but the other couldn't. I have to please Alexander however I can."

Was it *that* bad between her and Alexander? Of course he has my mother, whereas Elizabeth has nobody save her children.

"Is it that you don't love him?" Lee asked.

"That is a part of it."

"If you're in need of a friend, I'm here."

More quickly than an anemone, she withdrew; he could see the ice form in her eyes, on her face. So *cold*!

"Thank you," she said colorlessly, "but I don't need that."

He got to his feet and extended his hands to her, but she ignored them, rose unassisted.

"I'll be all right now," she said.

"Does that mean I'm at least forgiven for my rudeness?"

The ice melted briefly; she smiled with genuine feeling that lit up her eyes. "I have nothing to forgive you for, Lee."

"May I take you back to the house?"

"No, I'd rather be alone."

And she turned and walked away.

I will carry that smile with me all of my days.

TO HIS MOTHER he simply said, "Elizabeth will sail with you in February. She wasn't enthralled at the idea, but I gather that she's happier when Alexander isn't with her."

Brow creased, Ruby gazed at her son, puzzled. When had the change happened? Not this afternoon, surely! But somewhere along the time Lee had been back, he had grown from a boy to a man. It was just that she hadn't noticed it until today.

Aware that his mother had spotted some difference in him, Lee escaped without thinking to tell her that her role was to be that of Elizabeth's best friend on the coming expedition. And by the time that he saw her again, it had slipped his mind completely.

That night as she prepared for bed, Ruby underwent another enlightenment: that it was manifestly impossible for Alexander to have his cake and eat it too. Here in New South Wales, his affair with her was stale news, hardly worth commenting upon. But in London? Mixing in the highest circles, as Alexander did? No, it couldn't be. Nor would it be. Subject Elizabeth to humiliation and perpetual embarrassment because Alexander Kinross carted his wife and his mistress around in a *ménage à trois?* Never! So let Elizabeth go alone. That is the right thing to do. Alexander and I are a pair of children, we don't stop to think.

But how can I get her there without me? Did she know, she'd refuse to budge an inch from Kinross. So I'll make Jasmine and Peach Blossom my co-conspirators—why deprive them of the trip when three of their sisters are going? They can carry a letter to Alexander that will spell out my sentiments so pungently that even he will understand, the conniving bastard.

I'll pretend to board the ship—pretend to go down with seasickness before the ship slips her moorings—have Jasmine and Peach Blossom lock my cabin door and refuse to let anyone in, even Elizabeth. I'll find the ship's doctor and let him in on the secret—I'm sure he could do with an extra couple of hundred quid. By the time Jasmine gives Elizabeth my letter, it will be too late to return. Somewhere way out in the Indian Ocean. The die will be cast.

And Sung and I will be in Kinross to run the Apocalypse with Charles as a useful third. I've seen my jade kitten, spent a wonderful winter with him—the last of his childhood. When next I see him, the man I glimpsed today will be officially a man. Only what will I do if Alexander keeps him in England?

Eight

LETTERS

Kinross, January 1883

Elizabeth dearest,

If all goes to plan, Jasmine will have given you this when Ceylon is somewhere off the port bow. I suppose you could turn around and sail home again from Colombo, but it's the halfway mark. You may as well continue in a forward direction.

At the end of last July, when Lee left after breaking his news about this trip, I finally grew up. Alexander always says that it's the child in me he loves the most, and I understand what he means. My heart is so light, my sense of mischief and fun so pronounced that I have gone through everything, bad as well as good, airily dismissing the opinions of others as unimportant. Were I a respectable woman it might have been different, but you could say that I was born with nothing to lose. Never having had the good opinion of others, what mattered their good opinion? So I have waltzed around with Alexander shamelessly, including in Sydney. Of course I considered that I had the prior claim to his affections, and felt vindicated when he returned to me after his marriage to you. I am not a moral person, I really am not.

When Lee broke the news, all I could think about was seeing Alexander again. That he summoned us I took as a message that he does not intend to return to Kinross in the near future. My mind was filled with pictures of the life I would lead back in his arms, and they were comfortable pictures in that I knew you would not object, that I would be relieving you of Alexander.

And then I realized that perhaps he thought to go one better than Benjamin Disraeli by flaunting his mistress *and* his wife in the same open carriage. But that would never do. The scandal would rock London.

For myself, what's a bit of scandal? Whereas for you, awful disaster! As best I can imagine what went on in Alexander's mind, he intended to squire me around as your best friend, thereby not admitting to our true relationship. But people from Sydney trip back and forth to England, particularly to London, all the time nowadays. It wouldn't take long for the word to leak out, and Alexander is *not* the Prince of Wales.

That is why I have stayed home, dear. This is your hour, so seize it as my gift. You know, the trouble is that all three of us are products of small towns, and still live in a small town. Thanks to Apocalypse gold, we can do pretty much as we please. In Sydney, perhaps, but not in London.

Enjoy yourself, Elizabeth. Gad about, and the hell with Alexander. Just please say hello to Lee for me, and try to get on with him for my sake.

Much love, Ruby.

Ceylon, March 1883

Oh, Ruby!

I write this from Colombo, as there is a mail packet here en route to Sydney. It should reach you in about three or four weeks. So could I, if I had decided to turn around.

How artful you were! Dr. Markham, Jasmine and Peach Blossom fooled me completely. It never occurred to me that you weren't below decks suffering dreadfully, because I remember how ill Mrs. Watson was on the *Aurora* when I came out to marry Alexander. I was a little sick as we crossed the Great Australian Bight, but I am a reasonably good sailor. So, it turns out, are Nell and Anna. The Chinese girls have been worse, but the Indian Ocean is like a millpond, so they recovered after we left Perth.

Whether because the ship moves, I do not know, but Anna has decided to walk. She staggers a bit, but now that she has found out what legs are for, she never stops walking while she's awake. Her puppy fat has melted, she's turned quite trim and shipshape. Her favorite word is still "Lee!" said with a squeal, though she adds others at an accelerated pace—ship, shore, rope, smoke, man. Here in Colombo she has managed two-syllable words like sailor, harbor and woman.

I do thank you so much for your care of me, but Lee explained the situation very much as you thought it might be—you and I were to be best friends. My knees go weak at the thought of what he will say when he knows that you are not with us, but Jasmine gave me your message that you have written a letter to be given to Alexander when we reach England.

Dearest Ruby, I accept your sacrifice with a full heart, and understand your motive. I will pay my respects to Lee, I promise.

Much love, Elizabeth.

London, April 1883

My darling spoilsport,

No one would have known about us! Were Elizabeth not a very beautiful woman in her own right, people might have guessed, but provided I have a wife to introduce to all the best people, even if some of them found out about you and me, nothing could be proved and therefore no retaliations could be made. It is actually quite common here for the Best People to conduct the kind of *ménage à trois* that sees both wife and mistress members of the same social circle, though I admit that the mistresses are the wives of other men rather than *spinsters* like you.

Anyway, none of that now matters. I'll do my duty and escort my very beautiful wife everywhere without her best friend.

I miss you and love you, Alexander.

London, November 1883

Dearest Ruby,

The most extraordinary thing has happened! You must have had a feeling about it, to stay home, because had you come and word had leaked out about your true status, this could not have happened. Alexander had absolutely no idea of it, you see.

I am now Lady Kinross! Alexander has been made a Knight Commander of the Royal Order of the Thistle, which means he outranks Henry Parkes and John Robertson, relegated to St. Michael and St. George.

Queen Victoria bestowed the knighthood in person at a private ceremony. Of course Alexander bought me a suite of diamonds. One has to wear white, and have white ostrich feathers in one's hair. I felt like one of those bedizened white horses that drew Cinderella's coach to the ball. I imagine Alexander got the thistlehood because he's a Scot with a Scots wife. The old Queen loves the Scots, though rumor says she loved *one* Scot more than all the rest of us.

London is daunting but fascinating. The house Alexander has rented for us is huge and magnificent, furnished in much the same manner as Kinross House used to be—plush, gilt, brocade, crystal chandeliers. It has a telephone, can you imagine that? My two girls have their own wing, and Alexander has hired a tutor for Nell, the umpteenth son of a C of E canon. She doesn't like him, but admits that he is fairly knowledgeable. Anna can walk for a fair distance now, though Jade takes a device called a push chair with us—a canvas thing on four wheels with handles. We have to pad it because Anna still wets herself, but it has been many moons since she messed herself.

On the subject of Anna, she has been seen by all the great men of neuropathology, as they call it, in London, including Mr. Hughlings Jackson and Mr. William Gower. They examined her with great thoroughness, and, to quote Mr. Jackson, found "nothing focal" in her dementia, which is the term he used. From this, I gather that her whole brain is affected. However, the fact that she has acquired a tiny vocabulary and has started walking tell Messrs. Jackson and Gower that she will end in being "simple"—about on the same level as a village idiot. The worst of it is that Mr. Gower (a more approachable man) says that her body will continue to develop in a normal way, so she will have courses, breasts, everything. They blame it on her birth, not on heredity.

But I have lied to Alexander, who is so busy that he left me to see the neuropathologists. Mr. Gower told me that he did not think a third pregnancy—how formal their language is!—would result in eclampsia. He admits the possibility, but his amazing collection of machines that monitor the blood, the heart, the circulation and Heaven knows what else, tell him that my health has improved. He thinks that a strict diet of fruit, vegetables and brown bread without butter would see me through without a dropsy. But I just couldn't bring myself to tell Alexander this.

It's not that I don't want more babies, Ruby, it's that I cannot *bear* to resume my wifely duties. If he knew Mr. Gower's opinion, he would force me back to that life, and I would go mad.

Please, I beg, don't betray this secret! I just had to tell somebody, and there's no one but you.

Much love, Elizabeth.

Kinross, January 1884

Dearest Elizabeth,

Your secret is safe with me. It's to my advantage anyway, isn't it? Besides, Sir Edward Wyler said you wouldn't have a second eclampsia, and you did. Fine for them to talk, they're men, and men don't have babies.

You don't mention Lee. Have you seen my jade kitten? Jade tomcat, more like! But to me, always my little jade kitten.

Much love, Ruby.

Cambridge, April 1884

My gorgeous Mum,

Sir Alexander Kinross (phew, what a shock!) has endowed a new metallurgic laboratory, much to the joy of the university. As there is a train from Liverpool Street to Cambridge, he pops up to see me regularly; if there's racing at Newmarket on a Saturday, he comes to pick me up and we both go—more to look at the horseflesh than to bet, though when we do bet, we usually win.

I have had a visit from Lady Kinross. As I couldn't very well entertain her at my flat on Parker's Piece, I invited her to tea in the Caius common room, where she met all the chaps. You would have been proud of her. I know I was. She wore a lavender-blue silk dress, one of the new, smaller hats with a sprig of feathers tucked into its brim, matching kid gloves and the most elegant pair of boots. That I am a connoisseur of ladies' fashions is thanks to Carlotta, my bird of paradise, who can outspend a Spanish contessa at a modiste's salon.

I think Elizabeth has come out of herself a little, for she smiled at the chaps and produced sparkling conversation. By the time she left, they were all in love with her. This has already led to reams of bad poetry and an even worse piano sonata. As the Backs are a sea of daffodils, we took her for a walk down to the Cam before handing her reverently into her carriage.

I will finish my second year at Cambridge with top marks in all my subjects. I love you and miss you terribly, but I understand why you chose to remain in Kinross. You're a wonder, Mum.

All my love, your jade kitten, Lee.

Kinross, June 1884

Dear Alexander and Elizabeth,

I don't know whereabouts this will catch up with you now that you're traveling in Italy, especially as I believe that the Italian post is very unreliable. All those little states, and, like Germany, struggling with unification. I do hope that you do not get embroiled in some revolution or other!

Some bad news. Charles Dewy passed away at home a week ago, and was buried there. It was sudden, and, so Constance tells me, quite painless. His heart stopped while he was sipping a single malt whisky. He died with his favorite taste on his tongue and a look of bliss on his face. I am very cut up about it; my eyes are full of tears as I write. He was so jolly, got so much fun out of life. If heaven is anything like the place the Bible-bashers prate about, I think he'll be unutterably bored. As does Constance, who keeps making odd remarks about his whiskers.

We have a plague of flies here in Kinross, something to do with the sewage farm. When you have a moment, Alexander, you might bend your mind to the problem. Sung and Po are hopelessly uninformed about shit, though Po is importing some expert from Sydney. I wouldn't have thought anybody in Sydney knows more about shit than Po. Po—get it? Forget it.

Isn't my jade kitten a wonder? Though he says he won't come home once he has his degree—he wants to do a doctorate in geology at Edinburgh, he says. I miss all of you.

Much love, Ruby.

London, November 1884

Dear Auntie Ruby,

I am in trouble with my tutor, Mr. Fowldes, who has reported me to Daddy yet again. My latest crimes are: displaying no interest in deportment, social graces and religion; aspiring to calculus; cheeking him by proving that his mathematics were wrong and mine right—and gloating over it; saying "Oh, shit!" when I upset the inkwell; and deriding him for believing that God created the world in seven days. Now *that's* shit, Auntie Ruby.

He dragged me to Daddy's library by one ear and poured out my crimes in a terrible temper, then, having rid himself of that, he gave Daddy this *enormous* lecture on raising girls to think they can compete with men. God, he said, forbade that. Daddy listened solemnly, then asked him if he'd mind releasing my ear. Of course Mr. Fowldes had quite forgotten that he was still hanging on to it, so he let it go. Then Daddy asked me what I had to say for myself, which *outraged* Mr. Fowldes. I told Daddy that I was just as good as any boy at mathematics and mechanics, that my Greek, Latin, French and Italian were better than Mr. Fowldes's, and that I was fully entitled to make my own judgments about Napoleon Bonaparte, even if they did extol him more than they did the silly old Duke of Wellington, who couldn't have won Waterloo without the Prussians, and was a mediocre prime minister anyway. In Mr. Fowldes's book, the British are never wrong and the rest of the world is never right, especially the French and the Americans.

Daddy listened, then sighed and dismissed me. I don't know what he said to Mr. Fowldes, but it must have been more in my favor, since Mr. Fowldes has stopped trying to turn me into a *girl.* I was hoping that he'd send Mr. Fowldes packing and find me a tutor more like Mr. Stephens, but he didn't. Later on he told me that, as I went through life, I'd run up against a lot of men like Mr. Fowldes, so I may as well get used to them now. Ha ha, I got my own back! I short-sheeted his bed and smeared it with treacle. He was furious! That led to my first caning—it smarts, Auntie Ruby, I can tell you. But I just lifted my top lip at him and refused to so much as wince. I was tempted to tell him to get fucked, but even Daddy doesn't know I know that word, so I thought I'd better not. I'll tell him on my last day under his tutelage. I can hardly wait to see the look on his face. You don't think he'll be so shocked that he'll have an apoplexy and die, do you?

I'd far rather be in Kinross with Mr. Stephens and my pony, and that's the truth. However, Mum's friend Dr. Gower took me to see a museum of anatomical specimens, just the *best* treat I've ever had in my life. Shelves and shelves of jars full of organs, amputated arms and legs, embryos, brains, and even a two-headed baby. Oh, and two babies joined right down one side. If I was let, I'd put a bed in there and spend a year examining everything properly, but Daddy likes it better when I'm interested in rocks and electricity. He does rather grunt in disgust at anatomy.

He and Lee spent Lee's summer vacation investigating the new ideas in treating sewage, so I predict that Kinross will shortly have a new sewage treatment works. You won't forget to check on Chang and make sure he feeds my rats, will you? I like rats, such happy, clever little chaps. I like you too, Auntie Ruby.

Your loving friend, Nell.

London, April 1885

Dearest Ruby,

We are to come home at last—well, at the beginning of the autumn, anyway. Oh, I am so glad! Alexander has decided to sail with us, thanks to your ongoing correspondence about Po and the sewage situation. I agree, Po is a nice pun. There's a river in northern Italy called the Po—a splendid stream, very strong and wide, and not that far from the most peaceful and beautiful place I have ever seen, the Italian lakes. I like Italy more than any other country in Europe, including Great Britain. The people have such a sunny attitude to life, though they are pitifully poor. And they sing, sing, sing. So do the Welsh, but darkly.

It is very odd being Lady Kinross, though Alexander wallows in his knighthood. Well, I understand that. It vindicates him in the eyes of Scottish Kinross. Unfortunately Dr. Murray and my father were well and truly dead by the time he became Sir Alexander. Therefore Alexander now hopes that there *is* a life after death, just so the pair of them know he's a knight and can seethe about it. Whereas I believe that all Alexander's many honors and vast wealth have no power to impress Dr. Murray and my father, in this life or in the next. They would simply snort and say none of it can alter the fact that Alexander is not his father's child. As ineradicable as Original Sin.

I did not end in going back to Scottish Kinross. Oh, Ruby, I quailed at the very idea of sweeping into that little town in all my French splendor and jewels! A petty action. Foolish I may be, but petty? Never! However, Alexander did take me recently to Edinburgh, as Lee goes up there in October to do his doctorate. In Edinburgh I met my sister Jean—Mrs. Robert Montgomery of Princes Street. I have never been able to forget how shabbily she treated Alastair and Mary when they took me to the London train. Yes, I have forgiven her, but that is not the same. So I asked Alexander to invite Alastair and Mary to Edinburgh and put them up in magnificent style. Foolish, Ruby. They were two fish out of water, hideously uncomfortable and terrified of making a faux pas. Why is it that we commit our worst sins in a spirit of charity? Though for their sake I admit it was nice to rub Jean's nose in my ladyshipness. Alexander says that her husband is too fond of young men, and that all of Edinburgh knows it. So poor Jean. No wonder there have been no children. She is brittle in manner and drinks too much.

Nell has turned nine and Anna eight. Nell has these shocking conflicts with her tutor, who can't control her and can no longer teach her—she's outgrown the extent of his knowledge. Anna has discovered four verbs—need, want, play, gone.

The Chinese girls have had a wonderful time. I make sure that they have plenty of holidays, which, when we're in London, they spend at Madame Tussaud's or at the zoo.

I am sorry I haven't seen much of Lee, but he's so busy. I imagine you're thrilled that he's graduating with First Class Honors. An extremely sophisticated and charming young man whose nickname is, inevitably, "The Prince." Enough of his fellow Proctorians have attended Cambridge to guarantee that.

I will write again, of course, but I did want you to know as soon as possible that we're coming home.

Much love, Elizabeth.

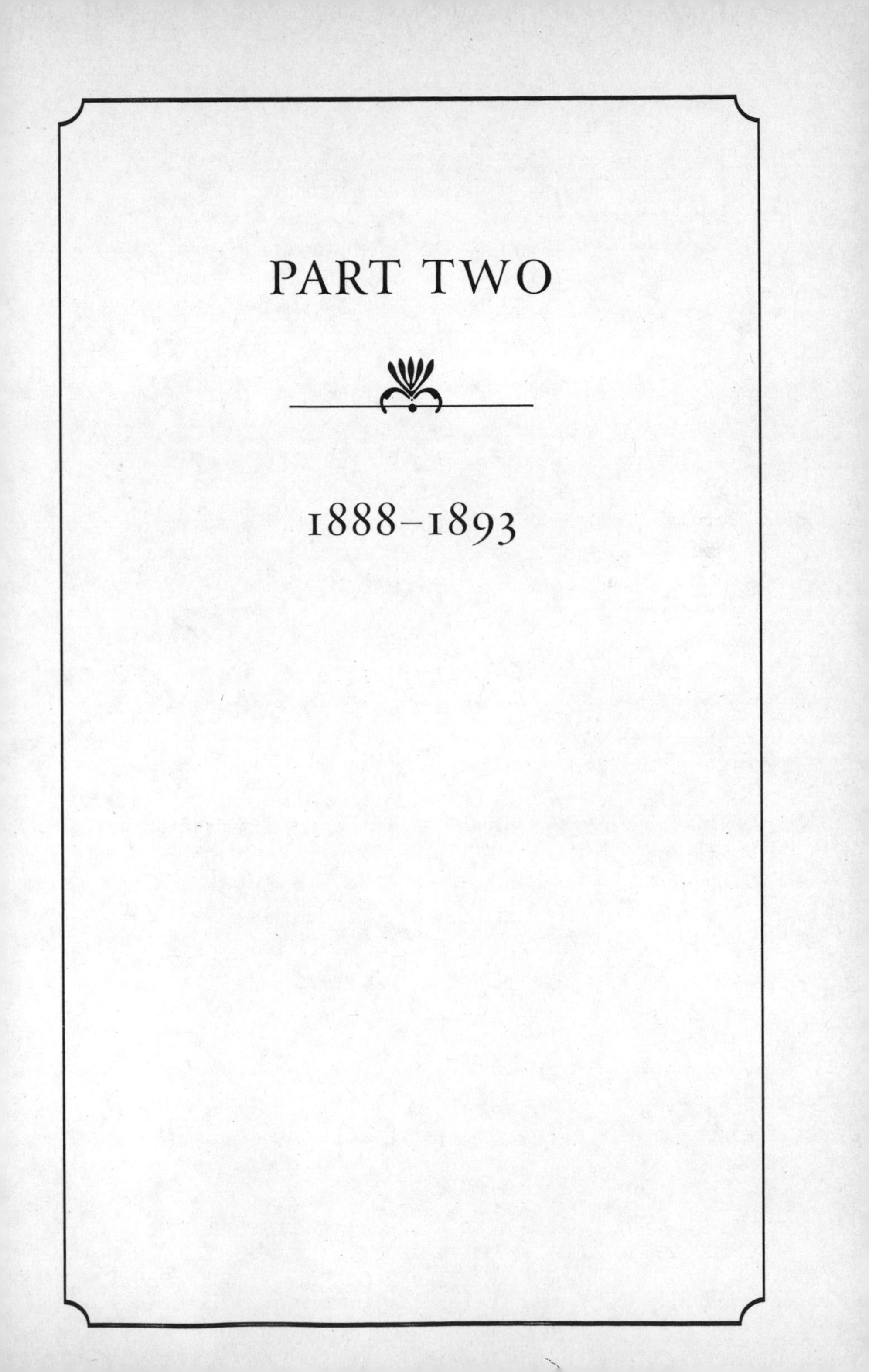

PART TWO

1888–1893

One

TWO BUDDING YOUNG WOMEN

NELL TURNED twelve on New Year's Day of 1888, and shortly thereafter began to menstruate. As she owned her father's long, lean physique, her breast development was rudimentary, a fact that had allowed her to ignore this first evidence of maturity. But the arrival of her courses could not be ignored, especially with Elizabeth for a mother.

"You can't romp around anymore, Nell," said Elizabeth to her, trying to remember all the things Mary had said to her when her courses had begun. "From now on you have to behave like a young lady—no more adventures into the mines and workshops, and no more being chummy with the men. If you have to pick something up off the floor, you keep your legs together and bend at the knees in a way that takes your whole body down. Under *no* circumstances do you sit with your legs apart or kick them up in the air."

"What on earth are you talking about, Mum?"

"Modest behavior, Nell. And don't look at me like that."

"It sounds like utter rubbish! I have to sit with my legs *together*? I can't kick them up in the air?"

"Not anymore. Your drawers might be stained."

"Only when I've got my courses," Nell said mutinously.

"You don't know when you might have them—they're quite irregular at first. I'm sorry, Nell, but playtime's over," said Elizabeth in an iron tone. "You'll remain in short dresses for another two years, but you *will* behave like a young lady."

"I don't believe this!" Nell cried, gasping theatrically. "You're cutting me out of Daddy's life! I'm like his son!"

"You are his daughter, not his son."

Nell stared at her mother in dawning horror. "Mum! You—you haven't *told* him?"

"Yes, naturally I told him," said Elizabeth, thrown on to the defensive. "Sit down, Nell, please."

"I can't!"

"When Anna was a baby," Elizabeth began, forced to explain herself, "I didn't see as much of her as a mother should, so I thought she was just a little backward, not mental. It was you who asked your father what was the matter with Anna, and he who realized Anna was mental. And I got into a lot of trouble with him over it."

"You deserved to!" said Nell, snarling.

"Yes, I did deserve to. But ever since then I've made very sure that I tell your father about everything that happens to Anna or to you."

"You're a *dreadful* woman!"

"Oh, please, Nell, be reasonable!"

"It's you who isn't reasonable! You just want to spoil my life, Mum! You just want to keep me from Daddy!"

"That's unfair and untrue," Elizabeth protested.

"Piss off, Mum! Just piss off!" cried Nell.

"Mind your manners and your tongue, Eleanor."

"Oh, I'm Eleanor now, am I? Well, I refuse to be Eleanor! My name is Nell!" And off Nell stormed to howl out her rage in the privacy of her room.

Leaving Elizabeth limp and at a loss. That didn't turn out as I intended—did I react the same way when Mary dealt with my courses? No, I listened obediently and behaved as Mary said I must from that moment on. Was she kinder than I've just been? More tactful? No, I don't believe so. What I do remember was feeling as if I had just been admitted into some secret society, and rather treasuring my membership. Why did I assume Nell would react as I did when she's so clearly not like me? I was hoping that I'd make a friend of her in this women's conspiracy, yet all I've done is antagonize her. Doesn't Nell realize that from this time on she's a target for men? That every time she goes where there are a lot of men, she's running the risk of inviting their attention in ways a child doesn't dream exist?

THOUGH ALEXANDER didn't mention the matter to her, Nell was far too clever not to see the change in him between one day and the following one. He eyed her differently, with a mixture of awe and grief. As if, she thought, burning with embarrassment, she had suddenly turned into someone he didn't know and couldn't trust. Never having esteemed the lot of women, Nell hated the fact that Nature had just reminded her that she was a woman. Especially because Daddy now regarded her as a stranger. Very well! If she was to be a stranger to Daddy, then he would become a stranger to her. Nell withdrew from him.

Luckily Alexander understood the reason for Nell's withdrawal enough to confront her.

"Do you think that I want you to turn into a prim and proper young lady, Nell?" he asked from his favorite easy chair in the library, she sitting opposite him with her legs clamped together in case her drawers were stained.

"What other choice is there, Daddy? I'm not a boy."

"I never thought you were a boy. You must forgive me if I've been a little distant these past few weeks—it's a shock to realize how swiftly time flies, is all. My wee friend is growing up, so I feel old," he said.

"*Old?* You, old, Daddy?" she demanded, outraged. "It's just that our fun is over! Mum doesn't want me to go into the mine with you, or to the workshops, or—or anything! I have to stop acting like a tomboy, but I don't want to stop being a tomboy! I want to go with you, Daddy—with *you*!"

"And you will, Nell. But your mother asked me to give you a little breathing space to get used to things."

"She *would*!" said Nell bitterly.

"Don't forget that her upbringing was very strict," Alexander said, quite as annoyed with Elizabeth as Nell was—how dared she try to frighten this most beloved child into abandoning him? "To her, once you're a woman in fact, you must learn to be a young lady in the full sense of that phrase. Mothers tend to think of their daughters as prey for the attentions of men, whereas I believe that they're pretty safe provided they don't encourage attentions. And I can't see you doing that, Nell," he said with a smile. "I do not intend to lose my best friend—you."

"So I can still go with you to the mine and the workshops?"

"Try and stop me taking you!"

"Oh, Daddy, I love you!" she cried, climbing on to his lap and throwing her arms about his neck.

Alexander had had a lecture from Elizabeth too, been informed that from now on he wasn't to let Nell sit on his knee or behave like a little girl rather than a young lady. But, he thought, arms tightening around Nell's still childish body, Elizabeth is mistaken. Why is it that her sort of upbringing always assumes the worst of people? Am I suddenly supposed to lust after my own flesh and blood, simply because she's growing up? What ridiculous nonsense! I'm damned if I'll deprive Nell of the overt affection I've always given her! And can Elizabeth really believe that any man would try to plunder Sir Alexander Kinross's virgin daughter? Were Nell a Ruby—and that, she'll never be!—no man would dare to make overtures to her. My name and power protect her.

ONCE NELL was readmitted into her father's life on the old footing, the only lasting effect of her menarche was to widen the gulf between Alexander and Elizabeth, who didn't—couldn't—approve of Alexander's decision to keep on treating Nell as he always had. Elizabeth's sense of propriety told her that this time she was in the right of it, Alexander in the wrong. Her sole comfort was that Nell continued to be dismally plain. Her hair was thick and black and by far her chief glory, but her brows were equally thick and black—and were pointed, devilish. A rather big nose sat above Alexander's too-thin mouth, and her long face held cheekbones so stark that they rendered it cavernous. The eyes, such a vivid blue, looked out of their deep orbits with a steady, slightly derisive expression. In fact, Nell had the mien of someone prepared to go to the stake for what she believed in, and that was not a comfortable look for a young lady.

In the schoolroom she ruled the roost. Her time with Mr. Fowldes in London had taught her that there was no point in trying to be submissive, because that only led to contempt; it was far better to be caned, to be dragged before her father, to cock a snook no matter what punishment might be dished out. For the only punishment that might have made Nell knuckle under was one that her father would never condone: the termination of her education in favor of one more suitable for young ladies.

With no son of his own, Alexander had pinned his hopes on Nell, who worshiped him so much that she couldn't bear to tell him what she really wanted to be—a doctor of medicine. It was, besides, an impossible ambition, even for Sir Alexander Kinross's daughter. Women were banned from Sydney University's medical faculty, and always would be. Oh, she could go abroad to study, or even go to Melbourne University, but Daddy wanted an heir of his own blood to succeed him, and that meant mining and metallurgy in the faculty of Engineering. Which had never admitted a female student either, but didn't contain a law forbidding the enrollment of a female, as Medicine did. An oversight due to short sight: no one could credit that a female might want to do engineering.

However, the change in Nell's body did lead to some changes in the way she looked at things, especially the situation between her mother and her father. It was the one area Alexander never spoke to her about, yet the one area she burned most to know about. Always her father's partisan, Nell blamed her mother, who, the moment Alexander hoved into view, retreated into an icy display of impeccable manners. Daddy's response to being shut out was to assume an air of faint displeasure that often deteriorated into witty barbs, snapped rejoinders. Natural responses for him; his was the more stormy temperament, less patient, not long-suffering. What Mum was underneath, no one knew, least of all Nell. Daddy called her a melancholic, whereas Nell, who read everything she could find of a medical nature, didn't deem her mother either a melancholic or a neurasthenic. Instinct said that Mum was just desperately unhappy, yet how could that be? Auntie Ruby and Daddy?

Nell never remembered not knowing about Auntie Ruby and Daddy, the most open of relationships. No, it couldn't lie at the base of Mum's unhappiness, because Mum and Auntie Ruby were extremely close friends. In fact, they were a lot closer to each other than Mum was to Daddy.

But it was here that Nell's oddly sheltered life to date could not help her. Never having gone to a regular school, she had no idea that this curious play of emotions between Daddy, Mum and Auntie Ruby was not only socially unacceptable, but also utterly bizarre. Queen Victoria would have refused to admit that it could exist.

"But I can't talk to her," said Elizabeth to Ruby after the business of Nell's courses. "I've burned my fingers enough. You talk to her, Ruby. She respects you more than she does me anyway."

"The trouble is, darling Elizabeth, that every time you look at Nell, you see Alexander." Ruby sighed. "Send her down to the hotel for lunch and I'll try."

THE INVITATION was unusual enough to pique Nell's curiosity, so she set off wondering what was in the wind.

"It's time," Ruby began once a lunch of Chinese food had been devoured, "that you became more fully acquainted with the situation between your mother, your father, and me."

"Oh, I know all about it," said Nell nonchalantly. "You and Daddy have sex together because Daddy doesn't have sex with Mum."

"Doesn't that strike you as peculiar?" asked Ruby, eyeing Nell in fascination.

"*Is* it?"

"Yes, very."

"Then you'd better tell me why, Auntie Ruby."

"For one thing, because married people aren't supposed to have sex with other people, just between themselves. *Sex,*" said Ruby thoughtfully. "You're very explicit, Nell."

"That's what the books call it."

"I'm sure they do. However, your mother is forbidden to have more children, so she cannot fulfill her sexual duties."

"I know that. So you help out," said Nell with aplomb.

"Jesus! Why should I *have* to help out?"

Nell frowned. "Actually, Auntie Ruby, I have no idea."

"Then I'll tell you. Men cannot be continent—that is, men find it impossible to do without sex. The Catholics delude themselves that men can keep a vow of what they call celibacy, but I doubt that very much. In fact, if a man could be celibate, I'd say he was crazy—you know, mad."

"So Daddy needs to have sex."

"Precisely. Which is where I come in. But your father and I are not a vulgar expedient, though most people think of us that way. There is love between Alexander and me, there has been since before he met your mother. But he couldn't marry me because I was already sexually experienced with other men."

"That doesn't seem logical," said Nell.

"I couldn't agree more," said Ruby a trifle grimly. "However, what it really boils down to is that women who are sexually experienced are deemed incapable of being faithful to one man, even to a husband. And men want to be sure beyond a shadow of a doubt that the children they have are in fact their children. So they want to marry women who are virgins."

"My mother was a virgin when she married Daddy?"

"Yes."

"But he loves you, not her."

"I'd rather say that he loves both of us, Nell," Ruby labored, wishing Elizabeth to perdition for inflicting this task on her.

"He loves her for his children, and you for the sex."

"It's not quite that cold-blooded, dear, honestly! The three of us are a bit of a muddle, and that's as close to the truth as I can get. The most important thing is that we get along together, we like each other, and we—well, we sort of share out the duties."

"Auntie Ruby, why are you telling me this?" asked Nell, face a study in concentration. "Is it because outsiders don't approve?"

"Exactly!" Ruby cried, beaming.

"Frankly, I don't see that it's any of their business."

"The one thing you can always be sure of, Nell, is that outsiders love to make everything their business. For that reason, you can't speak of this to outsiders. Understand?"

"Yes." Nell got to her feet. "I have to go to classes." She kissed Ruby on the cheek, a smacking salute. "Thanks for the lesson."

"Just don't mention our conversation to your father!"

"I won't. It's our secret," said Nell, and bounced off.

Bugger! she said to herself as she boarded the cable car. I know that Daddy loves Auntie Ruby and that Auntie Ruby loves him, but the one thing I forgot to ask is who Mum loves. Daddy? She might if she can't have sex, but Daddy needs it.

Better equipped to investigate, Nell set out to discover if her mother loved her father. And saw very quickly that Mum loved no one, even herself. If Daddy touched her, even accidentally, she acted like a snail withdrawing into its shell, a flicker of disaste in her eyes that said her reaction was not due to being forbidden to have intercourse. And Daddy *knew*! Mum's reaction made him angry, so he would lash out with one of his biting remarks, recollect himself, and disappear elsewhere. Nell wondered if, in fact, Mum even loved her children.

"Oh, yes," said Ruby, applied to a second time.

"If she does, she certainly doesn't know how to show it," Nell said. "I'm beginning to think Mum's a tragedy."

"If to bottle everything up constitutes a tragedy, then you are quite right," Ruby said, tears in her eyes. "Don't give up on her, Nell, please. Take it from me, if your mother saw someone point a gun at you and shoot, she'd step in front of the bullet."

* * *

BY THE TIME she turned ten, Anna had grown into a beautiful replica of her mother; an anguish for everyone, especially Jade, who was thirty-three. Tall and graceful, Anna walked effortlessly now and could speak in simple sentences. She also stopped wetting herself, but then transformed this victory into an omen of early maturity by developing breasts.

On her eleventh birthday her courses appeared, a nightmare. Like many poorly mentated children, Anna was overly terrified of blood, which she seemed to view as a depletion of self, be that self Anna or someone else. Perhaps the fear arose out of an experience she had had in Sam Wong's kitchen at the Kinross Hotel, when one of his helpers cut himself down to the bone of an arm, spraying blood everywhere as the arteries spurted, and screaming shrilly in a panic that made it difficult to get hold of him to apply a tourniquet. No one remembered that the nine-year-old Anna was standing there until it was all over and her shrieks were finally heard above the cook's.

So when her courses appeared, Anna screeched in terror, had to be held down while she was fitted with a towel. And no amount of time or repetition managed to lessen her terror. The only way that Jade and Elizabeth could get Anna through those five days of bleeding was to sedate her heavily with chloral hydrate and, if that didn't work, with laudanum.

If all of Anna's life had been a torment, that was as nothing compared to the ravages her menarche wrought on her, for there was just no way anyone could explain to her that the bleeding was normal and natural, that it would get itself over, that all she had to do was accept its monthly recurrence. Anna couldn't accept it because of the horror it inspired in her and the shortness of her attention span. Nor was she regular, which meant she couldn't be prepared for each episode ahead of time.

Between her periods she was quite happy unless she saw blood, when she would scream and blunder about in a panic. If the blood were her own, titanic struggles took place.

Finally, after a year that saw eight periods, Anna had taken in enough about her courses to start fighting the moment someone tried to undress her—she equated being undressed with bleeding. Which led to one benefit; Anna suddenly learned to undress herself, and to wash herself. Once Elizabeth and Jade were satisfied that her ablutions were adequate, they left her alone in that one respect.

"Perhaps her courses are a blessing," said Elizabeth to Nell. "I didn't think we'd ever teach her to wash and change."

OF COURSE the maturation of both her daughters made Elizabeth feel very old; a curious sensation given her actual youth. But here she was at thirty years of age with two budding young women on her hands, and no real idea of how to handle either of them. If she had known more, had wider experience, they would have helped overcome the difficulties; as it was, she had to fumble along as best she could and resort to Ruby when necessary. Not that Ruby was able to help her with Anna; no one could help with Anna save Jade, loving and patient, unflagging in her devotion.

Fourteen years into her marriage in March of 1889, Elizabeth had taught herself not to feel, and thereby attained a measure of content. In many ways, she reasoned, the life she led so far from home was not unlike the one she would have led caring for her father and then as maiden aunt to nieces and nephews; though a vital necessity, she was not the center of anyone's existence. Nor did she wish to be the center of anyone's existence. Alexander had Ruby and Nell, Nell had Alexander, and Anna had Jade. The years were flying, and nothing changed between her and Alexander. As long as he didn't touch her, she could keep up the façade for the sake of her one observant child, Nell.

Oh, there were nice moments! A laugh shared with Nell over Chang the cook; some point on which she and Alexander were in complete agreement; delightful chats with Ruby; Constance's visits to ease the loneliness of her widowhood; riding into the wonderland of the bush; some book that held her enthralled; a duet with Nell on the piano; privacy when she wanted it, which was often. And if she thought of The Pool, if the image of Lee at The Pool still haunted her, at least it had lost its sharp edges as time mellowed it, smearing the golden haze of the sun and his skin together with the inexorable thumb of an unrepeated memory. Time had even permitted her to return to The Pool, to enjoy it without really dwelling upon Lee.

TO ALEXANDER, his house had suddenly become cloyingly feminine, for though he nobly continued to take Nell with him on his rounds whenever she wasn't in the schoolroom, he had to admit to himself that it wasn't quite the same as it used to be. Not her fault, but his—and Elizabeth's fault too, with her oft-reiterated remarks about Nell's being a young woman now, and the target of *men.* So try as he would, he found himself checking his employees to make sure they weren't gazing at Nell in lust, or—worse, as Elizabeth kept saying—dangling after her with a mind on how much money she was worth. Common sense said that Nell was not a femme fatale nor was likely to turn into one, but the possessive father in him was sufficiently shaken to, for instance, suddenly decree that Nell might not go off alone with Summers, or with any other man of mine or workshops. He even visited the schoolroom to ascertain what the relationships were there—*that* was when he apostrophised himself a fool! Nell was obviously no more and no less than one of the boys. The three white Kinross girls who had begun with her had departed when they and Nell had turned ten, for reasons that varied from boarding school in Sydney to being needed at home.

It was Anna's maturation tipped the scales, made him yearn to flee. Even Ruby couldn't impart enough sanity to his life while he was tied to Kinross. Getting away was more difficult than of yore, thanks to Charles Dewy's death and Sung's slow slide into purely Chinese matters. Yet what had once been a gold mine was now an empire requiring his personal attention all over the world; Apocalypse Enterprises had expanded into industries and areas far removed from the mining of gold. It had interests in other minerals from silver-lead-zinc to copper, aluminum, nickel, manganese and trace elements; interests in sugar, wheat, cattle and sheep; factories that made steam engines, locomotives, rolling stock and agricultural machinery. There were tea plantations and a gold mine in Ceylon, coffee plantations in Central and South America, an emerald mine in Brazil, and shares in half a hundred thriving industries in the U.S.A., England, Scotland and Germany. Since the company was still privately owned, no one save its board of directors knew quite what Apocalypse Enterprises was worth. Even the Bank of England had to hazard a guess.

Having realized that he had an unerring eye for antiquities and art, Alexander had gotten into the habit of combining business trips abroad with the acquisition of paintings, sculpture, objets d'art, furniture and rare books. The two icons he had given to Sir Edward Wyler had been replaced and added to; the Giotto had been joined by two Titians, a Rubens and a Botticelli before he fell in love with the nonrepresentational works of modern painters based in Paris, and bought Matisse, Manet, Van Gogh, Degas, Monet, Suerat; he had a Velásquez and two Goyas, a

Van Dyke, a Hals, a Vermeer and a Bruegel. The guides at Pompeii would sell a priceless Roman mosaic floor for five gold sovereigns; in fact, the guides anywhere would sell anything for a few pieces of gold. Instead of putting them in Kinross House, Alexander occupied himself for a few short months in building an annex on to the house where all but a few favorite works hung or stood or loomed inside glass cases. It was an interest, something to alleviate his boredom.

Travel was another, yet he was tied to Kinross. In one part of Alexander's mind he was still following in the footsteps of Alexander the Great, curious to see everything the world had to offer. And now he was stuck in a house redolent with the sounds and smells of *women.* Never more so than after Anna joined the feminine club with a cacophony of shrieks and screams.

"Pack your trunks!" he barked at Ruby in June of 1889.

"What?" she asked blankly.

"Pack your trunks! You and I are going abroad."

"Alexander, I'd love to, but how can I? Or you, for that matter? There'd be no one to look after things."

"There will be in a few days," said Alexander. "Lee's coming home. He docks in Sydney in a week."

"Then I'm not going anywhere," said Ruby, looking mutinous.

"Oh, you'll see him!" Alexander snapped. "We'll meet him in Sydney, you can have your reunion, then we're off to America."

"Take Elizabeth."

"I'm damned if I will! I want to *enjoy* myself, Ruby."

The green eyes regarded him with something bordering on dislike. "You know, Alexander, you're growing very preoccupied with yourself," said Ruby. "Not to mention arrogant. I'm not your lackey yet, good sir, so don't growl at me to pack my trunks just because you're fed up with Kinross! I'm not. I want to be here if my son is coming home."

"You'll see him in Sydney."

"For five minutes, if you have anything to do with it."

"For five days, if you like."

"For five years, I would like! You seem to forget, my friend, that I've hardly seen my son in donkey's years. If he really is coming home, then home is the only place I want to be."

No mistaking the iron in her voice; Alexander abandoned his imperiousness and managed to look both contrite and beguiling. "Please, Ruby, don't desert me!" he begged. "We won't be away forever, just for long enough to shake the cobwebs out of my mind and off my shoes. Please, come with me! Then I promise you and I will come home and home you can stay."

She softened. "Well . . ."

"Good girl! We'll spend as long as you like in Sydney with Lee before we sail—anything, Ruby, as long as I'm out of here and with you! I've never taken you abroad—wouldn't you love to see the Alhambra and the Taj Mahal, the pyramids and the Parthenon? With Lee here, we'll be free. Who knows what the future holds? This might be our last chance, my dearest darling! Say yes!"

"If I have time in Sydney with Lee, yes," said Ruby.

He kissed her hands, her neck, her lips, her hair. "You can have anything you want as long as we're out of Kinross and I'm out of Elizabeth's clutches. Since the girls have grown up, she's done nothing but nag, nag, nag."

"I know. She has a bit with me, even," Ruby agreed. "If she could, I think she'd put Nell and Anna into a convent." She made a small purr of pleasure. "Oh, she'll get over being so clucky, it's just a passing thing, but it might be nice not to be one of her targets."

WHEN ELIZABETH heard an expurgated version of this from Ruby the following day, she looked aghast.

"Oh, Ruby, surely I'm not that bad!" she protested.

"Very nearly, and it's not like you," said Ruby. "Truly, Elizabeth, you have to get over this obsession with protecting the virtue of your girls. The last eighteen months have been a hard time of it. I know it isn't every mother has two girls turn into young women so quickly, but they're perfectly safe in this town, I can assure you. If Nell were a flibbertigibbet you might have some cause, but she's absolutely level-headed and not a scrap in love with love. As for Anna—Anna's a grown-up child! Your constant carping has driven Alexander away, including from Nell. Who won't thank you if she finds out why he's in such a lather to leave."

"But the Company!" Elizabeth cried.

"The Company will manage," said Ruby, suddenly reluctant to impart the news that Lee was coming home.

"And you're really going with Alexander?" Elizabeth asked, sounding wistful.

Ruby gasped. "Don't tell me you're jealous!"

"No, no, of course I'm not jealous! I just wondered what it would be like to travel with someone I adored."

"One day," said Ruby, kissing Elizabeth on the cheek, "I do so much hope that you find out."

IT WAS A VERY chastened Elizabeth who farewelled Alexander and Ruby at the train station. She has gone back into her shell, thought Ruby sadly, and isn't it an indictment of Alexander and me that her only venture into the world of reality has been due to concern over her girls? The worst part is that it's misplaced—neither of her girls is in need of her concern.

"Did you tell Elizabeth that Lee's coming home?" Ruby asked Alexander as the train drew out.

"No, I assumed that you had," he said, surprised.

"I didn't."

"Why?"

Ruby shrugged. "If I knew that, I'd be one of those newfangled clairvoyants. Besides, what does it matter? Elizabeth takes absolutely no interest in the Company—or in Lee."

"That upsets you, doesn't it?"

"Bloody oath it does! How can anyone not like my darling jade kitten?"

"Since I happen to like him very much, I honestly don't know."

WITH ALEXANDER gone, Nell immersed herself in her books, determined now to matriculate at the end of next year and go up to university at the very early age of fifteen. An ambition that appalled her mother, who opposed it adamantly. To be told that it was really none of her business.

"If you want someone to pick on," Nell flared, "then pick on Anna! In case you hadn't realized it, Anna's getting very naughty lately—give her half a chance and she's off."

As this was a legitimate criticism, Elizabeth bit her tongue and sought Jade to see what could be done to discipline Anna.

"Nothing, Miss Lizzy," said Jade gloomily. "My baby Anna is not a baby anymore, she doesn't want to be kept to the house. I try to go with her, but she's so—so cunning!"

Who ever would have thought it? wondered Elizabeth. Anna had become curiously independent, as if learning to wash and dress had sprung some secret door in her mind that, once opened, told her that she was able to look after herself. Between her courses she was a happy child, and not difficult to amuse; give her a jigsaw puzzle or some building blocks and she would play with them for hours on end. But once she turned twelve, which she did that year Alexander took Ruby away, she began a game of eluding her keepers, scampering off into the garden and hiding. Only her inability to keep her glee to herself—she chuckled very loudly—enabled Jade or Elizabeth to find her.

Elizabeth, however, was smarting from Ruby's judgment that she was over-protective, compounded when Alexander also gave her a piece of his mind just before he left.

"All she does is go into the garden, Elizabeth, so leave her alone, let up on her a little!"

"Unless she's curbed, she'll wander farther afield."

"When she does is time to act" was Alexander's verdict.

Now, three weeks after Alexander and Ruby had departed, Anna had been found down at the poppet heads just as the noon shift was changing. Recognizing her because Elizabeth still took her to church on Sundays, the miners kindly yet firmly turned her over to Summers, who brought her up to the house.

"I don't know what I'm going to do with her, Mr. Summers," Elizabeth said, wondering if a hard slap would do any good. "We try to keep a constant eye on her, but all we have to do is turn our backs for an instant, and she's off somewhere."

"I'll spread the word, Lady Kinross," Jim Summers said, hiding his exasperation; his time was precious, he had better things to do than police Anna. "If anyone sees her wandering, they're to bring her to me or to you here at the house. Will that do?"

"Yes, of course. Thank you," said Elizabeth, relinquishing the slap-for-punishment alternative as worse than useless.

And so it had to be left. With both Alexander and Ruby away, Summers was the man in authority.

BUT NOT FOR long. Elizabeth was marching an unrepentant and giggling Anna back to the house when Lee walked around the hedge from the cable car landing. She stopped in her tracks, staring as if mesmerized. Anna emitted a squeal and slipped from Elizabeth's slackened grasp.

"Lee! Lee!" the girl called, running to him.

The scene looked a little like a man trying to restrain a gangling hound-sized puppy, thought Elizabeth, gladder to see Lee than she had ever thought possible. She moved across the grass, a smile plastered to her mouth.

"Down, Anna, down!" she said, achieving a laugh.

"It is a bit that way, isn't it?" Lee asked, laughing too.

Jade appeared to take custody of Anna, who was reluctant to go at first, then submitted to the inevitable in her sunny way.

The youth was definitely a man now—he must have turned twenty-five a month ago. Though he had that smooth Chinese skin that resists ageing, there was a small sharp crease on either side of his fine mouth that hadn't been there when last she saw him in England, and his eyes seemed wiser, sadder.

"Dr. Costevan, I presume?" she asked, holding out a hand.

"Lady Kinross," he said, taking it and kissing it.

That she hadn't expected, didn't quite know how to react; she removed it from his clasp as casually as she could and began to walk toward the house with him.

"I take it that was Anna?" he asked.

"Yes, that was my problem child."

"Problem child?"

"She runs away every chance she gets."

"I see. That must be very worrying for you."

Someone on *her* side! Elizabeth stopped to look at him, then wished she hadn't; she had forgotten what looking directly into those extraordinary eyes was like. Rather winded, she took an audible gulp of air before replying. "Jade and I are beside ourselves," she said. "It wasn't too bad when all she did was hide in the garden, but recently she had to be returned from the poppet heads. I suppose next it will be Kinross town."

"And you can't have that, I agree. Are you short of Wong sisters, is that it?"

"Jasmine and Peach Blossom have gone with your mother, but I have Jade, Pearl and Silken Flower as well as Butterfly Wing. It sounds a lot, but the trouble is that Anna knows them all so well. What I need is someone she won't take any notice of. Jade suggested the youngest Wong, Peony, but I can't ask a twenty-two-year-old to take responsibility for Anna."

"Leave it to me, then. I'll ask my father for a woman Anna doesn't know and who won't fall for her tricks. Unless Anna has changed since England, once she gets used to having what seems a block of wood in her vicinity, she'll behave as if she were alone," said Lee, holding the door open.

"Oh, Lee, I would be so grateful!"

"Think nothing of it," he said, and turned to go.

"Aren't you coming in?" Elizabeth asked, dismayed.

"I don't think so. You have no chaperone."

"Oh, really!" Elizabeth cried, color flooding into her face. "Considering what my husband and your mother are up to at this moment, that's ridiculous! Come in, sit down with me and have a cup of tea, for pity's sake!"

His head went to one side as he regarded her through half-closed eyelids, then Ruby's dimples popped out in either cheek and he laughed. "Just this once, then."

So they sat in the conservatory over tea, sandwiches and cakes while Elizabeth plied him with questions. After all that, he had taken a doctorate in mechanical engineering, he told her, though he had also done some geology.

"And I worked for a while in a stockbroking firm in an attempt to understand how the share market functions."

"Is that useful?" Elizabeth asked.

"Not a scrap," he said cheerfully. "I discovered that there is only one way to learn business, and that is by doing it. My real education happened at Alexander's hands, going around with him whenever I had a chance. Now he trusts me to administer the Apocalypse and Apocalypse Enterprises in his absence, though I gather that Sophia Dewy's husband is also very shrewd in business, and has just been employed by us."

"More on the accounting side," said Elizabeth, pleased to be able to contribute something. "He works out of Dunleigh rather than Kinross—poor Constance has never recovered from Charles's death, and her daughters are very protective of her."

"He can take the books home, that's true, but if Sydney's telephone exchange would only join the march of progress, he could do far more from Dunleigh," Lee said.

"We do have telephones in Kinross, but with no telephones in Bathurst or Lithgow, it's purely local."

"Trust Alexander to be in the forefront of the march!"

When he rose to go Elizabeth looked regretful. "Will you come to dinner?" she asked.

"No."

"Even if I produce Nell as a chaperone?"

"Even if Nell is there, no, thank you. I also have to keep an eye on my mother's hotel."

She watched him walk across the terrace with an ache in her breast, as if some wonderful treat had suddenly been snatched from her without warning. Lee was back, but had made it clear that he didn't intend to spend any time in her company. Just when she had found sufficient confidence to thaw a little. Just when she felt sure enough of herself to treat him as a friend rather than the dangerously alien creature who had invaded The Pool. Oh, it was too bad!

HE WAS, however, true to his word; he sent her Dragonfly, an elderly Chinese woman as inscrutable as all Orientals are supposed to be. Wherever Anna was, there also was Dragonfly, so unobtrusive that within two days Anna forgot her presence.

"A perfect watchdog," Elizabeth said to Lee over the telephone, since she saw nothing of him at the house. "I can't thank you enough, Lee, truly. Dragonfly gives Jade and me a much needed rest, so that when she has her days off, we're quite capable of taking over. Please come to morning tea sometime."

"Sometime," he said, and rang off.

"Sometime, never," said Elizabeth to herself with a sigh.

AS FAR AS Lee was concerned, "never" was the word that said it all. When he had come around the hedge and seen Elizabeth grimly shepherding a younger edition of herself, Lee's hopes that he had finally shaken free of Elizabeth vanished as if they had never been. The feelings rolled over him like a wave—love, pity, desire, despair. Not trusting himself, he had refused to drink tea with her, only to come to a sudden understanding of her loneliness that forced him out of common decency to say yes. It was there in her eyes, in the set of her face, in the way she held herself—terrible loneliness! Yet that one pleasant tea with her found him teetering on the brink of a declaration that he knew she would reject with fear and finality. Therefore he couldn't see her again unless others were present, and such occasions were rare with Alexander away.

He hadn't wanted to come home, but acknowledged Alexander's right to command him; after doing all that could be done at a distance, it was high time that he proved himself at the nucleus of the Apocalypse Enterprises network. Alexander was forty-six and clearly seeking a successor who would free him to travel, to perform a less onerous duty for the Company.

When his mother and Alexander had met him in Sydney, he saw their transparent happiness at being together, at the prospect of going far away together, and his heart smote him. By now he knew Alexander's story—the ostensibly legitimate birth that hid his bastardy, his mother's unresolved secret, his utter determination to acquire wealth and power, the pleasure he took in that wealth and power. But of his relationship with Elizabeth he said nothing worth hearing; all Lee knew was what his mother had told him, that Elizabeth could not be allowed to have children and thus lived in Alexander's house as his wife without actually being his wife. But that didn't answer the mystery; in a town with so many Chinese, Lee knew that either Alexander or Elizabeth could have found a way to enjoy conjugal relations without pregnancy. Though they were famous for multiplying, the Chinese also knew how not to multiply if they so chose. Especially the educated ones. Certainly Hung Chee at the Chinese medicine shop. Nature was rich in abortifacients, if not in things that prevented conception.

His love for Elizabeth had sensitized him to Alexander's every unspoken expression of face, eyes, body, when he talked of his wife. And those unspoken expressions were of bewilderment, of pain. Not of an all-pervasive love, no—Alexander felt that for Ruby, Lee had no doubt of it. Yet he wasn't indifferent to Elizabeth. Certainly he didn't hate her or loathe her. Lee was always left with the impression that Alexander had given up on Elizabeth, which meant that the nature of their relationship must stem from her. No man could be indifferent to her, she was too beautiful for that—inside as well as outside. Beautiful in a way that drew men rather than repelled them; her aura was of unattainability, and that brought out Man the Hunter, Man the Conqueror. But not in Lee, who ached for Elizabeth in a less primitive way. Underneath the aloof composure he had twice glimpsed a panicked creature caught in a trap. What he yearned to do was set her at liberty, even if freedom meant she continued to regard him as the nothing she had once called him.

Oh, but she had been glad to see him! Glad enough to speak out against his going. To beg him to visit again. Well, that was the result of her loneliness, and wisdom had dictated his refusal. He must continue to refuse. Alexander was his friend and mentor; to betray Alexander's trust in him was unthinkable.

So Lee went about his Apocalypse business removed from the house on the mountain and Elizabeth, burying himself in his work.

Two

DISPUTES, INDUSTRIAL AND OTHERWISE

A MUCH REFRESHED Alexander returned home in April of 1890, just in time to celebrate his forty-seventh birthday; that the trip hadn't been longer was due to Ruby, who liked the concept of travel more than she did the actual sensation.

"Or perhaps," she said to Elizabeth before she so much as removed her hat, "it's that Alexander is such a ruthless sort of traveler—he hardly stops. There were times when I offered to every god in creation for a pair of wings. San Francisco, then on a train to Chicago, another train to Washington, Philadelphia, New York, Boston—and the United States was just the start."

"Which is probably why he left most of the tripping around to me and a guide when I went with him," said Elizabeth, very pleased to see Ruby. "Did you get to the Italian lakes?"

"I did. Alexander stayed in Turin and Milan—business as usual! I mean, here we are just off the train, and he's touring the workshops and the mine with Lee."

"Did you like the Italian lakes?" Elizabeth pressed.

"Gorgeous, my dear, gorgeous!" said Ruby, at a loss.

"I loved them. If I had a choice, I'd live on Lake Como."

"I hate to be a spoilsport, but I'd sooner the Kinross Hotel myself," said Ruby, kicking off her shoes. She shot Elizabeth an enquiring green glance. "Have you managed to get on better with my jade kitten?"

"I've seen virtually nothing of him, but he's been very kind to me," Elizabeth answered.

"In what way?"

"Anna took to disappearing off the property after you and Alexander left, even got as far as the poppet heads—she's so cunning, Ruby! You know Jade, so you know how carefully Anna's watched. But the little wretch was more than a match for Jade and me combined."

"And?" asked Ruby, looking up at Elizabeth.

"Lee found us Dragonfly, who is perfect. You see, Anna knows us and is clever enough to distract our attention, then slips away like lightning. Whereas Dragonfly is a block of wood—there, yet not there. She can't be shaken off. I tell you, Ruby, Lee took an enormous weight off my mind."

"I'm tickled that you're finally getting on with him. Ah, tea!" Ruby exclaimed as Peach Blossom brought in the tray. "I know you're a bit on the short side, Elizabeth, but do sit down. I'm dying of thirst—no one abroad makes a decent pot of tea. Well, outside of England, and that was a long time ago."

"You've put on a bit of weight," said Elizabeth.

"Don't remind me! It's all those delicious custardy things they make on the Continent."

A small silence fell that Elizabeth broke. "What are you hiding from me, Ruby?"

Startled, Ruby stared at her. "Jesus! You've grown very perceptive."

"Hadn't you better tell me?"

"It's Alexander," said Ruby reluctantly.

"What about him? Is he ill?"

"Alexander, ill? Not in a fit! No, he's changed."

"For the worse." Elizabeth didn't make it a question.

"Definitely for the worse." Ruby scowled, drained her cup and poured another. "He's always had a tendency to be arrogant, but nothing that I for one couldn't put up with. It even had a sort of charm. Sometimes I deserved to be slapped down." She giggled. "Metaphorically, of course. Though once I slapped him!"

"*Did* you? In my time, or before me?"

"Before you, but don't try to change the subject. These days he hob-nobs with industrial barons and top-of-the-tree politicians—Apocalypse Enterprises is a power almost everywhere. It seems to have gone to his head, or maybe it would be more accurate to say that he listens to some pretty ghastly men."

"What ghastly men?"

"His fellow tycoons. You never met such a hard lot, sweetie-pie! They don't care about anything except making money, money, money, so they treat their employees shabbily and resort to all kinds of nasty tricks to curb what's called the 'labor movement'—you know, trade unions and suchlike."

"I didn't think Alexander was susceptible to that," Elizabeth said slowly. "He's always taken great pride in treating his own employees magnificently."

"In the past," Ruby said ominously.

"Oh, Ruby! He wouldn't!"

"I'm not so sure. The trouble is that times are getting hard and all businesses are feeling it. There's a general agreement among the better-off that it's all because of some book that's just come out in English—its German title is *Das Kapital.* In three volumes, but only the first has been translated, and it's more than enough to set the cat among the pigeons, if I'm to believe Alexander and his cronies."

"What's it about? Who wrote it?" Elizabeth asked.

"It's about something called 'international socialism' and its author is a man named Karl Marx. I think there's another chap involved as well, but I forget his name. Anyway, it damns the well-off, especially the industrialists, and something called—um—capitalism. The idea is that wealth should be equally distributed so that no one's rich and no one's poor."

"I can't imagine that has any chance of working, can you?"

"No, people are too different. It says the workingman is shamelessly exploited, and demands a social revolution. The labor movements everywhere have grabbed it like a drowning man a spar, and are even talking about entering politics."

"Dear me," said Elizabeth placidly.

"I tend to agree with you, Elizabeth, but the trouble is that Alexander and his cronies seem to take it very seriously."

"Well, that's over there. Now Alexander's home where he belongs, he'll settle down."

LEE DIDN'T agree. It hadn't taken his mother to tell him that Alexander had changed; he saw it for himself as they walked from mine to workshops to Lee's pride and joy, the new plant to separate the gold from its ore by immersion in a weak solution of potassium cyanide and precipitating the gold out on to zinc plates and shavings.

For one thing, the new Alexander harped constantly on the worldwide decline in prosperity, and for another, he looked at everything in a different way than of yore—how to cut costs, even if that meant cutting corners.

"You can't economize in a cyanide process if there's safety involved," said Lee. "Potassium cyanide is lethally toxic stuff."

"Yes, if it's highly concentrated, but not at point-one of one percent, my dear young man."

Lee blinked. Alexander was *patronizing* him!

"One still starts off with the pure cyanide salt," Lee said, "so you can't let just anybody mix the solution. It's a job for intelligent, highly responsible men—men I've budgeted for in our wages accounts."

"Needlessly."

And so it went. There were too many hands in the locomotive workshop because servicing of the iron horses was too frequent—why hadn't Lee moved to automate the delivery of coal to the steam engines?—there was no reason to retire those old coal cars from the Lithgow-Kinross line—*he* hadn't seen any fault in the number three bridge when he came through.

"Oh, come, Alexander!" Lee expostulated, astonished. "You'll have to examine the bridge from underneath to see the fault!"

"I refuse to believe that it necessitates rebuilding the entire structure," Alexander said curtly. "That would put the railway out of action for weeks."

"Not if we do it as Terry Sanders suggests. A week at the most, and we can stockpile coal."

"You're a good engineer, Lee, but not a businessman's rear end, that's obvious" was Alexander's verdict.

"I FEEL AS if I've been savaged by a tiger, Mum," Lee said to Ruby when they met for a drink that evening.

"He's that bad, my jade kitten?"

"That bad." Lee took Scotch whisky instead of sherry, and didn't dilute it. "I know I'm not all that experienced, but I don't agree that I've spent money needlessly, which is what Alexander says. Suddenly safety isn't important. I could accept that if it didn't mean imperiling the lives of some employees, but it does, Mum, it does!"

"And he's the major shareholder," said Ruby. "Shit."

"Exactly." Lee laughed, helped himself to a second whisky. "I'm in the shit over shit as well! The sewage treatment plant desperately needed some work that I authorized, only to be told that it isn't necessary. I never thought of Alexander as a miserly Scot in all the time I've known him, but that's what he is now."

"Because he's taken bad advice overseas. He listens to men who'd shave a shilling if that meant saving a farthing for every hundred pounds. Dammit," said Ruby, leaping to her feet, "we're so *profitable,* Lee! Our overheads are negligible compared to how much we make, and there are no shareholders to satisfy—just the four original partners. None of us has complained. How could we, for Christ's sake?" She too resorted to the Scotch. "Well, we can inform him at the next board meeting that we don't approve."

"And he'll ride roughshod over our protests," said Lee.

"I don't feel like going up the mountain for dinner."

"Nor do I, but we have to go, if only for Elizabeth's sake."

"She tells me," said Ruby, draping a fluffy feather boa about her neck, "that you've been very kind to her."

"It would take a monster not to be kind to her." He eyed the boa with amusement. "Where did you get that mad thing?"

"In Paris. The trouble is," she said, kicking her train to fall behind her as she turned, "that it molts like an old chook." A chuckle. "Still, I am an old chook!"

"You'll always be a spring chicken to me, Mum."

THE DINNER started off well considering that just the four of them sat down. Some of Alexander's bonhomie had returned, so Elizabeth tried to keep the conversation light.

"You'll be tickled to know, Alexander, that this colony's ongoing war between its various religions has been complicated by the arrival of three new sects—the Seventh-Day Adventists, the Methodist Mission and the Salvation Army."

"And there's a group drawn from every religion," Lee said a little feverishly, "who call themselves Sabbatarians, and demand that all activities cease on Sundays, even visiting museums or holding cricket matches."

"Huh!" said Alexander. "None of them will be welcome here."

"But Kinross does have plenty of Catholics, and they're not too happy with Sir Henry Parkes since he stripped State aid away from their schools," Elizabeth said, passing the salad. "He thought, of course, that the move would force Catholic children into the State school system, but that hasn't happened. They battle on."

"I *know* all that!" Alexander snapped. "I also know that the Grand Old Man of Politics is a Protestant bigot who despises the Irish, so shall we change the subject?"

Elizabeth went crimson, put her head down and ate salad as if it had a dressing of hemlock. Furious with Alexander, Lee longed to reach out and squeeze Elizabeth's hand in comfort. Not able to do that, he changed the subject.

"I take it that you're aware of the federation situation?"

"If by that you mean that the colonies have agreed to join as something called the Commonwealth of Australia, yes, of course," Alexander said, face lightening; apparently he preferred talking to Lee than to Elizabeth. "It's been on the table for years."

"Well, it's definitely going to happen. The big debate is when it's going to happen, but the latest news is that it will be the dawn of the new century."

Ruby looked quizzical. "Nineteen hundred, or nineteen hundred and one?" she asked.

"Ah, that's the big stumbling block," Lee said, smiling and deciding to go for a laugh. "There's a group who say the new century begins in nineteen hundred, another that it doesn't begin until nineteen hundred and one. It all depends, you see, whether there was a Year Nought between One B.C. and One A.D. The church people plump for no Year Nought, whereas the mathematicians and atheists say there had to be a Year Nought. The best argument I've heard is that if there was no Year Nought, then Jesus Christ didn't have His first birthday until December twenty-fifth of *Two* A.D., and was actually only thirty-one when He went to the cross eight months before His thirty-three A.D. birthday."

Ruby roared, Elizabeth managed a smile, but Alexander looked scornful. "Claptrap!" he said. "They'll federate in nineteen hundred and one no matter what year Jesus Christ was born."

After which the conversation died.

"He hates being home," said Ruby to Lee in the cable car.

"I know, but it's the outside of enough when he takes out his spleen on poor Elizabeth, Mum. She just curled up."

"He's bored, Lee, frightfully bored."

"He's a boor!"

"Put up with him, please! He *will* settle down," said Ruby.

LEE PUT UP with Alexander's frightful boredom as best he could, which was by handing over all financial decisions to him (Alexander had demanded that he do so anyway) and staying as far out of reach as he could. If Alexander was in the mine, Lee was at the sewage treatment plant, and if Alexander was in the cyanide refinery, Lee was rebuilding the railway bridge. He had had a victory there; even in his new mood of economizing, Alexander could see that the structure was too weak to be repaired.

For Elizabeth it was harder because she couldn't get away from her husband in the evenings. He had quarrelled with Ruby, who taxed him over his treatment of Lee and got told to mind her own business, namely the Kinross Hotel. She retaliated by barring him from her bed. Elizabeth's lot was made harder by Nell, who was overjoyed at Daddy's return and stuck to him like glue outside school hours. Nell and her mother had been getting along together better while Alexander was away, now that vanished. Chiefly due to Elizabeth's protesting strongly against Alexander's intention to send Nell up to university to commence engineering in March of next year, when she would be a mere fifteen. Of course Nell was avid to go, fell all over her father when he said she could, and didn't possess sufficient tact not to crow about it to her mother.

"It's cruel to send a child into a man's world at fifteen," Elizabeth said to Alexander when she thought he was in a good mood. "I know she's bright enough to top the state in her matriculation exams this year, but she's four years too early. It wouldn't do her any harm to stay here another year."

"You're such a Job's comforter, Elizabeth. Nell is raring to go, and I need her qualified as soon as possible now that Lee is such a disappointment."

"Lee, a disappointment? Alexander, that's unfair!"

"No, it's bloody not! If I let Lee have his way, Apocalypse Enterprises would turn into a beneficent society for international socialism! It's all the workers this, and the workers that—my employees get paid better wages than anyone else's, live in a better and cheaper town—they're home on the pig's back! And what thanks have I received? None!" Alexander said, snarling.

"This isn't like you," Elizabeth said dully.

"It's like the new me. We're in for mighty hard times, and I do not intend to go under."

"Lee aside, I beg you not to let Nell go up next year."

"Nell is going up next year, and that's that. I'm having her and the Chinese boys taught to defend themselves—Donny Wilkins too. They'll be properly housed and absolutely safe. Now go away, Elizabeth, and leave me alone!"

AND SO MATTERS stood until that July of 1890, when everything seemed to happen almost at once.

It began with Dragonfly, who developed heart trouble and was told by Hung Chee in the Chinese medicine shop that she must not work for at least six months. With Alexander in a permanent bad temper—he still hadn't managed to climb back into Ruby's bed—Elizabeth knew that she couldn't apply to Lee for a replacement; she had no choice but to apply to Alexander. Who looked at her as if she were mad.

"I'm sure Dragonfly has been a great help—she's taken all the load of Anna, which has freed you and Jade up, hasn't it?" he asked, voice biting. "Well, back to work the pair of you go. There was never any need to pay an extra wage for yet another minder—this house costs a fortune to run!"

"But Alexander, Dragonfly became someone Anna didn't even see, that's why Dragonfly was so successful!" Elizabeth protested, feeling tears gather and determined not to shed them. "When Jade and I supervise Anna, she tricks us—truly, she's cunning! And she can't be allowed to wander. What if she has an accident?"

"How far can the girl go?" Alexander asked, brows raised in his devil's look. "I'll issue orders that anyone who sees her at the poppet heads or in town is to return her to Summers or you."

"I'm so sorry, Jade," Elizabeth said a few minutes later. "You and I are back on patrol with Anna."

"She'll escape," said Jade miserably.

"Yes, she'll escape. Still, I daresay Sir Alexander is right when he says she can come to no harm."

"Miss Lizzy, I'll make sure she doesn't trick me!"

"I just worry that she'll take a fall in the bush and break something. Oh, for Dragonfly!"

* * *

TWO DAYS LATER Alexander held a board meeting; only Sung, Ruby and Lee were present, Sophia Dewy's husband too far away to get to Kinross in time. Alexander did not intend to have more opposition than necessary.

"I'm reducing Apocalypse Mine production by half," he said in the tone that brooked no argument. "The price of gold is falling and it's going to fall even lower as time goes on. In view of this, we pull in our horns before someone chops them off. If you include the coal mine, we have a work force of five hundred and fourteen. That will go down to two hundred and thirty. The town employs another two hundred, almost all Chinese. That will go down to one hundred."

For a long moment no one said a word, then Sung spoke.

"Alexander, Apocalypse Enterprises can survive a worldwide slump for many years. The gold is a relatively insignificant part of our profits these days, so why can't we continue to mine it? We have vaults here, we can stockpile it if necessary."

"And deplete it for the future? No," said Alexander.

"How does stockpiling it deplete it?" Sung asked.

"Because it's coming out of the ground."

Lee folded his hands on the table, striving to maintain his calm. "One of the purposes of expanding Apocalypse Enterprises into so many different avenues was to sustain certain of our companies and holdings through bad patches," he said levelly. "If the Apocalypse Mine needs to be sustained now, we should do it."

"You don't run enterprises at a loss," said Alexander.

"Not if you cut production by half, I agree. But our work force is so skilled, Alexander! We have the best men in the gold-mining business. Why lose them for a temporary expedient? And why destroy goodwill? We've never had difficulties with the trade unions—in fact, our employees are so well treated that they don't bother joining trade unions."

The look on Alexander's face didn't change, but Lee struggled on. "I've always prized the fact that we have never treated our employees like second-class citizens. There's no need for greed, Alexander. Apocalypse Enterprises is quite capable of supporting our present life-styles even if we run the mine at a loss."

Ruby butted in. "Lee's right, but he doesn't go far enough. The Apocalypse and Kinross were the beginning of it all, Alexander, we owe everything we are to them. I for one won't consent to cuts that are a drop in the bucket when you consider the extent of the Company. I mean, it's everywhere! The mine and Kinross are your *babies*! You've put so much of yourself into them. Now you act as if they've committed a crime, and that's criminal."

"Sheer sentiment!" Alexander snapped.

"I agree, it is," said Sung, "but good sentiment, Alexander. Your people and my people have a good life here. It must go on being a good life, and that means preserving goodwill."

"You're over-using the word 'good,' Sung."

"And I do not apologize for over-using it."

"So I take it, since you own the majority share, Alexander, that you're about to sack two hundred and eighty-four mining men and one hundred town employees?" Lee asked.

"Correct."

"I register my disapproval."

"And I," said Sung.

"And I," said Ruby. "I also register Dewy disapproval."

"None of which matters a hoot," said Alexander.

"Do you intend to do anything for those you let go?" Lee asked.

"Of course. I'm not entirely a Simon Legree. They'll all receive severance pay according to years of service, skills and even size of family."

"That's something," said Lee. "Does it extend to the coal mine as well?"

"No. Just to Kinross employees."

"Jesus, Alexander, it's the coal miners will make the most trouble!" Ruby cried.

"Which is precisely why they won't benefit from my generosity."

"You sound like the mill owner from Yorkshire," said Ruby.

"Alexander, what's gotten into you?" Lee asked.

"Awareness of the gulf between the Haves and Have-nots."

"A more stupid answer would be hard to find!"

"That's bordering on impudence, young man."

"Not so young at twenty-six." Lee got up, face set. "I do realize that everything I am I owe to you, from my education to my share in Apocalypse Enterprises. But I can't continue to give you loyalty if you persist in such unkindness. If you do persist, I'm done with you, Alexander."

"That's absolute bullshit, Lee. With the labor movement organizing itself to go into politics and the unions feeling their oats, industrial giants like this Company are threatened from all sides. If we don't act now, it will be too late to act. Do you want some tom-fool clique of socialists running businesses from banks to bakeries? Labor has to be taught a lesson, and the sooner, the better. This is *one* of my contributions," said Alexander.

"*One* of your contributions?" Ruby asked.

"I have others. I do not intend to go under."

"How can Apocalypse Enterprises go under?" Lee demanded. "It has so many irons in so many fires that a genuine apocalypse couldn't smash it to smithereeens."

"I've made my decision, and I stand by it," said Alexander.

"Then I stand by mine." Lee walked to the door. "I hereby resign from the board, and from all participation in the Company."

"Then sell me your share, Lee."

"In a pig's eye, I will! That you gave my mother in trust for me, and that she transferred to me when I turned twenty-one. It's pay-back for the services my mother renders you, and it's not negotiable."

Lee quit the room quietly, leaving Alexander chewing his lip, Sung contemplating the far wall, and Ruby glaring at Alexander.

"That was not well done, Alexander," Sung said.

"I think you're off your head" from Ruby.

Alexander gathered his papers together briskly. "If there's no more business, the meeting is over," he said.

"THE TROUBLE IS," mourned Ruby to Lee, "that Alexander has begun to form a crust of—of—oh, I don't know how to explain it! His altruism is gone, thanks to chumming up with his fellow tycoons. Profits and power have come to mean more to him than human beings do. He's losing sight of *people,* he finds his joy—no, his excitement—in manipulating vast numbers of people for his own ends. When I met him, he was full of idealism and high principles, but not anymore. If he'd had a happier marriage and a couple of sons of his own, things would be different. He'd be busy teaching them ideals and high principles."

"There's Nell," said Lee, leaning back with eyes closed.

"Nell is female, and I don't mean that in a derogatory sense. Only that she's inherited Alexander's steel in a feminine way. She'll never rise to head Apocalypse Enterprises, I know it in my bones. Oh, she'll excel at engineering and she'll try hard to please him because she adores him. But in the end it will come to nothing, Lee. It can't do else."

"Mum the prophet."

"No, Mum the exponent of reality," said Ruby, serious for once. "What do you intend to do, Lee?"

"As I'm certainly not short of money, I can do anything that I fancy," said Lee, opening his eyes and gazing at her with the look she always associated with her little jade kitten. "I might travel in Asia, visit some of my friends from Proctor's."

"Oh, don't leave Kinross!" she cried.

"I have to, Mum. If I don't, Alexander will come down on me like a ton of bricks. Let him reap the whirlwind he's busy sowing."

"That will sour him even more."

"Then don't stay to see it, Mum. Come with me."

"No, I'll stay here. Quite honestly, one trip was one too many. I'm two years older than Alexander, and I feel those two years as if they were twenty. Besides, he's going to fall down with a crash, and if I'm not here to pick up the pieces, do you think Elizabeth will?"

"I have no idea," said Lee, "what she would or would not do."

UNLIKE ALEXANDER, Lee did not set much value on possessions, so packing was quick and easy. Just one large and one small case—less, did he not feel that he might need evening dress, suits for different occasions. Though it was queer not to look forward to meeting Alexander somewhere.

On his last morning he walked up the snake path and into the bush. The sun had a winter smolder to it, a dull glare that reddened the soft pink unfolding leaves of this year's new crop of eucalyptus foliage. Spring was around the corner already, the boronia budding and the northeast side of scattered rocks bearing exquisite creamy spikes of dendrobium orchids. So beautiful. Everything was so beautiful. And always hard to leave.

He sat down amid the clumps of orchids on a huge boulder and folded his arms around his knees.

The one thing I cannot eradicate is my love for Elizabeth, which goes on shaping my life. Nomadic, solitary, free. Yet I would not be free. I would have Elizabeth if I could. I would give everything I own and am for the chance to have Elizabeth. Her body, her mind, her heart, her very soul.

He climbed to his feet like an old man; he had to go and say goodbye to his beloved.

Whom he found in a distracted mood. Anna had gone missing.

"What happened to Dragonfly?" he asked.

Her eyes widened. "Don't you know?"

"Apparently not," he said, but gently.

"She had trouble with her heart and Hung Chee says she can't work for six months. Alexander said hiring her was ridiculous anyway, and forbade me to replace her."

"What *is* the matter with the man?" Lee cried, fists clenched.

"His age, I think, Lee. I suspect he feels old, and there are no more worlds to conquer. But it will pass."

"I'm going away for good," he said abruptly.

Her skin was always white, but it seemed suddenly to empty to an eerie transparency. Lee's response was instinctive; he reached out and took her hands, held them strongly. "Are you well, Elizabeth?"

"Not very, this morning," she whispered. "I worry for Anna. It's Alexander, isn't it? He's forced you to go away."

"Until he comes to his senses, yes."

"He will, though I hate to think of the price he'll pay. Oh, Lee, your mother! This will break her heart."

"No, only Alexander can do that. My going will make it far easier for her to reconcile with him, you know."

"It's not right! He needs you, Lee."

"But I don't need him."

"I understand that." Her eyes fell to her hands; without his realizing it, Lee's thumbs were moving on the inside of her wrists in small, caressing circles. She seemed fascinated.

Drawn there by the fixity of her regard, Lee looked down and saw what he was doing. He put a smile on his face, lifted one of her hands and then the other to kiss them lightly.

"Goodbye, Elizabeth," he said.

"Goodbye, Lee. Look after yourself."

He walked away without turning to see her, and she stood in the middle of the lawn watching him go, no thought of Anna in her head. Lee filled it, just as her eyes were filled with tears.

"YOU KNOW," said Alexander to her in the drawing room that night before dinner, "you improve with age, Elizabeth."

"Do I?" she asked tranquilly, guard up.

"Yes, definitely. You've turned into what I glimpsed once in the middle of cursing you for a mouse—a quiet lion."

"I am sorry that Lee is gone" was her answer.

"I'm not. It was inevitable. We came to the parting of the ways—he wants peace at any price, I'm spoiling for a fight."

"An unquiet lion."

"How would you describe Lee?"

The line of her jaw changed as she put her head back, a movement of such grace that he felt a flash of desire. Down went her lashes as her mouth tilted up in an enigmatic smile. "As the golden serpent in the Garden of Eden."

"Was the serpent golden?"

"I have no idea, but you asked me for an animal metaphor."

"It's apt, he does have a serpentine quality. You've never indicated whether you like him, come to think of it. Do you?"

"No, I've never liked him."

"Do you like anyone, Elizabeth?"

"Ruby . . . Sung . . . Constance . . . Mrs. Surtees."

"And your children?"

"I *love* my children, Alexander. Never doubt it."

"But not me, like or love."

"No, not you, like or love."

"Do you realize that you've been married to me for just about half of your entire life?"

Her head came down, her eyes opened wide to stare at him. "Is *that* all?" she asked. "It seems an eternity."

"Did I say a quiet lion?" Alexander pulled a face. "An eternity with me has turned you into a bitch, my dear."

RETRENCHMENT AT the Apocalypse Mine might have taken place without much fuss if it hadn't been for Sam O'Donnell, a miner who hadn't been on the job for long enough to merit more than a token sum when he was paid out. Nor did he have a wife or children to augment this. Even in his worst moments of parsimony Alexander retained a healthy self-preservation that told him it was prudent not to fire his workers without compensation, though there were no laws or statutes thus to compel him. Had he been on speaking terms with Ruby, she would have told him that when push came to shove he had too much heart to be a complete robber-baron, whereas Elizabeth might have said he was too vain to like being cursed as a complete robber-baron. There was some truth in both. His misfortune was that he couldn't care about his colliery workers in the same way as he did the Apocalypse gold men; they were simply dismissed with two weeks' pay. Generous, compared to some.

Sam O'Donnell went straight to the Amalgamated Miners' Association, the most militant section of which looked after the interests of coal miners. Most of the Australian colliers were Welsh immigrants and the mines, like Alexander's at Lithgow, were privately owned.

When Sam O'Donnell came back from Sydney, he was accompanied by a rising young political light in the labor movement, Bede Evans Talgarth of the New South Wales Trades and Labour Council. Though Australian born, Bede Talgarth, as his name suggested, had Welsh roots. He was more formidable than a simple agitator or union negotiator; self-educated to a high degree, he understood account books and economics, and had already, at the age of twenty-five, made a reputation as a wonderful orator. Soaked in the new gods Marx and Engels, he burned to disband the Legislative Council, which was the for-life unelected upper house of the New South Wales parliament, and destroy the influence of the British Government in all Australian affairs. He hated England passionately. Despite which, he had a cool head and a great deal of subtlety.

An interview on the first day of August with Sir Alexander Kinross proved to be the irresistible force colliding with the immovable object; the two men, alike in their humble beginnings, had each chosen a very different path in life and faced each other in no mood to concede the tiniest point. Since their conditions and wages had been so good over the years, Alexander's miners and refinery workers had never bothered to join a union. Except for Sam O'Donnell, a member from Gulgong days. Therefore Bede used him as his wedge by demanding that the man be reinstated.

"He's a troublemaker and a whiner," said Alexander, "and as such, the *last* of the men I've laid off who would be reinstated. In fact, if at some time in the future I were to hire again, I'd not hire Sam O'Donnell."

"The price of gold is falling, Sir Alexander. This is a ploy to keep your gold in situ until its price rises again."

"'In situ,' eh? Such an elegant phrase for a shirtsleeves demagogue! What you suggest is ridiculous. I'm laying off because I can't afford to continue full production, that simple."

"Reinstate Mr. O'Donnell," said Bede.

"Go to hell," said Alexander.

Bede Talgarth walked out.

The only accommodation in Kinross was at Ruby's hotel, where Bede had rented the smallest, cheapest room. Scrupulous about using union funds, he preferred whenever possible to pay his way out of his own pocket, which he filled, scantily, by writing for the *Bulletin* and a new labor paper, the *Worker,* and by passing a hat around after one of his stirring speeches in the Sydney Domain on a Sunday afternoon. What he hoped was to stand successfully for the next New South Wales parliament, whose present members had resolved that after the next elections all sitting members would be paid a handsome salary. Until now, a parliamentarian was unpaid, which meant poor men couldn't afford to belong to the elected lower house. In future poor men could.

A little above average height at five feet nine, Bede was heavily built, a legacy from the Newcastle coal face—he had started working alongside his Welsh-born father at twelve—and from far better nutrition than his father had ever enjoyed as a child in the Rhondda Valley of Wales. Despite his bulk, he was very trim, though he walked like a sailor due to the musculature of his thighs. His thick, waving hair was dark red, his skin was faintly freckled, and his eyes were the same black as Alexander's. People didn't call him handsome, but women found his square but regular features attractive and, if they chanced to see him with his sleeves rolled up, stared at his massively developed arms in awe. Ruby was more forthcoming when he encountered her in the hotel foyer after his meeting with Sir Alexander.

"What a bonny boy you are!" she said, her green eyes peeping coyly from behind an ostrich feather fan. "If the bit I can't see is like the rest of you, I'll amend boy to stallion."

His nostrils flared; he reared back as if she had struck him. Bede reverenced women as vulnerable servitors, and deemed vulgarity in them intolerable. "I don't know you from a bar of soap, madam, and if that's an example of your style of conversation, I don't want to know you."

Her answer was a guffaw. "A prude! A Bible-basher too, eh?"

"I fail to see what God has to do with women who talk smut."

"So you are a Bible-basher."

"As a matter of fact, I'm not."

Ruby dropped the fan and produced a dimpled smile of such glee that it was hard to resist. "You're the Trades and Labour Council man, Bede Talgarth," she said. "Typical of the breed too—full of fire to free the downtrodden workingman, yet determined to keep women in their place—childing, cooking, cleaning, forever pegging out the washing. I'm Ruby Costevan, proprietor of this hostelry and ardent enemy of the double standard."

"Double standard?" he asked blankly.

"You're a man and at liberty to say fuck, I'm a woman and not at liberty to say fuck. Well, sport, fuck that!" She strolled up to him and linked her arm through his. "You'll go farther faster if you accept women into the race of Man as equal. Though I'm of the opinion that not many men are my equal."

He was softening, quite why he didn't know, except that she was so extraordinarily beautiful yet managed to radiate good humor. In the end he suffered her arm and let her lead him into the hall. Of course the moment she said her name he knew who she was: the mistress of Sir Alexander Kinross and a director of Apocalypse.

"Where are we going?" he asked.

"To have lunch in my private dining room."

He stopped. "I can't afford it."

"Be my guest—and don't give me any of that shit about you and I being on opposite sides of the fence and you won't eat off the proceeds of Mammon! You're a stiff-necked young labor Turk, and I'll bet you've never had a meal with a millionairess. Now is your chance to find out how the other half lives."

"More accurately, the other one-hundredth of one percent."

"I stand corrected."

There was a clatter and a thump in the foyer; Ruby and Bede turned to see a female form spread-eagled on the floor.

"Oh, bugger!" the female form said as Bede helped her to her feet. "I *hate* these bloody long bloody dresses!"

"This is Bede, Nell. Bede, this is Nell, who is fourteen and a half and just out of short skirts," said Ruby. "Unfortunately we haven't been able to persuade her to put her hair up yet, and she won't wear a corset for love or money."

"You're the union man," said Nell, accompanying them with a swish of the abominated skirt. "I'm Alexander Kinross's elder daughter." Her bright blue eyes threw him a challenge as she sat down opposite him at the small round table.

"Where's Anna?" Ruby asked.

"Not to be found, as usual. Anna," Nell informed Bede, "is my younger sister. She's mentally retarded—that's a new phrase I've just found in the literature, Auntie Ruby. I like it better than mental, which implies the ability *to* think rather than an inability to think."

Mind reeling, Bede Talgarth proceeded to have lunch with two women of a kind he had never before encountered. Nell's vocabulary was less salty than Auntie Ruby's, but he suspected that was only because she was a little shy of him and didn't trust him, her father's enemy by definition. Not that he blamed her for filial loyalty. How like him she was to look at! But what sort of foul nest did Sir Alexander Kinross inhabit, that his own daughter lunched with his mistress? Called her *Auntie*? For as Nell chattered he became uncomfortably aware that the girl was fully acquainted with Ruby Costevan's status. It horrified him, for all that he thought himself a free spirit, emancipated from religion and the hidebound conventions it incorporated. Decadence, that's what it is, he decided. These people have so much money and power that they're like the ancient Romans, depraved and degenerate. Yet Nell didn't seem depraved or degenerate, even if she was quite shockingly outspoken. Then he realized that her head was stuffed with brains of a quality he couldn't hope to match.

"I'm going up to Sydney University to do engineering next year," she told him.

"Engineering?"

"Yes, engineering." She sounded patient, as if she talked to an idiot. "Mining, metallurgy, assaying and mining law, actually. Wo Ching and Chan Min are doing it with me, but Lo Chee will do mechanical engineering and machine construction. Donny Wilkins—he's the C of E minister's son—will do civil engineering and architecture. That way, Daddy has three of us for his chief interest, mining, one for his engines and dynamos, and one to build bridges and design his opera house," said Nell.

"But you're a girl and three of the others are Chinese."

"What's wrong with that?" asked Nell, sounding dangerous. "We're all Australians, and all entitled to as much education as we're able to cope with. What do you think rich people do with their lives?" she asked truculently. "The answer is that we do exactly the same thing as poor people do—fritter away our days if we're lazy, or work our arses off if we're industrious."

"What would you know about poor people, young miss?"

"About as much as you know about rich people—very little."

He changed tack. "Engineering isn't a profession for women."

"Poop to that!" Nell snapped. "I suppose you think we ought to deport Wo Ching, Chan Min and Lo Chee too?"

"Since they're already here, no. But I do think that Chinese immigration has to be stopped. Australia is a country for white people earning white men's wages," Bede said rather pompously.

"Jesus!" said Nell on a gasp. "The Chinese are a damned sight better immigrants than the lazy, drunken lot who flock here from all parts of the British Isles!"

An interesting skirmish that didn't become outright war due to Sam Wong's entry with the first course. Nell's face lit up, and to Bede's amazement she began to talk to him in Chinese, her face aglow with affection.

"How many languages do you speak?" he asked her after Sam disappeared. He tasted his prawn-filled pastry rolls drizzled with a sweet sauce and found gastronomic heaven.

"Mandarin Chinese—all our people are Mandarin rather than Cantonese—Latin, Greek, French and Italian. When I go to the city I'll have to find a tutor in German. A lot of engineering papers and texts are written in German."

"Our people," he thought, walking through Kinross later. "Our people" are Mandarin rather than Cantonese. What on earth does that mean? I always thought a Chinaman was a Chinaman. We will have great opposition from Sir Alexander Kinross when the *real* push to ban Chinese immigration begins. It's a natural federal law so it has to wait for federation, and all our white businessmen will be opposing it because they can pay newly arrived Chinese less than half what they pay white men. Yes, it's Labor will have to force the law through a federal parliament. That means our need to organize ourselves politically is even more vital than our union business.

Oh, and why has this Kinross situation blown up now, when we have a dangerous situation in Queensland, and the New South Wales squatters have formed their wretched Pastoralists' "Union"? If—no, *when*—the shearers go on strike, it's going to be a powder keg. And I'll be needed in Sydney, not in this backwater, for all its gold. Bill Spence is under such pressure from the shearers that he's going to have to insist on all-union labor in the wool sheds, and if he succeeds in bringing the Sydney wharf laborers on side, we're in for a hell of a time. But where is the strike pay to come from? We gave thirty-six thousand pounds to the London dockers last year and enabled them to win. But we are skint. And here I am in Kinross.

Bede wished he could like Sam O'Donnell, but the more he had to do with the man, the less he could bear to like him. Though Bede was more inclined to call him a shiftless charmer than a genuine troublemaker. The fact that he had plenty of friends among the refinery and shop workers and none among his fellow miners suggested that he irritated those alongside him. However, Bede was determined to use O'Donnell's best features to the hilt. The man was handsome, supple when he moved, smooth-spoken. And he hated the Chinese, about whom he was a valuable source of information. Kinross and the Apocalypse Mine were a mystery to the Trades and Labour Council. Not that Sir Alexander had favored the Chinese in his retrenchments. Their jobs had gone too, and in about the same proportion as white jobs.

An application to Sergeant Thwaites of the Kinross police for permission to speak in public in Kinross Square next Sunday afternoon was received with wary suspicion, but a telephone call to Sir Alexander fixed that.

"You can speak, Mr. Talgarth, and so can any other man if he wants. Sir Alexander says that free speech is the foundation of true democracy, and he won't oppose it."

So the rumors are correct, thought Bede, striding away with that sailor's gait. Alexander Kinross did spend time in America. No Scot born and bred who hadn't been there would use phrases like "true democracy." Even mention the word "democracy" to a stout supporter of the British in Sydney, and he reacted like a bull to a red rag—arrant American nonsense! All men were *not* equal!

Damn, where was O'Donnell? They had agreed to meet at the hotel just after lunch, but the afternoon wore on without a sign of the fellow. Finally, coming on dusk, he appeared looking a trifle disheveled.

"What have you been up to, Sam?" Bede asked, picking burrs off O'Donnell's coat.

"A bit of slap-and-tickle," said O'Donnell with a chuckle.

"You were supposed to be with me so you could introduce me to the laid-off workers, Sam, not off philandering."

"I wasn't phil-whatever," O'Donnell said sulkily. "If you saw her, you'd understand."

DURING THE six days he was in Kinross, Bede Talgarth began to make inroads among the laid-off workers who were boilermakers, fitters, turners, mechanics or laborers in the refinery and the many other workshops affected by a cut in gold production; the train would now run only once a week, as coal consumption was well down. Only one in every four coal miners at the Apocalypse colliery in Lithgow still had their jobs.

The gold miners, Bede learned, were impossible to woo for his cause. Extremely well paid, working a six-hour shift once in each twenty-four hours for five out of each seven days with additional compensation for night shifts, they stood at a clean mine face illuminated by strong electric light and well ventilated from air shafts equipped with electric-driven fans. Blasting was safe and no man entered the blast area before the dust had fully settled. Into the bargain, they were heavily outnumbered by colliers in the Amalgamated Miners' Association, which they deemed a union for colliers. Finally came a point that Bede Talgarth, ex-collier, had never taken into account until he came to Kinross: gold miners looked down on coal miners as inferior beings because gold miners were better paid and did cleaner work in better conditions, didn't come off a shift black with coal dust and coughing their lungs out from silicosis.

His speech in Kinross Square on Sunday afternoon went down very well. He had had a bright idea, and brought in a big group of colliers from Lithgow to swell that part of the audience willing to cheer. Feeling vindicated, he discovered that the Lithgow contingent also contained men from the brickworks, the ironworks and Samuel Mort's freezing works. Too clever to rail against Sir Alexander Kinross alone, Bede concentrated upon how little the employees made from Apocalypse's colossal profits, and painted a verbal picture of utopian days wherein wealth would be equally distributed, no man living in a mansion, no man living in a slum. Then he proceeded to the Chinese, who threatened the livelihood of every white Australian worker; cheap labor was a vital part of the capitalist equation, witness the kidnapping of black Melanesians to work as virtual slaves on the Queensland sugar plantations. They were yet another reason why Australia had to be a white country, all other races excluded. For, said Bede, the human species was naturally exploitative, so the only way to prevent exploitation was to make opportunities to exploit nonexistent.

The speech made Bede Evans Talgarth famous overnight in Kinross, and on the Monday he walked about surrounded by admirers. The Lithgow contingent begged him to speak in Lithgow the following Sunday, and even some of the Apocalypse gold miners patted him on the back. More, he admitted to himself ruefully, because they had enjoyed listening to a superb orator than because they intended any industrial action. That two-faced bastard Sir Alexander was also doing some speaking, but to small groups, and to the tune that he had always been a good employer, therefore they should believe him when he said he couldn't afford to keep up production. Bede still had a lot of work to do in Kinross.

WORK THAT was not to be done. On August 6 a telegram from the Trades and Labour Council recalled Bede to Sydney. News had come that the Pastoralists' "Union" was shipping non-union bales of wool from the country to Sydney to be loaded aboard overseas-owned ships. The Sydney Wharf Labourers' Union declared the wool "black" and refused to load it. In the midst of which a dispute blew up between the shipowners and the maritime unions, starting with the Marine Officers' Association and going all the way down the pecking order. The Newcastle colliery owners then locked their miners out, so the miners on every other coalfield in the state struck in sympathy. Industrial chaos even extended to the Broken Hill silver mines, where the owners suspended all work due to the fact, they said, that bullion couldn't be shipped.

The strikes spread like wildfire and eventually involved over 50,000 workers of all kinds. A brawl in Sydney saw the Riot Act read out, and bitterness grew in pace with the privations the strikers began to suffer. Thanks to that huge donation to the London dockers in 1889, union funds couldn't meet the demand for strike pay on the home front.

The strikes, which had begun early in August of 1890, rolled on until the end of October, when the unions crumbled in the face of more than obdurate employers and lack of money; the whole continent was now feeling the escalating economic crisis. By mid-November the wharf laborers, coal miners and others were forced to return to work with their demands unmet. Employers won a great victory, for they came out of those terrible three months with the right to hire non-union labor, even in industries that until now had been closed shops. The last to yield were the shearers of sheep.

Alexander had closed the Apocalypse Mine completely when the silver mines at Broken Hill shut down, pleading the same excuse: he couldn't ship his bullion. About the colliers at his Lithgow mine Alexander didn't care, but he was too astute to punish his Kinross workers, to whom he paid a subsistence wage slightly higher than union strike pay. Luck had been on his side; when the nation went back to work, Alexander's economy measures seemed pale.

KINROSS HAD become a distant memory for Bede Talgarth. He licked his wounds along with the rest of the labor movement, and turned his attention to the next elections for the New South Wales Legislative Assembly, which was the elected lower house. They weren't due until 1892, but now was the time for planning. The three-month nationwide strikes had crippled many families on the breadline, and he was going to be one of the men who, by legislation, would take them off the breadline.

A forward-thinking man, he considered the Sydney electorates wherein a Labor candidate stood a chance; they were many, as Sydney now held almost half a million people. Inner-city venues like Redfern, almost certain to return a Labor man, were so hotly contested by senior Labor men that Bede knew he'd lose the race to be Labor's official candidate. Therefore he would stand for a more marginal seat, and decided to go just southwest of the dreary industrial wastelands around the filthy rivers that trickled into Botany Bay. Here he thought he'd get enough votes in the Labor pre-selection ballot, then enough votes in the state elections themselves to be returned as a Member of the Legislative Assembly. Mind made up, he moved to his chosen electorate and worked with indefatigable energy to become a well-known figure there—warm, passionate, caring.

THE MOMENT the strikes were over Alexander packed his trunks and took ship for San Francisco. Much to his displeasure, Ruby flatly refused to go with him.

Three

DISASTER

NELL'S FIFTEENTH birthday was, in her opinion, a disaster. A letter had come from her father that told her he had undergone a change of mind; she would now wait until 1892 to commence engineering at Sydney University. The four boys, older than she, would also wait out this year of 1891 in Kinross so that the five of them would, as originally planned, go up together.

"I think it's important that I be in Kinross and Sydney when you start at university," said his neat, straight up-and-down handwriting. "Of course I realize that this postponement won't come as a joy to you, but button down your feelings and accept my decision, Nell. It's made in your best interests."

Nell went straight to her mother brandishing the letter like a rioter a flaming torch.

"What did you say to him?" the girl demanded, face scarlet.

"I beg your pardon?" Elizabeth asked blankly.

"What did you say to him when you wrote to him?"

"Wrote to whom? Your father?"

"Oh, for Christ's sake, Mum, stop acting the fool!"

"I don't care for your tone or your language, Nell, and I have absolutely no idea what you're talking about."

"This!" Nell cried, shaking the letter under Elizabeth's nose. "Daddy says I can't start engineering this year, I have to wait until I'm sixteen!"

"Oh, thank God for that!" said Elizabeth, sighing in relief.

"What an actress you are! As if you didn't know! Well, you do know! It was you made him change his mind—what did you say?"

"You have my word, Nell, that I have said nothing whatsoever."

"*Your word!* What a laugh! You're the most dishonest woman I know, Mum, and that's a fact. The only pleasure you get out of life is making mischief for me with Daddy!"

"You are mistaken," said Elizabeth woodenly, withdrawing. "I cannot pretend that I'm not glad you have to wait, but it's not of my doing. If you doubt me, go and talk to Auntie Ruby."

But the tears wouldn't be stemmed another instant; Nell ran from the conservatory bawling like a six-year-old.

"Her father has spoiled her," said Mrs. Surtees, an involuntary witness of this outburst. "It is a pity, Lady Kinross, because she is a nice girl at heart. Very unselfish."

"I know," said Elizabeth, looking despondent.

"She'll get over it," Mrs. Surtees said, and departed.

Yes, she'll get over it, Elizabeth thought, but she won't like me any better once she does. I can't seem to find the key to Nell. The trouble is, I suppose, that she's so far on her father's side that I am to blame for anything and everything that doesn't meet with her approval. Poor little thing! She topped the state in her matriculation exams last November, so what on earth can she do to keep her mind occupied for another year? I think that Alexander came to this decision not so much for Nell's sake as because he must have realized that the four boys aren't up to it yet. And if they don't go, Nell can't go. But why didn't he explain that to her? If he had, she'd surely not blame me. A rhetorical question, really. Alexander does whatever he can to keep Nell and me apart.

Nor was it any use going to Ruby for comfort; she had made it up with Alexander, albeit at a distance. When he did come home they would fall into each other's arms like Venus and Mars. A shiver of fear rippled down Elizabeth's backbone. With Ruby to come home to, Alexander might well return earlier than planned.

WITHIN TEN minutes of that encounter with Nell, Elizabeth confronted another member of her feminine family. Jade.

"Miss Lizzy, please may I speak to you for a moment?" Jade asked, standing in the conservatory doorway.

How peculiar! thought Elizabeth, staring at her. Pretty, eternally youthful Jade looked ninety years old.

"Come in and sit down, Jade."

Jade sidled in, perched herself on the edge of a white cane chair and squeezed her hands together in her lap, trembling.

"My dear, what is it?" Elizabeth asked, sitting beside her.

"It's Anna, Miss Lizzy."

"Oh, don't tell me she's run off again!"

"No, Miss Lizzy."

"Then what is wrong with Anna?" It was not an anxious query; only yesterday, during her shift with Anna, she had thought how well the girl looked—clear skin, lustrous eyes. At thirteen and three-quarters, Anna was settling into physical maturity far more easily than Nell. If only she didn't behave so atrociously while she had her courses!

Jade managed to speak. "I suppose it's all the fuss we've had in the last few months—strikes—Sir Alexander going away—" Jade stopped, licked her lips, started to shake rather than tremble.

"Tell me, Jade. Whatever it is, I won't be annoyed."

"Anna hasn't had her courses in four months, Miss Lizzy."

Eyes wide, jaw dropped, Elizabeth gazed at Jade in dawning horror. "She's missed *three times?*"

"Or four. As best I can remember, Miss Lizzy. I dread her courses so much that I don't want to think of them. My sweet baby held down, fed opium, screaming—I put them out of my mind! Until today, when she said, 'Anna no bleed anymore.'"

Chilled to the bone, a weight on her chest heavier than lead, Elizabeth got to her feet and flew up the stairs, forcing her pace to a walk as she neared Anna's room.

The girl was sitting on the floor playing with a heap of daisies she had gathered out of the lawn; Jade had taught her to poke a slit in their stems and thread them together to form a chain. Elizabeth surveyed her through new eyes. Anna is a woman in full bloom. A beautiful face and body, a beautiful innocence because the mind belongs to a three-year-old. Anna, my Anna! What have they done to you? You're *thirteen*!

"Mum!" said Anna cheerfully, extending her daisy chain.

"Yes, it's lovely, dear. Thank you." Elizabeth looped the flowers around her neck and went to Anna to lift her to her feet. "Jade just found a tick in the daisies—tick! Nasty old bitey tick. We have to see if you got a tick on you, so will you take off your clothes?"

"Erk! Nasty tick!" said Anna, who remembered the occasion when she had had a tick embedded in her arm. "Calamine!" she squealed. A three-syllable word of great importance to Anna, who knew that it took the itch and sting out of hurties.

"Yes, Jade has the calamine. Take off all your clothes for me, dear, please. We have to look for the tick."

"No want! Anna no bleed."

"Yes, I know that. For the tick, Anna, please."

"No!" said Anna, looking mutinous.

"Then let's see if we can find the tick where you don't have any clothes. If we don't find it, we'll play at taking off your clothes a bit at a time until we do find it. All right?"

And so it went until even Anna's drawers came off, her clothes folded neatly in a pile as Jade had taught her over years of patient persistence.

The two women looked first at the naked Anna, then at each other. A beautiful body whose ordinarily flat belly was definitely starting to swell; full and perfect breasts whose nipples had turned dark brown, engorged.

"We should have continued to bathe her no matter how much she objected," Elizabeth said dully. "But one doesn't see into the future." She kissed Anna on the forehead tenderly. "Thank you, dear. You were lucky. No nasty bitey tick. Put your clothes on, there's a good girl."

Clothes on again, Anna went back to her daisies.

"How far along do you think she is?" Elizabeth asked Jade outside in the hall.

"Closer to five than four months, Miss Lizzy."

The tears were streaming down her face, but Elizabeth didn't notice them. "Oh, my poor baby! Jade, Jade, what can we do?"

"Ask Miss Ruby," said Jade, weeping too.

Anger came, so violent that Elizabeth shuddered. "I knew Alexander was wrong! I knew we had to replace Dragonfly! Oh, what *fools* men are! He actually thought that he could throw the mantle of his power over my beautiful, desirable, innocent child! Damn him to hell!"

Nell came down the hall in time to hear this, looking as if her temper had cooled enough to believe that her mother wasn't the cause of her deprivation. "Mum, what is it? You're not crying because I shouted at you, are you?"

"Anna is pregnant," said Elizabeth, wiping her eyes.

Nell tottered, held herself up by leaning on the wall. "Oh, Mum, no! It can't be! Who would do that to *Anna*?"

"Some filthy mongrel who deserves to have it cut off!" said Elizabeth savagely. She turned to Jade. "Stay with her, please. Nell, you're reinforcements. She's not to be let wander."

"Maybe she ought to be let wander," said Nell, white-faced. "Then we might catch the bastard."

"I'd say he's gone. If he didn't abscond weeks ago, he'd certainly see her pregnancy for himself now and be off."

"What are you going to do, Mum?"

"See Ruby. Perhaps we can get rid of the thing."

"It's too late!" Nell and Jade cried in unison to Elizabeth's back. "It's too late for that!"

WHICH WAS what Ruby said after a fierce bout of lurid cursing. "What on earth got into you and Jade?" she asked, fists clenched. "How did you let her miss so many times, for God's sake?"

"In all honesty, I think because it's such a nightmare when she has her courses—we dread them so much that we don't want to think about them, let alone expect them. Besides, she does miss from time to time, she's not regular," said Elizabeth. "And who would—who would ever have dreamed of this? It's *rape,* Ruby!"

"*I* would have dreamed of it!" Ruby snapped.

Somehow it mattered to have Ruby's good opinion; Elizabeth battled on. "Things have been so hectic, and Alexander so hard to live with, between his arrogance, Lee's defection, his wanting to get away, and the friction between him and you—"

"Oh, I see! It's my fault, is it?"

"No, no, it's my fault, entirely my fault! I'm her mother, she's my responsibility!" Elizabeth cried. "I blame myself, no one else! Poor Jade is beside herself."

"And so are you," said Ruby, calming down enough to go to the sideboard and pour two large cognacs. "Brandy, Elizabeth, and no arguments. Drink."

Elizabeth drank, felt a little stronger. "What do we do?"

"Put getting rid of it out of your mind, for one thing. If she's closer to five months than to four, she could die. You get rid of them at six weeks—even ten weeks is risky. And thirteen is so young! Though Sir Edward Wyler's son might be willing to operate. He did take over his father's practice, didn't he?"

"Yes. Simon Wyler."

"I'll telegram him, but don't hold out any hopes. I doubt a medical practitioner in good standing would consent to do it, even given the circumstances." Ruby drew in a breath. "And Alexander will have to be told, even if he decides not to come home for the birth of his first grandchild."

"Dear God! He'll be livid, Ruby."

"Oh, yes, he'll be livid."

"What torments me most is what the baby might be like."

"The baby might be quite normal, Elizabeth, if Anna is the way she is because of her birth." Ruby gave a snort of hysterical laughter. "Jesus, what an irony! Alexander might get his male heir from his mental daughter and some filthy fucking shit-arsed mongrel who preys on defenseless children." Her laughter grew wilder, she shrieked with it until the tears came and she bolted into Elizabeth's arms to howl herself into heaving silence. "My dear, my so very dear Elizabeth," she said then, "what else is left for you to go through? If I could, I'd take it all away from you and bear it myself. You've never harmed a fly, I'm a whore pushing fifty."

"There's one other thing, Ruby."

"What?"

"Finding the man who did this."

"Ah!" Ruby sat up, found her handkerchief and mopped at the remains of her grief. "I doubt we ever will, Elizabeth, because I've never heard so much as a whisper that anyone was interfering with Anna. This is a small town, and I sit at the heart of it. Between the public bar, the saloon bar and the dining room, I hear everything. I can't credit that he's a local—no local would dare, he'd be lynched. Everyone local knows her age! My guess is a commercial traveler—they come and go so often that it's hard to keep track of them, never the same man for the same company twice in a row. Rifle salesmen, saddlers, hawkers and hustlers of everything from ointments and tonics to bottles of scent and gimcrack jewelry. Yes, a commercial traveler."

"He should be found and prosecuted. *Hanged!*"

"That's not sensible." The green eyes grew severe. "Use your brains, Elizabeth! Your private sorrow would become everybody's business and rags like *Truth* would have a field day with Sir Alexander Kinross's dirty washing."

"I see," Elizabeth whispered. "Yes, I see."

"Go home. I'll send a telegram to Dr. Simon Wyler and get out the code book to send a cable to Alexander. This is one item of news he won't want spelled in English. Go, dear, please go! Anna needs you."

* * *

ELIZABETH WENT, still shattered, but feeling that she could now cope with this disaster. The brandy had helped, but not as much as Ruby had. Practical, immensely experienced, down to earth. Though Ruby hadn't seen this coming either; if she had she would have spoken up. That's a comfort. We trust too much, we think that all the world will pity and protect these poor unfortunates as we do. It is no fault of theirs that they are what they are. But what a world is this, that it holds monsters who care only for their carnal satisfaction, who can think of a female human being as no more than a vessel. My darling child, a mere thirteen years old! My darling child, who won't even know what has happened to her, nor understand when we try to tell her. We must get her through this—how, I do not know. Do cows and cats have any comprehension of what is happening to them when they conceive? But Anna isn't a cow or a cat, she's a damaged thirteen-year-old, so I can't hope that she will deal with her labor the way cows and cats do. The pregnancy, perhaps. Knowing Anna, she'll simply think she's getting fat—or does she even know what getting fat is?

"We will treat it as if it's natural and nothing to worry about," Elizabeth said to Jade and Nell when she returned. "If she complains about finding it hard to move around, we'll tell her that it will pass. She's had no vomiting, Jade?"

"None, Miss Lizzy. If she had, I might have wondered sooner."

"Then she's carrying very easily. We'll see what Dr. Simon Wyler says, but I doubt she's pre-eclamptic like me."

"I will find out who did it," said Jade grimly.

"Miss Ruby says that's not possible, Jade, and she's right. It was some commercial traveler who's long gone. No local man would interfere with Anna."

"I will find out."

"None of us is going to have the time for that. Our job is caring for Anna," said Elizabeth.

Nell found it hardest to accept Anna's plight; for all of her conscious life Anna had been there, no sisterly companion, yet in her way something more. A helpless creature harder to train than a pet animal, utterly lovable because all of her that was, was gentle, sweet, smiling. Anna never had moods, and the only thing that upset her was bleeding. Kiss Anna, and she would kiss you back. Laugh, and she would laugh.

Perhaps it was Anna had inspired Nell to concentrate on the brain in her reading; so many mysteries to plumb! But there had been discoveries, and there would be many more. Maybe one day there would be a cure for people like Anna. How wonderful if she, Nell, could be a part of that cure! Which didn't stop Nell going to her room and weeping desolately. Anna's loss of innocence was the loss of her own.

DR. SIMON WYLER was rather different from his father; less suave, more abrupt. But clever enough to know instinctively how to deal with Anna. First he did what Elizabeth, Jade and Nell had avoided doing: question her about what had happened.

"Did you meet someone when you ran away, Anna?"

A frown, a look of bewilderment.

"Walking, Anna, in the bush. You like to walk in the bush?"

"Yes!"

"What do you do in the bush?"

"Pick flowers. See kangaroos—jump, jump!"

"Just flowers and kangaroos? See anyone else?"

"Nice man."

"Does he have a name, the nice man?"

"Nice man."

"Bob? Bill? Wally?"

"Nice man, nice man."

"Did you play with the nice man?"

"Best play! Cuddles. Best cuddles."

"Is the nice man still there, Anna?"

She grimaced, looked unhappy. "Nice man gone. No cuddles."

"How long?"

But that, Anna couldn't say. Just that the nice man was gone.

Dr. Wyler then proceeded to persuade Anna to show him how she and the nice man had cuddled; to her mother's horror she lay on her bed and let Dr. Wyler remove her drawers, spreading her legs apart without his encouragement.

"Pretend I'm the nice man, Anna. He did this—and this—and this, didn't he?"

The examination was gentle and kept as much as possible to Anna's definition of cuddles; if Elizabeth had thought that her appalled mortification could grow no worse, she was mistaken as she watched her thirteen-year-old daughter begin to writhe with pleasure and moan.

"All done, Anna," the obstetrician said. "Sit up and put on your drawers."

His eyes encountered Jade, and he shivered as if touched by a dead and icy hand. Then Jade rushed to the bed, helped Anna to put on her drawers.

"She's about five months, Lady Kinross," Dr. Wyler said as he sipped gratefully at his cup of tea in the conservatory.

"You won't get rid of it?" Elizabeth asked, face flinty.

"No, I can't do that," he said gently. Who could blame the poor woman for asking?

"She—enjoyed it, didn't she?"

"It would seem so. The fellow must have been an adept at seducing young virgins, and had some intelligence." He put the cup down and leaned forward, grey eyes compassionate. "Anna is a complete contradiction. Her mind is that of a toddler, but her bodily responses are those of a maturing young woman. He taught her to like what he did, even if perhaps the first time wasn't all that pleasant for her. Though that may not have been. Anna knows nothing of what women fear, so may not have experienced any pain. Especially if the man was an adept."

"I see," said Elizabeth, throat tight. "Are you trying to tell me that, once this business is over, Anna will seek it?"

"I honestly don't know, Lady Kinross. I wish I did."

"How do we deal with her labor when it comes?"

"I think I have to be here. Luckily my father is still very capable of practicing, and I don't think any of my patients will object to his attending them in my stead."

"And what of the baby? Will it be like Anna?"

"Probably not," said Simon Wyler with the air of someone who has already considered the question carefully. "If Anna delivers fairly easily, the baby ought to fare well. Everything is quite as it should be at this stage, certainly. Were I a betting man, I'd take a punt on a healthy baby with an intact brain."

Elizabeth refilled his cup and pressed a petit-four on him. "If indeed Anna should seek—pleasure—in time to come, is there any way to prevent her falling pregnant again?"

"Sterilization, you mean?"

"Do I? It's not a word I know."

"To sterilize Anna, Lady Kinross, I would have to perform very major surgery—open her abdomen and remove her ovaries. The risk is extremely high. We do Caesarean sections nowadays if no other alternative is available, and perhaps half the women live. Sterilization would be done well after childbirth, but it isn't as easy as removing a baby from a womb. The ovaries lie deep. Anna is young and strong, but I would advise against sterilization, madam."

"The alternative is a kind of imprisonment."

"Yes, I know. You will have to make absolutely sure that Anna is accompanied on all her excursions. In my view, vigilance will be as effective as sterilization."

And with that, Elizabeth had to be content. Dr. Wyler was right, she couldn't subject Anna to such a surgical risk, nor put her behind genuine bars. We must be vigilant, always vigilant, and I will have Dragonfly back no matter what Alexander says about economizing. Oh, Alexander, come home! How can I explain all of this in a coded cable at one shilling per word?

Ruby greeted her with Alexander's response to the earlier cable when Elizabeth reached the hotel. "He says we're to handle it. *He* can't leave whatever it is he's doing. Fucking bastard!"

"Would you mind encoding this?" Elizabeth handed over two pages of her handwriting, small and cramped. "I know it's terribly long, but I need Alexander's advice on Dr. Wyler's report. If I decide on a course without consulting him, he'll be furious."

"I'd code the Bible for you, Elizabeth, you know that." Ruby took the sheets and read them swiftly. "Jesus, it goes on and on, doesn't it? Poor, poor Anna!"

"We'll come through it, Ruby. But I'm not going to have Alexander say we didn't explain every ramification."

"I suspect from the tone of his first answer that he's very shaken, though he won't admit it." Ruby put the papers down and lit a cheroot. "How, I don't know, but the word of what's happened to Anna is out," she said. "People are boiling about it—I've never seen such a mood of anger. Even the ministers of religion have forgotten the bit about turning the other cheek. If we did know who it was, he'd be lynched. I've had Theodora in tears, Mrs. Wilkins asking me how to word a leaflet to be distributed to every family with young girls, and Sung sharpening his beheading axe. White or Chinese, everyone is foaming at the mouth." She emitted a gush of smoke, looking very dragonish. "But no one can come up with a name. Usually in situations like this—no, I mean in situations that create such outrage—some poor coot is tagged as the culprit for no good reason except he's disliked. But not this time. Kinross doesn't have one of those perverts who try to kiss or fondle girls, so, like me, the general consensus is that it was a commercial traveler who hasn't been back."

"There's one thing wrong with that," said Elizabeth. "Surely to give poor little Anna so much familiar pleasure in what he did, he had to have done it many more times than once. Commercial travelers never stay more than two days."

"Yes, but they're a club. The word about Anna might have spread among them—her 'nice man' might have been a dozen 'nice men,'" Ruby said, keen on this theory.

"I don't believe that. I believe it's someone local, and so does Jade," said Elizabeth, looking stubborn.

JADE DID INDEED believe that Anna's molester was someone from Kinross. Though Anna was Miss Lizzy's baby, both had been so ill that it had fallen to Jade to be Anna's mother. Unmarried she might be, but Jade was not without some sexual experience that dated back to early years before taking service with Miss Ruby in Hill End. Prince Sung had decreed that she go into service with Miss Ruby, and had chosen Pink Bird from among the seven Wong sisters to be his concubine. Had Jade asked for a husband, one would have been found for her, but after weighing the alternatives, Jade had decided on service as the easier life. Then Miss Lizzy had come along, and she transferred from Miss Ruby to Miss Lizzy, a kinder mistress. Having Anna as her own was like having a baby without the pain of birth or the awful nuisance of a father. No amount of hard work or long hours could matter to Jade, who loved the feeble, mewling little scrap as her own from the first day of Anna's existence. Nor did it ever occur to Jade to condemn Miss Lizzy for those first months of indifference to Anna; Miss Lizzy had had a hard time of it, and Mr. Alexander was not the husband or father of her choice. How Jade knew that was a mystery, for at no time had Miss Lizzy said anything, or given away what she felt by some facial expression. She also knew—again, how was a mystery—that Miss Lizzy was attracted to Lee, and that Lee was in love with her. Considering that Jade's life went on in Anna's domain, it was remarkable how much Jade knew.

Nothing in a household can be hidden from its old retainers, who are a part of the family in every way. Jade was the oldest and most faithful retainer, more attached to Anna than even Butterfly Wing was to Nell. And Jade knew what Elizabeth couldn't bear to know: that Anna's fate hung in the balance. Anna had a father, a father as powerful and imperious as Prince Sung, and he would see what had happened to Anna in a very different way from the way of women. Under the eternal law of all races, he would make the decisions. When Anna turned out to be mental, he had been so understanding, so merciful. But that was twelve years ago, and Mr. Alexander was not the same man he had been then. If Miss Lizzy had loved him—but Miss Lizzy did not. He would sit as a judge in a high elaborate chair removed from the sphere of women, and consider the case with the utmost dispassion, his intent to make a reasonable and logical decision according to the lights of men. How then to say that a reasonable and logical decision could break hearts? How to prevent him from committing Anna to an asylum?

Too beside herself to weep, Jade lay at night in her bed in Anna's room listening to the soft breathing of her grown-up baby, and resolved that she would find the man who had destroyed Anna's world, Anna's chance at happiness as one of the innocents.

"Miss Lizzy," she said to Elizabeth after Dr. Wyler's visit, "I need a holiday. Hung Chee in the Chinese medicine shop says I have a broken-down heart and must undergo the needles. I've spoken to Butterfly Wing, who is happy to take over my duties—Nell doesn't need her much, and she feels it badly."

"Of course, Jade," Elizabeth said, then looked fearful. "I hope you are still paid for your holidays? Mr. Alexander hasn't been himself about wages lately."

"Oh, yes, Miss Lizzy, I will be paid."

"Out of curiosity, how much are you girls paid?"

"More than Mr. Alexander's mining supervisors. He says we're harder to find and must be looked after."

"Thank God for that! Do you have any idea where you'd like to go for your holiday?"

Jade looked surprised. "Into Kinross, Miss Lizzy. I have to be treated with the needles. I'm going to stay with Miss Theodora, who is going to paint her house. I can help."

"That is *not* a holiday, Jade."

But Jade had gone, jubilant at how easily her first task had been done. She packed a valise and took the cable car down to the town, where a slightly bewildered Theodora Jenkins awaited her.

Though the days of giving piano lessons at Kinross House were in the past, thanks to Nell's outstripping her teacher and Elizabeth's loss of interest after Anna's birth, Theodora Jenkins had settled very comfortably into her Kinross life. Dear Sir Alexander gave her a generous pension—quite what for, she had no idea—and still allowed her free tenancy of her beloved little house. She gave piano and singing lessons when she felt a child showed promise, played the magnificent organ at St. Andrew's, and belonged to every club and society in town, from gardening to amateur dramatics. Her bread was famous and carried off first prize every year at the Kinross Show, though, gentle and grateful creature that she was, she gave the credit for her baking to the cast-iron cooking range Sir Alexander had placed in her kitchen.

He was such a mixture, Sir Alexander. Theodora suspected that if he liked you, he would do anything for you, but that if he did not like you, or you were just one of a large number of employees, he would do nothing for you beyond ensure that the town you lived in, namely Kinross, was superior to every other country town. And that was still true, despite the cut in Chinese workers who kept Kinross town looking good and functioning well.

Jade had come to her and asked if she might stay for a few days while Hung Chee in the Chinese medicine shop treated her broken-down heart. The request had surprised Theodora, who wondered why Jade hadn't gone to Ruby at the hotel, or else just went up and down the mountain on the cable car. However, Ruby had a reputation as a hard mistress, and perhaps having dozens of needles stuck in you made trips on the cable car an unpleasant experience. Whatever. Theodora Jenkins only knew that no one was ever going to stick *her* full of needles!

"Such a terrible business, Jade," she said over a scratch supper of bubble-and-squeak. "I'm not surprised it's affected you so badly, dear."

"Hung Chee says I would improve if we found out who did it," said Jade, who loved bubble-and-squeak.

"I know what he means, but, alas, no one has any idea, none at all." Theodora looked at Jade's empty plate. "My goodness, cooking for one means I never cook enough for two! Would you like some fried bread, Jade? Or some buttered pound cake?"

"Buttered pound cake, please, Miss Theodora. Tomorrow I'll cook Chinese pork and egged rice, and coconut bean curd for our dessert."

"What a delightful change! I look forward to it."

"You must know everyone in Kinross, Miss Theodora, and better than Miss Ruby does too. She sees the men who go to the hotel for a drink, but there are a lot of people who can't afford to eat in her dining room, even on special occasions, and Miss Ruby doesn't go to church on Sundays either," said Jade, scoffing cake thickly slathered with butter.

"That's true," said Theodora.

"Then you must think, Miss Theodora. Think about every single person who lives in Kinross or visits regularly."

"I have already, Jade."

"Not hard enough," said Jade, sounding inexorable.

She left it at that and let Theodora proceed to discuss the painting of her cottage, which turned out to be its exterior.

"Sam has agreed to do it for me—cream with a brown trim. I have the paint and the brushes and the sandpaper for him, just as he asked. He starts tomorrow."

"Sam?" Jade asked, frowning. "Sam who?"

"Sam O'Donnell. He was one of the miners dear Sir Alexander let go last July. The rest moved to Broken Hill or Mount Morgan, but Sam decided to stay here. Well, he's single and not a drinker—goes to Evensong on Sunday nights at St. Andrew's and sings *beautifully* in alto. Scripps the painter is hopeless—so sad, Jade, to think that some men would rather guzzle drink than look after their own families! So Sam paints houses he can manage on his own, and does odd jobs when he hasn't any houses to paint. He'll chop wood, dig your potatoes, lump coal." Theodora turned pink, tittered. "He's always happy to do things for me because I give him a loaf of my bread as well as the few shillings he asks for his work. He asks twenty pounds to paint a house and do it properly—you know, burn the old paint off and scrape all the boards down, then sand them. Very reasonable. Since dear Sir Alexander lets me live here, I feel that it behooves me to care for the place at my expense."

"Where does Sam live?" asked Jade, trying to picture him.

"He camps out by the dam, I believe. He has a big, strange-looking dog named Rover, and the two are inseparable. You'll meet Sam and Rover tomorrow."

The name had finally found a reference in Jade's memory. "Sam

O'Donnell. Isn't he the one who brought in that union man, Bede Whatsit, just before the big strikes?"

"I wouldn't know, dear, though I understand that the miners don't like him. Everybody else does—I mean the women of Kinross, who often find it hard to dig their potatoes or chop wood. Sam is indispensable to a lot of women, particularly those like me who do not have a husband to help."

"It sounds as if Sam likes to charm women," said Jade.

Theodora took on the mien of an agitated fowl. "No, no, it isn't like that!" she cried. "Sam is an absolute gentleman—for instance, he would never come inside a woman's house, just leans through the kitchen window to get his tea and bikkies." Horror dawned. "Jade! You're surely not thinking that *Sam* is the one? He isn't, I swear he isn't! Sam is very kind to women and very respectful, but I always have the feeling that he's not—well, *interested* in women, if you know what I mean."

"Young men? Little boys?" asked Jade.

Theodora squawked and fluttered madly. "Jade! *Really!* No, I do not mean that! I mean that he's happy with his life the way it is, I suppose. There are several widows who have made—er—overtures to him, but he turns them aside so tactfully that no one is hurt. Mrs. Hardacre is quite young and pretty and has a considerable amount of money, but Sam wouldn't even paint her house."

"You defend him so well, Miss Theodora, that I must accept your judgment of him."

Theodora got up to clear the dishes, suddenly sorry that she had allowed Jade to stay with her. What if Jade was nasty to dear Sam, or asked impertinent questions? The last thing in the world Theodora wanted was to drive away her house painter and odd-job man. Oh dear, oh dear!

WHEN SAM O'DONNELL turned up at seven the next morning to start stripping the old paint off Theodora's house, Jade was by Theodora's side to welcome him.

Very handsome in a white man's way, she decided. Tall, a graceful mover with the overly long, sinewy arms of someone who had shorn sheep for a number of years, fair hair, and endowed with a pair of twinkling eyes whose color changed—blue, grey, green. They slid over Jade without lighting up as the eyes of a man who lusts after women do, and not because she was Chinese. Jade was still a beautiful woman, and the white blood in her gave her large, well-opened eyes the look of a deer—she knew she was as attractive to white men as she was to Chinese. But Sam O'Donnell was unmoved. His manner toward Theodora, who had turned twittery at the sight of him, was impeccable. He gave her no hope whatsoever, yet was warmly friendly.

In his wake stalked a big dog of the very new kind specially bred to heel cattle—a dappled blue-grey coat and a black head containing a large brain pan. The animal's amber eyes were alert, watchful, slightly sinister. As if it knew it had to behave, but some primitive instinct inside it hungered to tear throats.

Sam checked what Theodora had assembled, nodded and unearthed a blowtorch from his tool bag. "Thanks, Miss Jay, she's apples," he said, beginning to fill the blowtorch's reservoir with spirits.

Obviously they were dismissed. Theodora went back into the house, Jade following her with a backward look. But Sam O'Donnell was not staring after them; he was still preparing his blowtorch. No, sighed Jade to herself, I don't think it's Sam O'Donnell.

For seven days she prowled the town, including the Chinese village and Sung's pagoda city hill, talking to every person she encountered, even if some of the whites and Chinese didn't want to talk to her. Prejudice from both races was a part of Jade's inheritance, so her skin was thick and her persistence oblivious to lack of co-operation. Probe, pick, push. Jade on this errand was not to be deflected.

She asked about Sam O'Donnell, with mixed results. The wives of miners spoke of him scathingly, whereas most Kinrossians not concerned with actual mining spoke of him favorably. The Reverend Mr. Peter Wilkins, caught titivating the altar, knew Jade well as Anna's attendant who always stood outside St. Andrew's church gate and waited for morning service to be over. He was happy to discuss the subject of Anna's seducer, but had nothing to offer. Of Sam O'Donnell he said,

"A good chap, always comes to Evensong rather than the morning service. Despite his actions when the miners were laid off, he *is* a good chap. He used to be a shearer, and they're always militant in union matters, Jade."

"Do you think he's a good chap because he goes to Evensong?" Jade asked, her humble tone stripping the question of offense.

"No, I don't," the minister said. "Sam's a good person. I had a plague of rats in the rectory just after half the town employees were laid off, and he got rid of them in two days. We've not seen a rat since. He fulfills a necessary function in Kinross by doing all the odd jobs one cannot find a Chinese to do. No insult is intended, Jade. The Chinese like permanent work."

"I understand, Mr. Wilkins. Thank you," said Jade.

Even so, she kept a wary eye on Sam O'Donnell as he assaulted the exterior of Theodora's house, working so hard that Jade wondered why some miners called him lazy. Perhaps, she thought, Sam O'Donnell had liked the money gold mining had paid him, yet hated to be underground? So after the union man Bede Whatsit left, Sam discovered a niche in Kinross that no other man wanted. He was in the fresh air, he could have his dog at his side all the time, and, if Theodora Jenkins was any guide, he ate better than campers usually did. Even the dog was the recipient of scraps and bones from the butcher. If he had a fault, it was that suddenly he would exclaim that he had to nip over to Mrs. Murphy's or Mrs. Smith's to help her for a couple of hours, but he'd be back. He didn't lie; Jade followed him and verified that he did help them. Vexatious for Theodora, perhaps, in that his absences meant his work for her suffered a little. Not that Theodora complained.

Jade became used to the sight of him leaning in the kitchen window at ten in the morning and there in the afternoon, sipping at his enamel mug of steaming tea and crunching on the bikkies Theodora baked; for his lunch he took another mug of tea and two huge bread-and-butter-and-cheese sandwiches and ate them in the shade of a tree in Theodora's backyard. At the end of each day Theodora gifted him with a loaf of her wonderful bread, and off he would go, Rover at his heels, his tool bag in his hand, to walk the five miles back to his camp at the dam.

Never once, she thought as she took the cable car back to Kinross House at the end of her "holiday," had Sam O'Donnell or any other likely suspect given her an indication of guilt by word, look, or action.

AND SO THINGS might have stood forever were it not for Jim Summers, growing sourer and dourer with each passing year. His home life, it was common knowledge, was bitterly unhappy, Maggie Summers having retreated into a state bordering on dementia; at times she didn't know who Jim was, at other times she knew him and would fly at him tooth and nail. Summers had also witnessed his own eclipse in Alexander's estimation, especially after the advent of Lee. With Lee's defection, Alexander remembered that the faithful Summers existed, and had asked for his company on this latest trip when Ruby said no. But Summers had had to refuse; he couldn't leave Maggie unless he put her in an asylum, and that the poor fellow just could not bring himself to do. Her life had been a series of disappointments, and though Alexander argued that she was too far gone to know where she was, Jim Summers remembered the asylum in Paris where he and his mother had visited her demented sister. When he wouldn't budge, Alexander was not pleased.

Just when Jade's suspicions shifted from Sam O'Donnell to Jim Summers she didn't know, save that a tiny succession of events finally added up to his guilt. The first, that she caught him trying to rape her second-youngest sister, Peach Blossom, who escaped with her virtue intact thanks to Jade's intercession. The second, that she saw the expression in his eyes when he watched Elizabeth walk in the garden. The third, that he looked at her, Jade, with hatred for spoiling his fun with Peach Blossom. And the fourth, that he was a little too familiar with Nell while helping her to mount a fractious horse; Nell had retaliated by lashing his face with her riding crop.

Jim Summers! Yes, why not? Why should years of constant service preclude him? He had access to everything, to every part of Mount Kinross, from its forests and bridle paths to the house itself. He had once lived on its third floor. His wife had once been housekeeper. And now his wife was incapable of fulfilling her marital duties, yet he didn't dare avail himself of the doxies who lived in a big house on Kinross's outskirts, and teetered there precariously as the town became more and more respectable, more and more at the command of God's moral police.

So Jade set out to stalk Jim Summers while ever he was on the mountain rather than at the works below. It was easier to do this because the rudderless Butterfly Wing grabbed eagerly at the offer to share custody of Anna, Dragonfly was back, and Elizabeth too took her turn in the nursery.

THE NURSERY had turned into a childing room, Dr. Wyler having insisted that everything be ready in case Anna went into an early labor. The most competent of the Wong girls, Pearl, had learned to drip chloroform on to a gauze muzzle at the right rate to ensure anesthesia but not asphyxiation, and Dr. Burton had been instructed in the new technique in case Dr. Wyler wasn't there. Kinross also boasted a midwife these days,

Minnie Collins, who was, in Dr. Wyler's opinion after he talked to her, more equipped to deal with a difficult birth than old Doc Burton. Thus the room had a glass cabinet full of shiny instruments sitting in carbolic, as well as another cabinet containing bottles of chloroform, carbolic and alcohol. Carbolic-reeking drawers held linens and swabs as well as a number of gauze muzzles.

Anna herself was more patient with her condition than anyone had expected; as her body swelled she became proud of it, would display it on the slightest provocation. When the baby kicked inside her, she shouted in glee. But she had taken against Nell, a painful business for Nell, who wanted desperately to help, to be a part of Anna's pregnancy and delivery.

Tired of mathematics, history, novels and anatomy, Nell moped until Ruby came to her rescue.

"It's high time you got some experience in the affairs of Apocalypse Enterprises," Ruby said to Nell in that tone that brooked no argument. "If Constance can learn to take Charles's place and Sophia's husband to take over the books, then you can certainly start learning to take Lee's place. You have a brain stuffed with theory, but now is the moment to learn to deal with facts. Sung, Constance and I have agreed that you should work five days a week—two in the town offices, three inspecting the mine, the refinery and the workshops. They aren't exactly new to you because Alexander used to cart you along whenever he could. If you're going to survive engineering at the university, you'd better know first what handling men who resent you will be like."

For Nell, salvation. She had soaked up engines and mines at her father's knee, then at his side, and, clad in a pair of baggy overalls—*shocking!*—soon proved to the men who eyed her in outrage that she knew one end of a locomotive from the other, and everything there was to know about cyanide refining. She could use a wrench with the best of them, didn't mind being covered in the new lubricating oils, and had an ear for flaws in metal as she tapped and clanged around a machine or train wheels. What had been male ire turned to admiration, the more so because Nell ignored the novelty of her sex and appeared to regard herself as one of the boys. She also had Alexander's innate authority; when she gave an order, she expected it to be obeyed because it was the right order; and if she didn't know the answer, she asked.

A boon for Elizabeth, who worried more about Nell than she did about Anna. It was Nell going into a man's world, and Nell who had the intelligence and sensitivity to suffer when she was repulsed. Though she had all of Alexander's steel, she had some of Elizabeth's enigmatic diffidence too, and while she wasn't close to her mother, Elizabeth understood her far better than Nell knew—or would have wanted. Daddy's girl, that was Nell, in exile because Daddy wasn't here. So to know that she was busy at Daddy's business was a relief.

AS ANNA approached her eighth month, which was March of 1891, her heaviness curtailed those long walks the women had insisted she take; there were no signs of pre-eclampsia, but the weight she had to carry around now made her fretful and difficult to entertain.

Jade's favorite place to put Anna when she was in attendance was the rose garden, in full late summer flower. There, after a short and gentle walk, Anna could be ensconced in a cane chair and kept amused by trying to guess the color of the roses. Though she understood the concept of color, she couldn't give a specific color a name. So Jade would make a game of it and have her giggling at the way she spoke the names of those colors.

"Maaaauve!" Jade would say, pointing to a bloom. "Piiiiink! Whiiiite! Yellllow! Creeeeam!"

Anna would repeat the sounds, but never remember which rose was mauve, which pink or cream. Still, it passed the time and kept her mind off her condition.

They were playing this game in the rose garden when Summers walked across the lawn some distance away; in his wake strolled a big blue cattle dog. Jade had heard that he now owned a dog, apparently for company; his wife liked the animal, a bonus.

Suddenly Anna squealed with joy and stretched out her arms. "Rover!" she cried. "Rover, Rover!"

The day went dark, as if the moon had drifted across the face of the blazing sun; Jade stood amid the roses and felt the full force of this innocent betrayal, discovered the awful difference between suspicion and certainty. Anna knew the name of Sam O'Donnell's dog.

But Anna didn't know Sam O'Donnell! During her week in the town, Jade had questioned everybody as to whom Anna met if she wandered into the town, who talked to her, who took charge of her and notified Kinross House. Suspicious of Sam O'Donnell, she had asked specifically about him, but he was not on the list of Anna Kinross's acquaintances. If she did get as far as the town, she headed for Ruby at the hotel or the Reverend Wilkins at the rectory. Was *that* where? When O'Donnell had been getting rid of the rats? Not according to the minister, anyway, and he would remember. Yet Anna knew the name of Sam O'Donnell's dog, and that meant she knew Sam O'Donnell very well.

"Rover! Rover!" Anna was still calling, arms extended.

"Mr. Summers!" Jade shouted.

He came over, the dog at his heels.

"Is this Rover?" Jade asked as the dog, an amiable creature, went straight to Anna and responded to her ecstatic greeting with slurps and whipping tail wags.

"No, its name's Bluey," said Summers, whose expression didn't alter. "Bluey, Anna, not Rover."

Summers did not know the name of Sam O'Donnell's dog. Feeling as if she waded through a syrupy lake, Jade let Anna make a fuss of the dog, let her wave goodbye to Summers as he went on his way, and continued to play with Anna until lunch time. When Jade saw that Anna was becoming susceptible to the sun, for as they went inside she complained that her head was "sore."

"You're more patient with her when she's sick," Jade said to Butterfly Wing, hovering anxiously with a draft of laudanum. "Do you mind staying with her? I need to go into Kinross."

While Butterfly Wing administered the potion to Anna (who rather liked it, a blessing), Jade went to the bottle cabinet and took one marked CHLOROFORM. Then, as Butterfly Wing settled on the edge of Anna's bed to lay a cold wet cloth on her brow, Jade took one of the gauze muzzles from its drawer. It was all done so quickly that Butterfly Wing never looked around, even when Jade, burdened, closed the door too loudly.

How many times in her mind she must have thought about this! Every move had been plotted, every complication sorted out. Jade went about her purpose with the smooth ease of familiarity, from the nursery to a shed in the backyard wherein, years ago, Maggie Summers had determined Jade would live. After that it had been transformed into a temporary prison for an assistant cook who went mad and had to be confined until he could be manacled and taken off to an asylum, and a detention cell it had remained just in case. So its windows were barred and shuttered, its walls thickly padded with straw-filled canvas, and its bed was a heavy iron affair bolted to the floor. The bed had been stripped to its mattress, but Jade had brought linen with her, and made it up neatly. A table, a chair and a beside table with a drawer in it, all of iron bolted to the floor, completed the furnishings. Though scrubbed out many times, it retained a faint odor of feces and vomit; Jade opened all the windows and lit thin sticks of incense in an old jam jar on the table. Back and forth she trotted to the house kitchen, where Chang and his assistants thought nothing of her conduct, too used to her comings and goings. She took a small spirit stove fitted with a copper kettle for boiling water, some Chinese tea bowls and a packet of green tea.

The backyard was deserted, as this wasn't a washing day and all Chang's attention was focused on preparing dinner. Once she was satisfied at the appearance of the shed, its window shutters now closed and the room equipped with six kerosene lamps, Jade stole inside and went to her quarters. There she put on her most attractive dress, a slim tube of embroidered peacock-blue silk split up both sides of its skirt to enable her to walk. Under normal circumstances no Chinese woman would have worn such a dress in a white town, so Jade donned an overcoat despite the heat. She took a small bottle of laudanum from her bathroom cabinet and slipped it into one coat pocket.

Then, bold as brass, she asked for the cable car and went down into Kinross; it was nearly four in the afternoon, and she knew that Theodora Jenkins would be at St. Andrew's practicing on the organ for a special Sunday service, the last before the start of Lent. The mining shift wouldn't change until six, so she had the car to herself, noting that the poppet heads were relatively deserted. At the bottom she walked swiftly, avoiding Kinross Square, to the house of Theodora Jenkins.

Sam O'Donnell hadn't changed his schedule, which was to work until five every day, Monday to Friday; if he popped off to see someone else, it was always just after lunch, so he would be back. The dog growled before Jade came into view, so when she turned the corner Sam O'Donnell already knew someone was coming, and stood, brush in hand, expecting Theodora. When he saw Jade in an overcoat his brows flew up quizzically and he grinned, put the brush down carefully athwart his can of paint.

"Aren't you roasting in that?" he asked.

"Terribly, like being baked in an oven," said Jade. "Would you mind if I took my coat off, Sam?"

"Go ahead."

He hadn't thought Theodora's Chinesey friend—a half-caste, for sure—

attractive, but the moment she shrugged the coat off and revealed that incredible dress, he experienced a shaft of want he hadn't felt since he last saw Anna Kinross. The slut was really gorgeous! Her waist was tiny, her breasts pertly upright, and her legs shimmered in silk stockings to lacy garters above her knees, then displayed a tantalizing hint of sleek bare thighs. And her hair—straight, black, thick, as full of light as a racehorse's hide—hung down her back, tucked behind each perfect little ear. There were only two kinds of women appealed to Sam O'Donnell: virginal young girls and amateur sluts.

"Where are you off to in that?" he managed to say.

"Prince Sung's village, which is why I'm dressed like this. But I should have taken the pony trap, it's just too hot. So I thought I'd get a drink of water from Miss Theodora and go home."

"Miss Jay's not here, but her door's open."

For answer she put a delicate hand to her head, gasped and swayed as if about to faint. Sam O'Donnell caught her, held her, felt her trembling. Mistaking this revulsion for desire, he kissed her. Jade kissed him back in a way he had never experienced, for he was not a whoring man—was this what Chinese girls were like? What had he been missing all these years, thinking of them with contempt? A tight little cunt, if what they said about Chinese men was true—on the small side. What he couldn't know was that Jade had worked for Miss Ruby in her brothel days, and had heard—sometimes seen—everything.

"I want you," he whispered. "Jade, I want you!"

"And I want you," she whispered back, fingering his hair.

"I'll finish for the day and take you back to my camp."

"No, I have a better idea," she said. "I'll go home in the cable car, while you follow me on the snake path. I live in a shed in the backyard of Kinross House, not far from where the snake path ends. The staff will all be inside, so all you have to do is use the backyard buildings as a cover until you see my door—it's bright red, the only one that color."

"It would be safer at my camp," he demurred.

"I couldn't walk that far, I'm too frail, Sam." She put her tongue in his ear, then swept it across his jaw to his lips and invaded them. "I love white men," she said at the back of her throat. "They're so *big*! But I'm in service at Kinross House, so men are forbidden to me. Yet here I am, breaking the rules for you. Sam, I want you! I want to put my mouth *everywhere*!"

That sounded as if she was indeed an amateur slut, but she was definitely sweet and clean; Sam O'Donnell suppressed his scruples and nodded. "All right," he said.

She put on her coat and turned drab, hair tucked inside it, legs concealed, breasts nonexistent. "I'll be waiting," she said, and hurried away.

On fire with want of her, he packed up for the day and set off for the snake path, the dog slinking in his rear as if it knew what business he was on; it probably did.

UNDER ORDINARY circumstances Sam O'Donnell was a continent kind of fellow who liked to be on good terms with women yet didn't want to plunder them sexually. He was, as he phrased it to himself, a fussy bugger, and the one thing that flattened his desire was a virtuous woman over twenty—or, he amended, a raddled whore like the bitches in that house of ill fame on the outskirts.

Born near Molong, a very small country town farther west, his destiny was decided by his circumstances: father scraping a living share-cropping or shearing, mother bearing babies. When he turned twelve he went to the wool sheds with his dad and learned to shear, a backbreaking, hideous job in the foulest of conditions. The shearers were housed in something euphemistically termed a barracks, slept on naked stretchers, and were fed food the feral dogs wouldn't eat. No wonder that shearers were the most militant of unionists! He stood it as long as his mother lived, then went off to Gulgong and the gold mines, where he learned the trade. After that, closer to forty than to thirty, he drifted to Kinross and was hired by the mining superintendent; he had never met the high-and-mighty Sir Alexander Kinross, even when Bede Talgarth came to town.

His head was filled with dreams of a better life for working men, of fairer conditions and considerate bosses, hence his joining the Amalgamated Miners' Association. It was active in Gulgong, and he had expected it to be active in Kinross; that it was not was due to Sir Alexander's cunning. Good conditions, good pay, a clean, cheap and pleasant town to live in. Which only made Sam O'Donnell hate Sir Alexander Kinross more. There *had* to be an ulterior motive, even if he couldn't figure it out. When the Apocalypse employees took their dismissal tamely, he set off for Sydney and secured the best demagogue in the business, Bede Talgarth. Yet still the sheep wouldn't turn into wolves! They took their redundancy pay and moved on. Why he hadn't done the same, he knew very well.

It went back to the day after he was dismissed, at the very beginning of July; Sir Alexander had laid off his men in groups, and Sam O'Donnell was in the first group. The furious Sam cooled his ire by hiking up on top of Sir Bloody Alexander Bloody Kinross's no-trespassing mountain. And there, not far from the cable car terminus but in the opposite direction from Kinross House, he stumbled upon a vision. The most beautiful very young girl he had ever seen, wandering through the ferns humming to herself. Old Rover, usually averse to people other than Sam, made a sound of pleasure, bounded up to the girl and leaped at her. Instead of screaming and pushing the dog away, she squealed with delight and accepted its embrace. Then as Sam O'Donnell approached, a conciliatory smile on his face, she looked out of her grey-blue eyes at him and extended her welcome to him.

"Hello," he said, and to the dog, "Rover, down! Down, Rover!"

"Hello," said the vision.

"What's your name?" he asked her, astonished that she seemed to feel none of the fear that was inculcated into all young girls at sight of a strange man in an isolated place—a fear that had foiled his intentions more than once in the past.

For answer she crouched down to pat the fawning dog, rolled over on its back and groaning.

"Your name?" he asked again.

She looked up, grinning.

"Your name?"

"Anna," she finally said. "Anna, Anna, Anna. I Anna."

Light dawned; this was Alexander Kinross's mental daughter, a poor dim-witted creature who, they said, went to church on Sunday with her mother but otherwise was only seen in Kinross when she had wandered too far. But he had never laid eyes on her there, had no idea that Anna Kinross was so beautiful, so desirable, so lush—and yet the very personification of innocence. No wonder they had the word out to pick her up whenever she went too far! She was every man's most fabulous, impossible wish.

He hunkered down beside her, some instinct of preservation telling him that he mustn't give her his name. But he had used the dog's name when he commanded it down, and Anna, instantly in love with the animal, had one of her rare attacks of memory.

"Rover!" she said, still patting the dog. "Rover, Rover!"

"Yes, that's Rover," he said, smiling.

It went from there, the most exhilarating and triumphant experience of Sam O'Donnell's life, interrupted only by a two-day trip to Sydney to fetch Bede Talgarth.

Patient and calm, he gradually coaxed the girl into small indecencies—a kiss on the cheek, a kiss on the mouth, a kiss on the side of her neck that evoked a grown woman's response. The gentle unveiling of her breasts, her gasping pleasure when he kissed and sucked their nipples. A hand sliding delicately into her drawers, and she curling up to arch and writhe like a cat in heat. And slowly, slowly, slowly he brought her to an almost slavish willingness; every day she appeared in the same place, eager to pat Rover, then eager to be kissed, fondled, caressed, aroused to a beating frenzy that turned her into some glorious big moth desperate to immolate itself in the fire it didn't know. Breaking her maidenhead was a nothing; she was so excited that she didn't even notice, and when he came to climax, so did she.

What made the seduction of Anna Kinross so amazing lay in who she was, who he was, and the exquisite secrecy that enfolded them. And the identity of her high-and-mighty father.

Early in July he remade his life in a way that he found, to his surprise, suited him perfectly. Self-employment! No more bosses, no more thankless toil in a stinking shed or confining mine, cut off from the sun and the outside air. Since Scripps the painter had become a drunk no one wanted to hire, he took on painting house exteriors—no big jobs that would turn *him* into a boss, however!—and doing odd jobs in between. He also began to go to Evensong at St. Andrew's every Sunday night. Helped the minister out with his rats. Always very polite. Never going inside a woman's house. He moved out of his boarding house and camped at the dam to give no one any idea of his movements, and held his odd jobs, painting jobs and good deeds as part of the secret of Anna Kinross, making out to one woman that he was just going to another woman's house to do something—oh, he was *clever!* In fact, Sam O'Donnell felt invulnerable. Did Sir Alexander Kinross delude himself that he was smart? Compared to Sam O'Donnell, he was less than a slug crawling in the slime. Anna was *his:* his private property, his groveling bitch-dog, his sexual heaven. Absolutely no inhibitions, yet as pure as the driven snow. Anna was the answer to a highly fastidious man's wildest fantasy.

Early in December, when they had been meeting for five months, Sam O'Donnell realized that Anna was pregnant; she had the same look his mother used to, and her belly wasn't quite flat anymore. Oh, Jesus Christ! That was his last trip to the mountain; he had no idea whether Anna still looked for him, just prayed that he and she never came face-to-face.

His luck held. When, early in the New Year, the news hit Kinross that some mongrel had gotten at that poor child Anna Kinross and made her pregnant, Sam O'Donnell resolved to ride out the storm. If he left town, they'd wake up to him, so he would sit pat. Not that he changed his habits. He was too crafty to cease those sudden "Back in three hours, Mrs. Nagle, got to give Mrs. Murphy a hand!" excursions. Simply, they became realities rather than fabrications. Sam O'Donnell had no illusions. If they pinned the guilt for Anna Kinross on him, he would be lynched.

SO HE WALKED the snake path to Jade Wong's shed feeling all the eagerness of a starved man glimpsing a loaf of bread. Maybe day-old bread compared to Anna, but nice bread nonetheless, and urgently needed; Sam O'Donnell was genuinely starving for, as he had put it to Bede Talgarth, "a bit of slap-and-tickle."

Even so, he took his time. He had worked hard for most of the day and didn't want to expend any more of his strength than was necessary on climbing a thousand-foot slope back and forth. So the sun was perched on the summit of the western hills when he reached the top and saw immediately that Jade had told him the truth. The backyard was deserted; Chinese talk and gales of laughter came clearly from the kitchen. With a curt gesture that told the dog to stay outside, he lifted the latch on the red door and slipped inside. The place smelled peculiar, of exotic aromas overlying something more unpleasant; the smell of a Chinese room, he supposed. Why couldn't she open the window shutters? Because light would be seen? That made no sense if she lived in this hovel.

"What's on the walls?" he asked Jade, staring at the padding.

"I don't know," she said, replacing the lid on a teapot. A steaming kettle on a spirit stove sat nearby on the same table.

"Why are there bars on the windows?"

"This is the home of a tiger."

A swift look around convinced him that she was joking—why didn't she open the window shutters instead of burning a lamp? She was odd, but he concentrated on how she looked without that overcoat—beautiful, really beautiful! As if reading his mind, she put a foot shod in a high-heeled slipper upon the chair and adjusted the seam of her stocking. His hand was there at once, moving across the tissue-fine sheath, then up above the garter to the naked flesh, even silkier. Probing higher, to discover a moist bare slit. No prim drawers for Jade Wong. She leaped and jerked, smiled at him with a pout, and gently removed his hand.

"No, Sam, everything in its place. First we drink tea—a part of custom," Jade said, lifting the teapot and pouring a straw-pale liquid into two small bowls. One was held out to him.

"It's got no handle, I'll burn myself," he objected.

"The tea is cooled to the right temperature. Drink, Sam," Jade cooed, sipping at her bowl. "You must drink it all or there will be no magic in our night together."

Oho, a Chinese love potion! Though it didn't taste as good as proper black Indian tea, it wasn't too bad; Sam drank, even swallowed a second bowl when she poured it.

After which he got his reward. Jade unbuttoned a placket in the side of her dress and gathered it in pleats to pass above her head. Awed, he watched the unveiling of her body from legs on up: downy black pubic hair, lovely belly, delicious breasts.

"Keep your stockings on," he said, fumbling with his own clothes, fingers clumsier than usual.

"Of course," she said, stalked to the bed and stretched out on it, one thumb in her mouth, its lips forming a crimson O as she sucked audibly, her doelike eyes fixed on him without blinking.

"Let me see your cunt, China girl," he said.

As she spread her legs obediently he shuffled to the bed, naked himself, but not as stiff and upright as he ought to be—oh, Jesus, what was *wrong*? The air seemed to gush from him as he slumped on to the side of the bed and collapsed as if pricked. He struggled to keep his eyes open, tried to pinch Jade's nipple, couldn't. His eyes closed—a bit of a nap first, then he'd ram her until her teeth rattled. Yes, a nap . . .

Jade waited for several minutes, then reached into the tiny drawer beside the bed and took out the gauze muzzle and the bottle of chloroform. When she put the muzzle over his mouth and nose and started to drip the fluid on to it, he began to struggle, but the laudanum held him still enough until the anesthetic took effect and he went completely limp.

A few more drops to make sure, then Jade let the muzzle slip from his face, busy unearthing a heavy leather jacket from beneath the bed. Working with the wiry strength of a woman in the pink of health, she maneuvered his arms and trunk into the device, buckled its straps tightly across his back and attached it by other straps to the iron struts connecting the top of the bed to the foot. After which she took stout leather cuffs and wrapped them tightly around his ankles, buckled them and tied them to the bed frame.

All of this was done in a way that saw Sam O'Donnell fixed in a semi-recumbent posture, his shoulders and upper chest elevated on several hard bolsters so that, if he had been conscious, he would have looked down on himself lying on the bed. One last task: Jade took a needle and thread, picked up one eyelid, pulled it back until it touched the brow, then sewed one to the other with a dozen quick stitches. She sewed the second eye open.

Around the room she went to light all the lamps, their wicks trimmed to give off brilliant flames without any smoke. She dressed herself in her ordinary black trousers and jacket, and sat on the chair to wait. He was breathing, but stertorously, and the open eyes were oblivious, unseeing. It took half an hour for him to rouse, which he did retching. But he hadn't eaten since lunch time and his digestion was excellent, so the retching remained dry.

He came to stupidly, thrashing vainly for leverage until his eyes encountered Jade sitting on the chair. Quietening, he let his hands and fingers fiddle inside the home-made straitjacket, wondering fuzzily why he couldn't seem to free them from restraint. In all his life he had never seen a garment like the one that now wrapped him around from neck to waist and confined his arms inside sleeves that crossed over each other, blind ends sewn together so there was no way out. Nor could he free his legs, their ankles tethered to the bottom of the bed. Or blink his eyes—*why couldn't he blink his eyes?*

"What?" he gasped, trying to focus on Jade. "What?"

She rose to her feet and stood over him. "You have to answer, Sam O'Donnell."

"What? What?"

"It is too soon," she said, and returned to the chair.

Only when he opened his mouth to scream did she move again. She popped a little cork ball between his lips, then tied a piece of cloth across his mouth to keep the ball inside it. Screaming was impossible; he had to save all his energy to breathe through his straining, flaring nostrils.

Back to the bed came Jade with a thin filleting knife. "You ruined my baby," she said, fingering the knife. "You took an innocent little child and raped her, Sam O'Donnell." She sneered. "Oh, yes, I know what you'd say! That she asked for it, that she wanted it. And her with the mind of a little child. You raped an innocent, defenseless child, and you will pay."

Frantic mumblings poured from his gagged mouth while his head rocked from side to side and his body heaved, but Jade took no notice. She lifted the knife, passed it many times in front of his gaze, and smiled the smile of the tiger.

His horrified, bulging eyes could only watch—what had she done to them, that he couldn't close them? Instead of closing them, he had to follow her movement as she went down the bed two feet and picked up his genitals in her left hand. She took a long time to perform the amputation, teasing his flesh with the knife, beading a red bubble, withdrawing, teasing again, cutting off the scrotum first, then the penis as he thrashed and silently howled his anguish to nothing, to no one. Jade let her grisly trophy bleed out on to his chest, then stepped back, penis and scrotum in her left hand, the knife in her right dripping blood on to the floor. Blood spurted, but not with the crazy jet of a severed arm or leg; powerless, Sam O'Donnell could only look at the red pit in his groin where his genitals had grown and watch his life force drain away until sight was stripped from his still open eyes.

All night Jade sat holding her sticky prize while Anna's seducer slowly bled to death. Only when light stole through the cracks in the shutters did she move, get up from the chair and go to the bed to look down on the ravaged face of Sam O'Donnell, his eyes rolled back in his head, the gag soaked with his saliva, tears and snot.

Then she left the room, closed the door behind her and looked for the dog. There! Stiff and stark, it lay beside the poisoned meat she had left for it. Goodbye, Sam. Goodbye, Rover.

She took the snake path down to Kinross and walked into the police station to slap the knife and the genitals on the counter.

"I have killed Sam O'Donnell," she said to the paralyzed constable on duty, "because he raped my baby Anna."

Four

BIRTH AND DEATH

HOW DOES an ordinary sergeant of the country division of the New South Wales Police go about this? asked Sergeant Stanley Thwaites of himself as he stared at the jellified mess on the station counter, more fascinated by it than by the knife or the Chinese girl, now sitting on a bench in the corner. The testicles in their sack were nondescript, whereas the penis was unmistakably what it was. Finally his eyes lifted and turned to Jade, whose head was down, her hands folded peacefully in her lap. Of course he knew who she was: Anna Kinross's nursemaid. Patiently waiting outside St. Andrew's every Sunday for Lady Kinross to reappear with her mental daughter in tow. He knew her name was Jade Wong.

"Are you going to give us any trouble, Jade?" he asked.

She looked up, smiled. "No, Sergeant."

"If I leave the manacles off, will you try to get away?"

"No, Sergeant."

Sighing, he went to the wall and plucked the telephone earpiece from its cradle, then depressed the cradle several times. "Put me through to Lady Kinross, Aggie," he shouted.

Too public, he thought; Aggie listens in to everything.

"This is Sergeant Thwaites. Lady Kinross, please."

When Elizabeth came on the line he simply asked if he could come and see her immediately. Let Aggie stew a while longer!

He assembled his party efficiently; if there was a body, he would need at least two other men—oh, and Doc Burton just in case Sam O'Donnell was still alive. Kinross had no coroner, that function relegated to Dr. Parsons in Bathurst, where the district courts were located.

"There's been an accident at Kinross House, Doc," he said above the sound of Aggie's heavy breathing. "I'll meet you at the cable car—no, there isn't time for breakfast."

So the party set off bearing the hollow covered stretcher of the dead, Jade in their midst, to find Doc Burton waiting grumpily at the terminus; while they ascended, Thwaites informed the doctor of Jade's confession and the proof she had slapped down on the police station counter. Flabbergasted, Doc stared at Jade as if he had never seen her before, but she still looked what he had always thought she was: a loyal and loving Chinese servant.

They went first to the house, where Elizabeth received them.

"Jade!" she exclaimed, bewildered. "What's the matter?"

"I killed Sam O'Donnell," Jade said calmly. "He raped my baby Anna, so I killed him. Then I went to the police station and gave myself up."

There was a chair nearby; Elizabeth sank on to it.

"We'll have to look, Lady Kinross. Whereabouts, Jade?"

"In a shed in the backyard, Sergeant. I'll show you."

The dog lay dead not far from the red door. "Its name was Rover," Jade said, poking it with a foot. "I poisoned it." No fear or remorse on her face, she led the way inside.

Only one of the two constables had had breakfast; that he lost the moment he saw the contents of the bed, which had soaked up Sam O'Donnell's blood so greedily that the only traces on the floor had dripped off Jade's knife. The smell had worsened, incense and old excreta now intermingled with stale blood. Hand over his mouth, Doc Burton leaned over the body briefly.

"He's dead as a doornail," said the doctor, and remembered a word from student days. "Exsanguinated."

"Ex-what?"

"Bled to death, Stan. Bled to death."

Another huge sigh erupted from the sergeant. "Well, there's no mystery involved, as the murderer has confessed. If you're happy to write a report for the coroner in Bathurst, Doc, then I suggest we slide him into this here dead man's stretcher and take him to Marcus Cobham's funeral parlor. He'll have to be buried quick or all of Kinross will smell him. No air in here." He turned to Jade, who hadn't taken her eyes off Sam O'Donnell, nor stopped smiling. "Jade, are you sure you killed him? Now think before you answer, because there are witnesses."

"Yes, Sergeant Thwaites, I killed him."

"What about the—er—missing bits at the station?" asked Doc Burton, whose own private parts felt numb, shrunken.

The sergeant rubbed the side of his nose reflectively. "I daresay that as they belong to him, they should go to Marcus as well. Can't be stuck on again, but they're still his."

"If he really did molest Anna, he deserves this," said Doc.

"That we have to find out. All right, Doc, you and the boys take the body back down the mountain. I'm taking Jade to see Lady Kinross and try to get to the bottom of this." One hand detained Constable Ross. "When it's done, Bert, better go out to O'Donnell's camp by the dam and see what you can find. Like evidence that he knew Miss Anna. After that, all of you can take turns to question everybody in Kinross."

"They'll know," Doc Burton said.

"Of course they'll know! What difference does it make?"

Jade walked beside Sergeant Thwaites across the backyard and led him into the house through a service door, thence to the library, where Elizabeth waited. This was the first time she had ever used Alexander's domain for her own purposes, but somehow she couldn't bear to see Jade's face in the brighter light of the other rooms. The sergeant too felt the significance of the business, and was grateful for the dimness.

Jade sat on a straight chair between Elizabeth and Stanley Thwaites, her face enquiring.

"You say that Sam O'Donnell molested Miss Anna Kinross," the sergeant began, "but how do you know that for certain, Jade?"

"Because Anna knew the name of his dog. Rover."

"That's pretty thin sort of evidence."

"Not if you know Anna," Jade answered. "She doesn't learn names unless she knows people awfully well."

"She never gave a name to her attacker, Lady Kinross, did she?" Thwaites asked.

"No, she did not. She referred to him as 'nice man.'"

"So the only thing you had to go on was the name of his dog? Rover? It's about as common a name for a dog as Fido."

"A blue cattle dog, Sergeant. When Anna saw Mr. Summers's blue cattle dog, she called it Rover. Its name is Bluey. Sam O'Donnell's blue cattle dog was called Rover," said Jade firmly.

"The breed is quite new," Elizabeth ventured. "In fact, as I didn't know this Sam O'Donnell or his dog, I thought that Mr. Summers's Bluey was the only specimen in Kinross."

"There must be *something* else," said Thwaites, despairing.

Jade shrugged, unimpressed. "It was all the proof I needed. I know my baby Anna and I know that man raped her."

Though he persisted for a further half an hour, Sergeant Thwaites could get no more from Jade.

"I can hold her in the Kinross cells tonight," he said to Elizabeth as he prepared to leave, "but tomorrow I'm going to have to send her to Bathurst, where she will be charged. There are facilities for women prisoners at the Bathurst Gaol. You'll have to apply to the Bathurst authorities for bail, but there's no resident judge, just three stipendary magistrates who can charge her, but can't otherwise deal with a capital crime. What I do suggest, Lady Kinross, is that you engage a legal firm to help you and Miss Wong." Sudden formality.

"Thank you, Sergeant. You've been very kind." Elizabeth shook his hand, then stood at the front door watching his burly bulk roll across the lawn toward the cable car, Jade's slender little figure walking passively beside him.

A telephone call to the Kinross Hotel told her that Miss Ruby was on her way up the mountain.

"Jesus, Elizabeth!" Ruby cried, erupting into the library, where Elizabeth was still ensconced. "The news is all over town that Jade cut off Sam O'Donnell's private parts, stuffed them in his mouth and forced him to eat them before giving him the Chinese Death of a Thousand Cuts! Because he raped Anna!"

"The essence is true, Ruby," said Elizabeth calmly, "though the deed wasn't quite as macabre as that. Macabre enough. She did cut off his private parts, but took them to the police station and confessed to murder. She's convinced that it was Sam O'Donnell got at Anna. Did you know him?"

"Only in passing. He never drank at the hotel—didn't drink at all, people are saying. Theodora Jenkins is a cot case—he was painting her house, and she thinks the sun rises out of his arse. Denies he could have had anything to do with Anna. A real gentleman, wouldn't even come inside to wash his hands. The C of E parson is up in arms too, prepared to go to the stake that Sam O'Donnell was an absolutely upright citizen."

Ruby's hair was falling down, so hastily had she dealt with it, and she hadn't stopped to lace her corsets; did I not know what a wonderful woman this is, thought Elizabeth, horribly detached, I would deem her a blowsy tart, mutton dressed up as lamb.

"Then there will be trouble in all directions," she said.

"It's dividing the town down the middle already, Elizabeth. The miners and their wives are on Jade's side, all the spinsters, widows and Bible-bashers have lined up behind Sam O'Donnell. The refinery and workshop people are going either way. Not everyone has forgotten that he tried to stir up trouble here last July and August," said Ruby, rubbing a shaking hand across her face. "Oh, Elizabeth, tell me that Jade killed the right man!"

"I am convinced of it because I know how close Jade's always been to Anna. Every look, every word, every gesture that Anna makes tell Jade stories that even I cannot plumb."

She went on to tell Ruby about the dog, upon which Jade had based her decision to kill its owner.

"That won't impress a judge," said Ruby.

"No, it won't. Sergeant Thwaites—he was very kind, Ruby—recommended that I engage a legal firm immediately, but I don't even know the name of Alexander's lawyers—do I need solicitors, or barristers? And don't firms specialize?

"Leave it to me," said Ruby briskly, glad to have something concrete to do. "I'll cable Alexander, of course—he's at his gold mine in Ceylon—and I'll have the Apocalypse lawyers depute the right firm to care for Jade's interests." She stopped in the doorway. "It may be that they decide to send the poor little bitch to Sydney for trial if they feel that a jury drawn from a pool of locals would be prejudiced. In my opinion a city jury would be worse"—she snorted—"but then, I'm prejudiced."

NELL FOUND out as she was witnessing the removal of dynamite from the explosives shed, and raced up the snake path, too impatient to wait for the cable car. All the grief and horror that Elizabeth was too controlled to show sat upon Nell nakedly as she stared at her mother, tears making visible runnels down her dirty face, her slight breast heaving under the stained overalls.

"Oh, it can't be true!" she cried after Elizabeth told her the story. "It can't be true!"

"What can't be true?" Elizabeth asked levelly. "That Jade killed Sam O'Donnell, or that Sam O'Donnell was the one who got at Anna?"

"Do you ever feel, Mum? Do you *ever* feel? You're sitting there like a mannequin in a shop window—Lady Kinross to a tee! Jade is my sister! And Butterfly Wing is more my mother than you've ever been, God knows! My sister has confessed to murder—how could you let her do that, Lady Kinross? Why didn't you clap your hand over her mouth if you could shut her up no other way? You let her *confess*! Don't you understand what that means? She won't be tried at all! You only try someone if there's a doubt of guilt. That's the jury's job—the jury's only job! A man or woman who confesses and doesn't recant is simply put in the dock to be sentenced by a judge." Nell turned on her heel. "Well, I'm off to the police station to see Jade. She has to recant! If she doesn't, they'll hang her."

Elizabeth heard it all, heard the hatred—no, not hatred, dislike—in her daughter's voice, and turned the bitter words over in her heart acknowledging their truth. Someone has put a stopper in the bottle that holds my spirit, my soul, and glued it there for all eternity. I will burn in Hell, and I deserve to burn in Hell. I've been neither wife nor mother.

"I suggest," she called after Nell, "that you have a bath and change into a dress if that's where you're going."

BUT JADE REFUSED to recant. Sergeant Stanley Thwaites would never have dreamed of forbidding Miss Nell to see the prisoner, so Nell was allowed into the one cell saved for violent offenders, sequestered from the half-dozen cells wherein drunks and petty thieves were incarcerated.

"Jade, they'll hang you!" Nell cried, weeping again.

"I don't mind being hanged, Miss Nell," Jade said gently. "What matters is that I killed Anna's raper."

"Rapist," Nell corrected automatically.

"He ruined my baby Anna, he had to die. No one else would have acted, Miss Nell. It was my job to kill him."

"Even if you did kill him, Jade, deny it! Then you'll have a proper trial, we can bring up all the extenuating circumstances, and I'm positive that Daddy will engage barristers who could—who could get Jesus freed by Pontius Pilate! Deny it, please!"

"I couldn't do that, Miss Nell. I did kill him, and I am proud that I killed him."

"Oh, Jade, nothing is worth a life, especially your life!"

"That is wrong, Miss Nell. A man who tricks a little child like my baby

Anna into serving his disgusting wants and fills a little child like my baby Anna with his stinking slime, is no man. He deserves everything I did to Sam O'Donnell. I would do it again, and again, and again. I live it in my mind as joy."

And from that stand Jade would not budge.

The next day at dawn she was put into the police wagon and taken to Bathurst Gaol, one constable driving the team, another sitting beside her. They feared her yet did not fear her. When Sergeant Thwaites decreed no manacles they thought him foolish, but the journey passed without incident. Jade Wong was delivered into captivity at about the same moment as the body of Sam O'Donnell was interred in the Kinross cemetery, the cost of his burial borne by Theodora Jenkins and several other grieving, distraught women. The Reverend Peter Wilkins gave a moving eulogy at the graveside—best be sure not to offend God by having the body in the church in case he *had* interfered with Anna—and the mourners picked their way between the wreaths, sobbing behind their black veils.

Though the police searched O'Donnell's camp and the ground around it with admirable zeal and thoroughness, they found nothing to connect the fellow with Anna Kinross. No items of feminine clothing, no trinkets, no initialed handkerchief—nothing.

"We opened his tins of paint and emptied them, we took his brushes apart, we unpicked the seams of his clothes, we even made sure that he hadn't hidden anything between the leaves of bark on his humpy roof," said Sergeant Thwaites to Ruby. "My word of honor, Miss Costevan, we looked everywhere. It wasn't as if he lived slipshod, either. Neat as a pin for a camping man—had a clothesline rigged up, a washing tub, his food all in old bikkie tins to keep the ants out, boot polish and boot brushes, clean sheets on his palliasse—yes, neat as a pin."

"What will happen now?" Ruby asked, looking every year of her age.

"I understand that the stipendary magistrates have been authorized to charge her, and that bail will be refused as it is a capital crime."

BY NOW THE news had broken in Sydney, where the newspapers printed all the gory details without actually mentioning what parts of Sam O'Donnell's anatomy had been severed and stuffed in his mouth, though they implied that he had been forced to eat them. Editorials tended to concentrate upon the hazards of employing Chinese servants, using the death of Sam O'Donnell as additional proof of the inadvisability of permitting the Chinese to immigrate. The yellower dailies and weeklies were all in favor of mass deportation of Chinese already resident in the country, even if they had been born in Australia. The fact that the demure little nurserymaid proclaimed her guilt proudly was taken as evidence of total depravity. And somehow Anna Kinross was described as "slightly simple"—a state of mind that readers assumed meant that she could add up two and two, but not thirteen and twenty-four.

The cable found Alexander on the west side of the Australian continent, though he hadn't yet notified his fellow board directors of his imminent arrival. He had lost none of his secretiveness with the passing of the years. His ship docked in Sydney a week after Jade was charged, and he was faced with a jostling crowd of journalists swollen by men from interstate and by stringers for the big overseas papers from the *Times* to the *New York Times*. Nothing daunted, he held an impromptu press conference on the wharf, fielding questions with the constantly reiterated plea that as yet everyone in Sydney knew more than he did, so why were they bothering?

Summers was there to meet him, shepherd him to his new hotel in George Street, far removed from those wretched steam trams.

"What happened, Jim?" he asked. "I mean, what's the truth?"

To be addressed as "Jim" was novelty enough; Summers blinked several times before replying, then said, "Jade killed the fellow who interfered with Anna."

"The fellow who *did* interfere with Anna, or just the fellow she thought interfered with Anna?"

"I've no doubt in my mind, Sir Alexander, that Sam O'Donnell was the man. I was there when Anna called my dog Rover. I saw her face—she was as happy as a sandboy, and looking for its master. If I'd only known that Sam O'Donnell owned a blue cattle dog named Rover, I'd have understood at once. Jade understood because she'd met O'Donnell and the dog at Theodora Jenkins's house. He was painting its outside. But I didn't tumble, so Jade stole a march on me."

Alexander studied his face, sighed. "It's a pickle, isn't it? I take it that no other evidence has come to light?"

"None, sir. He must have been very careful."

"Can we get her off, do you think?"

"Not a hope, sir, even with you on her side."

"So it's a matter of putting up a good show for the sake of my family and preparing them for the worst."

"Yes, sir."

"If only she'd reported her suspicions to you or Ruby!"

"Perhaps," said Summers diffidently, "she knew even then that it would boil down to his word against Anna's, and decided it was better not to involve Anna."

"Oh, yes, I'm sure of that. Poor, poor Jade! I owe her a great debt."

"I don't think that's ever crossed Jade's mind. She did it for Anna, only for Anna."

"Who have Lime and Milliken recommended?"

"Sir Eustace Hythe-Bottomley, sir. An elderly chap, but a Queen's Counsel and the most eminent criminal barrister in—well, all of Australia wouldn't be far from the mark," said Summers.

BEFORE HE LEFT Sydney for Kinross, Alexander had done what he could. In conjunction with Sir Eustace (who could foresee no other decision than the death penalty unless the accused were to recant), he had used his connections to ensure that the presiding judge would be a reasonable sort, and that the sentencing hearing would be held in camera in Bathurst rather than in Sydney. And as quickly as possible. Sir Eustace traveled in Alexander's private car as far as Lithgow, where it was detached to be coupled to the Kinross train, then went on alone to Bathurst in a first-class compartment with his numerous staff still jammed into one second-class compartment, there to mull over the Laws of England as they applied to the colonies.

His interview with Jade in the Bathurst Gaol was a futile business. Coax, cajole and sing like a bird though he did, she remained obdurate: she would not recant, she was proud of what she had done, her baby Anna was avenged.

WHEN ALEXANDER arrived at Kinross station, only Ruby was on the platform to welcome him.

The sight of her was a shock—do I look as suddenly old as she does? Her hair is still that unique color, but she's put on so much weight that her eyes are disappearing into a pudding of flesh, her waist is nonexistent and her hands like podgy little starfish. But he kissed her, linked his arm through hers and walked with her through the waiting room.

"Your place or mine?" he asked outside.

"Mine for the moment," she said. "There are things we have to talk about that you won't be able to talk about with either Elizabeth or Nell."

The town, he was relieved to see, looked exactly as it ought despite the halving of its work force. Its streets were clean and tidy, its buildings well kept, Kinross Square's flower beds awash with dahlias, marigolds, chrysanthemums, all the proper blooms of late summer. A riot of yellow, orange, red, cream. Good! Sung Po's gardeners had done what he ordered, excavated an artificial bank to insert a gigantic mechanism that drove the ten-foot hands of a flowering clock through the twelve hours of each half day, brightly colored leaves and tiny blossoms picking out the Roman numerals, the disc of the clock face, the ponderous hands. What's more, the thing was correct: half past four in the afternoon. And the bandstand was freshly painted—had O'Donnell done it, or that sot Scripps? The trees that lined the streets had grown, crepe myrtles in vivid bloom, melaleucas with bark like multiple layers of peeling paint—oh, come, Sir Alexander, think of metaphors that have nothing to do with paint!

How he missed the place that bore his name, yet how he longed to be free of it the moment he was in it! Why wouldn't people do as they were supposed to do, live their lives with logic, reason, common sense? Why did they fly around like thistledown in the eddies and surges of a hot summer's day? Why couldn't husbands love wives and wives love husbands and children love everyone? Why did the differences between people always outweigh the things they shared as one? Why must bodies grow older than the minds that fuel them? Why am I so surrounded, yet so alone? Why does the fire burn as brightly yet the flames grow ever dimmer?

"I'm fat," she said, sinking on to a sofa in her boudoir and fanning herself with an accordioned affair the color of bile.

"You are," he said, sitting opposite.

"Does it irk you, Alexander?"

"Yes."

"Then just as well that this business is proving extremely good for my figure."

"We had a monster in our midst."

"A very cunning monster who half the town is convinced was no monster, but a harmless odd-job man."

"The idol of fools like Theodora Jenkins."

"Of course. He had her measure, got a kick out of charming her into adoring him—didn't desire elderly virgins or widows, but probably masturbated on making them wet their drawers."

"How is Elizabeth? Nell?"

"Elizabeth's much as always. Nell is dying to see her daddy."

"Anna?"

"Due in about a month."

"At least we know the pedigree of the child."

"Are you sure of that?"

"Summers is positive that the man was Sam O'Donnell. He was there when Anna thought she recognized the dog, and I think he saw more of Anna's face than Jade did."

"Bully for Summers!"

"More importantly, Ruby, how do I tell Elizabeth that Jade will hang?"

Her face changed, squeezed itself up into grosser folds. "Oh, Alexander, don't say that!"

"It has to be said."

"But—but—how can you be so *sure*?"

His fingers groped in a pocket, fished out a cheroot. "Are you not smoking these days?"

"Yes, give me one! But how can you be so sure?"

"Because Jade is a political pawn. Both the Free Traders and the Protectionists—not to mention the trade unionists, who are now beginning to call themselves Labor—need to make the people see that they're opposed to the Chinese, that they'll obey the people when the time is right and get rid of the Chinese. How better to soothe feelings now than by hanging one poor little half-Chinese girl, Australian born though she may be, for what is seen as an unspeakable crime? A crime against *men,* Ruby. Castration. Amputation of manhood! The man she did that to was white, and of evidence against him there is none beyond my mental daughter's recognition of his dog. Can Anna be called into a court and made to testify, even if the court is a closed one and there is no jury? Of course not! The judge may call for any testimony he likes before passing sentence, but to call Anna would be seen as a travesty."

Her tears seemed to ooze out of unbaked dough; he felt ill, couldn't think of her with desire. Don't leave me with no one! he cried silently, but to whom he cried it, he didn't know.

"Go, Alexander," said Ruby, stubbing out her cheroot. "Just go, please. She's Sam Wong's eldest daughter, and I love her."

He went straight to the cable car and took it up to the top of the mountain, facing, as all the seats did, Kinross below. A lake of shadows blue and lilac and pearl, the smoke of its chimneys adding a layer of the somber North Sea grey they were painting the new iron warships that, it seemed in another existence, had so fascinated him scant months ago.

Elizabeth was sitting in his library, something new; he did not remember her ever choosing it. How old was she now? Thirty-three in September. His own forty-eighth birthday was only a few weeks away. Now they really had been married for more than half of her life. An eternity, she had called it. And so it was, if eternity were flexible, and who was to say that it was not? What was the difference between the span of eternity and how many angels could dance on the head of a pin? A philosophers' squabble.

Elizabeth was thinking that Alexander improved with the years, and wondering why iron-grey hair streaked with white was so very attractive on a man, yet so ugly on a woman. His trim, slender body hadn't sagged or shrunk, and he moved with the graceful ease of a youth. Of Lee. The lines graven on his face were not evidence of age but of experience; she had a sudden wish to urge him to have a great sculptor craft a bust of him in—bronze? No. In marble? No. In granite. That was the stone for Alexander.

His black eyes held a new expression, of weariness, sadness, a grim determination fueled more by disappointment than by success. This won't break him because nothing can. He will weather every tempest his life throws at him because his core is granite.

"How are you?" he asked, kissing her cheek.

"Well," she answered, the pain of this peck driving through her like a javelin.

"Yes, you do look well, all considered."

"Dinner is some way off, I'm afraid. I wasn't sure when you would arrive, so Chang has planned Chinese food he can cook in a few minutes." She rose to her feet. "A sherry? A whisky?"

"Sherry, please."

She poured two full-sized wineglasses almost to the brim, carried one to him, took one back to her chair with her. "I've never understood why sherry is served in such small glasses, have you?" she asked, sipping. "One is forever jumping up and down to replenish it. This way, one doesn't have to jump up and down."

"A brilliant innovation, Elizabeth. I thoroughly approve."

He studied her over the brim of his glass, savoring the keen aroma of the amontillado before taking some into his mouth and letting it rest upon his tongue. Feeling the anticipation of its course down his gullet like a caressing ember. Her beauty grew; each time he saw her again it was with amazement at some new and perfect addition to her beauty, from a change in the way she held her head to a tiny crease at each corner of her mouth. Her figure in the smoky mauve dress was shading to voluptuousness without a trace of fat, and the hands that bore his rings looked like sea flowers, bending, swaying, borne by the currents of her mind.

Her mind he didn't know. She would never admit him to it. An enigma, that was Elizabeth. The mouse had become a quiet lion, but not remained that. What was she now? He had no idea.

"Do you wish to discuss Jade with me?" he asked, finally letting the sherry slide down his throat.

"I imagine that you've discussed it with half the world, so I'd rather let it lie, if you don't mind. We both know what must happen, and words once said can never be snatched back, can they? They are all there somewhere, ringing like bells." A glitter of tears filmed her eyes. "It is unbearable, that's all." Then the tears were gone; she smiled at him. "Nell will be here in a minute. Do compliment her on her appearance, Alexander. She's so desperate to please you."

As if on some director's cue, Nell came in.

What Alexander saw was himself in a feminine mold. Not a new experience, yet utterly novel. During the six months of his absence Nell had grown up, passed from girl to woman. His dark hair was piled up on top of her head, his wide but thin-lipped mouth looked as sensuous as determined, tinted with some pinkish substance she had also smeared faintly along her cheekbones. His long and slightly cavernous face was alluring on her, yet told the world that she wasn't to be trifled with. Imperious. Her skin was clear and healthily tanned as far as the bottom of her neck, ivory below it. Like her mother, she had abandoned the bustle in favor of a skirt that was fuller at the back than the front, of peau-de-soie silk the color of storm clouds. Not a busty, strapping young woman of Ruby's ilk, nor perfectly proportioned like her mother, but at ease with her rounded spareness. And she did have Elizabeth's long, swanlike neck.

Alexander put the glass down, walked to her quickly, held her first at arm's length, smiling, then folded her against him. Over his shoulder Elizabeth could see her face, its chin tucked into his coat, its thick-lashed eyes closed. A portrait of bliss.

"You look superb, Nell," he said, kissing her tenderly on the lips, then led her to a chair near his own. "Some sherry for my grown woman?" he asked.

"Yes, please, Daddy. I've turned fifteen, and Mum says I should learn to drink a little wine." Her eyes sparkled at her father. "The trick is never to drink more than a little."

"Which is why you're getting sherry in a sherry glass." He lifted his own glass in a toast, so did Elizabeth. "Here's to our beautiful daughter Eleanor. May she always prosper."

"May she always prosper," Elizabeth echoed.

Always sensitive to atmosphere, Nell made no mention of Jade or their troubles. Instead she concentrated upon regaling her father with tales of the job Ruby had given her, able to poke fun at herself, eager to tell him of this blunder, that mistake, what a pleasure it was to work with men once they stopped thinking of her as a woman.

"That happens in an emergency," she said, "when the only one who sees the solution is the trusty Nell Kinross."

From this she passed to an animated discussion with Alexander that embraced the technical difficulties they were experiencing in the cyanide refinery, then to a hot argument about the respective merits of direct and alternating electrical current. Exponents of the latter were newer, younger men; Alexander thought alternating current overrated and wasteful.

"Daddy, Ferranti has proved that an alternating current can work harder! Power bigger things than telephones and light bulbs! Electric motors are poor things, but I swear that soon, using alternating current, there will be electric motors powerful enough to run our cable car!" Nell said, face alight.

"But you can't store it in batteries, my girl, and you have to store it. Alternators mean running the dynamos all the time, which is shockingly wasteful. Without storage batteries, the whole production of current ceases the moment a dynamo breaks down, and they're notorious for that."

"One of the reasons for that, Daddy, is that the idiots wire the alternators in series when it's obvious they should be wired in parallel. Wait and see, Daddy! One day industry will need the kind of high voltages and transformers only alternating current can supply."

The good-natured argument raged on while Elizabeth sat listening to this truly extraordinary young woman whose grasp of mathematics far exceeded her father's, and whose knowledge of mechanics was phenomenal. At least in Nell, Alexander had a kindred spirit; she had the key to unlock his essence. Granite and granite. Later, Elizabeth mused, their battles will be titanic. All Nell needs is time.

Pleading his late arrival as a valid excuse, Alexander put off seeing Anna until the next morning.

"Anna's not happy," Elizabeth explained as she walked with him to the nursery. "She wants Jade, and of course we can't make her understand why she can't have Jade."

The sight of his younger daughter shocked him. The beauty, which he had forgotten, the sheer normality of her face, which his imagination had transformed into something more stigmatic, and the swollen belly bulging under a loose robe.

But at least she recognized him, said "Dadda!" several times, then began to howl for Jade. When Butterfly Wing tried to soothe her, she was pushed away rudely. As the howls and wails increased Alexander walked out, unable to bear the overwhelming smell of a gravid woman who took no care of herself nor, in her present mood, would let anyone else care for her.

"What a business," he said in the hall.

"Yes."

"When is young Wyler coming up?"

"In three weeks. Sir Edward is looking after his practice in Sydney."

"Is he bringing a midwife?"

"No, he says Minnie Collins will do very well."

"I understand that Anna won't let Nell see her."

Elizabeth gave a deep sigh. "That is so."

ANNA WENT into labor two days after Dr. Simon Wyler arrived toward the end of April, screaming her way through every cycle of pain, fighting and thrashing around so strongly that the obstetrician was obliged to tie her down. Neither he nor Minnie Collins could get it into poor Anna's head that she must co-operate, bear down, follow orders. All Anna knew was that she suffered agonies entirely alien to her, and protested against them shrilly, wildly, incessantly.

When her labor entered its last stage Dr. Wyler resorted to chloroform, and twenty minutes later withdrew a big, strong baby girl from the birth canal. Her color was pink and healthy, her lungs in excellent condition. Elizabeth, in attendance, could not help but smile down at this new human being, so unwanted and, until now, so unwelcome. But the dear wee scrap couldn't help her parentage, nor should she be punished for it.

Informed of the successful outcome of Anna's travail, her father simply grunted.

"A name?" Elizabeth asked.

"Call it whatever you want," Alexander answered curtly.

Elizabeth decided on Mary-Isabelle with a hyphen, a name that lasted only as long as Anna lay half conscious and exhausted. Which wasn't for more than six hours; no matter how inadequate her mental equipment, Anna was physically sturdy and in perfect health. Worst factor of all, her milk was coming in copiously.

"Give her the baby to nurse," said Dr. Wyler to Minnie.

"She won't know what to do!" said Minnie with a gasp.

"We can but try, Minnie. Do it."

Drawing the swaddlings back, Minnie handed the bundle to Anna, lying propped up in her bed. Looking amazed, Anna stared down into the tiny, working face, then gave a huge smile.

"Dolly!" she cried. "Dolly!"

"Your very own dolly, Anna," said Dr. Wyler, blinking away tears. "Put Dolly to the breast, Minnie."

Minnie loosened the neck of Anna's nightgown to expose one breast, pushed Anna's arms upward, and guided the baby and Anna toward each other. When the baby's mouth groped for and found the nipple, began to nurse, Anna's face underwent a transformation.

"Dolly!" she cried. "Dolly! My Dolly! Lovely!"

It was the first time she had spoken an abstraction.

The watching Elizabeth and Butterfly Wing gazed at each other, heedless that they wept. Anna would forget Jade now; Anna had her very own dolly, and the bond was made.

So when Sir Alexander Kinross registered his granddaughter's birth at the Kinross town hall, he entered her name as Dolly Kinross. Against the slot for the father, he wrote "S. O'Donnell."

"It seems I'm cursed with bastards," he said to Ruby when he called in to see her at the hotel on his way home, and shrugged wryly. "Not to mention cursed with girls."

She had taken the hint and was losing weight, but too fast; stripped of some of its youthful elasticity, her skin sagged under her chin and beneath her reappearing eyes. How long now will I hold him? she had wondered every day when the mirror showed her the turkey neck, the fine, crepey wrinkles on her upper arms and cheeks. But her breasts hadn't wavered from their high, firm stance, nor her buttocks subsided. As long as they are all right, I will hold him, she thought. But my menses are dwindling and my hair is thinning. Soon I will be an old hag.

"Tell me what you did abroad, where you went," she said to him after their lovemaking, which he seemed to enjoy as much as ever. "You were even more secretive than usual before you left."

He sat up in the bed and linked his hands around his knees, his chin on them. "I went on a quest," he said after a long pause. "A quest to find Honoria Brown."

"And did you succeed?" she asked, dry-mouthed.

"No. I'd hoped, you see, that I might have quickened her, that she might have borne me a son on her hundred-acre Indiana farm. But the people who have it now had bought it from people who used to have it, and they in turn had bought it from earlier owners. No one remembered Honoria Brown. So I put a Pinkerton man on it, told him to find her. The news caught up with me in England. She'd married some fellow and moved to Chicago in 1866, and was childless at that time. There have been children since, but she died in 1879 and her widowed husband married again a year later. Her children scattered because they didn't like their new stepmother, I gather. When the Pinkerton man asked if I wanted their whereabouts located, I said no, and paid him out."

"Oh, Alexander!" She got out of bed, pulled on a frilly robe. "And what else did you do?"

"I've already reported it to the board, Ruby."

"Most impersonally." Her voice wobbled when next she spoke. "Did you hear anything of Lee?"

"Oh, yes." Alexander began to dress. "He's doing very well for himself, mostly by dropping in on his old school chums at various Asian localities. I'd been planning to import a tribe of Indians from the Himalayan foothills to work in the Ceylon mine, but Lee nipped in first and set them to prospecting for diamonds in their own neck of the woods. The local rajah's son was most helpful in securing his father's agreement to this—for a price, of course. Fifty percent of the profits, which isn't bad. From there he went to England, saw Maudling at the Bank of England—these British institutions don't believe in retirement ages, do they? Maudling must be almost as old as the bank. He's on the board now, thanks to his activities with Apocalypse Enterprises. Like me, Lee's interested in the new iron battleships, especially their engines. There's a man named Parsons has a new sort of steam engine in development—he calls it a turbine."

Ruby had finished with her hair, drawn back more severely from her face than of yore; she had discovered that this pulled the skin of her face tighter, lessened the wrinkles. "Sounds as if Lee's busy trying to pip you on the post, Alexander."

"Have no doubt of it, he is! But surely you know all this, Ruby. He must write to you."

She grimaced, whether because of the difficulty of climbing into her dress or on Lee's behalf, Alexander wasn't sure. "Lee writes with clockwork regularity, but two or three lines to tell me that he's well and on the move from some queer place to another queer place. It's almost as if," she added wistfully, "he hates to be reminded of Kinross. I'm always hoping he'll write to say he's engaged, or married, but he never does."

"Women," said Alexander cynically, "are putty in his hands." He looked at her and frowned. "You've changed the way you dress, my dear. I rather miss those sumptuous satin affairs."

She looked at herself in the full-length mirror and pulled a face at the dress, which had a skirt that didn't sweep and a waist that didn't need to be wasped and a covered bosom. Plain and rather tailored, it was admittedly of silk grosgrain, but in that wretched bile color that had become so fashionable. "At my age, dear love, I'd look ridiculous. Besides, no one's wearing bustles anymore, feathers are out, necklines are rising, and leg-o'-mutton sleeves are all the go. Revolting things! Except for the poshest evening functions, it's all wool, tweed, grosgrain if you must wear silk. An old tart can't afford to look an old tart."

"It's my opinion," said Alexander, smiling, "that women's fashions are a sign of the times. The times are bad and will get far worse. We are in a commercial decline, not limited to this part of the world. So women are dressing more austerely, in dull colors and extremely ugly hats."

"I accede to the plain dresses and the dull colors, but I absolutely refuse to wear an ugly hat," said Ruby, linking her arm through his.

"Where are you going?" he asked, surprised.

She looked innocent. "Why, up the mountain with you! I've not seen Dolly since yesterday." Suddenly she stopped. "Did you send a message to Jade about the baby?"

"Elizabeth did the moment she was born."

"Is it hard to get messages to her?"

"Not if they come from Sir Alexander Kinross's family."

"How long will it be before her hearing?"

"July."

"And it's scarcely May. Poor little soul."

"Indeed."

THE NEWSPAPER reportage about the Kinross's Chinese nurserymaid and her crime hardly impinged upon Bede Evans Talgarth, galvanized by a turn of events that had the labor movement in a ferment. The Trades and Labour Council, pushed by a shrewd and dedicated Lancastrian named Peter Brennan, had just come around to seeing a political future for Labor and had started to compile a draft of Labor's platform when the huge strike of August 1890 intervened. However, the crushing defeat of the unions involved in the strike only spurred the Labor leaders to seek parliamentary representation for the ordinary white workingman. A by-election in West Sydney took place in October of 1890; Labor contested it with a union-approved candidate who swept to victory. The stage seemed set for the New South Wales general election to be held in 1892, far enough away to ensure that Labor would be properly prepared, with all the internecine strife about the identity of its candidates well behind it.

The Trades and Labour Council finished its official Labor political platform in April of 1891, a full year before the next elections. It included the abolition of electoral inequalities, universal free education, the achievement of union objectives, a national bank, and various measures to discourage the Chinese from manufacturing in Australia. On taxation the delegates were more divided, some arguing for a land tax, others for a single tax covering everything and everybody. Having extended the platform to encompass reform of local government, a new political party emerged. Its name was the Labor Electoral League, the word "Labor" spelled without the British "u" in it. In time it would become the Australian Labor Party. Labor in Latin meant "work, toil."

Then potential disaster struck. The New South Wales lower house saw

Sir Henry Parkes's Free Trade Party succumb to a vote of no confidence. This led to the Governor's dissolving the parliament and calling for new elections, which were set for the three weeks between June 17 and July 3 of 1891. Almost a year earlier than expected.

Labor scrambled frantically to sort out candidates for each electorate, no easy task in a state 300,000 square miles in extent. Not of course that electorates stuffed with affluent people were worth contesting, but that still left very many that were. The more remote country electorates had to be contacted by telegram or visited by central committee members doomed to several days on trains, coaches, even horseback. For that reason, the elections were spread over a period of three weeks.

The Bourke electorate, days away from Sydney, didn't care a hoot about city problems. Its chief concern was the importation of Afghans and their camels, which were stealing the entire haulage business from white Australian bullockies and their massive drays. The Labor political platform as drawn up by the city slickers and the coal miners didn't mention Afghans or camels, but in Bourke they *mattered.* The resulting quarrel with Sydney was fierce, but Bourke was forced to submit—no camels in the platform.

Neither the Free Trade Party nor the Protectionist Party took the Labor Electoral League seriously, thus conducted their usual leisurely, complacent campaigns, which mostly consisted of taking businessmen to lunch or dinner and ignoring the working classes completely. The Free Traders wanted no tariffs or duties upon imports, the Protectionists wanted local industries shored up by tariffs and duties upon imports. Both parties viewed the non-gentlemen of Labor with utter contempt.

Working furiously in his chosen southwestern Sydney area, Bede Talgarth succeeded in gaining nomination as Labor's official candidate, then went to work visiting those who would vote. He faced the polling period with trepidation, but also with a degree of confidence; he couldn't see why ordinary workingmen would want to vote for men who despised them when they now had a better alternative in the workingman's very own politicians.

As his electorate was a Sydney one, he knew his fate quickly. Bede Evans Talgarth found himself an M.L.A—a Member of the Legislative Assembly. As the results gradually came in for the 141 electorates in the state, thirty-five of them went to Labor. So did the balance of power in the parliament. Not that it was all joy for Labor; sixteen of the M.L.A.s were representing city electorates, nineteen country electorates. The city men (women weren't allowed to vote, let alone stand for parliament) were mostly staunch unionists, whereas the country men, apart from a group of coal miners plus one shearer, were not union-affiliated at all. Only ten of the Labor M.L.A.s were Australian born, only four were over fifty, and six were under thirty. It was a bench full of young men eager to change the face of Australian politics forever. Eager, yes, but also inexperienced.

What the hell! thought Bede Talgarth, M.L.A. The only way to gain experience is to jump in at the deep end, boots and all. The words that had been able to thrill a huge crowd in the Sydney Domain would now echo around a chamber growing very tired of Parkesian rhetoric. But the Grand Old Man managed to hang on to his position as Premier, forced now to court these presumptuous Labor buffoons (some of them were, alas) if he wanted to win a vote. A task made more difficult by Labor's internal complexity, governed by hideous amounts of that foul American entity, democracy; about half the Labor members were for free trade, the other half for protectionism.

So in July, when it was far too late to matter, Bede Talgarth remembered that day in Kinross when Sam O'Donnell hadn't showed up at the hotel after lunch. "A bit of slap-and-tickle," he had explained with a sheepish grin when he did show up hours later. Oh well, as evidence it was even thinner than the dog. It would not have persuaded the judge to amend his decision that Jade Wong, spinster of the town of Kinross, aged thirty-six, should hang.

FEARING MASS demonstrations if Jade were brought to Sydney, it was decided that she would be hanged on a specially constructed gallows in Bathurst Gaol, and that the execution would not be open to journalists or the public.

The judge, a member of the New South Wales Supreme Court, had been more than fair, but Jade stoutly maintained that she had killed Samuel O'Donnell in the manner described, and was glad she had killed him. He had ruined her baby Anna.

"I have no choice," the judge said during his address to the few still, attentive people permitted to be present. "The crime was indisputably premeditated. It was planned and carried out with a degree of cold-blooded calculation I find almost unimaginable in the light of Miss Wong's past history and career. Nothing was left to chance. Perhaps the most sickening aspect of the deed was Miss Wong's sewing the victim's eyes open. He was forced to witness his own mutilation and destruction. Nor has Miss Wong at any time expressed in words, or otherwise shown, a sign of any remorse." His lordship took a small black cloth from his bench and draped it on top of his full-bottomed wig. "Prisoner at the bar, I hereby sentence you to be taken to a place of execution and there hanged by the neck until dead."

Only Alexander came from Kinross to hear him. Jade's face didn't change, nor her smile lose its spontaneity. No fear in the big brown eyes, no sign of contrition. Jade was patently happy.

THE EXECUTION took place a week later, at eight o'clock in the morning of a bitter, rainy July day, with the mountains around Bathurst covered in snow and an icy wind blowing to whip Alexander's coat around his knees and prevent his using an umbrella.

He had seen her in her cell the day before to give her four letters: one from her father, one from Ruby, one from Elizabeth and one from Nell. From Anna he gave her a lock of hair, and that she loved more by far than anything the letters could say.

"It will go against my breast," she said, kissing it. "Is the baby well? Dolly?"

"Blooming, and it seems quite normal for ten weeks. May I do anything for you, Jade?"

"Look after my baby Anna, and swear to me on Nell's head that you won't ever put her in a home."

"I swear it," he said without hesitation.

"Then I have done what I set out to do," she said, smiling.

JADE WAS LED out clad in her black trousers and jacket, her long hair pinned up in a bun on top of her head. The rain didn't seem to bother her; she looked tranquil and walked without faltering. No minister of religion was present; Jade had refused spiritual comfort, insisting that she had not been baptized and was not a Christian.

The warder escorting her positioned her on the center of the trapdoor while another warder tied her hands behind her back and bound her ankles together. When they went to put a hood over her head she shook it violently until they desisted. Then the hangman stepped forward and dropped the noose around her neck, adjusted it so that the knot lay just behind her left ear, and tightened it. For all the interest she displayed, Jade might already have been dead.

It seemed over in a second, yet to go on for an hour. The hangman tripped the lever and the trapdoor collapsed with a loud clunk. Jade fell the short distance calculated to break her neck without decapitating her. There were no jerks, writhes, tremors. The black-clad figure, so tiny, so harmless, twirled a little, its face as peaceful as it had been from the beginning.

"I never saw a condemned person with that much courage," said the warden, standing with Alexander. "Awful business."

The arrangements had been made. Alexander was to receive the body after the coroner had confirmed death; it would be cremated at Sung's facility, but the ashes would not be sent home to China, or given to Sam Wong. Sung, who had kept completely out of the affair for fear of retaliation against his people, had had an inspiration he thought Jade would approve of. Alexander also approved. In the middle of the night, Sung himself would steal into the Kinross cemetery and dig Jade's ashes into the big mound of soil over Sam O'Donnell's body. For all eternity—or as much of eternity as mattered—Sam O'Donnell would have his murderess leaching into his thin, cheap coffin.

"I would like Miss Wong's letters back, please," Alexander said to the warden.

"Let's move in out of this rain," the man said, starting to walk. "Want to read them, eh?"

"No, I want to burn them unread by anyone. They were for her eyes only. You will oblige me in this, I hope? I wouldn't like to read a transcript of them in a newspaper."

The warden recognized the iron fist inside the velvet glove, and abandoned his plans at once. "Certainly, Sir Alexander, most certainly!" he said heartily. "There's a fire in my sitting room where we can dry off. A cup of tea while we wait, eh?"

Five

A MAN'S WORLD

WHEN NELL started engineering at Sydney University in March of 1892 at the very young age of sixteen, Alexander did what he could for her. The school was located in a single-storied white building intended as temporary but reasonably roomy accommodation until the proper school of Engineering could be built. It lay on the Parramatta Road side of the university and had a verandah in front of which grew tomatoes. Not seeing the point of subtlety, Alexander had simply told the Dean of Science and Professor of Engineering, William Warren, that he would contribute large sums for building purposes *if* his daughter and her Chinese colleagues were not victimized by their teachers. Heart sinking, Professor Warren assured him that Nell, Wo Ching, Chan Min and Lo Chee would be treated like his white male students—but that they would not be favored, oh, dear me, no.

Alexander had grinned and raised his pointed brows. "You'll find, Professor, that neither my daughter nor the Chinese boys are in need of special favors. They'll be your brightest students."

He bought them five little adjoining terraced houses where the Glebe impinged upon Parramatta Road and brought in contractors to create free access between them from inside; each of the five students (the extra one was Donny Wilkins) had his or her own quarters, with room for servants in the attics. For Nell, that meant Butterfly Wing, of course.

Orientation Week saw the female student viewed with outrage by the non-Kinrossian freshmen; the attitude of the twenty-odd more senior students at first bordered on insurrection, but an irate delegation to Professor Warren went away smarting.

"Then," said Roger Doman, due to graduate with a Bachelor of Science in mining engineering at the end of the year, "we'll just have to force her out unofficially." He pulled a menacing face. "Not to mention the Chinks."

Wherever Nell went she was booed and hissed; whatever she was deputed to do in the laboratory was sabotaged; her notes were stolen and defaced; her textbooks disappeared. None of which rattled Nell, who soon demonstrated in class that she was head and shoulders above the rest when it came to intelligence, knowledge and ability. If they had thought they hated her during Orientation Week, that was nothing compared to how the white male students felt after she displayed no compunction in humiliating them before Professor Warren and his tiny group of lecturers. It gave her immense satisfaction to correct their calculations, to demonstrate that their conclusions were wrong, and that they didn't know one end of a steam engine from the other compared to her. Or the Chinese boys, an additional mortification.

The most mortal insult to white male supremacy was Nell's invasion of the school's lavatories, in a separate building and never intended for women. At first the users bolted when she appeared, but then Doman and his cohorts decided that it was better not to bolt, but to behave grossly: display their penises, shit on the floor in front of her, foul the stalls, remove their doors.

The trouble was that Nell didn't play fair, or even female. Instead of bursting into tears, she retaliated. Doman, wiggling his penis, received a vicious slap on it that had him doubled up. Her scornful remarks as to penis size—was *nothing* sacred?—soon had the urinators scrabbling to hide their members the moment she walked in. The filth she dealt with unscrupulously by going to Professor Warren and escorting him on a tour of the lavatories.

"You're asking to be fucked silly!" Doman snarled, catching her alone soon after the men had been commanded to scrub the premises and behave properly in future.

Did Nell flinch, either at the language or the concept? No. She eyed the ringleading senior student up and down contemptuously and said, "You couldn't fuck a cow, Roger. You like sucking cock, you pervert."

"Cunt!" he spat.

Her eyes danced. "Ditto, brother smut," she said.

So there didn't seem to be any way of driving Nell Kinross out short of brute strength; the bitch was as foul-mouthed as any bullockie and utterly ruthless in revenge. She didn't play by the rules, and she certainly didn't act like a girl.

The plot to beat her and the Chinks up was hatched a month after classes started. Carefully planned, it necessitated lying in wait for them as they walked home along a deserted path amid a grove of trees where, later on, a university sporting oval would sprawl. The only difficulty was Donny Wilkins, a white man; in the end the would-be attackers decided that he had demonstrated where his allegiances lay, and would have to take his punishment too. The assault party, twelve strong, was armed with cricket bats and sandbags, but Doman carried a horsewhip that he intended to apply to Miss Nell Kinross's naked back after she and her yellow friends were subdued.

But it didn't work out that way. Pounced upon, Nell, Donny and the three Chinese boys countered like—like—

"Whirling dervishes" was the only way Roger Doman could put it as he tended his wounds afterward.

They kicked, whacked with the sides of their hands, wrested the bats and sandbags away from their attackers with ridiculous ease, sent bodies flying through the air to land flat and be stomped on, wrenched shoulders out of their sockets, broke an arm or two.

"Face it, Roger," said a panting Nell when it was over in a few seconds, "you're not up to our weight. As a mining engineer, you'd better bite the bullet or my daddy will see that you never get a job anywhere in Australia."

Which was worst of all. The bitch had power and wasn't a bit afraid to use it.

So by the time that the new students were sent to various workshops in Sydney's industrial areas, student opposition to the female in their midst had died a shameful death, and Nell Kinross was famous from Arts to Medicine. When she turned up in overalls to tackle dirty jobs, no one said a word. A fascinated Professor Warren—no advocate of women in engineering, any more than were his lecturers—admitted to himself that *some* women were just too strong to succumb to the traditional ways men had of getting rid of them. She was, besides, by far the most brilliant student he had ever encountered, and her grasp of mathematics entranced him.

One might have been pardoned for thinking that Nell would become a heroine to the university's tiny contingent of militant women, out to get the vote and equal rights for females. But that didn't happen, chiefly because, once her difficulties were over, Nell Kinross displayed no interest whatsoever in these women, all enrolled in the faculty of Arts. A man's woman to the core, Nell found women boring, even if they were, as they called themselves, feminists, with very legitimate complaints.

That first year of Nell's saw a worsening in the economy that meant some of the engineering students had to count their pennies and worry about whether their parents could afford to keep them in the relative leisure of a degree course exhaustive enough to prevent part-time work. But a word from Nell saw her father offering scholarships to those engineering students unable to continue. That should have earned her gratitude, but of course it did not. The scholarships were accepted, but Nell loathed even more for having the connections and power to create them.

"It isn't fair!" cried Donny Wilkins to her. "They should be down on their knees thanking you. Instead, they've gone back to booing and hissing whenever you appear."

"I'm a pioneer," said Nell, unbowed and unimpressed. "I'm a woman in a man's world, and the men know I'm the thin end of the wedge. After me, they'll never manage to keep women out, even women who don't have Sir Alexander Kinross for a daddy." She laughed, a delightful sound. "One day they'll have to put in a women's lavatory. And *that,* Donny, is the end of resistance."

THE "PRACTICAL WORK," as it was called, required the students to pick up skills on the shop floor. Textbooks and theory were not enough; Professor Warren's principle was that an engineer had to be as capable of welding, brazing and treating metal as any tradesman, and if a mining engineer, capable of working at a mine face, of blasting, drilling and dealing with the product, be it coal, gold, copper or any other mined substance. Practical work in mining for the mining engineers wouldn't happen in this first year; practical work for first-year students consisted of shop floor experience in factories and foundries.

In Nell's case, the industrial proprietors had to be apprised of her sex in advance and agree to accept her. Not a difficulty in premises that had—or hoped to have—custom from Apocalypse Enterprises, but impossible otherwise. Which didn't slow Nell down until toward the end of that first year, when she wanted desperately to spend some time on the shop floor of a factory in southwestern Sydney where new mining drills were being made—by new, of a design that promised to revolutionize drilling into hard rock faces. Because Apocalypse was a big customer, she got permission, only to be told that the metalworkers' union, which ran a closed shop there, refused to have a woman inside the doors, let alone prancing around the machinery.

This was not a problem Sir Alexander could fix; Nell was on her own. Her initial move was to seek an interview with the shop steward, who served as liaison between the factory's metalworkers and their union's headquarters. The meeting was rancorous and didn't go as the shop steward had imagined, thinking to send the capitalist bitch packing in floods of tears. He was a bigoted Glaswegian Scot who regarded Sir Alexander Kinross as a traitor to his class, and swore solemnly to Nell that he would die before he'd see *any* woman on his shop floor. Instead of tears he got unanswerable questions, and when, exasperated, he swore at her, she swore right back.

"She's worse than a woman," he said to several cronies after Nell had stalked out, "she's a man in woman's clothing."

Where to now? Nell asked herself, steeled to win no matter what the cost. Old goat! Shop stewards were notorious as the laziest or least competent among union employees, which was why they sought the union liaison position. It protected them and freed them from too much hard work. Angus Robertson, you'll suffer me no matter how hard you fight against it!

After perusing Labor journals like the *Worker,* she saw her next move: enlist the help of the local Labor M.L.A., an avowed republican and dedicated socialist. His name was Bede Talgarth.

Bede Talgarth! She *knew* him! Or at least, she amended, she had once had lunch with him in Kinross. So off she set for his parliamentary office in Macquarie Street, only to be refused an audience because she was neither one of his constituents nor connected to the Labor movement. His secretary, whom he shared with a number of other Labor backbenchers, was a stringy little man who sneered at her and told her to run away, have a few babies like a proper woman.

A few enquiries at the parliamentary library revealed that Bede Talgarth, previous profession collier, marital status single, born on May 12 of 1865, lived in Arncliffe. This was a sparsely populated working-class suburb inland from Botany Bay, and not very far from the drill factory. Since she couldn't see him in his offices, she would beard him in his domestic den. Which was a small sandstone house dating back to convict days, set in about an acre of ground that no one tended.

When she marched up to its peeling dark green door and plied the knocker, no one answered. After several more tattoos and ten minutes of waiting, she abandoned the front door and walked all the way around the house, eyeing its grubby curtains and grimy window panes, the overflowing garbage can outside its back door, revolted by the stench coming from an outhouse at the bottom of the neglected backyard.

Since she detested inactivity yet was determined to wait until Bede Talgarth came home, she began to pull out the weeds around the house. Hard to grow flowers or vegetables in this poor and sandy soil, she thought, piling the weeds into a heap that soon grew into a small hill.

It was dusk before Bede came through the battered gate in the paling fence that separated the grounds from the unsealed pavement outside. The first thing he noticed was the smell of uprooted plants, the second, that impressive heap of them. But who was the gardener dedicated to such a thankless task?

He found her around the back, a tall, spare girl in a dark grey cotton dress that fell almost to her ankles, had no shape worth speaking of, a high neck and long sleeves which she had rolled up above her sharp, bony elbows. He didn't recognize her, even when she straightened and stared straight at him.

"This place is a disgrace," she said, wiping her dirty hands on her skirt. "It's not difficult to see that you're a bachelor who'd be happy eating off a packing case and sitting on an orange box. But if you're short of money you could grow vegetables with a bit of cow manure to help the soil, and the exercise would be good for you. You're growing a little pot belly, Mr. Talgarth."

Since he knew this fact only too well and was exasperated by it, her observation rankled. But he had recognized the voice, crisp and autocratic, and stared at her in astonishment.

"Nell Kinross!" he exclaimed. "What on earth are you doing here?"

"Weeding," she said, her blue eyes traveling over his navy-blue three-piece suit, the celluloid collar and cuffs, the clubby M.L.A. tie and links. "Gone up in the world, eh?"

"Even Labor members of the parliament have to conform as to dress," he said defensively.

"Just as well it's Friday, then. You can put on some old clothes and spend the weekend among the weeds."

"I spend my weekends going the rounds of my constituents," he said stiffly.

"Accepting bikkies and sugary tea, probably scones with jam and cream, and later on, big mugs of beer. You'll be dead before you're forty, Mr. Talgarth, unless you reform your ways."

"I fail to see that my health is any of your concern, Miss Kinross!" he snapped. "I suppose you want something—what?"

"To go inside and have a cup of tea."

He winced. "It isn't—er—very clean or tidy."

"I didn't assume it would be. Your curtains need a wash, so do your windows. But tea is made on boiling water, so I will undoubtedly survive it."

She stood waiting, her pointed brows raised, that bony face looking derisive save for its eyes, which twinkled wickedly.

He heaved a sigh. "Be it on your own head. Come in."

The back door opened into a scullery that contained a pair of concrete washing tubs supplied with water by a tap.

"At least you have water laid on," she said. "Why do you still have a long-drop down the backyard?"

"The sewer hasn't been connected," he said shortly, leading the way into a small kitchen that had another sink, a four-burner gas stove and a big deal table with one wooden chair tucked under it. The walls were a dingy, yellowed cream so sprinkled with the peppery dots of fly excrement that they made a kind of design statement. The table itself bore the larger droppings of cockroaches, the floor pebbles of mouse and rat droppings.

"You really can't live this way," said Nell, pulling out the chair and seating herself; she extricated a handkerchief from her large leather holdall and flicked it across the table to make a clean spot for her elbows. "The parliament pays you a good salary these days, doesn't it? Hire someone to clean."

"I couldn't do that!" he snapped, growing angrier with each of her disparaging remarks. "I'm a *Labor* man, I don't condone servants!"

"Rubbish!" she said scornfully. "If you want to argue from a socialist point of view, then you'd be offering employment to someone probably desperate for a little extra money, and sharing your own prosperity with one of your constituents—a woman, most likely, therefore not empowered to give you a vote, but I'm sure her husband would give you his."

"Her husband would most likely already give me his."

"One day women will vote too, Mr. Talgarth. You can't subscribe to all this equality and democracy stuff without seeing that women are citizens too."

"I am absolutely opposed to the concept of servants."

"Then don't treat her like a servant, Mr. Talgarth. Treat her as what she actually is—an adept at her trade, which is to clean. There's no disgrace in that, is there? You pay her well and on time, you thank her for her wonderful work, and make her feel wanted, needed—it won't do you any harm with your voters to have a woman singing your praises as a democratic employer to all her friends. Men vote, yes, but women can influence their votes, and I'm sure often do. So you hire a woman to keep your house clean, and set aside enough time in your grounds to keep that pot belly at bay."

"You have a point," he conceded uneasily, pouring boiling water into his teapot. The sugar bowl was dumped on the table. "It's got cockroach doings in it, I'm afraid, and I don't have any milk."

"Buy yourself an ice chest. Arncliffe must have an iceman, and there's no reason why you have to lock him out if you're not here—there's nothing worth stealing. You'll have to get rid of the cockroaches, they live in drains, sewers, anything filthy, and they sick up what they've eaten—see it all around the rim of your sugar bowl? It's a death trap. I'll bet there's a lot of typhoid in Arncliffe, not to mention smallpox and infantile paralysis. You're in the parliament—get the slugs on to the sewerage. Until people learn to be clean, Sydney's a dangerous place. Get rid of the rats and mice too, or one day there'll be an outbreak of bubonic plague." Nell accepted the mug of black, sugarless tea and drank it gratefully.

"You're supposed to be an engineer, aren't you?" he asked feebly. "You sound more like a doctor."

"Yes, I'm finishing my first year in engineering soon, but what I really want to be is a doctor, especially now they've opened Medicine to women."

Fight it though he did, he found himself liking her; she was so businesslike, so logical, so free from self-pity. And, despite her criticisms, not in the least repelled by his bachelor habits. Nell Kinross liked to produce sensible answers. Such a pity she's on the other side, he thought. She'd be a valuable addition to our forces, even if behind the scenes.

Her joy was complete when he produced an orange box and sat on it—just as she had suspected, he didn't care about material things. How much it must irk him to wear a suit! I'll bet when he goes out on weekends to visit his constituents, he's back in dungarees and rolled-up sleeves.

"I have a good idea," she said suddenly, holding out her mug for more tea. "Instead of eating bikkies and scones with jam and cream when you're making your calls, you could offer to dig holes, chop wood, shift furniture. You'd get exercise, and not have time to stuff your face."

"Why," he asked, "are you here, Miss Kinross? What is it you think I can do for you?"

"Call me Nell and I'll call you Bede. Such an interesting name, Bede. Do you know who he was?"

"It's a family name," he said.

"He was the Venerable Bede, a monk of Northumberland, who is said to have walked all the way to Rome and back again. He wrote the first real history of the English people, though whether he was a Saxon or a Celt isn't known. He lived in the seventh and eighth centuries after Christ, and was a very gentle, holy soul."

"That leaves me out," he said lightly. "How do you know all this sort of thing?"

"I read," she said simply. "There wasn't much else to do in Kinross until Auntie Ruby put me to work. That's why engineering is so easy for me—I know the theory backward, and the actual business, especially mining, very well. I just need a degree."

"You still haven't told me what you want."

"I want you to talk to a cantankerous old Scot named Angus Robertson, who is the union's shop steward at Constantine Drills. I need to get some experience on the shop floor there, and the owners gave me permission. Then Robertson said a flat no."

"Oh, yes, the metalworkers. I don't see why they should feel threatened by women—I can't see any woman, even you, wanting to drill and weld and hammer and rivet and whatever steel."

"No, I want to learn how to turn steel on a metal lathe. No engineer worth his or *her* salt can design steel stuff without understanding what a metal lathe can and can't do."

"I agree that shop-floor experience is essential." He turned the corners of his mouth down, frowned into his own undrunk tea. "All right, I'll talk to Angus. But I'll also talk to the union leaders. They can exert more pressure on him than I can."

"That's all I ask," said Nell, rising to her feet.

"How can I contact you?"

"I have a telephone in my house. It's in the Glebe. If the answer's yes, you can come to dinner and eat *healthy* food."

"By the way, how old are you, Nell?"

"Sixteen and—um—eight-tenths."

"Jesus!" he said, breaking into a cold sweat.

"Stop panicking," she said scornfully as she departed. "I can look after myself."

I'll bet you can, he thought, watching her cab disappear down the road. Jesus! Jail bait, and he'd had her inside his house! Still, no one knew, so what had it mattered?

And she was right, of course. Everyone in his electorate pitied him as a bachelor in a dreadful house, incapable of caring for himself. Hence the food he was always offered as he did his rounds. How could he explain to these people that the parliament put on a tip-top lunch every day it sat? That the Trades and Labour Council had food too? He would get into the grounds with a hoe and hire—for a decent wage—a desperately poor woman to clean for him. Set rat- and mousetraps, lay down poison for the cockroaches, and buy flypapers to twirl from the ceiling and trap the flies on their sticky, toxic surfaces. I don't want to die before I'm forty, he said to himself, but I've noticed that my gut isn't all it ought to be. If the place is cleaner, maybe I won't get those bilious attacks. Nell Kinross, all of sixteen in years and all of sixty in sheer gall.

THE ANSWER was yes, on one condition: that Nell rivet two steel plates together. If she could do that, then she could learn to work the metal lathe. Much though he hated to admit it, Angus Robertson announced that she could rivet well. But when she returned three days later for her lesson, she found the whole workshop idle.

"Steam engine's down," said Angus Robertson with quiet triumph, "and our steam engineer's crook."

"Dear, dear," said Nell, walking across the floor to where the engine stood producing steam and brushing the three men around it aside to peer at it. "How crook? Not a fever, I hope?"

"Nay," said Angus, watching in fascination as she studied the governor assembly that regulated the amount of steam passing through the slide valve into the combustion chamber. "Rheumatics."

"Tomorrow I'll bring you in some sachets of powder that you can pass on to him. Tell him to take one sachet three times a day and wash it down with plenty of water. It's an old Chinese remedy for rheumatic pains and fevers," said Nell, one hand groping for a tool that wasn't there. "Pass me that socket wrench, please."

"Some Chinky *poison?*" Angus recoiled, gasping dramatically. "I'll no' give Johnny anything like that!"

"Oh, rubbish!" snapped Nell, brandishing the wrench. "It's mostly willow bark ground up with other beneficial herbs—not an eye of newt or toe of frog in sight!" She indicated the governor assembly with the air of someone who found it hard to believe that the problem hadn't been solved. "The weights are cockeyed, Mr. Robertson. Two broken straps, which won't take long to fix."

Within two hours the governor fly weights—brass balls the size of Ping-Pong balls—and the riser assembly were back in place, the straps holding the weights brazed on to the crown and riser. The balls spun out with centrifugal force, the slider valve opened to let sufficient steam into the combustion chamber, and the fly wheel began to turn, permitting all the machinery that the steam engine powered to work again.

Bede Talgarth had turned up to watch; so had the junior partner of Constantine Drills, Mr. Arthur Constantine.

"Is there anything she doesn't know, or can't do?" Arthur Constantine asked Bede.

"I'm as ignorant about her as you are, sir," said Bede with the formality suitable to an encounter between a capitalist and a socialist, "but I gather that her father is a hands-on sort of chap, and that she's been his offsider since she was little. Professor Warren, who is Dean of Science, says that she'll top her class so easily that it's hardly worth examining her."

"A frightening prospect," said Arthur Constantine.

"No, a warning bell," Bede said, "and it tells me that out there in the weaker half of our population there are women being wasted. Luckily most women are content with their lot. But Nell Kinross is a message that some women despise their lot."

"Then let them go nursing or teach school."

"Unless their talents lie in engineering," Bede sniped, not because he was converted to women's struggle for equality, but because he wanted to make this sleek man uncomfortable. He and his kind spent an increasing amount of their hours worrying about their workers, so why not add the spectre of women workers?

"I suggest, Mr. Constantine," said Nell, coming to join them, "that you invest in a new governor assembly for your steam engine. Those straps have been brazed up a dozen times, so they're going to go again. It's true that one steam engine can power all your machine tools, but only if it works. You've lost three hours of production today, and no manufacturer can afford that when he's employing just the one steam engineer."

"Thank you, Miss Kinross,"Constantine said stiffly, "the matter will be attended to."

Nell winked at Bede and strode away in her overalls shouting for Angus Robertson, who scuttled to her side with the mien of one who had been bested—temporarily at least.

Grinning, Bede decided to stay and watch Miss Kinross make even finer mincemeat of Arthur Constantine, Angus Robertson and the metal lathe, which she took to like a duck to water.

There's a certain poetry of motion about her, Bede thought; she moves with such certainty and fluid grace, expression rapt, oblivious to everything outside the sphere of what she's doing.

"I CAN'T get over how strong you are, Nell," he said to her when he came to dinner at her house. "You heft steel around as if it weighed a feather."

"Lifting is a trick," she said, unimpressed by this token of admiration. "You know that, you have to. You haven't always worn the seat of your trousers shiny sitting on a parliamentary bench or negotiating with employers."

He winced. "What I really like about you," he said, "is your tact and diplomacy."

The meal, he discovered when he arrived, was not a cosy tête-à-tête, but a cheerful, noisy repast shared by the three Chinese and Donny Wilkins. Delicious Chinese food, good company.

Yet none of them is in love with her, he realized; they're like brothers with a bossy older sister, though she's the youngest.

"I have a message from Angus Robertson," he said when the meal was over and the "brothers" had gone to their books—final exams were looming.

"Crusty old Scots engineer," she said affectionately. "I brought him round, didn't I? By the time I'd learned the lathe, he was eating out of my hand."

"You proved your worth in a man's world."

"What's the message?"

"That your Chinese powders worked a treat. The steam man is back at work feeling a box of birds."

"I'll drop Angus a line to tell the chap that he can buy more of the powders at a Chinese herbalist's in the Haymarket. Though if he's going to take them regularly, he should wash them down with milk rather than water. It's terrific stuff, but it's hard on the stomach. Milk is the answer to that for any medicine of any nationality that's hard on the stomach."

"I'm beginning to think that for all your engineering skills, Nell, you'd make an even better doctor," Bede said.

She ushered him to the door, more pleased by that statement than by any compliments he had paid her. "Thank you for coming."

"Thank you for asking me," he reciprocated, hopping down a step without trying to touch her. "After your exams are over and before you go back to Kinross, will you come to dinner at my house? Believe it or not, I'm a good cook when I have a reason to cook. In our family, all the children had to take a turn in the kitchen. The place will be cleaner, I promise."

"Thank you, I'd like to come. Just phone me through the exchange," she said, and closed the door.

He walked away toward Redfern thoughtfully, not sure of his feelings. Something about her attracted him strongly—that fearless, indomitable quality, perhaps. The way she went straight for what she wanted, yet never moved before the right time. I wonder does her father know that she hankers to be a doctor? Medicine is the most strenuously defended male bastion, probably because, when you think about it, medicine is a perfect career for a woman. But Sir Alexander wants her with him in the business, and he's used to getting his own way. On the other hand, so is little miss Nell.

THEY HAD no contact between that dinner and the end of the exams, which Nell flew through, even more confident because her "practical work" had been so varied and satisfactory. In one corner of her mind she was wondering whether her teachers would try to cut her down to size by marking her down, but if they did, she was prepared. She would subpoena her examination papers and insist that they be marked again by someone at Cambridge who did not know her sex. A court order would not please the faculty of Science or its engineering branch.

But perhaps Professor Warren and his lecturers sensed how far this dreadful girl was prepared to go, or perhaps they longed for large donations from her father; whatever pushed them, pushed them to mark her fairly. Which, in a discipline like engineering, where the answers were mostly either right or wrong, meant that Nell topped her class with a frightening margin between her and Chan Min, who came second just ahead of Wo Ching. Donny Wilkins topped civil engineering and architecture, and Lo Chee topped mechanical engineering. Total victory for the Kinross students.

Nell wrote to Bede at his home address and said that she was free to have dinner at his house if he still wanted to entertain her. Bede wrote back with the day and the time.

One of the things about Nell that puzzled Bede was her reluctance to show off her wealth; when she turned up promptly at six o'clock two Saturdays later, she had caught the tram and then walked the several blocks from the shopping center. Yet she could have hailed a hackney outside her door and been driven to Arncliffe in comfort. Her dress was another grey cotton thing without shape, its hem a good four inches above her ankles—very daring had the dress been a scarlet one or even festive in a less damning color. No hat on her head—another solecism—no jewelry, and her habitual big leather hold-all that rested on a strap over her left shoulder.

"Why are your dresses so short?" he asked, meeting her at the front gate.

Nell was too busy looking at the acre of ground in delight. "Bede, you've weeded it properly! And do I see a vegetable plot in the backyard?"

"Yes. I also hope you see that the pot belly has gone," he answered. "You were right, I needed exercise. But why are your dresses so short?"

"Because I can't abide dresses that sweep the dirt," she said with a grimace. "Soiling the bottom of one's shoes is bad enough. Soiling something that one can't wash every time it's worn is even worse."

"Does that mean you wash the soles of your shoes?"

"Of course, if I've been somewhere nasty. Think of what gets on them! The streets are slimed with spittle—mucus from some fellow blowing his nose with his fingers—disgusting! Not to mention vomit, dog turds and rotten garbage."

"I understand the spittle. We've had to introduce a fine for spitting in tramcars and train carriages," he said, walking her down the path to the front door.

"The curtains are clean, so are the windows," she said, sounding pleased.

Ushering her into the house wasn't something he did with pride, as he hadn't any furniture to speak of: one old sofa with herniating springs visible between its bottom and the floor, a bureau, and a big, battered old desk with a chair drawn up to it. The kitchen table, however, now boasted two wooden chairs, and the orange case had gone. The floors were either bare boards or cheap linoleum, but someone had scrubbed the fly dirt off the walls and there were no rat or mouse pebbles to be seen. Or any cockroach droppings.

"Though I haven't gotten rid of the wretched things yet," he said, sitting her at the kitchen table. "They're immortal."

"Try saucers of red wine," said Nell. "They can't resist it, and they drown in it." She chuckled. "That would please the Temperance League, wouldn't it?" A polite cough. "I presume you rent rather than own?" she asked.

"Yes."

"Then try to persuade the landlord to fence the property with six-foot palings. Then you could keep a dozen chooks, have eggs from them, and at the same time have outer defenses against cockroaches. Chooks love to eat cockroaches."

"How do you *know* all these things?"

"Well, we live in the Glebe, which is full of cockroaches. Butterfly Wing eliminates them with saucers of red wine and a backyard full of wandering chooks."

"Why don't you wear a hat?" he asked, opening the oven door and peering inside.

"Smells delicious," she said. "I just hate hats, that's all. They're of no earthly use, and every year they're getting uglier. If I'm out in the sun for long periods, I wear a Chinese coolie hat—it's sensible."

"And, I noticed at Constantine Drills, overalls on the shop floor. It's no wonder old Angus objected to you."

"The last thing any factory or workshop needs is some fool woman getting her skirt caught in a fly wheel. The overalls are not exactly come-hither, so what does it matter?"

"True," he admitted, tending pots on top of the stove.

"What's for dinner?" she asked.

"Roast leg of lamb, potatoes and pumpkin roasted around the joint, some nice little butternut squashes, and murdered beans."

"*Murdered* beans?"

"Cut into thin shreds. Oh, and gravy, of course."

"Bring it on! I could eat a horse."

The food was traditionally British, but very good; Bede had not exaggerated when he said he could cook. Even the murdered beans weren't overdone. Nell tucked in and ate quite as much as her host did.

"Do I have to save room for pudden, or can I have a second helping?" she asked, wiping the last of the gravy off her plate with a piece of bread.

"I have to watch that pot belly, so it's a second helping," he said, smiling. "Judging from your appetite, you don't suffer from a tendency to fatness."

"No, I'm like my father—on the skinny side."

After the meal was done and cleared away—he refused to let her wash or dry the dishes, said they weren't going anywhere until he felt like doing them—he produced a good pot of tea and two porcelain cups and saucers with silver spoons. The sugar bowl was spotless and the milk chilly from incarceration in the new ice chest. Whereupon, with a plate of Mrs. Charlton the cleaning lady's oatmeal cookies between them, they settled to talk about many things that always returned to his passion, socialism and the workingman. Nell often didn't see eye to eye with him, and gave him good arguments, particularly about the Chinese. Time flew by unnoticed, for both of them were people who lived inside their minds, had suppressed what he would have called his carnal urges and she her romantic dreams.

Finally, when he at least became aware that it was very late, he dared to bring up a subject he felt—the why eluded him—*entitled* to know about.

"How is your sister?" he asked.

"Very well, according to my mother," Nell said, her face darkening. "You won't know this, but Anna has taken against me, so I haven't bothered going home during the vacations, I've done practical work on the shop floor instead."

"Why should she take against you?"

"That's a mystery. You must understand that her thought processes are extremely limited and unpredictable. The newspapers at the time said that she's slightly simple, but the truth is that she's very mentally retarded. Her vocabulary consists of about fifty words, mostly nouns, an occasional adjective, a rare verb. That fellow could manipulate her as easily as he did his dog. Anna is very good-natured in almost all circumstances."

"So you believe it was Sam O'Donnell?"

"Absolutely," she said emphatically.

"And the baby?"

"Dolly. That's what Anna called her, thinking her a doll. So my father registered her name as Dolly. She's eighteen months old now, and—isn't it ironic?—very bright. She walked early, talked early, and, my mother says, is beginning to be a trouble." The darkness in Nell's face grew more somber still. "I must go home on Monday, because something is going on that my mother isn't willing to discuss in her letters."

"It's a difficult burden to carry, isn't it?"

"An unusual one, at any rate. So far I haven't been called upon to carry an ounce of it, but that isn't right. Nor are other things I feel, but can't tell you about because they aren't facts, just instincts. I *loathe* instincts!" said Nell savagely.

Its greenish glow enhanced by one of the new ceramic mantles, the gas light on the wall played on his thick, unruly mass of hair and turned its copper hue to old bronze. His eyes, as black as Alexander's, were deeply set in their orbits and rather narrow; unfathomable, thought Nell, suddenly intrigued. One only knows what he is from what he says, never from how he looks, especially those enigmatic eyes.

"You'll grow more respectful of instincts as you get older," he said, and smiled at her with white, even teeth. "You've built your world on facts—not unusual in a mathematician. But the great philosophers have all been mathematicians, so they have the kind of brain can conceive abstract ideas. Instincts are abstract emotions, but not entirely thoughtless. I always think of mine as based on events or experiences I haven't consciously valued, yet somewhere deep down another part of me values them."

"I didn't think Karl Marx was a mathematician," she said.

"He's not a philosopher either. He's more akin to some researcher into human behavior. Mind, not soul."

"That bit about instincts—are you telling me that I should go home as soon as possible?" she asked, a tinge of regret in her voice. "That you have an instinct about it?"

"I'm not sure. However, I'll be sorry to see you go. It's been a great pleasure to cook for an appreciative eater, and I was looking forward to doing it again."

Yet he wasn't signaling her with any man-woman stuff, for which she was grateful.

"I've enjoyed the evening," she said, sounding stilted.

"But you've had enough." He rose to his feet. "Come on, I'll walk you up to the main road and find you a hackney."

"I can catch the tram."

He withdrew his watch from a pocket, flipped its lid open and consulted it. "Not at this hour, you won't. Do you have money for a hackney?"

"Oh, lord, yes!" Her eyes danced. "It's just that hackneys are like instincts—I dislike being cooped up in such a small, smelly place. One never knows who was in there before one."

"Let me pay your fare."

"Indeed you will not! With a cleaning lady and a new ice chest to add to my sins? How much is a block of ice twice a week, threepence? Six-pence?"

"Fourpence, actually. But I am quite well off these days—members of parliament, including the Labor ones, tend to dispense salaries and privileges liberally. So I've saved a lot." He drew a breath, put his hand under her elbow to guide her to the front door. "As a matter of fact, I'm seriously thinking of finding out how much the owner wants for this property. If it's anything like a reasonable price, I'd like to buy it."

Alexander Kinross's daughter considered the statement with half-shut eyes and a pursed mouth. "You should be able to beat him down to under two hundred. It's a full-acre block, yes, but in an industrial area that's encroaching on it. Unsewered. He'd not get much for it from someone intending to build a factory on it, and the speculators interested in housing have moved closer to the coast. Terraces are out, brick semi-detached are in, and this is the wrong shape to stick half a dozen semis on. Offer him a hundred and fifty and see what he says."

Bede burst out laughing. "Easy for you to say, impossible for me to do! I don't have a haggling bone in my body."

"Nor did I, I thought," she said in a surprised tone. "But I like you, Bede, so I'd haggle for you."

"That's nice to hear. I like you too, Nell."

"Good," she said, flapping a hand at a hackney. "What luck! I hope he'll take me to the Glebe."

"Tip him threepence and he'll take you anywhere. And don't be tempted to let him go at Parramatta Road. There are gangs of larrikins about."

"A symptom of hard times, my father would say. Jobless youths in need of some outlet for their energies. Therefore a good time to offer for property." She climbed into the tiny conveyance. "I'll write from Kinross."

"Do," he said, then stood until the tired horse geed up and the carriage rattled away. "But you won't write," he said to himself, sighed and turned to walk the few yards home again. It wouldn't be any good anyway: a Welsh coal miner's socialist son and the daughter of Australia's richest capitalist. A child not yet seventeen. On the verge of life, not riding its crest. A man of principle—and he was that—would let her get on with her life far from his ken. So be it. Goodbye, Nell Kinross.

BUT NELL didn't get home to Kinross until after the New Year and her seventeenth birthday. Her father and Auntie Ruby appeared in Sydney to "do the town," as he put it: theater, museums, art galleries, exhibitions, even the pantomime. Thoroughly enjoying herself, Nell forgot her—and Bede Talgarth's—instincts.

Six

ANNA'S DOLLY

I COULDN'T VERY well ignore Daddy's wishes," Nell said to her mother defensively.

"Of course you couldn't," Elizabeth answered, apparently not aggrieved. "In fact, it was probably for the best. Looking back on it, I think I made too much of things."

"What things?"

"Anna got annoyed with Dolly, and hurt her."

Nell lost color. "Mum, no!"

"It was only the once, about six weeks ago."

"How did it happen? *Why?*"

"I honestly don't know. We never leave Anna alone with the baby, but Peony wasn't actually watching them, she was busy with some mending. Then Dolly gave a shriek of pain and began to cry really hard. When Peony got up to see what was wrong, Anna just wouldn't let her near. 'Bad Dolly! Bad Dolly!' she kept saying." Elizabeth looked at Nell helplessly, a plea in her eyes that Nell had never seen. "She had hold of Dolly's arm, and she was pinching it, screwing it. The poor child was struggling and howling—I was coming down the hall and heard her, which was just as well. Anna wouldn't let her go, kept on pinching and calling Dolly bad. It took Peony and I combined to make her let go, and ages to calm Dolly, who developed a nasty bruise and wouldn't go near Anna for days. That put Anna in a bad temper. You know Anna, she's never bad-tempered! Just unmanageable when she has her courses. Anyway, eventually we decided to give Dolly back to her for a little while, and the bad temper disappeared at once. Luckily Dolly didn't protest—I think she'd gotten to the stage where the memory of being hurt didn't matter as much as being kept away from Anna."

"Which one is Peony?" asked Nell, frowning.

"A Wong girl. Ruby sent her when Dolly began to walk and talk. Not exactly to replace Jade, more to give me some help."

"Is she in Jade's league?"

"Perhaps not, but she's very devoted."

"I should have ignored Dad and come home," Nell grumbled. "Let's go and see them, Mum."

The nursery might have served as an artist's model, it looked so perfect in every detail. The new Wong sister was huddled close to Anna, who had Dolly on her lap; two different heads of black hair, one straight, one curly, bent together over an exquisite little fair child, plump and dimpled.

The last time Nell had seen Dolly she was still a baby, but this was a toddler almost two years old, with a thatch of flaxen ringlets above a round, cherubic face in which were set two eyes the color of aquamarines. Her brows and lashes were brown, perhaps suggesting that the hair would darken as she grew older, and she had a look to her that didn't suggest Alexander or Elizabeth—her father, no doubt.

When Anna glanced up and saw Nell, her face broke into smiles; she flung Dolly away as if she were a lifeless doll—not a new action, Nell deduced, as Peony was ready to catch the child, put her on the floor unharmed.

"Nell! Nell! Nell!" Anna cried, arms outstretched.

"Hello, my darling," said Nell, hugging and kissing her.

"Dolly! Where Dolly?" Anna demanded then.

"Here," said Peony, handing her over.

"Dolly, my Dolly!" said Anna to Nell, beaming.

"Hello, Dolly. You don't remember me, do you?" Nell asked, taking one little hand. "I'm your Auntie Nell."

"Auntie Nell," the child enunciated clearly, and smiled.

"May I have her, Anna?"

A frown came; Anna considered her sister from under her fine dark brows, and for a moment both Elizabeth and Nell wondered if she would reject Nell as she had before Dolly's birth. Then she plucked the child off her lap and threw her carelessly at Nell. "Here!" she said, the impulse of denial dying.

Half an hour with Anna and Dolly left Nell more exhausted than contending with white male university students, but it also left her steeled to say what had to be said. Preferably to both her parents at one and the same moment.

"Mum, Dad," she said in the library, where the three of them gathered for a sherry before dinner, "I have something to discuss that won't wait."

Sensing what was coming, Elizabeth shrank into herself at once, whereas Alexander merely lifted his eyes from contemplation of his drink and raised his brows in an unspoken question.

"It's Anna and Dolly."

"What about them?" Alexander asked, stifling a sigh.

"You're going to have to separate them."

He looked aghast. "*Separate* them? Why?"

"Because Dolly is a flesh-and-blood child whom Anna treats like a rag doll. Don't you remember what happened when she was given a puppy years ago? She squeezed it too hard, it bit her, and she dashed its brains out against the wall. The same fate is in store for Dolly, who's become big enough and independent enough to strive for a little freedom. Freedom Anna isn't willing to allow. Rag dolls are at beck and call, you can chuck them away into a corner and pick them up whenever you feel like it."

"Surely you exaggerate, Nell," said Alexander.

"Indeed you do," said Elizabeth. "Anna *loves* Dolly."

"Anna loved the puppy too, and I do not exaggerate!" Her voice rose, sharpened. "Dad, did Mum tell you how Anna pinched Dolly's arm a few weeks ago? Left it black-and-blue?"

"No," said Alexander, putting down his drink.

"But it was only the once, Nell," Elizabeth protested. "I told you, it was only the once! There's been nothing since."

"Yes, Mum, there has! It happens all the time, but you're refusing to see it. Dolly gets flung around every day as if she were inanimate, but between Peony—a very good girl!—and her own instincts for self-preservation, she manages to avoid being hurt." Nell went across to her father and sank down at his knee, her hand on it, her cornflower-blue eyes fixed on his face. "Dad, the situation cannot be allowed to continue. If it does continue, then Dolly is going to be seriously injured. Either Peony won't be close enough to catch her, or Anna will refuse to give her up if she's punishing her 'bad Dolly.' The same goes for you as for Peony, Mum. Neither of you is half as strong as Anna."

"I see," said Alexander slowly. "Yes, I see."

"We'll redouble our efforts," Elizabeth said, casting this traitorous daughter a look of loathing. "They are mother and child! Anna nursed Dolly for eight months! If we tried to pull them apart, Anna would pine away and die."

"Oh, Mum, do you think I haven't considered that?" Nell cried, head turned toward her. "Do you think saying all of this gives me any pleasure? Anna is my sister! I love her! I always have, I always will. But she's changed since Dolly's birth—maybe that's easier for me to see, because I haven't been here for such a long time. Her vocabulary has lessened, so has her ability to string words together. Anna's always been infantile, but she's steadily regressing. After Dolly's birth she was so gentle, treated Dolly as if she understood that it was living flesh she cuddled. But now she doesn't. And her moods are worsening. She's become—oh, petulant and domineering—probably because she's been so spoiled all her life. No one has ever slapped her for being naughty, or tried to remonstrate with her."

"She never needed slapping! Which is more than I can say for you, madam!" Elizabeth snapped.

"I agree," said Nell, remaining calm. Her attention returned to her father. "Dad, you *must* act."

"It's always you who sees the truth, Nell, isn't it? Yes, I must act."

"No!" Elizabeth shouted, jumping to her feet in a flurry of spilled sherry. "No, Alexander, I won't permit it!"

"Go away, Nell," said Alexander.

"But Dad—"

"Not now. Just go away."

"The final phase has come," Alexander said as soon as the door closed. "I started as Dadda, then I became Daddy, and now I'm Dad. Nell has grown up."

"Into your living image—cold and hard-hearted!"

"No, into her amazing self. Sit down, Elizabeth."

"I can't," she said, beginning to pace.

"You *will* sit down! I refuse to have a serious discussion with someone swishing around in an attempt to avoid the truth."

"Anna is my child," Elizabeth said, sinking into her chair.

"And Dolly is your grandchild, don't forget that." He sat forward, his hands clasped loosely together, and pinned her on his unblinking ebony stare. "Elizabeth, for all that you dislike me, for all that I disgust you, I am the father of your daughters, and Dolly's grandfather. Do you honestly believe that I am so insensitive that I can't plumb the depths of this tragedy? That I didn't suffer for Anna when I learned she was so afflicted? That I didn't suffer for Jade, who paid the price? Do you think that, if I could, I wouldn't somehow alleviate the pain and sorrow that has surrounded Anna for all her fifteen years of life? Of course I would! I'd shift heaven and earth, if shifting heaven and earth would help her. But tragedies don't cease being tragedies. They run their course to the terrible end. Just as this tragedy will. Perhaps no child could be as gifted as Nell without some kind of counterbalance. But you can't blame Nell for being who she is, any more than you can blame me—or yourself!—for what Anna is. Accept the facts, my dear. Anna and Dolly have to be separated before the tragedy worsens."

She listened, tears pouring down her face. "I have hurt you dreadfully," she said through sobs, "although I never meant to. If this is a time for truth, I know how little you deserve what I've done to you." Her hands writhed, fingers screwed together. "You have been kind and generous, and I know—*I know!*—that if I had behaved differently toward you, none of the bitter things would ever have been said. Nor would you have needed Ruby. But I cannot help myself, Alexander, I cannot help myself!"

Handkerchief out, he rose from his chair and went to her, pushed the linen into her hand and held her head against a thigh. "Don't weep so, Elizabeth. It's not your fault that you can't love me or even like me. Why rack yourself with guilt over something you can't help? You're a slave to duty, but I made you one when Anna was a baby." His hand closed on her hair. "It's a pity that my natural affection for you isn't returned. I'd rather hoped that with the passing of the years, you'd grow closer. Instead, you just move farther away."

Her sobs had quietened, but she said nothing.

"Feeling better?"

"Yes," she said, using the handkerchief.

He returned to his chair. "Then we can finish. You know as well as I do that the deed has to be done." A peculiar pain came into his face. "What you don't know is that I swore an oath to Jade that I would never commit Anna to an asylum. I daresay she knew far more than she ever told us. That she saw this coming, or something similar. So we have two things to do. The first is to separate Dolly from her natural mother, who can mother her no longer. The second is what to do with Anna. Do we keep her here, a virtual prisoner, or do we send her elsewhere to imprison her?"

"Could it work if she were kept here, always locked up?"

"I think Nell would say no. For one thing, she would still be in fairly close proximity to Dolly, and there is a streak of cunning in her—witness how she could elude all her minders when she had her trysts with O'Donnell."

Elizabeth pressed the little buzzer on the table beside her. "Mrs. Surtees," she said when the housekeeper came, "would you ask Nell to come back to the library, please?"

The moment Nell appeared, chin up, Elizabeth went to her and held her, kissed her brow. "I'm sorry, Nell, truly sorry. Please forgive me."

"There's nothing to forgive," said Nell, sitting down. "It was shock, I know that."

"We need to talk to you about Anna," Elizabeth said.

Alexander leaned back, his face in shadow, while Elizabeth labored on. "We have agreed that Anna and Dolly must be separated, which means we have to decide what to do with Anna. Should we keep her here under lock and key, or send her away?"

"I think she has to be sent away," said Nell slowly, eyes misty. "O'Donnell opened a door for Anna that cannot be closed. I believe that has accounted for some of her deterioration. No, she doesn't know what it is she misses, yet she misses *something* that she once had and once enjoyed. There's an element of—of—of frustration in her behavior that she's taking out on Dolly. It's all so hidden, so mysterious! We don't know anything about how the mentally retarded view their world, or what kinds of more subtle emotions they experience than rage and happiness. I can't help but think they live in a more complex way than we assume."

"What did you see today, Nell?" Alexander asked.

"An element of spite directed at Dolly—honestly, Dad, Anna does fling her around quite viciously. And the fact that Dolly can cope with it suggests that it happens all the time. But that it didn't happen before she grew old enough and clever enough to evade injury. It's Dolly who matters more, because Dolly has a future. She's a dear little girl with a normal brain. How can we allow her to be exposed to Anna? Yet if we keep the pair of them here, Anna will find her."

"Are you suggesting," Elizabeth asked, "that Dolly not be told Anna is her mother? That, for instance, I should become her mother?"

"For as long as the fiction can be maintained, yes."

Alexander had been only half listening, part of his mind engaged in finding a way out of his oath to Jade. "What if we send Anna not to an asylum but to a secure private house? Her minders will have to be women, given O'Donnell. A place that has a big courtyard where she can walk and play in a garden, that has the feel of a home? Would Anna learn to forget us, Nell? Would she learn to love at least one of her minders instead?"

"I'd rather that than asylum care, Dad. I'd rather that than try to keep her here. If you can find a suitable building in Sydney, I'd be willing to police her care."

"Police it?" Elizabeth asked, alarmed.

Alexander Kinross looked out of his daughter's eyes. "Yes, Mum, her care will have to be policed. People can be so deceptive, especially the assortment of people who care for the helpless. They are natural victims for petty cruelties and needless inhumanities. Don't ask me how I know that, I just do. So I'll police the place—drop in unexpectedly, look for injuries, see how clean she's kept, all that sort of thing."

"It will tie you down," said Alexander with a growl.

"Dad, it's high time I contributed something to Anna. Mum has had to do it all so far."

"I've had good help," said Elizabeth, in a mood to be just. "Imagine what it would have been like if I couldn't have afforded help. There's a family in Kinross with the same problem."

"But unlikely to have a Dolly from it. Their girl is very stigmatized—harelip, cleft palate, stunted growth," said Nell.

"How do you know that?" asked Alexander, astonished.

"I used to see her when I lived here, Dad. She interested me. But she won't live nearly as long as Anna might."

"And that's a mercy," said Alexander.

"It won't be to her mother," Elizabeth said abruptly. "Or to her brothers and sisters. They love her."

A WEEK LATER Anna broke Dolly's arm and attacked Peony when she tried to rescue the frantic child. Suddenly no one had the time for remorse as the fighting, kicking Anna was subdued and her child permanently removed from her. Until an alternative in Sydney could be found, Anna was relegated to a guest suite owning a tiny entrance foyer that could be locked before unlocking the rooms themselves. Worst of all, the windows had to be fitted with bars, as the suite was on the ground floor.

Alexander and Nell hurried off to Sydney to look at houses, an ideal opportunity for Nell to put her proposals to him during the journey. Though the train was approaching Lithgow before she summoned up the courage to begin.

"I think," she started, "that eventually we'll have to build a house, Dad. No one puts a courtyard at the center of a house, and we have Donny Wilkins to design it for us. That keeps it in the family, don't you agree?"

"Go on," said Alexander, eyeing his daughter with a mixture of amusement and skepticism.

"There are big tracts of land going down to the harbor in Drummoyne and Rozelle that I hear are going to be sold thanks to hard times. A lot of the men who could afford mansions in huge grounds are declaring bankruptcy now that the banks are crashing right, left and center. Is Apocalypse in trouble, Dad?"

"No, Nell, nor will be."

She heaved a sigh of relief. "Then that's all right. Am I correct in thinking that harborside land is a good investment?"

"Yes, you are."

"So if you bought one or two bankrupt estates, you wouldn't lose on them?"

"No, I wouldn't. But why concentrate on the backwaters of the harbor when there are equally grand mansions going for a song in Vaucluse and Point Piper?"

"They're posh suburbs, Dad, and posh people are—funny."

"I assume that you don't consider us posh?"

"Posh people don't sequester themselves in isolated places like Kinross, they like to be where they can entertain royalty and governors. Put on the dog," Nell said, using a new phrase.

"So what are we, if we're not posh and don't put on the dog?"

"Filthy rich," she said gravely. "Just filthy rich."

"Dear, dear. Therefore I should buy my vast tracts of land containing mansions in pedestrian suburbs like Rozelle?"

"Exactly!" She beamed.

"Well, it's actually quite a good idea," Alexander said, "save for one thing. You'd find it difficult to get from the Glebe to Rozelle to police Anna."

"I wasn't thinking of putting her somewhere like Rozelle yet," Nell temporized. "Later, when the mansion could become the nucleus of a hospital. Not an asylum, a *hospital.* Somewhere that good work could be done to find a cure for the mentally afflicted."

He was frowning, but not direfully. "Just where are you going, Nell? Finding an avenue of philanthropy for my filthy riches?"

"No, not really. It's more that—um—well . . ."

"Get it off your chest, girl."

She gulped and took the plunge. "I don't want to continue in Engineering, Dad. I want to do Medicine instead."

"Medicine. When did you decide that?"

"I really don't know, and that's the truth," she said slowly. "It's always been there, you see, right back when I used to cut open my dolls and make organs for them. But I never thought I'd be able to—Medicine was the only faculty that banned women. Now they've started to admit women into Medicine, and women are *flocking* to do it!"

He couldn't help it, he began to laugh. "And how many lady medical students constitute a flock?" he asked, wiping his eyes.

"Four or five," she said, laughing back.

"How many men students are there?"

"Almost a hundred."

"Still, you've had a worse trot in engineering and survived."

"I'm used to being a woman in a man's world." A wriggle, a jump. "Quite honestly, I'm more afraid of how I'll manage to get on with the women medical students than the men."

The train was coming into Lithgow, its speed slackening; for perhaps five minutes they sat facing each other and said not a word, Nell in anguish, Alexander in thought.

"We've never spoken," he said finally, "about you and your expectations, have we?"

"No, we haven't, but I suppose I assumed that I was to do engineering so I could join the firm, maybe help to run it."

"That's true, but not what I meant. I mean your inheritance. Which is seventy percent of Apocalypse Enterprises."

"Dad!"

"It's a difficulty that I've never sired a son," Alexander said, forcing himself to keep looking at her, "but in you I sired a daughter with a prodigious brain. A brain capable of any kind of technical or mathematical reasoning. And as you grew, I began to believe that, your gender notwithstanding, you would prove as good an administrator as any father could hope for in a son.

To have you graduate in mining engineering is a way to prepare you for your inheritance. What I hope is that you'll preserve your good sense and marry a man who will complement your own genius, who will be a partner for you in every way."

She got to her feet and went to a window, opened it and put her head and shoulders out to watch the activity as the Kinross train was shunted to its siding and their car uncoupled. "The Bathurst train is late," she said then.

"It's easier to talk without the racket." Alexander got out a cheroot and lit it. "I'll make a bargain with you, Nell."

"What sort of bargain?" she asked warily.

"Finish Engineering and I won't oppose your doing Medicine. Then you'll have at least one degree. There may be more women in Medicine than there are in Engineering, but I won't have the same influence with your professors that I do with factory owners." His eyes twinkled through the smoke. "I suppose I can dangle the bait of a new building or two, but I suspect I'm going to have to save some of my filthy riches for that mental hospital."

Nell extended her hand. "Done!" she said.

They shook solemnly.

"The Professor of Physiology is a Scot, Dad. Thomas Anderson Stuart. The Professor of Anatomy is another Scot, James Wilson. Most of the teaching staff is Scottish—Professor Anderson Stuart keeps bringing them out from Edinburgh, which irritates the Senate and the Chancellor mightily. But Anderson Stuart won't be denied—does that sound familiar, Dad? When he arrived in 1883, the medical school was in a four-room cottage. Now it has a huge building all to itself."

"And who's the Professor of Medicine?"

"There isn't one," said Nell. "Shall we walk on the platform a little, Dad? I need to stretch my legs."

The air was hot, but that didn't stop Nell from clutching her father's arm and snuggling against him as they strolled up and down. "I love you, Dad. You're the best," she said.

And that, concluded Alexander, is really all one can ask of one's children. To be loved and deemed the best. Her news had come as a bitter disappointment, but he was too fair a man to want to force her where her heart didn't want to go. Well did he remember those dissected dolls! The thumbed pages of his precious Dürer. A growing collection of medical books that she had ordered from his London bookseller. All there staring him in the face for years. And she was a woman, she would go where her heart wanted to go. Strange creatures, women, he reflected. Nell wasn't a bit like Elizabeth, and yet her composition was half Elizabeth. Sooner or later that half would show itself.

From Nell his mind veered to Lee.

I have always sensed that Lee was my natural heir, right from the beginning of knowing him. Now I have to find him and get him back. Even if that means I bend my stiff neck and apologize.

ALEXANDER AND NELL had a busy two weeks in Sydney. They found a forty-year-old house on Glebe Point Road not far from Nell's abode and decided it would do. Built of plastered sandstone blocks, it was roomy enough to accommodate Anna and six attendants in comfort, plus a cook, a laundress and two cleaners. Because it sat in half an acre of ground, Alexander had an exercise yard constructed just outside Anna's own quarters, only a door between.

Finding suitable attendants was more difficult. Alexander and Nell interviewed them together, Nell going so far as to sniff at each applicant's breath. The scent of cloves was as significant as the reek of liquor, Nell told the fascinated Alexander.

"The chaps chew cloves if they've been on a bender the night before lectures," she explained.

Alexander was in favor of a beaming, patently motherly woman as the chief attendant, whereas Nell held out for an austere soul with whiskers on her chin and spectacles perched on her nose.

"She's a battleship in full sail!" Alexander protested. "A dragon, Nell!"

"True, Dad, but we need someone like that in charge. Let the nice ones fuss and cluck over Anna to their hearts' content, so long as the starchy one has the power. Miss Harbottle is a good person, she'll not abuse her authority, but she will insist on running a tight battleship. Or a decent dragon's den."

AND IN APRIL, when everything was ready, a heavily sedated Anna was conveyed from Kinross to her new home in the Glebe. Only Elizabeth, Ruby and Mrs. Surtees wept. Anna's Dolly was too busy exploring a whole new world, Alexander had gone abroad yet again, and Nell was back at university doing engineering.

PART THREE

1897–1900

One

THE PRODIGAL RETURNS

A YEAR IN Burma had yielded Lee rubies and star sapphires, as well as the useful fact that here too petroleum leaked to the surface. As yet it was used only for the manufacture of kerosene after an arduous journey from the highlands in earthen jars. A year in Tibet yielded no diamonds, but spiritual riches of greater import than a Koh-i-Noor. And a year among Proctorian friends in India had commenced with a search for diamonds, then branched into something of more benefit to the maharajah's people. The production of iron from immensely rich ore deposits was hampered by a smelting technique that hadn't changed in literal millennia, depending as it did on charcoal, in short supply thanks to felled forests. Funding new methods through the sale of manganese, Lee shipped coal from Bengal and put the principate on a strong industrial footing. When some members of the British Raj protested at his gall, he answered that he was simply the maharajah's servant, that the maharajah still ruled (albeit with British consent), and what were they complaining about? The Empress of India would get her share, he was sure.

After that he skipped rather hastily to Persia to see his best friends from Proctor's days, Ali and Husain, two sons of Shah Nasru'd-Din, who seemed likely to rule from the Peacock Throne for fifty years, a jubilee he would celebrate in 1896.

Curiosity drove Lee into the Elburz mountains to see for himself the petroleum soak-wells and tar pits that Alexander had described. They were still there, still undeveloped.

Sitting his Arab horse with one booted leg across its withers, he nibbled at a nail and let his eyes roam almost sightlessly over the rugged terrain. "Elburz," he had discovered, was a misnomer dumped upon all the mountain ranges of western Persia by European geographers; the actual Elburz lay around Tehran, towering peaks under perpetual snow. What he looked at were just—mountains. No name at all.

A pipeline to the Persian Gulf . . . One well per five acres . . . A way for Persia to extricate itself from hideous debt, and a way for him to make his own fortune. Petroleum was finding more and more uses—lubricating oils, kerosene, paraffin, better tar than coal tar, vaseline, aniline dyes and other chemicals—and as fuel for a new engine that vaporized it inside the working parts with a degree of efficiency that steam couldn't rival. Hadn't the maharajah told him how artificial indigo was ruining India's trade in the natural dye?

Making up his mind, Lee returned to Tehran and sought an audience with the Shah.

"Iran possesses great wealth in petroleum," he said, using the proper name, his Farsi improved enough to dispense with an interpreter, "but no local knowledge to exploit that wealth. Whereas I have the knowledge as well as the funds to exploit it. I would very much like to be granted permission to do this, in return for an agreement giving me fifty percent of the profits plus whatever moneys I outlay in equipment and apparatus."

He labored on in a language that had no technical words, Ali and Husain helping where they could.

Another man sat listening: Nasru'd-Din's probable heir, Muzaffar-ud-Din. He was serving as the governor of Azerbaijan, a Persian province bordering the Caucasus that was at constant loggerheads with the Turks and the Russians. Because of the rapid development of Baku as a source of petroleum for Russia, Muzaffar-ud-Din was very interested. He was also anxious that Iran shouldn't be shouldered aside in any race to control ground on—or in—which a valuable resource might be located. To the Shah's family, Lee represented a relatively benign party, in that he had no territorial ambitions nor other axes to grind than Mammon. Mammon they understood, Mammon they could cope with. The old Shah had sunk into an executive torpor, hamstrung by the system of privileges and entitlements that all too often saw the wrong men gain the power. But Muzaffar-ud-Din was just past forty years of age, and as yet had not developed the grave illness that would later dog him. It was not the Turks who most worried him, but the Russians, always intriguing to gain access to the oceans of the world without running the gauntlet of someone else's sea and formidable navies. Iran was highly desirable.

So, after months of dickering, Lee Costevan emerged with the right to exploit petroleum in western Persia over an area of 250,000 square miles. Peacock Oil had to be gotten up and running, which was a matter of hiring disgruntled wildcatters in America, buying drill rigs that pumped pressurized water through hollow casing to the latest toothed rotating bits, and setting up steam engines to provide power.

His difficulties were many, none actually technical. He had to get used to being accompanied by a battalion of soldiers because the mountains were full of untamed tribes that did not subscribe to Tehran's rule; the daunting heights turned road-making, even of the most elementary kind, into a nightmare; of railroads there were virtually none; and, worst of all, the whole country was desperately short of burnable fuel, coal or wood.

Therefore, Lee decided, I start with what's feasible under the existing circumstances. So he confined his first wells to Laristan, where a railroad connected the city of Lar to the Gulf, and where, around Lar, there was coal. His wildcatters, he soon learned, had noses for oil as well as great experience; Lee listened and accumulated practical knowledge to back up his degree in geology from Edinburgh. A pipeline was clearly, as he said to himself in a wry pun, a pipe dream, but the oil could travel by rail tankers, and the British policed the Gulf, which they regarded as theirs. Port facilities were primitive, seagoing tankers scarce. Undaunted, sure that petroleum was coming into its own more and more with every passing year, Lee battled on to see Peacock Oil viable. Luckily the Shah and his government were so impoverished that a return of £10,000 was a fortune.

In 1896 old Nasru'd-Din Shah was assassinated scant days before his fiftieth jubilee; the assassin, a humble Kerman, said he was acting under orders from Sheikh Kemalu'd-Din, who had thanked his kinsman the Shah for great kindness by preaching sedition and then seeking refuge in Constantinople. Extradited to face charges (the assassin was hanged), Kemalu'd-Din died en route, and Iran settled down quite peacefully under the rule of Muzaffar-ud-Din. The new Shah commenced his reign in a promising way by regulating the copper coinage and abolishing the ancient tax on meat, but beneath the surface the usual plotting went on.

For Lee it was an anxious time; a little oil was getting through and he was showing a profit, but not the millions that he knew would come.

UNAWARE THAT the new Shah was sickening, in 1897 Lee decided to visit England. He had been away from Kinross for nearly seven years and had deliberately dropped out of sight; letters to Ruby were given to a traveler passing through to post in some European city, and never revealed his whereabouts. So Alexander, searching for him, had not managed to locate him. The reason was simple: it didn't occur to Alexander that Lee might go into the petroleum business, especially somewhere like Persia. Once Lee hurried out of India, he became the invisible man.

Only two items from Kinross accompanied him: photographs of Elizabeth and Ruby. His mother had sent them to him in India together with one of Nell, but somehow looking at a feminine version of Alexander didn't please Lee, so that one he dropped in a pile of burning leaves. Taken early in 1893, just three years after his departure, they still came as a shock. Ruby's, because she had aged so much, and Elizabeth's, because she hadn't aged at all. Like a fly in amber, he thought when he first saw it; not life finished, but life suspended. Though the ache was old, something that he didn't feel unless inadvertently he put a hand on it. So the photograph was carried on his person but not looked at very often.

Mr. Maudling had finally gone the way of all flesh, to be replaced by an equally courteous and competent gentleman, Mr. Augustus Thornleigh.

"How much have I got left?" Lee asked Mr. Thornleigh.

Augustus Thornleigh studied him in fascination. The tale of Alexander Kinross's first appearance at the Bank of England was still retold—the tool box, the buckskins, the battered hat—and here was another to add to it, the banker thought. Smooth skin weathered to the color of light oak, that bizarre pigtail, the darkness of the face and its strange light eyes. He wore a chamois suit surely pretty much like the one Sir Alexander had, but no hat, and the upper garment was more a shirt than a coat, open halfway down a chest the same color as his face. Yet his accent was elegantly pear-shaped and his manners impeccable.

"Something in excess of half a million pounds, sir."

The fine black brows flew up, strikingly white teeth showed in a grin. "Dear old Apocalypse earns on!" Lee said. "What a relief. Though I must be the only Apocalypse shareholder who keeps withdrawing rather than depositing."

"In one way, Dr. Costevan. Deposits do come in your name regularly from the Company." Mr. Thornleigh looked mildly enquiring. "May I ask what your personal investments are?"

"Petroleum," said Lee tersely.

"Oh! A coming industry, sir. Everyone is saying that the horseless carriage will replace the horse, which has the farriers and horse breeders in a fine fit of despondency."

"Not to mention the saddlers."

"True, true."

They chatted on until a teller brought Lee the bank notes he had asked for, then Mr. Thornleigh rose to escort his client off the premises.

"You just missed Sir Alexander," he said.

"He's in London?"

"At the Savoy, Dr. Costevan."

DO I, OR DON'T I? Lee asked himself as he hailed a hackney. Oh, what the hell, why not?

"The Strand—the Savoy, actually," he said, climbing in.

Having nothing smaller, Lee gave the driver a gold sovereign which the man pocketed in a flash and pretended was a shilling for fear that the coin was a mistake. Not that Lee was there to witness this charade; he walked into the hotel and demanded a room from a smooth fellow in butler's gear who was parading up and down the foyer.

Oh, bother! thought the fellow, how do I go about explaining in a tactful manner that this peculiar chap can't afford us?

At which moment Alexander walked down the stairs wearing a morning suit and top hat.

"Complete to a tee, Alexander!" Lee called. "What a fop you've turned into in your old age!"

The Great Man seemed to cover the thirty feet in one bound, took the peculiar chap in a hard hold and kissed his cheek.

"Lee! Lee! Let me look at you! Och, far rather what you're wearing than this pox doctor's clerk's outfit!" Alexander cried, smiling from ear to ear. "My dear boy, you're a sight for sore eyes! Are you staying anywhere?"

"No, I was just asking for a room."

"There's a spare one in my suite if you'd honor me."

"I'd be glad to."

"Where's your luggage?"

"Don't have any. I lost all my European clobber in a little skirmish with some Baluchis about a thousand years ago. What you see is what you get," said Lee.

"This is Dr. Lee Costevan, Mawfield," said Alexander. "One of my fellow directors. Be a good chap and ask my tailor to come around tomorrow morning, would you?" Then off he went toward the stairs, an arm flung around Lee's shoulders.

"No lift?" Lee asked, absurdly pleased to see him.

"Not these days. I don't get enough exercise." One hand groped for the pigtail and flapped it. "Have you ever cut it?"

"I trim the ends from time to time. Weren't you going somewhere important?"

"Fuck important, you're important!"

"Why do we all pick up my mother's bad language? How is she?"

"Very well. I've just arrived from Kinross, so it's a mere six weeks since I last saw her." Alexander grimaced. "She won't travel with me anymore, says it wears her out."

His mouth went dry; Lee swallowed. "And Elizabeth?"

"Also very well. Absorbed in Dolly—did you hear about poor Anna? I can't remember exactly when you disappeared."

"You'd best tell me all of it again, Alexander."

SO IN THE END no apology was tendered because none was needed; the two men sat over a long lunch in Alexander's suite as if they had last met yesterday, yet last met a century ago.

"You're needed, Lee," Alexander said.

"If I can be part-time, yes, I'm happy to be needed."

Which led to a description of Lee's activities in Persia and his hopes for the petroleum industry. Alexander listened intently, intrigued by the fact that his own reminiscences of Baku had led Lee into this field.

"I didn't realize at the time," he said, "because I couldn't speak any of the languages, that the locals had discovered how to refine the crude oil sufficiently to fuel their engines. But of course they couldn't crack it to separate the best fractions, and Dr. Daimler hadn't come along with his internal combustion engine either. Such a simple thing! Making the fuel work inside the cylinder instead of externally. I swear, Lee, that raw materials come along at exactly the right time to make some new invention not only feasible, but practical."

But Alexander wasn't in favor of the Persian enterprise. "I don't know much about the country, but it's bankrupt, volatile and very much at the mercy of the Russians. Thornleigh at the Bank of England says that Russia is going to try for control through banking, or a bank. Persia's in need of loan money, and Britain's behaving a bit like a girl who's been proposed to once and confidently expects to be proposed to several more times, so why not say no for a while? Keep on with it as long as you can, Lee, but my advice is to get out the moment you can do so without losing your shirt."

"I'm rapidly inclining to the same viewpoint," said Lee with a sigh, "yet there's more money in petroleum than in gold."

"And being in on the ground floor is an advantage. However, I think you've made your move just a little *too* early. I've gone in a different direction—not petroleum, but rubber. We now have thousands of acres planted with Brazilian Para rubber trees in Malaya."

"Rubber?" Lee asked, frowning.

"It's becoming ubiquitous—used for almost anything. Motor cars need tires made of rubber, preferably a rubberized canvas outer tire and an air-filled inner tube of pure rubber. Bicycles have leaped ahead since pneumatic tires. Springs, valves, washers, waterproofed fabrics and overshoes, rubber sheets for hospital beds, cushions, gas bags, machine belts, inked stamps, rollers—an almost endless list. They make electrical cable insulation of rubber now instead of gutta-percha, and there's a rock-hard rubber called vulcanite that resists corrosion by acids or alkalis."

He was away; Lee leaned back, stomach replete with a juicy steak, and watched the play of emotions cross Alexander's face. He hadn't really changed; he probably never would. Like most sinewy men, he had looked old when he was young and would look young when he was old. As thick as ever, the hair was almost white and gave him a leonine cast because he still wore it down to his shoulders, and the eyes had lost none of their obsidian fire; despite his insistence that he needed to climb stairs for exercise, he hadn't put on an ounce.

Though his nature had softened again, perhaps due to the business with Anna and Dolly—Lee wasn't sure. Just that the arrogance and imperiousness that Lee had seen in Kinross had now crumbled to reveal the old Alexander. As dynamic as ever, still possessed of that unerring instinct for what was the right thing to go into—rubber, for pity's sake! Yet softer, kinder, more—merciful. Something had taught him humility.

"I have a gift for you," Lee said, fishing in his shirt pocket. The photographs had to come out, and before he could transfer them to the opposite pocket Alexander had leaned across to pluck them from his hand. Still *some* imperiousness!

"Your mother I can understand, but Elizabeth?"

"Mum sent me three to India," Lee said easily. "Of her, of Nell, and of Elizabeth. I lost Nell somewhere."

"Ruby's more tattered than Elizabeth."

"I look at her far more often."

Alexander handed the photographs back. "Will you come home, Lee?" he asked.

"First—here it is."

A look of awe on his face, Alexander studied the coin. "An Alexander the Great drachma, and a very rare one! Superb condition—I would say, mint, except that's impossible."

"It was given to me by the present Shah of Persia, so who is to know? It might have sat untouched since your namesake left Ecbatana—the Shah said it came from Hamadan, which was Ecbatana."

"My dear boy, it's priceless. I can't thank you enough. So will you come home?" he pressed.

"In a little while. I want to look at the *Majestic* first."

"So do I. They say she's the best battleship in the world."

"I doubt that, Alexander. What possesses the Royal Navy to keep on putting their twelve-inch guns in barbettes instead of turrets? I think the American navy goes one better with turrets."

"Whichever, the things are too slow—fourteen knots! And the Krupp steel is better armor than Harvey's. Kaiser Wilhelm is beginning to build battleships too," said Alexander, savoring his cheroot. "Personally I think that the Royal Navy is eating up too big a portion of the British Government's money."

"Oh, come, Alexander," said Lee gently, "I may have been out of things for four years, but I doubt the British are hard up."

"They have the Empire to rape, yes, but the business slump we've been enduring in Australia is worldwide. The truth of the matter is that building battleships is keeping men employed, for there are no ocean liner keels in the shipyards of the Clyde."

"How are things in New South Wales?"

"Grim. Banks have been collapsing one after the other since 1893, though that was the worst year. Foreign investment capital was pulled out in a hurry. I tried to tell Charles Dewy years ago not to deposit in Sydney, but he wouldn't listen. As well that Constance has two sons-in-law of shrewder disposition than Charles was." The black eyes twinkled. "Henrietta is still unattached. I don't suppose you're looking for an excellent wife?"

"No."

"Too bad. She's a good girl destined, I fear, to be an old maid. Like Nell, she's too fussy and too pushy."

"How is Nell?"

"Doing medicine at Sydney University, if you believe that." Alexander scowled. "Graduated with First Class Honors in mining engineering, then enrolled in second-year Medicine. Women!"

"Good for Nell. Medicine must be hard going for a woman."

"After engineering? Rubbish!"

"She's your daughter, Alexander."

"Don't remind me."

"And what of federation?" Lee asked, changing the subject.

"Och, it's a foregone conclusion, though New South Wales isn't keen. I think that's because Victoria is. There's no love lost between those two colonies. Victoria will gain."

"And the trade unions?"

"The shearers and general laborers have joined together to form the A.W.U.—the Australian Workers' Union. The miners—coal, naturally—are as pugnacious as ever, and the Labor Electoral League is dying to try its luck in a federal parliament."

"Which leads me to a burning question—whereabouts is the capital of the new nation to be?"

"By rights, in Sydney, but Melbourne won't countenance that. The most anyone will concede is that the capital should be in New South Wales *somewhere.*"

"Anywhere but in Sydney, eh?"

"Too easy to make it Sydney, Lee. Oldest settlement, et cetera. I've heard every town from Yass to Orange. Still, one must be thankful for small mercies. Sir Henry Parkes can't be the first prime minister because he died last year."

"Good lord! There passes an era. Who's the new Great Man?"

"No one. In New South Wales, a fellow called George Reid. In Victoria, Turner, though he'll not be prime minister. It's for all the world like the rivalry between England and France."

"The French are well in the lead with the motor-car."

"That won't last," said Alexander cynically. "They don't have the experience with steeling iron that the Americans and the British do. They can precision engineer, but Germany pinched all their metallurgists, industrial plant and Alsace-Lorraine after the Franco-Prussian War. The French have never recovered."

"I'm surprised you don't have a motor-car yet, Alexander."

"I'm waiting for Daimler to produce something really worth having. The Germans and the Americans are the best precision engineers in the world, and the engine design is so simple. The wonderful thing about a motor-car, Lee, is that you don't need a degree in engineering to fix it. A little mechanical aptitude and a few tools, and Mr. Motor-Car Owner can fix it himself."

"It will decrease the amount of noise on the roads too. No iron-bound wheels on the vehicles, no iron-shod hooves on its horses. Easier to turn, easier to drive than a horsed carriage. I'm surprised that you haven't gone into manufacturing it."

"Someone in Australia already is—they're going to call their horseless carriage the Pioneer. But no, for the time being I'll stick to steam," said Alexander.

AFTER LEE had been provided with suitable apparel, the pair set out for the naval dockyards in Portsmouth armed with letters of introduction, there to prowl all over the *Majestic*.

"You're right about her speed, Alexander—she's slow. The American ships are doing eighteen knots with heavier armaments, though admittedly with thinner armor plating." Lee eyed the coal hatches thoughtfully. "She takes two thousand tons, they say—enough to sail five thousand miles at twelve knots. But I'd be willing to bet that it's older ships will sail the oceans. At her cost, she'll be kept in the North Sea."

"I read your mind as if it were sending flags up a mast, Lee. They're putting the Parsons steam turbine engine into liners and merchant ships, and I've even heard that the Royal Navy has put it into a few torpedo boats. When they put it into one of these fifteen-thousand-tonners and change from barbettes to good rotational turrets, they'll have a *real* battleship." Flashing Lee a grin, Alexander trotted down the gangway with a twirl of his amber-headed cane and a wave in the direction of the bridge. "Let us," he said as they walked into a misty rain, "keep an eye on developments, eh?"

"I read your mind as if it were sending flags up a mast," said Lee gravely.

OF COURSE the engineering works of Mr. Charles Parsons had to be inspected, together with several other factories producing innovative machinery, but by August they were on a ship for Persia and the Peacock oilfields. There Lee found that his Farsi-fluent American second-in-command had done well in his absence, and would go on doing well. No more excuses; he had to go home.

Half of him had expected that Alexander would decide to visit his plantations of Brazilian Para rubber trees in Malaya en route, but no. They boarded a fast steamer in Aden that was heading straight for Sydney.

"That is," said Lee, "via Colombo, Perth and Melbourne. I think therein lies the reason for Sydney's unpopularity as the national capital. Perth may as well be on another continent, but ships get to Melbourne first. It's another thousand miles up to Sydney, so a lot of ships don't bother going on to Sydney. Now if some way could be found to approach Australia from the north, Sydney would be far more important than Melbourne."

He did a lot of rather feverish talking during that voyage, unwilling to give Alexander the slightest hint that he dreaded returning to Kinross. How would he manage to behave normally to Elizabeth, especially given that Alexander was determined to keep him closer than ever before? He could live in the Kinross Hotel, yes, but since Anna's departure Alexander had moved all of his administrative duties and paperwork to his own house; the offices in town had been partially converted to a research facility under the aegis of Chan Min, Lo Chee, Wo Ching and Donny Wilkins. Lee was to work with Alexander at all times, and would certainly have to eat lunch at the house, if not dinner.

The years had been lonely, only bearable because of what he had learned from the monks of Tibet; were it not for Elizabeth, Lee believed that he might have elected to stay there, abandon all the training and precepts his mother and Alexander had instilled in him for a life that had a hypnotic element to it, a communal synchrony governed by the soul. The

Oriental in him liked that, could have been happy living on the top of the world removed from time, pain, yearning. Except that Elizabeth mattered more, and that was a mystery. Not one look or gesture of encouragement, not one word to give him hope. Yet he couldn't banish her from his mind, or cease to love her. Is it that some of us do genuinely have a soul mate, and, having found that soul mate, are borne along helplessly on the tide forever striving to engulf and dissolve in the soul mate? Make one out of two?

"Have you told Ruby and Elizabeth that we're on our way?" he asked Alexander as the ship neared Melbourne.

"Not yet, but I can actually telephone them from Melbourne. I thought that was the way to go," said Alexander.

"Would you do me a favor?"

"Of course."

"Don't tell anyone that I'm with you. I'd like to surprise them," said Lee, trying to sound offhand.

"It shall be so."

BUT THAT LED to complications. There were visits to be made in Sydney: to Anna, and to Nell. Would Nell keep the secret?

"She's living in Anna's house these days," said Alexander as they took a hackney to the Glebe. "After the boys finished their degrees and returned to Kinross, she couldn't live alone in their digs, so when she suggested that I build her a little flat on to the back of Anna's place, I was relieved. She has privacy, but she's also there to make sure Anna is nursed properly."

"Nursed?" Lee asked, frowning.

"You'll see," said Alexander cryptically. "Some things I didn't tell you because they're hard to describe."

Anna shocked him. The beautiful thirteen-year-old he had known in Kinross—she was just getting started with O'Donnell when he left—had become a slobbering, shambling, grossly fat young woman who didn't recognize her father, let alone him. The grey-blue eyes wandered, and one thumb was raw and bleeding from being sucked.

"We can't break her of it, Sir Alexander," Miss Harbottle said, "and I agree with Nell, we shouldn't tie her arm down."

"Have you tried painting the thumb with bitter aloes?"

"Yes, but she spits on it and rubs the bitter aloes off on her dress.

There are less soluble compounds, but they're quite poisonous. Nell thinks that she'll eventually chew the thumb down to bone, at which point it will have to be amputated."

"And she'll start on the other one," said Alexander sadly.

"I am afraid so." Miss Harbottle cleared her throat. "She is also having fits, Sir Alexander. Grand mal. That is, they involve her whole body."

"Oh, my poor, poor Anna!" The eyes Alexander directed at Lee shone with tears. "It isn't right, that someone so harmless must suffer all this." He squared his shoulders. "However, you care for her wonderfully well, Miss Harbottle. She's clean, dry and obviously contented. I assume that food is her great pleasure?"

"Yes, she loves to eat. Nell and I agreed that she should be allowed to eat. To restrict her food would be as cruel as it is to restrict the food of a dumb animal."

"Is Nell in?"

"Yes, Sir Alexander. She's expecting you."

As they walked through the big house Lee noticed how well it was organized, and how many women there were to help nurse Anna. The atmosphere was cheerful, the premises spotlessly clean and well decorated—more these days, Lee thought, to keep the staff happy than the oblivious Anna. Though that's not Alexander's doing—it wouldn't occur to him. Therefore it must be Nell's.

Her flat was accessible through a door painted yellow; it stood ajar, but Alexander called to warn her that he had arrived. She came out of an inner room at a sedate walk, her black hair screwed up into a tight bun, her spare figure clad in a plain olive-drab cotton dress that had no waist and finished inches short of her ankles. Her feet were shod in sensible brown boots tightly laced to above her ankles. A second shock for Lee: her likeness to Alexander was now striking, for the softness of her girlhood had passed from her face to leave it stern, unflinching and just a trifle mannish. Only the eyes were her own, grown bigger because she herself was thinner; they were like two high-powered blue rays that cut through anything in their path.

At first she saw only Alexander, went to him to hug and kiss him unself-consciously. Oh, yes, they were close! Like twins. Grumble about her doing medicine though he did, Alexander was enslaved, putty in her hands.

Then, withdrawing from her father's embrace, she saw Lee, jumped a little, smiled. "Lee! Is it really you?" she asked, pecking him on one cheek. "No one said you were back."

"That's because I don't want anyone to know I'm back, Nell. Keep the secret for me, please."

"Cross my heart and hope to die."

Butterfly Wing had made a simple lunch: fresh bread, butter, jam, cold sliced beef, and Alexander's favorite dessert, custard tarts topped with nutmeg. Nell let the men eat, then made a pot of tea herself and settled to talk.

"How's medicine?" Lee asked.

"Everything that I had hoped."

"But difficult."

"Not for me, but then, I get along with my instructors and professors fairly well. It's harder on the other women, who just don't have my knack of dealing with men. The poor things can be reduced to tears, which men despise, and they *know* that they're being deliberately marked down because they're women. So they mostly have to repeat each year. Some are failed twice for the same year. Still, they battle on."

"Have you been failed, Nell?" Alexander asked.

His own face looked scornful. "No one would dare! I'm like Grace Robinson, who graduated in 1893 without failing a single year. Though she should have been awarded honors, and wasn't. You see, women's schools don't prepare them for chemistry and physics, nor even mathematically. So the poor souls really have to start from scratch, and the lecturers aren't prepared to teach the basics. Whereas I'm a graduate engineer. That gives me a lot of clout with the faculty." She looked sly. "Lecturers are very sensitive about being shown up, especially by a woman, so they tend to leave me alone."

"Do you get on with your fellow women?" Lee asked.

"Better than I had expected to, actually. I coach them in the sciences and maths, but some of them never seem to catch on."

Alexander stirred his tea, tapped the spoon on the side of his cup, then put it in the saucer. "Anna. Tell me, Nell."

"The mental deterioration is accelerating rapidly, Dad. Well, you've seen that for yourself. Did Miss Harbottle tell you she's having epileptic seizures?"

"Yes."

"She's not long for this world, Dad."

"I feared you'd say that when Miss Harbottle didn't talk of the years to come."

"We keep her warm and out of drafts, and try to make her do a little walking, but she's increasingly reluctant to exercise. It may be that she'll go into a status epilepticus—one fit after another until she dies of sheer exhaustion—but it's more likely that she'll catch a cold, it will go to her chest, and she'll die of pneumonia. If one of the staff has a cold, she doesn't come to work until the coughing and sneezing is over, but someone is bound to infect her before they even know they have a cold. I'm surprised it hasn't happened already. They are all very good to her, you know."

"Considering what thankless, unrewarding sort of work it is, I'm pleased to hear you say that."

"A woman with the temperament to nurse finds satisfaction in the most thankless work, Dad. We chose our staff well."

"Which would be the easier death?" Alexander asked abruptly. "Pneumonia or continuous fits?"

"Continuous fits, in that consciousness is lost with the onset of the first one, and never regained. It looks frightful, but the patient doesn't suffer. Pneumonia is far worse—a lot of pain and distress."

A silence fell; Alexander sipped steadily at his tea, Nell played with her cake fork, and Lee sat wishing that he was anywhere other than here.

"Has your mother been visiting?" Alexander asked.

"I've forbidden her to come anymore, Dad. It does no good, since Anna doesn't recognize her either, and to watch her—oh, Dad, it's like looking into the eyes of an animal that knows it's dying. I can't even begin to imagine her pain."

Lee reached for a custard tart—anything was better than having nothing to do, even chewing at sawdust. "Have you a boyfriend, Nell?" he asked lightly.

She blinked, then looked grateful. "I'm too busy, I really am. Medicine doesn't come as easily as engineering."

"So you're going to be a maiden lady doctor."

"It looks that way." Nell sighed, then assumed a wistful expression that sat strangely on such a determined face. "Years ago I knew a chap I rather fancied, but I was too young and he was too honorable to take advantage of me. We went our ways."

"An engineer?" Lee asked.

She burst out laughing. "I should say not!"

"Then what was he, or is he?"

"That," said Nell, "I'd prefer to keep to myself."

IT WAS NOVEMBER, and a cicada year; even above the huffing locomotive and the clickety-clicking of the wheels it was easy to hear them shrilling deafeningly in the bush that came so close to the line. A hot summer for coast and inland alike, a vicious monsoon season in the north, that was what cicadas meant.

Alexander was edgy during the trip from Sydney to Lithgow, only seemed to relax when their car was coupled to the Kinross train, back to running four times a week. What Lee couldn't know was that Alexander sensed his reluctance to return, had prepared himself for a sudden announcement that Lee was sorry, but he'd changed his mind and was off back to Persia. So when they were heading for Kinross on a train that didn't stop, Alexander felt better, more confident.

He more than liked Lee; he loved him as the son he'd never had, Ruby's child who was also a link to Sung. When he had dragged Lee to see Anna, he was hoping that a spark would kindle between Lee and Nell. To see that pair marry would put the finishing touch on his life. But no spark had passed between them, not even the vaguest kind of attraction. Brother and sister. And he simply couldn't understand it, when Nell was so like him, and Lee's mother loved him. *Surely* they were meant for each other! Then Nell started waffling about some fellow she had hankered after, and closed up like a clam, while Lee sat patently unaffected. The bastardy had long ceased to be an issue; Alexander had grown so far beyond that old hurt that he now regarded Lee's birth as the ultimate irony. His heir would also be a bastard. Yet he wanted some of *his* blood in Lee's issue, and that wasn't going to happen. If Lee ever married at all. A nomad. Perhaps on his Chinese side he harkened back to some footloose Mongol only at ease roaming the steppes. Women literarlly swooned over him, trying to catch their breath inside tightly laced corsets, threw him lures of all sorts from utterly blatant to diabolically cunning, but Lee never took a scrap of notice. He always had a woman tucked away somewhere, be it in Persian Lar or an English town, but his attitude was pure Oriental: a Pekinese prince in need of a concubine—someone who played and sang, spoke only when spoken to, had studied the Kama Sutra backward, frontward and sideways, and probably jingled when she walked.

What had Elizabeth called him? A golden serpent. At the time the metaphor had startled him, but he appreciated her reason for choosing it. The sort of wretched animal that crawled into a hole for four years and swallowed its own tail—how he had searched for Lee! Even Pinkerton's hadn't been able to find him, nor the Bank of England trace the tortuous route Lee's hefty withdrawls took en route to his pocket. Dummy companies, dummy accounts, Swiss banks . . . Nothing was bought in his name, and who would have connected him to something called Peacock Oil? Everyone assumed it was the Shah.

Sheer luck that when the golden serpent crawled out of his hole, he had been there to catch his tail. And hang on grimly. Entice the slippery creature back to his home. Now they were in the home stretch, and he was finally beginning to believe that he had his prodigal son firmly in his grasp. Time was fleeting; he himself was fifty-four, and Lee was thirty-three. Not that Alexander expected to die before he had logged up at least his threescore years and ten, but a seven-year interruption in the training program was a handicap.

KINROSS HAD changed greatly during the seven years of his absence; Lee's admiration began on the railway station platform, which was equipped with waiting rooms and lavatories in a smart yet cottagey building trimmed with cast-iron lace; baskets and tubs of flowering plants stood everywhere, with a garden bed beneath the two big signs that said KINROSS, one at either end of the platform. The original opera house had been converted into a theater, and a new, grander opera house reared on the opposite side of Kinross Square. Every street was tree lined and lit by electricity; both gas and electricity were laid on to every private dwelling. There was a telephone connection to Sydney and Bathurst now as well as the telegraph. Pride of ownership blazed everywhere.

"It's a model town," said Lee, hefting his bags.

"I hope so. The mine is back at full production, of course, which means the coal mine is too. I'm starting to come around to Nell's opinion that we'd be better off with alternating electrical current, though I intend to wait until Lo Chee has a better design for a turbine generator—he's brilliant," said Alexander. He moved toward the cable car. "Ruby's coming up for dinner, so I'll leave you to have your surprise all to yourself. You can bring her up later."

I must remember, Lee said to himself as he entered the hotel, that she is now fifty-six years old. I can't betray my grief, for there's bound to be grief. Alexander didn't say it, but I couldn't help but gather that she's aged more than he expected. It must be terrible for a beautiful woman to show her years, especially someone like Mum, who has always depended on her beauty. And hasn't walled herself up in a blob of amber like Elizabeth.

Yet she was just as he remembered: bold, voluptuous, oddly elegant. Yes, there were a few lines around her eyes and mouth, a little sagging under the chin, but she was still Ruby Costevan from the mass of red-gold hair to the wonderful green eyes. Expecting Alexander, she was clad in ruby-red satin with a thick choker of rubies around her neck to hide the loose skin, rubies on her wrists and in her ears.

When she saw him her knees gave way and she sank, billowing, to the floor, laughing and crying. "Lee! Lee! My boy!"

It seemed easier to get down to her level, so he knelt to take her into his arms, crush her close, kiss her face, her hair. I am home again. I am back inside the first arms I ever remember, her perfume coiling inside my head, the wonder who is my mother.

"How much I love you!" he said. "How much!"

"I'll save all the stories for dinner time," he said later, after Ruby had repaired the ravages of overwhelming joy and he himself had changed into evening dress.

"Then we'll have a drink together before we start—the car won't be down for half an hour," she said, moving to the row of decanters, a soda siphon and an ice bucket. "I have no idea what you drink these days."

"Kentucky bourbon if you have it. No soda, no water, no ice."

"I have it, but that's a potent tipple on an empty belly."

"I'm used to it—it's what my wildcatters drink when someone else is buying. Of course the country's Mohammedan, but I import it quietly and make sure no one drinks outside the camp."

She handed him a glass and sat down with a sherry. "It gets mysteriouser and mysteriouser, Lee. What Mohammedan country?"

"Persia—Iran, they call it. I'm in the petroleum business there in partnership with the Shah."

"Jesus! No wonder we couldn't find hide nor hair of you."

They sipped without talking for a few minutes, then Lee said, "What's happened to Alexander, Mum?"

She didn't attempt to prevaricate. "I know what you want to know." She sighed, stretched her legs out and looked fixedly at the ruby buckles on her shoes. "A number of things . . . The quarrel with you, because he knew that he was in the wrong. After he came down off his high horse, he didn't know how to mend the fences his high horse had kicked over. By the time he'd decided to swallow his pride and go to you, you had disappeared. He searched for you quite desperately. In the midst of that came the business with Anna, O'Donnell, the baby—and Jade. He saw her hanged, you know, and that took a terrible toll. Then Nell wouldn't do what he wanted, and Anna had to be separated from her child. A different man would have hardened more, but not my beloved Alexander. All of it combined served to pull him up—not with a jerk, but gradually. And, of course, he blames himself for marrying Elizabeth. She wasn't much older than Anna—right at the age when impressions set in stone, and stone is what she's become."

"But he's had you, whereas Elizabeth has had no one. Can you wonder at her turning to stone?"

"Oh, bugger that!" she snapped tartly, cut where she was vulnerable. His glass was empty, so she got up to replenish it. "I just keep hoping against hope that one day Elizabeth will be happy. If she met someone, she could divorce Alexander for his perpetual adultery with me."

"*Elizabeth* in a divorce court airing her dirty linen?"

"You don't think she would."

"I can see her running off into obscurity with a lover, but not standing in front of a judge and a room full of journalists."

"She won't run off into obscurity with a lover, Lee, because she has Dolly to care for. Dolly's forgotten all about Anna, she thinks Elizabeth is her mother and Alexander her father."

"Well, that alone would predicate against divorce, wouldn't it? The whole Anna-and-the-unknown-man scandal would be dug up again, and Dolly's what—six? Old enough to understand."

"Yes, you're right. I should have thought of that. Fuck!" She underwent one of her lightning changes of mood. "And what about you?" she asked brightly. "Any wife on the horizon?"

"No." He glanced at the gold wrist-watch Alexander had given him in London and drained his glass. "It's time we went, Mum."

"Does Elizabeth know you're here?" Ruby asked, rising too.

"No."

When they reached the cable car platform, Sung was waiting; Lee stopped suddenly, shocked. His father, now close to seventy, had transformed himself into a venerable Chinese Ancient of Days—the wispy beard straying over his chest, the inch-long fingernails, the skin like old, smooth yet sallow ivory, the eyes narrowed to slits in the midst of which two black beads slid in synchrony. This is Papa, yet I think of Alexander as my father. Oh, how far have we come on this incredible voyage, and whence will we sail when the wind next blows?

"Papa," he said, bowing and kissing Sung's hand.

"My dear boy, you look wonderful."

"Come on, all aboard!" said Ruby impatiently, hand ready to press the electric bell that signaled the engine room high above.

She's hungry to have us all together, thought Lee, helping Sung into the car. My mother just wants everybody to love everybody else, and everybody to be happy. But that is impossible.

IT WAS ELIZABETH at the door to welcome them in, and Ruby, dying to see Elizabeth's reaction to the unexpected guest, pushed Lee in front of her and Sung.

How is it to see the one woman after so long? For Lee, it was pure pain, a twisting of everything inside him that sent agony and grief and sorrow and despair winging to his mind, so that he saw a blurred phantom composed of all those emotions, not Elizabeth.

Smiling, he kissed the phantom's hand, complimented her on her appearance, and passed on into the drawing room to leave her greeting Ruby and Sung. Alexander and Constance Dewy were there, Constance coming to kiss him, squeeze his hands, look at him with a speaking sympathy that puzzled him. Only when he was safe in a chair did he realize that he had not *seen* Elizabeth.

Nor did he, really, at dinner; with only six sitting down, Alexander elected not to fill the end places, so Lee was at one end of his side and Elizabeth at the other. Sung was between them, Alexander opposite him, Constance and Ruby beyond.

"Not socially acceptable," said Alexander cheerfully, "but in my own home I'm at perfect liberty to put the men together and leave the women to their feminine conversation. We won't linger here for port and cigars, we'll go out with the ladies."

Lee took more wine than was his custom, though the food, as excellent as ever—Chang was still master of the kitchen, he was told—kept him reasonably sober. Back in the drawing room for coffee and a choice of cigars or cheroots, he foiled Alexander's plans for a seating arrangement by pushing his chair back from the others, isolating himself from the merriment. The room was glaringly lit, the Waterford chandeliers now equipped with electric bulbs instead of candles, the gas wall sconces converted to electricity too. It's so harsh, thought Lee. No lovely pools of shadow, no soft greenish glow from the gas mantles nor caressing gold light from candles. Electricity might be our fate, but it isn't—romantic. Merciless, more like.

From this position he could see Elizabeth with startling clarity. Oh, so beautiful! Like a Vermeer painting, brilliantly illuminated, every detail defined. Her hair was still as black as his, its soft waves coaxed into a huge bun on the back of her head without the rolls and puffs that had come into fashion. Did she ever wear a warm color? Not in his memory, at any rate. Tonight she was in a steely dark blue crepe dress whose skirt was fairly straight and lacked a train. Most such were beaded, but hers was plain and devoid of tassels, held in place by straps across her shoulders. The sapphire and diamond suite of jewels sparkled around her neck, in her ears, on her wrists, and the diamond engagement ring dazzled. The tourmaline, however, was gone; her right hand was bare of any rings.

A spirited conversation was going on between the others; Lee drank in her face and spoke to her.

"You're not wearing your tourmaline," he said.

"Alexander gave it to me for the children I would have," she said. "Green for the boys, pink for the girls. But I didn't give him any boys, so I took it off. It was so heavy."

And, to his amazement, she reached into a silver box on the table next to her chair, withdrew a long cigarette and groped for the box of matches encased in a silver jacket. Lee got up and took it from her, struck a match and lit her cigarette.

"Will you join me?" she asked, her eyes lifted to his.

"Thank you." There were no messages for him in that glance, just courteous interest. He went back to his chair. "When did you begin to smoke cigarettes?" he asked.

"About seven years ago. I know ladies don't, but I think your mother has rubbed off on me—I find that I don't care very much what other people think these days. I confine them to this after-dinner sojourn, but if Alexander and I are in Sydney and eat in a restaurant, I smoke my cigarettes, he smokes his cheroots. It's rather amusing," she said, smiling, "to watch the reactions of the other diners."

And that was the end of their talk. Elizabeth smoked her way down the cigarette with dainty enjoyment while Lee studied her.

Alexander had collared Sung and was talking shop.

Flexing her fingers unobtrusively, Ruby prepared to go to the piano; an annoying stiffness was creeping into her hands, an ache that was worst in the morning. But Alexander and Sung had come to some contentious point and wouldn't thank her for playing at the moment, and Constance sat dozing over her glass of port—she was acquiring elderly habits. Having nothing better to do, Ruby stared at her jade kitten with an enormous rush of love. He was gazing at Elizabeth, who had turned to listen to Alexander and Sung, presenting Lee with her flawless profile. Ruby's heart crashed to the bottom of her chest so tangibly that her hand went to it, clutched her waistband. Oh, the look in Lee's eyes! Naked longing, total want. If he had gotten to his feet and begun to tear Elizabeth's clothes off, that would not have been any clearer a statement than the look in his eyes. My son is utterly in love with Elizabeth! For how long? Is *that* why—?

With a lunge that woke Constance up and terminated the talk between Alexander and Sung, Ruby got up and went to the piano. Strangely, she found power and expression in her fingers that she had thought gone forever, but this wasn't an occasion for Brahms, Beethoven or Schubert lieder. This called for Chopin, Chopin in a minor key, those poignant ripples and glissandi so full of what she had seen in her son's eyes. Unfulfilled love, haunting love, the yearning that Narcissus must have felt as he tried in vain to capture his own image in the pool, or Echo as she watched him.

So they stayed late, entranced by the Chopin, Elizabeth smoking an occasional cigarette that Lee always lit for her. At two o'clock Alexander asked for tea and supper sandwiches, then insisted that Sung should stay the night.

He walked with Lee and Ruby to the cable car and started the engine—its boiler always stoked—himself rather than summon the stoker ahead of time.

In the car Ruby took Lee's hand in hers.

"You played so beautifully tonight, Mum. How did you know I felt like Chopin?"

"Because," said Ruby bluntly, "I saw how you looked at Elizabeth. How long have you been in love with her?"

His breath caught; he expelled it in a gasp. "I didn't realize I gave myself away. Did anyone else notice?"

"No, my jade kitten. *No one* noticed but me."

"Then my secret's safe."

"As safe as if I didn't know it. How long, Lee? How long?"

"Since I was seventeen, I think, though it took time for it to sink in."

"That's why you've never married, why you don't stay here for very long, why you ran away." Ruby's cheeks glistened with tears. "Oh, Lee, what a bitch!"

"That's putting it mildly," he said dryly, fishing for his handkerchief. "Here."

"Then why did you come home now?"

"To see her again."

"Hoping that it had gone?"

"Oh, no, I knew it hadn't gone. It rules me."

"Alexander's wife . . . But how detached you are. When I said he might divorce her, you didn't seize on that, you demolished my argument instead." She shivered, though the air was summer warm. "You'll never be free of her, will you?"

"Never. She means more to me than my life does."

She turned to him and flung her arms around him. "Oh, Lee! My jade kitten! I wish there was something I could do!"

"There isn't, Mum, and you must promise me not to try."

"I promise," she whispered into his waistcoat, then gave a throaty chuckle. "There'll be rouge all over you, cuddling me. That will lead to gossip in the laundry."

He hugged her closer. "My dearest mother, it's no wonder that Alexander loves you. You're like a rubber ball—always able to bounce back. Truly, I'll be all right."

"But are you going to stay this time, or run?"

"I'm staying. Alexander needs me, I knew how badly when I saw Papa. He's abdicated from all save his Chinese identity. No matter how much I love Elizabeth, I can't desert Alexander. I owe everything I am to you and to him," Lee said, then smiled. "Fancy Elizabeth smoking!"

"She needs the whatever-it-is in tobacco, but cheroots are a bit too strong. Alexander has her cigarettes made at Jackson's in London. It's very hard for her. All she has is Dolly."

"A nice child, Mum?"

"Very sweet, and with just enough intelligence. Dolly won't be a Nell, she'll be more like the Dewy girls. Smart, vivacious, pretty, educated to a level appropriate for a female of her rank. So she'll marry some eligible young man Alexander will heartily approve of, and perhaps give him some male heirs at last."

Two

ENLIGHTENMENT

THE SIGHT of Lee after so many years came as a profound shock to Elizabeth, who hadn't dreamed that he was back. Admittedly her husband had been in a jaunty mood when he arrived, but she put that down to a successful trip away, to some alluring new venture germinating in his fertile brain. A part of her was curious as to what he was up to now, but she didn't ask him when he breezed in. He sought his bathroom to remove the travel stains, then lay down for a nap before he changed into evening dress for dinner. While he was thus occupied she gave Dolly her supper, bathed her, put her into her nightgown, and read her a bedtime story. Dolly loved stories, and promised to be a reader.

She was such a dear little girl, exactly right for Elizabeth—not terrifyingly clever like Nell, nor backward like Anna. Her hair had indeed darkened to a streaky pale brown, but it had kept its ringlets, and her big aquamarine eyes were windows on to a tranquil soul. She had dimples in her cheeks that turned into adorable tiny pits when she smiled, which was often. A kitten had come as an experiment to see how she would treat it; when Suzie (actually a neutered male) proved a success, it was joined by Bunty, a neutered male dog of small size, floppy-eared and yearning to please. They went to bed with Dolly every night, snuggled one on either side of her—not a sight that impressed Nell, who talked of ringworm and roundworm, fleas and ticks. To which Elizabeth replied that the animals were bathed regularly, so when these afflictions appeared she'd start to worry, and she hoped that when Nell had children of her own they wouldn't be smothered under a blanket of hygiene.

Caring for Dolly had melted Elizabeth a little; she just couldn't maintain that rigid self-control when faced with all the dramas of a basically happy child's life, from grazes and cuts to the death of a pet canary. Sometimes she had to laugh, sometimes she had to hide tears. Dolly was maternal heaven.

She didn't appear to remember Anna at all, called Elizabeth "Mummy" and Alexander "Daddy" unself-consciously, though Elizabeth suspected that somewhere inside her mind hid memories of those days with Anna, for occasionally she betrayed knowledge of Peony that definitely went far back into Anna's time.

The worst of it was that Dolly couldn't go to school in the town. Did she, some spiteful or thoughtless child would be sure to tell her about her real mother and debatable father. So for the moment Elizabeth tutored her. Next year, when she turned seven, she would have to have a governess. No matter what our children have been like, Elizabeth reflected, we have never been able to send them to an ordinary school, which is a tragedy. Even Dolly has the Kinross taint: too different to blend in.

Telling the child of her real parents haunted Elizabeth, who tormented herself with questions no one could really answer—not Ruby, and certainly not Alexander. What was the right age for such a hideous shock? Did one do it before puberty, or after? Common sense said that no matter what age was chosen, Dolly would be scarred. That was all right, but what if she warped rather than scarred? And how do you tell a sweet, harmless girl that her mother was mentally retarded and the victim of a monstrous man who fathered her? That her mother's nursemaid murdered him in the most horrific way, then was hanged for it? Many a night saw Elizabeth's pillow wet with tears as she chewed and fretted over when, where, how she could ever tell Dolly what Dolly *had* to know before the cruel world got in first. All she could do was to love the child, build a foundation of security and unconditional love that would serve as a support against the awful day. And Alexander, grant him that, had been equally caring, far more patient and forthcoming than he had been with his own daughters, even Nell. Nell . . . A lonely young woman, hard, tough, sometimes ruthless. No place for boyfriends in that life! When she wasn't slaving over her medical textbooks or enduring the sarcasm of her teachers, she was supervising Anna's imprisonment. Elizabeth suffered for her, yet was aware that Nell would despise her for suffering. To be an Alexander was one thing, but to be him in a female guise was quite another. Oh, Nell, choose *some* personal happiness before it's too late!

As for Anna—that was unbearable. When Nell had banned her from visiting the house in Glebe Point Road, Elizabeth had fought back fiercely, only to come up against all of Alexander's steel. A losing battle, just as her life with Alexander had been a losing battle. But to lose it was made infinitely worse by the knowledge that, underneath, she was pathetically grateful to be banned. Oh, the relief of not having to see what Anna had become! Yet the grief of admitting that she, Elizabeth, was never strong enough.

SO ELIZABETH went downstairs ahead of Alexander to make sure that his instructions about the table seating had been followed. If they were dining alone or only Ruby was joining them, they did not bother to dress, but Constance was here, and Sung was coming plus one other as well as Ruby; Elizabeth had dressed. Rather indifferently; there were plenty of new costumes in soft pastels in her wardrobes, but out came the dark blue crepe, out came the sapphires and diamonds.

One of the latest innovations in the house was an electric buzzer that sounded when the cable car reached the top; usually Alexander answered it by going to the door to wait, but tonight he still hadn't come down when the buzzer sounded. Elizabeth went to stand watching Sung and Ruby coming up the steps, someone behind them. Then suddenly the mystery guest was in front of them, eyes fixed on her—blindly? Lee. At times like this—but had there ever been a time like this?—Elizabeth's long, self-imposed training in outward composure clamped down, put a polite smile on her face, kept her backbone straight. But it was the thinnest of veneers; beneath it the emotion expanded like the huge billow of dust that followed a blast in the limestone quarry, and with the same sense of utter upheaval. She knew that if she moved she would rock on her heels, that her legs would fail her, so she stood absolutely still while she said something inane to welcome him, saw him pass on to greet Alexander, coming down the stairs, stayed on that same spot to exchange pleasantries with Sung and Ruby, let them go past her. Only then, as they clustered around her husband, did she try to move. One foot forward, then the other; her legs worked, she could continue.

And thank God for Alexander, who had placed her on the same side as

Lee, but not next to him; she concentrated upon Ruby, opposite her and bubbling over with joy at Lee's return. All Elizabeth had to do was interpolate an occasional yes or no or mmm. That generous soul Constance Dewy apparently felt the same way, for she too let Ruby rattle on.

While Ruby rattled on and Constance listened eagerly, Elizabeth tried to come to terms with the realization that she was totally, desperately in love with Lee Costevan. In her private thoughts she had always deemed what she felt for him as an attraction, something that didn't really matter. Everyone experienced attractions from time to time, why shouldn't she? But the moment she saw him after seven years of not seeing him, Elizabeth understood herself at last. Lee was the man she would have chosen of her own free will to marry, the only man. Yet had she not married Alexander, she would never have met Lee at all. Oh, life is cruel! Lee is the one man, the only man.

Even afterward in the drawing room, when Lee elected to sit removed from everyone, the turmoil inside her did not let her see anything in him that might lead her to hope—oh, what was she thinking, *hope*? Thank God he was indifferent! In that lay her salvation. If he had loved her back, it would have been the end of many worlds. Though why did Ruby play Chopin, and only his yearning, exquisitely sad pieces at that? With a feeling and a dexterity her arthritic hands should not have allowed her. Every note fell through Elizabeth as if she had been made of cloud—or water. Water. I met my fate at The Pool, and for fifteen years I haven't known it. Next year I will be forty, and he is still a young man who lives to seek adventure in distant lands. Alexander has dragged him back to take the place of the sons I didn't have, and his sense of duty has forced him to obey. For though he feels nothing for me, I can tell that he isn't happy to be here.

When he looked at Ruby, which he did for long periods, she could look at him with the delicate clarity that admitting her love had given her. But there was no one to see how she looked at him; her chair did not permit the others to see her face. Once she had called him a golden serpent to Alexander, but now she understood all the nuances in that metaphor, and why she had chosen it. It wasn't accurate, it sprang from her own suppressed feelings and had nothing to do with what he really was. He was the personification of sun and wind and rain, the elements that made life possible. The odd thing was that he reminded her of Alexander: the colossal masculinity that knew no self-doubts, the keen and technical brain, the restlessness, the radiated power. Yet the one she couldn't bear to touch her, the other she hungered to have touch her. The greatest difference between them was her love, withheld from the one entitled to it, given to the other without hope of its ever being returned.

She didn't sleep that night, and at dawn crept into Dolly's room with a soft "Ssssh!" to the animals, which stirred when Dolly didn't. Peony slept elsewhere these days, worked reasonable hours and had plenty of days off. Drawing up a chair, Elizabeth sat beside the little bed to watch the day steal across that sweetly sleeping face, and resolved that this was one child who would never go through what Nell or Anna had. Therefore no breaking the news of her parentage to her before maturity. Dolly would enjoy an idyllic childhood of laughter, ponies, the gentle lessons that produced good manners and thoughtfulness—no bogeys, no old men to terrify her, no thankless toil. Just hugs and kisses.

Only then, watching that sweetly sleeping face, did Elizabeth finally come to understand what her own childhood had done to her, and admit how right Alexander's judgment of Dr. Murray had been. I will teach her about God, but He will not be Dr. Murray's god. Nor will I ever permit some dreadful picture of satanic evil to color her life. And suddenly I see that something as trivial as a picture on a wall can do as much damage to a young life as the truth about Dolly's parentage. We shouldn't need to be frightened into being good little children, we should be led to goodness by parents who mean so much to us that we cannot bear to disappoint them. God is too intangible for a child to comprehend; the onus rests on parents to make themselves people their children love and value above all else. So I will not spoil Dolly, or give in to her in everything, but when I stand firm against her, I will do so in a way she respects. Oh, my father and his stick! His contempt for women. His *selfishness.* He sold me for a small fortune, not a farthing of which he ever spent. Mary had his measure. When Alastair inherited the money, Mary spent it on a few frivolities and many important things. All her children were educated on it, the boys to university standard, the girls sufficiently well to be schoolteachers or nurses. She was a good mother, and Alastair a good father. What harm is there in jam on the table for every meal?

I should have refused to be sold, though it was Alexander's fault too, for offering to buy me. All my father wanted was the money, but what exactly did Alexander want? Oh, so long ago! I have been married to him for twenty-two years, and still I don't know. A chaste wife, certainly. Children, especially sons, yes. To cock a snook at my father and Dr. Murray—that too. But what else? Did he think that duty would lead to love? Did he think himself capable of turning duty into love? But he wasn't willing to cast every particle of bread he had on the waters of our marriage; he kept Ruby's loaf on the shore just in case. That poor woman, so terribly in love with him, so unsuitable as a wife. And he took what she said about never wanting to marry anyone as the truth because it was what he wanted to hear. Fool! *I* know that had he asked her, she would have said yes, yes, yes! And they would have loved each other madly, probably had half a dozen sons. But he didn't see the queenly chatelaine inside the shady lady until it was too late. Ruby, Ruby, he ruined you too.

When Dolly awoke she found her mummy there and held out her arms for those hugs and kisses. How lovely she smelled after a peaceful night! Oh, Dolly, be happy! Accept the truth when you hear it as something that doesn't matter one iota as much as love.

WHEN SHE went down to breakfast in the conservatory Lee was there with Alexander. This was the Lee she liked best, in old dungarees and an old shirt with its sleeves rolled up.

"Why," she asked, sitting down and accepting a cup of tea from Alexander, "don't you men cut the sleeves off your shirts?"

They both stared at her blankly, then Alexander began to laugh, his arms above his head as if in triumph.

"My dear Elizabeth, an unanswerable question! Why don't we, Lee? It makes perfect sense, like sherry in big glasses."

"We don't, I think," said Lee, smiling with that touch of the inscrutable Chinese, "because it's always been mandatory that, upon meeting a lady or a bank manager or a solicitor, we must roll our sleeves down immediately to look like gentlemen."

"In this kind of clobber? I'm game to chop mine," said Alexander, offering his wife the toast rack.

"If you are, I am." Lee rose to his feet. "I'm off to the cyanide plant—there are problems with the electrolysis, we're losing too much zinc. Elizabeth, your servant."

She inclined her head and muttered something; once Lee had gone she buttered a slice of cold toast and made a show of eating.

"What do you intend to do today?" Alexander asked, taking a fresh pot of tea from Mrs. Surtees. "Here, this is hot."

"Spend the morning with Dolly, then perhaps ride."

"How's the new mare?"

"Very nice, though it's hard to replace Crystal."

"All creatures must go," he said gently, wondering how he was going to tell her that Anna would die soon.

"Yes."

"What do you call this one, since it's a dappled grey?"

"Cloud."

"I like it." He got up, frowning at her. "Elizabeth, you aren't eating. Last night you pecked, this morning you're not getting far with that toast. I'll ring for fresh."

"Please don't, Alexander. I prefer the butter unmelted."

"It doesn't look like it to me."

But, having said his piece, he departed, and Elizabeth could abandon the toast. The tea she drank, as always without sugar; when she stood up her head whirled. He was right, she wasn't eating enough. Lunch. If Lee's busy down in the cyanide plant, he won't be here, so maybe if I tell Mrs. Surtees to have Chang make something I really like, I'll be able to eat.

Mrs. Surtees came in while Elizabeth was still steadying herself and went to support her. "Lady Kinross, you're ill."

"I'm all right, just light-headed. I can't seem to eat."

Mrs. Surtees poured another cup of tea and loaded it with sugar. "Here, drink this. You won't like it, but it will make you feel better. I'll put a jug of orange juice on the table at lunch. It's amazing how long our oranges last if they're left on the trees." Satisfied that Elizabeth had drunk enough of the tea during this little homily, she smiled and went to the kitchen.

The sweet tea had worked; Elizabeth went to find Dolly, not having discussed the lunch menu. Which didn't matter. Chang and Mrs. Surtees were quite capable of deciding menus. And I have to think of things that don't involve Lee . . .

Who succeeded in manufacturing excuses for not dining at the house: either the refinery needed his attention, or the research center geniuses had struck a problem, or this, that, the other.

A puzzle for Alexander, who liked to talk business with Lee over lunch, but accepted all the reasons Lee produced in good faith; to Alexander, they were symptoms of how difficult it had been to run the Apocalypse smoothly in Lee's absence. Gone were the days when he had found fault with everything Lee said or did; these days Alexander admitted that Lee was knacky, competent, knew about everything and *did* have a business head. Having learned that Lee usually found the time to lunch with his mother at the hotel, since it didn't involve a time-consuming trip to the top of the mountain, Alexander decided to lunch at the hotel too.

Constance Dewy had gone back to Dunleigh; Elizabeth had the house to herself. If she wondered why she hadn't seen Ruby, she put that absence down to Lee, sticking to Kinross town and the foot of the mountain like a burr to a fleece.

SUMMER CAME in very hot and very dry, a weight of motionless air that pressed down so remorselessly that there was no escape from it anywhere, inside or out.

Alexander took the time off to build a shallow pool for Dolly in the shade of some trees the cicadas didn't like, and taught her to swim.

"But it's a small volume of water, easy to change when it grows algae and whatever else," he said to Elizabeth, who was enormously grateful for his thoughtfulness. "I've got Donny Wilkins working on the concept of public swimming baths—how to keep a huge volume of water clean and healthy. I mean, we solved the sewage problem with one of the new treatment works, so why not give the town swimming baths?" He grinned rather diabolically. "But I insist on *mixed* bathing—won't that upset the Methodists? I fail to see why the pleasure of cooling off in public baths should be constrained because a family can't frolic together. Think what a thrill it would be for a young fellow to see a girl's erect nipples through a wet bathing costume!"

Elizabeth couldn't help smiling. "That's the sort of thing you should save to say to Ruby," she said, no sting in her voice.

"Where do you think I got it from? Only she went further—thought the girls would get just as big a thrill from seeing the young men with wet costumes plastered against their—er—"

"Disgusting!" said Elizabeth, laughing. "Soon there will be no mysteries left."

He also installed big fans at either end of the house attics to draw in cooler air and pull out hot air. Elizabeth was amazed at the difference that made, even to the ground floor. No doubt the Kinross Hotel was getting the same treatment, all the bigger buildings, and probably sooner or later the houses with at least a crawl space above their ceilings. Apocalypse subsidized the town's electricity and gas supplies, so it was feasible. He could never rest, Alexander, he was always looking down new avenues. But would Lee be the same when Alexander was gone? Elizabeth genuinely didn't know. Still, that was for the far future, one that she knew how to face. Dolly would be grown up and married, so there would be nothing to hold her here. At long last she would be free to go elsewhere, and she knew where she was going—to the Italian lakes. There to live in peace.

NELL ARRIVED home for Christmas.

Her appearance shocked her mother and father. *Shabby!* The awful dresses were even more awful—completely shapeless, of much laundered cotton in dull browns and greys. Colors that did not suit her, didn't bring out the striking blue of her eyes or the creaminess of her skin. She didn't own a single pair of shoes, just flat-heeled brown boots that laced up past her ankles; she wore thick brown cotton stockings, cotton underwear, short white cotton gloves. The only hat she owned was Chinese coolie.

"We're much of a muchness except for height," Elizabeth said on Christmas afternoon, with a crowd coming for Christmas dinner. "I have a brand-new lilac chiffon that you'd find very comfortable, and Ruby sent up a pair of shoes because she says you have the same-sized feet. A pair of sheer silk stockings too. You needn't wear corsets—the new fashions don't require them if you don't like them. Oh, Nell, you'd look so lovely in lilac chiffon! You—float. I noticed it first thing."

"That's because I walk without wiggling my hips or bottom," said this unimpressionable child. "I call it a disciplined walk. You can't wiggle and wobble around a hospital ward—every HMO would crucify you."

"HMO?"

"Honorary Medical Officer—the big boys in private practice who are apportioned the beds. Can you imagine it?" Nell demanded wrathfully. "I've seen the foyer of Prince Alfred Hospital jammed with a *hundred* poor men, women and children waiting for a bed, and only *one* bed available because the HMOs hog them for their paying patients! Some of the poor die still waiting."

"Oh," said Elizabeth limply. She tried again. "Wear the lilac chiffon, Nell, please! It would make your father happy."

"No, I bloody won't!" said Nell fiercely.

Though she did make an effort to be pleasant during dinner; Elizabeth had seated Lee on one side of her and Donny Wilkins on the other, deciding that if all else failed, the three of them could talk mining shop. But Nell looked so odd, so drab and—well, *mannish.*

It was Ruby who went to the heart of the matter as soon as the dinner guests rose and repaired to the large drawing room. She herself was looking magnificent in a soft, flowing marmalade silk gown and beltlike links of gold set with amber. Since Nell had always loved her, she made no objection when Ruby pounced on a pair of armchairs, shoved Nell into one and plumped herself in the other, green eyes gone a little yellow from so much orangish gold. Her figure, the clinical Nell had to admit, had gone back to superb after that temporary weight explosion; Ruby wasn't at all likely to die of apoplexy. In fact, Ruby had probably worked out how not to die at all.

"It wouldn't have killed you to tart yourself up a bit," said Ruby, lighting a cheroot.

"Those things will kill *you*" was Nell's rejoinder.

"Don't avoid the issue, Nell. You know what your trouble is? It's simple. You're trying to turn yourself into a man."

"No, I'm just trying not to remind anyone that I'm a woman."

"Same difference. How old are you now?"

"Twenty-two on New Year's Day."

"And still a virgin, I'll bet."

A deep flush stained Nell's cheeks; her lips tightened. "That is none of your bloody business, Auntie Ruby!" she snapped.

"Yes, it is my business, little Miss Medicine. You know what all the parts look like, you know how all the parts work. But you don't have a fucking *clue* what life is all about because you don't live a life. You're a grind, Nell. A machine. I'm sure you're brilliant at all the things that please your teachers. I'm sure that they respect you even if they'd rather not, given your sex. You've carved your way through your chosen career the way your father carves into this mountain. Every day you see death, every day you see tragedy of some sort. You go home to that flat in Glebe Point Road and there's your dying sister, one more horror. Yet you don't live a life of your own. And if you don't, Nell, there's something lacking in how you regard your patients, no matter how kind and compassionate you seem to them. You'll miss something vital that's been said to you, some tiny human fact that could make all the difference to a diagnosis."

The vivid blue eyes were looking at her, startled and confused, as if at a statue that had come to life. But Nell said nothing, her anger ashes on the cold dark hearth of reality.

"Darling Nelly, don't retreat into a mold so masculine that it will end in ruining your career. I agree that what you wear is absolutely suitable for hospital and laboratory work, but it isn't suitable for a young, vital woman who should be proud of her femininity. You've crashed the barriers, but why give fucking men the victory by becoming one yourself? The next thing you'll be wearing trousers—again, sensible in certain environments—but you can't grow a prick, no matter how big your balls are. So make a few changes before it's too late. You can't tell me that there aren't medical school parties and balls, times when you can remind the bastards you're a proper woman. Remind them, Nell! And keep the practical gear for practical occasions. Go out with a few blokes, even if you don't fancy them. I'm sure you can fight them off if they get too stroppy. And if there is one you really fancy, pursue the relationship! Get *hurt*! Suffer a little on your own behalf! Go through all those ghastly self-doubts when the affair breaks up and you're convinced it's you, not him, it has to be you. Look in your mirror and weep. That's living a life."

Her mouth was dry; Nell swallowed, licked her lips. "I see. You're quite right, Auntie Ruby."

"No more 'Auntie' stuff, it's just Ruby from now on." She extended her hands, clenched and unclenched them, glared at them. "The fingers aren't behaving tonight," she said. "Play for me, Nell. But not"—she drew a breath—"Chopin. Some Mozart."

It was her one relaxation; Nell hadn't neglected the piano. So she smiled at Ruby and moved to the grand piano in her awful brown dress, there to entrance the company with merry Mozart and tzigane Liszt. Later Ruby joined her to sing operatic duets, and Christmas night ended with all the guests singing their favorite songs, from "I'll Take You Home Again, Kathleen" to "Two Little Girls in Blue."

So when Nell's birthday dinner came around on New Year's Day she wore the lilac chiffon. It was too short for her, but Ruby's silk stockings and stylish lilac shoes turned that into an advantage; what showed of Nell's legs was shapely. Her hair was arranged to flatter a long face that revealed the skull beneath, and Elizabeth's amethysts glittered around her graceful neck. Content, Ruby watched the astounded admiration on Donny Wilkins's face, and the delight on her father's. Good girl, Nell! You've saved your bacon, and just in time. I wish Lee looked at you the way Donny does, but his eyes are on your mother. Jesus, what a business!

NELL LEFT two days later, but not before she had talked to Elizabeth about Anna. Consultation with her father had been a heartache, though perhaps it fell into Ruby's definition of suffering on her own behalf, and was therefore living a life.

"I hate to put the burden on you, Nell," Alexander said, "but you know all too well how things stand between your mother and me. If I tell her what's going to happen to Anna, she'll withdraw into her shell and not have any companionship in her grief. If you tell her, there's at least a chance that she'll be able to give vent to her grief."

"Yes, I know, Dad." Nell sighed. "I'll do it."

And do it she did, weeping herself, which gave Elizabeth the chance to enfold another body in her arms, do the mourning and keening that goes with terrible, helpless, hopeless grief. Nell's greatest dread was that Elizabeth would ask to see Anna, but she didn't. It was as if, in that eruption of sorrow, she had closed a door.

Lee took Nell down the mountain to the train; Alexander was committed to blasting, something he still liked to do himself, and Elizabeth had drifted off, a shady hat on her head, apparently to commiserate with the roses still surviving the heat.

Nell had never really known Lee very well, and found his alien kind of attraction a little reptilian. Which, if she had known of Elizabeth's metaphor, would have made more sense. Even wearing his working clothes, he was a gentleman to his fingertips, his vowels as rounded as a duke's; yet underneath there worked something dangerous, fluid and coiling, dark yet dazzling. Very much a man, but of a kind she didn't understand and couldn't like. Her prickly reaction to him negated any chance to see his softness, his unbending honor and fidelity.

"So it's back to the hospital grind?" he asked as they went down in the cable car.

"Yes."

"Do you enjoy it?"

"Yes."

"But you don't enjoy me."

"No."

"Why is that?"

"You put me in my place once—Otto von Bismarck?"

"Dear me! You must have been all of six. But you're still conceited, I see. That's a pity."

They didn't speak again until they reached the train station and he carried her bags into the private compartment.

"This is grossly sybaritic," she said, gazing about. "I can never get used to it."

"It will go in the fullness of time. Don't grudge Alexander the fruits of his labor."

"What do you mean, 'go in the fullness of time'?"

"Just that. Eventually taxation will prohibit all such—er—sybaritic grossness. Though there will always be a first-class and a second-class."

"My father loves you to death," she said abruptly, sitting.

"I love him to death too."

"I disappointed him, doing Medicine."

"Yes, you did. But not in a spirit of vengeance. That would have cut him far deeper."

"I *should* love you. Why can't I?"

Lee lifted her hand and kissed it. "I hope you never find out, Nell. Goodbye."

And he was gone. Nell sat as the whistle blew and the train emitted the cacophony of noises that heralded its imminent departure. Frowning. What did he mean? Then she burrowed into her carry-all and found her materia medica textbook; within a minute both Lee and the sybaritic nature of her father's private compartment were forgotten. This coming year was her third-last, haunted by examinations that fully half the students would fail. Well, Nell Kinross wasn't going to fail, even if that necessitated not living a life. Bugger boyfriends—who had time?

THE SUMMER continued at its relentless peak until its very last gasp, which happened on the fifteenth of April, 1898.

Anna died in a status epilepticus early in the morning of the fourteenth, aged twenty-one. Her body was conveyed to Kinross for a tiny funeral held at the graveside on top of the mountain, attended only by Alexander, Nell, Lee, Ruby and the Reverend Mr. Peter Wilkins. Alexander had chosen the site, not far from his gallery wing, shaded by immense gum trees with pure white trunks; they could have been a row of pillars. Elizabeth didn't go; instead she looked after Dolly, who frolicked in her pool on the far side of the house. Nell assumed that the door was closed forever.

But later, after Lee, Ruby and Mr. Wilkins had gone down the mountain and Nell sat with her father in the library, Elizabeth went to the mound of sweet-smelling, freshly turned earth and laid all the roses she could find upon it.

"Rest in peace, my poor innocent," she said, turned and walked into the bush.

The northern sky was a soaring mass of mighty indigo storm clouds, their edges curling over in icy white billows like terrible waves roaring in from the sea; summer's last gasp was going to be a cataclysm. But Elizabeth never even noticed as she pushed into the undergrowth, thinned and sticked by lack of rain, deserted by its denizens for fear of the coming tempest. Her mind was devoid of conscious thought, it simply hummed with a thousand thousand memories of Anna that shut out the sky, the bush, the day, the image of herself.

The storm rolled closer; an eerie darkness fell, redolent with a sulfurous glow and the sickly-sweet stench of ozone. Without any prelude, lightning and thunder flashed and cracked together. Elizabeth didn't notice. She came back into herself when she was drenched to the skin by what seemed a waterfall, and then only because the path she had been following had turned to a brook under which lay mud so slippery that she couldn't keep her feet. This is how it should be, she thought dreamily, crawling forward on her hands and knees, blinded by the rain. This is how it should be. How it must be.

"THANK GOD the weather's broken," said Nell to Alexander as they watched the storm commence from the library's bay window.

He gave a convulsive start. "Anna's grave!" he cried. "I have to cover it!"

And off he ran into the rain while Nell went kitchenwards and shouted at people to help him.

When he returned he was soaked and shivering; the temperature had dropped forty degrees in half that many minutes, and the wind was rising to a howl.

"Was it all right, Dad?" Nell asked, giving him a towel.

"Yes, we covered it with a tarpaulin." His teeth chattered. "The odd thing is that it was already covered. With roses."

"She came after all," said Nell, wiping at tears. "Go and change, Dad, or you'll catch your death."

No risk of bushfires from lightning strikes in this downpour, thought Nell, going to find her mother.

Peony was giving Dolly her supper—is it that late? Nell wondered. The storm had twisted time, blotted out the sun.

"Where's Miss Lizzy?"

Peony looked up; Dolly waved her fork cheerfully.

"I don't know, Miss Nell. She gave me Dolly—oh, a good two hours ago."

As Nell walked down the hall Alexander came out of his rooms looking worn but curiously relieved; with Anna's death, the worst was over. All of them could breathe a little more easily.

"Dad, have you seen Mum?"

"No, why?"

"I can't find her."

They searched the house from attics to cellars and then explored the sheds and outbuildings, but in vain. Elizabeth was not to be found.

Alexander had begun to shiver again. "The roses," he said slowly. "She's wandered off into the storm."

"Dad, she wouldn't!"

"Then where is she?" Suddenly looking every day of his age, Alexander went to the telephone. "I'll notify the police station and we'll get a search party together."

"Dad, not now! It's almost night, and raining like buggery. You'll only end in getting half the search party lost—no one knows the mountain except us!"

"Then Lee. He knows the mountain. So does Summers."

"Yes, Lee and Summers. And I."

By the time that Lee and Summers arrived in mackintoshes and sou'westers, Alexander had assembled compasses, miner's lamps, spare flasks of kerosene and whatever he thought might be needed; dressed himself for the weather, he was standing over a survey map of the mountain while Nell prowled up and down looking frustrated.

"You're half a doctor, Nell, I need you here," he had said to her when she begged to search too.

Inarguable, but having nothing to do didn't suit Nell.

"Lee, you take the farthest perimeter, which means you'll ride my horse," said Alexander. "Summers and I will search closer to home because I doubt she'll have gotten very far between the storm and her state of mind. Brandy," he said, producing hip flasks. "Luckily it's warming up again, but we'll need it."

Lee looked peculiar, Nell thought as she paused in her pacing; his strange eyes wide and almost black, the fine full mouth quivering slightly.

"We'd best find her tonight," said Summers, hoisting his pack. "This rain is setting in, the river will be a torrent, and it might be that tomorrow everyone is too busy fighting a flood to mount a big search party. We'll catch her before she gets too far, that's the ticket, eh, Sir Alexander?"

Cold comfort, thought Nell, left to watch the three men go while she, a half-trained doctor, was left behind. Oh, how much she admired her father! Everything had been taken care of while he waited for Lee and Summers; the night shifts in the mine had been canceled, all employees told to go home, Sung Po alerted that a flash flood was likely, volunteers called to fill sandbags in case the river broke its banks. When he had tried to get through to Lithgow, he had found that the line was down, which meant no communication with Sydney.

Oh, Anna, thought Nell, piling her textbooks up on a table, what did life do to you that your going is so fraught with pain?

Mrs. Surtees came in, trying to conceal her anxiety. "Miss Nell, you haven't eaten anything. Can you manage an omelet?"

"Yes, thank you," said Nell calmly. "I'd appreciate that." No point in being too faint to deal with whatever the men brought in—pray that Mum's all right!

ALEXANDER'S HORSE was a pretty chestnut mare these days, docile and strongly built. Lee hadn't gone very far before he shed the mackintosh and sou'wester, folded them into a packet and slipped them into a saddlebag. The wind had turned to blow from the northeast, which had sent the temperature up enough to take the chill out of the rain; it was easier to scan the ground without that wretched hat flapping in his face, the mackintosh lifting with each gust. The miner's lamp, optically adjusted to give out as narrow a beam as possible from a burning wick, hadn't been designed for wet weather, but hurricane lanterns were too dim for this kind of work. He kept it sheltered from the rain by capping it with his broad-brimmed work hat and swung it tirelessly from hand to hand as he nudged the horse along at a snail's pace.

The news that Elizabeth was missing had struck him like a killing blow, except that this was slow dying, not a quick death. He hadn't seen her that afternoon when they buried Anna, though he had scented something on the wind that had nothing to do with the looming storm. As if fear, guilt and bewilderment were in the air. All he knew was what Ruby had told him: enough. They had had many talks since she had caught him out, talks that filled in the huge gaps in Lee's knowledge of that sad, doomed marriage.

Her mind had snapped, he was sure of it. So had Ruby been, farewelling him outside the hotel.

"The poor thing has gone mad, Lee, and vanished into the bush to die like a wounded animal."

But she couldn't die! She mustn't die! Nor could he let her go mad. Exchange Elizabeth for Anna in that barred cell? No, not if he had to give up his own life to prevent it! Only how would that benefit her, who liked him well enough these days, but only as a fairly distant friend?

Several times he dismounted to track some faint movement that didn't look like wind-tossed foliage, but found nothing. The chestnut mare, a good and willing goer, plodded on without complaint. An hour went by, another, yet another; he was now two miles from the house, and still no sign of her. Alexander had decided to use dynamite as a signal that she had been found, but Lee doubted that he would hear it above the wind, the rain, and the grumbling of the trees. Pray Alexander or Summers had come upon her closer to the house! If she had gotten this far, she might be ten feet away from him and not be visible.

Then, sweeping the lamp from hand to hand across the horse's head, he saw something fluttering on one of the those thorny shrubs that made walking in the bush unpleasant for the ignorant. He could reach it by leaning in the saddle, plucked it off. A shred of thin cotton fabric. White. She had been wearing a white dress, Nell said, one of the few encouraging facts they learned before setting out. It probably indicated loss of mind rather than loss of the will to live. Had she been determined on dying, she would have worn something as dark as the night.

He had come out of the thicket on to a bridle path that led to the pool he had swum in an eternity ago, and wondered now if she had been following it almost from the time she left Anna's grave. There were more signs of her progress, at the end on her hands and knees if the muddy grooves where the path was thickly sheltered from the elements were anything to go by.

WHEN HE saw her huddled on a rock by the pool the gladness drove all else from his brain, for she wasn't dead; she was sitting hunched over with her arms around her knees and her chin on them, a small white creature come to the end of its tether.

He slid from the horse, tied its reins to a branch and came up to her quietly, not sure how she would react to his presence, terrified of startling her into blundering off again. But she didn't move, even after a sudden rigidity told him that she knew someone was there.

"You've come to take me back," she said, very tiredly.

He didn't answer because he didn't know how best to answer.

"It's all right, Alexander, I know I can't escape. But I needed to come to The Pool. I suppose you think I've gone mad, but I haven't. Not really. I just needed to come to The Pool."

He edged close enough to have touched her, but settled next to her instead, cross-legged, his hands dangling limply off his knees. Oh, the relief! She sounded exhausted, but, as she said herself, not mad.

"Why did you have to come to the pool, Elizabeth?" he asked above the wind and the rain.

"Who is that?"

"It's Lee, Elizabeth."

"Ohhhhh," she said, drawing it out. "I'm still dreaming!"

"It *is* Lee. You're not dreaming, Elizabeth."

The reservoir of the miner's lamp was almost empty, but it shed a wan light from where it sat on the rock at his knee that barely reached his hands; she turned her head to study them.

"Lee's hands," she said. "I'd know them anywhere."

His breath caught, he began to tremble. "Why?"

"They're so beautiful."

One of them reached out to unlock hers from about her legs, its arm sliding across her back to turn her toward him. "They love you," he said, "along with the rest of me. I've always loved you, Elizabeth. I always will, forever and ever."

So little light, yet it seemed to blaze like a sun, showed the look in her eyes before they closed to feel his first kiss, soft and tentative, as befits a moment waited for half a lifetime.

Too terrified of losing her and the moment to think of going to the saddlebags, wherein lay blankets, a mackintosh, a supply of kerosene, he put her down on his clothes, and she was so exalted that she knew nothing beyond his mouth, his hands, his skin. When he eased her shoulders out of the dress to bare her breasts and gather them against his chest, a huge stab of some utter pleasure shook her to the marrow and wrenched a groan from her. Yet it went on and on and on. . . .

Who knows how many times they made love on that hard bed amid the rain? Certainly not the lamp, whose flame diminished to a pinpoint and snuffed itself out.

But finally Elizabeth lay in an exhausted sleep, and Lee, wide awake with the wonder of it and her, was forced to remember reality. Though it physically hurt to leave her, he groped to the patient horse to extricate the spare kerosene and his watch: three in the morning. It would be a late dawn because of the heavy skies and the rain, but not more than two hours off. Since he had found her, the others had not, and a frantic Alexander would be ready to go at dawn with that part of Kinross not needed to stem a flood. The level of water in the pool had risen considerably, and would continue to rise; he would have to move Elizabeth anyway. And how were they going to deal with this? The one thing he could not let happen was to have Alexander find them still entwined like the lovers they had become.

Lee slipped the saddlebags from the mare and carried them back to the rock, unscrewing his flask of brandy.

"Elizabeth! Elizabeth, my love! Elizabeth, wake up!"

She stirred but muttered mutinously back into sleep; it took him several minutes to persuade her to sit up, but once she had taken a little brandy she roused fully, shivering.

"I love you," she said, a hand on either side of his face. "I have loved you forever."

He kissed her, but pulled away before the whole thing could start again; she was chilled to the bone, only sustained by the night's excitement, the warmth of his body.

"Put your clothes on," he said—not an order, but a plea. "We have to go before Alexander mounts a full-scale search."

It was too dark to see her face beyond a blur, but he could feel the anxiety and tension flood into her at the mention of that name. On went the clothes; he wrapped a blanket around her and put the mackintosh over that, then refilled the lamp and lit it to guide them.

"Do you have any shoes?"

"No, I lost them."

It was a struggle to get her across the horse's withers; still, once he was in the saddle and had a good hold of her, they could talk as he rode, curbing the mare, which sensed home and a warm stable in this direction.

"I love you," he started, not wanting to start anywhere else.

"And I love you."

"There's more to it than that, though, dearest Elizabeth."

"Yes. There's Alexander," she said.

"What do you want to do?" he asked.

"Keep you," she said simply. "I couldn't bear to let you go, Lee. It's too precious."

"Then will you go away with me?"

But reality had asserted its claim on her too; he felt her shrink against him, felt her sigh. "How can I, Lee? I don't think Alexander would let me go. Even if he did, I still have Dolly to look after. I can't desert Anna's child."

"I know. Then what do you want to do?"

"Keep you. It will have to be a secret, at least until I can think more clearly. I'm so tired, Lee!"

"Then our secret it is."

"When will I see you again?" she asked, alarmed.

"Not until the rain's over, my sweet love. If we have floods, a week at least. Let's make it a week anyway."

"Oh, I'll die!"

"No, you'll live—for me. We will meet at the pool seven days from this coming dawn. That will mean an afternoon, won't it?"

"Yes."

"Do you think you'll be able to keep our secret?"

"I've kept myself a secret since I married Alexander, so why should this be any different?"

"Go to sleep."

"What if something happens and you can't come?"

"You'll know through Alexander, because I'll be with him. Go to sleep, my dearest."

* * *

WHEN LEE rode toward the house shortly before dawn shouting that he had found Elizabeth, her sleeping form was gently handed down to a white-faced, shaking Alexander, who carried her into the house and Nell. When he emerged, brimming with gratitude, it was to find that Lee had given the mare to Summers and taken himself home to Ruby.

"That's rum," said Alexander, frowning.

"Oh, I dunno, Sir Alexander," said Summers with superb logic, "the poor coot was wet through, and he's a much heftier man than you. Your clothes won't fit him, will they?"

"True, Summers. I'd forgotten that."

So it was about thirty-six hours later before Lee had to endure Alexander's fervent thanks, delivered at the hotel after what Alexander said had been a visit to old Brumford, his lawyer.

"Is Elizabeth all right?" Lee asked, feeling that to express anxiety was natural under the circumstances.

"Surprisingly, yes. Nell's a bit flummoxed. She was all set to deal with anything from pneumonia to a brain fever, but after a twenty-four-hour sleep, Elizabeth woke up this morning fresh as a daisy, then ate an enormous breakfast."

Alexander, however, looked anything but fresh; his eyes were red-rimmed, his face drawn. Though he was clearly trying to look jaunty, it wasn't working.

"Are *you* all right, Alexander?" Lee asked.

"Oh, lord, yes, perfectly! It just gave me a bit of a fright, coming out of the blue like that. I really can't thank you enough, my boy." He looked at his gold wrist-watch. "I have to take Nell to the train. What a grand girl! With you at my side again, I can wish her well in Medicine."

Nothing that Lee wanted to hear, though it relieved him that Nell was leaving Kinross. A grand girl, yes, but as sharp as a tack and no friend to him—or, he suspected, to her mother.

I hate it! thought Lee. All this subterfuge and sneaking around. There's only one thing worse than having Elizabeth this way, and that's not having her at all. I can't even tell my mother what's happened.

He didn't have to. The moment he walked into the hotel trailing water all over the carpet, Ruby knew.

I have lost my son. He's given himself to Elizabeth. And this is the one subject I dare not bring up with him. He hates it but loves her. To want is one thing, to get what you want is quite another. Oh, pray this doesn't kill him! All I can do is light candles at that abode of sanctity, the Tyke church.

"My goodness, Mrs. Costevan," said old Father Flannery (he always accorded her the dignity of a married title), "you'll be coming to Mass next!"

"Fuh—bother that!" snarled Ruby. "Don't get your hopes up, Tim Flannery, you old soak! I just like lighting candles!"

And perhaps she does at that, thought the priest, clutching the fistful of notes she had thrust at him. He had enough here to drink the finest Irish for months.

ELIZABETH AWOKE into a whole new world, one that she hadn't—couldn't have—known existed. She loved and was loved. The dreaming phases of her sleep had been filled with images of Lee, but to wake and know they were real—! Some twist in her mental processes had blotted out all memory of visiting Anna's grave, of the roses, of walking into the bush with the blind drive of an animal seeking its home, intent only on reaching The Pool. What she remembered was Lee finding her there, and all the wonderful, beautiful, glorious emotions and sensations that had followed. To have lived as a married woman for twenty-three years and never to have understood what true marriage was!

Her body felt different; as if it truly belonged to her soul, rather than was a cage imprisoning her soul. No aches or pains plagued her when she woke, not even a tiny stiffness. I was dead, and Lee gave me life. Almost forty years of age, and this is my first taste of pure happiness.

"Well, you're finally compos mentis!" said a brisk voice: Nell moved to the bed. "I can't say you had me worried, Mum, but you've slept for almost twenty-four hours."

"Have I?" Elizabeth yawned, stretched, made a purring sound.

Her daughter's shrewd eyes were fixed on her face, and wore a puzzled look; had Nell only known it, this was one of those situations Ruby had referred to, when her own ignorance of life rendered her blind to what someone more experienced would have seen immediately. "You look absolutely splendid."

"I feel it," said Elizabeth, the shutters beginning to come down. "Did I cause much trouble? I didn't mean to."

"We were frantic, especially Dad—he had me very worried. Do you remember what you did? What you were thinking of?"

"No," said Elizabeth, speaking the truth.

"You must have gone miles. Lee found you."

"Did he?" Her eyes looked up at Nell with mild curiosity, nothing else. Elizabeth was an expert at secrets.

"Yes. He took Dad's horse—it never occurred to any of us that you'd move at the speed of light in that weather, so Lee had the least likely alternative. Dad would rather have found you himself." Nell shrugged. "Still, it doesn't matter who found you—the important thing is that you were found."

No, thought Elizabeth, the important thing is that Alexander didn't take the horse. Then it would have been Alexander who found me, and I would still be his prisoner.

"I suppose I was a mess?" she asked.

"That's putting it mildly, Mum! You were caked in mud, slime, God knows what. It took ages for Pearl and Silken Flower to get you clean."

"I don't remember being bathed."

"That's because you were sound asleep. I had to sit at the top of the bath and keep your head out of the water."

"My goodness!" Elizabeth swung her legs out of the bed. "How is Dolly? What does she know?"

"Only that you've been ill, but that you're all right now."

"Yes, I am all right. Thank you, Nell, I'd like to dress."

"Do you need help?"

"No, I can look after myself."

An inspection of her body in two big mirrors revealed cuts and bruises galore—strange, that they didn't hurt a bit—but nothing that betrayed what had happened at The Pool. She closed her eyes, sagged in relief.

Alexander came in a little later. Eyes wide, Elizabeth gazed at him as if she had never seen him before. How many times had he made love to her between her wedding night and the onset of her illness when she became pregnant with Anna? She hadn't counted, but many times. Yet never once had she seen him naked, or wanted to. He had known that much, and not forced the issue. But only now, because of what she and Lee had done together, did she understand. Where there is neither love nor physical desire, said her newfound insight, nothing can ever happen to improve matters. And yes, Alexander had done his best to change that. But he was a driving, straightforward man whose physical desires reflected his nature; by no means unsubtle, but *learned.* I never shook with want for him, she thought. There is nothing in him, nothing he could do to me, that could lift me to that exalted, ecstatic state I have just known with Lee. I could no more have borne to have a shred of clothing between my body and Lee's than I could have sent him away from me. I wouldn't have cared if the whole world watched, or if it ended, with Lee's hands on my skin and my hands on his. When he said he had always loved me and always would, it was like coming home. Yet how can I tell this man any of that? Even if he could bear to listen, he wouldn't begin to understand. I don't know what happens between him and Ruby; with no other yardstick than Alexander and me to go by, how could I? But from today everything has changed, everything is different, everything is a source of wonder. I have undergone a miracle, I have lain with my beloved.

Alexander was staring at her as if at someone he knew he ought to know, but didn't. His face was lined and looked older than she remembered it—how long ago seemed Anna's death! To her he seemed to have lost essence, but she gazed at him with all her usual tranquillity, and smiled.

He smiled back. "Are you hungry enough to eat breakfast?"

"Thank you, I'll be down shortly," she said serenely.

So they settled together at the table in the conservatory, upon whose transparent, white-ribbed roof the rain beat down so steadily that the panes ran in shimmering ripples.

"I *am* hungry!" said Elizabeth in amazement, wading her way through grilled lamb chops, scrambled eggs, bacon, fried potatoes.

Nell had joined them; she was going back to Sydney shortly.

"You must thank Lee, Elizabeth," said Alexander, not hungry.

"If you insist," she said, swallowing toast.

"Aren't you grateful to him, Mum?" Nell asked, surprised.

"Yes, of course I am." Elizabeth reached for the chops.

Alexander and his daughter exchanged a rueful glance, then abandoned the subject.

Having eaten her fill, Elizabeth went to see Dolly; Nell, about to accompany her, was detained by her father.

"Is she right in the head?" he asked. "She's so unaffected by what happened."

Nell considered the question, then nodded. "I think so, Dad. At least, as right in the head as she's ever been. You used the correct word—Mum is fey."

* * *

WHEN HE REALIZED that Elizabeth had gone missing, Alexander suffered a shock of such magnitude that he knew a part of him would never get over it. For most of the last twenty-three years he had thought of Elizabeth as a thorn in his side—a staid, prim, frigid creature whom he had married for all the wrong reasons. He'd taken the blame because the wrong reasons belonged to him, not to her, and tried to make amends. But her ever-growing distaste of him had wounded him to the quick, set off a chain of reactions founded in pride, resentment, self-esteem. The love of her that had come so soon after their union she had rejected, so he attributed the unhappiness that clouded both their lives more and more as time went on to her and her rejection of the love he had offered. Convinced himself that his love had died. Well, how could it not die, when it was planted in such unforgiving soil? And somewhere along the way he had lost sight of anything except his own thwarted impulse to conquer. All the while calling her a pillar of ice. Yet how could one conquer a pillar of ice? Grasp it, and it melted away into nothing one could take hold of.

But as he searched for her in a frenzy of fear and guilt, he saw for the very first time in their long relationship how terribly he had failed her. All the things he had given her, she didn't want; all the things he hadn't given her, she craved. He equated love with fabulous gifts, immense luxury. She did not. He equated love with fantastic sexual satisfaction. She did not—or, if she did, he was not the man who could give her that. A fire did burn in her, he was sure of it now, but it didn't burn for him. And what he asked himself over and over as he searched for her was where and why the erosion of her esteem for him had started. But his panic was too great to see the where, the why. He could get no further than the realization that the love for her he had deemed dead for many years was not dead after all. A poor emotion, unreturned, so injurious to his sense of self that he had blotted it from his mind. Now here it was, risen to the surface again, thrust there by the horror of imagining her mad and dead. His fault if she was. His fault, no one else's.

And there was Ruby. There was always Ruby. Once, he remembered, he had asked her if a man could love two women at once; she had turned the question aside with a trace of malice, but it was in her own interests to do that. Yet she must have known that he loved both of them, for she joined herself to Elizabeth as a confederate. He had thought she did so in a spirit of charity, as the victor. Now he understood she had done so as a sure way to keep that part of his love that belonged to her. If he hadn't loved Elizabeth, the two women in his life would still have become friends, perhaps, but more distant ones. He was, he admitted, a man who liked to have his cake and eat it too. Ruby meant more; Ruby was romance, sex, intimacy, an illicit thrill, and that curious combination that a beloved woman becomes to her man, of lover, mother, sister. But he had lived his life with Elizabeth, fathered her children, gone through the torments of Anna and Dolly with her. And that took love, else he would have let her go.

So when Lee rode across the lawn and gave her back to him, Alexander underwent an enlightenment that brought him lower than a surrendered captive. He owed his wife a debt he couldn't hope to pay with any coin save one: open the cage and let the bird fly.

AFTER FIVE DAYS the rain blew out; Kinross, so close to flood, gave thanks. If Alexander had been a less careful custodian and left the river as it had been after the mining of the placer, flooding would have been inevitable, but he had shored the banks and returned the stream to a proper course dredged deep enough to take the overflow.

Seven days after her disappearance, Elizabeth mounted Cloud and set off for her customary ride. Once she left the immediate vicinity of the house she swerved into the saturated bush and let the mare pick its way between boulders and hazards for a full mile before returning to the bridle path that led to The Pool.

Lee was there, waiting, came to Cloud and held out his arms to receive her. Kisses wilder and more passionate, a degree of starvation that even she hadn't gauged; she couldn't wait for him to touch her, to bare her body, to take it. And always those alien sensations of ecstasy, a pouring forth of everything she was into the crucible of love. Then he took her into The Pool, and made love to her in what seemed their natural habitat, water.

When they were dry she unbraided his hair, enchanted by its length and thickness; played with it, entwined it among hers, led it over her breasts, buried her face in it. And told him of how she had seen him swimming in The Pool, and never managed to banish the sight of him from memory.

"I didn't know it could be like this between a man and woman," she said. "I have entered a whole new world."

"We can't stay here much longer" was his answer: why was it always he who had to remind them of reality? Then he asked her what had haunted him since he found her. "Elizabeth, dearest love, you're not supposed to do this. I know we *can* do it, but only after I've seen Hung Chee, who knows the table of the woman's cycle. So far we've taken no precautions, and you can't be let conceive. That's a death sentence."

She laughed, a carefree sound echoing its joy around the forest. "Darling Lee, there's nothing to worry about! Truly, nothing! No child I bore to you would hurt me. If I am lucky enough to conceive, there will be no eclampsia. I am as sure of that as I am that the sun will come up tomorrow morning."

Three

ALEXANDER IN CONTROL

THE ENTIRE burden of what had happened between Elizabeth and him fell upon Lee, who hadn't realized the enormity of its weight until he met Elizabeth at the pool seven days after he had found her. From the moment when she laughed and ridiculed his fears for her safety in the event of a child, he understood everything that he had pushed from his mind for a week. All that had filled it was Elizabeth, the incredible fact that she loved him, had loved him for as long as he had loved her. The qualms he suffered he had assumed would vanish when they met again and could talk the matter through—surely there was an honorable answer! But she wasn't interested in answers, she didn't see the point of answers; she had found her answer in him, and nothing else mattered to her.

He had gone to their meeting determined it would have no physical side because he remembered his mother explaining that sexual intercourse was a death sentence for Elizabeth. He knew it was not: conception was. His mother knew that too, which was why she had never fallen pregnant to Alexander. But they were tied to the Chinese nobility, weren't ignorant like Europeans.

Oh, but let there be no issue of that one unforgettable ascent into paradise! It might be forgiven him, as he hadn't intended it or imagined it could happen, but now they had to wait. Then she had slid from her horse into his arms and he saw her, smelled her, felt her, tasted her. The power in her overwhelmed him, he just couldn't stop himself. Then, when he had raised the subject of conception, she had gone into fits of laughter!

Time! Where had it gone? They hadn't discussed more than a small fraction of what had to be discussed before she was back on her dappled mare and riding off. They were to meet again at the pool in four more days; she had begged for an earlier tryst, but he had managed to stand firm. They were on a collision course with disaster, as he well knew and she ought to know. But for all his experience with women, Elizabeth represented the one and only love, so he had no idea how single-minded women in love were, or how ruthless, or how indifferent to any factor save the preservation of that love. He had thought that they would be as one about sparing Alexander as much pain as possible, but she didn't care one iota about sparing Alexander. Dolly, yes. Only Dolly held her immobile. It was he, Lee, who cared about Alexander, who saw what they were doing as a kind of treason to the man responsible for Lee's good fortune, career, opportunities. His mother's most dearly beloved. Elizabeth feared Alexander; for the rest, he didn't exist.

She had ridden away obviously convinced that they could keep their secret forever if necessary, and hugging that secret to herself as if it were a trophy in some ongoing war against her husband. For Lee, on the outside of this very long marriage, it was shrouded in mystery. Only now could he appreciate that even his mother did not fully understand it. Probably Alexander was as much in the dark as he was, for the fulcrum on which it turned was Elizabeth.

So Lee went back to Kinross down the snake path in the face of the dying sun more confused and rudderless than ever. All he knew was that he didn't possess the duplicity or furtiveness to maintain a secret relationship with Alexander's wife. For a week he had believed that she would betray it in all innocence by a chance remark, an imprudent reference to him, but now he realized that she never would. Even if she swelled up with his child, she would preserve her silence.

This thought, rising to the surface of his mind as he passed the poppet heads and waved at their attendants, made him stop in his tracks. Oh, Jesus! No, no, no! Not for anything would he do that to Alexander! He knew the story, told to him in a tiny coffeehouse in Constantinople: Alexander's mother had had a lover whose identity she had refused to disclose, and her husband had known that the child wasn't his. To let the wheel describe that particular full circle was manifestly impossible. Sneaking around was bad enough; repeating history was intolerable. To humble such colossal pride, to reduce a life's work to insignificance, to impose upon Alexander his titular father's fate—no, and no, and no! Unthinkable!

Ruby was waiting for him as he entered the hotel, the worry she felt not written on her face, which smiled at him even as its eyes quizzed him.

"Where have you been? People kept ringing up for you."

"I've been on the mountain looking at ventilation shafts."

"Is that important?"

"Oh, Mum, and you a director of Apocalypse Enterprises! It always is, but Alexander's planning a big blast where the old vein's run out in number one tunnel—he says there is another vein twenty feet in, and you know his nose for gold."

"Huh! His nose for gold!" Ruby snorted. "He might have a Midas touch, but he never seems to remember that the original King Midas died of starvation because even his food turned to gold." But that wasn't what she was thinking. My son looks dreadful. The incubus of this affair is so tight around his neck that it's strangling him. It's time I went to see Elizabeth and wrung the truth out of her. "Dinner?" she asked.

"Thanks, but I'm not hungry."

No, what you're hungering for is another man's meat. But is it still a going thing? Is that why you're so tormented, my jade kitten? She can't run the risk of a pregnancy, so probably what you're going through is hunger pure and simple. My poor Lee.

Lee went up the stairs to his own room. It wasn't very large because he wasn't a personal possessions kind of man—the clothes he had to have for all occasions, a few hundred treasured books, little else that mattered. Photographs of Alexander, Ruby, Sung. None of Elizabeth.

For a while he sat in his armchair and looked into nothing, then got up and went to the phone.

"Lee here, Aggie. Sir Alexander, please." No need to tell Aggie whereabouts; she knew exactly where he was at all times, just as she knew that X was eating dinner at Y's house, that Z was on the sports oval training his new dog, that M was in Dubbo visiting his mum, and R stuck on the lavatory with diarrhea. Aggie was the spider at the center of the Kinross telephonic web.

"Alexander, when do you have a moment? I need to speak with you privately as soon as possible."

"Privately as in privately?"

"Definitely."

"Tomorrow morning at the poppet heads. Eleven?"

"I'll see you there and then."

The die was cast. Lee went back to the armchair and wept his goodbyes. Not to Elizabeth yet—Alexander might consent to divorce her, even give her Dolly. No, Lee wept for Alexander. After tomorrow morning, they would never meet again. The break would be cruelly complete, for neither man believed in half measures. And how hard that would make things for his mother! Somehow he had to fix it so that she at least didn't suffer from the repercussions.

ALEXANDER TOOK the cable car to the poppet heads, Lee walked the snake path. The day, April 24, was one of those mid-autumn idylls that sometimes follow a summer that had lasted too long and been too harsh; a sweet-smelling breeze off the freshly washed and pungent bush, a gentler sun, a few puffy clouds wandering through the sky as if lost.

At this hour the poppet heads were almost deserted. Alexander was standing beside a massive air compressor powered by a steam engine, which was why it couldn't be put inside the mine—too much smoke, too much poisonous gas. When he had switched from hand drills to pneumatic percussion drills for boring the charge holes and from picks to pneumatic percussion hammers for breaking down the rock face, he had had to devise a way to supply compressed air to these air-powered machines, located as far away from the compressor as a quarter or a third of a mile. A large steel pipe inside a slightly bigger hole pushed the air down to a cylindrical steel tank six feet in diameter and twelve feet long that sat on the gallery floor; from this, sections of steel pipe led to the drills and hammers.

Drilling and blasting didn't happen every day by any means, however, nor was it ever done in more than one tunnel at a time. Alexander's inclination lay to electrically powering the air compressor, but that was for a future when electric motors were adequate. For the moment, steam was the only way to go, so the compressor was one of, if not the largest, in the world.

"Your private talk can wait" was Alexander's greeting. "I want to go into number one tunnel for another look."

They took a cage and traveled down 150 feet to the vast main gallery, brilliantly lit by electricity; men appeared regularly, pushing small ore-laden skips on rails to the open side of the gallery, where there was a fifty-foot drop down to the big skips in the main adit. A small skip on reaching the edge was tilted by a lever and cascaded its contents into a big skip below. An engine outside the adit hauled the big skips out by a steel cable to where they could be hitched to a locomotive and towed off to the sorting and crushing sheds. Dust hung in the air, which otherwise was fresh, fed in and sucked out by electric fans. All around the blind three-quarters of the gallery walls the tunnels dived into the mountain, some traveling straight, some upward, some downward, the newer ones branching many times.

Together they walked into number one tunnel, the oldest and most exploited, their way lit by electricity; as mining in it had ceased, they met no one. Typical Alexander, it was more than adequately shored up by massive beams, though Lee knew that the granite in this part of the mountain didn't have enough greywacke to make a collapse likely.

It was a thousand-foot walk, punctuated by the wet, sloshing suck of their boots and the slow, steady dripping of water the crushing pressure of the mountain squeezed out. In this climate, no danger of the water's turning to ice and acting as a wedge to split the layers apart. That could only happen when blasting, the most delicate and demanding of all mining operations—which was why, if the blast were a big or unusual one, Alexander preferred to do it himself.

Finally they reached the blind end of number one tunnel, to find some preparations already assembled for the blasting: a spool of insulated wire, an Ingersoll pneumatic drill perched on a tripod, the last section of steel pipe leading from the cylinder of compressed air in the gallery, a box of tools. One end of a heavy rubber hose was clamped by steel cuffs on to the steel pipe, the other on to the drill. Dynamite and detonators would not appear until it was time to set the charges, and then in proper custody. The magazine wherein the explosives were kept was a concrete bunker with only four keys: one each for Alexander, Lee, Summers and Prentice, the blasting supervisor.

"This blast is a bit of an experiment," Alexander said after both of them had run their hands down the relatively smooth rock face as sensitively as if they caressed a woman's skin. The lights blazed on it, throwing every fault line into prominence. "There's no more gold for at least twenty feet, so I want to bring down more rock than usual. Start at the middle on that fault there, then explode the rest of the charges concentrically. Each group wired in series. I'll drill the holes myself."

Lee listened in some bewilderment; no one knew this art as Alexander did, but he wasn't being very forthcoming.

"How much rock do you intend to bring down?" Lee asked, a frisson of fear streaking down his spine.

"Quite a few tons."

"If you were anyone else, I'd forbid it, but I can't very well do that to the master."

"You certainly can't."

"But you are *sure?* You haven't discussed it with me."

"This is dear old number one. She likes me, the bitch."

They turned to plod back to the gallery.

"When do you plan to blast?"

"Tomorrow, if it's as nice a day as today—no winds to fuck up the ventilator shafts." He gestured at a cage. "Up or down?"

"Up."

There could be no more procrastination. Lee gulped, trying to find enough moisture in his mouth to talk. A thousand recitations through the night, choosing or discarding the words that he must use. Rehearsing the most important speech of his life.

"Now what's this private matter?" Alexander asked briskly.

The steam engine powering the compressor was big enough to drive a freight locomotive, so it made a lot of noise as it forced the compressor to supply air to the gallery cylinder and its lines. Off to the far side the poppet heads engine chugged more gently, a stoker leaning on his grimy shovel, another man checking dials.

"Over here," said Lee, leading Alexander to a spot on the parapet of the limestone shelf away from the engines, poppet heads and personnel on duty. There was nowhere to sit, so he hunkered down with his buttocks resting on his heels, Alexander following suit.

A leaf lay on the ground; Lee picked it up as if examining it, began to pick its dry fragility to pieces. And in the end, of course, every rehearsed word vanished from his mind. All he could do was get it out.

"I have loved you better than my father, Alexander, but I've betrayed you," he said, shredding the leaf. "Not a plotted and planned betrayal, but a betrayal all the same. I can't bear to live with a lie. You have to know."

"Know what?" Alexander asked, as calmly as if what Lee had to tell him would turn out to be a minor peculation, a tiny fraud.

The leaf was gone; Lee lifted his eyes, swimming with tears, to rest them on Alexander's face, his lips moving soundlessly as he groped for words. "I'm in love with Elizabeth, and when I found her eight days ago, I—I betrayed you."

Some unnamable emotion flared briefly in the black eyes, which then went dull, opaque. Alexander's face didn't change. Nor did he say anything for what seemed an age, just squatted in the laid dust with his wrists propped on his knees, his hands as loose and relaxed as they had been before Lee spoke.

"I thank you for your honesty," he said at last.

That immense dignity which had so drawn Alexander to a child eight years old was still very much at Lee's core, and it kept him from pouring out excuses, self-exculpatory explanations, all the protestations of virtual innocence that a lesser man would have tripped over himself to make. If a lesser man could have screwed up the courage to confess to someone like Alexander.

"Easier to tell you than to live a lie," Lee said. "I am to blame, not Elizabeth. When I found her she wasn't herself, she was—was terribly distressed. But it happened, and it happened again yesterday. Elizabeth believes that she loves me."

"Why shouldn't she?" Alexander asked. "She's *chosen* you."

"It can't be, I know that. So I should have broken it off yesterday. But I didn't. I couldn't."

"Does she know that you're telling me this, Lee?"

"No."

"Does your mother? Is she in on this too?"

"No."

"Then it's our secret."

"Yes."

"Poor Elizabeth," said Alexander on a sigh. "How long have you loved her?"

"Since I was seventeen."

"Which is why you dreaded coming home to Kinross. Why you once disappeared off the map."

"Yes. Though you must understand that I never expected or intended to do anything about it. I have always loved you too much to hurt you, but it happened when I had no defenses and she had no defenses. She was in no condition to resist. I caught her with her guard down."

"That's a victory," said Alexander dryly. "I've never caught her with her guard down. If it had been me to find her instead of you, her guard would have stayed up. That's the story of Elizabeth and me. I live with someone bled of all vitality. A ghost. I'm just so pleased that the fire does burn."

He was taking it like the strong, honorable, unflinching man he was, Lee told himself. Which only made Lee's suffering worse. The hideous hurt had to be there, but Alexander wasn't about to show it.

"Anyway," said Lee, "I have put her at great risk. She shouldn't have children, I know that, yet I couldn't help myself. Yesterday I went to talk to her, just talk to her, but it didn't work out that way. And when I spoke of the danger, she laughed!"

"Laughed?"

"Yes. She refuses to believe there's any danger."

"There probably isn't." Alexander got up, extended a hand to Lee. "Come, we'll walk a bit. I want to go up to the spot that lies over the end of number one tunnel. I like it there, my soul or spirit or whatever you want to call it communes with my gold mountain there."

To the engine hands they looked what they were, the mine's owners having some deep discussion about its future; of great interest to all employees.

"I couldn't live a lie," Lee said again when they reached the spot and perched on a couple of rocks.

"You're too honorable, my boy, that's your trouble. But she was happy to live a lie, wasn't she?"

"Not because she's naturally deceitful, honestly," said Lee, laboring. "I think it's how she's organized herself over the years. And she so dreads your finding out. Oh, she's aware of your kindness, your respect for her. Yet she's afraid of you, and that is a complete mystery to me."

"Not to me," said Alexander, stroking the surface of his rock. "I'm an incarnation of Satan."

"I beg your pardon?"

"Elizabeth is the victim of two twisted, evil old men. They are both dead, but their influence will always be with her. I've been a way station for her, someone who sired her children, someone who houses her and shares her food. And there's your mother, whom I'll love until the day I die. Which Elizabeth well knows. My dear Lee, we can't force other people to be or do what we want, though it's taken me fifty-five years to find that out. For many reasons I don't intend to go into, Elizabeth can't bear me. A physical thing too. If I touch her, I can see her flesh crawl. I ceased to love her years ago," he lied—spare Lee everything you can, Alexander—"if I ever did love her. I used to think I did in the beginning, but perhaps I was simply in love with the idea of what we might have been to each other if she had loved me. Is her love for you very recent?"

"She says not," Lee answered, hating this detached, quite passionless interview for its very detachment. He wanted—he *needed!*—to be roared at, punched, kicked. Anything but this!

"Then both of you have suffered, yet you've remained loyal. That counts for much with me."

"I know today's an end, Alexander. I'm prepared for that."

"Your bags are packed, you mean."

"Metaphorically, yes."

"And what of Elizabeth? Are you going to sentence her to yet more years of living with a man she can't bear?"

"That depends on you. She won't go without Dolly, and Dolly is your only grandchild. A court would award her to you—*if* Elizabeth could face a court branded an adultress."

"Adultery is the only suitable ground for divorce. Cruelty is also a ground, but it doesn't apply, and there's many a judge beats his wife. However, she could divorce me for adultery with Ruby."

"And wouldn't that look wonderful? The divorced wife of the famous man then marries her former husband's mistress's son. A half-caste Chinese. The press would have a field day."

"If she loves you enough, she'll do it."

"She does love me enough. But the scandal would follow us for years unless we moved abroad. Perhaps that's the answer."

"Yet I need you here, Lee, not abroad."

"Then there is no answer!" Lee cried wretchedly.

Alexander changed tack. "Are you positive that she doesn't know you intended to see me?"

"Yes, absolutely positive. She's walled herself up in a new secret compartment, and she's happy there."

"And you're just as positive that Ruby doesn't know?"

"I am. It's always been my habit to talk to her about anything, including my love for Elizabeth. A more worldly woman than my mother doesn't exist. But I haven't told her about this new development. She can keep a secret as well as Elizabeth, but I—I just couldn't bring myself to tell her."

Alexander lifted his head to look straight into Lee's eyes. "I need time to think," he said. "Give me your word that you'll not mention this to anyone, even Ruby or Elizabeth."

Lee got up from his rock and held out his hand. "Word of honor, Alexander."

"Then that's set in stone. Tomorrow, after the blast, I'll give you my answer. Will you be there?"

"If you want me there."

"I do, I do. Summers has ten thumbs and Prentice puts me off. He's fine if he's doing the blasting, but when I do it he hops up and down like a jumping bean."

"I am aware of all that," Lee said gently.

"I'm aware you're aware. It's just that I'm a bit knocked off center by your news. I thank you for your candor, Lee—very much. I knew I wasn't mistaken in you, and I want to apologize to you for the way I treated you back in 1890. I'd grown too big for my boots." He stamped the ground, which sounded a little hollow. "Now I wear the right-sized boots again. No man could ask for a loyaler or more capable second-in-command, and you'll make a fine commander-in-chief one day." He cleared his throat, looked wry. "But I'm drifting off the point, which is that I have to work out a way to keep you yet free Elizabeth."

"I think that's impossible, Alexander."

"Nothing is impossible. Eight tomorrow morning in the main gallery. I'll probably still be in number one tunnel, but don't go inside. Powder monkey's orders."

And he swung in the direction of the cable car, while Lee headed for the snake path.

Suddenly Alexander called out. "Lee!"

Lee halted and twisted to look at him.

"It's Dolly's birthday today. Four o'clock at the house."

I HAD FORGOTTEN Dolly's birthday, thought Lee wearily as he donned a dark suit; with the festivities due to start at four, no evening dress, though of course the adults would sit down for dinner after the birthday party. Constance Dewy would be there.

He encountered Ruby coming down the corridor from her rooms, and waited for her. How beautiful she was! Her figure had improved, if that were possible, its bones carrying a little less weight than in his childhood, when voluptuousness was in fashion and men could indulge their natural preference for it. Her dress was of French crepe as green as her eyes, its bodice and leg-o'-mutton sleeves inlaid with pink and its knee-length skirt cut in long teeth ending in tassels. The under-dress, all the way to the ground, was pink, and her kid gloves were pink. A small green hat with a curled brim sat on her red-gold hair, its front adorned with pink roses.

"You look good enough to eat," he said, kissing a silken cheek with eyes closed to savor the scent of gardenias.

She gurgled. "I hope Alexander thinks the same."

"You shouldn't say things like that to your son."

"Well, at least you know what I mean, which augurs well for your birds of paradise."

"My birds of paradise prefer the thrill of diamonds."

They traveled up in the cable car to find Alexander, Elizabeth and Constance in the small dining room, decked with bunting. Everyone had to wear a party hat. Constance had brought them from Bathurst, where an enterprising Chinese shopkeeper had taken advantage of the Chinese skill in making tissue-thin colored paper; he sold streamers, party hats, fancy paper tablecloths and napkins, exquisite wrapping paper for gifts.

When Peony led Dolly in on some pretext they commenced a chorus of happy birthdays and showered the delighted child with presents. But it was a sad birthday party too: Dolly didn't know any children around her own age. What does one give a seven-year-old? Lee had found a nest of Russian dolls that appeared, ever smaller, each from inside a bigger one. Ruby produced a German porcelain doll with jointed arms and legs, clad in the latest fashion, with a mop of real hair, real eyelashes around striated blue eyes that closed, and red lips parted to reveal teeth and a tongue that actually wobbled when it was pushed. From Alexander, a tricycle, and from Elizabeth, a gold bracelet of linked hearts that bore its first charm, a golden horseshoe for luck. Constance handed over a huge tin of bonbons.

Dolly blew out the seven candles on her cake, lovingly made by Chang and iced in her favorite color, pink.

"She'll undoubtedly spend the night being sick," Constance said as they repaired to the drawing room after games and a visit to the stables to see Dolly's main gift, a Shetland pony.

"Never mind," said Elizabeth comfortably. "Peony will dose her with some of Hung Chee's magic bilious potion after she's sicked up the worst of so much sweet stuff, and she'll settle for a good sleep."

Not even Alexander could have detected that his wife was conducting an affair, Lee thought. Not once did she let her gaze rest on him for longer than was proper.

The dinner was somewhat sparser than usual; birthday cake and fairy sandwiches do not make a good beginner. The moment the main course was cleared away, Alexander rose.

"If you'll excuse me, I'm going to the mine. I have some work to do."

"I'll go with you and lighten the load," Lee offered.

"Thanks, but this is *my* party. A solitary one."

"Not even Summers?" Lee asked.

"Not even Summers."

"How is his poor wife?" Constance asked.

"Mad as a hatter, but remarkably healthy."

"A sad business."

"Indeed," said Alexander, and disappeared.

LEE'S CONFESSION had come out of the blue, and though he had listened imperturbably, Alexander's mind reeled. He had never dreamed that Elizabeth was in love with Lee. She has good taste, he remembered thinking as Lee talked; this is a completely honest and decent man. Nor had Lee been crass enough to mention Alexander's mother and her secret, though obviously it worked on him powerfully. Love was supposed to be blind, yet Lee's love was perceptive enough to see Elizabeth's liking for secrecy. If a child did come and Lee had said nothing, Elizabeth would have kept the secret of its father to the bitter end. Because she was all bound up in secrets. That was what happened when youthful confessions were punished without mercy, when the confessions were not seen as a wish to tell the truth, and therefore were not deemed praiseworthy. So she had learned not to confess; instead, she had learned to keep secrets so well that she hardly knew even her own motives.

And he, Alexander, had not made a friend of her. Too busy outfitting her appropriately, showering her with jewels, training her to be his chatelaine. When he had talked to her, it had been as a teacher upon subjects far from her ken—geology, mining, *his* ambitions. The sons they would have to share *his* interests. What did she care if this cliff was Permian and that layer Silurian? Yet that was what he had talked about on the journey to Kinross. Not things she could respond to, but things that *he* loved. Oh, to turn the clock back! To have only known that he was the very image of old man Murray's drawing of Satan! And she had come to the marriage bed so utterly unprepared, even if she had been informed of the mechanics. Young girls in rural Scotland were so sheltered, so ignorant. Between the description, probably outlined by some misanthropic bitch, and the act, lay a gulf bridged only by long preparation.

Preparation he hadn't bothered with. He hadn't wooed her, but had simply claimed her. A gold mine ready to dig. There should have been a period of quiet dinners together, of flowers rather than diamonds, of kisses given after permission to kiss, of a slow awakening that predisposed her to greater intimacies. But no, not the great Alexander Kinross! He had met her, he had married her the next day, and climbed into her bed after one kiss in the church. There to prove himself an animal in her eyes. One mistake after another, that was the story of his relationship with Elizabeth. And Ruby had always meant more.

But it was only in the aftermath of Elizabeth's disappearance that he really understood what he had done to her. The pain, the disappointment. She hadn't had the chance to choose for herself.

It's no wonder she disliked me from the first. It's no wonder she was so ill when she carried my children. She didn't want me as their father, though she hadn't found a man she did want. Now that I know about Lee I am *positive* that she can carry babies, even at her age, without a scrap of trouble. I'm so glad I learned about Lee before today! He's perfect for her.

NUMBER ONE tunnel was a refuge that he had completely to himself; the shift wasn't due to change until midnight and the miners, in number five and number seven, knew he was working number one. Unless he summoned a man, he would be left alone.

The compressor was a beauty; it delivered sufficient air pressure to the drill even at such a distance, and he was delighted at the performance of this particular Ingersoll drill. Almost new, it had been run in very smoothly.

He had intended to bore his charge holes twelve feet in, positioning them as he had mapped out several days ago; for that reason he had refused Lee's help. Lee would have queried him—he knew too much. Anyway, he didn't need help, he knew exactly what he was doing, and he could do it better, faster. Then, on the first hole, the drill bit punched into a void at eleven feet—he was right, there was a fault in there! But he continued the holes, each time punching into that void around eleven feet in. And as he kept on drilling, he kept on thinking.

What a grand life I've had! What a vindication! They're an effective recipe for success, are hard work, intelligence and ambition. I haven't put a foot wrong in any of my ventures from gold to rubber, and if there has to be a failure, I'd rather it was in my private life. Sir Alexander Kinross of the Thistle—didn't I look braw in my robes? How much I've enjoyed myself! The triumphs, the travel, the wild adventures, the gold piling up in the Bank of England, the satisfaction of building a model town a generation ahead of its time, the knowledge that all public men have a price, and the pleasure of buying them, the rapacious fools. What does money matter, if in taking it a man sells himself as another man's creature? Yes, I've had a grand time of it for fifty-five years.

He paused to tie a bandanna around his forehead, then went on working, each movement sure and fluid.

For all the misery that marriage had caused Elizabeth, she had gifted him with a wonderful daughter who would go far in her chosen profession—if, that is, she didn't choose to turn into a crusader instead. Nell, he had noticed, was an altruist, and that she had to get from her mother. The only goal he hadn't achieved was a son and heir of his own blood. He should never have sent to Scotland for a bride; he should have married Ruby, the wife of his heart, for she held it along with his mind in that busty, lusty body. But not because of that busty, lusty body. Because of her bawdy sparkling wit, her trenchant wisdom, her sense of the ridiculous, her gargantuan zest for life. One in many millions, Ruby. He had failed her too, as great a grief as knowing he had failed Elizabeth. Loved both, failed both.

But he owed Elizabeth a debt, and it was high time he paid it. To love her yet fail to make her happy was inexcusable. At least Ruby was happy. Lee was perfect for Elizabeth, yes, but could he deal with her secretiveness? He was fathoms deep in love with her, but it was that courtly love of medieval times, a hopeless pining at a chaste distance. Could he make the transition from no hope to hope fulfilled? Was the Elizabeth he had dreamed of for seventeen years the Elizabeth he'd have to live with? That, Alexander couldn't know. Didn't want to, either.

Sung popped into his mind. Good old Sung! No man had ever had a better partner with whom to start such a massive enterprise. That was where Lee got his sense of honor from, of course. Odd, when the father hadn't personally supervised his half-caste son nor indeed taken much interest in him at all. Sung's Chinese sons were, if anything, more foreign than Sung was—a different upbringing entirely. Alexander was inclined to think that Lee had had the best of the bargain. Things would get worse for the Chinese after the colonies federated, but Alexander was sure now that those already in Australia would stay in Australia. How stupid, to ignore the brains and talent in the non-white world!

Anna came and went like an instrument of torture, muddled up with Jade, Sam O'Donnell, Theodora Jenkins. Now *she* was a case of what love could do to ruin a life! The foolish woman had left Kinross and now existed in abject poverty in Bathurst taking in mending and teaching piano. All because she wouldn't see the truth about her charming handyman. Jade, a little black body twirling gently at the end of a rope, ashes soaking into Sam O'Donnell's cheap coffin. Clever of Sung, that had been. After this record rain, O'Donnell's moldering bones would be locked in the webby embrace of his executioner.

What was there to make of Anna? Poor, innocent wee mite. A tragedy as inevitable and inexorable as a mass of ice grinding down a valley. For that alone he was in debt to Elizabeth, who had borne the brunt. Well, he had to give her her chance and pray that it hadn't come too late. Lee was hers to the death, but would she want that once she had him? Would he too start to pinch and constrain her? Not, he thought, if she can give him children. They'll be the babies of her heart. I wonder if one will look like Ruby? I'd like that!

THE HOLES were done. Alexander trudged down the tunnel to where Summers had just arrived with a four-wheeled dolly that held a case of dynamite, a paste of salts, gun cotton, platinum wire and detonators. How time flies! Alexander thought, looking at his watch. Its hands were mated at half past six. Nine hours to do the drilling. Not bad for an old man.

"Your note *did* say a full case of the sixty percent, Sir Alexander, but isn't that rather a lot?"

"Far too much, Summers, but I wasn't happy with the stuff in the open case. Here, let's have a look." He prised the stout wooden lid off the case and stared at the orderly rows of brown sticks, lifted one to feel it and smell it, nodded. "This lot is fine. I'll take it in on the dolly."

"I wish I wasn't such a duffer about explosives," Summers said dolefully, and started to pull the dolly into number one.

Alexander stopped him. "Thank you, Summers, I can manage."

"What about the Ingersoll? Dismantling the air pipe?"

"I moved the Ingersoll myself, and dismantled the air pipe."

"You shouldn't, Sir Alexander, you really shouldn't."

"At my age, you mean?" Alexander said with a grin, and began to pull the dolly.

Summers stood watching his figure dwindle in the brilliant light until the tunnel curved and he disappeared.

Back at the rock face again, Alexander took a stick of this maximum-strength explosive and slit its wrapping up one side with a sharp knife. He pushed it into the hole fairly easily, picked up the very long tamper bar and rammed it all the way to the void. Then another stick, another, another, working now as quickly as he could, filling the hole until there was room for one more stick only. To its end he crimped the fulminate of mercury detonator cap, a primer of salts, and two wire terminals connected by a platinum filament atop a bed of gun cotton. And on to the next hole.

The sweat rolled off him, his muscles screamed from the exertion, but he placed his charges as he wanted, each hole trailing a length of wire, until 156 sticks, each containing 60 percent nitroglycerin, lay inside the rock face. Then he stripped six inches of insulation from each wire and twisted them together to make just one bundle. After that he stripped the insulation from the end of the wire that he would soon unroll as he went back to the gallery, where it would be connected to the terminal that would trigger the blast. There! Done. He gazed at his work with approval, nodded.

Kicking the spool of wire ahead of him, he trod the sloppy ground to the gallery. Summers, Lee and Prentice were waiting for him; Prentice brought the spool to the terminal and bent to cut the wire, intending to do the connecting himself. Alexander took the wire from him, stripped it, and connected it. What a fussy, cantankerous bugger he is! thought Prentice. Has to do it all himself, just as if no one else could.

"She's ready to go, dear old number one," Alexander said crisply, smiling at them. He looked dirty and dog-tired, but jubilant.

Prentice sounded the siren that warned everyone a blast was coming; when finally it ceased its howl, Alexander flipped the switch on the terminal and the ammeter said current was flowing. They stood with their hands over their ears, as did forty other men, but no blast came. The maw of number one tunnel sat dark and empty, its lights now disconnected.

"Fuck!" said Alexander. "There's a break in the wire."

"Wait!" Lee cried sharply. "Alexander, wait a moment! It might be a hang fire."

For answer Alexander switched the current off; the ammeter needle slumped to zero. "I'll fix it," he said, took a lamp and started into the tunnel. "This is *my* blast. All of you are to stay right where you are, is that clear?"

This time he covered the ground at a lope, grinning, filled with power and purpose. What the men behind him didn't know was that the current still flowed; he had wired a bypass inside the terminal, activated when he had thrown the switch to its off position. It bypassed the ammeter too.

The two wires lay on the ground, their naked copper ends pinkly glittering in the light of the lamp. He put it down and picked up the wires in either hand.

"Better this by far than living to piss on my shoes," he said, and touched the wires together with fierce pleasure.

The whole tunnel erupted, chunks of rock flung three hundred yards as the mountain, fatally flawed eleven feet beyond the rock face, tried to collapse in on itself as the force of the massive amount of explosive drove it apart. The first shock of shrieking air was followed by the shattering noise; the men in the gallery were tossed about like bubbles in boiling water as the space was deluged in flying particles and a huge pall of dust rolled through it, up the shafts to the poppet heads, down into the skip tunnel and out the adit. The roar was heard in Kinross, heard faintly on top of the mountain. Yet when it was over and Lee picked himself up, ears ringing, he saw that the gallery stood undamaged. The outside sirens were screaming and men came running from the town—oh, Jesus, not a cave-in! Who was dead, how many tunnels and shafts were under tons of rock?

The first thing was to ascertain safety; when Lee, the mining engineers and the supervisors made their inspection, they found that nothing had come down except number one tunnel. Elsewhere there wasn't a crack in a beam, a rent in a canvas sheet, a buckle in a skip rail. The entire force of the blast was confined to number one tunnel.

The man's a genius, Lee thought dully as he and Summers went as far into number one as they could—about ninety feet of what had been a thousand feet. Alexander had set his charges to wreak maximum havoc in minimum space. Not one part of the Apocalypse had suffered apart from his original tunnel. "Dear old number one. She likes me, the bitch."

Summers was howling like a small boy and most of the men in the gallery were weeping, but Lee couldn't. While Prentice and the other supervisors started to get ready to try to dig Alexander out, Lee walked unobtrusively to the terminal and pulled out the cable connecting it to the generator shed. Turning it over in his hands, he unscrewed the bottom plate and saw what Alexander had done. *You never missed a trick, did you?* No one was watching him; Lee dismantled the bypass and tucked it into his pants pocket, then reassembled the device. When someone thought to examine it, test it in the laboratory, it would behave exactly as it ought. I'll bet you even worked out that it would be me to find this. Because, Alexander Kinross, you wanted to die in an accident—luck's caprice, no one's fault. I'll aid and abet you. I owe you that, and much, much more.

They would never find him, of course. He hadn't been on his way back to the gallery when his world ended, he was right there at the rock face with naked wires in his hands. You're entombed forever, Alexander Kinross. The king in his golden mausoleum.

"Jim," he said to Summers, still howling, "Jim, listen to me! I can't stay here, there are women to be told. The men can dig in a hundred feet if they want, but no farther. If he's not in this hundred feet, he's dead. He's dead anyway, we all know that. But they can try for a while, they'll feel better if they do. I'll be back as soon as I can."

And Summers, who had responded to authority all his life, wiped his face, blew his nose, stared at Lee out of drowned eyes. "Yes, Dr. Costevan, I'll see to it."

"Good chap," said Lee, patting him on the shoulder.

DOWN THE mountain, or up the mountain? Down, he decided. His mother would hear the rumors first, so it was she who would have to be told first.

What did Alexander say yesterday, toward the end of our talk? Something about he'd have to work out how to keep me yet free Elizabeth. Yes, something like that. But who would have guessed what his solution would be? Who else was ruthless enough, determined enough to go straight to the marrow of it? The women will never know that it wasn't an accident, so no guilt for Elizabeth, no hatred for Ruby. If my mother knew that he'd committed suicide as the best way out of an impossible situation, she'd blame and hate Elizabeth forever after. And that would mean a new, different fracture. This way, what passed between Alexander and me is our secret. He died in a mine accident. They happen all the time. Oh, it will be talked about! How did the charges detonate when the current wasn't flowing? Why was the blast so enormous? Why wouldn't Alexander let anyone else into number one tunnel? But no one will know for certain except me—and Alexander.

When Ruby, waiting anxiously on the verandah, saw Lee coming from the cable car, she had to hang on to an awning post to stay upright. As he grew closer she saw his face—set, hard, stern. Whether because of it or through some more mysterious agency, she suddenly knew beyond a shadow of a doubt that Alexander was dead. One hand came out, the other clung to the awning post as if to a crutch. Lee took the hand, chafed it.

"There's been an accident in number one tunnel. Alexander is dead, has to be dead."

The big green eyes held the same look a cat's did when its kittens had been taken away to be drowned: sorrow, bewilderment, inchoate pain. Soon, thought Lee, she will begin to search for him inside the corners of her poor crushed mind, sure that there has been some mistake.

"His big blast?" she asked.

"Yes. It miss-fired, so he went to fix the break."

She swayed; he put an arm around her and led her inside, to a chair and a brandy.

"That's not like him, to miscalculate anything to do with explosives or blasting. He's been doing it for thirty-five years," she said, a little color returning to her skin.

"Maybe that was the trouble, Mum. He grew careless."

"That's not in his nature, and you know it."

"I'm just trying to explain it, including to myself."

"A widow at last!" she said in tones of wonder. "At least I feel like a widow. Trust Alexander to leave two of them."

"Will you be all right now, Mum? I have to tell Elizabeth."

"She won't mourn him. Now she can have you."

"That isn't fair to anyone, Mum."

"Oh, go, go!" she said tiredly. "It's the shock talking. Tell Elizabeth I'll be up later in the day. She'll be all right until then, with Constance staying there. All widows now."

The adit skips were working overtime as half the town tried to remove the densely packed rocks from number one tunnel; Lee went up in the cable car to find Elizabeth and Constance sitting drinking tea in the conservatory. The two faces lifted to his were untroubled until the women absorbed Lee's appearance—caked in dust, running sweat, expression the same one Sung assumed when some major transgression had occurred among his people.

"What's happened?" Elizabeth asked. "We heard a faint boom."

"A terrible accident. Alexander is dead."

Constance's teacup crashed to the floor; Elizabeth put hers down carefully and adjusted its handle to complement the pattern of flowers on the saucer. Her white skin had gone even whiter, but a long moment passed before she looked up at Lee. Her eyes were a terrifying mixture of grief and joy as the two emotions warred within her. And when they are worked through, thought Lee, she is going to feel nothing but relief. Alexander's wife will not mourn him. It is my mother will do that. In which he did his beloved an injustice; twenty-three years of any kind of union, no matter how bitter, must lead to deprivation, and thence to mourning.

"Ruby," she said, her mouth quivering. "Does Ruby know?"

"Yes. I told her first because the town was talking. The explosion down there sounded what it was—terrible."

"I'm so glad you told her first. Thank you," Elizabeth said gently. "He mattered far more to her. Oh, poor thing!"

Constance was weeping, wringing her hands.

"Don't cry," said Elizabeth in that same soft voice. "It's better this way, to die in his prime without any expectation that death was coming. I'm glad for him."

"Mum says she'll be up later. Will you get hold of Nell?"

"Yes, of course."

"Have they found his body?" Constance asked.

Lee's unsettling eyes looked straight at her. "No. They will never find his body, Constance. It's hundreds of feet down a tunnel that's not there anymore. He's a part of the Apocalypse forever." He moved to the door. "I must go, I'm needed."

Elizabeth accompanied him across the lawn, burgeoning after the rain. "He didn't know about us, did he, Lee?" she asked.

"No, he didn't," Lee said, suddenly realizing that this was one lie he would have to live with all of his days. "All of his energies were concentrated on his blast. Accidents happen, even to men who are blessed. A mine is a dangerous place." He passed his hand across his eyes. "I just never thought of this lying in wait for Alexander. He was the king."

"In the end the burden must fall on the king," Elizabeth said cryptically. "It's the price he must pay for ruling."

"Is there still a place in your heart and life for me?"

"Oh, yes, always. But it will have to wait a little."

"I can wait. Just as long as you know that I'm here for you whenever you need me. I love you, Elizabeth. Alexander's death has no power to change that."

"And I love you. I think it would please Alexander to know that I've found someone to love." She lifted herself on tiptoe to kiss Lee's cheek. "You're in charge now. Come whenever you can."

DOES NOTHING ever change? asked Ruby of herself when she met Elizabeth at the house that afternoon. Here she was, Alexander's official widow, as composed, cool and withdrawn as ever. Even her eyes were tranquil, though not happy. She goes away, no one knows where. Alexander always said that of her.

Dolly had been told, and lay sobbing on her bed with Peony clucking and soothing; and Elizabeth had telephoned Nell, interrupting her ward rounds at the Prince Alfred Hospital to tell her that her father was dead. She was on her way, said Elizabeth to Ruby in that calm, detached, gentle voice.

Lee came back in time for dinner, bathed and changed into clean work clothes.

"We've agreed to suspend the search," he said, sitting down like an old man and accepting a Kentucky bourbon from his mother. "All the engineers have agreed that to try to excavate the tunnel one more foot might lead to another, more massive cave-in. There was no sign of Alexander's body. It's inside the mountain."

What seemed to chew at Elizabeth was the absence of a body, as she betrayed when she asked, "What do we do, Lee? He can't be officially buried, can he?"

"No."

"But he has to have a *grave*!"

"He can," Lee said patiently. "There doesn't have to be a body in it, Elizabeth. He can have a grave anywhere you like."

"Next to Anna. He loved the top of the mountain."

Ruby sat silent, still too far into shock to weep. By unspoken consent all three women seemed to have decided to go into black—severe grosgrain dresses high to the neck and starkly unadorned. Did they, Lee wondered, always have something like that tucked away just in case? Though no one had worn mourning for Anna. It had been too merciful an end to don black.

"A statue," said Ruby suddenly. "A bronze statue in Kinross Square of Alexander in his fringed buckskins, riding his mare."

"Yes," said Constance eagerly. "By someone very good."

Three pairs of eyes swung to Lee; they want me to organize it, he thought. I have taken Alexander's place, but do I want to? The answer is, no. But I seem to have no choice. Alexander's death has pinned me more firmly to Kinross than Caesar was to his concept of Rome.

He slept that night in the house, though not in Alexander's bed. In the little guest suite that had served as a temporary prison for Anna. And in the middle of the night he woke from a nightmarish sleep to find Elizabeth beside him. A part of him recoiled in horror, yet his chief reaction was gratitude. She was wearing a nightgown, so she hadn't come seeking sexual solace. He rolled on to his side to embrace her, and she clung to him with soft kisses.

"How did you know I needed you?" he asked into her hair.

"Because you loved him."

"Did you ever, in the most secret part of you?"

"No, never."

"How have you borne it?"

"By walling myself off from it and him."

"You won't need to do that with me."

"I know. But it will be hard at first, dearest Lee."

"It can't not be. You have to take down the walls a brick at a time. Not by yourself. I'll be there to help you."

"It seems too unreal to be true. I thought Alexander would live forever. He seemed that sort of man."

"He did to me too."

"When can we let people know about us?"

"Not for months, Elizabeth, unless you can survive a scandal."

"I can survive anything if you're with me, but you'd be much happier if there was no scandal. You loved him."

"Yes, I loved him."

AS THE CORONER sat in Bathurst, the enquiry—it could hardly be called an ordinary inquest—was held in Bathurst. The room was full of journalists, for the presumed death of Sir Alexander Kinross was international news.

Summers gave evidence that Sir Alexander had asked for an unopened case of 60 percent dynamite, two hundred sticks of it, and was able to produce the note thus instructing him. Then confessed that he was a real duffer about explosives, was lucky to know one end of a stick of dynamite from the other, if indeed there was a difference between the two ends. He could swear that Sir Alexander had most definitely turned the current off at the terminal, for he had seen the ammeter needle fall to zero. No one had turned it on again after Sir Alexander went back up the tunnel, he was prepared to swear to that too.

Prentice gave evidence that he had taken the spool of wire from Sir Alexander and cut it, but that Sir Alexander had seemed annoyed, had snatched the wire, stripped it, and connected it himself. He explained that he had sounded the blast siren and that all the miners on duty had emerged from their tunnels to wait in the gallery. With his own eyes he had seen Sir Alexander flip the switch on, seen the ammeter register a flowing current. And he testified very positively that he had watched Sir Alexander switch the current off again before entering the number one tunnel to fix the break in the wire, which was what all of them assumed had happened.

Lee gave evidence that confirmed the evidence of Summers and Prentice as to who had attached the blast wire to the terminal and who had triggered the switch, first on, then off—Sir Alexander. He produced the terminal in court and explained how it worked, explained too that it had been thoroughly tested in the laboratory and found to be working properly—it was not a complicated piece of equipment. If the Coroner needed more evidence on this point, the engineers who had tested it were in court.

Quizzed as to how, then, the blast could have happened, Lee could only shake his head and say he didn't know. Applied to, Prentice also shook his head and said he didn't know. Dynamite was an inert substance until detonation, and even if one detonator had gone off, not all the charges would have exploded because not all were wired in series. The usual technique was to fire the first charges, inspect the results, and then decide whether to continue to blast. No, it was never the intention of a powder monkey to bring down a whole rock face; the bulk of it was done with pneumatic percussion hammers after the blast had produced apertures and split the rock along its fault lines.

Recalled, Lee admitted that Sir Alexander had been excited over this particular blast, which he had called "experimental." Recalled, Prentice confirmed this.

"Have you any theory at all, Dr. Costevan?" the Coroner asked at the end of the evidence.

"One, your honor. That there was a large fault just behind the rock face that Sir Alexander didn't know about, and that the blast triggered a major collapse of the granite around the fault. I can't see how else it could have happened. Though it doesn't mean much to a layman, when I went up on the mountain a few days ago, I found a depression right over the spot where the end of number one tunnel used to be. To a geologist, that indicates a fault that has collapsed, considering that there was no depression there before the accident."

"Could that cause a huge explosion, Dr. Costevan?"

"It depends, your honor. I don't think any of us who were in the gallery that morning could tell you whether the noise we heard was an explosion, or the tunnel coming down. Both cause intense sound waves on the ear drums," said Lee, deliberately scientific.

The Coroner brought in a verdict of death by misadventure; Sir Alexander Kinross was now officially dead.

Ruby and Elizabeth hadn't attended, but Nell did, even though it had meant yet another trip from Sydney that would be extended because of her father's memorial service and the reading of his last will and testament. She walked out with Lee, her face grim.

"I think all of that was claptrap," she said as Lee ushered her into the train from Bathurst to Lithgow.

"In what way, Nell?" he asked, sounding mildly enquiring.

"My father didn't make mistakes."

"I agree, he didn't."

"So?" she asked, looking dangerous.

"So it's a mystery, Nell. I don't have any answers."

"There's one somewhere."

"I hope you can find it. I'd rest easier if you did."

"My mother doesn't give a damn."

"Oh, I think she does. She finds it hard to show what she feels, you should know that better than I."

"No one better," said Nell bitterly. "Ruby mourns more."

"She has more reason to mourn," he said bluntly.

"We're an odd couple, Lee, you and I."

"Embroiled in the peculiar relationships of our parents."

"Well put. You're perceptive, for an engineer."

"Thanks."

She leaned her cheek against the compartment window and fixed her eyes, a dimmer blue than usual, on Lee's face. He was subtly changed—surer, older, far more determined. Is it that he expects to be my father's major heir? But Dad told me that I was. I don't want to be—*I don't!* But no, it isn't that working in Lee. There is another reason for the change. He's never attracted me, yet all of a sudden I can see his attraction. Great integrity, and honor, and sensitivity. My mother and his mother both look to him as to their only salvation in this awful time. Oh, isn't that typical? Lee's a *man.* Neither of them gives a hoot whether I'm there or not.

In Lithgow they changed to the Kinross train, having lapsed into a silence each was unwilling to break.

Then he said, "Between Anna's death and this, Nell, you must have missed quite a lot of classes. Will you be all right?"

"I think so. The exams at the end of the year are on materia medica, clinical medicine, surgery, a bit more physiology and anatomy. I'll pass because I already know my stuff, and there's no hard-and-fast rule about attendance, particularly if one is absent with good reason." Her long face was growing enthused. "I'll be all right next year too. It's my final year, 1900, that will be the hardest. There's so much of it devoted to things I don't regard as medicine—medical jurisprudence, for instance. I'm doing a doctoral thesis as well, so I hope to graduate as a genuine Doctor of Medicine, not a mere Bachelor of Medicine."

"What's your thesis on?"

"Epilepsy."

Anna, he thought. "Are you planning to marry?" he asked with a charming smile that robbed the question of offense.

"No."

"A pity. You're all of Alexander's blood left."

"I don't believe in that sort of thing, Lee. It's antiquated and unimportant. And there's Dolly."

"Sorry," he said, not sounding it.

"Unless *you* want to marry me," she said, eyes challenging.

"Not in a million years."

"Why?" she demanded, affronted.

"You're too scratchy and aggressive, and I'm not the right man to round your corners off. My taste runs to gentle women."

"Got one picked out, have you?"

"No. One doesn't pick a woman out. She does the picking."

Warming to him, she leaned forward. "Yes, I think that's true," she said.

"Whatever happened to the anonymous fellow you fancied?"

"Oh, that was so many years ago that I was a mere sixteen. He nearly had a stroke when he found out how young I was. So it fizzled out before it really started to burn."

"Can't you rekindle the spark?"

"No! Especially not with Dad's passing. I'd be a traitor."

"How so?"

"The bloke happens to be a Labor member of the New South Wales parliament. Head as far up socialism's arse as Dad's was up capitalism's." She sighed and actually looked a little misty. "Oh, but I did like him! A lot shorter than you, but he'd give you a run for your money in the ring, I'd bet."

"Only," said Lee, grinning, "if he knew all those Chinese tricks you learned to defend yourself."

ALEXANDER'S LAST will and testament was a new one, made two days after Anna's death—well before Lee's confession, a great relief. Lee couldn't blame himself for anything it contained, though he did wonder why Alexander hadn't changed it once he had been apprised of Lee's conduct with his wife. Six of Alexander's seven shares in Apocalypse Enterprises were left outright to Lee; the seventh was left to Ruby, which meant that the thirteen shares totaling the Company's whole were now seven for Lee, two for Ruby, two for Sung, and two for Constance Dewy. Lee was the major shareholder and indisputably the boss.

Elizabeth, Nell and Dolly were each left an income of £50,000 a year to be paid out of profits or from trusts, as the board saw fit to decide.

Jim Summers got £100,000, the Wong sisters £100,000 each, and Chang £50,000. Alexander expressed a wish that Sung Po should continue as town clerk, and bequeathed him £50,000. Theodora Jenkins received £20,000 and the deeds of her old house.

The 10,000 acres of Mount Kinross were the property of the Company, but Elizabeth was to have tenure of them until her death, after which they would return to the board. All the cash bequests were to be free and clear of legacy duty, to be picked up out of Alexander's own funds.

His private fortune, his art collection, his rare books and all properties in his name were left for any children Elizabeth might have after his death, a clause that no one understood, even Lee. What had Alexander sensed, for know about them he did not when he made that will? Was it his way of telling Elizabeth that he was sorry, that she was free to marry again?

"I'm so glad it's you copped the burden, Lee," said Nell.

"I'm not. I really didn't expect to."

"You're tied hand and foot to Apocalypse Enterprises now. I suppose when I did medicine he washed his hands of me."

"As the custodian of his achievements, yes, but I wouldn't call fifty thousand pounds a year washing his hands of you."

"You don't know about my hopes that he'd endow a hospital for the mentally disturbed."

Lee forced a smile. "If you told him you wanted to do that, it's reason enough to deprive you of the opportunity. Alexander would deem that tilting at windmills, Anna or no Anna."

"Yes, he would, wouldn't he? A total pragmatist."

"Oh, I don't know—look at his bequest to Theodora."

"I'm glad he remembered her."

"So am I."

"How big *is* his private fortune, Lee?"

"Enormous. The bequests and legacy duty won't even dent it."

"To any children Mum might have after his death . . . But he knew—we all know!—that she can't have any children! So what happens to his fortune if she doesn't have more children?"

"A nice point. Since it's in the Bank of England, it will probably go into chancery after her death, there to stay for years while lawyers wrangle and feed off its corpse like vultures," Lee said. "If you have children, you could sue for it on their behalf, I imagine."

"Mum, to start having children at *her* age?" Nell looked as if she expected the world to end before that happened. "Though I do admit," she went on thoughtfully, "that eclampsia probably wouldn't be a danger."

"Why not?" asked Lee, clutching at straws.

"I suspect she's in much better health than she was then."

"Even at her age?" he asked, tongue in cheek.

"Well, yes, theoretically she's still fertile, I suppose."

And there Lee left it.

AT LEAST HE left it as far as Nell was concerned, but Lee soon discovered that he was perpetually caught in Alexander's web. Ruby was the next one.

"He must have known about Elizabeth and you before he made his will," said Ruby when they returned to the hotel.

"Believe me, Mum," he said very earnestly, holding her hands, "Alexander did *not* know about Elizabeth and me when he made his will. If he had, he would never have left me the major share, and you know it."

"Then why—?"

"All I can put it down to is a premonition, or perhaps to a feeling that with his death, Elizabeth's life would take a new turn. That more children wouldn't harm her," Lee said, unable to express what he only sensed.

"But he was set to live forever! How could he know that—that within a week of drawing up the wretched thing, he'd be dead in a mine cave-in?" she demanded, pacing.

Lee sighed. "He always called Elizabeth fey, but he was as much a Scot as she. His instincts were uncanny. Truly, I believe that he had a strong premonition."

"I suppose it can't have been anything else, but it leaves so much unanswered!" Suddenly she laughed, not hysterically, but in genuine amusement. "Bugger the man! He made that will for a purpose. Just because he's gone doesn't necessarily mean that he's going to stop tormenting us."

"Sit down, Mum, have a cognac and a cheroot."

She lifted her balloon to him; he lifted his to her. "Here's to Alexander," she said, and tossed the spirit down.

"Alexander. May he never stop tormenting us."

Not until after dinner did Ruby return to the subjects that were chewing at her.

"My dearest jade kitten, what about Elizabeth?"

"I shall marry her at the appropriate time."

"Do you *swear* to me that he didn't know?"

"No, I won't! What an idiotic request, Mum! Use your common sense," he said sharply. "Can we *please* leave this subject alone?"

She took the rebuke with equanimity, then said, "He must have been down in old Brumford's office making the draft of the will while Elizabeth was still sleeping, and he signed the final draft straight after breakfast on that second day, Brumford told me. And Alexander said that Nell was sticking to her mother like glue." Ruby huffed. "He hadn't seen you, so he couldn't have known."

"Oh, please, Mum, change the subject!"

"Nell is going to hit the ceiling when she finds out about you and Elizabeth."

"As long as *you* understand, I don't care about Nell."

"Oh, I understand! I can't blame either of you." And off she went again. "That's all sustains me over this will business—if he had known, he'd not have made you his major heir. That's inarguable, even to Nell. Alexander didn't love Elizabeth, but he wouldn't have tolerated anyone poaching on his preserves."

"Mum, I love you, but I'm going to murder you."

"I know you love me, and I love you too, jade kitten." The tears began to run down her face, but she managed to smile. "I miss Alexander desperately, but I'm so happy for you. With any luck, I might have some horribly rich grandchildren. She won't have any trouble having them, I know it in my bones."

"She says the same thing. So does Nell."

The phone rang. Lee got up to answer it, the look on his face telling Ruby who the caller was.

"Certainly, Elizabeth. I'll get her," he said for Aggie's benefit. "Mum, Elizabeth would like to speak to you."

"Is everything all right?" Ruby asked the receiver.

"Yes, Nell and I are fine. But I wasn't sure how fast Lee was planning to move on Alexander's statue, so I thought I'd best ring now and tell you what I think," said the disembodied voice.

"Alexander's statue?" Ruby asked blankly.

"Not in bronze, Ruby. Please, not in bronze. Tell Lee that I want it in granite. Granite is Alexander's stone."

"I'll tell him."

Ruby hung up. "She wants Alexander's statue to be made in granite, not in bronze. It's his stone, she says. Jesus!"

Indeed it is, thought Lee. He's entombed under thousands of tons of it. There's a dimple in the mountain now right over the end of number one tunnel, just as I told the Coroner. He hit a fault—a big one. And he knew it was there. He even teased me by dragging me up there to finish our talk, and stamped on the ground. Hollow. But I was too beside myself to listen. I am the only person who can ask what he can never tell me: Was he planning his suicide before he knew that Elizabeth was unfaithful with me? Did her disappearance provoke more than a natural fear and anxiety? Did he think that he should give her her freedom while she was still young enough to bear more children? Usually he discussed every aspect of a blast with me, but not this one.

ELIZABETH HAD taken to sitting in the library with only the desk lamp switched on; her chair was far from it, shadowed, of no use for any purpose save thinking.

A month since Alexander's death. It had dragged. With the inquest verdict in, the memorial service over and the will read, the life of Sir Alexander Kinross had finally come to its end. In an odd way Lee seemed to have retreated, not of himself, but inside her own mind. The time was split as with a wedge between Alexander alive and Alexander dead. Her future and her freedom were assured, yet she couldn't get beyond thoughts of Alexander. Who had, she knew as surely as if he materialized before her and told her, committed suicide. As deliberately, thoughtfully as he did everything. Since she didn't know that Lee had told Alexander about them, she presumed he hadn't known about her and Lee, which meant that some other reason lay at the root of it. But what that reason was, she had no idea.

"Mum, you shouldn't sit here alone in the dark," said Nell, coming in. "Dinner's in half an hour. Can I get you one of your enormous sherries?"

"Thank you," Elizabeth said, blinking in the dazzle as Nell went around switching on more lights.

"Can you eat? Should I have Hung Chee make you up a tonic?"

"I can eat." Elizabeth took the glass and sipped. "But a tonic from Hung Chee? Hasn't modern medicine got something more effective? From Hung Chee, it might have anything in it from powdered beetles to dried dung to shivery grass seeds."

"Chinese medicine is brilliant," said Nell, sitting opposite her mother with her own enormous sherry. "We tend to go to the chemistry lab and manufacture something, whereas they go to Mother Nature. Oh, a lot of what we manufacture is excellent, can do things no Chinese medicine can. But especially for minor or chronic complaints, Nature has a wonderful pharmacopoeia. After I graduate, I intend to collect old wives' remedies, cure-alls of custom and tradition, and Hung Chee's recipes for gout, dizzy spells, rashes, bilious attacks and God knows what else."

"Does that mean you're not going into research anymore?"

Nell scowled. "There won't be a post for me in research, Mum, that much I've learned. But I'm not brokenhearted about it—and that's rather surprised me. I want to go into general practice in some desperately poor part of Sydney."

Elizabeth smiled. "Oh, Nell, that pleases me!"

"I have to go back to Sydney tomorrow, Mum, or I'll have to repeat Med IV, but it worries me to leave you here alone."

"I won't be alone for long," said Elizabeth placidly.

"I beg your pardon?"

"I'm going away for a while."

"With Dolly? Where?"

"No, I'm sending Dolly to Constance at Dunleigh. Sophia's children are there, so are Maria's, and it's time Dolly learned to mix with children around her age. The Dewy girls haven't discussed Dolly's parentage, and Dunleigh is a long way from here. They have an excellent governess. Constance suggested it."

"That's splendid, Mum. It really is. And you?"

"I'm going to the Italian lakes. I used to dream of them," Elizabeth said in a slightly eerie voice, "whenever I planned to run away. But I never could run away. First there was Anna, then came Dolly. Do you remember them, Nell? The Italian lakes?"

"Only that they were beautiful," Nell said through a choked throat. "Did you plan to run away often?"

"Whenever I found life here unbearable."

"Was that often?"

"Very often."

"Did you hate Dad that much?"

"No, I never hated him. I didn't love him, and that grew into dislike. Hatred says that you can never find a reason for what you feel, it's too blind, but I was always able to see the truth. I was even able to see Alexander's point of view. The trouble was that it lay a world away from mine."

"He did love you, Mum."

"I know that now that he's dead. But it doesn't change anything. He loved Ruby more."

"Bugger Ruby Costevan!" Nell snapped.

"Don't say that!" cried Elizabeth, so loudly and sternly that Nell jumped. "If it weren't for Ruby, I don't honestly know what I might have done. You've always loved her, Nell, so you mustn't start blaming her now. I won't hear a word against her."

Nell was trembling. *Passion* in her mother's voice! And for the one person society said she should detest! "I'm sorry, Mum. I was wrong."

"Just promise me that when you marry—you will!—you marry for the right reasons. Liking, most of all. Love, of course. But also for the pleasures of the body. It isn't supposed to be mentioned, as if it were something the Devil invented rather than God. But I cannot tell you how important it is. If you can share your private life with your husband wholeheartedly, nothing else will matter. You have a career of your own that's cost far too much to abandon, and you mustn't. If he wants you to abandon it, don't marry him. You'll always have sufficient income to live comfortably, so you can be married and still continue to practice your career."

"Good advice," said Nell gruffly, beginning to see many things about her mother and father.

"No one can give better advice than someone who has failed."

A silence fell; Nell studied her mother through different eyes, with a wisdom that had grown since her father died. Always Dad's partisan, always exasperated with Mum's passivity, that air of being somewhere else. What she had loathed about her mother was the martyr element, but now Nell saw that Elizabeth was not, nor ever had been, a martyr.

"Poor Mum! You just never had the luck, did you?"

"No, I didn't. But I hope to have some luck in the future."

Nell put down her glass and rose, went to kiss her mother on the lips—

a first. "I hope you do too." She held out her hand. "Come, dinner will be ready. We've laid the bogeys to rest, haven't we?"

"Bogeys? I'd rather call them demons," said Elizabeth.

LEE ACCOMPANIED Elizabeth back to the house after she saw Nell off on the train and followed her into the library feeling a little lost. The only physical contact they had had since Alexander's death was that passionless, pathetic interlude in Anna's temporary prison bed. Not that he condemned her for this withdrawal; on the contrary, he understood it very well. But to him it was Alexander's presence that hovered between them, and he couldn't find the right incantation to banish it. What frightened him was that he might lose her yet, for though he loved her and believed that she loved him, their relationship was thus far built on sand, and Alexander's death had shifted that sand in many ways—his inheritance—his ignorance of how her mind worked. If Alexander didn't know after so long, how could he? Through his love for her, said his instincts—but logic and good sense were not so sure.

Even now, with the library door firmly closed and the dark curtains drawn, she gave him no sign that she wanted him to come to her, take her into his arms, *love* her. Instead she stood pulling her black kid gloves through her fingers as if to torture these inanimate reminders of bereavement. Head bent, watching what she did with total absorption. Alexander is right, she goes away and leaves no key to the maze she wanders.

Minutes went by. Finally word burst from him: "Elizabeth, what do you want to do?"

"Do?" She lifted her head to gaze at him, and smiled. "I would like the fire lit. It's cold."

Perhaps that's it, he thought, kneeling with a taper at the grate to touch it to the carefully laid paper and kindling. Yes, perhaps that's it. No one has ever fussed over her, considered her comfort and well-being. The fire lit, he took her gloves from her, unpinned her hat, led her to a comfortable chair drawn up to the hearth, smoothed her hair where the hat had disarranged it, gave her a sherry and a cigarette. Her eyes, black in the gloom, reflected the leaping flames when they turned in the direction of the fire, but only if he was there. Otherwise they followed his movements until he settled on the carpet beside her knee and leaned his head against it. She picked up his pigtail and wound it around her arm, though he couldn't see what her face said. It was enough to be here with her like this.

"'How do I love thee? Let me count the ways,'" he said.

She picked it up. "'I love thee to the depth and breadth and height my soul can reach.'"

"'I love thee to the level of every day's most quiet need, by sun and candle-light.'"

"'I love thee with the breath, smiles, tears, of all my life!'"

"'And, if God choose,'" he ended, "'I shall but love thee better after death.'"

They didn't speak again; the small sticks were glowing, so he rose to put dry old logs upon them, then sat on the floor between her knees, his head back to rest upon her stomach, his eyes closed to savor the feel of her hands stroking his face. The sherry stood undrunk, the cigarette burned itself to ashes.

"I'm going away," she said a long time later.

His eyes opened. "With me, or without me?"

"With you, but separately. I'm free to go, free to love you, free to want you. Just not here. Not in the beginning, anyway. You can take me to Sydney and put me on a ship to—oh, it hardly matters! Anywhere in Europe, though Genoa would be best. I'm going to the Italian lakes with Pearl and Silken Flower. We will wait there for you, however long it takes." A fingertip traced the contours of an eyebrow, feathered along his cheek. "I love your eyes. . . . Such a strange and beautiful color."

"I was starting to fear that it was all over," he said, too filled with happiness to move.

"No, it will never be over, though one day you may wish it was. I'll be forty in September."

"There's not that huge a gap between us. We'll be old together, and middle-aged parents." He sat up and twisted to look at her. "Are you—?"

She laughed. "No. But I will be. That's Alexander's gift to me. I can't imagine he did it for anything less."

He gasped, knelt up. "Elizabeth! It's not true!"

"If you say so," she said, smiling a secret smile. "How long will it be before you can join me?"

"Three or four months. Woman, I love you! That's not nearly as lyrical as the poet, but it's said with just as much feeling."

"And I love you." She leaned to kiss him fiercely, then sat back in the chair. "I want us to be everything we can be, Lee. That means starting to live together somewhere that has no memories for either of us. I'd like us to marry in Como and honeymoon in the villa I find. I know that we'll have to come back here, but by then we will have exorcised all the demons. And houses only become homes when they're soaked in memories. This house has never been a home, but it has many memories. It will be a home, I promise."

"And the pool will remain our secret place." He got up, pulled a chair close enough to touch her if he wanted, smiling at her in a vague, dazed way. "I can hardly believe it, my dearest Elizabeth."

"What do you have to do to get away?" she asked. "Can the Company manage without you?"

"It's an entity with a life of its own—you might say, almost self-perpetuating. Sophia's husband will be my second-in-command, so it's time he earned his spurs," said Lee. "Besides, the world is shrinking, my darling, and your late husband was one of the men who did the shrinking."

"And my next husband will go on shrinking it, I suspect." She finally sipped at her sherry, but when he offered her another cigarette she shook her head. "I don't want one anymore. Do get yourself a bourbon, dear heart."

"I don't want one anymore. I'm switching to sherry."

He kept putting more logs on the fire, thinking that this was what life with Elizabeth was going to be like: peace and passion, complete communion. Just sitting with her beside the hearth at the end of each day, feeling delighted to set eyes on her, missing her when she wasn't there.

"By nature I'm a homing pigeon," he said in a surprised tone. "How strange, when I've spent so much of my life wandering."

"I'd like to see some of the places you've wandered to," she said dreamily. "Perhaps on our way home from Italy we could see your oilfield in Persia?"

He laughed. "My barely profitable oilfield! But Alexander and I had the same idea at the selfsame moment as to how I could get rid of it with a very large profit. We were inspecting the *Majestic*—a battleship—in Portsmouth at the time, and he said, 'I read your mind as if it were sending flags up a mast.' Then I echoed him. We didn't need to say anything else, we both knew."

"In some ways you're very like him," she said, displaying pleasure rather than pain. "What was this simultaneous idea?"

"It won't come to pass tomorrow—or next year, for that matter. But within ten or twelve years the British are going to want oil-fueled turbines in their battleships. If Britannia is to continue to rule the waves, she has to have battleships that can carry enormous guns, very thick armor plate, and still do more than twenty knots. Without a gigantic cloud of smoke. Oil—thin, pale smoke. Coal—a black pall. The rub, my darling, is that the British don't have any oilfields. I intend, when the time is right, to sell my share of Peacock Oil to the British Government, which will please the Shah mightily. He'll be able to fend off the Russian bear if he's partners with the British lion. Though," Lee ended thoughtfully, "I'm not sure which of those two predators is the more dangerous."

"Well, it sounds like a happy ending to me," she said. "My love, Alexander chose very well in you!"

"Alexander chose very well in *you.* If he hadn't imported a bride from Scotland, I would never have met you, and that doesn't bear thinking about. I'd still be a wanderer."

"And I would be a maiden aunt in Scottish Kinross. I'm glad Alexander imported me." A tear fell. "I'd change nothing except for Anna."

To which he made no reply, just reached to hold her hand.

Four

THE LADY DOCTOR

THE DEATH of her father made a big difference to Nell's career in medicine; suddenly her marks went down, and not because her work had fallen off. She passed Medicine IV, but her professors chose to give her a bare pass—she had had too many absences, was their excuse. And in Medicine V and Medicine VI—her final year—nothing she did impressed them, though she knew very well that she should have been at the top of her class. Honors, even Second Class, were now out of the question, though she didn't think they would dare to fail her. Or, put it this way, she dropped hints that if they did fail her, she'd go straight to the juicier newspapers, which had lots of digs at the faculty of Medicine for its discrimination against women. So they passed her—without honors, even Second Class—and she graduated a Bachelor of Medicine and Bachelor of Surgery. Her doctoral thesis on epilepsy had been set aside as too abstruse and vague, unsupported by clinical evidence. It was not, besides, a fashionable disorder. So Sir Alexander Kinross's daughter sent it to Sir William Gower in London and asked if it was worth a doctorate. Signing herself "E. Kinross."

She was still waiting to hear back from London when her graduation day came around early in December of 1900. A time of curious excitement and more curious fears; federation of the colonies was about to take place and the Commonwealth of Australia would come into being. Still very much tied to Great Britain; her citizens would carry British passports and be British subjects. Australians per se did not exist. It would be a second-class country, its identity British, its constitution—very long—devoting itself to the rights of the federal parliament and the states; the People only got one mention, in the short preamble. No bill of rights, no sense of individual freedom, Nell thought resentfully. British-style democracy for the preservation of institutions. Well, we started out as convicts, so we're used to being sat on. Even the Governor of New South Wales can refer to our "birthstain" in his first message to the people. Go to buggery, Lord Beauchamp, you superannuated English fool!

She was sitting on a bench outside the Gothic glory of the medical school eating a cheese sandwich lunch, in no mood for commingling or commiserating with her fellow female medical students, none of whom had done any better than she. And the male students, despite her dolling up to go to parties and balls, still tended to avoid her as an emasculating bitch. The news that she was worth a cool fifty thousand a year for the rest of her life had stirred some interest in the more predatory among them, but Nell knew exactly how to emasculate such importunate idiots. They had retired smarting; nor did it help her marks when an unmarried senior lecturer threw his hat into the matrimonial ring. Never mind, she had made it, and that was a great victory. She hadn't failed a single year.

"I thought it was you," said a voice as its owner sat down beside her with the thump of a heavy body.

The face Nell turned the intruder's way was scowling, its eyes blazing. Then the eyes widened; Nell's mouth dropped open. "Jesus!" she exclaimed. "If it isn't Bede Talgarth!"

"The very same, and no pot belly," he said.

"What are you doing here?"

"I was in the law library doing some reading."

"Why? Are you doing Law?"

"No, just boning up for the federal parliament."

"You're in it?"

"Sure as eggs are eggs."

"Your platform is lousy," she said, swallowing the last of her sandwich and brushing the crumbs off her hands.

"You call one person, one vote, lousy?"

"Oh, that's well and good, but inevitable, as you are aware. Women have the vote, and they will even in New South Wales by the time there's another state election."

"Then what's lousy?"

"Total exclusion of colored and other undesirable races from immigrating," she said. "Undesirable, indeed! And anyway, no one is really *white*! We're pink or beige, so we're colored too."

"You'll never give up on that, will you?"

"No, never. My stepfather is half Chinese."

"Your stepfather?"

"Surely your head isn't so far up your socialist arse that you failed to notice that my father died two and a half years ago?"

"I have a glass window in my stomach, so if I unbutton my coat I can see," Bede said gravely. "Truly, I am sorry. He was a very great man. So your mother has remarried?"

"Yes. In Como, eighteen months ago."

"Como?"

"Don't you know any geography? The Italian lakes."

"Then we meant the same Como," he said smoothly; he had perfected the political sidestep. "Did it displease you, Nell?"

"Once it would have, but not these days. I can't be anything but glad for her. He's six years younger than her too, so with any luck she won't be a widow for quite as long as most women are. She's had a hard life, she deserves some happiness." Nell giggled. "I have a half brother and a half sister twenty-four years younger than I am. Isn't that wonderful?"

"Your mother had twins?"

"Heterozygous twins," said Nell, showing off.

"Explain," he said, another political sidestep: you're safe to profess ignorance if the matter is an esoteric one.

"Two different eggs. Identical twins come from one egg. I daresay she decided that at forty-plus she'd better reproduce in multiples. The next lot will probably be triplets."

"How old was she when she had you?"

"Not far past seventeen. And yes, if you're fishing for my age, I'll be twenty-five on New Year's Day."

"I remember your age, actually. There I was, an up-and-coming politician, with an unchaperoned sixteen-year-old in my house." He eyed her ringless fingers. "No husband? Fiancé? Boyfriend?"

"No bloody fear!" she said scornfully. "How about you?" That popped out before she could suppress it.

"Still an unattached bachelor."

"Still living in that ghastly house?"

"Yes, but it's improved. I bought it. You were right, the landlord sold it to me for a hundred and fifty pounds. And with typhoid, smallpox and the latest epidemic, bubonic plague, sewers are going in everywhere. So

I'm on the sewer now. I grow the most magnificent vegetables where the long-drop used to be."

"I'd love to see the improved version." That popped out too.

"I'd love to show it to you."

Nell got up. "I have to race over to Prince Alfred Hospital, I'm due to attend in the operating theater."

"When do you graduate?"

"Two days from now. My mother and stepfather have come back from abroad for it, and Ruby's coming down from Kinross. Sophia is bringing Dolly, so the whole family will be reunited. I can't wait to see my wee brother and sister."

"May I come to see the lady doctor graduate?" he called.

She turned her head to shout back. "My bloody oath!"

He stood watching her flying form diminish, its black academic gown flapping wildly. Nell Kinross! After all these years, Nell Kinross. He had no idea by how much her father's death had enriched her, but at heart she was the worker to end all workers. A short, dark grey bag for a dress, black boots as clumping as any miner's, hair screwed into a tight bun, not a scrap of rouge or powder on that creamy skin. His brows lifted, a rueful grin curled around his mouth; without realizing that he did, he put up a hand to rumple his auburn thatch—a gesture that told his fellow parliamentarians that Bede Talgarth was making a far-reaching decision.

Some people are utterly unforgettable, he thought, wending his way to the trams. I have to see her again. I have to find out what's happened to her. If she's just graduating in Medicine now, she must have finished her engineering degree—unless, as some of the more progressive dailies blatted, they had failed her at least once for every year of Medicine she'd done, something they did to women students.

Most of Nell had forgotten him a hundred yards beyond the bench, but he lurked at the back of her mind in some compartment that added a small, warm glow to her animus. Bede Talgarth! How right it seemed to resume a friendship that mattered, she admitted, a great deal more than she had realized.

THE OPERATION went on forever, but finally, a little after six, she was free to go to the hotel in George Street where her mother and Lee were staying. For once she took a hackney, kept yelling through the roof hatch at the driver to get a move on. How strict was Mum with her new babies?

Would they still be up so that they could meet their sister, or would they be asleep?

Elizabeth and Lee were in the drawing room of their suite; Nell burst in, stopped dead. *Was that Mum?* Oh, she had always been beautiful, but not the way she was now! Like the goddess of love, radiating an assured, unconscious sexuality that was—was almost indecent. She looks younger than I do, thought Nell, a lump in her throat. This is the marriage of her heart, and she has bloomed like a dark and dusky rose. And Lee's arresting handsomeness was more marked, though less epicene; his eyes, Nell noted, searched for Elizabeth all the time, weren't content unless they rested on her. They're like one person.

Elizabeth was coming to kiss her, Lee to hug her; she was put into a chair, given a sherry.

"I'm so glad you came back," Nell said. "It wouldn't have been the same if you weren't here to see me graduate." She gazed about. "Are the twins asleep?"

"No, we kept them up to say hello," said Elizabeth, taking her hand. "They're with Pearl and Silken Flower next door."

They had been born eleven months after Lee and Elizabeth had married, and were now seven months old. Nell stared at them with such a rush of love that tears sprang to her eyes. Oh, the *darlings*! Alexander looked like both his parents, black hair with some of Lee's straightness yet some of Elizabeth's wave, an oval, ivory-skinned face like Lee's, Anna's grey-blue eyes fringed with her impossibly long, curly lashes, Elizabeth's cheekbones and Lee's fine, full mouth. Whereas Mary-Isabelle was the image of Ruby, from red-gold hair to dimples to wide green eyes.

"Hello, weeny brother and sister," said Nell, kneeling. "I'm Nell, your biggest sister."

They were too young to talk, but both pairs of eyes looked at her with intelligence and interest, both mouths opened to laugh, four chubby little hands clasped hers.

"Oh, Mum, they're gorgeous!"

"We think so," said Elizabeth, picking Alexander up.

Lee went to Mary-Isabelle. "This one's Daddy's girl," he said, kissing her cheek.

"You weren't concealing anything when you wrote that you had an easy birth?" Nell asked anxiously, doctor to the fore.

"Carrying them was difficult toward the end—I was so huge and heavy," said Elizabeth, stroking Alexander's flyaway hair. "Of course I had no idea that there were two of them. Italian accoucheurs are highly skilled, and I had the best. No tearing, nothing beyond the usual discomfort. I found it very strange—when you and Anna were born, I was unconscious, so there I was, going through what was, for me, a first labor. Such a surprise after Mary-Isabelle was born, when they told me there was another one to come!" Elizabeth laughed, squashed Alexander gently. "I *knew* I'd have an Alexander, and there he was."

"While I was pacing up and down in the traditional way on the far side of the door," said Lee. "I heard Mary-Isabelle cry—I'm a father! I thought. But when they told me about Alexander, I passed out."

"Which one is the boss?" Nell asked.

"Mary-Isabelle," the parents chorused.

"They're very different in nature, but they like each other," said Elizabeth, handing Alexander to Pearl. "Bed time."

RUBY, SOPHIA and Dolly arrived the next day; Constance Dewy was too poorly to make the journey. At nine years of age Dolly had grown into her plain stage; that isn't going to last, thought Nell. By the time she turns fifteen she'll be a budding beauty, but her two and a half years at Dunleigh have done her the world of good. She's more sprightly, more outgoing, more assertive, and yet she hasn't lost her sweetness of nature.

Though she clearly liked Mary-Isabelle, at that first meeting Dolly gave her heart to Alexander. Because, Nell realized with aching breast, he had her real mother's eyes, and something in the child remembered Anna's eyes. Exchanging a glance with Elizabeth, Nell saw that her mother noticed it too. It's in our very blood to recognize our mother, no matter how long ago and far away the memories are. She will have to be told soon, or some malign worm will wriggle there first. But she'll be all right, will Anna's Dolly.

Ruby hadn't gone to seed after Alexander's death; it would have seemed a betrayal. Though she dressed in the fashion, she contrived to make its basic ugliness elegant and soignée. With half the British Empire off to South Africa to fight the Boers—or it seemed like half—those who set the fashions appeared to suffer such guilt that even birds of paradise had turned into dabchicks. And skirts were shortening; Nell didn't stand out so much these days, though, it had to be admitted, the shorter skirts looked far better on Ruby.

Change is in the wind, Nell thought; the new century is here, and within one or two years a woman medical graduate will be awarded an honors degree. It should have been me.

"You look different, Nell," said Lee to her as they sat in the hotel lounge over coffee and after-dinner drinks.

"In what way? Scruffier than ever?"

His white teeth flashed—Jesus, she thought, he really is something to look at! Just as well my taste runs in another direction entirely.

"The spark's rekindled," he said.

"You *are* perceptive! Though it isn't exactly rekindled—at least, not yet. I ran into him yesterday at uni."

"Is he still a parliamentarian of the wrong persuasion?"

"Oh, yes, but federal. I tore into him about Labor's anti-immigration of colored races platform," she said with a purr.

"But that didn't put him off you, did it?"

"I doubt anything could put him off anything if he gets his teeth stuck in. He's a bit of a bulldog."

"That should suit you. Think of the fights you'll have."

"After living with my mother and father, I'd prefer a life of peace, Lee."

"They rarely fought, that was one of their problems. You're Alexander's spitting image, Nell, you'll relish a fight. If you didn't, you'd never have finished Medicine."

"Point taken," she said. "Do you and my mother fight?"

"No, we don't need to. Especially with two babies in our nest, and another—one, I hope!—on the way. Barely, but she says it's definite."

"Jesus, Lee! Can't you leave it inside your trousers for a while? She needs time to recover from bearing twins."

He laughed. "Don't blame me! It was her idea."

Ruby was burbling to Sophia about Mary-Isabelle. "Another me!" she crowed. "I can't wait to teach the scrumptious pet to call a spade a fucking shovel. My new jade kitten."

"Ruby!" gasped Sophia. "Don't you dare!"

NELL GRADUATED with two other women and a far greater number of men. Watching in decent obscurity, Bede Evans Talgarth waited until the new lady doctor had been hugged and kissed by her small crowd of relatives. If that was her mother, Nell certainly had not inherited the beauty or the cool, calm manner. And her stepfather, a striking man, wore his hair in a Chinese pigtail. If he had not, it would have been hard to tell exactly which touch of the tar brush he had. Each carried a baby, the mother a boy, the father a girl; two pretty Chinesey women in embroidered silk trousers and jackets stood nearby with two perambulators. And there was Ruby Costevan—how could he ever forget that day in Kinross? Picking Nell up off the floor and lunching with her and a millionairess, as Ruby had called herself. What fascinated him today was to hear Nell's stepfather call her "Mum."

They all looked expensive, but they didn't have that high-society air that so many of the graduates' parents exuded as they strutted with their round vowels and the Australian twang buried underneath. Words like "Mafeking" and "Uitlanders" came faintly to Bede's ears; his lip curled. Second-hand jingoism. It was the Boers in the right of it. Why didn't we in Australia have a revolution like the Americans and throw the British out? he asked himself. We'd have been a damned sight better off.

He edged up to Nell's group nervously, aware that, despite his good suit, his stiff-collared and stiff-cuffed shirt, his parliamentary tie and his soft kid shoes, he looked what he was—a coal miner's son who had worked the coal face himself. This was insane! She'd never fit into his life!

"Bede!" Nell cried in delight, taking his outstretched hand.

"Congratulations, Dr. Kinross."

She performed the introductions in her customary blunt way, first her family to him, then, "This is Bede Talgarth," she ended. "He's a socialist."

"A pleasure to meet you," said Lee in *real* round vowels, shaking Bede's hand with genuine warmth. "As the head of the family, welcome to our capitalist coven, Bede."

"Care to have lunch with a millionairess tomorrow?" asked Ruby, ogling him.

The Chancellor and the Dean appeared, sniffing money and possible endowments.

"My wife, Mrs. Costevan," said Lee to the Chancellor, "and my mother, *Miss* Costevan."

"They asked for that!" said Nell, doubled up with laughter as the pair scuttled away. "I'm a *woman* doctor, so I can't even get a residency in a hospital, but do they give a shit? No!"

"Then you'll be hanging out your shingle somewhere?" Bede asked. "In Kinross, I suppose?"

"With bubonic plague in Sydney, rats by the millions, and so many people who can't afford to call a doctor? No, not I! I'm hanging my shingle out in Sydney," said Nell.

"Then how about hanging it out in my electorate?" he asked, taking her elbow and drawing her a little apart. "There's not an income in it, but I daresay you don't need to earn an income."

"True, I don't. I have fifty thousand pounds a year."

"Christ! That tears it," he said gloomily.

"I don't see why. What's yours is yours, and what's mine is mine. The first thing I have to do is buy a motor-car. So much better for house calls. One with a tonneau in case it rains."

"At least," he said, laughing, "you'll be able to fix it when it breaks down, as I believe they do all the time. I can't even change the washer on a tap."

"That's why you went into politics," she said kindly. "It's the perfect profession for people with ten thumbs and no common sense. I predict you'll end up prime minister."

"Thank you for the vote of confidence." His eyes lost their amusement, became bold yet caressing. "You look very nice today, Dr. Kinross. You should wear silk stockings more often."

Nell blushed, which mortified her. "Ta," she muttered.

"I can't have lunch with you tomorrow because I'm lunching with a millionairess," he said, ignoring her confusion, "but I could make roast leg of lamb at my house any night you care to name. I've even got some new furniture."

"NELL," SAID Elizabeth, sounding very pleased, "is going to be all right after all."

"There's someone for everyone," said Ruby comfortably. "He's a working-class bigot, but she'll soon knock that out of him."

Five

ALEXANDER RIDES AGAIN

WHEN ELIZABETH and Lee returned to Kinross, they brought Alexander's statue with them in a gigantic wooden crate. In the end it had been fashioned from marble rather than granite, for an unexpected reason: the Italian sculptor Lee commissioned insisted that, if this masterpiece was to be a masterpiece, it *must* be in marble! Not any old marble, but a special block that he had found at Carrara and reserved for just such a work as the statue of Sir Alexander Kinross. This would not be one of those shoddy public monuments city councils erected, Signor Bartolomeo Pardini declared with scorn. This would be a masterpiece! Up there with Rodin, though why that man chose bronze—pah! As for granite—pah, and pah again! A substance for gravestones.

Impressed by such Latin passion, Lee talked to Elizabeth and they agreed that the great Pardini should be let have his way.

Some superstition that neither understood forbade Lee and Elizabeth to see the finished work before it was crated; let it be put in place first. There would be no solemn unveiling, none of those pretentious ceremonies the statue's subject had personally loathed. Alexander would simply be put on his dark brown marble plinth in Kinross Square by a team of men and a crane, and when he was in place—why, everybody could see him anytime.

It *was* a masterpiece. The block of stone had the layered qualities of cameo shell or agate; the mane of hair was white, the face a pale tan, the fringed buckskin suit a darker tan, and the horse, a mare, was amber-brown. The effect was startlingly lifelike, so much so that strangers would get as close to it as they could to see if it had been painted or glued together, and marvel when they discovered it had not. Alexander rode his proudly stepping steed bareback like a Roman emperor, one hand up in a salute, the other loosely by his side. Lee had asked for a western saddle, but when he saw Signor Pardini's masterpiece on its plinth in Kinross Square, he conceded that the artist does know best. Alexander would have loved himself. Ruler of all he surveyed, just like his ancient namesake.

Ruby more than loved it. If she had nothing better to do, she sat on her upstairs verandah staring at Alexander in profile, for since he faced the town hall, he was sideways to the Kinross Hotel. Only Elizabeth found the statue upsetting. Whenever it intruded on her sight, she averted her gaze. Perhaps that was because Alexander had eyes; the sculptor had inserted two orbs of white marble inlaid with glassy black obsidian. Kinrossians swore that those eyes followed you as you walked by.

IT WAS ONLY after the statue was erected that a miner, at the rock face of number seventeen tunnel with his percussion hammer, felt as if someone watched him, and turned his head. To see Sir Alexander close behind his shoulder. A hand reached past, plucked at a friable piece of glittering ore, rolled it between fingers of solid flesh right down to the dirt beneath their nails. The leonine head, white hair like crystal in the brilliant light, nodded; up went the pointed brows.

"Good! We'll get a fair whack out of this vein," said Sir Alexander, and vanished, not into thin air, but more as if he rolled backward without moving his feet, faster than lightning.

After that he was often seen deep down in the Apocalypse, walking abstractedly, or supervising a miner, or inspecting a set of charge holes. It became tradition that if he walked or supervised, the Apocalypse was right and tight, but that if he checked the charge holes, he was warning them that an accident was likely. The miners were not afraid of him. Somehow it was a comfort to see Sir Alexander going about the only business he had really loved.

If Lee was in the mine, he was sure to be there, and at times the poppet heads men would see him walking the mountain with Lee, who had a habit of visiting the dent below which lay the end of number one tunnel; whenever he did, Alexander would appear to sit with him.

He also sat with Ruby on the upstairs verandah of the Kinross Hotel gazing at his statue.

But he never showed himself to Elizabeth.